MY
BROTHER'S
KEEPER

BOOKS BY

Marcia Davenport

MY BROTHER'S KEEPER
EAST SIDE, WEST SIDE
THE VALLEY OF DECISION
OF LENA GEYER
MOZART

MY
BROTHER'S
KEEPER

By Marcia Davenport

CHARLES SCRIBNER'S SONS   NEW YORK

COPYRIGHT, 1954, BY
MARCIA DAVENPORT

LIBRARY OF CONGRESS CATALOG CARD NO. 54–6300

PRINTED IN THE UNITED STATES OF AMERICA BY
KINGSPORT PRESS, INC., KINGSPORT, TENNESSEE

For
C.D.B.

PART I

PART I

I never knew the Holt brothers, which seems strange because within a few weeks of their deaths I felt that nobody else could have known them so well. I never saw Seymour Holt at all. What I saw of Randall Holt was as gruesome a sight as a man could meet in a lifetime. By the day when they found Randall Holt I had already learned a great deal about that gentle man, and it became all the more harrowing and ghastly to have to watch while they scooped up the unspeakable thing from the rotting floor and carried it away in a covered basket.

Like the rest of the world I first knew of the Holt brothers through the newspapers which made them a sensation. Scarcely anybody has forgotten how Seymour Holt was found dead in that derelict house crammed from cellar to roof with one hundred and seventy tons of hoarded rubbish; and how, after twenty-two days' search by the police, Randall Holt's body was found buried in one of his own booby-traps, in the same room where Seymour died.

Day after day the story ran on the front pages of the New York newspapers, and I followed it in their European editions which reached me by air in Milano. The *Corriere* of course reported it too; their very able American correspondent made the most of a drama sure to grip Italian imaginations. So one heard the thing discussed everywhere. I was then winding up an eighteen months' stint on exchange service from our bank, while the Credito Settentrionale had sent my opposite number to my place in our Foreign Department in New York. It was a good arrangement. I learned more than I could have done in any other way and I had a delightful time besides. I am afraid I will never again get used to a gobbled sandwich and a gulped cup of coffee at a counter or off the corner of my desk, instead of the restful two-hour luncheon where I learned to eat and drink perhaps too well, and to enjoy the company of my Italian friends with the comfortable knowledge that there was nothing else to do with the time: every office and place of business was closed like ours. This comes at first as a surprise to Americans working on the Continent, but I notice how quickly we adapt ourselves to it and stop mumbling about inefficiency and wasted time.

Gianfranco Pozzi and I had just returned from such a lunch at Gino e Biki, whose cooking is one of the higher pleasures of Milanese life, when I was pitched head first into the sensation over the Holt brothers. This might be all in the day's work for a newspaper reporter or a doctor or a lawyer, but it seemed very far off course to me. We had been reading the New York papers while we drank our espresso after lunch; that was the first of a series of days in which they itemized the junk which came crashing through an upstairs window of the Holt house as the police inched and dug their way through ceiling-high tunnels of bundled newspapers and heaved mountains of stuff out into the back yard. I can still see Gianfranco's face, pop-eyed with amazement, while I read aloud and translated: electric generators, old bicycles, gas chandeliers, dressmakers' forms, toys, a trombone, a buggy-top, automobile parts, old opera programmes, kerosene stoves, women's hats and corsets, innumerable tattered suitcases, a pair of oars, a guitar, a checkerboard . . . the time came when I saw the inside of the house, and all this was as nothing compared with what remained there. That day, however, I was still dumbfounded by what we had been reading, so it seemed the more incredible a quarter of an hour later that the dead hand of Seymour Holt should reach across the Atlantic to touch myself, of all unconcerned people, in a Milanese bank.

Commendatore Nerini, one of the senior officers, called me to his desk and himself was much too Italian to take a dry banker's attitude towards the letter he picked up from a cluster of papers clipped to an envelope which had apparently just arrived by air from New York. He handed me the letter, saying, "Here is an extraordinary thing, Veecherly, *molto strano*. Look at this." His English was pretty good, carefully spoken and heavily accented. I always felt apologetic for the trouble I caused those good-natured Italians with a name like Wycherly.

The letter was from Bowen Dugdale, the head of our Trust Department, and had been written four days before—two days after the body of Seymour Holt was found. It informed us that Seymour Holt had been a client of our bank which, together with Holt's lawyer, was named executor of his will. The will, wrote Dugdale, contained a provisionary bequest which would necessitate the obtaining of immediate, certified information. Seymour Holt had stipulated that if one Renata Tosi, last heard of in San Bernardo di Bellagio, could furnish incontrovertible proof of the identity of the father of her son, known as

Sebastiano Gandolfi, the said Renata Tosi was bequeathed a life income from the bulk of Seymour Holt's estate, with the principal to go outright to Sebastiano Gandolfi after the death of the said Renata Tosi. If Renata Tosi should predecease Seymour Holt, Sebastiano Gandolfi must himself furnish proof of the identity of his father in order to inherit the legacy.

I stopped reading and looked at Commendatore Nerini. He was staring at me with an expression which struck me, surprisingly, as shocked. His lower lip was thrust forward and his brows knitted.

"*Cosa dice?*" he asked hunching his shoulders.

"Fantastic."

"Fantastic. Even without the sensation of 'ow this 'Olt died and what manner of man he was. But, for this affair to create another *scandalo* here—" His face became a question-mark.

"But Commendatore," I said, "why? Some obscure woman, an illegitimate son . . . it happens anywhere . . . every day . . ."

"But preferably not to a distinguished man."

"Oh." I laid the papers on the desk and thought for a moment. Names unless they are widely known in one's own country do not mean much when one is a stranger elsewhere. But almost at once I began to realize why Nerini seemed so concerned. "You think," I asked him, "that this could be *Professor* Gandolfi? The—"

"The scholar," he agreed. "The physicist. The Council Minister. One of the most respected men in Italy, in Europe. A patriot—"

"The Nobel Prize," I murmured, as the details fell into place in my mind. "But why do you think it must be he?"

"He comes from that Comune, he has one of those *cognomi* by which half the peasants in the district call themselves, and he is the only Gandolfi known to the world. How can it be any other?"

"But—" I picked up the letter again. It was unnecessary to point out that the great man's name was apparently not Gandolfi at all.

"Exactly," agreed Nerini. "And you may be the one who has the very awkward task of informing him, or of asking him to admit the fact if he knows it already."

There did not seem to be any way that I could refuse. Bowen Dugdale had asked that I be sent to obtain the information since I was so soon anyway to return to New York, where the findings would have to be filed before Seymour Holt's estate could be administered.

Dugdale had added, "We cannot make inquiries through Seymour Holt's brother Randall, because Randall Holt has not been seen since before Seymour Holt's body was found. Randall Holt closed his checking account with us in 1913, and our bank has had no dealings with him since. Unless he is proved to be dead there is not much we can do in that quarter now."

I suppose Nerini, watching me read all this, must have seen that I was not too sure of my ability to get the information for Dugdale. But we agreed that I had to try, and I said, "I only hope my Italian is good enough."

"It is good enough. Of course I can send somebody with you if you like, but—"

"I see."

"First you must find the woman if she is alive, and whatever she may say, she will be more reluctant to say it to two men than to one. And if she is dead—"

"I hope not."

"I too. *Dunque,* you will go tomorrow?"

The mission was a failure. I had to return almost empty-handed to Milano from my strange and frustrating day in a remote mountain village high above the Lake of Como, and cable my report to Bowen Dugdale. Next day he rang me up on the transatlantic telephone.

"Better catch the first plane over, Dick," he said. "They've reamed tons of stuff out of that house and I've been through enough of it to find the woman's name all over the place."

"Are they still chucking the junk out of the window?" I asked.

"No, that's been stopped. You come back here and help sort it out and then take the tangible proofs back to Italy and try to force the issue with them. That's the only way to do it."

So I left at once for New York. I have always thought that if it had not been for that suspended twenty-four hours with nothing to do but sit cramped in the plane, unable to sleep, the Holt brothers might never have taken such a grip on my imagination that for a good many weeks I scarcely thought about anything else. I have flown the Atlantic—and the Pacific too, for that matter—so many times that the trip has become no more extraordinary than a ride in a taxi. But that flight from Milano to New York seemed to me like a witch's broomstick, rushing me through the air to the most grisly objective that a journey might have. The plane landed in the early afternoon and, having almost no luggage, I was out of Customs and into a taxi in less than half an hour. Bowen Dugdale had suggested I go to his club, where he was putting me up, and have the bath and the nap which are all one can usually put one's mind on when arriving from a long flight; he would join me there for dinner.

But leaving the airport I took a sudden decision and told the cab driver to take the Midtown Tunnel and go to the address in Chelsea of the Holt brothers' house. I was not only curious about it; I felt a powerful compulsion to see it. The driver grumbled about a helluva break to have to go to such a part of town in the worst time of day, but I told him it would be worth his while and counted myself lucky that he was not one of those garrulous characters; I wanted to think undisturbed. He was silent while we were inching our way across town behind prodigious truck traffic to reach Tenth Avenue so that we could come back, eastbound, on Twenty-fourth Street. As we turned into that block I saw the driver scratch the back of his head and he said, "Say, mister, ain't this here number we're headin' for that house full o' junk where the fella was found dead?"

"Maybe," I said. But before we could creep within several hundred yards of the place, I saw the crowd gathered in the street. "I might as well get out here," I said, and tipped the man well enough to satisfy his temper if not his curiosity. He had no idea of passing the house without stopping to rubberneck at it.

Carrying my small travelling bag, I walked slowly along the pavement. The house was in one of those famous Chelsea terrace rows, set far back from the sidewalk behind spacious front yards almost half a block deep. Nothing on Manhattan Island is more obscenely derelict than the few of those yards that remain, abandoned to filth, trash, rats and the savage stray cats who hunt them; to the ruin wrought by the most wretched type of slum which seems infinitely uglier and crueller than the vilest railroad tenements of the lower East Side or dark Harlem. These Chelsea houses were once dignified and beautiful, homes of which gracious people were proud, homes which they loved in much the same way as the children they raised in them.

There must have been three hundred people in the crowd standing on the sidewalk and spilling over into the street. They were largely silent, and I could see that many of them had been there much of the time since this dreadful scene had become the centre of public attention; this was the ninth day since the discovery of Seymour Holt's body. The onlookers were apparently the drab and raddled people of the neighborhood. I had read that a mob of more than a thousand had watched on the day when the police had dumped all that rubbish out of the window, but when that was stopped the spectators had obviously thinned out to this assemblage of regulars. They were not allowed inside the front yard, which was cordoned off by the police, and guarded by two officers who were looking thoroughly bored. I saw more policemen on the high front stoop, whose sandstone steps appeared to be sagging crazily, and other men inside the house. The front door stood open. I stopped for a time on the curbstone, craning to see past the people.

Nothing could ever again look so ominous to me as the tall bleak façade of that rotting house. One could see all over it the marks of long cumulative decay. Chunks of the streaked brown sandstone cornice and the ornate window-facings had broken off, leaving rude gaps in the design, uniform with the whole row, which had been the pride of some forgotten architect of the 'Fifties. The neighboring houses were in no better repair but there was an eloquent difference between them and the desolate home of the Holts. The other houses had all been broken up into warrens inhabited by turbulent, drifting slum-dwellers whose crazy variegations of dirty torn curtains, milk bottles, tin cans, stunted plants, cats and dogs, soiled bedding, and ragged laundry filled the windows. The Holt house there in the middle of all this was a sepulchre, uniform and lifeless from the cellar windows to the roof. I stood and looked at it for a long time. Every window had once been covered by a drawn blind whose original color nobody could guess; but these blinds were all in shreds and tatters and behind each it was impossible to discern just what filled the crusted window and formed a solid black block. I found out soon enough. I could even imagine, standing there. But once I went inside I never again had that awful sense of disembodiment, as if I too were a ghost, hovering there on the pavement, watching a sharp autumn wind whip and fling dirty things—old paper, rags, a broken Piccadilly collar, the brim of a straw hat—across the black grit of that hideous front yard.

I stopped musing, deciding to waste no more time; and making my way through the crowd, I explained my errand to the first guard of police, so that I was quickly passed along from one group to the next, until I was standing at the entrance doorway.

I have thought hard how to describe the smell which was the first, the constant, and the inescapable impression of that house. Merely by thinking about it now I can feel the nausea moving up my gullet. Perhaps it is enough to say that my outfit of the Third Army was the one that broke open Buchenwald in April, 1945. It was we who found the ceiling-high piles of unburned bodies stacked like logs between the gas chambers and the crematory ovens; we who had to do something about the train of open freight cars overflowing with corpses, abandoned there on the railway siding in the sunshine. That was the unholiest possible exaggeration of what such a stench could be. But I was appalled to find the Holt house different only in degree. The smell of death and rot and vileness was the same, yet in its way even fouler, because as everybody knows, the place was a solid impacted block of massed paper and trash, pierced only by those terrifying tunnels. Never in thirty-five years at the least had a window been opened. In fact the only unobstructed window in the entire house was the one at the second floor rear near which Seymour Holt had sat, paralyzed and blind, until he died there. That was the window which the police broke open after receiving a mysterious telephone call suggesting that they investigate the Holt house; the window to which they set the fireman's ladder that was their first means of access, and their only way of carrying out the body of Seymour Holt. Every other window was solidly obstructed. No wonder the detectives working inside the house kept the front door open behind them; but that made little difference.

The policeman at the door cupped his hands and shouted into the foetid black hole. I waited, almost retching at the stench, and presently there appeared two men in dirty coveralls. One came from a black cave to the right, where all I could see were stacks and piles and masses of I did not yet know what, except for bundles of crumbling newspapers; and the second man came cautiously down the stairs, lighting his way with a strong electric torch and watching his footing. He did not touch the banister which had once, apparently, been a handsome turned rail and was now leaning crazily out over the hall, with some of its posts dangling and the rest missing altogether. He shook his head slowly as he joined me and stepped outside for some air and a cigarette.

"Glad to meet you, Mr. Wycherly," he said. "Mr. Cullom said you'd probably be here today." Cullom was Seymour Holt's lawyer. "My name's Deering. My partner here is Sam Blyfeld." Each man pulled a soiled work glove from his right hand, making a disgusted face; we shook hands and Deering said, "Some mess, eh?"

"How do you know what you're doing?" I asked.

Deering shoved a denim cap to the back of his head and took a deep breath of the outside air. "God, I wish I did know," he said.

"We think we're looking for Randall Holt," said Blyfeld.

"Any clues?"

Both men shook their heads. Deering answered. "Just a hunch, but we've all got the same one. Cullom too. He's had lines out all over any place the man might be. So has the Department. But you ask me, he's right in there."

"The stink," said Blyfeld. "That's enough for me. Old Seymour's been out of there nine days and the stink's just as bad as ever. Got to be a reason."

They explained why the search had to be so slow and so cautious. It was on account of the booby-traps. The rooms, insofar as they had been able to get into them, had been filled up by a consistent plan, a weird example of methodical madness. There was a groundwork of objects, beginning with the furniture which had first belonged in each room, buttressed by a wild assortment of things such as had been thrown out of a second-storey window and listed in *The Times* the day I had read it all out to Gianfranco Pozzi. Between and around and on top of this mass were the bundled newspapers, tightly jammed all the way to the ceiling, and solidly from wall to wall, except for the tunnels that had been built to thread them. There was no recognizable plan about the tunnels, they existed as the only means of getting through or across the rooms; sometimes they were curved, sometimes short and straight and turned at sharp angles. Everywhere they were punctuated by booby-traps, horrible, cunning contrivances of string and wire and old automobile parts and pieces of broken furniture. Deering and Blyfeld explained that some of the traps were just alarms, rigged up with empty tin cans and old bottles intended to tumble down with a hellish noise and warn the brothers of intruders. But other traps, said Deering, were deadly—connected with ropes which would pull over into the tunnel half a ton of bundled newspapers and block it entirely.

"Does anybody know why all the newspapers?" I asked. I had been wondering how that had started.

"Sure," said Blyfeld. "Old Randall wasn't such a mystery around the neighborhood here. Some of those folks out there used to know him. They say he'd sit out on the stoop dressed in a funny kind of brown velvet lounging-jacket, all worn out, and a pair of striped pants and a cap he always wore turned around backwards. And he'd talk to people if he felt like it. He used to talk about his brother."

"Do you suppose he made sense?"

"Depends on what you call sense, I guess," said Deering. "Look inside here and you know the poor devil was nuts. Listen to what they say he said, and you feel real sorry for him. Funny the way we talk as if he was dead for sure—but I bet he is."

"About the papers," said Blyfeld, "that makes you feel kind of sorry for him, but it sure shows he was cracked. He took care of old Seymour like a baby and Seymour seems to be the reason for a lot of all this. He was blind, I guess you heard that. And Randall had this one damned notion, stubborn as a mule. He said he was sure he was going to cure Seymour's blindness, and after he got his sight back he'd want to read all the papers so he'd know everything he'd missed in thirty-five years. Can you tie that?"

Deering looked at his watch. "We might as well call it a day," he said to Blyfeld; and to me, "Mr. Cullom says you'll be around while we're doing this on account of the things the bank is looking for. If you mean to get very far inside that place—" he gestured at the foul-smelling cavern behind us, "you'd better wear an outfit like ours. This beats anything I've ever had to do, and I've done plenty. Me for a bath, boys— a couple of baths. So long."

Next day I really joined the search. Before it ended I had been twelve whole days in that house with Deering and Blyfeld and their helpers from the Police and the Sanitation Departments. They looked for Randall Holt and I looked for anything which would induce Renata Tosi to meet the conditions of Seymour Holt's will. That, at least, was my first objective. I might have had more peace of mind since, and much more time for my own work, if I had been able to confine my interest in the Holt story to the matter of Seymour's will. That became quickly impossible, not only because of the drama and the pathos and the horror, but because much of what I looked for concerned Seymour and most of what I found concerned Randall. Then there were the objects of decayed rubbish which, as we found them, emerged to more and more vivid identifications. If I list them here, they move back into the bewildering hodgepodge which is all they actually were. But follow if you can what was happening in my reasoning as we dug out a series of pianos—two, three, seven, fourteen finally; or trunks full of mouldering but still spectacular women's clothes; the chassis of an automobile; masses of printed and manuscript music with hair-fine scribblings on the disintegrating margins in the hand which I soon learned to know was Randall's; or a cookery notebook kept by the mother of the Holts, where there were irrelevant entries in a different hand, the meaning of which was a startling clue to some of what I learned. What should I think of a thing they told me was a Kiddie Kar of the earliest vintage; or a nursery icebox and a baby's bathtub and I forget how many prams of various kinds? I knew the reason for the boxes and crates full of newspaper clippings about the Opera early in the century, but why the dozens of unopened bundles of unsold tickets to a church picnic on Staten Island? Why the moth-eaten rocking-horse, with the receipted bill for its purchase from Schwarz glued to its saddle? Why did the house contain so many market baskets, all alike, all of a certain odd, rounded shape and one of them, found inside the belly of a rusted kerosene stove, with a shred of once-pink ribbon tied to its handle? Some of my questions were questions no longer, after the day near the end of the search when we had dug our way into what had once been the sole bathroom of the house, but which the Holts apparently never used; they used no plumbing or sewerage; no gas, no electricity. The deep tin bathtub of the early 'Seventies was rusted through in ugly holes, and lying face down in the bottom of it there was a child's desk, to which had been affixed a heavy brass tumbler lock. The thing was covered by masses of refuse layered between old plush portières, burst bed-pillows, and rags. A rat leaped from the mess as the men poked at it, and vanished into the rotten wall. That little desk when we broke it open held too many of Randall's secrets for their discoverer to shrug them off and go his way.

Nobody could help brooding about all this, and wondering, and putting together the immense mass of tangible evidence which proved what the lives of the Holts had been. But brooding leaves me just where I have been for a long time, preoccupied, haunted, compelled beyond my will to follow those twisted lives from their youth to their desolate age. It is not the facts, fantastic as they are, which drive and prod at my imagination; but how these human characters were the causes and the victims of the facts and of their own fates. This gives me no peace. If I were a writer, I would get it out of my mind by making a book of it.

But I am not a writer, and up to now the strange story with its crazy embellishments has gone on revolving and evolving and developing in my mind, leaving me stranded for lack of the skill to transcribe it. I am sure I know what happened to those people and how and why they became in the end what they did. I have the instinct to follow the workings of cause and effect, and also the instinct to make order. This is the habit of my training in my own work; we must be precise, we must keep order of everything entrusted to us, we must cleanly finish off the details of each thing that we undertake. In this case I am baffled and so I believe forced to ponder about the lives of the Holt brothers instead of winding up their affairs and dismissing them as I would ordinarily do. The result of all this is that I see and feel the story that I would write if I could, but it never gets outside the limits of my imagination. Inside these limits it is clear and very real and it leads me on and on. This is the way it seems to me, this is what I think, what I sense, what my imagination weaves out of what I have seen. . . .

PART II

CHAPTER 1

Seymour thought Grandmama must have forgotten that he was there in his favorite play-place under the round table with the twisting legs and the thick fringed plush cover which hung down to the carpet. Inside it was dark and warm and secret. Seymour could pretend this place to be whatever he chose—a robbers' cave, a railway tunnel, the coal-hole of a ship. This afternoon it had been a mine, like the inside of the mountain where Curdie worked with his father. Of course Seymour did not believe all that magic, all the things that goblins and witches did, which made Randall's eyes grow so big and round, and gave him nightmares after Nana put the light out. Seymour was not afraid of all that since he was four years older than Randall. But he knew that a mine really was full of gold and silver and wonderful colored jewels, and there in the dark, scrambling on his hands and knees between the heavy legs of the table, he could scratch and pick at the patterns and colors in the carpet, pretending he had found rubies or a lump of gold or a handful of diamonds. He was busy picking out diamonds, the white threads in the pattern of the fancy carpet, when he heard Papa's heavy step crossing the room. It stopped beside Grandmama's chair near the window.

"Why, John," she said, "you are home early today."

"Yes." Seymour heard a soft creak as his father sat down in the tufted armchair opposite Grandmama. "Yes, I suppose. I rather thought I would be in time for tea with Lily."

"She is in the drawing-room," said Grandmama's tight, cross voice. "She did not have tea with me today."

"Yes, I heard her playing. I came straight upstairs."

"Lily is too old to take piano lessons," said Grandmama. "I think you are foolish to permit it."

"She loves music," said Papa.

"She can hear music at the Opera like everybody else. There is no need for her to take these ridiculous lessons. It is unsuitable for a married woman, and who is this Mr. Malvern, this person who comes here?" Grandmama's voice was low but very sharp.

"Oh, Mother, I don't think it matters. Just a music teacher." Sometimes when Papa spoke in that dragging way Seymour watched for his eyes to close as if he were going to fall asleep.

"I *thoroughly* disapprove," said Grandmama. "This is not the first time I have spoken about this, John. I think you should put a stop to her nonsense."

Seymour had forgotten about his mining now. He simply sat cross-legged and listened.

"Mother," he heard Papa say in his 'patient' voice. Seymour was clever about voices, he had learned how much they can say almost without words. "Mother, don't you think you are a little hard on Lily? She is so young—"

"Too young," snapped Grandmama. "And it's high time she grew up. She'll make a fool of you, John. You'll have brought it on yourself, to be sure—what can have made you do it!"

"I love her." Papa spoke slowly.

"That's perfect nonsense. One doesn't marry for such a reason. You were quite old enough to know better—you had me to warn you. Now that you've got a flighty, silly creature on your hands, you will have to put some sense into her."

"Lily is artistic," said Papa. "She loves music."

"Music! It's that foreign blood, that's what it is. You never should have married her."

"Mother, please. You do exaggerate so. You had nothing against Lily before, you've said so yourself. The Randalls were always our friends, and one French grandmother—must we go over all that again?"

"You were well enough off as you were." Seymour had to inch forward and put his head down to the fringe of the plush table-cover to hear that. He felt choked and hot, but he would not try to go away now; he would not dare to.

"Please don't say that again, Mother. It's a pity we can't all be quite happy together. You love the boys."

"Very much," said Grandmama in a tone so hard that eight-year-old Seymour flinched. "That is why I think Lily might well stop being so 'artistic' and devote herself more to her responsibilities."

Seymour waited a long time before he heard Papa say, "I wonder if you know how little chance you give her."

"John!"

"It's true, Mother. I've tried to say it before. Lily hasn't got a house to run, or anything to be responsible for, not even the boys, between you and Nana."

"Nana. Did you think I would let a twenty-year-old girl choose a nurse when Seymour was born?"

"No. I didn't think so. But if you don't let Lily run the house or manage her own children, what is she to do?"

"She can do as I say. She can learn from me."

"She has tried." Seymour knew from the tight feeling in his own throat that Papa must be trying not to say something. Seymour could hear the loud, slow breathing that Grandmama always made when she was cross. He began to feel worried about Papa. He wished too that he dared crawl out and go away but also he wanted to hear what was coming next. And something dreadful would happen if he should let them discover that he had been there under the table all this time. He held his breath and crouched there hugging his knees. He heard Papa cough and say quickly, "Sooner or later we'll have to change all this, Mother. I—we—Lily and the boys and I—ought to have a house of our own."

Seymour listened even more closely. This was a surprising idea. He heard his grandmother say, "And what about your promise? You haven't forgotten it, of course, so I take it your fool of a wife has been at you again. I'll not hear of it, John. Not another word."

Then Seymour had to wait a long, long time. He knew exactly how Grandmama and Papa were sitting there, stiff and angry, looking so much alike with their narrow foreheads frowning, and their mouths shut tight. They would be sitting up straight in the slippery red chairs which gave Seymour gooseflesh if he touched them, staring out the bay window at the long back yard where the snow was too old and slushy to be fun any more. That was why Seymour had been kept indoors this afternoon. He waited and waited and at last he heard Papa stand up and say, "Well, I'm going upstairs to see the boys."

"Yes," said Grandmama. Seymour knew exactly how she would look down her nose at her left shoulder, where a gold watch hung from a fleur-de-lis pin. She was always looking at the watch and she had taught Seymour to tell time by it and also how to say fleur-de-lis. "Yes," she said, "it's almost time for their supper. I must go and see whether this new cook has made their broth properly."

Seymour heard the loud rustling of her skirts as she rose from her chair. He was quite frightened. They were both going up to the day nursery and when they found he was not there, someone would go at once to look for him. He mustn't be found here. And while he was wondering what to do, he thought quickly of Mama. Somehow she seemed in more danger than he. He had a feeling that he wanted to run and warn her. He held his breath while he listened to Grandmama and Papa leaving the room and starting up the stairs. When they were nearly at the top, Seymour scuttled from under the table, ran across the room and down the thickly carpeted stairs to the drawing-room, as fast as he could. He was very quiet. He heard the piano as he slithered down the stairs. He did not know just what he was going to say to Mama, but he knew he wanted to rush to her and throw his arms round her and whisper, "Be careful, watch out. Be careful of Grandmama."

He opened the door and slipped into the drawing-room, shutting the door behind him. He ran towards Mama at the piano. He was in a hurry to tell her. But he stopped. She was sitting there with Mr. Malvern on a chair beside her, and Seymour was startled to see that she had Randall on her lap. She was guiding Randall's right hand and nodding and smiling as his tiny fingers struck the keys. "You see?" cried Mama, turning to Mr. Malvern. "It is true, don't you see? See how he takes to it."

Seymour wanted to cry out, "Mama!" But he could not. He stood there and watched her and that man with the bushy whiskers nodding and beaming over Randall, and it didn't seem to matter any more that he had something to tell Mama. He could scarcely remember what it was. He stood and stared at them, at Mama's left hand with the thick gold ring, holding Randall on her lap, and her right hand supporting Randall's wrist. She was humming softly as Randall's fingers picked out the notes. Sometimes she turned her curly brown head towards Mr. Malvern and smiled.

Seymour gathered his feet tight together and bent his knees and jumped as high as he could in the air, coming down with a crash on his copper-toed boots. At the same time he shouted "BOO!"

Mama shrieked. Mr. Malvern jumped to his feet. Randall began to cry.

"Seymour!" cried Mama. "How you frightened me." She left her piano stool, setting Randall on his feet, and went across to Seymour.

"Boo!" he roared again. "Boo! BOO!"

Mama knelt beside him and put her arms round him. "Hush," she said. "Stop that, Seymour, it's naughty." Randall was wailing in the corner. "You've frightened Brother. And you're very rude." Her face was sad and Seymour remembered that he was sorry for her, but he shouted, "I don't care."

Mama shook her head. "Now tell Brother you're sorry." She held out her right arm to Randall, who hung back, crying, with his finger in his mouth. "Come here, Baby," she said. "That's a good boy." She stared reproachfully at Seymour and said, "I ought to punish you."

"But you won't!" cried Seymour. "You wouldn't—" he stopped, with his mouth open. The door was flung wide and Grandmama stood there tall and scowling, looking at Lily kneeling with her arms round the boys.

"What is the meaning of this?" asked Mrs. Holt. Her long face was red and angry. "Lily, why did you bring the children downstairs? It's past their suppertime. What have you done to Randall?"

Seymour watched anxiously. Mama bit her pale lips and said, "I'm sorry, Mother Holt."

"Why did you bring them down here?"

Lily did not answer. She was wiping Randall's nose with her pocket handkerchief and smoothing back Seymour's hair.

"Please answer me at once!" said Mrs. Holt.

Seymour shouted, "Because she wanted to!" His grandmother strode forward, wrenched him from his mother's arm, and pushed him towards the door. "Go upstairs and stay in the night nursery alone until I come for you." Seymour stood still, his mouth shut tight. "Go at once!" said Grandmama.

"Go, darling," whispered Mama. Seymour marched off, with a glare at his grandmother as he passed her. She was seizing Randall by the hand, preparing to take him away upstairs. Seymour climbed the first flight slowly, peering down between the banisters into the drawing-room. Grandmama was dragging Randall away, but she stopped at the door and said, "Lily, I think there has been enough of this nonsense about music lessons. This bringing the boys into your—your—" Grandmama made her pinched-up nose at Mr. Malvern. "This is too much." She started to follow Seymour up the stairs, dragging Randall who was still wailing. Seymour hurried. Grandmama had to go slowly because Randall's legs were so short.

John Holt had been there beside the bed for over an hour, trying to calm Lily and induce her to stop sobbing. He had never known her to cry so; it seemed as if her sobs must rip her lungs to pieces. He had pleaded and soothed, cajoled, caressed, and whispered all the tender words and phrases he knew, but the shuddering and heaving, the great gasping sobs continued. On the marble-topped stand at his elbow there were sal volatile, a vinaigrette, and a bowl of ice-water out of which he wrung folded handkerchiefs to bathe her swollen face. He tried clumsily to hold the cold compresses over her red, streaming eyes, but she turned and tossed too much, rolling over to lie on her face and weep into the pillows. He stroked the back of her neck, put his cheek down on her matted curls, and whispered another plea to try to be quiet. "You must," he said, "dearest, darling Lily, please try to stop crying."

Gradually the fit-like gasping subsided. John sat down on the edge of the high-headed walnut bed, and lifted up his wife so that she lay with her face hidden against his waistcoat. "That's better," he whispered. "That's a good girl. You're feeling better now." He ignored the frantic shaking of her head. "Oh, yes you are," he said in an artificial, soothing tone which made him feel clumsy and foolish whether it reassured her or not. "You're feeling much better."

But she shook her head violently. "No!" she said. She twisted herself up and looked straight at him. Her poor pretty face was raddled and puffed, her curly bangs all gone to strings round her forehead. "Take me away, John," she said. Her eyes were heartrending. He felt as if he had punished an innocent small animal. "You must take me away. Away from her."

"Try to be quiet now," he whispered, kissing her.

She pulled herself up and sat, bracing herself with her hands. "It's no use to talk like that," she said, gasping between the words. "You must promise me now." She stared so hard at him with her reddened, glassy eyes that he felt cowardly for looking away; but he could not look into her eyes. He sat gazing dully at the dark, heavily-furnished room dimly lighted by a single gas-jet above the rosewood bureau. "You've promised me before," she said. "Many times. You've put me off that way. Haven't you?"

He bent his head and she sat watching the dark blush which swept slowly to his forehead. He kept his eyes on his hands which were gripped together on his knees. He felt his wife's cold fingers closing upon the sides of his face. She leaned forward and said slowly, gasping less now, "It's true and you know it. You promised to take me away. When will you do it, John? When?"

She watched his face. All these things he had just said, all his pleading, echoed in her mind. "Anything," he had said, begging her to stop crying. "Whatever it is, but please, darling . . . please, Lily. . . ." And now she watched his face and saw it troubled, irresolute, abashed. An older woman, wiser, and longer a wife would have seen and become resigned to the hopeless truth. But she was twenty-eight and he was forty-seven.

She shook his head a little between her hands, and her voice turned shrill to force his attention. "Why don't you take me away, John? Why did you promise?"

"I shouldn't have."

"But *why*? You know we can't go on like this. Why?"

He had no answer. Lily was trembling in little starts, still breathing unevenly. "Why can't we have the house you promised me, all to ourselves?"

"—not easy to understand," she heard him mutter.

"But I have to know! You've got to tell me. Why can't we just— just leave?"

"Money," he murmured, still avoiding her eyes.

"But you're rich. Father told me so." She was artless.

"Mother is. It's hers, you see. And she told me, I mean she made me—"

He felt Lily's hands stiffen against his head and then fall heavily away. He raised his eyes, prompted by uneasy shame, and saw her face turn pale, her eyes grow round and wide. "Oh," she breathed. "Oh. You promised her first, you promised her long ago. You said you'd never leave her, you said we'd all live with her. *John!*" she cried in a voice of pure terror, "how could you do such a thing?"

He could not answer, he sat silent. Lily raised her hands to her temples and pushed back the tangles of her hair, eyeing him with fear and bewilderment. "You did that," she breathed. "You did that to me and those little boys." He felt her trembling; she was shaken by long, slow tremors quite different from her mindless hysteria of before. He raised his head and saw that she had begun to weep again, but in a manner altogether different, without violence and without sound. Her eyes remained wide and staring, and from them there rolled large tears, sliding one after the other slowly down her cheeks. He saw with pain that this was her defeat; there would be no more storms of useless protest. She sat drawn away from him, weeping, with her square white hands cupped piteously in her lap. He turned his head slowly away.

"You knew you were doing this," she whispered. "You knew it and you lied to me and you've lied all these years. You never told the truth until now. I never knew you were cruel," she breathed, speaking the words with slow spaces between them. Amazement and revulsion began to contort her face. "Cruel—oh!" She raised the back of her left hand to her eyes as if to shut out the sight of him.

"Oh, Lily, no! No!" He tried to take her other hand but she shook him off. They both shrank as they heard a tap at the door.

"What is it?" asked John roughly.

The waitress stood there. "If you please, sir, Mrs. Holt sends word it is past dinner-time. She is waiting in the drawing-room."

"Tell her we are sorry, Nora. Mrs. John is not well and will not be down for dinner. Ask my mother not to wait for me."

The door closed and John Holt watched Lily turn away in dull revulsion. She lay down quietly on her left side, with her back towards him. He sat confused and wretched and uncertain. What did one do, what could one do, in such a situation? Without a penny of one's own, how could one buy or even rent a proper house for a family like his? He had never made money, he had never seen the need to do so, his mother had held that a gentleman should not. His stipend as the least of the partners of his old-fashioned law firm could not meet a fraction of what it would cost to maintain his family by himself. His mother had always managed everything, as well she might between her own ample fortune and her outright life tenure of her husband's money. John's father had died when his son was a child. And only now, with sudden perverse surprise, did the son dare ask himself how such a state of things could have come about. Would it not have been more natural for his father to have arranged that he receive his inheritance on coming of age? Why this? And what—John Holt felt almost dizzy with the unfamiliar sensation of inquiring coldly into the hitherto unquestioned—could his mother have done to assure his father's making such a will?

His mother had taken good care that he should never find out. All his life he had accepted her rule. He had not failed to see that others found it harsh, but she had been good to him within the narrow confines she allowed. Not until his marriage had he ever overstepped them and perhaps not even now, except for Lily's terrible distress, would he have had the resolution to rebel. But his mother had made the error of driving him to a choice. He made it, with a sense of purpose so unfamiliar as to feel extraordinary. He leaned forward and put his hand on Lily's shoulder.

"Lily dear," he said. She twitched away. "No, please. Listen to me, dear. I've got to tell you something."

"I won't believe it," she said, her voice like lead.

"You must."

"You'll tell me you will take us away. John, I can't believe you," she said, flinging her arm across her eyes.

"I know, I know, I don't deserve to be believed. I've been—I was weak, Lily. But I've made up my mind now. Truly I mean it."

"And when will we go?" she asked. "How will you get the money?"

He did not dare say that he did not know. Also he did not want to lie to her again—not that he had ever intentionally lied, but words came too easily when it was not going to be possible to implement them.

"I'll change my work," he said. This had never occurred to him before. And having said it he felt bathed in relief, for he knew that he had not blurted out something he could not live up to. "I'll get a partnership in another firm, some newer one." (The sort of firm his mother would call 'upstarts,' he thought.) "I don't have to stay with Wright and Pettengill."

Lily turned slowly, rolling her slight body across the wide mattress until she lay on her right side, facing him. Her cheeks did not seem in the dim gaslight so waxen pale as a little while ago. Perhaps she had taken heart, he thought. She looked at him and presently said, "Do you really mean it, John?"

"Oh, I do. Believe me." He bent over to touch her with his lips. "I can't bear the way I've made you suffer—"

The door was flung open behind them. They both jumped, tense, Lily with a sharp gasp.

"John!" Mrs. Holt stood in the doorway, her stiff black taffeta gown sharp and bulky as a monument in the gaslight from the hall. "You are an hour late for dinner."

Lily's hand closed on his arm as if to tell him not to rise to his feet. He had not intended to do so. He said, "I am sorry, Mother. I sent word by Nora that Lily is not well."

"She was perfectly well this afternoon, quite well enough to play the piano. She can—"

"She is not well now."

"What is the matter with her?"

"I think you can see for yourself, Mother. Lily is upset."

"She has brought that on herself. You spoil her and indulge this nonsense with your pampering. There is nothing the matter with her."

John held Lily closer in his left arm and said, "In any case, she does not want any dinner. And I asked you not to wait for me."

"I will decide when I wish to dine."

"Very well, Mother, but I am not coming down this evening. Nora can bring me up a cup of soup or something."

"I give the orders in my house, John."

He felt Lily cringe against his shoulder. "Just as you say, Mother. It doesn't matter, I am not hungry at all. Please don't wait dinner for me any longer."

Mrs. Holt turned as if to leave the room, but stopped again. He had known that she would. She said, "I want to see you in the library, John."

"Not this evening, Mother, please. I don't want to leave Lily."

Even in shadow he could see the angry tightening of his mother's jaw. He could hear her loud, almost whistling breathing, reflected in the sharp rise and fall of her bosom as she stood silhouetted against the lighted hallway. "I am shocked," she said, in her hardest, coldest tone. "Shocked at your disloyalty. To me and to your home."

"It is all very regrettable, Mother, but it cannot be much of a surprise. Only this afternoon I tried to tell you that we will have to go away and live in a house of our own. I have promised Lily that we shall."

"*You* have promised? On the strength of what, may I ask?" The old woman's scorn should have confounded him, but instead he found himself stimulated by the surprising thought that she sounded rather ridiculous. It struck him that he had been listening all his life to remarks which he might have heard in some set, stagey drama at Daly's. Lily clasped there in his arm gave him warmth and courage. Perhaps it was true, as he had often heard and read and never dared to prove, that one strong assertion could dispel the power of a bully. His mother did not wait for his answer, as if to show by her contempt that she knew he could not have one. She only said, "Let Lily find out what your promises are worth," and shut the door behind her with a thud.

The little boys sat up stiffly at table as they had been taught to do, Seymour on Grandmama's right and Randall, perched on a volume of the Encyclopaedia, on her left. Their soft fair hair, Seymour's straight and Randall's curly, was sleek and a little damp from Nana's brushing, when she had washed their hands and faces and straightened their clothes and re-tied their full necktie bows before sending them downstairs for Sunday dinner. From her place between Randall and John at the head of the table Lily watched the children thoughtfully and wondered whether they were too young to sense that this Sunday was different from all the others which had preceded it in the rigid ritual that had been fixed by Mrs. Holt years before John Holt could first remember.

Sunday never varied. It began with a heavy pancake breakfast, followed by the ceremonial drive to St. George's, where the family pew was the scene of a discipline military in its precision and its alert obedience to the silent commands of its head. Mrs. Holt did not hold with any such nonsense as having small children slipped out and taken home before the sermon. They sat, heads up, hands folded, no fidgetting, inhumanly controlled. Church over, there followed the lengthy rite of greeting the Rector at the door and one's friends in the porch and on the pavement, as the families stood waiting in their bulky finery for their carriages to roll up one by one, and carry them home to their enormous midday dinners. The traditional menu might vary from one house to another, but within each sacred enclave it was almost certain to remain unchanged every Sunday of the year. The Holts ate a thick soup and roast beef with mashed potatoes and a sweet chosen expressly for the children, since this was the only meal of the week which they ate with their elders. Lily who loathed all milk puddings had suffered through years of Caramel Custard or Floating Island, which she was not permitted to refuse: Mrs. Holt commanded that she set an example to the boys who were required to eat everything that was put before them.

How different life would be, and, Lily dared to trust at last, how soon! In the short space of little more than a day she had built up a whole world in imagination, whose details were so clear to her that this morning as she sat watching her little boys suffer in church, she had resolved suddenly to move her family from St. George's as soon as they moved from Mrs. Holt's house. They would attend her own family's church, the Ascension, which she had scarcely entered since her marriage there, for Mrs. Holt had made that quite impossible since the death of Lily's parents. Perhaps if Eugene Randall had not lost his money and left his daughter a person not worth having married . . . had Lily really overheard Mrs. Holt say some such thing or was her imagination at work to help her through the ordeal of Sunday dinner?

She smiled at her silent, wide-eyed little boys. They looked much alike, but Seymour's face was longer than Randall's and showed already the length of jaw and upper lip which was the basis of the strong resemblance between John Holt and his mother. Randall's face was rounder and its softer contours, the wider cheekbones and the slightly cleft chin, were more a likeness to Lily than the mere unformed outlines of babyhood. Lily still thought and spoke of Randall as Baby, though he was past four, and Mrs. Holt had lately been reproving her for this. It was a habit difficult to break, for when Lily looked at Randall, she was seized by a sense of passionate tenderness evoked by the sight of his soft white neck fringed with delicate golden curls at the nape. She watched him carefully putting into his mouth spoonfuls of the cut-up roast beef, the potato, and the vegetables which had been prepared for him. He had a small appetite and sometimes there was trouble if he did not want to finish his food. Lily thought with ecstasy that after tomorrow when John should start to put his new decisions into effect, her children would begin to be her own. Soon they would be settled in their own house, away and safe from Mrs. Holt; Lily herself would sit at the foot of her own table with her sons on either side of her and her husband at the head. She could hardly dare to believe it true, but all of yesterday had gone into making plans with John, who had scarcely left her side since Friday night when the miracle, as she thought of it, had happened. It was not that she had really doubted his devotion before, only that fear and suspense and disappointment had made her feel as if she had. Even today, quite sure at last that John meant to carry out his plans, it seemed beyond belief that she was to be freed from her sufferings. In church she had fervently thanked God, she had whispered into her gloved hands a spontaneous torrent of gratitude.

"May I carve more beef for you, Mother?" asked John.

"No thank you." Mrs. Holt's voice was low and curt.

"Lily?"

"No, dear." She gave her husband a tender smile to tell him that she was too happy to have much appetite.

There was silence again. Nora came, with her heavy tread and her sullen face, to remove the platter in front of John and change the plates. The children watched her, their eyes round and solemn. When they had finished their caramel pudding, eagerly spooning up the last drops of brown syrup from their plates, their grandmother sat for a moment as if to reimpose the full force of her authority on her family. Then she rose from her chair with a sweep of black skirts and led the silent procession in file up the stairs from the basement dining-room to the drawing-room on the floor above. There in the doorway she bent down stiffly to offer the angle of her harsh chin to be kissed, by way of dismissing the children to the nursery for their naps. But instead of moving along to the next flight of stairs, Seymour stood still. He was waiting for his mother who was just reaching the ground-floor hall landing, followed by John. And Randall as usual did what Seymour did. The little boys wanted to kiss their parents too, they were still of the age when every parting and every greeting must be marked by a kiss.

"Go upstairs, children," said Mrs. Holt.

"Yes, Grandmama," said Seymour, echoed by Randall. But they ran towards their parents.

"Seymour!" said Mrs. Holt from the drawing-room doorway.

"We're going," cried Seymour. But he had his arms round his mother and Randall was jumping up and down, waiting his turn.

Mrs. Holt took a step forward. John Holt moved past Lily and the children and with a slight bow gestured his mother into the drawing-room.

"The children are to go straight upstairs to Nana," she said.

"The children want to kiss their mother first," said John. Lily, with Randall's warm arms hugging her and Seymour clinging to her skirts, felt a great lurch of joy. She could scarcely believe this, she was overcome, her legs felt weak beneath her. She buried her face in Randall's neck to hide the tears that she could not restrain, though she knew that the sight would infuriate Mrs. Holt. Oh, she thought, what does it matter, what can it matter now, when we are so soon to be free. She dried her eyes quickly as she bent over the children, whispering to them to mind their grandmother and run upstairs at once for their naps.

But in the drawing-room, sitting over after-dinner coffee with John and his mother, in silence as oppressive as the maroon plush draperies and the inlaid ebony furniture, Lily had a frightening thought. Always on Sunday afternoons John took the boys for a walk after their naps. This was an old Chelsea custom which Lily knew he greatly enjoyed. He had often told her of his father and himself, a little boy of five, dressed in their Sunday best, walking sedately west on Twenty-third Street as far as the pleasant green bank of the river, where most of their friends and neighbors also promenaded, taking the air and greeting one another with stately bows and sweeps of their high beaver hats. John had many reasons, Lily knew, for keeping affectionately to this custom; not the least must be, as it had been for his father, the pleasure of an hour's freedom from the iron regimen of Mrs. Holt; perhaps from Mrs. Holt herself? Lily would have enjoyed her own daring in pursuing such a thought, except that she had become so worried about what was to happen this afternoon. She was afraid to stay alone in the house with Mrs. Holt after John and the boys had gone out. She wished she could go with them. But the weather was bad, grey and lowering, and the streets impossible for her. The pavements were thick with slush and melting snow. John and the boys could wear high cloth-topped galoshes, but Lily could not manage her skirts in such conditions, and did not even own any footgear designed for walking such as no lady would have occasion to do.

Once again John surprised her. He set down his coffee-cup and broke the silence to say quietly, "Mother, it is so bad underfoot today that I wonder if you would mind my taking the horses and driving out? Then Lily could go with us too."

Lily's heart pumped hard under her tight dove-colored basque.

Mrs. Holt's nostrils narrowed and she said, barely moving her lips, "This is Reilly's afternoon off."

"I know. I don't need him. I thought I could hire a buggy at the stables and drive our horses in it myself."

Lily watched Mrs. Holt anxiously. She saw that the old lady wanted peremptorily to refuse; yet to do so before Lily would be to put herself in a position so unreasonably disagreeable as to be untenable even for her. She only said, "Well, I suppose . . ." and rose abruptly to leave the room. John stood up and escorted her to the door; then he returned to stand beside Lily's chair, looking down at her.

"Oh, John!" she said, clasping his hands and holding them to her breast, "how sweet of you! You understood!"

He smiled. His face wore an expression of calm and of something which Lily would later remember as a strength that she had never known in him before. She did not realize how much assurance he had gained in the brief time, not two full days, since he had faced the truths about his mother and his family and himself, and found the determination to act like a man. He had even told Lily last night of his feeling that once he had made the break and established himself independently he would for the first time have won his mother's real respect, and he believed that she would turn over to him sufficent funds, which were rightly his, to make their new life comfortable. He bent over Lily and said, "I thought we might drive over to Murray Hill and have a look at some of those new houses going up there. We'll just drive past them today, to get a general idea . . ."

She held his hand to her cheek and caressed it. "It's too wonderful," she whispered. "Too good to be true. You darling!" She looked up at him with wet eyes. He kissed her and patted her shoulder.

"I'll walk over to the stables," he said, "and be back with the buggy in a little over half an hour. You be downstairs here, all ready with the boys."

The children, pink-cheeked from their naps and blissfully excited at the prospect of the drive, were all dressed to go out, standing at the drawing-room window watching eagerly for their father. Lily hovered behind them, feeling in her own joy and excitement like a child herself. But she must remember to be watchful, there were so many rules to obey, so much to fear . . . "Darlings," she whispered, gently placing the boys' mittened hands close to their sides, "remember not to touch the curtains . . . *don't* press your noses to the glass . . . **you** know Grandmama doesn't like you to look out the front windows . . ."

"But we have to watch," cried Seymour, craning his neck. "We have to watch for Papa."

"Watch for Papa," echoed Randall, standing on tiptoe.

"Yes of course . . . yes. He'll be here in a moment."

But Lily looked at the tomb-shaped onyx clock on the mantel. It was fifty minutes since John had left for the stables. He should be here. Perhaps it had taken longer than he expected to arrange for the livery buggy. She was uneasy, but principally, in some gnawing way, about Mrs. Holt. This plan for the afternoon had seemed from the very first too good to be true and Lily was haunted with the fear, until now unrecognized, that somehow Mrs. Holt intended to spoil it. Oh dear, she thought, I mustn't worry, I must stop worrying. She put an arm round each of the boys and asked them, "Shall we go over to the piano and sing a song while we wait for Papa?"

Randall clapped his hands but Seymour shook his head. Then Randall, seeing his mistake, shook his curly, capped head too. "No," they cried, "we have to watch for Papa!"

The ten minutes to the full hour had flown. Now Lily felt real fear. Where was John? She had been hoping he would arrive and take them out before Mrs. Holt should find some reason for leaving the library at the second floor back, where she sat when she was alone, to come downstairs with some purpose in mind which would prevent their going out after all. As if to confirm her fear, Lily, listening hard for the horses in the street outside, heard instead the heavy, even step of Mrs. Holt upstairs. She heard it pace from the library at the other end of the house, along the second-floor hall. Crouching there with an arm round each of the boys, Lily held her breath and listened in acute suspense. Would she hear the horses, would they come trotting quickly, quickly as she was praying? Would Mrs. Holt by a miracle go along the passage to her bedroom overhead at the front of the house, instead of down here to wreak some malice against Lily?

No. Lily's heart lurched sickly as the footsteps attacked the stairs, deliberately, relentlessly. Down they came, one by one, while Lily held the boys, one in each arm, and prayed almost aloud for John to hurry. She strained harder than ever to hear the first sound of the horses trotting up the street. Mrs. Holt was halfway down the stairs, then she was almost at the bottom, when Lily started with a low cry. There was a sound outside in the street, but not the trotting of horses; Lily heard a man running. Mrs. Holt's footsteps passed before the closed door of the drawing-room and Lily peered sickly through the window to see a youth running all out of breath, as fast as possible, straight to the gate, through the yard, up the high front steps. . . .

"What's that?" cried Randall, and Seymour said, "Where's Papa?"

"Sh— sh—" Lily did not know that the children could feel her trembling in monstrous terror. "Sh—" She strained to listen. She heard the heavy front door opened by Mrs. Holt. She heard the breathless gasping voice of the man, a flood of something in a heavy brogue. She moved across the room with clumsy, stumbling steps, dragging the children, clutching their shoulders. It was Seymour who reached out and opened the drawing-room door. Lily stood there, gazing at the tall black figure of Mrs. Holt, sharp and solid in the open doorway, with the panting man facing her on the threshold.

"Accident?" the cold heavy voice of Mrs. Holt was asking. "An accident?"

"Yes mum. T'was that roan o' Mr. Duryea's. Bolted, it did, acrost the yard and Mr. Holt, mum, he tried to stop it." The man's voice wavered and broke. "Oh, Mother o' God, mum!"

"Control yourself! What happened?" Mrs. Holt's tone was like a blow in the face.

"He—he slupped, mum. There's ice round the trough, he was standin' there waitin' while we harnessed, and this roan broke out, ugly like, rearin' right up in Duryea's gig . . . ye see, mum? Ye see how t'was?"

Lily swayed on her feet, clinging to the children. "Was?" she heard Mrs. Holt say. "You mean. What do you mean? My son?"

"Och, God forgive me, mum, it's tryin' I am to tell ye—he's—he's— t'was his head, mum, got kicked. He's—"

"No!" shrieked Lily. She howled like an animal. "No, oh no. No . . . No . . ."

CHAPTER 2

It was hot, Seymour thought, walking home from school; as hot as July. It did not seem like May at all. The suffocating heaviness of New York's summer had already closed in like a hot lid clamped over a stewpot, and Seymour as he trudged along was thinking of freedom and Hare Island. He could smell the good salt air in imagination, and instead of this drooping, dusty yard, his mind's eye was full of dories, dinghies, masts, barnacled rocks and lobster-pots. His steps lagged as he turned in along the path through the front yard, counting up the weeks and then the days until the fifteenth of June. He had better hurry these last few steps, in order to stay out of trouble; he had turned in at the gate at the stipulated minute of half past three. His grandmother always sat waiting for him in her red satin chair in the bay window of the library at the back of the house, but she knew to the instant when he arrived home. She had Nana or a maid posted to watch for him. The front door always swung open just as he started to climb the high stoop.

It was out of the question for him to be late, but he would have liked it today. He had spring fever, he felt both listless and restless, and dreadfully disinclined for the daily rite of reporting to his grandmother. He wanted to dawdle and waste time and whack at things with a switch. He would have liked even better to go over with Tom Berry and Willy Dean to the shore of the river where he used to go walking on Sundays with Papa. Some boys teased Seymour for not being allowed to go where he pleased and play as he liked; others advised him to ignore his grandmother.

"What can she do to you?" asked Willy Dean. "Give you a licking? What do you care, she couldn't hurt much, an old lady like that. You ought to feel my Pa's right arm." The inference was that a boy of thirteen was rather fortunate to be without a father who could exercise his authority in the coal cellar or the wood shed.

"Aw, no," Seymour had to reply. "It's just that—" He could not explain. Sometimes he wanted not to be able to explain to himself. It

[34]

always came round to Mama and the way it was with her and Grandmama. If Seymour were late from school Grandmama could actually find a way to blame it on Mama. Seymour was wise far beyond his age in ways of keeping the dubious peace. When there were scenes he preferred not to be the cause of them, and once they had started, it was only the course of prudence to prefer to be on Grandmama's side.

He dragged his feet, moving up the front walk. He was disgusted at the thought of the afternoon which yawned before him. While he was playing some baby game with Randall in the back yard, with Grandmama watching from her window, Tom and Willy would be wading in the rocky shallows of the river bank, or fishing from Old Rory's Pier where they were strictly forbidden to go; and when they left the river to start home they would stop at Mickle's Ice Cream Parlor on Tenth Avenue, also forbidden, and eat three-colored ice cream out of wobbly-footed tin dishes with spoons that even Mama said, shuddering, were probably never washed. And Mama did not often get in a word about such matters.

Seymour climbed the high steps of the front stoop, watching the door swing open for him. But instead of Nana or Minnie standing behind it, there was Mama peering round the edge of the door with her finger to her lips. She was smiling at Seymour and bending down for his kiss and his hug. But he held back. He had the familiar sensation of creeping uneasiness which presaged some kind of trouble, and he said, as he laid his round school cap on the hall table, "Mama, you mustn't, you know that. You'd better go back to Randall." He waved at the open door of the drawing-room, which ought to be closed, with Mama and Randall working at the piano together until Grandmama should give the signal for the boys to go out to play.

"I only wanted to meet you, darling," said Lily. Her high voice was more like a child's than Seymour's.

"She doesn't like it, Mama. If she doesn't hear the piano—" He thrust his head into the drawing-room and signalled Randall to play and play hard. Then he started for the stairs. Lily stood there, pouting. "But you haven't kissed me," she whined. Seymour pecked quickly at her cheek and hurried up the stairs. He did not look behind him, he knew that if he did he would see his mother standing there moping, her eyes full of tears.

As usual his grandmother was sitting straight and stiff in her chair, with her back turned to the door as Seymour opened it. She said, "Good afternoon, Seymour."

He did not miss the rasp in her voice.

"Good afternoon, Grandmama." He went round to stand before her. There was no nonsense about kisses here. Seymour was pronounced too old for such sloppiness except at bedtime and breakfast time.

"Why did your mother open the door, Seymour?"

"I don't know, Grandmama—she just—"

"Just. Either she practises with Randall or she doesn't."

It went through Seymour's mind for the thousandth time that his grandmother ought not to say such things to him, but he knew very well why she did say them. He had only to glance at the plush-covered table to recapture the sensation that he was eavesdropping while she talked to his father, and this felt also as if he were eavesdropping upon himself. His grandmother talked to him with the same mixture of intimacy and command, but she never treated him as her equal any more than she had Papa, a grown man. Seymour stood before her the picture of deference, but his bland expression concealed the thought: she never looks a day older, she's seventy-six years old and she may live forever. I wonder what would happen if I simply quit obeying her. He knew very well why he was not prepared to quit, though he had never pursued all the reasons, it was really unnecessary. They all led to his mother and Randall.

"Did you bring home the corrected Latin exercise, Seymour?" There had been trouble about that yesterday.

"Yes, Grandmama." He opened his school satchel, and handed her the copy-book. She can't understand a word of it, he thought. But he had to admire her for acting as if she could. She sat frowning over the pages and, nodding at the teacher's notations, gave him back the book. Then she looked at her watch while Seymour anticipated each of her actions.

"It is time for Randall to stop," she said. "You may go and tell him. Take him out and play at something quiet, in the shade of the ailanthus tree. The sun is hot today."

"Very hot." Seymour wished he dared speak as sourly as he felt.

His grandmother moved her head slightly, with the upward tilt which was the signal for dismissal. Seymour left the room, torn between relief and the prospective dullness of the hour ahead. He went down to the drawing-room and, without concern for interrupting Randall in the middle of a passage, told him it was time to go out.

Lily raised her hand to hold Seymour off. Most of the time she acted like a frightened lamb, but curiously, when she was practising with Randall she became as determined as Mrs. Holt herself. She motioned Randall to keep on, and Seymour stood there for a moment watching the two. Randall worked willingly; his fingers which should be stiff and grubby like any small boy's, were agile and clean, and his hands moved silkily up and down the keyboard, their backs motionless, only the fingers working with the fluid facility which was the result of talent and good teaching and hard work. He was working on a passage of *Gradus ad Parnassum*. Seymour, who had no great opinion of Randall's capacities in any other respect, who often thought him a tiresome baby, had to admit that Randall already could play the piano better than anyone Seymour had ever heard; and he knew that this was the second of his grandmother's two reasons for allowing Randall his music lessons and so much of his mother's time and company. The first lay in the realm of all that Seymour, with shrewdness far beyond his age, did not admit to himself. He stood listening to Randall and watching his mother, lightly poised on the edge of her chair, one hand raised and its forefinger flicking off the first beat of every measure. Seymour wondered how on earth she could keep this up, day after day. He had heard Professor Mundt say that much of Randall's progress was due to his mother's exacting supervision of his practising. It seemed to Seymour a great fuss about a lot of nonsense. It always had seemed so; he remembered innumerable moments when sheer boredom had goaded him to interrupt the practice session by some kind of outbreak for which he might expect to be drastically punished. Since, however, all punishments were his grandmother's absolute dictature, nothing much happened if Seymour broke out in this way. Except the time he burned the piano.

He ought to yell at them now, he thought. Letting them finish their page wasn't worth the trouble there would be if Grandmama did not soon see him and Randall going out to play in the back yard. He was just opening his mouth for a real sound-off when he was saved the trouble by a long, startling roll of thunder. It was so dim in the heavily-curtained drawing-room that he had not noticed the sudden darkness which had blanketed the glaring afternoon. Hooray! he thought. He had not counted on such luck as a thunderstorm. His mother jumped up, squealing; she was afraid of storms and horses and water and fire and almost everything else. Randall stopped practising and Lily ran to Seymour and threw her arms round him and buried her face in his neck.

"Oh!" she cried. "Oh, Seymour, I'm so frightened. Mama's so frightened."

"Pshaw," he said roughly. "It's nothing, Mama." He patted her shoulder. The rain began to fall in splashing sheets.

Inevitably the door opened and Mrs. Holt said, "You will not be able to play out of doors, boys." She stood watching Lily clinging to Seymour. "You," she said to him, "may go down and work at your workbench."

Seymour's polite reply was smothered by a tremendous clap of thunder; lightning blazed past the windows and Lily screamed and quivered.

"Now, now," said Mrs. Holt. "Don't be stupid, Lily. Seymour, you may go."

"Oh, leave him here," wailed Lily. She was on her knees with her arms round Seymour's neck and her face buried against his shoulder. "Please leave him here!"

"Nonsense, nothing is going to hurt you." Mrs. Holt took a step forward and Seymour unconsciously held his mother closer. "I want you to take Randall upstairs to Nana, Lily, and if you cannot control yourself, at least remain in your own room until the storm is over."

Lily clung to Seymour; he felt her stiffen and hold her breath as another flash and thunderclap shook the house. Randall had slid off his piano-stool and was hovering near Lily and Seymour, also trying to comfort his mother. "Don't be frightened, Mama," he said in his small, high voice. He patted her arm. "We won't let it hurt you, will we, Seymour?"

"Never mind, Randall," said Mrs. Holt. "Nor you, Seymour. Go and do as I say."

She spoke rather more gently than usual, and Seymour wondered if she could be feeling sorry for his mother. He disentangled himself from Lily's arms and said, "Yes, Grandmama. Would you like me to take Randall upstairs first?" He knew this was a ridiculous suggestion,

Randall was perfectly capable of walking upstairs by himself. Nine years old!

"Never mind," said Mrs. Holt.

Seymour left the room and went down the basement stairs to the corner of the cellar where his workbench had been set up, close to a window-grating which gave him light from one of the high windows opening on the back yard. There was also a gas-jet directly overhead at a height that he could easily reach. Since last year he had been permitted to light the gas instead of asking somebody to do it for him. He lit it; then he took off his jacket with a whistle of relief and flung it on a canvas-covered hulk standing in the corner.

He should have hung the jacket neatly on the hook provided for it, but there was satisfaction in not doing so, or any of dozens of other equally trifling things, if he could get away with it. He stood for a time eyeing the model which he was in the midst of building, the model of an imaginary ferry-boat which should be an ingenious improvement over the clumsy bloated side-wheelers that he had seen all his life, plying the river to the Jersey shore and back. Ever since he could remember he had had this knack for making odd and original boats out of bits of wood and tin and string and wire, and it was an established habit in the house for everybody to save such odds and ends for Seymour. Some of his ideas came from watching the stream of shipping which moved up and down the Hudson only two blocks west of the house, where he went to watch and dream and idle whenever he could contrive to drag Nana or Mama, and inevitably Randall, on the walks which alternated with those dreary stupid hours in the back yard. But his favorite boats were suggested by the wonderful riches of Hare Island; the ugly efficient sword-fishing craft, the dories of the lobstermen, the graceful classes of sailing boats, racing sloops and yawls and little skidoos; and best of all the beautiful yachts that belonged to the Newport swells, which moored in the harbor in full sight of the house when they were out on cruises.

On a shelf above his bench stood a finished two-masted schooner yacht in full sail, one of the best boats he had ever made. Usually he gave his boats to Mama when they were finished and she kept them proudly in her room and treasured them. This schooner belonged to her too, but Seymour had brought it back to his workshop because he meant to make a change in the rigging. That was intricate work and he was not always in the mood to do it. Today he found he did not much want to go on with his new ferry-boat either. He stood at the bench turning over the model in his hands, measuring and re-measuring a piece of the hull that did not fit properly, and trying to get up the will-power to take the whole thing apart and cut the central piece over again. But his attention wandered. He thought about all sorts of things . . . whether Tom and Willy had got caught in the storm out on Old Rory's Pier . . . whether Mama was feeling better now and whether Randall had really been sent up to Nana or allowed to stay with her . . . whether (and here he tried very hard not to think any more) he oughtn't to hang up his jacket instead of leaving it where it was. Actually he was not thinking about the jacket at all, but about the old piano underneath it, muffled in canvas. He hated it to be there and that was exactly why it was there. "That will be your punishment," Grandmama had said. "That piano will stay there in your own corner of the house and it will stay as long as the house stays. You will keep it and never throw it out and it will have taught you something, Seymour."

She ought to have thrown it away. She ought at least to have sold it to the old cabinetmaker who had said there was quite a bit of useful rosewood in it. It was only the inside that was burnt out. And she hadn't had any right to decide about it anyway, for it belonged to Mama, it had been one of her wedding-presents from her father; Mama had told Seymour how he had bought it for her only a few months before he lost all his money and died. Seymour wished that all the men in his family had not got such a way of dying and leaving every-thing in control of Grandmama. He had never known either of his grandfathers; he had only heard vaguely of an Uncle George, Mama's brother who had died long ago; and Seymour remembered all too vividly Papa's death only five years ago. Randall was already very vague about Papa and knew him mostly as a name because Mama so often spoke it, but Seymour remembered him perfectly and often tried to act as if Papa were not dead at all, but only away for a time. One of Seymour's favorite notions was a scene that repeated itself often in his imagina-tion. Papa was all dressed and ready to go away on some journey; his valises and travelling-rug stood ready in the front hall, where Seymour himself was standing with Mama in the open drawing-room doorway, while Grandmama stood in the vestibule cutting off their full view of

Papa while she said good-bye to him. Then Seymour would walk forward and politely bow Grandmama aside, and Papa would say, "That's right, Seymour, you must be the man here while I am away. Take good care of Mama and Grandmama and Randall, and see that everybody. . . ." But Seymour was never very clear after that just what his father would have had everybody do. Move to the different house that Papa had talked about that afternoon when Seymour had been hidden under the library table? Not very well without Papa.

He began slowly to separate the glued parts of the ferry-boat. His fingers worked accurately even though he wasn't thinking much about the change he was going to make in the hull. The dark heavy rain fell with a sullen splash outside. Seymour liked the sense of being safely shut away down here, released from the boredom it would have been to have had to play out of doors with Randall. There were moments when he liked to be with Randall but they had to come about of themselves and not be decreed by Grandmama or Nana . . . He had got the glued ferry-boat apart now and stood turning over the pieces and trying to feel interested enough to start over again, but this was one of those times when that looming bulk in the corner made him think about one thing when he really wanted to think about another. . . .

It was only a couple of years ago, a winter afternoon just before school closed for the Christmas holidays. He was still too young to walk back and forth alone and Nana always took and fetched him. He had finished at school a Christmas present for Mama, a small album in which he had copied out in shiny white ink *The Night Before Christmas*. The pages of the album were of bright red paper, and each one was elaborately decorated with pictures and snow-scenes illuminated with sticky white crystals scattered onto glue; the horns of the reindeer were carved from tiny slivers of wood, and Santa Claus's beard was a delightful blob of real white wool, surreptitiously picked from the nap of a blanket. Seymour was very proud of it. As soon as Nana opened the front door he made a rush for the drawing-room, he could not wait to give his present to Mama. Nana called him back; Seymour knew he should obey her and besides she was perfectly right when she said he should put his present away and save it to give to Mama on Christmas morning. But at the moment he did not care, not even when Nana said, "Your grandmother first, Master Seymour. Go straight upstairs to the library."

"I won't," he answered, which was a dreadful naughtiness, and ran to his mother sitting at the piano with Randall. He thrust the album at her but she only smiled a little, shook her head, put her finger to her lips, and pointed to the ceiling to remind Seymour to go up to report to Grandmama. Randall kept on playing. It was some kind of silly exercise which sounded like three notes struck over and over again. Seymour hated it. He hated every single thing he could see and feel and hear, the room, Mama, Randall, the piano, all of it. He stood for a moment beside Mama but she paid no further attention to him and presently he turned and went away, slamming the door behind him.

Then there was trouble with Grandmama for what he had done, and he was sent to spend an hour alone in the night-nursery, standing in the corner with his face to the wall. He had hidden the album inside his jacket, and standing there he took it out and tore his beautiful present to the smallest bits he could. When that was done and the floor around him littered with shreds, he stood and listened with the sharpest care in order to place each person in the house. Grandmama was still in the library, one always heard her heavy step along the hall when she left that room. Randall had finished practising, Seymour heard him coming into the day-nursery with Nana. That meant that Mama would have gone to her own room. It was quite late in the afternoon, but not yet so nearly dark that Minnie would go through the house drawing the thickly stuffed curtains and lighting the gas chandeliers. But Seymour knew that she soon would do that and he began to think. All his life he had seen Nora or her successors lighting the gas cocks of the chandeliers with thin wax tapers attached to the end of a long wooden pole that stood in a corner of the pantry. The tapers were kept in a drawer nearby, and so were a lot of big sulphur matches.

Everything seemed to be on Seymour's side. Nobody saw him slip through the halls and tiptoe down the flights of stairs to the pantry. Minnie was not in the pantry when he pushed the swinging door open a crack and peered in. He crept to the drawer, seized a handful of wax tapers and several matches and crammed them into the waistband of his blouse. Still unnoticed, he went to the drawing-room and silently closed the door behind him. He laid open the lid of the square piano. Then he took the bunch of tapers, scratched a match—the most strictly forbidden of all forbidden things—lit the tapers, and flung the whole bunch together with the rest of the matches right into the insides of the piano.

Out of all the confusion afterwards, Mama's cries and wails, Randall's terrified screaming, the yelping prayers of the servants to Holy Mary and all the saints, the sickening acrid smell of burning varnish and felt, Grandmama's most awful voice, the lowest-pitched but loudest she ever used, Reilly slinging buckets of water into the smouldering piano, the final wreck of the drawing-room, its maroon plush and festooned gimp and crimson wallpaper and podgy chairs and sofas dumped on their backs or waving their silly feet in the air, Seymour remembered most vividly the way it had ended, with Grandmama standing before the marble chimneypiece, whose swagged plush drapery hung crazily awry dripping pink water on the hearth. The servants had been dismissed and there was nobody in the room but Grandmama and Mama and the boys. Lily was whimpering and trying to edge towards the door, with Randall's hand clutched in hers.

"No," said Grandmama, in that voice like something out of the Bible. "You are to stay here, Lily. Randall too." Randall only looked up at her with great blue eyes swimming with bewilderment. Seymour stood as far from her as he could go, off in the corner by the windows, staring at the toes of his boots. He knew that if he looked up he would see Mama's hurt and puzzled face, reproachful but not angry; she had never been angry with him or with Randall, and Seymour knew very well why not. Grandmama's anger was as much as any house and any family could contain.

"Now why," she intoned at Seymour, "did you do this wicked, this unspeakably evil thing?"

There was silence. Seymour stared stubbornly at his feet, pressing his lips together and grinding his back teeth. He knew that his ears must be fiery red; he could feel them tingling.

"Answer me!"

Seymour remained silent.

"Seymour!" Such a tone must be audible from the cellar to the roof.

Seymour began to feel very queer, as if his head were swelling up and likely to snap from his neck and sail away like a freed balloon. He swallowed, he drew long breaths through his nose, and he did not say a word.

Then Mama said, in a trembling whisper, "Answer Grandmama, Seymour."

For Mama's sake he would have spoken if he could think of anything to say. They were all watching him, he felt their eyes piercing and boring and trying to take him apart. He licked his lips quickly, several times, and then pinched them shut again.

"Please," he heard his mother gasp, and he knew she was trying to hold off Grandmama.

He raised his head and stared at the sodden wall—why had they got the whole room in such a mess, anyway?—and said through his teeth, "I don't know."

"That is no answer," said Grandmama. "You will answer my question. Why did you try to burn up the piano?"

Seymour kept his head bent and made it clear to all of them that this was neither shame nor abasement; it was defiance. He said nothing more. He heard his mother try again to plead with him, then Grandmama snapped, "That will do, Lily. I am here." To Seymour she said, "You will tell me at once why you did this thing. You will give me your reason."

He jerked his head up and opened his mouth and shouted, "I DON'T KNOW."

He saw his grandmother's long, wrinkled face harden into a shape he had never seen before, a jagged oblong like the faces of the stone animals carved on the buildings of the Zoo. She seemed to have turned the color of stone, too; she looked a strange shade of grey. Seymour was desperately frightened and he had known the feeling in varying degrees before. But for the first time he also felt something else, a sharp sensation like a knife-thrust through the sick lump of fear settled in his gorge. This was a sense of unexpected triumph, the last thing in the world he could have looked for today. If he stuck to his guns and refused to answer her question he could win hands down over Grandmama no matter what she resorted to in the effort to make him speak. Let her beat him, which she almost never had, for she was proud of her principle that she could train and mould children by force of will and character alone, without resorting to physical punishment.

"This insolence," she said, "is going to cost you dearer than all your shocking mischief. I will have your answer, Seymour, and you will remain in total disgrace until you have given it. Nobody will speak to you or notice you or act as if you were in the house. You will sit with your hands folded, on a straight chair in the night nursery and you will sit there exactly as long as you fail to answer my question."

"He—he—" whispered Lily.

Grandmama turned to her and said, "Go upstairs, Lily. Go away and take Randall with you."

Seymour watched them go. He ought to feel more frightened than before to find himself all alone with Grandmama but instead he found he did not care very much. He listened indifferently while she said, "I am going to have your answer, Seymour, your reason for destroying Randall's piano—"

"It wasn't Randall's," he muttered. "It was Mama's."

"Do not contradict me. All this will be taken account of in your punishment. It was Randall's, and he is to have a new one, a better one. The best piano that can be bought."

Seymour stood looking at Grandmama with dull disinterest. What was it to him if she bought another piano, or a dozen pianos? He could not care about any of it any more.

"And you are going to pay for it," said Grandmama. Seymour stared as if to point out the silliness of ordering him to buy a piano on his allowance of five cents a week.

"That is insolence too," she said. "I see the expression on your face. I tell you you will buy Randall a new piano, and when you are older you will see what I meant. Money has no meaning to you now. One day it will. You will find out when—"

"It was Mama's piano!" cried Seymour. To interrupt Grandmama was a terrible thing, and he did it without even hesitating. "I'll buy *Mama* a new piano!"

"Go upstairs!" said his grandmother in a thundering bellow. "Do as I said. Sit on that straight cane chair in the corner of the night nursery and if you move a muscle I will be there to deal with you."

He started to walk stiffly from the room.

"And," she said, "in case you think buying Randall a new piano with money that has no meaning is not much of a punishment, you may think about the piano you have just destroyed. It is going to remain where you will have to think about it."

That was when she had decreed that the burnt-out wreck was to stay in Seymour's work-place in the cellar, a disgusting reproach to his memory and his eyes. At the moment that too had not seemed like the dire punishment she said she meant it to be. He had learned in fact to ignore it most of the time; it was just a lumbering bulk standing there in the corner. But sometimes like today he felt cranky and snarling and confused, sometimes he had a sense that Grandmama when she punished him was trying in fact to punish Mama—but for what? And why all this fuss about a piano, any piano, and what difference whose piano it was supposed to be? Seymour stood at his bench, studying the separated parts of the new boat, trying to get into the mood to carve down the hull so that it would fit better when he put the boat together again. But he could not feel interested, his attention wandered everywhere that he hated it to go instead of staying here to do what he wanted. He felt jumpy and rough. Each of his thoughts—Grandmama, Mama, Randall, pianos, boats, making things, doing things—was more annoying than another. Suddenly he seized the beautiful finished schooner from the shelf and holding it in both hands he brought it down with a crash on the edge of the old burned piano. The smashed pieces fell around his feet on the cement floor and Seymour raised his right foot and stamped on them with his heel, over and over again.

That day when Seymour burnt the piano Lily for the one time in her life forced the courage to try to intercede with Mrs. Holt. Seymour had been sitting upstairs for hours, sullen and defiant in his refusal to give a reason for what he had done. Between the intervals when the old woman had gone up to interrogate him, Lily had been hovering outside the night nursery, hoping to help him, but too frightened to disobey the order that forbade her to speak to him. She wanted to advise him to say anything rather than drag out the stupid punishment. She understood the explosive mixture of rebellion and jealousy which had driven him, but she herself could not have justified it in words: how could a child?

She knocked on the library door and entered, trembling, to face her mother-in-law. Mrs. Holt was sitting stiffly in her chair by the fire, staring at the coals. She raised her bushy eyebrows as Lily appeared, but her manner was rather less harsh than usual as she said, "Well?"

Lilly swallowed apprehensively and tried to keep her voice calm. "I thought," she said. "I wanted—"

"Sit down."

Timidly she took the other red satin chair across the hearth. She was about to speak, but Mrs. Holt anticipated her. She said, "I suppose you want to talk to me about Seymour?"

Lily nodded, with her eyes cast down. She said, "You know, it really was my piano, Mother Holt. He was very naughty, but—"

"I know it was your piano. Have you the money to buy another for Randall?"

Lily shook her head; her lips trembled and she said, "I wish I had. If it would make any difference with you about Seymour."

"Not the least difference, Lily. He must be punished. I can perfectly well buy another piano. But I wonder whether I can root this terrible streak of temper and destructiveness out of Seymour." She spoke thoughtfully.

Lily looked up, drawing a long breath and praying for courage. "Are you sure this is the way to do it?" she asked. Her heart beat wildly. Oh, she thought, how I hope I don't set her off. "Is it possible you could be too strict with him?" She was frightened at her own temerity and afraid it would desert her. To her great surprise the old woman, instead of lashing out at her, said slowly, "In the circumstances I don't think so." She paused as if considering something; then she said, "Seymour has too many qualities like my husband."

"Oh." Lily had never before heard John Holt's father mentioned. She sat back and looked at the old woman and tried to imagine what she meant. For a long time there was no sound but the faint spurt and hiss of flaring coals. Lily murmured at last, "John never spoke to me about his father."

"He scarcely knew him. My husband died when John was six years old. And I had no wish to keep his memory alive."

Lily had never known Mrs. Holt in such a mood, never could she have thought her human enough to venture a confidence. Many questions passed through her mind but she did not dare ask them. Her silence appeared to placate the old woman. They sat in a phenomenal moment of comity, which they had never once shared; and though Lily was a silly and unreasoning creature she grasped, beyond her fears and her anxiety for Seymour, that the old woman perhaps unconsciously was invoking her understanding if not her sympathy. It had never occurred to her that this rigid, bitter character could ever have been pliant enough to suffer hurts such as she habitually meted out.

"My husband," said Mrs. Holt slowly, looking into the fire, "was a dissolute, passionate, violent-tempered rotter. I did not know it when I married him. I found out afterwards."

"Did you," asked Lily softly, "were you—?"

Mrs. Holt sighed. It was like the silly fool to think in such terms.

"Of course I was in love with him," she answered brusquely. "I was young once too. And nobody remembers it now, but I was thought handsome and clever. It was supposed to be a very good match."

"He—I suppose he was well off?"

"Very. Rich, splendid to look at. I expected a good life." She paused and knit her brows, while Lily wondered whether she would go on talking. She said, "Within six months of our marriage I scarcely ever saw him. He was always away, racing or gambling, always with men like himself and the women they consort with. There is nothing," she said, her craggy face contorted, "that I do not know about such men and what they do to their wives and children. He was away on a debauch for a whole week when my son was born."

Lily sat forward, dumb with surprise. It was not the story which amazed her so much as Mrs. Holt's startling capitulation to the impulse to tell it. Once having breached her reserve the old woman went on talking. "So perhaps you can understand," she said, "that the single purpose of my life has been to make of my own son, and now of your two, men who could not resemble a hair of my husband's head. For that one needs authority—and my husband was in no position to deny it."

So that, thought Lily, is why he had to leave her all his money and nothing directly to John. I wonder if he could have known what the result would be. She did not know what to say. She had it on the tip of her tongue to ask whether John or either of her own boys had ever given Mrs. Holt real reason to suppose they could resemble her husband. Merely these outbreaks of Seymour's temper? And surely not Randall, that angelic sweet-natured little boy. She thought of her John, and said mildly, "You couldn't have worried about John. He was so good, so gentle—"

"Because he never had a chance to be otherwise."

Lily wondered. The old woman went on. "It would have been better had he not married. I never meant him to."

"I know that. I've always known you didn't like me."

"I should not have liked better any wife of John's."

"But I loved him so much," said Lily, as if such a reason could at this date have softened her mother-in-law. Mrs. Holt's face tightened; she glanced witheringly at Lily. To Sabina Holt the word "love" had long been a synonym for damnation. If love be pure, it must be eloquent of her own sufferings; if impure, the symbol of her husband's depravity. This sentimental fool here could not grasp that, nor realize that John Holt's death, however tragic, appeared to his mother a vindication of her dictum that he must never leave her, least of all at the importuning of a wife. If he had had no wife he would not be dead. What was the use, thought the old woman. She was beginning to regret already having talked so freely to Lily. Perhaps it had been a mistake. But having done it, she would leave matters as they were.

"You may go upstairs to Seymour," she said, looking away, "and put him to bed. I know why he burnt the piano; I thought it necessary to make him say."

"I truly don't believe he can, Mother Holt. He won't do such a dreadful thing again."

"If he does, he will go through with his punishment."

When Randall was left in the drawing-room with Mama and Grandmama he listened with delight to the heavy drumming of the rain outside. It meant that he would not have to go out this afternoon and it might even mean, with luck, that he could stay in Mama's room for a while instead of in the day nursery. This might take a little doing. For a moment he wished Seymour were here to help; they had their own understandings about how to manage certain things. But then he thought, no; when it has to do with Mama, Seymour can be almost as bad as Grandmama. Mama was still trembling and whimpering on account of the thunderstorm, and instead of continuing to pat her shoulder and comfort her, Randall walked over quietly to the piano to put his music away. He was very neat. Everything was arranged just so in the music cabinet and he kept it that way without supervision. He put the Clementi and the Czerny and the Schumann away in their alphabetical places and closed the cabinet and the piano, and put the piano stool exactly where it belonged, and Mama's small chair back in the spot where it always stood grouped with its mates around a gilded bamboo whatnot. He did all this with grave attentiveness, as if he were unaware that Grandmama was watching him. Then he said, his innocent blue eyes very childlike, "What do you wish me to do now, Grandmama?"

"Why—" Randall felt a ripple of satisfaction; this was a good sign. It came only when one asked Grandmama for orders instead of having them thrust at one. "Have you finished your French for tomorrow?"

"Not quite." As a matter of fact he had not only read and translated *Le Corbeau et le Renard*, he had memorized it, just as he made all his best efforts for any of his work supervised by Mama. Grandmama had long since given up the empty gesture of teaching French words to the boys, because there was no denying that Lily had been brought up to speak it well. Let her teach it to Randall along with music, a soft unmanly thing he had inherited from her. Seymour was of different fibre; one could expect to make something of him.

"Well then," said Mrs. Holt to Randall, "you might as well finish your Fable for tomorrow. Lily, you are quite all right now, are you not?"

"Oh, yes, Mother Holt." Lily spoke with eager brightness which deceived neither her son nor the old woman. "I feel splendidly. I'm sorry I—I'm so sorry—"

Mrs. Holt shook her head as if to dismiss the subject and proceeded heavily from the room. "I shall be waiting for you and Seymour punctually at five-thirty in the library," she said to Randall. That was the half-hour when she read them the Bible every evening before their supper.

"Yes, Grandmama," said Randall demurely, following the two billowing, rustling sets of skirts up the stairs. Mrs. Holt disappeared into the library and Lily continued to the next floor, followed by Randall. Each knew that the other, but for the old woman there behind the door she had just closed, would have broken into a run and flown up the stairs to the refuge that they could scarcely wait to reach. But they moved sedately. Lily's room was the large double one at the third floor front, which she had shared with her husband, and which to the very least detail she kept exactly as it had been when he was alive. She slipped inside the room now, and Randall behind her, as if they had been conspirators; the door was no sooner shut behind them than they ran into each other's arms swiftly and fervently like lovers who had been kept apart for days. Lily held Randall clasped to her bosom and stroked his fair curls and kissed his temples and his eyelids and Randall kissed her pale cheeks and hugged her and whispered, "Dear Mama, please try to forget about her, don't think about her."

"Yes, yes," she whispered. "Oh, Randall, dearest, what would I do without you!"

For a time they made a show of going through Randall's lesson, sitting close together on the divan, her left arm round his shoulder, their cheeks touching as they bent their heads over La Fontaine. But he knew his Fable already; soon they put the book aside, and Randall curled up close to her, with his head on her shoulder. Sometimes she sang to him in these stolen moments and sometimes she talked, dwelling on her few treasured memories of happiness, which Randall knew well how to evoke. He knew that she loved him to open one or another of the drawers, cupboards, or boxes where she kept every token of memory which had ever come into her possession. Her room was therefore crowded and though superficially neat, actually a series of small concealed clutters, each of which was the touchstone of some sentimentality intensely significant to her. So Lily and Randall, sitting there with an open photograph-album on the table before them; or a box full of yellowed ball-programmes with faded ribbons and tarnished gilding; or the small top drawer of Papa's dressing-stand filled with collar-buttons, moustache-shapers, brushes, pomatum, and manicure implements, would lose themselves in talk which thawed the frost of fear where they existed.

Today Randall had taken down from a shelf an album which was one of a series of what Lily in her girlhood had called her "memory books." All her friends had kept such books, velvet-covered volumes with blank pages of slotted cardboard, into which they slipped the daguerreotypes and sketches, the souvenirs, the notes, the invitations to balls and other parties, the flowers pressed in mica envelopes, which marked the thrilling time between one's début and one's marriage. There were later albums too, the sacred one full of wedding memories, the treasured mementos of the honeymoon, the precious volume which began with the birth of Baby and was followed by as many more books —each covered in pale pink or blue satin hand-painted with winged cherubs and garlands of forget-me-nots—as there were successive

Babies. But Randall liked best the early albums which told how beautiful and gay and charming Mama had been, and what lovely parties she had gone to when she was young.

"But," he asked, "why is it that you only went to parties until you were married? Don't married people go to parties?"

"Why yes, darling, of course."

"But you never go now. You never have parties here."

"Well you see, I am a widow, and without Papa—"

Randall could not remember clearly the days when Papa had been alive but he was quite sure there had been no parties then either. "Were there?" he asked. "Did you and Papa go to parties then, or give them here?"

"Not—not exactly."

"Why not?"

"Well, you see, Grandmama . . . we didn't like to go out and leave her alone."

Randall might have asked why Mama and Papa had not, then, invited their friends to parties here at home, but he could not imagine a party, the sort of thing Mama described, with dancing and beautiful gowns and music and flowers, here in the same house with Grandmama.

"Will I go to parties when I am older?" he asked.

Lily laughed. "I should hope so. Young men have the best time of all, they say. And you will have more wonderful things to do than most boys, you will be going to Europe to study—"

"You always say so, Mama, but how can you be sure?"

"What do you mean, darling? Of course I am sure!" Lily opened her eyes wide and held Randall by the shoulders. "You must go."

"Yes, I know, but—"

"But what? Don't you *want* to?"

"Of course I want to, if you say so."

"Professor Mundt says so too. You must go to Vienna, he says, when you are older, that is the only place, and you will have lessons with some great teacher, perhaps Leschetizky, and hear all the wonderful concerts and operas and make lots of lovely friends and—"

"But—" Randall had a worried pucker on his forehead. "What about you, Mama? Aren't you going with me?"

"Of course! We'll have a flat, or a little house somewhere with a garden and—"

Randall nodded eagerly; none of this was new, they had talked about it many times before. Some of it was like practising, something he knew letter-perfect before he began to go through it all over again. This time, however, he asked a new question. "What about Brother?" he blurted, in such a way that Lily saw he had been making up his mind for a long time to say this. Randall had a way of calling Seymour 'Brother' at certain moments and with a kind of secret emphasis; he said 'Brother' only to Seymour himself or to Lily, never in the presence of his grandmother.

Lily paused and weighed Randall's question, and he saw a vague look come into her eyes as he watched her face anxiously. "What about Brother?" he asked again.

"Oh," said Lily, "why—why he won't want to go, darling. I mean, that is, he—Grandmama would never let him go."

"But this will be when I am big," said Randall. "Is Grandmama—" Lily watched him nervously—"is she going to live forever, Mama?"

"Sh—" Her face turned pink in a sudden blush. She glanced quickly at the door. "We mustn't, you oughtn't . . ."

"That's not naughty," whispered Randall. "I only said she's very old and she is. Don't you ever think about that, Mama?"

"Oh, darling." How could she cry, 'If you only knew!'

"Well—suppose she—she—you know, suppose there were just the three of us? Wouldn't we all be together?"

"Of course we would." Lily found herself for the first time confronted by a thought so obvious that how could she possibly not have had it many times before? She could dream and hope; she had prayed for years for freedom; and now, if she should be freed, the prospect startlingly held a problem of its own when heretofore it had shone clear and glorious like the gate to Heaven itself. Yet what exactly was this problem? Lily could not name it; it took the shape of some unimaginable obstruction to her dearest hope. And nine-year-old Randall had been the one to point it out.

"Oh," she said, "there's lots of time, darling. It will all come out beautifully, I am sure."

Randall jumped lightly away from her as they heard a tap on the door and Lily, closing the album before them, cried brightly "Come in!"

It was Seymour. He was munching a piece of bread-and-butter-and-brown sugar and Lily gave a conspiratorial giggle when she saw it.

"Shut the door quickly," she whispered. Seymour did so, with cool deliberation which was pure bravado.

"How did you get it?" she asked, for eating between meals was forbidden by Mrs. Holt and it was not easy to obtain anything from Cook or Minnie. The old lady kept track of all the food in the house, eyeing cut roasts of meat, and cakes and puddings and anything from which it was easy to notice a stolen slice. But bread and butter and sugar were more difficult to trace. "They weren't in the kitchen," said Seymour succinctly. "I guess they're upstairs changing their uniforms." He knew very well, and Lily knew that he knew, exactly when the maids left the kitchen empty, and when and where to place every happening and every object in the house which had the remotest interest for him.

"Want some?" he asked Randall. "I'll go and fix it for you." This was more bravado and Lily knew it. She wondered what had got Seymour into this mood.

Randall shook his head. He would have liked just one bite of Seymour's snack, but he was not hungry enough to want a whole piece for himself. He said so. Seymour said, "Oh no. You can have your own but you can't have any of mine."

Lily raised her eyebrows as if to ask an explanation, but such a trifle was not worth talking about when she had a moment to enjoy both boys together. She patted the divan on her right and when Seymour sat down there, flung an arm about each boy and hugged them both. Seymour submitted with a show of patience, eyeing the closed album on the small table before them.

"Up to that stuff again," he said. "Don't you ever get tired of thinking about the same old things? Old pictures and dead flowers and stuff."

"It's no worse than all that rubbish of yours in the cellar," said Randall.

"Why, darling!" Lily's face was quite shocked. "What a thing to say!"

"I don't care," said Seymour, swallowing the last of his bread and butter. "If he's too stupid to see what I do with things—"

"*Sh.* Stop squabbling, boys. Let's have a few happy minutes together while we can." Lily drew the children close to her, hugging each by the shoulder until their cheeks were resting against hers. "Wouldn't it be wonderful," she sighed, "if only we were always—"

They all jumped a little. They had heard Mrs. Holt's voice downstairs; the library door must be open and Mrs. Holt giving some order to Minnie for whom she had rung. Lily's eyes, together with Seymour's cool grey ones and Randall's wondering blue globes, turned to the crystal clock ticking fussily on her bedside table. It said twenty minutes past five.

"We have ten minutes," said Lily anxiously.

Seymour shook his head, drawing away while she tried to hold him closer.

"Mnh, mnh," he sounded, with his lips closed. "She wants to know if we're upstairs getting washed." He pulled himself away from his mother and stood up. "Come on, Ran."

"Oh, dear." Lily hugged Randall closer and looked up at Seymour with a babyish, pleading expression. Seymour's face was quite stern, he wore that look which Lily could never quite believe, setting his little-boy face in severe lines utterly unrelated to his soft skin and fine fair hair.

"It's no use, Mama. Do you want to get us in trouble?"

Lily sighed and let Randall go. He stood up and then threw his arms quickly round her neck and gave her a hug and a kiss.

"I told you to come on, Ran," said Seymour, watching them. "He's too old to be babied like that, Mama." Lily looked at Seymour with her most docile expression, and Randall said, "He's not Grandmama. You don't have to obey him too."

"I—I'd rather, darling. He's only trying to keep us out of trouble, don't you see?"

"Well," said Randall with prim deliberateness, "I guess I do. I'm coming, Brother," he said, as Seymour started towards the door. "Have you got anything to show her?" he asked anxiously, as they slid quietly through the hall to their own rooms. Their grandmother usually demanded an accounting of their time after an afternoon like this; she would require to see what Seymour had made and to hear what Randall had memorized. They got into the night nursery and gave each other a confiding grin. Nana was not there, probably down in the kitchen at her everlasting tea, and they hurried to wash their hands which she would be here to inspect before sending them down to the library.

"Have you?" asked Randall again.

Seymour snickered. "What makes you so sharp today?" he asked, drying his hands. He put the towel away and began to feel in his pockets.

Randall giggled too. He pointed to Seymour's right shoe, whose heel had apparently got glue on it, for a tangle of white string and shreds of cloth had stuck to the shoe. Seymour looked down at it and then at Randall. "Gee," he said, flushing. "Thanks." He sat down on the floor and cleaned his shoe and put the wadded-up mess in the waste-paper basket. Then he looked Randall over to insure quick approval at inspection. Then he pulled a piece of whittled wood from his pocket and said, "This'll do. It's a thingummy."

"A *what*?"

"A thingummy. Oh, I'm going to tell her it's the deck-housing of a coal barge."

"Is it?"

"What do *you* think?"

"What will she think?"

"Here's Nana," said Seymour, making a face. "We're all ready, Nana," he said sweetly. "Come on, Ran. And take a long time over your French when she asks for it, will you?"

They filed past their old nurse who stood looking after them with her heavy, horselike gaze. Like a horse she was conditioned by years of driving to a set of automatic, obedient reactions and also like a horse she knew a master when she saw one. "It's herself," she said, as the boys' thick boots clumped down to the library. "Another wan just like herself."

She shook her head, well satisfied that a new place with younger children was to be found for her at the end of this year. Master Seymour, if she knew anything, would soon be a job she wouldn't care to handle. And Master Randall—too much of that piano-strumming and nonsense in his head like that poor weak whiny one.

CHAPTER 3

Seymour had just won the Saturday afternoon Class A race, his sixth straight victory, bringing him within two weeks of the Season Cup. He was full of happiness and excitement as he brought his boat in to its mooring. He came about, dropped the mainsail, and slid round in one smooth manoeuvre as Randall up forward neatly hooked the dinghy. Seymour could never have enough of sailing, especially after he had waited years for the supreme joy of owning his own boat. But Randall if anything was the more proud. He said, as they went to work furling, "That was a beauty today." He grinned at Seymour with overflowing admiration. "You really are a sailor."

"Oh, I guess it's the boat. And you're a good hand." They were trying to outdo each other in generosity. It had been a fine race. There was a big spanking breeze outside and tacking had been a very tricky job. The Crawley and the Richmond boats had both been disqualified, and they were sailed by older men who had been racing for years. But Seymour had only received his boat two months ago, in June, as a grand cumulative present to celebrate several major events: his eighteenth birthday last winter, his graduation with honors from school, and his behaving with good grace about his grandmother's insistence that he go to Columbia next autumn and live at home, instead of going away to The Massachusetts Institute as he had hoped.

"I guess it's worth the price," he said to Randall, throwing him a sweater and adding, "Put that on, Kid." He motioned with his chin across the harbor to their lawn, where they could see Mrs. Holt standing bulky and black-clad as always, with her telescope to her eye.

"I had the cold," said Randall wearily. "Weeks ago."

"I know. But you think I want a harangue about you this evening?"

"I thought you were going to the Milburns' beach party this evening."

"I am—I hope. That's why I don't want any trouble beforehand."

Randall pulled the sweater over his head and went on with his work.

"This spinnaker's too wet to stow," said Seymour. "Let's take it to the house and dry it there. I won't be around later to come out if we leave it drying over the boom."

"I could come," said Randall.

"Oh, no. There'd be a fuss. They never used to let me row out alone after supper when I was crew for Mr. Jarrett, they'd be the same about you. And you think I want—"

"Never mind," said Randall with a laugh. "You're right. What's it like on those beach parties, Brother?" His fine fingers were making short work of the mainsail stops, and his face was wistful.

"It's fun. You'll be old enough to go pretty soon. Grand things to eat, and sitting around a big driftwood fire. And toasting marshmallows later, and singing, and tonight there's going to be a moon."

Randall knew too what else Seymour was anticipating but you didn't talk about that. It was part of the reason why Seymour seemed so changed lately and so far away. They had finished making everything shipshape; they dropped the spinnaker into the dinghy and sprang in after it, cast off, and Randall asked to row in. Seymour said, "Better not. You know." It was Mama they had to consider now; she was always trying to make Randall promise not to row and get his hands calloused. They shot across the harbor and Randall said, "Look, Brother, there's Dorothy Bayliss waving at you."

He watched Seymour's face, and the careful, blank expression which came over it. Seymour looked over his shoulder and saw that his grandmother had left her lookout post; then he waved quickly and casually towards the Bayliss place and bent to his oars again.

"I guess she's trying to congratulate you about the race," said Randall. "You'll see her at the party, won't you?"

"I suppose."

"Everybody says she's the prettiest girl on the Island."

"Aw—" Seymour thought better of what he had been about to say. If he tried to shut Randall up the kid would only harp more on the subject. "There are lots of others."

Randall knew better than to say anything more about this now. They had reached home anyway, and there was no more time to talk. They climbed the slope to the sprawling "cottage" of brown weathered shingles, where Mrs. Holt had spent her summers ever since her husband had built the house when she was a bride. Hare Island was a thoroughly conservative place, duller and stuffier than Newport which was at that time a sleepy little town not yet dreaming of its own spectacular future. Hare Island people were smug, satisfied, and free from the proddings of restlessness and vulgarity which, they would one day say, had laid Newport open to the barbarian invasions of the new millionaires. In truth the Hare Island colony were not and never had been rich enough to score; they were old-fashioned families descended in a sound blue line from the English settlers of New York. This was the reason for the one seeming inconsistency in Mrs. Holt's rigidity: the vast difference for the boys between their New York winters and their Hare Island summers. They were allowed in summer the only freedom they ever knew, because their grandmother supposed that they could not come to harm or fall under bad influences on an island miles out at sea, tightly colonized by people she had always known.

Lily, whose silly romantic views occasionally proved disconcertingly realistic, was less sure than her mother-in-law of Hare Island's impermeability to life and the outside world. She was still young enough to see Seymour as she was sure he appeared to his contemporaries, superbly handsome, with a fascinating tendency to silence made provocative by his finely modelled features and deep grey eyes. What Seymour felt or even more rarely, said, was worth waiting to learn. Randall was the ingenuous one who had not yet developed in the kiln of Mrs. Holt's exactions the hard and undeniably attractive glaze of the instinct for shrewd self-preservation. Sitting now at tea with her mother-in-law as the boys surged up the porch steps outside, Lily had to restrain the impulse to rush out and throw her arms about them and make the fuss which Seymour's victory deserved. Instead she waited until they came in, bronzed and panting, and flung themselves upon the bread-and-butter and cake.

"It's too wonderful," cried Lily, wishing she dared run over and hug Seymour. "Tell us all about it."

"Oh—not much out of the usual," he said, with his mouth full. "Thank you, Grandmama." He took the cup of tea she had poured out for him. "Some of them had a little trouble at the Cat and Kittens."

"But Seymour did it *this* way!" Randall illustrated with his hands the series of quick tacks that had brought their boat through ahead. "And Mr. Jarrett was awfully nice, he hailed us and saluted Seymour."

"Edwin Jarrett is a fine man," said Mrs. Holt.

"A sportsman," said Seymour.

Mrs. Holt raised her eyebrows as if to remind Seymour that her pronouncement was intended to be the last word. Lily had nothing to add to the conversation, she sat smiling brightly at the boys and surreptitiously glancing at the mantel clock. It was after five and Seymour, she knew, was supposed to be at the post-office at six, where the party were to meet to ride out in hay-wagons to Barren Beach. Whenever Seymour was about to go out to enjoy one of the privileges which his age and his good behavior had wrested from the reluctant old woman, Lily suffered torments of suspense until he was safely out of the house. She loved Seymour to go out, she loved in imagination to follow him as he met with the jolly group of young men and girls, who, she knew, admired him and liked him, the girls for his good looks and the boys for his prowess as a sailor. There had been times this summer when Lily, alone with him for a moment, had whispered, "Do be careful. Oh, Seymour, I'm so afraid sometimes that she'll—you know."

He had patted his mother's cheek reassuringly. "If I haven't learned to watch my step by now, Mama, I'd really be a fool." He laughed.

To her relief he was dismissed from tea in time to go upstairs to change his clothes. Lily saw that Randall yearned to tag along; he wanted to watch Seymour get ready for the party, his only way of vicarious participation in pleasures that seemed centuries away. Lily knew how hard it was for him to be dropped from things after years of living in tandem with Seymour. She longed to find something for him to do to make up for his disappointments now, but Mrs. Holt made that impossible. There was nothing at Hare Island to take the place of the concerts that Lily and Randall were allowed to hear in New York, because Mrs. Holt considered those part of Randall's education and could not conceive of music as pleasure. Lily sighed. She could only offer Randall a game of dominoes after supper, with Mrs. Holt sitting nearby knitting in the lamplight.

Seymour ran downstairs and came into the sitting-room to say good night. Lily tried her hardest not to gaze at him with loving admiration; she had been scolded for that, and such a scolding now might mount up to ruining Seymour's evening. But he was so handsome! His fair hair, sun-bleached and cropped short, sprang in a crisp line from his bronzed forehead; his cool grey eyes were doubly striking in his sun-browned face, and he wore his white flannels and striped blazer with an easy grace which reminded her poignantly of her husband, whom she had not even met until he was almost twenty years older than Seymour was now. But John Holt had kept all his life the youthful grace of figure and movement which made Seymour so charming to look at. Lily began to re-live the past in a reverie which kept her apparently pre-occupied or, more fortunately for Seymour, somewhat indifferent, as he stood for a moment between her chair and Mrs. Holt's.

"Eleven-thirty sharp, Seymour," said the old lady. At the age of eighty-two her voice if anything was more rasping and dictatorial than ever.

"Yes, Grandmama."

"And stop the clock when you come in." That was her way of policing him, an infuriating humiliation of the sort it was impossible to keep secret from his friends. One had to be tough-fibred to rise above that. At least, however, he was now spared reporting to her in her bed-room as he had had to do last year when he was first allowed to go out in the evening.

"Good night, then." His grandmother tilted towards him the angle of her whiskery chin. He kissed it, kissed his mother's cheek, who breathed, "Have a good time, darling," and gave Randall an affectionate slap on the shoulder. Then, holding his breath, he was out safe and free on the front porch, and down the steps in a bound. He took his bicycle from the shed, carefully secured his trousers with spring clips, and sped down the road, conscious of the glorious flavor of liberty, as if it were the taste of a rare delicacy. When he whizzed into the post-office square the three big hay-wagons were there, filling with the laughing, chattering party, the girls in fluffy muslin dresses which they wrapped, giggling, round their ankles as they were helped up to the high banks of fresh hay. His friends hailed him with calls and shouts of congratulation, and several of them cried from their perches, "Here, Seymour! We've saved a place for you!"

But he knew that there would be a place next to Dorothy Bayliss, without any remark about it. Many others knew it too, but he did not care. Nearly everybody had his special arrangement of this sort, but Dorothy was popular and there was competition. He sprang into the wagon where she was seated, shyly smiling at him, and dismissed with modesty the chorus of congratulations on the race today.

"It really was wonderful," said Dorothy softly. "I was out with Papa in the judges' boat and saw it all."

"I saw you," said Seymour.

"You didn't! You were working so hard you didn't see a thing."

"Blind as a bat," agreed Seymour. "I didn't see you waving from your lawn when you got home, either."

"Anyway, you were splendid," sighed Dorothy happily. Seymour looked at her small, pretty hands folded in her ruffled pale blue lap. He would have liked to take one of them and hold it just for a minute, but that was unthinkable. Dorothy looked at him and her bright face turned pink in a sudden blush. Seymour leaned over and said something to George Parsons about a tennis game tomorrow; and while George was reminding him, to his discomfiture, that Seymour could not play tennis on Sunday but would Monday do, the last of the guests swarmed into the wagons and in a chorus of shouts the big teams hauled off for the two-mile ride to Barren Beach.

The clambake had been under preparation all day and when the wagons stopped on the bluff high above the long shingle of Barren Beach, the delicious smell of driftwood smoke, broiling lobsters and steaming clams rose on the rich salt air. There was a sharp descent down a stony trail from the top of the bluff to the beach, and Seymour, in a private understanding with Dorothy, left her to go down with somebody else while he went to help Mrs. Milburn and carry some of her wraps and rugs. Dorothy would save a place for him at supper.

This was laid on long white canvas cloths spread on the sand, round which the thirty-odd guests sat on cushions and steamer rugs. Seymour found his place and sat down cross-legged beside Dorothy, with John Borden on her other side and Edith Lincoln beyond Borden. Seymour knew that all this had been previously arranged by Dorothy and Edith, her best friend. John Borden was Edith's special beau and Dorothy needn't pay much attention to him.

Seymour felt afloat on a tide of happiness. What a day! And though these famous clambakes of old Nezer White's were a Hare Island tradition, familiar as bread and butter to everybody, they never tasted less delicious, and the appearance of each course, served by a crew of Nezer's fishermen assistants, was greeted with hungry shouts. First they drank mugs of boiling clam broth and ate alongside huge heaps of steamed clams, dipping them with their fingers in tin dishes full of melted butter. Then followed the lobsters, grilled as nobody but Nezer could do, on driftwood coals, and eaten with giggling apologies for licked fingers and buttery chins which were all part of the fun. Then from the barrels where the clams had steamed in spicy seaweed came halves of little chickens, and from underneath the driftwood coals, black baked potatoes, flaky white inside and permeated with pungent smoky flavor. Then there was a rest, while they watched the clear evening light deepen slowly, and the sea, lazy and good-natured today, roll in gentle breakers on the beach a few yards away. The great bluff at their backs made a perfect windbreak; this shallow cove, old-timers always said, had been designed by Nature to make the perfect setting for beach-parties.

"Oh, I'm having such a good time!" The girls picked daintily at chicken bones and shook their heads with little cries of protest as more food was offered.

"Have another! Have two!"

"I *couldn't*. I'd *burst*!"

"I'm going to have some more!"

"Oh, Mary, no."

"I will too!" Poor Mary, the inevitable fat girl seated between Mr. Milburn and Ronny Cole, who stuttered and wore thick glasses.

"Oh, look! Here comes the corn!" Now their appetites were renewed, and they fell to work on the fat, steaming ears of Country Gentleman corn, shining with butter. Seymour had felt ravenous when the supper began, but a little food had filled up the crevices and he did not want any more. Dorothy had not eaten much either. He tried to join in the laughter and the talk but all he wanted was to sit still and look at Dorothy and wait for her to speak. Her laughing brown eyes and curly hair and short, freckled nose might have been ordinary in anyone else, but in her seemed bewitching. He loved her small wrists and ankles and the quick lightness of her movements. But best of all, he believed, he liked her speaking voice which had a surprising quality of depth and quietness. Most girls spoke in a high, bubbling stream, pretty enough but to Seymour meaningless, while the velvety gentleness of Dorothy's low-pitched speech stirred him every time she said a word. He could not quite remember when this lovely voice of hers had emerged from the blur of small childhood, for he had known Dorothy ever since they had played, along with most of these friends of theirs, at sandcastles and toy boats while their nurses sat in a row on camp-chairs holding umbrellas over their heads.

"I don't want any more to eat," she said.

"Neither do I." Seymour looked up and down the two long rows of laughing, sunburned faces, with Mr. and Mrs. Milburn at the ends of the party and their son and daughter, Charlie and Grace, on opposite sides in the middle. "Why do you suppose we never have fun like this in the winter?"

"I don't know. New York parties are stiff. And you don't seem to—" Dorothy paused, a little embarrassed.

"I know." It was unnecessary to bring in Mrs. Holt. Seymour had not been sent to dancing-school when everybody else was, and had scarcely ever been allowed to go to parties in town.

"But next winter will be different, won't it?" Dorothy smiled shyly. "Will you come to my coming-out party?"

"I should think so! After all, I'll be at college."

"It will be fun, won't it?"

"I hope so. Of course that's not why I'm going there."

"I didn't mean that. I meant me—coming out."

"Will you like it so much?" Seymour spoke uneasily. "Will you—" he paused.

"What?"

"Oh, nothing." How could he say he hoped she would not like it too much, not allow herself to be distracted by too many beaux. He wanted to feel he had first place and could be sure of keeping it. Dorothy laughed. He supposed she knew what he meant.

After a time, when the food was finished, the canvas cloths were rolled up and the fire down the beach was renewed with great beams and chunks of driftwood. The party moved to settle themselves in a broad semicircle round the landward side of the fire. The late summer dusk was deepening to a beautiful starry night. They sat and watched the sea and the sky turn darker until the horizon disappeared in cobalt velvet, the sea marked by its eternal voice and the sky by its jewels, as if their casket had been flung open and the diamonds inside strewn high and wide with wildest extravagance. Everybody here had seen this sight innumerable times, but they exclaimed and marvelled as they watched it, for this was one of the ancient wonders which had the magic to seem always new.

Someone started a song and soon by threes and fours the others joined in, until the whole party was singing. They all knew the repertoire; the songs, like the hay-wagons and the menu and old Nezer and the sounds and smells, were all part of the tradition. Some could harmonize and some could just sing and some could barely carry a tune, but they all chimed together. They sang "After the Ball" and "Sweet Rosie O'Grady"; "Sweet Adeline" and "I've Been Working on the Railroad." But Seymour's favorite of all was "Juanita":

"Nita, Juanita,
 Ask thyself if we must part. . . ."

Dorothy's low voice rang in his ear, the soft contralto he loved to hear. He stopped singing to listen to her. His eyes were fixed on the sparks and the leaping blue and orange flames of the great fire against the magnificent sky.

"Ask thyself if we must part. . . ." Without turning his head Seymour moved his right hand quietly across the steamer-rug on which they were sitting, and took Dorothy's small left hand and hid it, holding it tight, in a fold of the rug. He found his breath short, he felt choked. Those words echoed through his head and his throat and gave him courage to grip Dorothy's hand, feeling its small bones and its delicate warm skin. He wanted to draw her closer, but that he could not do; the air seemed to speak of the feelings like his own which throbbed through all these girls and young men and held them pulsating against the barriers of convention and good taste. How easy it would be, he thought, to move only a little, to draw Dorothy only a bit closer, until he could slide his right arm round her waist as he longed almost painfully to do. But never, except on the few occasions when he had danced with her this summer, had he so much as touched her hand before; and now that he had grasped it he must be content. He wondered what she felt; he waited, pressing her hand and moving his thumb across its smooth palm, for some response from her. And when it came, when her small fingers closed hard for a moment on his, he could only stare more fixedly at the fire, swallowing, not trusting himself to look at her.

He wanted the party never to end; he had kept his grasp of Dorothy's hand, and in spite of his reticence, moved as close to her as he dared, before the hour of singing by the driftwood fire had spun itself out. It was time to start home. There were sighs, here and there a giggle as some girl was swung to her feet, calls of "Where's my sweater?" and "Let me help you," and "I'll carry that," as they moved slowly and regretfully up the beach to the path where kerosene lanterns had been placed to light the way. They climbed up the bluff and got into the hay-wagons again and settled down for the ride back. The moon had risen and was high now, startling white, and the sandy road looked like a trail of cream poured out between the dull dry green of the dunes on either side. Seymour settled Dorothy in the wagon and then contrived, with boldness of which he himself was afraid, to let his arm fall behind her and around her shoulders as he took his place beside her. He held his breath, he was unsure of himself and now anxious lest she take offense and in trying to draw away make them both conspicuous, the last thing he wished to bring about. But she did nothing. She sat quietly with her hands in her lap, and under cover of the bustle made by the others climbing into the wagon, Seymour breathed more easily. He leaned back, and when he summoned the courage to look at her she smiled, with gentle uncertainty.

"You are sweet," he whispered, and doubted if she heard him. The wagon was starting in a chorus of cheers and then there was the long, pleasantly jolting ride in the brilliant moonlight, with everybody else, he knew, feeling just as he and Dorothy did; and finally the arrival back at the post-office square. The clock under the white steeple of the church across the way said twenty minutes past eleven. Seymour's heart sank. This was a dreadful blow. There was no possibility that he could walk to her house with Dorothy and himself get home inside of ten minutes. He scowled and bit his lip. Dorothy said, "You'd better not try." It made the ignominy all the worse for her to know his dilemma. "I can walk home with John and Edith," she said. The Lincoln cottage was next door to the Bayliss's.

Seymour felt his face burning; he swallowed and turned his head sharply, defiant and decided. "Nonsense," he said. "Of course I'm going to take you home."

She did not say anything. He jumped down from the wagon, held up his arms to help her jump, and felt as if the whole party must hear his pounding heart as she swung for an instant in his arms. They went over to thank Mr. and Mrs. Milburn and say good night, and Seymour turned to walk home with Dorothy.

"Your bicycle," she said, laughing.

"By golly, that's right." He was crestfallen. He did not want to push the bicycle alongside while he walked with her, but there was nothing else to do. He dared not take the extra time to run back to the post-office for it, doubling on his tracks in the direction away from home. He muttered something that Dorothy was not intended to hear, but she laughed softly and said, "Oh, come along."

They took a footpath across the stretch of dunes that lay between the post-office and the broad harbor ringed with cottages where their homes lay perhaps a third of a mile apart. The colony of houses was scattered all along their way, and as they walked slowly, their friends in groups and couples moved before and behind them, turning off with calls of "Good night!" "Good night!" until Seymour found himself almost alone with Dorothy, since the Bayliss house was farthest out towards the edge of the harbor. Edith Lincoln and John Borden disappeared inside the door of her house. Seymour knew that Mrs. Bayliss would be waiting for Dorothy. His moment of magic was so limited that as they moved past a clump of bay shrubs he stopped in their shadow, laid down his bicycle, and stood looking at Dorothy in the moonlight. She seemed surprised. Her lips were parted and her eyebrows raised as if to ask a question. But it was Seymour who spoke and when he did he felt a fool. He only said, "Dorothy."

She was silent. He took her hand slowly between his two and held it for a moment and said, "You see . . ." Then he had nothing more to say.

"I've had a lovely time," she said.

"So have I." He wanted to draw her closer and he felt the nerveless yielding of her hand and arm, but he had not the courage.

"Don't make yourself late, Seymour," she whispered. Now instead of shame that she should know the mortifications of his existence, he felt a plunging relief. He wanted her to understand, and she did.

"It—" he spoke with hesitation and then blurted, "It won't always be like this, Dorothy."

"Of course not."

"And sometimes I want to ask you—ask—"

"What?"

"If you—you don't mind—well, waiting. I know I can't be much fun the way things are. But some day—"

"I know."

"Yes, but in the meantime, you're going to be meeting lots of new people and you know how much trouble I have in New York. It's hard enough here, but in the winter, well—"

"But, Seymour," she said, and her low voice throbbed in his ears. "The others, the new ones, they wouldn't—" He stared at her small delicate features etched in the moonlight and saw the deep blush which swept over them while she hesitated. "They wouldn't matter," she whispered.

He stood clinging to her hand, surprised to find that he was trembling. For a moment he could not speak. Then he swallowed and said, "Dorothy—you mean that I do?"

She bent her head and if she answered he could not hear.

"Oh," he said softly, "I didn't dare hope. Because I feel, I've felt for such a long time—" he paused and something made him say, "You didn't think me silly? Did you just—*understand*?"

Again she nodded shyly without speaking. Seymour's hands held her forearms, and drew her back into the shadow of the shrubbery. They stood close together, Seymour so much taller that he bent down to see her face, and to look into her eyes which for the first time looked straight into his, wide and tender with what she had not the words to say. "Oh," he said, "Dorothy. Do you mean you would, do you think some day . . . all that waiting . . . you wouldn't mind?"

She shook her head slowly, looking at him. Then she raised her face and Seymour touched her lips with his own. His arms moved to go round her and for an instant he could feel her, warm and trembling a little, as he held her. But she drew away, whispering, "We must go, Mother's waiting for me, too."

"I know. I—oh, Dorothy, do you really mean it?"

Once more he felt her lips, delicate, shy, velvety as he imagined a butterfly's wing must be. She turned her head and Seymour, though he longed to embrace her with all the strength which suddenly flared through him, gently let her go. They stepped quickly round the shrubs onto the path leading to the house and as they hurried up the steps, the door was opened by Mrs. Bayliss who stood there smiling.

"Did you have a good time?" she asked, as Dorothy kissed her.

"Lovely! It was just wonderful."

"A grand party," said Seymour.

"Quite a day for you," said Dorothy's mother. "Mr. Bayliss says you handled your boat splendidly in the race, Seymour. You're sure to win the Season Cup."

"Oh, thank you. It's nothing, really."

"Of course it is! I'm not going to ask you in, it's getting late. But we'll see you soon."

"Good night," said Dorothy softly.

"Good night, Dorothy. Good night, Mrs. Bayliss."

"Thank you for bringing Dorothy home. Good night."

The door closed. Seymour sprang down the steps, seized his bicycle and pedalled home furiously, not only because he was so late, but because his blood was racing and driving him along and he felt from sheer excitement almost as if he had the power to fly. He could not really believe it yet; he did not realize what he had said or Dorothy had said; but she was his girl, he had kissed her, she liked him better than anybody else, and she expected to keep on doing so and to like him more as time went on. He had dreamed of this without imagining that it could happen, and now it had. It was too good to be true, but it was true, and with this to live for a chap could endure even the maddening troubles of his existence.

He let himself in at the side door which had been left unlocked for him, and tiptoed across the hall and the sitting-room to the fireplace. The moonlight was so brilliant that it was unnecessary to light a candle. Seymour stood looking at the mantel clock, listening to its reproachful ticking while he also listened with all the acuteness of his years of practice for any other sound in the house. There was none, and the clock said fourteen minutes past twelve. Seymour opened the glass face of the clock and took the pendulum in his fingers and stopped it. Then he stood there hesitating. More sharply than before he listened for a sound in the house. He bent down suddenly and took off his sneakers and moved in his stocking feet to the bottom of the stairs and stood listening there. The house had the hollow but penetrating quiet which told him that everybody upstairs was sound asleep. He went back to the clock and stood and looked at it. For a matter of forty-four minutes he might find tomorrow morning that some crushing chastisement had fallen on him, some catastrophe whose extent he could not, or dared not, imagine. Never before had he done what he weighed doing now, but never before had the necessity arisen. He had, however, thought of this; there was very little in the realm of self-preservation which had not already occurred to Seymour. Deceit was a risk and he disliked it thoroughly, but he had to weigh it now against far more urgent dangers. Still listening with ears sharpened by anxiety, he put out his hand, trying to ignore the pounding of his own pulse, and slowly set the stopped clock back. When, with his mechanical fingers he had placed both hands of the clock, they said two minutes past eleven-thirty. Seymour closed the clock face, took his sneakers in his hand, and sure that he was not making a sound, crept up to his room.

When he came down to breakfast on the required stroke of eight, his grandmother and Randall were already seated at the table. Mrs. Holt in her usual black sat behind the silver coffee pot at the head of the table, facing the door. Above her high collar her jowled, frowning face, instead of looking at Seymour, was slightly bent over the bowl of porridge which she ate every morning. Seymour walked to his chair and, standing behind it, inclined his head and said "Good morning, Grandmama." This salutation had been substituted, as a mark of his superior age, for the morning kiss which he had dreaded all his life; Randall was still expected to kiss the old woman every morning and privately expressed his opinion about that to Seymour. Randall, who detested porridge and for whom breakfast was therefore a daily ordeal, gave Seymour now a sidelong look of such meaning that Seymour reacted with instant alarm: there was trouble. His grandmother had not answered his greeting, so Seymour took his place and stared at his own oatmeal with loathing. How could he choke down such stuff when he was already strangling with uneasiness? At that moment he heard his mother's light steps running down the stairs and into the dining-room. She came in crying, "Good morning, Mother Holt. Good morning, boys."

Automatically the brothers stood up and Randall held out his mother's chair. They both kissed her quickly and went back to their places. Mrs. Holt had not said a word nor looked up. Lily glanced at her for a moment, then at Seymour, and then he saw the color drain from his mother's face. She sat back, nervously wiping her lips and trying not to look again at Seymour. When matters stood in this condition one never knew quite what to do, if like Lily and Randall one were an innocent party. Sometimes it was better to try to make a little meaningless conversation, but that took more heart than this morning's atmosphere allowed. Seymour sat, pretending to eat, and trying to catch the waitress's eye so that she would relieve him of his dish as quickly and unobtrusively as possible.

"Was it—" his mother began lightly to speak, in her nervous anxiety to mask the awful silence; and then she paused. She could not ask about the party, something had happened to Seymour which had to do with last night. "Was it nice weather?" Lily asked lamely.

"Fine," said Seymour. He had got rid of the bowl of porridge, which might of itself have raised a preposterous, childish issue. He sat waiting for his coffee, which his grandmother always poured. She continued to ignore him. The rest of the breakfast appeared, the invariable Sunday pancakes, the bacon which in summer took the place of winter's sausages. Seymour could not have eaten a mouthful; his brain was already moving round and round in the circle which was to be a very long day's treadmill. The old woman knew, but how could she know except she had been wide awake last night and lain there without making a sound, watching, by her bedside clock, to trap him? He suppressed a sigh. He had had enough years' experience to know now that there was nothing better to do than to face it squarely, himself to put it up to the old woman. He sat waiting for his coffee, which she did not pour so that he had to ask her for it. She gave him an ugly look with her bagged, spectacled eyes and poured his coffee and handed him the cup without a word. He drank some coffee. Then, rallying his courage more to face humiliation before his mother and Randall than for the coming ordeal with his grandmother, he said, "May I speak to you before church, Grandmama?"

"You are not going to church," she said, in a thick tone eloquent of ill-suppressed rage.

Never had she said such a thing before. Lily sat back, with quick tears of terror in her eyes, and Randall gazed at the old woman in horrified bewilderment. What could she mean?

"You are not going out at all, anywhere," said Mrs. Holt, "until we leave for New York tomorrow."

Seymour's cup clattered into its saucer and he knew that his face must have turned brick red. It burnt so that his eyeballs stung. He sat rigid. There was nothing to say. He could ask her what she meant, but he knew what she meant. Memory upon memory broke over him in sickening waves, every sharp and scathing thing she had ever said about his mother, every scornful remark about his father's disastrous marriage. He need not even remember the early and indelible impressions of the things he had overheard: he knew. She had her spy, or spies; how or by what means he would never be able to find out; but if she had been every moment of last evening there beside himself and Dorothy Bayliss, she could not be more aware. Then the sheer loathsomeness of her venomous, twisted view, a vile travesty and abasement of his feelings, rose up as if to suffocate him. He had never known real anger of this kind before. For all his violent temper and the savage, destructive things it had driven him to do, he had never sensed what he felt now, a righteous rage so enormous that it swept down his lifelong habit of cowed, hypocritical deference. Without knowing it, he was on his feet, saying, "You are contemptible! A sneaking, spying—you've spied on me! You vile old woman!"

He did not know what he was saying, against the pandemonium of Lily's squealing sobs and Randall's heartbroken wail, "But the Cup! The Season Cup! He can't miss the Labor Day Race!"

"Silence!" bellowed Mrs. Holt.

"Silence is what you'll have," retorted Seymour. "I was going to grovel before you and confess like a child about the clock. Now I'm not. Nobody else would ever find himself in such a position. You'll have your silence. Move us back to your prison in New York. I can't do anything about that. But silence is all you'll ever get from me, if you beat me to death for it."

He picked up his cup and saucer and flung them across the room where they smashed on the hearth. Then he kicked back his chair with a crash and strode from the room.

CHAPTER 4

For the ninth time Randall started again at the red mark where the second theme of the Larghetto began. This was deceptively simple, actually very difficult and more demanding of expressiveness, of what Professor Mundt called *Innerlichkeit* than the rest of the wonderfully poetic movement. "It iss for *diss* dat you play diss concerto *beim Konzert*," he said. Randall was working hard to have it ready for the Students' Concert, the day before Thanksgiving. For several years he had played at each of these concerts which took place three times during the winter, but this was his first concerto, to be played with a small orchestra of real Philharmonic players. Randall had chosen the concerto himself and begged for it in spite of Professor's doubts. The Mozart C Minor, to which Professor taught him to refer as *"Köchel vier hundert ein und neunzig"* was too serious and difficult for him, his teacher thought; and Randall not mature enough. But Professor believed in letting his students follow their tastes.

Yet Randall was having trouble. He tried to make the wistful, transparent melody reflect the mood of sad anxiety which permeated the house and surrounded his mother and himself like a mist. One must not be too personal in these efforts at interpretation, he knew; they must not be forced. But here with every reason to make it possible; with no real technical difficulty, music that he adored, and the desire to draw all he felt from the yearning theme, he could not bring it alive. He tried for a moment, sitting still, to evoke the mood of the plaintive woodwinds who opened the passage, so simple as to be nothing but five little notes made immortal by genius. Last winter when he had heard Paderewski play the concerto this passage had drawn tears to his eyes. Now he could only feel the inner wish to evoke the same feeling; he could not make his hands do it. He was suddenly overcome by discouragement and the sense that he ought not to have undertaken this. He laid his arms on the edge of the music rack and put his head down on them and sat there wishing he were not too old to cry.

He heard the door open and close and he looked up and found Seymour standing near him. The room, except for the gas-mantle lamp

by the piano, was quite dark and Randall realized that it must be past
six, over an hour later than Seymour usually arrived home after his
trip by the Hudson River Railroad from the University. Seymour said,
"What's the matter, Kid?"

Randall gestured at the music. "Oh—nothing! It's hard. Say, aren't
you home awfully late?"

Seymour shrugged. Randall knew he had been calling at the Bayliss's, which was the only motive urgent enough to induce Seymour to
defy this year's rule that he be home on the stroke of five o'clock
every day. The old woman's control of Seymour had become something
of a mockery. The only real axe she could wield would be to refuse to
pay his tuition at Columbia. She could not physically imprison him in
the house but sometimes Randall wondered uneasily if she were not
capable of hiring some man, like a prison guard, to escort Seymour
daily to the University and back. From the sidelines, watching the
deadlock between the two, Randall felt as if he could divine better than
Seymour the vindictive lengths to which their grandmother might still
go. It was all very well to admire Seymour passionately, as Randall
did, for having the courage to hold to his vow. But the price of this
might be beyond computing; and it would not be exacted of Seymour
alone. Randall was thinking of this as he sat at his piano looking up at
his brother's handsome but gloomy and troubled face.

"Where's Mama?" asked Seymour, dropping into one of the fussy,
tufted parlor chairs.

Randall indicated upstairs with a tilt of his head. "You know." She
was almost always lying down these afternoons, with the blinds drawn
and a cold compress over her eyes.

"Has She—" They had their own way of pronouncing the pronoun
when they spoke about their grandmother. They never called her now
by any other name between themselves.

"Not that I know of, not today. Mama just said she didn't feel
well when I came in from school and I didn't need her here." Lily no
longer practised regularly with Randall. He was well enough drilled not
to require supervision during the long hours of scales and exercises and
technical studies. For the rest, old Professor Mundt said, he had either
developed enough musicianship to fix his own marks at which to aim,
or he would never have it.

Seymour sat humped in his chair, with his chin propped on his knuckles. He looked very unhappy. Randall began to wonder whether something was troubling him beyond the alarming situation here at home. He tried to find a tactful way to ask, and then gave it up. Seymour would confide in him if he wanted to, and never by any sort of possibility if he did not want to. Randall only said, "I think Mama is terribly worried."

"I know. That's the only part I mind. She isn't really ill all the time, she hasn't got headaches like she says."

"Of course not. She only does it to keep out of the way."

"The more she does it the likelier she is to believe herself when she says she feels ill."

"She's awfully unhappy, Brother."

"I know she is. So are you. So am I. But will you tell me if it was any better before? Now I've got the old bully checkmated, at least."

Once more Randall tried to find the courage to warn Seymour that this might not be so true, or so simple. He was in the house more hours of the day than Seymour, even though he spent that time shut up at the piano, and he was uneasy every moment. "It's something queer," he said, slowly. "Something going on."

"What?"

"I can't tell, that's the trouble. I have a feeling She—She does something to Mama when we're out."

"What can She do? Mama always stays in her room while you're at school, she always did. *She* never goes there, that's why Mama started shutting herself up like that."

"Maybe I'm all wrong," said Randall, with hopefulness which did not deceive Seymour. The boy was really worried. Now Seymour found himself uneasy even beyond his own anxieties which Randall did not know about.

"Maybe you're not wrong, too," he said. "If you mean—well, I haven't exactly admitted it to myself either, but there is a difference in Mama. I know what you mean."

Randall nodded, pulling down the corners of his mouth. "And a difference in Her too. She's sort of, I don't know—secret. Locked away. I wouldn't care if I didn't think it meant some kind of trouble. She used to make me go and do all that reporting to her in the library the way we always had to and now She doesn't send for me so much."

"Well, what are you kicking about?" Seymour laughed with an

acid rasp. "Haven't I done you a favor? I wish somebody'd done as much for me four years ago!"

"Maybe She's going to die," said Randall coolly. It took nerve to say the words and he felt pleased with himself.

"What else should She do by now?" Seymour got to his feet and looked at the old tombstone clock. "Dinner in a quarter of an hour. Come on, wash yer hands, Master Randall, and change yer collar, now." He spoke in the fussy, nasal brogue of old Nana, gone years ago, whom he had always liked to mimic. The brothers laughed and went away upstairs.

After dinner, when Seymour was trying to study in his own room, the calculus which was usually not difficult for him· turned intolerably hard. He was doing brilliantly at Columbia; the Dean said few freshmen showed such aptitude for mathematics and engineering. There was already every likelihood that Seymour could finish his undergraduate course in three years. After some graduate work in special engineering he would be ready to start work as a naval architect, the one thing he had wanted all his life to do. And he had seen clearly for a long time past that nobody could have stronger motives than he for wanting to be independent. He supposed there was a good deal of money tied up in the family, but little as he knew of the details he knew that his grandmother would use every possible device to keep him financially in her power whether she were alive or dead. He must make for himself the means to break away.

The figures swam and wriggled on the page before him. Seymour pushed away the textbook and with his elbow dashed to the floor his notebook, with its engraving-like notations and drawings in his small, fine hand. He sat with his head between his hands. Eight or ten weeks ago it had all looked quite simple. Beyond his inflexible intention to keep to the one declaration that he had vowed in his rage, from which he could not back down, he was prepared to be as reasonable as possible. He knew that if he stayed out of the house at hours outside his college day, his mother and Randall would have to take the punishment. So he had seen· almost nothing of Dorothy. He had resigned himself to that. He knew the situation could not continue forever. What troubled him most was that he never seemed to have a chance to explain to Dorothy, or to talk to her alone; he had never said a word about the precipitate departure from Hare Island. On his few calls at the Bayliss house over on Gramercy Park he had not once found Dorothy alone. Either her mother was receiving callers and Dorothy as the débutante daughter must assist; or some of Dorothy's own friends were there in a chattering, fluttering bevy, full of excitement about the season's parties which were beginning at Thanksgiving.

This afternoon was only the fourth time he had seen Dorothy since last August. Now when he could not study, when he was restless and probed by a twisting sense of imminent trouble, he thought back over every moment of the half hour he had spent in Mrs. Bayliss's drawing-room; then he began to compare today with his previous visits; and something cold and sickening clutched at his throat as he forced himself to admit, with puzzled pain, that Dorothy was changed. Not only was she changed, with a constraint which he had at first and now, he thought, mistakenly, taken for shyness; she was more changed each time he saw her. Seymour drew a long breath and found himself mopping his forehead with his handkerchief. Had he been utterly stupid not to have realized this, or would anyone else have been as slow to comprehend as he? But what was wrong? Seymour did not feel he had ever said a word to Dorothy, or held a feeling for her, which was not the expression of the best there was in him. From every imaginable aspect he examined his own heart, and all this measured by her own scarcely-spoken but unmistakable meaning the night of the beach-party, made him sure that neither of them had done or said or felt anything wrong. His conscience was clear, and he believed in her. She was not a flirt and she had not been playing with him. What had happened?

Today he had found her in the rear of the two adjoining parlors at her house, sitting with two girls whom he did not know well, girls who spent their summers at Newport. Mrs. Bayliss was pouring tea in the front parlor, chatting with some ladies, and Seymour was the only man present. Mrs. Bayliss had given him tea, and now as he sat carefully remembering and reconstructing every moment of the afternoon, he realized with another shiver of disquiet that she too was changed since last summer. He could still hear her pleasant voice in retrospect, thanking him that night for bringing Dorothy home and saying that they would ask him over soon; but no such words had ever been uttered since. She was calm and agreeable, but hardly cordial. When he had drunk his tea she had called into the other drawing-room, "Dorothy, Seymour is here to call," and had sent him in to join the three girls.

They were sitting round a low tabouret table, with long sheets of paper spread over it, and were going over, item by item, what Seymour knew at once was the invitation-list for Dorothy's coming-out ball. She looked up as he came through the archway between the two rooms and before she spoke at all, her face, at which he had been trying not to look too fixedly, turned quite pink.

Seymour sat now hunched in his desk chair, twisting his hands in sudden painful enlightenment. She had not blushed from shyness or pleasure when he appeared; she was embarrassed. Why?

"Good afternoon, Seymour," she said, holding out the dainty hand he loved. "I think you know Seymour Holt," she said to her friends. "Virginia Godwin. And Ellen Van Thuyl." He did know them slightly; he bowed, they murmured something, and he sat down on the edge of a chair.

"Isn't it exciting, all the parties," began Miss Van Thuyl. "We were just—"

"I'm afraid there will be too many," said Dorothy quickly. She had folded up the sheets of paper and put them under a book on the lower shelf of the table.

"Oh, there couldn't be too many!" The other girl was tall and boldly handsome, and Seymour could see her the centre of any ball. He laughed a little and said, "I shan't be troubled with too many, at any rate."

And Dorothy had said nothing. At the moment he had not immediately remembered her words of last summer, when she had asked him to promise to come to her ball, and had said how much fun it would be, and how she was looking forward to the parties this winter. But now it broke over him in a chilling wave. He had not heard her say a word about the party since; and he realized with a shock that he was not going to be invited to it. Tumbling in the wake of this came a flood of other and graver realizations. Dorothy was not being shy, and she was not trying to withdraw from a moment's sentimental yielding. Something more serious was happening. Seymour sat at his desk, staring at nothing, hours after he had heard Randall go to his room and turn in for the night.

Next afternoon he presented himself again at the Bayliss house, and was ushered by an expressionless parlormaid into a drawing-room unoccupied by anybody. The second parlor was also empty.

"Mrs. Bayliss is having tea upstairs in the library, sir," said the maid. "I will announce you."

"I—" Seymour had no chance to say he had come to call on Miss Dorothy. The maid had left the room. He waited, heartsick, with a galloping pulse, and suspense wrenching at the pit of his stomach. It seemed to him that the maid was gone an hour; she was in fact very long, with Seymour standing erect and motionless on the hearth when he could in his wretchedness have paced the nap off the carpet. At last the maid stood in the doorway and said, "Will you come up to the library, sir?"

Seymour followed her upstairs and passed the door she held open. Mrs. Bayliss was seated on one side of the library fire, and facing her, with his back to the door, Dorothy's father. Seymour realized with a start that this was Saturday. He had lost track of everything since last night, and had not expected to find Mr. Bayliss at home from his office. Dorothy sat in a low chair between them, pale and with trembling lips. Seymour saw that she had been crying and there rose above his own apprehension a surge of longing to comfort and reassure her. But nothing could be more futile, more impossible. He shook hands with Dorothy's parents and then with her, startled that her small fingers were icy cold.

"No, thank you very much," he said, as Mrs. Bayliss motioned him to a chair and began to pour tea for him. "No tea, thank you."

He remained standing, looking with a sinking heart from the gentle face of Dorothy's mother, clearly troubled, to Allan Bayliss who had known his father well and Seymour all his life. Dorothy had bent her head, a mild, resigned gesture which hurt him with a prescient pang. He could see only the top of her head, the crisp light brown curls shining in the firelight. Seymour thought for a distracted moment how he should love to touch her, to put one hand under her chin and raise her face so that he could see it again. But this was no moment for such dreaming, and he waited only long enough to sense that the answer to the question he had come to ask could be had only from Dorothy's father, or by way of his permission.

"I hadn't expected to see you, sir," he said, "but perhaps it's just as well. I wanted to ask if I might speak to Dorothy."

Allan Bayliss looked at his wife and then at Seymour, with an expression which was at once stern and full of regretful affection.

"I'm not surprised, Seymour. I know, I understand why you are here." He looked at Dorothy for a moment, sitting with her hands twisted round her fine handkerchief. "Don't you think, dear, it would be better if you and Mother go and leave Seymour and me here by ourselves?"

She started to rise from her chair; then she sat up straight and Seymour's eyes smarted as she said, her lovely soft voice dark with forced courage, "Seymour asked to speak to me, Father. I can—I will—" She choked. Her mother reached over and grasped the girl's hand and Seymour swallowed and said, "Dorothy, I'm awfully grateful but I think your father is right. Please go."

"Won't you sit down, Seymour?" asked Allan Bayliss when the door was closed. "Do you smoke, have you a pipe?"

"No thanks, sir." Seymour smiled lamely. "I've never smoked." But he sat down slowly in the chair facing Dorothy's father.

"I—this had to come, of course," said Mr. Bayliss. "But I wish I could spare you, my boy. And the worst of it is I've got to ask for your understanding with every word I say."

"I don't think it will be very difficult to understand, sir," said Seymour. In a streak of awareness as if a closed door had been flung open, he sensed what was coming.

"You have courage," said Bayliss. "You have many other qualities that I admire and—let's be completely frank here—that Dorothy would find it natural to love. You are both very young, but not too young to fall in love." He pulled thoughtfully on his pipe for a moment. Then he laid it on the table beside him and leaned forward and said, gently shaking his head, "That's what I've told Dorothy absolutely must not happen."

"But—but—I—we—" Seymour was trying to find a way to tell his feelings in a word of truth.

"Not yet," said Bayliss. "I saw exactly what was happening last summer. I was weighing then how I would feel if things took a serious turn. I talked to Dorothy after that evening, that night you brought her home. She told me everything that passed between you. There was no harm in that, none whatever."

"I'm glad you felt that way, sir."

Bayliss smiled sadly. "I did. I do. But the very next day I was forced to consider what Dorothy would be up against if I should let things take their course, let her see as much of you as you both would like." He paused and gave Seymour a look of complete frankness. Seymour waited a moment and said, "You can imagine how I felt."

"I can imagine, indeed. Your grandmother did a shocking thing, a thing which reflected not only upon you, but upon my daughter. Naturally nobody at Hare Island or any friends of ours could misunderstand. Unfortunately we all know her too well. And that's the crux of the matter, Seymour."

Seymour sat silent, wretched and not confronted with anything that he had not really known before. Bayliss did not speak for some time. Then he said slowly, "Of course there was always the chance that you would both outgrow a first love, people do, you know. But then there was the chance that you wouldn't."

"I really—well, sir, I never thought all the way into the future. I have to go through college, get to work—"

"Of course you do. And no man really wants to see his daughter tied up in a long-standing promise like that. But that is not my objection, Seymour, you should be perfectly clear about it. The objection is your grandmother. So long as that woman is alive, I will not let my girl have any chance to—to become attached to you. Nothing. No meetings with you at all, except on the most distant possible basis." He leaned forward in his chair, ready to exchange any glance, however painful, with Seymour; but Seymour was sitting with his head between his hands, staring at the floor. Bayliss felt wracked with regret and pity. Seymour said slowly, "My grandmother is over eighty years old."

"I know that, my boy. I follow you. But even after she is dead, I would still want time. Time to see what your upbringing has made of you, to put it frankly. Your father was a friend of mine, you know, he was only six years older than I. I have seen your grandmother's handiwork ever since I can remember—and I am not going to let my girl risk her whole life in such a danger." He paused and Seymour looked up slowly and saw that he was weighing something else; then he said thoughtfully, "I remember Lily Randall, too, when she married your father. I was at their wedding. She was—she was rather like Dorothy."

Seymour put his head between his hands again. Bayliss closed his mouth hard and blew his nose. A man would be, he thought, a stone not to be wrung literally to tears by this boy's plight. For Seymour it was dark; he sat with his eyes closed, his teeth clenched, and a hollow probing pain somewhere, anywhere, everywhere inside him. For the first time in his life he saw himself not as of the moment, not as of the years of childhood past, but as of the future; and his future seemed now a fearful and impenetrable space of endless darkness. Had he been deluding himself that by seizing the initiative, defying the old woman, stubbornly taking the first steps towards independence, he could hope to escape a fate which this kindly and admirable man clearly feared for him? Why, Seymour asked himself in silence; why is this so? Can I not begin to live even when she is dead? No matter how I try? And Bayliss's memory of his mother, a girl who resembled Dorothy, something which had never occurred to Seymour, rose now to invoke a whole new train of anxious thoughts about his mother, vague and frightened and silly and helpless. Where was this to lead him? What could he see but sorrow and emptiness and grief? He raised his head slowly, unashamed of his wet eyes and unafraid of Allan Bayliss, who in dealing him an extreme hurt had shown him more kindness than he had ever in all his life known.

"So there is really no hope for me at all?" asked Seymour, struggling to hold his voice level.

"How can I see into the future, my boy? I only know that I care more for my daughter and her happiness than anything in this world. I am trying to do the right thing, and it isn't—it hasn't been, easy. Nor for Dorothy either." He saw Seymour bite his pale lips. "She is a good girl and not a silly one. It is very seldom a girl will let herself be advised before it is too late."

"You are right," said Seymour. Bayliss thought his voice imposing in its control.

"I am very deeply impressed by you," said Bayliss slowly. "You have been more than manly about this. I cannot tell you how much I regret what I have had to do. I wish I could retract somehow—but my dear boy, I can't."

"I understand."

"That's what I told Dorothy. That's what I said she ought to count on when I advised her to write you that note."

"Note?" asked Seymour. "Dorothy wrote to me, Mr. Bayliss?"

"Why, yes." They stared at one another. "A week ago, I should think, when the invitations to her party were mailed." Seymour was gripping the arms of his chair. Bayliss saw his white knuckles. "We had to talk about this then, of course. It had to be made clear once and for all. I believed it would be easier for you not to be asked to the ball, and I told Dorothy it would be better and more honest if she should write and explain. Once for all," he said again.

"So—so—" Seymour was almost choking. "So naturally she didn't expect to see me yesterday." He rose quickly to his feet. Bayliss rose also. They stood for a moment on the hearth, exchanging a look of grave and appalled understanding. "You see what happened, sir," said Seymour. He put out his hand. "I'm afraid it only proves how right you are."

Bayliss wrung his hand. Seymour said, "Good bye, sir. I can't stay any longer."

Bayliss gripped his hand hard again, and when Seymour had left the room, shook his head slowly and stood staring sadly at the fire.

Seymour rang the doorbell at home with a long, angry peal. He had no latchkey, and when the new maid opened the door—the staff had been entirely changed when they returned from Hare Island—he strode past her without a word. He went straight upstairs and flung open the door of the library without knocking. His grandmother was sitting as usual in her ugly red satin chair, which with the curtains drawn and the gas lighted for the evening, was turned from the bay window towards the fire. He had not been in this room since last year. He closed the door roughly behind him.

"I want the note from Dorothy Bayliss that you intercepted," he said, in a tone ringing with fury.

"I burnt it," said the old woman. She might have been telling him the time.

"I expected that. I really came here to tell you I know what you have done. I told you last summer you are contemptible. If I had a worse word I'd use it now."

His grandmother laughed. Seymour's ears buzzed with the sound, augmented by his anger. "Words," she said, in her heavy, hatefully resonant voice. "Those are cheap and you make a fool of yourself spending them. You are a fool anyway."

"Yes. Ever to have let myself be bullied by you. That's all over. From now on I'm going to do exactly as I choose."

"More words. Don't waste them, Seymour. You are absolutely dependent and haven't any choice."

"Oh yes I have. I can move out of here tonight and get a job somewhere."

"And your education?"

"That would only be another thing you'd ruined, depriving me of that along with everything else."

"Oh, you ought to have your education." He could not tell whether she meant to be sardonic or, in some inscrutable way, reasonable.

"Then I'll have it on my terms. I'd say I would go away to Boston, to the Massachusetts Institute, except I can't leave my mother and Randall alone in the house with you. So you'll pay for it here. You'll give me a latchkey and an allowance, and if you refuse, I will move out and go to work instead."

"Leaving your idiot of a mother and that piano-thumping milksop here."

"Whatever they are, it's your fault."

"They haven't got the stuff you have," said the old woman amazingly. Seymour knew now that if he had treated her in this way years ago he could have saved himself and the others untold misery. "You may amount to something if you don't throw yourself away on some snip like that Bayliss girl."

"Be still! Don't mention her name, you wicked old woman. You may as well know that the Baylisses like the rest of us are marking time until you die. If I don't see Dorothy Bayliss meanwhile, that's because you don't know how decent people feel. And next summer at Hare Island—"

His grandmother interrupted him with a rough "Bah! Hare Island. I've sold the Hare Island house and put the money in the irrevocable trusts where you can't touch it."

Seymour stood with his mouth open, slowly grasping what she had said. Then he asked, wrinkling his forehead, "And my boat?"

"*Your* boat? I told you you are a fool. A minor has no title to property."

"You monster!" Seymour's voice broke out wildly. All the hurt and humiliation of this heartbreaking day came to a head in a scream of protest about his boat. For his real loss, for Dorothy, he could struggle to grieve like a man, in courage and silence. This was different. "You are the vilest person in the whole world. What harm did I do you with that boat? The only—" he paused and drew in his breath with a great gulp, fighting not to burst into a sob and give her the satisfaction of seeing him suffer. She sat staring coldly down her nose, as if nothing unusual were happening at all.

"Oh, I want you to know how I hate you," he said, when he could control his voice. "I want you to know all about it. All that I always knew, when I was a little tiny kid, about the way you treated Papa. And how you've made my mother suffer."

"That sniveling idiot," said the old woman.

Seymour's fists closed and he stood over her in her chair and said, "You *are* a monster, I said so. What's the matter with you? Why have you got this mania for wrecking people's lives? Why is every good and decent feeling poisoned when you touch it? Everybody hates you. Everybody is afraid of you—only I'm not any more. Not me. Everything I ever felt for you is one big hate. I hate you and I want you to die. I hope you die. Why don't you die?" he roared, leaning over her and shouting into her face. "Why don't you die?"

To his amazement, something happened to the face. One side of it went up, twisting and curling like a piece of lighted paper, right up into the frizzle of white hair round her narrow forehead; and the other side went down, dragged and going sidewise, into her jowl. Her eyes behind their spectacles moved off into two crazy unrelated stares. Then one eye slowly, foolishly closed in a kind of leer and the other remained wide open, glassy like the eye of a doll. A dribble of spittle drooled from the downward side of her twisted mouth. Seymour backed slowly away, observing with a shocked sense of no surprise at all her body twisted and crooked like her face, the hands and feet awry with everything high on the left side and dragged down on the right. She was making a gargling noise. Seymour stood up straight for a moment, watching her. Then he walked to the bell and rang it. When the maid came he said coldly, "My grandmother has had a stroke. Run and fetch Dr. Wharton." He remembered that the maid was new. He called after her, "Dr. Prentice Wharton. Three houses west, on this side of the street."

Mrs. Holt died on Christmas Eve, leaving a will which was read to Seymour and Randall and their mother following the funeral the day after Christmas. In the most ingenious possible way, and to the utmost extent of the law, the old woman had tied up all the money, her own and her husband's by means of which she had imprisoned her son John, in two trusts. Seymour was the eventual inheritor of the larger share, Randall of the lesser. Seymour's share was to remain in an irrevocable trust until he was forty years of age, Randall's until he was forty-five. While they were minors the brothers would not receive any income directly, but only small allowances in amounts to be determined by their Trustees. At the age of twenty-one they would receive a stingy portion of their funds, but the rest was to be reinvested. A further portion would be paid them at the end of ten years, but still not all. Neither, until he was past forty, would ever be able to put his hands on enough money at a time to make such a capital purchase as a house or other piece of major property. Meanwhile the house here in Chelsea was incorporated into the two trusts on a basis which forbade its sale; and at this point Seymour exclaimed, "But that's madness. The neighborhood is running down so fast, it changes week by week."

The lawyer who was reading the will gave Seymour a look which could be interpreted as an opinion that the whole will was madness, but he continued to read. Seymour's Trustees were the bank and this lawyer and another legal figure, a retired judge who could be expected to be more inflexible than Mrs. Holt herself. But in Randall's case the will held a surprise: after Seymour was twenty-one he was to become one of Randall's Trustees, his power limited to determining questions relating to Randall's education.

The brothers stared at one another in astonishment.

"Now what," said Seymour, "do you suppose she meant by that?"

"I don't know," said Randall, "but it's a good thing for me."

Their mother said nothing. The will was of no concern to her. She sat in a corner of the room with her hands crossed in her lap, pale and effaced and paying little attention. In her high-necked black dress she looked homely and dowdy. Neither she nor the boys had manifested the least sorrow as a hypocritical concession to the indifferent, transient servants or the few old family connections who had called out of a sense of duty or convention. Lily and the boys were wearing mourning because it had not occurred to them not to do so. They would observe the conventional period of mourning retirement for the same reason. But Seymour had already said, "Will you tell me what we are retiring from? How can you withdraw from withdrawal? Nobody ever invited us anywhere."

"Well," said Lily vaguely, "of course now they wouldn't anyway."

"They will," said Seymour with a grim face. "As soon as this business is behind us."

"Oh, darling," said his mother in her wiry, plaintive voice. "You aren't expecting to *entertain*?"

"Of course I am. Haven't we had enough prison all our lives?"

"I don't see—I wouldn't know—" Lily's hand fluttered to her lips.

"Oh, there's plenty of time," said Seymour. "First let's get used to being ourselves."

He found that the only provision for his mother was a direction by his grandmother to the Trustees to pay the bills for Lily Holt's absolute necessities and a preposterously small annual sum for her clothes, out of the incomes of the trusts. The house was to be run on the same basis. Things were intended to be as nearly as possible what they had been in his grandmother's lifetime. Seymour shut his jaw with a snap. "I'll change all that," he said to Randall, and when Randall asked how, he answered, "You wait and see."

He intended to start at once with changes sharp enough to jolt his mother and Randall out of the routine of years, which they were continuing to follow sheerly from habit. He dismissed the servants and then asked his mother to engage a new staff. She turned pale and murmured, "Oh, dear. Please, I, why must I—"

"Mama," he said, "I'm only asking you to do something in your own interest—and ours. We want people here who never had anything to do with Her. These last ones didn't care a straw for us—none of them ever did. Would you in their places?"

"But Seymour, I don't know how to find servants."

"You simply go to an agency and tell them what you want and then sit there and talk to the people they've got. At least I suppose that's the way it's done."

"Oh, dear," said Lily.

"And when you do get a new cook," added Seymour, "I wish you'd make sure there isn't a way in the world she can find out what Grandmama's meals used to be. No more Irish stew on Monday. No more pancakes or roast beef on Sunday. No more codfish on Friday. No more porridge for breakfast—ever again."

"Hoo-ray!" called Randall from the stairs on his way down to practise.

But it proved one thing for Seymour to give orders and quite another for his mother to carry them out. She could not carry them out and her efforts to do so kept the house in a turmoil. For a long time Seymour was very patient. He did not need Randall's rather timid advice to go slowly and give Mama a chance to get used to keeping house. He wanted to give her every chance and he made all sorts of suggestions which he thought would help her.

"Why don't we do over the library?" he asked her. "Change everything around and fix it up so you can use it for a sitting-room. You've never had a corner of the house for your own except—"

"Oh, *no*!" cried Lily. "Not the library. I wouldn't sit in that room for anything in the world!" She wrung her hands.

"But it would all be different," said Seymour patiently. "That's what I meant. Different curtains and chairs—we can shift the house all around. And get rid of those awful red satin armchairs," he added, scowling. The things invoked the old woman at every glance.

"Not the library," whined Lily. "Please."

"Very well." He controlled his irritation and his momentary impulse to snap at his mother. "Very well. I'll use the room myself. I don't see why I should study in my bedroom."

At moments like this he could have added that he did not want to study or live in the house at all. Columbia was by no means the ideal place for the engineering he needed, and he would have gone away to Boston with eager relief. But it was out of the question to leave his mother and Randall going round in their tracks here by themselves.

For a time they were all satisfied with the sheer luxury of Mrs. Holt's absence. They observed the first weeks of mourning with punctiliousness directly out of proportion to their real feelings; as Randall said, his blue eyes wide with ingenuous sincerity, "You know, we oughtn't to feel so pleased and relieved. Everybody thinks we're shut up here really mourning Grandmama."

"Don't you believe it," said Seymour. 'Everybody' to him was personified by the Bayliss family. He was waiting only for the right moment, which instinct would mark, to go and call at the Bayliss's and see how matters stood there now. "Everybody who knows us knows exactly how we feel. They'd be fools if they didn't."

He chose, finally, a Thursday afternoon the week after Lent began. The débutante parties would be over. Dorothy had had more than three months of such gaiety that even in his isolation Seymour knew she was ranked the prettiest and most popular débutante of the season. He had no reason to hope that he would be encouraged to see her, though surely he would not be forbidden now; every word of his talk with Allan Bayliss was as vivid as at the moment he had first heard it. He could be on probation for many reasons, but most of all because Mr. Bayliss would have to have time "to see what your upbringing has made of you." The challenge seemed to Seymour tremendous but not hopeless. It was his redeeming chance and he was determined to make the most of it. By comparison the handicaps of his youth and the long prospective years of college and work seemed quite secondary.

He found Mrs. Bayliss alone in her drawing-room. This was as great a relief as Dorothy's absence was a disappointment. Mrs. Bayliss greeted him cordially and asked for his mother, at the same time saying, "Dorothy is at the Sewing Circle this afternoon. All the girls, you know—"

Seymour wished he had known. But how should be remember that the Lenten Sewing Circle met on Thursday afternoons? He had forgotten it if he had ever heard it mentioned.

"How is Mr. Bayliss?" he asked. He felt awkward, if not a fool; he might as well have inquired outright for the measure of Mr. Bayliss's feelings now.

"Quite well, thank you."

Seymour drank his tea nervously, grateful that Mrs. Bayliss found small matters about which to chat. He could not have made a word of conversation when urgent feelings were pressing all sorts of unspoken questions which he could not bring out. Suddenly he found himself painfully afraid that Mrs. Bayliss would say something about Hare Island, or boats, or next summer; and then he realized for the first time that she and all the others must know what his grandmother had done. He struggled with a plunging wave of mortification, cruelly sharpened by his own stupidity in not having thought of this sooner. If he had, perhaps he would not have had the courage to call today. He took his leave as soon as he could, and was only faintly comforted when Mrs. Bayliss said kindly, "It was nice to see you, Seymour."

"Please—please give my regards to Dorothy," he said.

"Of course. And mine to your mother." She smiled and he bowed and went away. It had been nearly completely unsatisfactory, but Seymour was still not sure of the real state of affairs. Sitting in the Twenty-third Street horse-car he stared out at the dirty, mired slush of late February, the carriages lined up at the entrances of the department-stores, the vans and drays with their great steaming horses, the hurrying crowds on the pavements. Everything and everybody in sight seemed to have more purpose and be more alive than he. He sighed as the horse-car crossed Ninth Avenue and slowly approached his own corner. He could not remember just when it had begun to happen, but only a few years ago, he thought; Chelsea was turning into a bleak and ugly district, its fine houses one by one degenerating into rooming-houses, its pavements unmended, its trees unreplaced when they died. Many of the neighbors among whom he had grown up had moved away to other parts of the city, eastward and uptown. And here he was, with Randall, condemned to live in the Chelsea house no matter what Chelsea was becoming, unless he or both of them should earn enough money to go away and make what they chose of their lives, leaving the old house to rot if that was what its fate must be.

He walked from Tenth Avenue round the corner and eastward on Twenty-fourth Street, for their house was nearest the Tenth Avenue end of the block. As he approached the gate he was surprised to see a large van standing there, backed up with its doors open and two heavy planks running from the rear of the van to the street. The horses were stamping in the slush. Seymour peered into the van and found it empty; then he walked up the front path, eyeing the open door, and into the hallway of the house. An upright piano stood there, with four blue-jacketed men around it and Randall and Lily discussing where it was to be put.

"What is this thing?" asked Seymour. "Where did this piano come from?"

"It's from Hare Island," said Randall. "Look." He handed Seymour a piece of paper which, he said, had been brought by the man with the van. Seymour saw at a glance that the paper was a delivery order from Mrs. Holt's executors, which made it clear that the only thing which had not been sold lock, stock, and barrel with the Hare Island house was this piano. Seymour stood and glared at it. Randall said, "It's a pity. The piano's no good, the dampness at the Island, you know, and—" He paused and looked at Seymour with a sudden grimace of emotion. "I wish," he said, and choked.

Seymour asked by a gesture what Randall meant, and Randall said miserably, "I wish it were your boat."

"If ye please, mum," said the van boss gruffly to Lily, "wull ye be tellin' us where to put this pianney? We ain't got all day."

Lily said, "Oh," and looked helplessly at Seymour.

"Put it down in the cellar," he said roughly. "Down there." He pointed to the door under the stairs. "Put it by the other one that's down there."

He had not formed the habit of imitating the profanity of some of the young men he knew, but now, stamping into the library and slamming the door behind him, he stood in the middle of the room and swore.

About a fortnight later he knocked on his mother's door one day and after her faintly shrill "Come in!" he entered the room to find her nervously ruffling the pages of a blank-book. He could see that the pages were written in her vague, rather childish hand, and she closed the book with a little gasp as he came near enough possibly to see anything written in it.

"It's my housekeeping notebook," she said, a bit breathlessly. "Sit down, darling."

Seymour stood for a moment eyeing the room and wondering quite where to sit down. This clutter, this thing of furniture piled with small objects and boxes, or strewn ribbons, bits of lace, hat-trimmings, and unfinished scraps of knitting, had become much more noticeable in the past year or two. Mama's room had always been full of stuff like this, but it had been kept in a certain amount of order. Now it appeared as if the system, whatever it had been, had worn out and burst its seams.

Seymour pushed a pile of old photographs from one end of the divan and sat down.

"I'm glad you're really doing the housekeeping," he said with a smile. "It's not so very bad, is it?"

"Oh, yes!" Lily's mouth trembled, and she said, "I do try so hard to please you. That's why I—" she patted the closed notebook on her knee. "I copy receipts out of the Ladies' Journal and try to think of things to eat."

"Well, isn't the cook any help at that?"

Lily sighed. Then she said, "Oh, cooks are so *cold blooded*, Seymour. When I—sort of ask her—what it would be nice to have, she just stands there and says, 'That's for yerself to say, mum.' It makes me feel—

well, I think she's laughing at me, Seymour." Lily's eyes filled with tears.

"Oh, nonsense. You're just not used to her. We're getting along fine. And I wish you'd do something for me, Mama."

He looked at her with a smile, but she felt behind it something fixed and determined which made her realize beyond question that Seymour was no boy any longer, nothing at all like Randall who never showed this streak of hardness. Lily felt he never would; he was so gentle and so affectionate with her. She wished Seymour hadn't said he wanted something and she was uncomfortable because he sat waiting there for her to ask what it was.

She said timidly, "Well?"

"I wish you would write a note to Mrs. Bayliss and invite her and Mr. Bayliss and Dorothy here for Sunday supper next week."

Lily shrank down in her chair as if Seymour had said something to make her afraid. "Oh," she said weakly, "please—please not."

Seymour's jaw looked as if he had set it hard. He said coldly, "Mama, this is silly of you. We can't go on like this all the time."

"But—but it's too soon to entertain," she said.

"This is not 'entertaining.' Sunday supper in the middle of Lent can hardly be called that. I told you I want you to ask the Baylisses here— and I do."

To his annoyance, she began to cry. "I—can't," she sobbed. "It's too soon. I—I mean—"

"You don't mean anything that makes any sense to me."

"I—I'm—" Lily gulped.

"You're a little unused to it," said Seymour, in the gentlest tone he could. "I know that. But Mama, really you ought to see—it's not only that we have a right to be like other people—we've got all that lost time to make up for. And besides this makes a great difference to me."

His mother stared at him and nodded her head slowly, while tears slid down her cheeks, but she said in her querulous voice, "I see, but just the same I can't, Seymour. Not yet. I'm afraid."

"But of what? Certainly not of old friends you've always known?"

"I don't know," she wailed. "Stop badgering me. I just don't know. I'll try later on, truly I will. Please give me time." She put her hand on his arm and looked up at him. Her pale, puffy face with its red-rimmed eyes, her faded hair which straggled and no longer made those pretty curls above her forehead, her trembling lips and her nose which seemed to have lengthened to a different shape from the piquant short one of her early photographs, all went together into an unlovely blur which was part of this dim, cluttered room with its faintly musty odor and its aura of secrecy. "Please give me time," she begged again. "Don't make me do it now, Seymour, please. I can't." She put up her handkerchief to her face and sat there weeping. He stood up and said curtly, "Very well, then, we'll have to wait awhile. But remember I asked you, and somehow or other you'll have to get used to the idea. I mean it." He went away.

On Easter Monday Mr. and Mrs. Bayliss announced the engagement of Dorothy to Paul Parsons, the elder son of the Dorsey Parsons of Washington Square and Hare Island. The wedding took place in June at Grace Church. The groom was a rich young banker, seven years older than the bride, and the match was thought most suitable. Seymour, enclosing his mother's card with his own, sent a dozen salad plates from Tiffany's.

CHAPTER 5

Professor Mundt from his shabby armchair looked over the tops of his half-spectacles and nodded his white head slowly. Randall had finished the Waldstein Sonata and sat tired, with his hands in his lap. Sometimes at these moments he bent his head in a certain way which touched the old Professor and gave him at the same time a sense of anxiety. There seemed a meekness about Randall, a lack of assurance as if in silent pleading for approval, which was not part of the personality of an artist. Yet he played very well. His technique was good, his musical taste sound so far as it was formed, his keyboard mastery more than satisfactory for a student of his age, especially, thought the Professor, for one with a meagre musical background. Professor Mundt had always said that while Randall had talent and the essential quality which the old man called *echt Pianismus*, he could only develop the stature of an artist by intensive study and life in Europe, preferably in Vienna since that had been the old man's own birthplace and the Conservatorium his musical home. This idea had been so long taken for granted yet so vaguely suspended that to Seymour it had become a backdrop for Randall, undiscussed like the streaked purplish-striped moiré wallpaper in the drawing-room, about which something would one day have to be done. But his teacher knew that Randall's day had come now. The boy was nearly nineteen years old, there was no more time to waste.

"*So*," said the Professor. "*Es geht schon.* I haf finished vit' you."

Randall looked up with surprise. "What do you mean, Professor?"

"Just vat I said. I haf done all I am goot for, you go no farder vit' me. Now you go to Wien."

"It hadn't occurred to me just yet." Randall spoke with hesitation.

"It should. Now you finish your school, finish vit' nonsense, *entweder* you make now *das Künstlerleben, oder*—" The old hands went up in a gesture of finality. Randall rose slowly from the stool and stood in the bend of the piano with his hands in the pockets of his jacket. His teacher sat looking at him, unconsciously nodding a little at his own thoughts: it was a handsome lad, a beautiful one; look at that fine head with the golden curls, the wide blue eyes, the intelligent broad brow; the mouth and chin, however, a bit too soft? Too much of the mother there? *Ach*, the boy could grow a beard!

"How do I know I could get into the Conservatorium?" asked Randall. "Maybe I'm not good enough."

"I haf prepared you for the examinations. I tell you you pass, you leaf such t'ings to decide by me. The journey *undsoweiter* decides your brother, *nicht*?"

"Well—yes. Of course my mother—"

"Your mother has no authority." Not for nothing had the Professor been Randall's teacher for ten years. "Now already since last year can your brother give permission. You send him here, say I vish to talk vit' him."

"He's very busy just now," said Randall uneasily. "He's graduating from Columbia next month and grinding for his final exams."

"*Doch!* Und you? Also taking by your school *das Diplom, auch* you practise goot enough to play your lesson like today? You send your brother."

Seymour did begrudge Randall's affairs the necessary time and attention. No problem, he knew, was ever made less irksome by putting it off, but this one pushed its tentacles into so many different questions that he wished he could somehow chop it all down with one sharp blow. He knew perfectly well that Randall's plans must be made before the summer. Summers had been a nagging difficulty ever since the loss of the Hare Island house and all that went with it. There had been temporary expedients for Lily and Randall of summer boarding-houses at mountain or seaside resorts cheap enough to meet the stingy limitations of the Trustees, while Seymour stayed in town working as an unpaid apprentice in the offices of Grew and Minturn, the leading firm of naval architects. Beginning with this summer, after taking his degree, he had been offered a permanent post with the firm. The negligible salary did not much trouble him for he also received the small portion of his income stipulated after he should reach the age of twenty-one. In different circumstances, he often thought, with a quick effort to reject the creeping insinuations of disloyalty, he could now begin to make a thoroughly agreeable life for himself. A young bachelor could do very nicely on his means . . . with his mother and Randall away he could close this ugly, burdensome, oversized house and take a couple of rooms over on

Murray Hill . . . join a pleasant club where he could dine and find agreeable company . . . go out on cruises with clients of the firm whose yachts had problems to be solved . . . the prospect was so attractive that he had decided, on the hope of making it possible, to abandon the idea of graduate study in engineering, which Mr. Minturn had thought unnecessary . . . all he needed now was freedom. And walking slowly home from his talk with Professor Mundt he circled mentally round and round the core of the matter: freedom. It was within his grasp. And what was he to do about it?

He had begun to feel actual loathing for the bleary prospect of Twenty-fourth Street. Nowadays he had to make a conscious effort to remember what it had been like in the days when the block-long row of deep front yards had all been green and grassy, with bright beds of red and yellow flowers, and neatly painted wrought-iron urns on fancy pedestals, full of geraniums and trailing ivy. The street was not entirely and finally run down even yet; some places like their own were kept in a decent sort of order, but city smoke made good lawns and pretty flowers impossible. One thing led to another; that condition and the changing times made it difficult to find the old-fashioned sort of visiting gardener who kept the place up; makeshifting there meant makeshifting otherwise. Seymour scowled as he walked past the former Willetts house two doors from their own. In a couple of years it had gone utterly to pot. The unwashed windows were haphazardly curtained or not curtained at all; the front yard had lost the last of its grass to a crust of cinders; a broken bicycle stood rusting against the areaway where it had been for months; and the final degradation was proclaimed by a sign reading ROOMS, fixed in a front window. Seymour turned his head in revulsion as he passed the place and went along to his own low front gate. He had given up the struggle to keep flowers blooming in the two round beds on either side of the walk, but the lawn survived in some protest against the onslaught of grit. Seymour thought with a grimace of the dead hand which had saddled him with this incubus, after planning for years to tie him up in the maze of inexorable responsibilities which his mother and Randall personified.

He climbed the front steps slowly, and with a sigh let himself into the house. Professor Mundt's demands on behalf of Randall were right and necessary. But their price would have to be paid by Seymour, and this, he thought, was a bitter time to exact that price of him. He laid his hat on the hall table and stood for a moment outside the closed door of the drawing-room. Randall was practising as usual, his drilling, dogged repetition of a short difficult passage grating on Seymour's nerves. It was dark in the hall, and seemed even darker on coming in from the brilliant spring sunshine outside. Seymour put his fingers to his eyes for a moment because the sudden change of light had caused them to twitch and an illusion of sparkling beads to dance before them.

"Oh, Lord," he muttered, and started up the stairs. He found his mother sitting as usual on the cluttered divan in her stuffy, shadowy room, her lap full of the contents of some box she had turned out on it, and beside her an open old-fashioned valise into which she was dropping things as she pawed them through. She looked up at Seymour with an unnaturally bright smile, for more often than not she was vague and drooping, and she said, "Oh, Seymour darling, it's you." He kissed her cheek and stood for a moment watching her hands hover among the things in her lap. "I thought I'd start getting ready, you know," she said.

"Ready, Mama?" He smiled. "I hadn't quite thought about the summer yet."

"Oh, I didn't mean that!" said Lily eagerly. "I shall have so much to do getting ready for Vienna. I thought I could try to get started while you—"

He was actually surprised that his silence conveyed his chagrin to his mother. Her voice trailed away and she raised her face to him with a frightened stare; then her eyes filled with the inevitable tears. But she said, "Of course we ought to be leaving as soon as Randall—"

Seymour went through the awkward motion which had become a habit; he looked about for a place to sit down, then he lifted a mass of indeterminate objects from the divan, placed them on the floor, and sat down slowly beside his mother. He put his hand gently on her shoulder and drawing a breath said, "Mama dear, you aren't going to Vienna with Randall, you know."

She only looked at him with bewilderment. "Why," she mumbled, "why of course I'm to go. I've always—it was—"

"That was long ago," said Seymour, groping for kind and simple words in which to put this cruel statement. "It used to be a nice kind of dream for you and Randall to make together while Grandmama was alive and we all—" He touched his mother's cheek and tried in every way, with his eyes, the tone of his voice, to give her comfort while he spoke. "While we all needed to dream of something that would mean escape from her. I had my dreams too, you know."

"But it *wasn't* a dream," said Lily. "Randall and I are to go to Vienna and live in a nice little flat and go to the—"

For a moment Seymour turned away and there passed through his mind the swift and daring thought: suppose I let them go? Suppose I just do the easy thing? The life which he would then be free to make for himself opened like a prospect of Paradise before him; it was as if he could stand on the hilltop of his own freedom and look all about him, forward and as far as vision could reach, at the joys of all that he had always longed to do. Then the queer dead odor of the room bored at his nostrils; his throat caught in a dry knot, his head felt leaden. He looked at the windows with their perpetually drawn shades, a thing which had come about of Lily's imaginary headaches and become permanent nobody quite knew when. He looked again at his mother, whose features in her ageing, infantile face were blurred by the dimness in which she existed and now, he felt, somehow by his own eyes too. He thought, she is forty-four years old. She looks sixty—seventy—how do I know? She is an old woman but she can live on for half my lifetime. What shall I do? His was not a mind to muddle in a futile treadmill round that awful question. He knew and he gave himself the answer, aloud. While he did so he could feel the vitality drain out of him, he felt cold and presently, putting his hand to his forehead he found that his fingers really were frigid.

"Mama," he said, speaking slowly and he hoped with tenderness. "You must try to understand. Things are altogether different now. You dreamed of going to Vienna with Randall when he was a little boy and you couldn't imagine him as a man and able to be on his own. And we all, I just said so, we all had our dreams of getting away from Her." He paused. His mother was sniffling. He said, "But now you don't have to be afraid of Her any more. You are safe here, don't you see?"

He bent forward to see his mother's face and draw if possible a response of some kind from it, but she was already dissolving into high, whining tears, weeping into the handkerchief that hid her eyes and her nose which always reddened at the first sob.

"You have so much confidence in Professor Mundt," said Seymour, groping for some rational way of reinforcing his own opinion. "He feels that Randall should go, the sooner the better, we all know that. And he says that Randall must go alone."

Lily shuddered and Seymour heard her whimpering, "No, no, no" into her handkerchief.

He said "I'm terribly sorry to disappoint you, Mama dear. I don't want to hurt you and I don't want to be the one who puts his foot down. We've all had enough of that to last us the rest of our lives. But this is important. Somebody's got to decide."

Lily only wept in treble squeaks and after a series of gulps and chokes she got out, "He—he—he's too young. He needs me." After that Seymour thought he discerned, "—little boy. Can't go all alone."

He stood up suddenly, driven to make some quick motion to release a wave of irritation. He shoved his hands into his pockets and said, "Mama, stop crying and look at me." His voice was cold and lashing. Lily gave a gasp of astonishment and jerked up her head. Seymour stood there frowning. With that long downward pull of his mouth he bore sufficient resemblance to the source of all terror, for her, to make her crouch there, her mouth fallen open and her chin quivering below it. He said, "I'm sorry to be so hard about this, Mama, but you've got to understand once for all. Randall is not only not a little boy or a child any longer, he is a young man. He's got to get away from—from us and live the life of a music student since a musician is what he's going to be."

"But—but—he—doesn't know—" Lily's mouth moved up and down like that of a fish out of water, and Seymour knew all too well what she was trying to say.

"You don't have to talk about it, Mama. I know what you mean. And I am telling you that Randall is to go to Vienna alone and that is the end of it."

Lily crumpled again into noisy tears. Seymour said abruptly, "In case you think this is my own decision you'd better know that Professor Mundt feels even more strongly about it than I do."

"He *always* knew," wailed Lily. "He knew we were going together."

"Whatever he knew years ago, he knows now that Randall is to go alone."

"He *can't* go alone," Lily's silly voice rose and fell in reedy waves. "He's too little, he's too—"

"He is going alone," said Seymour, in a tone of voice that she had never heard before. "He is going alone or he isn't going at all."

Seymour turned to leave the room and found Randall just opening the door. The two stood face to face. Randall shut the door behind him and said, "I heard you."

"Well," said Seymour, "you can't be much surprised."

"No."

"There it is, then. You can start the day after you finish school."

Randall stood dumbstruck, looking at Seymour but listening to his mother. He moved as if to go over and comfort her and make the sort of affectionate fuss which was the only quick way to quiet Lily when she went into a state like this. But Seymour, standing with his arms folded and that alarmingly familiar look on his face, was a silent restraint. Randall moved his feet uneasily but did not go farther towards his mother. Lily's gasping ululations were all the sharper for the dead silence between the brothers. Finally Randall said, "I don't see how I can go," making a gesture at Lily.

"I'll be the judge of that." Seymour was finding in himself a capacity for hardness which he had never measured before.

"But," said Randall.

Seymour stared at him. "You heard what I said, Ran. I didn't think there was going to be any 'but' business from you. I thought you wanted to be a pianist."

"Well, I do."

They both looked at their mother, aware that this was no kind of talk to be conducting in her presence. Then Seymour shrugged as if to inform Randall that he had gone so far in telling Lily the truth that there would be no use in withholding anything further. One could not be quite sure anyway just how much she really understood.

"Then you've got to strike out and be one."

Randall's fair head drooped and he stood, unconsciously, in an attitude of weakness such as to rouse in Seymour a real sense of alarm. "He iss too soft," Professor Mundt had said this afternoon. "Too *kindlich*." The thick voice echoed in Seymour's ears. "So goot he iss, so gentle, *ja*, that makes sensitif the artist. But it iss not enough. *Kraft muss er auch haben*. He should struggle." Seymour had conveyed by a glance how much struggle had already been imposed on his brother and himself, but the old man who knew them well had shaken his head and said, *"Nein,* I mean different. Avay from you, from his Mama, *weit weg* must he go. He finds trouble, so *auch* he finds strength. Vidout diss iss no *Künstler."*

Seymour for a moment weighed the bitter contemplation of what it would mean to him should life somehow reverse his position and Randall's. To be sent away from all this, to be forced out upon the world, to be driven to act a man and to reckon with the consequences of a man's actions! Instead he stood here committed by his own conscience and the dead hand of an old woman, by the appalling spectacle of the ruin she had wrought, to responsibility whose limits he could not discern. All the responsibility, he thought bitterly, and none of the privileges. He watched Randall, as plainly swaying in the inner winds of uncertainty as a tree in a storm; and he looked at his mother, helpless and for all the problems she personified, curiously inert. There was nothing more to say now. He gave Randall a look of cogent meaning, and turned to leave the room. He went downstairs to the library and flung himself into the chair at his desk; he had hours of studying to do and nothing could so have unfitted him for it in mind and mood as the scene he had just left. He sat scowling at the difficult diagram on the open page before him, champing the stem of his pipe in his teeth. There was a quiet knock on the door and Seymour snapped, "Come in!" He had expected Randall.

"What do you want?" he asked brusquely as Randall closed the door. "You know I've got all this cramming to do."

"Of course I know." Seymour almost winced at the timidity in Randall's voice. "But I thought—I guess I thought—"

"What?"

"Oh—I don't know." Randall leaned across the desk and looked at Seymour with a pleading expression. "It's awfully hard on Mama, Brother. Can't you see?"

"Of course I can see! What do you take me for, a fool?"

"Then, why—"

"'Because there's no sense doing any more damage around here after all that's been done already. Mama is—you know what she is. Give it any name you like. The point is she will never be any less childish and helpless than she is now, and if one of us is going to be saddled with her—" Seymour ignored the shocked expression which crossed Randall's face—"it had better be me. I don't have to go to Europe on account of my work and you do."

"Maybe," said Randall uncertainly, "I wouldn't have to go either."

Seymour scowled. "What do you mean? You mean you're afraid to go?"

"Oh, no," said Randall quickly.

"Then what are you talking about? I've made it as plain as aces. You're going and you're going alone."

"I'd be perfectly willing to have her along." Randall was not looking at Seymour as he spoke. "She wouldn't be in my way."

Seymour slammed his book shut and met Randall's startled eyes with the cold stare which meant the rousing of his temper. "I'm getting sick of this," he said. "The whole point is that she is not to go with you, she is not going anywhere. She's going to stay here, damn it, where she's my responsibility, and you are either going to Vienna and make sense, or you are not. The choice is up to you. You are going to make the choice, and make it today. And once it's made it's going to stay made."

Randall turned slowly and went over to the bay window and stood looking out at the back yard. He had dreaded this issue for so long that now in the midst of it he felt as if he had already been through it in some past time and was dreaming and re-dreaming all that he had feared. He knew that Seymour was right. He wanted to agree with him; all his life he had drawn his strongest satisfactions from agreement with Seymour, or from acting together with him; most of all from letting Seymour make choices and take decisions for them both. Suddenly this strong framework appeared to be collapsing beneath Randall's feet. In its place there was nothing solid, nothing except the quivering tentacles of a question on which Randall knew he had always been insecurely impaled. Seymour in his place would face the veiled, wavering difficulty, square off at it, and close with it, resolving the issue once for all. But Randall, twisting a tassel of the heavy curtain-pull, only stood at the window looking at the drab back yard, acutely aware of Seymour's irritated impatience behind him.

"I'm going to—I want to—" Randall paused. Seymour gave him no help. "I'll tell you after dinner," Randall finished, forcing out the words.

"I won't be here."

"You won't?" Randall's tone asked the rest of the unspoken question.

"I'm going to take a woman to supper at Jack's," said Seymour, so harshly that he was almost shouting. "And afterwards I'm going to her flat with her. See? And it would be damned good for you if you did something of the sort yourself."

CHAPTER 6

"And you should never have come in the first place." Steingruber was a sour, sickly man with a wry expression and meaty hands thrusting from his soiled cuffs. He was pacing the end of the room while Randall sat mute at the piano. "More than a year already you study by me and first I think, well, yes, good enough. You learn good, work is good. You can play. But something is not there." He paused and scratched his short bristle of dusty grey hair. "Then I think, *nein, hoffnungslos,* he is like all the other English, he is too—too—"

"I am not English."

"I'm talking!" shouted Steingruber. "English, Amerikaner, *s'ist mir ganz Wurst. Es fehlt euch allen etwas.* Why do I speak German?" he screamed. "I know your stupid language."

"I see."

"*Ja.* You understand? Then why waste my time?"

"I didn't know I was wasting it." Randall's face was ashy. He had been biting his lips and keeping his hands clenched under the keyboard. He had to force his voice to make a sound.

"*Barmherziger Gott!* You don't feel? You don't know?"

Randall raised his head and gazed straight at Steingruber. "You think me a fool," he said, breathing loudly through his nose. "Will it be easier for you if I go on acting like one?"

"For me?" Steingruber shuffled down the room and leaned across the music rack to stare astonished into Randall's hurt blue eyes. "*Mein lieber Kerl,* why think about me? This is your life, not mine." His rough testiness was giving way to bewilderment. "Why care what's easy for me?"

"Because if it hadn't been hard you would probably have said this long ago—maybe right in the beginning."

"But you are supposed to protest!" said Steingruber, stupidly. "You are supposed to call me a brute or a fool who can't understand you. Then you rush away to somebody else, to Leipzig or Warsaw—"

"I don't think you're a brute. I guess you may be right." Randall had to make a stern effort to hold his voice from wavering. He sat exchanging with Steingruber the first truthful look that either had ever dared. The pinched bitter lines relaxed around Steingruber's long nose, and standing there he looked almost kindly.

"Tell me," he said. "This—is it what you really want?" He thumped the piano with his hand.

Randall did not answer at once. After a time he said, "In—in a way. It wasn't my idea in the first place. I just never thought about not doing it."

"*Ach, so.* Again the mama, *ja,* old Max Mundt wrote me. First I thought no, *ausgeschlossen.* We see this very often, you understand. Then he begs me at least to listen. Can I refuse? So I listen." Steingruber scratched his head again. Dandruff floated down on the piano. "So like I said, talent it is there. You pass the examinations. *Aber warum? Für welchen Zweck?* I must ask myself, I am an honest man, I cannot help it, I am sorry." He spread his hands with a flap. "*Es tut mir furchtbar Leid.*"

"That's all right," said Randall faintly. Steingruber leaned forward and peered at him.

"But how? What will you do? What becomes of you?"

"That's what I was about to ask you."

"*Me?*" The teacher's thick forefinger jabbed his breast. "*Um Gottes Willen,* why me?"

"Who else?" The good innocent blue eyes looked into his. "I—" Randall swallowed and took a long breath and said with much effort, "I don't want to go back to New York a total failure. Even if I didn't mind not being a pianist, it's the others, you see. They—they're the ones who care."

"The mother and—?"

"My brother."

"He is good? You love him?"

"Oh yes! Very much."

"He pays for this?"

"No, no. It's not a question of money."

Steingruber watched thoughtfully the faint color that mantled the boy's face and faded again, leaving him paler than before. How could they ever have been such fools, he thought. Soft and timid and so easily hurt, not one gram of the brass necessary for the brutal contests of the concert world. Maybe the mother and the brother could not know any better, but Mundt? Steingruber shook his head.

"So," he said slowly, "if you don't make a concert artist, you would prefer *trotzdem* something by the piano?"

Randall nodded, unconscious that the slow sagging of his shoulders told too clearly his relief, his anxiety, and his burden of shaken pride. Steingruber spoke thoughtfully. "It is true you are a good musician. Clean. Sound. *Sehr sympathisch.* You read wonderful. You would be a good *Begleiter*," he said. "Accompanist." He watched the boy closely to see whether this would appear a humiliation, a relegation to a subservient, even menial role. Randall gave no sign. Steingruber said hastily, "Some artists are almost made by their accompanists. You know that? Some singers are cattle with a voice until their accompanist, their coach, shows them what to do."

Randall did not say anything. Steingruber could not guess what he was thinking. Just as the teacher was casting about for some word, however empty, to mitigate the draught he had administered, Randall looked up and said quietly, "I should think there would be so many people like me in Vienna that there couldn't possibly be room for one more."

Steingruber nodded heavily. "A good *Bursch, bist Du.* Not a fool, not at all. You are right, what you said is true. But for those who stay in Wien! *Mein Gott,* even the good ones starve. You did not mean to stay in Wien, *aber?*

"No, oh no. Just to study."

"So. You work, you get experience, you get authority, by the Court Opera gives much prestige. Then you go to America, you get all the work you can do. *Glaube mir,* such a life is better than a bad virtuoso. Better than a teacher, too," he said sourly.

"Oh."

"*Ja,* 'oh'! Look at me," growled Steingruber, leaning sharply towards Randall and slapping himself on the chest. "You think *I* expected to be a Professor? You think anybody expects to? Ha! Each one is another Liszt, bigger than Liszt. Me. You. Everybody. Ten thousand Liszts! *Wunderbar!*"

Randall pushed back his piano stool and stood up slowly. He walked over to the green tile stove and leaned his shoulders against it, comforted by the mild warmth. Steingruber flung himself into an armchair near the piano and began to fill his long-stemmed pipe. Randall had never thought of him, much less seen him, as a natural person. He was known as a terror and students regarded their courses with him as their worst ordeal. Now it appeared one need deal with him on no terms but the simple truth. For the first time in a whole strange distorted year, Randall felt calm and almost happy.

"Herr Professor," he said, "would you be willing to help me do what you suggest? Go to the right place to learn?"

"*Natürlich*. Such a way you listened to me, you don't think I don't help you? Of course I help you. I will talk to Kippler at the Hofoper, maybe he soon even gives you a little to do, who knows?"

"Who is Kippler?"

Steingruber raised his shoulders and sighed with impatience that anybody, even a green American student, should not know who the leading musical personalities were.

"Kippler is Kippler. *Gott weiss*, I think he is called maybe chief correpetiteur, or head rehearsal superintendent, more words I have not got. By Kippler they prepare the singers for the orchestra rehearsals. How many young pianists they use, you could imagine—" He flapped his hands again.

Randall stood with his lips pursed and his eyebrows peaked. This idea was a startling relief from the dim fear of a future in which he had never truly brought himself to believe. He did not yet know what to think of Steingruber's proposal, but he was ready to learn what he could do about it. A few evenings in the top galleries of the Hofoper, dazzled more by the spectacle of royalty and beauty in the boxes than by the music from stage and pit, had not prepared him for the idea of working with singers. He said so.

"*Doch*," shrugged Steingruber, "where does everybody else begin? With one thing that he can do. Then he finds where to do it. Also will you. Go now," he said, looking at the cuckoo clock on the cluttered wall. "Go, the next poor devil is coming. *Ach!*"

Seymour did not read all of Randall's letter to their mother, only as much of it as would leave her in her dream. Lily Holt had become a dim and dusty wraith, willingly cut off from every contact with reality except in her obsession about Randall. Seymour's only insurance of peace or privacy for himself was to feed his mother continuous, judicious doses of enough good news of Randall to keep her content and busy in her imagined world, where Randall was now an important musical figure. It was easy to edit Randall's long letter in such a way that when Seymour read the blue-pencilled parts to Lily, Randall's move to the Hofoper had become the Director's search for a young pianist of genius, whom, for a reason conveniently left unstated, the Opera could no longer do without. Lily never even murmured a remark that Randall, without a day's experience in the musical theatre, should leap to the grandest one in Europe straight from the Conservatorium.

"Suppose she ever found out?" said Seymour to old Professor Mundt whom he had gone to consult beforehand.

"She finds out vat? Always she iss less able to understand. By der time she finds out it can also every vord be true."

This was unarguable. After reading the censored letter to his mother, Seymour put it carefully away and since he had no reason to reread the letter, he himself drifted into a half-belief that Randall at last was getting his feet firmly on the ground and might actually do as well as old Mundt speculated. A good many months went by while Seymour pursued a thoroughly pleasant life. He enjoyed his work immensely, he was gay, he could pick and choose among invitations, his evenings were allotted to a judicious mixture of masculine pleasures and feminine company. Best of all he liked the trial trips and shakedown cruises on new boats and yachts which the firm had built. He had found a steady, elderly Irishwoman to live with his mother on the third floor of the house, which Lily now never left; and for the rest Seymour was little at home. He usually looked in on his mother at the end of the day, just before he dressed to go out for the evening. Almost always he found her poring over the latest of Randall's letters, smoothing and petting it with her vague, restless hands while she sat treasuring the leather box in which she kept them all. Randall had been well warned not to ruin the illusion which Seymour had thought best to spin for Lily, and after a few protests, had drifted into the easy way, not of lying as to what he was doing, but of exaggerating the significance of what he did. Seymour relaxed in the unrealistic prospect that the future would somehow take care of itself. It was a shock beyond belief when he received a cable from Randall, which he read with alarm and amazement: MUST LEAVE VIENNA ADDRESS POSTE RESTANTE DRESDEN REPLY MY LETTER PROMPTLY.

What could have happened? Seymour dismissed his first impulse to cable and inquire; Randall had obviously written already. Seymour's imagination tormented him all through the two weeks until Randall's letter arrived. When it came nothing had prepared Seymour for the absurd escapade which had engulfed his meek and innocent brother.

It began at *Fasching*, Carnival time, after Randall had spent the winter studying hard with Anton Pachl, one of the staff correpetiteurs at the Hofoper, and a favorite accompanist of the singers at their *Lieder-abende*. Pachl, like Randall's previous teachers, could scarcely believe from his first impression how good a musician the youth really was, how much serious ability and proficiency lay behind the timid, too gentle personality. "You should get out more," Pachl advised him in the German which Randall now spoke well. Pachl was young himself and his advice was not theoretical. "Be frivolous, be like everybody else. This is Wien, after all—why live in it as if it were a convent?"

Why, indeed? Randall was ashamed to confess that he had no idea how to change the drab existence he had pursued ever since coming here. He could not relate his own austere and frugal life, his hours of practice in his gloomy room in the Riemergasse, to the dazzling splendors that he saw on the short walk from his lodgings to the Hofoper. He had heard that there was no spectacle anywhere to compare to the Kärntnerstrasse, and he supposed this must be true. Where else could there be such glittering turnouts, such preening human peacocks in uniform, such beautiful women so richly dressed, the ladies in barouches and victorias on their way to the Ringstrasse, the demi-mondaines strolling on foot? The shop windows burgeoned with jewels and furs and fantasies. The air was rich and ripe with perfume and the fat aroma of chocolate and coffee; one could feel the texture of leisure and laxness and mischief. But what had all that to do with him, he thought; and still less could he attain a sense of any relationship to the lives of the people at the Hofoper. He could not spend an hour at work in the obscurest rehearsal-room under the eaves of the opera-house without overhearing breathless whispers, without sensing the currents of intrigue and scandal which linked the singers and ballerinas to the male ornaments of the Court who had their headquarters across the street at Sacher's. Nor could he escape the gusty visceral humor and the affectionate teasing of the singers and other artists who had no reticence about anything.

He had barely become acquainted with some of them before their cheerful curiosity about his private life produced the astounding evidence that the lad was, apparently, quite chaste. Somebody joyfully dubbed him *der Keuscher* (the virgin); and this became inevitably Keuscherl or Keuschi, which caused him the agony of blushing scarlet whenever he was greeted. Pachl, however, said he should be delighted, nobody had such an original nickname and nothing remained now but to make fools of the people who took it literally. "So you will go to the Maskenball with me," he said, "and we will see what we will see."

"Oh—I couldn't!" Randall was really frightened. "Why—I've never been to a ball. I don't even dance."

"Then you are in the right place to learn."

"But not the ball," Randall pleaded. "People like—ah—us—we—don't go to balls."

"To the Musikverein goes everybody on Fasching. Everybody! You didn't hear once about Kaiserin Elisabeth?"

"No, why?"

"*Ach*, I forget, such a child, American too. Never mind, we go."

"But I haven't got—I couldn't afford—a costume."

"You think I do? We take something from the *Garderobe* here, like everybody else. *Ai-Gott!*" he exclaimed, pulling out his watch, "Lisl Dunkler is waiting for me." He licked his lips and made a derisive gesture at the piano. "She enjoys her work."

Randall sighed. He wondered how long he might stay in Vienna before he would cease to be shocked at the frank, genial promiscuity, the lively uproar in which people lived here. He tried to relate it to anything he had ever known of life and he could find no single point of contact except, to his surprise, the thought of Seymour. Seymour would know what to do here and would make the most of it; Randall would never feel like anything but a bewildered outsider.

Pachl dragged him to the Carnival Ball on Shrove Tuesday, after fitting them both to dominoes and masks in a wardrobe room at the opera house. The street as they stepped out on the Ring was a wonderland of lights, packed all its width with shouting, singing, dancing people, blowing horns and waving streamers as they pranced along. The Karlsplatz was beautifully decorated with banners and lanterns and the great doors of the Musikverein stood open in a blaze of light, welcoming all Vienna to the unique occasion of the year. Pachl hurried forward, dragging Randall by a firm grip on the elbow. Once inside, Randall saw the impossibility of escape. Never could there have been such a crowd, he thought, and surely never so good-natured a one. It was impossible to move as one chose, one felt oneself swept along in the main stream moving through the corridors to the great hall flanked by its accessory salons all brilliant with light. The crowd was so dense that it muffled the music. Randall was amazed when he could finally see the great augmented orchestra playing the irresistible *Wiener Blut*; only inside the ballroom could its full sonority be heard. He edged his way into a deep corner under the balcony, relieved at losing Pachl in the crowd, and fascinated by his first real view of waltzing Vienna, gayer than at any other time behind the secrets of its masks. He was lost in the spectacle when to his horror a woman's hand slid up his forearm under the loose domino sleeve, and a masked face pressed so close to his that he drew back in terror.

"*Nah!*" she whispered, putting her lips against his ear. She spoke in broad dialect. "Let's go and drink a little wine."

"Th—thank you," Randall gulped. "I'd rather—I'm not—"

"Nonsense. This is Fasching, you can't say no."

Alone he could never have wormed his way through that vast crowd and out of the ballroom and off into a maze of halls and stairs and corridors which became less and less crowded as his companion, clinging to his arm, firmly made her way. She knew where she was going and Randall shook with suspense and the helpless knowledge that he was trapped. Once he paused at the entrance to a refreshment-hall and said, "Here, let us stop here, the wine—"

But she went on as if she had not heard him, softly chuckling to herself. They came to a dingy passage papered in dark green wallpaper and dimly lit by a gas-jet. Randall coughed and said, "I think we've— there's a mistake, isn't there?" But she only laughed and stopped walking and, her eyes glittering through the slits of her mask, slid her left hand along a moulding while her right hand stayed tucked in Randall's arm. Behind her the wall opened. Randall stiffened and she snickered and said, "It's nothing, just a back door." And still teasing with her eyes she stepped backwards through the wall, drawing him with her. He found himself in a small room, quite commonplace, clearly the office or the studio of some functionary. There was a desk and a piano and a bookcase full of scores and a dado lined with plaster busts of the composers, and a narrow horsehair sofa.

"See?" she giggled, raising the black lace veil that hung from the upper half of her mask, and before Randall could stop her she had dropped onto the couch, clinging to him, and locked her mouth to his in a kiss of appalling authority. First he could not breathe and then he felt a tumult of other and more alarming sensations. He felt as if he were being wrenched apart, he loathed what was happening to him, he could have struck or roughhandled the woman to get free of her. But at the same time he liked it. In his mind he was ironbound, furious and fighting to get away. The rest of him at first did nothing, as if paralyzed, and then did what his companion intended, evidently to her pleasure for she was voluble about it. At last to his utter shame she sighed luxuriously, clinging to him, and whispered, "How should I believe it? It was true! *Keuschi!*" she cried, in unbridled delight, and sitting up with a jump, whipped off her mask.

"Oh. Oh, God." Randall heard his breath go out in a gargle. "Ott . . . Otti." He turned and shrank against the wall.

"*Ja!*" she cried, beaming like a jack-o'-lantern. "*Ja, was sagst Du!* Otti Kunz!" Her voice broke over him in shrill, delighted peals.

"Get—go—let me get out of here," he said. He was struggling in the maze of her skirts and ruffles and her big, muscular arms.

"Why?" she trilled. "Why go? *Solch'na'schaina Jungerl!*"

"Let me go," he said through his teeth. He could have slapped her but she had his hands pinioned while she embraced him with horrifying gusto.

"*Immer 'was neues!*" she cried happily. Her voice swirled up and down in excited, singsong dialect. "You don't escape from Otti!" she said, laughing. "This I promised myself already. I'm no fool."

"Oh, God," he mumbled.

She shook him gaily by the shoulders. "Silly! Stupid! What are you alive for? Without pleasure is what? *Komm—nochmal!*" and again she overwhelmed him. In his mind ran fragments of thought . . . you might as well . . . what have I to lose . . . Seymour would . . . how did she know . . .

Presently he asked her that. "*Gott*, what a child! You think a mask hides anything if you are looking for it?" She stretched herself like a cat. There was a clock ticking on the dado and she looked at it. "Now I let you go," she said. She shook her forefinger under his nose. "But not for long."

If he had ever imagined plunging into the maelstrom of careless pleasure in which the artists revelled, it could surely never have been with Ottilie Kunz. She was one of the half-dozen leading sopranos and would probably never have seen Randall at all, except that Pachl in the midst of the piano rehearsals for *Feuersnot* had caught a bad cold and Randall had been drafted to fill the gap for a week. He could not have known that the big prima donna had even noticed him. She was surrounded with the usual degree of obsequious fuss, but also there trailed in her wake a sizzle of gossip which Randall, if he understood it, was too naïve to believe. And now he was engulfed by her. Well—if he allowed himself to think at all, it was of Seymour who could never again hand down advice in sarcastic superiority. Randall was not given a chance to think much. He was busy, he found himself with extra work on his hands, and when he received a peremptory whisper or scribble from Otti, he did as she ordered. She had trapped him in his unwillingness to seem childish and a prude.

A note was slipped into his hand one spring evening when he had been listening backstage to *Die Walküre*, in which Otti did not sing. He sighed. He had about decided that he had had enough, and during the endless bore of Wotan's scene with Fricka, he had been cogitating how to shed Otti without making a fool of himself. The note said, "Come at once to Sacher's, Apartment 141. Bring along a score and tell the Concierge you are expected."

Randall went out to the passage and stood there hesitating. This looked like a bad idea. She could not be in Sacher's except at the instigation of somebody who belonged there, and why then had she sent for him? He was very uneasy. Some kind of prank lay at the bottom of this and he dreaded involvement. Then he thought, oh, what's the use— maybe this is the only way I'll ever see the inside of Sacher's—and how much harm can she do if I walk into anything so long as I've got a score under my arm? He went to the library and got out *Otello* and took it across the street to Sacher's.

Otti greeted him boisterously. He found her lolling in a cushioned bergère in the midst of a spectacle of luxury such as all the gossip about Sacher's had never led him to imagine. The room was a bonbon-box;

silk walls, gilt, wildly elaborate furniture, enormous festooned curtains, rose-shaded lights, a thick flowered carpet and—Randall noted queerly —not a breath of air. Otti sat chuckling, and twirling the neck of a champagne-bottle buried in a pail of ice while Randall stood dumb-struck, gaping at an alcove whose swagged damask curtains displayed, rather than concealed, a vast brass bed heaped with lacy and beribboned pillows. He turned his shocked blue eyes on Otti Kunz and had to watch her lift up those great thick arms and chortle, "Come, a kiss."

He drew back and said, "What are you doing here? Why did you send for me?"

"What am I doing here? *Ach*, it's a child. *Schluss* with the questions."

"So it's true," he said stupidly. "About Prince Werdenstein. This is his apartment."

"Of course it's true. Who's making any secrets? Come, give me a kiss."

"Certainly not. I'm going."

"*Ach*, what do you care? Not about poor Ludo, God knows. And you don't care like that about me."

"I certainly don't."

"Then come and drink some *Sekt* and don't be so stuffy. Here." She poured a glass and held it up.

"Otti, come to your senses. Have you no shame? Where's your—your—prince?"

"Not here, *selbstverständlich*. He sent word he was prevented at the last minute. So I got bored and sent for you."

"Well, I don't like it. Good night." Randall turned to leave the room. Otti Kunz bounded from her chair and wrapped him in her formidable arms. "Let me go," he mumbled while she tried to silence him with kisses.

She had got the better of him in every contest before and it was foregone that she would do it again. As usual it was easier to give in, and perhaps worth a moment's fun. He would certainly never play this game in quite this setting again, he thought.

They were in bed when they heard the key in the lock. Otti clapped her hand over his mouth as if she expected him to scream. With the other hand she waved wildly at the armoire in the corner. "*Dort—dort!*" she hissed. "*Schnell!*" But the salon door was flung wide by the bowing flunkey who had opened it and Randall, barely glimpsing the incredible figure which strolled through, dived under the blankets. He was rolled tight in a sweating ball, too terrified to feel anything, and he heard as if from miles away a cool, scornful voice sneer, "Well, Otti? A fool as well as a slut?"

There was a ghastly silence. Randall felt the bed shake with Otti Kunz's trembling. He began to pray for unconsciousness, he wished he could be found dead when that apparition should rip off the bed-covers as he was sure it would. Instead he heard the icy voice say, "I will have a word in the salon when your guest is ready to depart."

Randall heard the clashing brass rings as the alcove curtains were dragged shut. Rather than look at Otti Kunz he would eagerly have died; but somehow he crawled from the bed and made himself present-able, anxiously scanning the damask walls of the alcove for the usual small service door upholstered like the wall. He could see none. He stood dizzy with mortification. He heard Otti Kunz behind him breath-ing like a winded horse, apparently too terrified or too witless to pull herself together and get out of the bed. The situation was so mad, so impossible, so utterly without anything to do with him—Randall Holt, who had never asked to be part of anything happening in this room, this city, this country—that his very unrealness amidst it broke over him in an enormous wave. The actual image crossed his mind, the clean fierce decency of the American coast, the salty honesty of the air and the world where he belonged and where a thing like this could not hap-pen. But if it did, something nudged at him, if it did, who would know what to do? Who would tell him what to do now? Why, he thought, un-consciously straightening his shoulders and stiffening his back, why Seymour. Of course. What would he do in this fix? I don't know, but I'll try to act as if I did.

He walked firmly to the curtains, whipped them back with another brassy clash, and stepped forward, keeping his chin high. The Prince was standing with his elbow on the mantel, drinking a glass of cham-pagne. Randall had never had a good look at such a sight, he had only seen such figures in the distance. He took in the tight snow-white trousers, the pale blue tunic dripping with gold braid and lace, the medals and orders, the scarlet sash, the preposterous choker collar topped by a thin, vapid face wreathed in frizzy blond muttonchops and thinning fair hair. Why, thought Randall, you popinjay, you look like a damned fool. There can't be a man inside that get-up.

"Who are you?" asked Prince Werdenstein with the utmost insolence.

Randall did not answer. The Prince stared, produced an eyeglass, and screwed it into his right eye.

"It makes no difference at the moment who I am," said Randall in English, "and your view of the situation is quite correct. With your permission—" he stopped speaking because to his left he saw the inevitable small upholstered door in the wall, and it was opening. Why, he thought, couldn't it have been in that damned alcove?—and then he jumped at a squeal of panic from Otti Kunz in the bed behind him.

"Franz!" she shrieked. *"Du verdammter Idiot!"*

The prince and Randall gazed stupidly at the waiter who had entered carrying a tray with fresh glasses. Then they turned to look at Otti Kunz, scarlet-faced in the bed, her big pink bulk flapping like a wine jelly. Randall was bewildered but still intent on getting away; he even moved towards the door but a roar of "Stop!" from the Prince held him involuntarily. He turned to see the waiter wringing his hands and bowing and scraping before the Prince, gasping, *"Exzellenz!* Excuse! A mistake, a—"

"Who the devil is this man?" The Prince was standing over the woman in the bed. "What's going on? This man doesn't work here."

"Nein," moaned Otti Kunz. *"OGott-OGott-OGott-"* She was rocking herself in her arms.

Randall put his hand to his chin, narrowing his eyes at the waiter. Somewhere, something familiar . . . take away the apron and the striped waistcoat . . . somewhere around the Opera . . .

"It's her husband," he said.

"Donnerwetter! Is this true?" Otti Kunz waggled her bent head. The Prince threw a contemptuous glance at the terrified little man. "How dare you!"

"Excuse!" said the man again, half wailing. "I—would—I should explain. Believe me," he pleaded, grovelling, "it was not Your Highness, your most exalted Excellency. It was—that!" He made a gesture at Randall. "What is honorable, what is well understood—" he made another hand-wringing bow. "But *Exzellenz,* this—this Amerikaner—"

The Prince touched his frizzy whiskers. A shifty expression crossed his cold grey eyes. He gave Randall a sneering look, then bestowed one each upon the nasty little man and the woman in the bed.

"There seems to be some idea," he said in English to Randall, "that you should pay for your extremely ill-arranged entertainment."

"Well, I'm not going to."

The Prince pulled a musing, sardonic face. "I wonder." He turned to Kunz and said, "You had some such idea?"

"*Ach!*" said Kunz.

"Of course," said the Prince in his polished English, "if you were of any acceptable rank I should challenge you." He took a Russian cigarette from a jewelled case and lighted it delicately. "Not, naturally," he made a scathing gesture at Otti Kunz, "for that. But principle—honor—"

"Principle!" cried Randall. "Honor!" He looked from one corrupt face to the other, the highest and lowest of the type. "Now see here," he said. "I didn't want to come here, I was made a fool of too. I don't want your wife," he said to one man, "or your mistress," to the other. "All I want is to get away from this tart."

"Nobody will argue the epithet with you," said the Prince. "But *lèse-majesté—*"

"I'm an American. We don't recognize—"

"*Pssst,*" whispered Kunz, edging behind Randall. "*Exzellenz* is married to the Archduchess Franziska."

Randall could not see why a royal wife made any difference. He stared, and the Prince said, "You will leave Vienna at once?"

"Why?" As soon as he had uttered the word Randall realized his naïveté. The story would be all over the capital tomorrow and his continued presence would provoke a cyclone of ridicule around Werdenstein. Randall said, "I intend to stay in Vienna and finish the work I came here to do."

"Not if the Imperial Chamberlain has reason to arrange your departure."

Randall was opening his mouth for a retort which he hoped would prove defiant, when they all started at the noise of heavy knocking on the door. Otti Kunz cowered lower in the bed, the false waiter slunk towards a curtain, the Prince scowled, and Randall stood dumb.

"Go away!" shouted the Prince.

Instead there was another rough knock. A bass voice boomed, "*Hoheit,* it is I!" Without further ado the door opened and Randall gulped with amazement at the sight of a black-upholstered barrel of a woman, moustached and menacing, gripping in two thick fingers a lighted cigar. She took in the scene with furious eyes and boomed at Werdenstein, "Never has my hotel been shamed in such a way! Two impostors, canaille, have got into this apartment tonight. Never, never," she said again, snapping shut her teeth. She took a pull on her cigar.

"You are aware, Frau Sacher, that I had nothing to do with this. I was dealing with these riffraff in my own way when you had the effrontery to intrude."

"Intrude!" roared the old battle-axe. "In my own house—intrude!"

Randall expected the Prince to do something dramatic or peremptory. Instead the man turned coolly to a table, picked up his gold-laced képi and white gloves and without a further glance at anyone, strolled to the door. He turned there and said, "Since you choose to deal with the scum, pray proceed, Frau Sacher."

"Just one minute," said Randall, to his own surprise. "I've been called three dirty names already, and I warn you right now that's going to be the end of it." He followed the Prince to the door.

"End!" shouted Frau Sacher. "The police will bring this affair to an end!"

"Not so far as I am concerned," said Randall. He was quaking inside; his stomach, he was sure, was going to betray him. "You won't call any police or do anything more about this, because if you do, somebody from the American Legation is going to make it very embarrassing for this—his—eh—Highness." He stood with his hands in his pockets to hide their trembling. The Prince looked down his nose at Randall and then, furtively, at Frau Sacher.

"Probably," he said with a poor show at authority, "it will be better if this person merely leaves Vienna immediately."

"Probably," said Randall, and never remembered the moves by which he found himself again in the street.

"So you see, Brother," Seymour read, "I didn't know exactly what to do and for the time being I came here to Dresden. I suppose I could go on with the work I was doing in Vienna, the opera is very good here. But I don't feel much like it. To tell you the truth, now that I've told you so much of it already, I don't like Europe. I never feel as if I belonged here. I've tried hard. They all say I play excellently but I'm not a pianist. They tell me to work with singers and look what happened. If most singers are like the one I got mixed up with, I don't want anything to do with them. I guess I never realized that there is so much in a musical life besides music, and I don't like the parts that aren't the music. Anyway, I don't know what to do now and I wish you'd tell me what you think."

Seymour cabled Randall to come home.

CHAPTER 7

Randall stood on the pavement, looking at the house. Seymour watched him. He saw Randall's eyes turn up and down the street, confirming his first shocked reaction to the growing shabbiness of the neighborhood. Then the wondering blue eyes moved back to take in the drab front yard of the Holt house, not yet totally abandoned like its neighbors, but losing the battle with smoke and soot and the march of the town away from this district. The house itself stood out suddenly to Seymour's eyes as he saw, startled, what Randall saw: a forbidding sight. Seymour had drifted into the habit of not noticing it. Now he watched Randall gazing at the first and third storey front windows, whose blinds were all drawn like those of the fourth floor and the servants' dormers in the mansard. Only the second-floor windows looked as if the house were inhabited. Randall turned, puzzled and questioning, to Seymour and then paused at the sight of his brother, spruce and dashing with his sleek blond moustache, his smartly tailored clothes, and his expensive peccary gloves. Seymour said, "I suppose it does look queer when you're not used to it. I just haven't realized. But nobody uses all those rooms, Ran. Mama—you know—" He threw a glance at the third-floor windows. Lily had not let them be uncovered for years. "I use the second floor, that's why it's different. Grandmama's bedroom and the library."

"I guess you're hardly ever here."

"Well—" Seymour laughed.

They began to move up the front walk. Randall appeared increasingly troubled. Seymour knew that he was watching for his mother; would the door not fly open, and she be there on the steps? Seymour explained quietly why not. "She hasn't been downstairs since—well, you know when. It was long before you went away. She's terribly excited about your coming—more than is good for her, I'm afraid. But even that wouldn't be likely to bring her downstairs."

He was opening the front door with his latchkey. The entrance hall was very dark. Seymour apologized, lighting the gas. "I don't leave a light burning," he explained. "You can see why . . . dangerous . . ."

They stood at the foot of the stairs, and though Randall knew he ought to hurry straight up to his mother, he hesitated, with his foot on the bottom step. His face was very troubled. Seymour watched him and said, "I know, it's always queer to be away a long time. Makes everything seem smaller, doesn't it?"

"Yes, and—and it's so dark and empty, and somehow, it seems close, sort of stuffy."

"I suppose you're right. I'm afraid I haven't given it a thought. You ought to air a house once in a while even if you don't use all the rooms."

"Oh, well, you've got other things on your mind." Randall turned to mount the stairs.

"Say, Ran," said Seymour behind him. Randall heard uneasiness in his voice. He looked down and said, "What?"

"I guess I ought to tell you. It's meant to be a surprise, of course, but between you and me it will be a—a shock, to say the least. You'll carry if off better if you know."

"Carry what off? What surprise?"

"Don't blame me, anyway. Mama has bought you a piano."

"A what?" Randall let go the stair-rail and pressed his hands to his head. "Brother, you aren't serious!"

"I am, God help us."

"But what do you mean? What did she do? The place is full of—" Randall stood with his mouth open.

"Oh, I know," said Seymour miserably. "She bought a Steinway concert grand for you, the finest piano in the world, she says. And she put the one from the drawing-room up in her room so you can play for her sometimes."

"Oh," groaned Randall, "how horrible. Seymour, where did she get the money?"

"Sold her engagement ring. It was a big stone, you remember."

"And you let her do it? You let them deliver the thing?"

"I was away cruising on a new boat."

"Oh, no," said Randall wretchedly. "What on earth shall we do?"

"Nothing," said Seymour. "I talked to the doctor about it. He says if we're going to carry out this idea we've really got to do it. She's so happy about you, she thinks—"

Randall shuddered and passed his hand across his eyes. In the dim light Seymour saw that he was pale. "Horrible," he said again.

"It is," said Seymour. "It's one of those things you start without knowing how you're going to finish. Now we have no choice, we've simply got to keep on fooling her about you." He saw Randall wince again. "I mean," he added, "let her believe whatever she wants to believe."

Randall said, "This is pretty hard on me, isn't it?" His face was drawn.

Seymour made a sad attempt at a smile; a tremulous expression of tenderness crossed his face, and he moved up the stairs where he put his arm round Randall's shoulder. "I know," he said. "I wouldn't have put the whole burden on you, Ran. If I'd been anything she cared about in that way, I'd gladly have taken your place. But she's so helpless— Lord God, you know better than I!"

"I know."

"I'll help, Ran, believe me. There'll be lots of ways I can help. If you'll just do something at least on the fringe of what she believes—"

"Oh, I will. Of course I will. It'll take a little while to work it out." Randall turned and started up the rest of the stairs. At the top he stopped suddenly and looked down at Seymour and asked in a sharp tone, "Why is the house so empty? Where are the servants?"

"Why—you know all that. I wrote you."

"Oh. Did you?"

"Why, yes. What did I want with them, Ran? Mrs. Gerrity lives on the third floor with Mama and cooks for her there in a little kitchen I fixed up. I let them all go, somebody just comes in to clean."

"I see." Randall went on towards the next flight of stairs. Seymour looked up at his bowed, drooping shoulders. "It's all right," he called. "You can dine with me at the Club."

"When you're there," said Randall from the landing.

He was unnerved by every aspect of his homecoming. Putting off the meeting with his mother by talking to Seymour had only uncovered a maze of pitfalls through which he, carrying the whole burden of responsibility for his mother's condition, must grope his way. He had not hoped for much joy out of coming home, but he had not looked for all this trouble. Two and a half years away from Lily made it no easier to face her now. It was a long time since he had been able to turn to her for comfort or reassurance about anything. The minutes dragged while he stood there in the dark hall, painfully conscious of the few steps to his mother's door. He heard murmurs and muffled noises in the room beyond; then the door opened and his mother stood there holding out her arms.

"My boy! My wonderful boy!"

"Mama dear. How good to see you." The slight body in his arms was draped in nondescript shawls and veils, the blank pale face framed in queerly colorless hair. Randall tried for an instant to get a good look at Lily's face, but there was too little light in the dim room. Everything ran into a dark blur, the tomblike pieces of walnut and rosewood furniture, the heavy bed, the chairs and divan strewn with boxes, baskets, pictures, papers, ribbons and laces and slippers and clothing; the piano in the farthest corner by the heavy drawn curtains. She had opened the piano and raised its lid; Randall hid his grimace of revulsion by bending to kiss his mother.

"Wonderful!" she crooned. "Oh, darling Randall, how wonderful you are! You can't imagine how proud I am."

"It's nothing, Mama," he said, wishing she could know how much he meant it. "I haven't really done anything."

Lily laughed her tinkling, baby's laugh. "Don't be silly, now!" She chided him with a wavering forefinger. "Don't think I haven't hung on every moment of it!" She turned and made an unsteady dive for a shabby leather box tucked beside the pillows on her bed. "See!" she said, lifting and caressing the worn mass of his letters in the box, "just see how I've treasured these. You were so *good*, darling, so good to me. Such wonderful letters." She bent over the bed, handling and smoothing and folding the letters, murmuring to herself and visibly fading back into the mist in which she lived. She had forgotten that Randall was there. He stood hesitating, wondering what to do and whether he could slip away and pick up the thread some other time. He moved quietly to the door, but it swung open before he reached it and a stout authoritative woman came in, carrying a small tray with a glass and spoon on it.

"Well!" she said, too loudly for Randall's nerves. "Here we are! Now ain't it grand to have your famous boy home again, Ma'm?"

"Wha—why—" Randall watched his mother drift back to the scene. "Oh!" she exclaimed shrilly, "oh, yes! Wonderful. Randall, come here, look. It's here, you see, I had it brought up here." She clung to his arm, looking up into his face with her queer pleading eyes. "Didn't you see it?" She pulled him towards the piano in the corner.

"I—of course, Mama." He tried to speak heartily. "I was just too wrapped up in you to notice it at first. Yes, it's fine if you like it." He stopped uncomfortably.

"Ah, the grand surprise," said Mrs. Gerrity's heavy voice.

"Yes," said Lily, with hectic eagerness. "Of course you haven't seen it, you ran straight upstairs to me, didn't you? But wait till you see it, just wait!"

"What, Mama?"

"My surprise! Downstairs in the drawing-room, darling, oh, I'm so proud of you and they said it's the finest one they ever made and Paderewski was trying to buy it oh Randall you'll love it so and when you aren't practising for your concerts I thought you'd play to me here sometimes it's really the best, they said, the best one they ever—"

Randall saw the sign in Mrs. Gerrity's spectacled eye.

"It's fine," he said lamely. "Just fine. I don't know how to thank you—"

"You haven't seen it yet! You must go and see it. Try it."

"Yes, of course, I'm going." He drew a breath hoping for courage or the chance that he might say the right thing, and said, "Don't you want to come and see it with me, Mama?" He put his arm gently round her shoulders.

"I?" Lily shrank back, her face puckering and crinkling, her eyes clouding. "Why—oh," she breathed, looking round the dark clutter of her room and putting her wavering hands to her face, "oh—you see— I couldn't do *that*!" She turned to a chair and began pawing through the mess strewn over it. "I have so much to do, you see, I wanted to get everything ready—" Her voice trailed away in mutters.

Randall turned slowly away. The nurse gave him a signal with a tilt of her grey head, and he left the room and went in search of Seymour. The library was a reassuring relief. Seymour was working at his desk. When Randall came in he sat back, put down his slide-rule and pencil and took off his spectacles. He laid them down, rubbing his eyes and studying Randall's face to learn how he had taken the meeting upstairs. Randall sat down slowly and said, "See here, you haven't got a drop of brandy or something, have you?"

"Of course I have. Damned good idea, too."

Seymour rose and went to a cabinet for a decanter and glasses. Randall sat silent, too shaken to try to throw off his distress. Staring as one does, at such moments, at nothing in particular he noticed the spectacles that Seymour had taken off. Their lenses were extremely thick and so heavy that the gold frames were a peculiar shape in order to hold them. Seymour came over to sit opposite Randall, handing him a pony of cognac. Randall looked at him closely; his eyes appeared blank, exhausted.

"What kind of glasses are those, Brother?" Randall's tone was uneasy.

"What? Those?" Seymour took a pair of ordinary spectacles from his breast pocket and began to polish them. "Which?"

"Those." Randall pointed to the desk. Seymour shrugged and said, "Nothing special. Lots of people use them for close work, you know. Tables and blueprints . . . how do you find Mama, Ran?"

They sipped some cognac. Randall leaned back in his chair and rested his head against the cushion. He was still feeling the motion of the ship. In the first days out he had been seasick; now he felt desperately tired. He was silent for a long time. Then slowly he answered Seymour's question. "It's awful, Brother. She's simply—well—she's—"

"But you knew that. She'd been going that way long before you went to Europe."

"Yes. It's harder to believe when you haven't been with her, though."

"It must be."

Randall winced. Perhaps Seymour did not mean that as it sounded. "I don't quite understand why it's necessary to do all this fooling her," he said. "I should think she's so—what can you say?—so far gone already it couldn't make any difference."

"Doctor Slade says not. He says the shock if such people are jolted out of their illusions, or their obsessions, can be very dangerous. They're all right so long as you let them pretend what they want. The main idea is to keep them occupied, you see. Mama thinks she is terribly busy now that you're an important musical figure and will be giving concerts and all that."

"But I'm not!" Randall sat forward almost in panic. "I haven't said that. All we agreed to say was—you know what we said. I'll try to do some kind of work that will give us a leg to stand on, but not what will end in our making public fools of ourselves."

"It won't," said Seymour, trying to soothe him. "Take your time, Ran. Don't be so upset about it."

"Upset! You'd be upset if you had to start out deliberately being a fake—and if you had that damned new piano hung around your neck."

"That's too bad, it's true."

"It's horrible. When you think about the past and those—Brother, are those others still down in the cellar?" Randall watched Seymour's face closely. A cold shuttered expression seemed to close down on it.

"Why, I suppose."

"Well, let's get rid of them. At least we can make that much sense, don't you think so?"

Seymour answered reluctantly. "Well—no," he said. He gave Randall a sidewise look.

"No? Why on earth not? They're worthless, you know that."

"Not altogether. They're full of copper wire and steel tuning pins and stuff I could use . . ."

"Oh. Do you still make ship models?"

Seymour's brows drew together and Randall saw the hardening of his jaw, which meant tension. He said, "Sometimes I want to work a thing out with my hands instead of on paper . . ."

His tone warned Randall to drop the subject, and Randall sat wondering why. He had a sharp sense that something was being hidden from him. Seymour had changed very much in the years of Randall's absence; so had Randall himself. Each looked it and felt it and saw it in the other. Something like an enamel of cool assurance and confidence in his own attractiveness had formed a shell around Seymour; it had been plain from the first glimpse of him this morning. By contrast Randall, even with European clothes and the command of a new language and experience of a new milieu, still kept his pliant, docile ways. They were a fine-looking pair, the elder hardening in a distinguished angular mould, the younger almost beautiful with the suggestion of youth in bloom. They were silent. Randall looked at Seymour and thought, "He must be a devil with women," and Seymour thought, "The kid hasn't changed enough, he'll always be too easy to hurt."

Randall did not know what to do. Here it was, late on a December day, and when Seymour had not come home by half past seven he began to feel alarmed. The dinner party was at eight. Dressed in the tails which Seymour had forced him to have made, he stood in the front hall with his watch in his hand, listening for Seymour's step outside. At quarter to eight he was panicky, he must go now if he were to arrive on time, but how could he go without Seymour? What on earth could he say? That thought melted the last of the courage he had summoned to face the evening. At five minutes to eight he thought with horror that by now he should have sent a message to Mrs. MacRae, he could not imagine what sort of message except some spectacular lie, but whatever it might be, she should have had it by now. Damn this house, he said half aloud, without a servant in it to go on an errand or fetch a messenger-boy. He mopped his forehead with his fine handkerchief, bought at Seymour's insistence. He looked again at his watch to find it now twenty minutes to nine. Impossible. Surely he had not stood thirty-five minutes in this draughty hall, paralyzed for lack of knowing what to do? It began to occur to him that something might have happened to Seymour. Perhaps there had been an accident, perhaps Seymour was ill. Randall knew in the same moment that this was not so. He paced the hall, quite certain what not to think, but wildly bewildered when he tried to find an explanation. Then he began to feel angry. Seymour had made a fool of him. It's not as if I had wanted to go in the first place, he thought. I don't care if I never see these people or anybody like them. But why should Seymour be able to put me in such a position?

After a time he went up to his room, and wrenching off the new tailcoat, the white waistcoat, the stiff shirt and white tie with which he had had such a struggle, he pitched them into a corner. He pulled a jersey over his head and sat down stiffly on the edge of a chair. Now what should he do? It was long after nine, he was cold and angry and suddenly very hungry. He wanted something good to eat. He wanted something hot and filling and cosy like the Austrian food he had grown to like, *Beuschel mit Knödel* or *Kalbsgulyasch mit Nockerl.* He swallowed hungrily at the thought. He was sick and tired of the smart, well-served steaks and chops and roasts and oysters at Seymour's club or the restaurants where they ate occasionally He was more tired of the increasingly frequent evenings when he found himself alone, and of the only sort of restaurant where he ever ate alone, the dreary kind. Humble places in Vienna were easy and kindly and there had always been somebody from the Conservatory or the Opera at whose table he could sit down and eat his meal. Here he had some problem to face, some annoyance to swallow, with every bite of food.

Presently he went downstairs, wrapped his neck in a muffler, put on his overcoat, pulled a cap over his eyes, and went out. The cold leaped at him. He had never felt such cold; intense, stinging, hard as black ice. He dug his hands into his pockets and turned east. He had no particular place in mind, but Twenty-third Street was full of restaurants. He walked quickly, driven by the cold. He tramped east on Twenty-third Street and paused for a moment, attracted by the bright lights of Cavanagh's. It was a good place and the brothers knew it well. I guess I might as well go in, he thought, looking through the steamy windows at the big white tables, the comfortable chairs filled by heavy, well-fed trenchermen. One man was grinning at the biggest lobster Randall had ever seen. He put his hand on the door and then suddenly drew back. My word, he thought, I can't go in there, I haven't got a collar and tie on. He turned away. What's the matter with me, he thought? Why do I care what Seymour does? I ought to be relieved, I didn't want to go to the damned dinner or the ball either. He walked on, losing interest in food as he passed saloons and cheap eating-places, not knowing what he wanted, not knowing why he was so distraught. Damn, he thought, walking quickly but aimlessly, what's the matter with me, why can't I make up my mind? Just because I hate to eat alone?

He went home and downstairs to the gloomy derelict kitchen, which was used only in the morning when the cleaning-woman made a pot of coffee for the brothers' breakfast. Rolls were brought by the boy from the bakery on the corner of Tenth Avenue. And that was the extent of the housekeeping. Randall lighted a gas jet and shuddered to see the cockroaches scurrying away. He opened doors and cupboards, aware that he would find nothing, but doing it anyway. In a crock he found a roll, so stale that he could scarcely break it. In a tin there was a little tea. He shrugged disgustedly and put some water on the gas-ring to boil. The old kitchen range had not been lighted in years and the dank basement room was so cold that Randall did not take off his overcoat.

The only warm room in the house was the library and though he felt diffident about using it when Seymour was out, he went there to get warm. He poured coal on the grate fire and sat down in the chair opposite Seymour's, holding out his blue, chilled hands to the red coals. I shouldn't, he thought, it's bad for the hands; and then he fell into the long hopeless maze of what to do about these hands and the music which was all they were good for, and the blind alley of well-meant lies and timid experiments in which he was trapped. I'd like to read, he thought, sitting there and looking at the books which lined the old brown walls, I'd like to read and get my mind on something beside all this mess . . . . he watched the books slither and waver, the colors of the bindings run together . . . I don't want to go to sleep, I want to stay awake and be here to give Seymour hell when he comes in . . .

He woke violently, for Seymour had slammed the door. Randall leaped from his chair. Seymour was standing in the middle of the room, slowly swaying to and fro. Randall looked from his brother's white, exhausted face, the eyes narrowed, the mouth locked bitterly, to the mantel clock, and then at Seymour again. It was nearly half past three. Seymour still wore his hat, pushed back on his slightly balding forehead, and Randall had not removed the long woollen muffler from his neck. They gave one another contemptuous looks.

"Nishe shight we are, eh?" Seymour's voice was snarling and he reeked. Randall shuddered.

"You're drunk," he said.

"Shpoken like man of the world."

"I might have known. Gad, that was a rotten thing you did."

"Mished party. Made you mish party. Both mished party. *Shit*!"

"Seymour!" Tears of outrage stood in Randall's eyes. "Keep your filth for your—" he choked.

"Thash right. She doeshn't care. Never care. Never care about a goddam thing." He lifted the hat from his head and slung it across the floor. "Never care, shee? You either."

"Then why don't you leave me in peace? Go and make a pig of yourself. But leave me alone."

"Pig, hah! Bl—bl—PIG!" Seymour doubled over with a choking noise and hid his face in his hands. Randall went close to him, flinching and grimacing at the stench of alcohol. But he put his hand on Seymour's shoulder.

"You're ill," he said, concerned in spite of himself. "Let me help you to bed."

"Help, hell. Hold my liquor. Hold anything. Not like you." He swung away, throwing off Randall's hand.

"Well, hold it then." Randall felt angry again. "See you don't make a monkey of me when you do it, though."

" 'Sh too eashy. Monkey. No Aush'rian woman make monkey of me."

"Shut up!"

"Sh'up yourshelf. Grow up too. Li'l Randall, li'l goody. Mama'sh li'l—"

"You stop that!" Randall winced at the sound of his own voice, shrill and almost tearful. He took a long breath and forced his voice down in his chest and said, "Stop talking like that. Leave Mama out of it. You got me in this mess, with your lies and your selfishness, dumping the whole thing on me. Get out of here and go to bed. You're drunk and you stink."

"Thash sho," said Seymour slowly. He turned unsteadily and made his way across the room. Randall stood watching him with anger and disgust. Seymour paused at the door and jerked his chin at Randall and said, "Poor Randall." He shook his head several times. "Poor Sheymour. Know what I mean? Poor Sheymour . . ." He stumbled down the hall to his room.

Late that afternoon, Seymour Holt had come slowly down the steps of a brownstone house on Murray Hill. His face was almost hidden between the fur collar of his overcoat, wrapped high against the bitter cold, and his Homburg pulled over his forehead. He walked down Madison Avenue, watching for a hansom. He had none too much time to get home to dress for dinner at the Wellington MacRaes', who had also invited Randall. Later the party was going on to the Van Dreesen ball. Seymour had had a struggle with Randall to induce him to go. Randall was afraid of Society, he was shy, he said he would have no conversation for the dinner and no dancing for the ball. Seymour dismissed his arguments. Randall need only see himself in the eyes of hostesses, to whom a couple of years in Imperial Vienna would seem the final touch of lustre upon that desirable pearl, a fresh young bachelor.

"Yes," said Randall gloomily. "A couple of years in a back street and one ball where I—"

"Never mind. I said I'd bring you and you're going."

There was not a hansom in sight and the air was so cold that it pinched Seymour's nostrils. He would have to take the Madison Avenue street car to Twenty-third street and there the crosstown car to get home. And he would be very late. It was too bad about Randall, who would be upset, but at the moment that had not much urgency to Seymour. Nothing seemed real except the total blackness of the room he had just left, the soundlessness of the dark, the loud breathing of the man who sat so close to him, knees almost touching, eye-to-eye but for the barrier of clicking black instruments. Because his hands lay clasped in his lap Seymour had chanced to feel his own wildly irregular pulse. This is nothing new, he told himself, you know all about it by now, don't be surprised, don't let him take you by surprise. That's not the way to meet it. Don't let yourself be surprised.

And it was no surprise. He heard what he had been told before; was the last time four months ago? Six months the time before? Don't be surprised! A year ago. God damn you, he had cursed himself, don't you give a sign. He can't surprise you. He could not, indeed, for his words were only continuations of what he had said all those times before. "Progressive . . . some change in condition, Mr. Holt, but not as I had hoped. . . . very desirable to eliminate precision focussing . . . strongly advise you . . . result of consultation . . . Germany if you wish, but . . ."

"Have you any way of knowing how long?" Seymour asked. His voice was firm and cold.

"That depends largely upon you. If you could change your work entirely, eliminate all close application—indefinite time, possibly. Quite possibly."

And what, Seymour could have cried aloud had he not sealed the channels of expression, am I to do? What shall I become? I know the devil who is part of me, who will not hang meek upon this cross. What will he do when you take away my work and leave me idle in that house? Must I explain—how shall I explain—to my weak and helpless ones? He walked faster, bending his head to break the impact of the freezing air. He forgot to look for a cab and he forgot too that he had meant to take the street car. Presently he forgot that he had meant to go home. He walked very fast, stepping off each curb to cross the street without a glance in either direction. At Thirtieth Street he paused and turned eastward and walked until he came to the lights and the warm sour smell and raucous laughter of a corner saloon.

After his third whisky he asked the bartender if there was a boy about who could run an errand. There was, and Seymour scribbled a note on a leaf from his pocket notebook.

"Here," he said, giving the boy half a dollar, "take this to Lexington Avenue. Montagu Apartments, Miss Florrie La Brea. Personally, understand?" He leaned on the bar again.

Mrs. Gerrity more than anyone kept up the pretense about Randall, because it kept her patient occupied. Only the vaguest suggestion sufficed to satisfy Lily and start her off on a time-consuming fantasy woven round Randall's increasing distinction and importance, the number of his engagements, and the scope of his repertoire. Lily asked very few direct questions. A hint that Randall had out-of-town engagements postponed for a long time the question of when he would play in New York. Randall worried because he knew the question could not be kept forever suspended. He had become rather adroit at satisfying his mother without telling her anything, and when he felt matters approaching the danger-line he appealed to Seymour who always seemed to have some expedient to tide them over.

When Lily began to fuss in the belief that Randall would make his New York début at a Carnegie Hall recital before the season was over, Mrs. Gerrity diverted her attention by interesting her in clothes. Sure, she must be getting her wardrobe ready if she was to start going to concerts! Mrs. Gerrity brought in an old seamstress who was a friend of hers, in whose wake there came dressmakers' dummies, fashion-plate albums, and other paraphernalia. Since Lily had never in her life thrown anything away, trunks were found full of her débutante and bridal finery, the remodelling of which was strung out for many weeks. This absorbed her as the making of new clothes could never have done. For a time she was quite content. When Randall or Seymour stopped in for a moment, they found her surrounded by billows of faded, musty clothes, shaking out and caressing the ruffles, smoothing the satin bodices which still fitted her emaciated figure, posturing before the pier-glass in a way which made her haggard face and strings of dust-colored hair ghastly by contrast. It was a frightening thing, heavy with the portent of an ominous ending, but the brothers did not know what else to do. Randall sensed that the worst had happened when Seymour, after several evenings of evasive and brooding silence broke the bad news.

"She's been insisting that her clothes are ready," he said. "And when she listens to you practising downstairs she sits with a pencil and paper saying she's helping you make up your programme."

"It's queer that she's never once asked me to play for her on that piano she moved up to her room."

"Oh, I know. She's like that. If you let her have her way about a thing she sort of forgets and lets it slide. That was why we didn't oppose her about the piano before you got home. But now—" Seymour stroked his moustache doubtfully. "I don't know, I'm so afraid of doing the wrong thing."

"Have you done anything? Or what have you done?"

"Well—" Seymour looked up uneasily, filling his pipe while he spoke. "You understand, Ran—she pushed me awfully hard and I did ask Doctor Slade what I'd better say."

"I guess I know what's coming." Randall sank down dejectedly in his chair.

"Slade said there was nothing else to do. He told me to tell her you will play at Carnegie Hall and let her muddle along thinking she's getting ready for it."

"Lord almighty, what a mess."

"I hope not. It's very hard on you and I'm sorry— but we've just got to hope we can get by with it."

"Did you have to tell her a date?"

"Yes. She got pretty excited and insistent, that's always the danger line. So I told her the twenty-sixth of February—I don't know why. I just plunged."

"About three weeks from now. My God," said Randall, feeling a sick twinge. "This is worse than if it were really so."

"You're awfully good about it, Kid." Seymour gave him a pathetic smile. "I feel as if—as if I've got an awful lot to make up to you for. I'm sorry about that night, Ran. I've felt like a dog about it."

"Oh, that's nothing, Brother." Randall's blue eyes glistened suddenly. "Forget it." He forced a small laugh. "I never did want to go to those parties. But it's too bad about you and all those people."

Seymour made a face. "They're bores, mostly. It's just not having anything better to do at times."

"I really am worried about Mama, though," said Randall. "She'll probably insist on making all sorts of plans."

"Oh, she will. Slade says that. He's got other cases very like this one. He told me about old Mrs. Mattingley up on Fifth Avenue. She still gives her annual ball and her series of dinners, just as she used to do before she—before her mind failed. They go through all the preparations and arrangements—only of course nothing really gets done. They just treat her the way we do Mama."

Only because he knew this could Randall endure watching his mother's preparations for his "recital". She spent days on end choosing the guests who were to sit in her box. Two of the five were dead, but Lily had no idea of it. When at last she had written and copied and recopied the notes of invitation, she gave them to Seymour to post and he locked them away in his desk. Over and over she repeated her other wishes to Seymour: exactly what sort of carriage and what color horses she wanted from Grogan's Livery Stables (which had been gone from Ninth Avenue for years). She decided upon every part of her costume, but each day she changed her mind and had the question to decide all over again. It was when she began to talk about a small reception for Randall after the concert that Seymour became so alarmed that he consulted Doctor Slade once more.

"That's not the most difficult part," said the doctor. "Let her go as far as she likes about arrangements, provided you can intercept them. Let her get all ready the evening of the 'concert'. Give her her head. When she is ready to go out—I think it more than possible that she may go into a maze at that point and actually refuse to leave her room."

"Are you counting on that?" asked Seymour sharply.

"No, that would be rash. I only think it might happen. But if it does not, and she really insists on going out, then Mrs. Gerrity is to give her a warm tonic drink, telling her she needs it to keep up her strength for the evening. Of course the 'tonic'—" he raised his eyebrows significantly. "You need not worry about that, Mr. Holt. The sedative will be fast-acting as well as strong. When she wakes up the next day she will not remember any details at all. In fact she will probably be very happy, full of pride about the concert. It will keep her content for a long time."

Randall was miserable when the moment came actually to put on his loathed full-dress clothes and go through the ghastly farce of saying good night to his mother before "leaving for Carnegie Hall. You must be early, darling, not *too* early, but in plenty of time to warm your hands." Lily tried to press upon him an old sealskin muff in which to put his hands while driving uptown. "Nobody would see it," she pleaded, stroking his arm. "Please, darling." Randall thought it more realistic to refuse, but Seymour coming into the room gave him the flick of an eye, and Randall took the moth-eaten old thing and, under excuse of nervousness about the concert, cut his good night short. His mother clung to him and Randall had to force himself to kiss her "one last time, for luck." He had never known so dreadful a sense of depression and self-depreciation. All his efforts to justify the innocent deception as right and necessary disappeared in a gulf of revulsion from the strain and the lies and the fear of some dreadful unforeseen consequence. He escaped at last from the room and by prearrangement with Seymour went straight downstairs. His mother would listen for every sound he made until he was out of the house, but she would never go to a window to watch him drive away; the deepest-fixed of all her obsessions was her refusal ever to uncover a window or look out of one.

Nonetheless, Seymour had ordered a cab for Randall in case Lily should stand listening, which would be typical of her, for him to drive away. It had begun to snow heavily that morning, and now the streets were so thickly blanketed that a horse's hoofs could not be heard. So Seymour decided that it was unnecessary to order a second carriage for his mother's fictitious trip to Carnegie Hall. Once she was quiet for the night, he planned to pick up a hansom and hurry out to his club to join Randall for dinner.

The suspense became almost intolerable during the long hour that it took Lily and Mrs. Gerrity to get her dressed. Seymour paced the library, worrying about Randall, worrying about a slip in the doctor's plan, worrying with a sudden panicky afterthought, what he should do if his mother in the morning should demand to see the newspapers with the critics' reviews of Randall's début. Why had he not thought of this sooner?—but what could he have done if he had? At that moment his mother's door opened upstairs and she called in her high, whining voice, "Are you ready, Seymour? Is it time?"

He went out to the hall and looked up the stairs at his mother standing inside the open doorway of her room. God knows what she must have on, he thought, but it will be décolleté and I hope she doesn't catch cold before Gerrity gets her to bed. He said, "Yes, Mama, I'm coming," and went back to the library and poured a stiff drink and gulped it. Then he went upstairs.

"Is the carriage here, Seymour?" His mother was standing before her pier-glass, arranging and re-arranging an ostrich boa round her shoulders. Her face was twitching with strain and her eyes looked like pieces of cracked glass.

"In a minute, Mama. There's lots of time, it's really too early."

He looked uneasily at Mrs. Gerrity, who was more expert than he at judging his mother's condition and anticipating her actions. Would Lily want to leave her room at the end, or would she refuse? Mrs. Gerrity's heavy face was set and forbidding. Apparently she had no doubt that his mother really meant to go out.

This would be his signal to slip away and wait in the library until Mrs. Gerrity should have induced his mother to drink her hot broth or milk or whatever it was, and soon thereafter report that the drug had taken effect. "She'll drink it more willin', sir, if you've just told her it's too soon to go out and you'll be waitin' awhile yet."

The minutes crawled by. Seymour stood by the library door with his watch in his hand. Until the actual beginning of this evening's horrible comedy he had felt it could be carried off. Now he was squeamish with apprehension. It was a cold night and the room certainly not overheated, but Seymour felt the sweat breaking out on his forehead and damping the palms of his hands. He swallowed again and again, listening miserably for some sound upstairs which would tell him how things were going. Then he became acutely uncomfortable. Tension and fear had their natural effect, and Seymour hurried to the water-closet at the far end of the hall, next door to the bathroom.

Upstairs Lily ran, weaving and fluttering, from her mirror to the door to the thickly curtained window where she listened for her arriving carriage, back to the door again. Actually to pass through the doorway and go out to the hall was the great obstacle which her confused mind had not yet rallied the resolution to surmount. Several times she put out her stick-like hand, shaking in its crumpled long glove, and touched the doorknob; then she drew back with a shiver. She had no notion of time and could not tell how long this suspense had dragged out; to her it seemed hours but actually it was only the few minutes while Mrs. Gerrity in the kitchenette waited for a small saucepan to boil. Lily had forgotten about her and the drink she was preparing. Suddenly Lily grasped the doorknob, turned it, and smothering a gasp of fright, forced herself to step out to the hall. She paused there. The library door stood open downstairs; she could see the light from the room. She called Seymour and heard no answer.

"Seymour!" she called again, but not much louder. She had succumbed to a flash of uncanny suspicion. When there was no answer to her second call she stood terror-stricken at the top of the stairs. Then she seized her ruffled train in one hand and the banister in the other and pattered softly down the stairs. Her fear of the halls and stairs and the world outside her own room was swept aside by her greater fear of what they might be doing to her. Where was Seymour? Where was the carriage? In the second floor hall she paused, peered into the empty library and again bleated "Seymour!" All she heard was a noise of running water, which had no meaning to her. Seymour must be downstairs. She ran down the next flight; once on her way panic overrode everything else. Driven by frenzy she swept through the house. Where was Seymour, what was happening? Lily stood in the dark, draughty front hall, staring at her reflection in the old hatrack mirror by the flickering light of the single gas-jet. "Seymour!" she cried again softly, for now she was cunningly intent that Mrs. Gerrity should not hear her. There was no answer. From the mirror there stared at Lily a grey, ghastly face. For a moment she peered at it. Then she pointed, she saw the trembling arm go up, the loose kid glove flapping round it. "Ashamed!" she moaned. "They're ashamed. They don't mean to take you to Randall's concert."

She paused. Then she cried, "No! Seymour!" and turned like a snake to the front door. She opened it and was out on the snow-covered stoop. She peered down the walk, looking for the carriage. I'm too far, she thought, I can't see from here, I must go closer. Grasping her long train in both hands she slithered down the buried steps, plunged and stumbled to the gate. There was no carriage at the curb. There was not a living thing in sight. There was not a sound. "Seymour!" she screamed now, forgetting Mrs. Gerrity. "Where's my carriage? Where are you?" She looked right and left, up and down the street. She began to waver on her feet, whining and mewing. "My carriage. Grogan's carriage, my concert, my baby, I'll be late, what are they doing . . ."

All the while she was running, weaving and floundering through the deep snow. "Ninth Avenue," she gasped, bringing up great groans from her exhausted lungs. "Grogan's, Ninth Avenue, why haven't they sent my carriage, how dare they, what's . . . where's . . . stables how can they . . . stables I'm going . . . carriage two bay horses . . . Randall . . . "

An instinct to take cover must have seized her as her legs gave out, for when Seymour and Mrs Gerrity, shouting and pounding through the street, found her a little later she was lying in an areaway half buried in a drift of snow.

When she died of pneumonia a week later Randall was in a state of collapse. All alone Seymour dragged through six haunted days, drowning in self-condemnation, wretched, sometimes envying Randall the profound lethargy which had followed his single terrifying burst of hysteria as he left his mother's deathbed. He had gone quite wild, screaming at Seymour, beating and clawing the air, sobbing, "You killed her, you knew it would kill her, you and that murderer of a doctor, you let her die . . ."

"I didn't, Ran. We didn't." Seymour tried to put his arm round Randall's shoulder, tried to grasp his flailing hands. He looked helplessly at Slade who stood at the window measuring a dose of some drug into a hypodermic syringe. The doctor came over to Randall, who tried to fight him off, while Seymour said, "Please, Ran. I'm suffering too. Have pity on me, for God's sake. I was only trying to do the best thing, trying to keep her going. Listen to the doctor."

Randall said, "No, no, send him away, I won't listen." But it was only a few minutes until he turned slack and apathetic and the doctor treated him and told Seymour to keep him in bed and not allow him to go to the funeral.

Seymour decided not to let notice of his mother's death be published until after her funeral. Alone he rode in the single shrouded black carriage to the burial-place in Brooklyn. Alone he stood in the mired, melting snow, staring at the hideous, frozen yellow earth, the more hideous black granite shafts marking the graves of the Holts for a century past. Names and the dim grey faces which had belonged to them, many Holts, and Whetstone and Jones and Seymour and Randall, wives condemned to lives more awful than their awful deaths . . . are we damned, thought Seymour, against the obbligato of the clergyman's perfunctory murmuring, are we all damned? I too, my brother, are we damned? Do we live, do we live in any sense, or will we die more awfully than these? He looked up from his dreadful reverie because the murmuring noise had stopped, because the shiny black glove of an attendant had put something in his hand. Seymour looked at it, shrinking, narrowing his dizzy eyes. It was a lump of rock, no, of earth, that frozen yellow earth. Turning a little so as not to look, Seymour dropped it upon the coffin in the grave, and pushing past the shocked clergyman he ran, in a wavering course, to the gate where he had left the carriage.

Warned by that moment of dreadful prescience, as if swaying or the brink of a forbidding but irresistible gulf, Seymour pulled himself together within a few days and decided to tackle the warren which his mother's years of occupation had made of the third floor. Sooner or later the house must be cleared out anyway. Even if they could never get rid of the place, Seymour was beginning to feel that he and Randall must get away from it. What they would do, and how they would live were questions still darkly veiled. It was easier to try to foresee a future for Randall than to face the unfaceable about himself. For the moment he thought it best to begin with the nearest thing at hand. Randall was quite calm, still deeply lethargic, and had rested quietly in bed for several days past. Leaving him asleep in the early afternoon, Seymour went upstairs. He was determined to get through his task without yielding to the emotions which would have undermined and demoralized him had he not sworn beforehand to abjure that. He opened the door of his mother's room and lighted the feeble gas-jet hanging over the marble-topped bureau. Then he stood appalled more than ever before by the frightful mess and clutter. Lily Holt herself had detracted from the impact of this sight, with her intensity and her insistence. Now it was as if her silence and her absence had ceded to all these crazily amassed objects the articulation and the identity which she had given up. Not only where to begin, thought Seymour, but how? Look at that, and that, and that—what did one do with such things if one merely moved them from where they were?

He stood in the centre of the cramped room, dwarfed and feeling like a mouse when he looked at the piles of boxes and albums and ornaments and cases spilling out faded ruffles, ribbons, laces, baby-clothes, yellowed collars and faded fancy waistcoats of his father's, tarnished souvenirs of gaieties of long ago. My God, he muttered, my God, I never knew it was as bad as this. He made his way with the greatest difficulty across the room to the windows, pushing and moving things piled up on every side to obstruct him. He must begin by baring the windows and airing the room; he wondered, conscious of the suffocating atmosphere, how many years since that had been done. When he grasped the cord of the first pair of curtains the rope broke in his hand. He was standing there wondering how to reach the short end dangling far above his head, when he heard a sound behind him. He turned quickly, knocking over a pile of boxes. Randall stood barefoot in the doorway in his nightshirt.

"What are you doing?" he cried. His voice was shrill and grating. This was the first time he had spoken in a week.

"Why—you can see. I was about to air the room. You oughtn't to be out of bed, Ran. You'll catch cold."

"You stop that. Don't you touch anything here."

Seymour clambered over the clutter strewn in his way and got across the room to Randall. He put his arm round Randall's thin shoulders. "There's nothing to be excited about," he said, in the most soothing tone he could manage. "Don't be so upset, Ran. I just thought I ought to get on with this—you can see we'll have to clear all this out."

"No!" Randall's blue eyes glittered. "No. You leave her poor things alone, don't you touch her things."

"But—" Seymour tried to lead him away.

"No!" Randall stood shivering. "You get out of here. You leave her things alone."

Seymour sighed. "Very well," he said softly. The immediate thing was to get Randall back to bed. "All right. Come on downstairs, Ran. We'll just leave the room shut up for a while until you feel better."

He turned out the gas, shut and locked the door, and tenderly led Randall away.

CHAPTER 8

The Rector of St. Timothy's wanted the *Stabat Mater* of Rossini sung in Holy Week. He was extremely proud of the music at St. Timothy's and indifferent to the minority of his parishioners who chafed at his High Church practices and his ardent promulgation of the music of Rome. However, even the most disgruntled of the dissenters were gradually coming round to the view that there was something to be said for anything which drew crowds to St. Timothy's and brought it fame. After all, they reasoned, we only have these Roman Masses and Cantatas at festival seasons. Much of our everyday fare is Bach and he was a perfectly proper Protestant.

The *Stabat Mater* would mean the usual intensive extra rehearsing, long hours of work with the choir, and the engagement of soloists from the outer darkness of the operatic and concert world. This was Randall Holt's second year as assistant organist and choirmaster, in charge of the detail of preparing the choral works. He loved the job, but had no idea just how he had actually been chosen for it. Seymour took great care that he should not know. The idea had been Doctor Slade's. Randall ever since his mother's death had insisted that the tragedy had been the doctor's fault, and had refused to see or speak to the man.

"You mustn't talk like that," Seymour often told him. "Or really believe what you say. It amounts to putting the blame on me too."

"Well, why not? And between you you've both made a worse villain of me."

Randall turned with relief to an honest job and the satisfaction of knowing he could do it well. He liked the calm detachment of the choir-room in the parish house, the organ practice beneath the dim vaults of the church roof, the gentle personality and deep musical scholarliness of Merion Fitzhugh, the church's celebrated organist who had studied at the Thomaskirche in Leipzig and at Notre Dame in Paris. Looking back on his own tempestuous experience in Vienna Randall regretted his ineptitude which had stood in the way of his doing what he was suited for and had mixed him up with a crew of theatrical savages. Some of this he had timidly related to Dr. Fitzhugh, as his shyness began to wear off; and Fitzhugh said, laughing, "I'm very glad you had those months at the Hofoper, Holt. You're better equipped than I am to deal with these bohemians when we have to use them here."

Randall was not so sure of that when he met for the first time with the quartet of soloists engaged to sing the *Stabat Mater*. The two women and the tenor were from the Opera. The basso was Edward Ricker, a specialist in oratorio and sacred music. He was an Ohioan who had sung all over the world and learned in each place the choicest of its vices. He was as fat as Ho-Tai, he smoked strong cigars, he sometimes came to rehearsals straight from luncheon at Mouquin's or Delmonico's, belching a proud description of the meal which made Randall feel ill. The man should have dropped dead of gluttony. Instead he stood up and sang like the Angel Gabriel. When he was not singing he sat with his enormous belly spread over his lap, eyeing the pretty soprano whom the Opera had recommended (and of whose modest fee it would take its cut, as was the custom.) Her name was Renata Tosi. "She doesn't speak much English," the manager's assistant had explained, "but she's a fresh young voice, nice texture, just what you want. She knows the music. We brought her over last fall for small lyric parts and she's all right."

From the looks and gestures of Ricker and the shock-headed young Milanese tenor, Randall thought she must be more than 'all right'. The three apparently had some convulsing joke among themselves, for an aside from either man seemed enough to set the soprano's brown eyes dancing and once Randall saw her go scarlet and hiss *"Taci!"* at the tenor, who turned aside with a snicker. The only unconcerned member of the quartet was the mezzo-soprano, a heavy, fortyish Italian woman who looked like a very good cook and, in fact, was. Between her numbers she sat like a patient cow waiting for her next cue. Randall was flabbergasted when, as the second rehearsal was breaking up, she went over to him, expertly felt his bony arms and shoulders and said in her rich voice, *"Poveretto! Bisogna mangiare!"*

"*Sì*," boomed Ricker, nodding fatly. "Take her up on it quick, Mr. Holt. She makes the most glorious risotto in the world. *Vero*, Monguzzi?"

Monguzzi shrugged comfortably. Randall was wondering whether she really meant to invite him to dinner when they were startled by a shriek of laughter from Renata Tosi behind them. She was leaning on the piano in peals of mirth, holding her handkerchief to her face. Beside her the tenor was whispering into her ear and though she flapped one hand at him to shut him up, she laughed louder and louder.

Randall was embarrassed. This kind of hilarity was highly unseemly in St. Timothy's parish house and he supposed he ought to put a stop to it at once. But he could no more have summoned the authority to do so than he could have pitched Edward Ricker through a window. He bit his lip and looked uneasily at Tosi and the tenor, then at Ricker, perhaps hoping that as the only American present, he might understand and for the sake of propriety, help Randall out. But Ricker himself had joined the joke, whatever it was, and when he let out a great blast of mirth Randall paled. Between guffaws Ricker translated in gusts. "He says—Dino says—if she keeps on—tchk tchk—doing in American churches—what they have *castrati* do—tchk tchk—in Rome—tchk tchk—where is she going to—tchk—end up?" He wiped his huge moon face. "Only he says it in detail."

"But," said Randall, blushing yet anxious not to seem a hopeless prude, "they don't have—er—them—any more. I really think—"

"Drop it, Dino. Stop!" Ricker was coughing and blowing into his handkerchief, shaking all over. "Go," he said, giving the tenor a push. "*Via*, go home. *Basta 'sta porcheria*. Now he's talking about *ragazzi* instead. Boys."

Oh, Lord, thought Randall, are all opera-singers alike? He looked forward longingly to the peaceful weeks after the Rossini, when these licentious scamps should have gone back to their lair and left him to recapture the cloistered serenity in his work which he had grown to love. He was not to be allowed that, as he learned when Renata Tosi arrived for the next rehearsal. She was in no laughing mood, in fact she seemed upset. Her English was so limited that in her agitated state it consisted of isolated words strung between streams of Italian which Randall had to overlook since he could not understand it. He could follow her, though, when she said and repeated many times, "You help, yes? You help me?"

She thrust at him a slip of pink paper which he found to be a performance-notice from the Opera, with orders to report in some ten days for rehearsal. They had cast her as The Forest Bird in *Siegfried*.

"Me!" She clasped her hands across her lacy breast. "I tell no, I tell *impossibile, non parlo tedesco, non canto tedesco,* why they tell Wagner for me? *Pazzi! Cretini!*" She was even prettier angry than laughing, her large eyes swimming with unshed tears, her cheeks pink and her lips parted over exquisitely white teeth. She put her gloved hand on Randall's arm and pleaded, "You help, yes?"

"But what can I do?"

He found that she had been cast because of the manager's stubborn determination to mount a Wagner opera although he had only a few leading singers to put into it. He proposed to fill the smaller parts with anybody else and there was indeed no good reason why not. Any lyric soprano, he said, could sing The Bird, and he was right. When Tosi protested that she had never sung a note of German music he told her to report for coaching to the German director he had hastily hired to put on his one venture into Wagner. Tosi, who had just seen the fat-necked *brutto porco* (in her words) bellowing at the luckless Italian who had been tapped for Alberich, indignantly refused. She was told to submit or quit. She retorted that she would sing the part only if she were left alone to study it—here she made eloquent, flattering gestures which Randall tried shyly to deprecate—with somebody who really knew something, a cultivated person, her own correpetiteur who had worked in Vienna for Schalk and Mahler, *un artista molto raffinato e gentile*.

"Oh, no," Randall protested, scarlet with embarrassment. "I—really—"

"No? *Perchè* no? You know well this music, eh?"

"But, but—you say you don't know any German."

Renata Tosi threw back her head scornfully. "For such a part I learn that *porca lingua*?"

"No, but you have to learn enough words to sing this Bird."

"*Va bene—va bene*. You tell me noises, I make the same like you. Such a part nobody notice what I tell. I am hidden—" she winked at him. "Must be, how is *facile*?—easy."

"Then why," blurted Randall with hopeless simplicity, "did you make all this fuss?"

"*Madonna santa*! How I keep my—how you say?" She made impatient gestures to indicate pride. "*Sono una donna—basta!*" she cried.

Randall laughed. She said again, "You help, yes?"

"I suppose so," he said reluctantly. They made an appointment for the morning of Easter Monday. Like most of the operatic colony, she lived at the Ansonia Hotel. On the long ride in the street car up Broadway from Twenty-third Street to Seventy-third, Randall had plenty of time in which to wonder just what he was letting himself in for. There was an air of alarming frivolity about Signorina Tosi. Against his will he thought uneasily about Seymour's remarks an hour ago. They had left the house together, which was unusual, for Randall ordinarily did not go out in the mornings. He had drifted into the habit of making breakfast for Seymour and himself, since charwomen's coffee was undrinkable and their slovenliness a hateful setting in which to begin the day. After breakfast Randall usually practised for a couple of hours before going over to St. Timothy's to work at the organ there. So today when he started out with Seymour to walk to the street-car, it had been only natural to explain his errand. Seymour thought it a fine idea.

"Is she pretty?" he asked, swinging his cane and smiling as if at some unspoken joke. His grey eyes were unusually lively behind his gold-rimmed pince-nez attached to an elegant black silk cord. He was certainly a figure of a man, thought Randall. He answered, "Why—yes, I suppose so."

"Suppose? Don't you know?"

"Yes. She is very pretty."

"Aha. That's better." Seymour's long legs in their smartly-cut trousers clipped off like sharp shears the distance to the corner. "Point two?"

"She has a charming voice."

"Discussable. What else has she got?"

"What do you mean?"

"Well, you tell me she's young and pretty and a bit-player modest enough so your church can hire her. But she lives at the Ansonia. Randall, dear."

"Practically all the artists live at the Ansonia," said Randall stiffly.

"Including the impecunious young beauties? How charitable of the management."

"What are you getting at?" Randall knew irritably that he was not making a very good go of obtuseness.

"Just asking, to put it as delicately as possible, who is keeping the lady."

"You always have such vulgar ideas!" Randall felt himself reddening and, had he possessed Seymour's vocabulary, would have cursed.

"Vulgar?" Seymour raised his hat in a mock salutation. "Here is your corner. I may be vulgar, brother dear, but realism is not necessarily the same thing. Keep your eye peeled for a hot-tempered Latin in the panelling somewhere."

Randall's knock on Renata Tosi's door was answered by an enthusiastic, soprano "*Avanti!*" and he stepped into the room.

"*Già?*" he heard her exclaim, but he did not see her. The room was a burgeoning confusion of imitation French furniture, mussed cushions, lacy curtains, fading roses, here a slipper, there a trailing mass which must be a ruffled gown. On a bamboo stand there was a small tray with a used coffee-cup. There was an upright piano in the corner, carelessly piled with scores, a feathered hat, a handkerchief, a scent-bottle, and an open gold mesh handbag. Randall stood looking dumbly at the scene.

"You wait a moment?" cried Signorina Tosi from beyond a door slightly ajar. "Take a chair, *s'accomodi* . . ."

While he hesitated, looking for any chair upon which something was not flung or strewn, the door in the corner opened wider, admitting a waft of scented steamy air which informed him that there was the bath of this bed-sitting-room apartment. Behind the gilded screen in the other corner, over which something embarrassingly sheer and lacy had been flung, must be a bed. He had not, he thought, successfully enough obliterated certain memories of Vienna. He was standing with his hat in one hand and *Siegfried* in the other, wishing he had not come, when he heard a ripple of laughter and turned to see Renata Tosi, wrapped in a mass of ruffles, with her dark hair piled on top of her head in no shape at all. She must just have stepped from her bath, he thought, anxiously hoping he was not showing his embarrassment.

"You are so early arrive'!" she cried. "*Come mai?* They are only the ten o'clocks."

"But our appointment was for ten o'clock."

"*Pensa! I* said the ten o'clocks?" she pointed a finger at herself with such comic astonishment that Randall burst into a laugh and she joined him delightedly. "That is better," she said. "You must not give me the frighten, you make in first the face so serious."

"You say such funny things," said Randall. "I haven't really heard you speak English before."

"Yes, is no bad, eh? Only since few months, I must translate always from here." She tapped her ear and then her forehead. "Here is *italiano*, but from the mouth must come *inglese—Formidabile*, why I consent to such a thing?"

"English is easy," said Randall, knowing he sounded a fool. Seymour would have had something very different to say.

"For you! *Be'*, you teach me, you tell, I listen."

"That's not what I came for," he said, laying down his hat and proffering *Siegfried*. "Do you know any German at all?"

"I? *Per carità!*"

"Well, it doesn't matter, as we said. It's only a few lines. You can learn them phonetically."

"*Ecco*—like I say. Is easy, no?"

"They used to say so in Vienna. But I shouldn't think any Wagner would be easy."

"For me is easy or I not sing." She waved her hand carelessly and ran across the room to the bell. "First we drink *un caffè, poi vediamo*."

"You mean that's your way of deciding what you'll sing? If it's easy for you?" Randall stared.

"*Cosa vuoi?*" she shrugged. "You think it please me work hard?"

"The *Stabat Mater* is not easy music and you did that very well."

"*Ma che!* One aria, one duettino, *niente*."

"And five concerted numbers. I don't call that nothing."

"It was nothing," she insisted. "Something you know is nothing. *Non mi piace lavorare*." She made a face at the piano. "I don't like learn new parts."

"When did you learn the *Stabat Mater*?"

"In the *Conservatorio*. I was oblige'. Now I think I not be oblige' any more, *invece* this *cretino* want Wagner! Is no good enough Verdi? Puccini? *Ah, ecco il caffè!*"

She piled two lumps of sugar into an after-dinner cup, filled it, and handed it to Randall who had not been given a chance to say he did not take sugar in coffee. He almost choked over his first taste.

"*E' buono, no?*" she exclaimed, draining her cup at a gulp. Randall was still recovering from the hot, black, bitter-sweet, oily shock to his tongue. "You don't like?" she asked anxiously. "*Perchè?*"

"I guess I'm not used to it." He wondered how to force down the rest.

She stood laughing at him, her head thrown back a little, her young throat a swanlike arc. Her skin was white for an Italian, but not the blue-white of the dark-haired Irish type which she resembled. There was warmth in her robust pallor and in her richly colored lips, which

Randall had been too innocent to suspect of paint when he had seen her before. Now, unconcernedly emerging from her bath, her face was bare of any artifice and she quite at ease about it.

Randall did not want the rest of his coffee and he wished he had the savoir-faire to dispense with it and get on with her lesson. She stood there smiling at his irresolution. He became increasingly uncomfortable. Up to now he had lacked the boldness of imagination to own that the very appetizing creature alone with him here was obviously naked except for a ruffled peignoir, and that she saw nothing bizarre about the position at all. He had an idea that it would be better not to look at her any more, since every line of her bantering face was inviting him to do so. So he turned a little away, saying, "Hadn't you better— er—eh—just—I mean, wouldn't you rather I stepped out to the hall while you, ah, finish dressing?"

"No, no," she said, "*stia commodo*. Dress?" She looked down at herself as if in surprise at her own *déshabillé*. "Perhaps. *Va bene*, wait a minute." She ran to the screen in the corner and disappeared behind it. "Maybe you play me this music while you wait. Is *complicata, la melodia*?"

"Not a bit," he said, hugely relieved. "Just like this." He played, she began to sing by ear, and presently she was standing near him, very proper in a starched white shirtwaist and a braided black skirt. Randall went on playing, pointing to her entrances, but she shook her head and motioned at him.

"You tell," she said. "Give me a sign, *basta*. For what I read?"

"Is this the way you were taught?" he asked with asperity. "Just to sing by ear?"

"*Ma no!*" Her brown eyes rounded in astonishment. "In Milano? *Al Conservatorio*? You think we are *ignoranti*?"

"No," he said, irritated. "Of course not. That's why I expect you to read music."

"I told you I don't like to work," she said. "Read is work. *Vocalizzare* is *niente. Andiamo.*"

He sighed. She did not seem firm enough of purpose to account for this streak of obstinacy, but he knew that he was no judge of women. It struck him that her flippancy was assumed, that she was a good artist in spite of herself and her refusal to take her work seriously. Her voice was exquisitely fresh, more fragile than the lightest voices he had heard in Vienna, and she used it with grace and taste. She picked up The Bird's music in a few effortless repetitions. While she sang, repeating several times each phrase as he played it, she wandered round the room making desultory sorties at the disorder she had strewn. Some of the mess had disappeared into cupboards and drawers by the time Randall rose from the piano.

"Now about the text," he said. "Let's—"

"Now? Today? Absolutely, no."

"But—"

She came over to him and with the utmost delicacy she did a vulgar thing. She chucked him under the chin, faintly clicking the tips of her fingers and laughing up at him like a teasing child. He flushed and stood there fuming. "Really," he said stiffly, wishing he knew how to make her ashamed of herself. Instead he succumbed to a wave of the familiar mortification which, he thought, it seemed the horrid part of singers to arouse. He turned aside, plainly annoyed, and picked up his hat.

"Very well," he said, and walked towards the door. He heard her pattering after him; did this woman never walk? Whenever she had the least purpose in view, she ran.

"*Domani?*" she cried gaily. "Tomorrow?"

He turned and scowled at her. "I wasn't even sure you meant to keep on," he said. "And if you do—"

"Yes?"

"You haven't done enough work today to make it worth my time to come all this way. You may not like to work, but some people are in earnest."

"Oh." She stood with her mouth a little open and her dark eyes wide with surprise. Having said it, he felt better, less a fool. He had turned the tables. He watched the faint blush of embarrassment which tinged her lively face with its delicate bones, its slanted nostrils, and its low forehead from which the brown hair sprang so prettily. She looked like a flower on a slender stalk, her long neck wrapped in its high boned collar.

"I'm sorry," she said slowly. "I did not see from your view."

"Oh, that's all right."

"You come again tomorrow, yes?"

"Yes, I'll be here. Shall I leave the score in case you want to look at it?"

She bit her lip, still a little uncertain, then he saw her sense of mischief flash like a lighted match. She giggled. "You really think that?" she said. "You think I study?"

"It wouldn't hurt you."

She turned her head and tapped the lobe of her ear, a well-shaped ear but large in proportion to her small finely-modelled head.

"*Così* I learn," she said. "Believe me. I don't waste your time. I am, how is it, grateful. *Poltrona*, lazy, perhaps, but stupid, no."

"That's all right," he said again awkwardly. "I'll see you tomorrow."

She held out her hand and he took it and shook it and dropped it. Turning to leave the room he realized he should have kissed it. Oh God, he thought, am I always to be made a fool of by singers? He strode down the hotel corridor but not fast enough to escape hearing a laughing sotto-voce from her doorway.

"*Bello!*" she said.

That evening at dinner at the Marine Club Seymour asked Randall how his morning had gone. Randall ate several spoonfuls of mock turtle soup before answering.

"Well enough," he said.

"Was it amusing?"

"I didn't go to be amused, so naturally I wasn't."

"That is not corroborated by the gleam in your eye."

"I? Gleam?"

Seymour swallowed the last of his Little Necks and laughed quietly. "You've been as pleased as punch about something ever since we met half an hour ago. I told you your Italian lark would turn out to be a jaybird."

"She is not 'my' Italian lark, and I don't follow you. What do you mean, jaybird?"

"A tease. A flirt. Something tells me."

"I couldn't say."

"I never saw anything like the innocence of those blue eyes. Well, you and I are both odd ducks, but not that odd. Personally, I think you've probably stumbled onto something."

Randall sighed. "Could it possibly occur to you that a woman could be a singer and not a toy?"

"It could. But in this case it wouldn't. What did she have on?"

Randall could have dived under the table to hide the blush that swept across his face. "I've no idea," he said, making a stab at aplomb.

"I see. Waiter, this steak is overdone. Take it away and send the steward here."

"Oh, Brother, please don't make a scene." Randall was always embarrassed by Seymour's gastronomical intolerances. "I'd rather have the chicken fricassee."

"I know you would. But red meat is good for you and I ordered a very rare sirloin for two. We are going to have it."

Randall never cared as much as that about food and he could not share Seymour's enjoyment of roast beef and thick steaks oozing blood. But there was no point in arguing that subject now; he would rather hear Seymour do battle with the steward and the chef than continue to banter him about Renata Tosi. He sat crumbling bits of bread while Seymour laid down the law about beefsteak and the cooking in general. They had to settle down to a long wait while another steak was grilled. Anxious to keep Seymour's attention diverted, Randall told him that the roof over the rear part of their house was in need of repair. The cleaning-woman had told Randall that considerable dampness had worked into the attic rooms during the winter. "I suppose we ought to fix it," he said.

"I suppose. But it's so futile to spend any money on that old tomb. If we start with the roof they'll tell us something else is necessary and one thing will lead to another. You know."

"Of course. But don't you think we might as well make up our minds about the house altogether? The estate is supposed to pay for repairs, we don't have to. Are we going to stay on living in it the way it is?"

"I don't know." Seymour spoke slowly, thinking. "I've been the one who wanted to get us out of there and I still am—in a way. But—"

Randall said nothing and waited for Seymour to explain. Seymour said, "It's true, I've always wanted a nice small flat and we could afford one together. But I couldn't manage my share of that and have something else that I believe I want even more."

"What is that?"

"Don't be too surprised, Ran. I really want it awfully." Seymour smiled with the wistful expression of a small boy. He seldom had such moods and Randall said, "What is it you want, Brother? A boat?"

"No. A boat would cost more than I could possibly afford, at least any boat worth buying. No, I want an automobile."

"An *automobile*!" Randall gaped with astonishment, absently watching the waiter carve the beefsteak and arrange portions on each plate, alongside a massive baked potato. Randall began immediately to push the mealy inside of his potato onto the pool of crimson beef juice, soaking it up so that he would not have to look at it. "Isn't an automobile dreadfully dangerous, Brother?"

Seymour laughed. "Not so dangerous as expensive, I should say. They're not a curiosity any more, Ran, lots of people have them. I want one while—" he interrupted himself and began to eat.

"While what?"

"While they're still fairly experimental. You know I like to fuss with machinery."

"Yes, of course. But what would an automobile cost?" Randall was awestruck at the daring of this idea.

"About twenty-five hundred dollars, the one I want, the Stevens-Duryea."

Randall stared. "My word, that's a lot of money. Aren't there any cheaper automobiles?"

"Yes, quite a lot. But those wouldn't be interesting. It's the same as a boat, one's not worth having unless it's big enough for deep-sea cruising, and that would be completely beyond my means. But I could buy a good automobile if—" he raised his eyebrows with another boyish smile.

"If we stayed in the house. Well, I've never been as anxious to get out of it as you were. I don't particularly like it, but the way we've drifted into living, we're really not there very much. I'd as soon sleep and practise there as somewhere else." Randall knew that no matter where they lived he would always have the same problem, the dreary emptiness of the evenings and the meals when Seymour was engaged with his own concerns. The remedy for Randall was to find companionship of his own, but he shrank from that effort with the same timidity which caused him now to feel relieved that they need not make the break from the old house. He said, "Go ahead and buy your automobile, as far as I'm concerned. I see why you can't afford anything else besides —it will take about a year's income, won't it?"

Seymour nodded, swallowing some ale and wiping the edges of his moustache. "That's just it. If we stay in the house for about a year more, I can buy my motor car now and my salary will see me through the rest of things." He gestured at the dining-room. "It will be a tight squeeze, but—"

"I'll gladly give you some of my money," said Randall eagerly. "I never use it all up."

"I'd much rather you did use it," said Seymour with a smile. "Maybe you'll begin to one of these days. Anyway, after another year we can think about moving out of the house if we want to. And in four years more I'll get twice the income I have now. In eight years you will. So who knows?" His expression became remote. "One can plan, anyway." He shrugged.

Randall thought he detected a note of strain or bitterness in Seymour's last words, a long-familiar suspicion which the gaiety of Seymour's life made inconsistent. So once again he dismissed it. He only said, "By the time I'm thirty-one we'll have quite a handsome income between us, won't we?"

"Something over eight thousand. But it's not likely to stay between us. Suppose you marry, Ran?"

"Oh," said Randall, startled, "that's not likely! You're much more apt to marry."

"I shouldn't think so, you know. Since you ask me I don't think either of us is a good bet to marry. But particularly not me. I've got bored with correctness and convention and the romantic marriages that are part of it all. I suppose it depends on how you start out." His face was moody. "I've seen too much, I remember Papa too well and poor Mama. Good God, look at Dorothy Parsons after eight years. Stuffy as a duchess. That's cured me of romance."

"It's a pity to hear you talk like that."

"Lots of things are a pity. Well, we're settled anyway: we stay in the house. Do we spend any money on it—or ask the estate to? Frankly, I don't think it's worth it."

"But suppose the roof falls in?"

"Let's gamble that it won't for another year. After that we'll probably move anyway. The old woman made that preposterous will and I'd rather let the house stew in its juice. If we never ask to have any of the trust money spent on the house we'll be as rich as Croesus by the time the trusts terminate. And probably too old to enjoy it, too," he added.

Stilton cheese and celery were brought for Seymour and a meringue glacé for Randall. Seymour peered at it, holding his pince-nez towards the tip of his nose. He shuddered delicately and said, "How can you!"

"But I like it. The way you like that horrible bleeding meat."

"You picked up the tastes of a *poule* in Vienna. Sweets and chocolate and whipped cream."

"Then you should thoroughly enjoy dining with me." Randall grinned with uncharacteristic mischief. Seymour chuckled. "I'd not have thought it of you," he said. "Are you seeing your new toy again tomorrow?"

"Brother, I told you—"

"Tush. She sounds delightful."

"I haven't said a word about her, except for answering your tactless questions. You're determined to imagine things."

"Perhaps I am. For some reason she piques my curiosity."

"Not mine."

"You haven't enough. But you will, child, you will. It will be thrust upon you."

Randall walked home alone after parting from Seymour on the steps of the Club. Almost always Seymour had some late engagement which was kept a discreet blur, and Randall would not have dreamed of inquiring about it. Habit was so strong in him, and any departure from it such an effort that he went home automatically to the empty house without volition or intention. Once in a great while Seymour or some circumstance forced him to consider an alternative; perhaps a concert to which Randall knew he ought to go, or a careless suggestion from Seymour to come along and make a fourth at a late supper at Jack's or Mouquin's. There would be a pretty companion for him and if Seymour brought up the question, he had to scold Randall into joining such a party. Randall rarely did.

He walked through the gritty front yard, grateful for the dark which hid its pathetic efforts to respond to early spring. Last autumn in an impulse of protest against the increasing ugliness of the surroundings he had planted some hyacinth and tulip bulbs, and the hyacinths had come into bud during the past week. Their willingness and their optimism put him to shame; how could he have asked them to bloom in such a spot! He let himself into the dark house and lit the sputtering gas jet in the hall. He hung his hat and his light topcoat on the branching hatrack and turned to climb the stairs. The banister felt grimy under his right hand. Who knew how thoroughly the woman cleaned in the mornings?—nobody was there to check up on her and neither brother cared enough to involve himself in a matter that would surely be disagreeable. It was easier to ignore the question, like everything else in the house. Randall stood there looking up the dark stairwell. I wonder, he thought, if Seymour has ever been upstairs above the second floor since—since—his mind veered away from the memory of the days after his mother's death. More than two years had passed since he had stopped Seymour from turning out her room. Randall had never intended such a length of time to slide by, he had only not felt ready for the ordeal so soon after her dreadful death. But once Seymour locked the door it had stayed locked. Randall stood thinking about that now. He was quite ashamed. All their ways, his and Seymour's, were habits into which they had drifted without really noticing it. If he stood and thought about this house, room by room, he would be counting off more rooms locked and unused than he and Seymour ever entered. That was not their fault, they had not asked to be saddled with this cumbersome old pile. The only way they could live in it was to ignore the existence of the space that they could not use. But it must be an awful mess, Randall thought, with a twinge of uneasiness. We really ought to do something about it, I suppose. In fact, I guess I ought to go and look at those top-floor rooms where the roof has leaked. He only knew about it from Mrs. McBane, the charwoman; he had not been up there to look.

Why go now? he asked himself. He could not remember where the gas jets were; he would be stumbling and tripping all over the place. I could take a candle, he thought. You could also wait until morning. But I don't want to go up there in the morning. I want to—I am going out in the morning. It was a nice thought, a pleasant one, somewhat dampened by Seymour's teasing and his own disapproval of Signorina Tosi's laziness and flippancy, but still pleasant enough so that he did not want to dim it by tackling a disagreeable task beforehand. No, I'd better go now, he decided. He went to his own room, the small one beside Seymour's which had once been their grandmother's bedroom, and which, with the library at the back of the house, completed the second floor where the brothers lived entirely. The only other space they used was the ground-floor drawing-room where Randall practised; and Seymour's workshop in the cellar where nobody went except himself. It was a queer arrangement, Randall reflected, now that he had begun to think about it; but it was the natural outcome of their obligatory occupancy of the house.

He lit his bedside candle in its china holder, picked it up, and climbed the stairs to the third floor. On the landing he lit the gas. He stood for a moment looking at the closed door of his mother's room. We must open it, he thought; but he shrank with a twinge from imagining the dim pathetic clutter in which she had maundered out her life. He preferred to remember her young, as young as he could remember, and fixing his mind on that easier memory he went on to climb the next flight of stairs. He did not think he had been up to the fourth floor since he and Seymour, graduated from the nursery, had moved downstairs from it. By the light of his candle he found the hall gas-jet and turned it on to light it. He jumped, startled by a shrill squeal like the cry of a small animal. The gas-jet was full of air, it would not take the flame. He turned it off and holding his candlestick high, he climbed the steep flight of steps to the servants' garret under the mansard. It was pitch dark up here except for the feeble circle of yellow light thrown by his candle. He moved slowly to the rear of the house where he had been told the dampness had got in. He put his hand on a doorknob and was just turning it when he stopped. Inside the room, instead of the dead silence which held the rest of the empty house, he heard noise; scratching, scuffling. His hand felt clammy on the cold porcelain doorknob; a lump rose in his throat. It can't be rats, he thought, trying to reassure himself. Oh my God, I can't go in there if it's rats.

Somewhere he remembered having read that one could frighten them. He raised his foot in its strong boot and stamped heavily on the bare floor. He kicked the bottom of the door a couple of times. Then drawing a long breath he burst into the loudest shout he could utter, and threw open the door with a crash. His flickering candle showed only barren ugliness, but he also kept his eyes away from the floor. He moved with so much noise that he could not have heard them if they were there, scurrying away. He stood in the centre of the room, turning round in a circle with his candle high, to examine the ceiling and the walls. His nostrils clenched as if to shut out the evil and mouldy smell of the room, compounded of damp and dirt and something related to the noises whose cause he had been determined not to see. The roof, he decided, had not leaked so badly after all. People like that McBane woman always exaggerated such things. There was one corner where the ceiling and the wall were stained and streaked, but the plaster seemed intact and it would be a long time before anything worse happened. Long before it did, he thought, flinching from the vile air, he and Seymour would be gone. He turned towards the door, shutting out the sight of the two narrow iron cots and the thin, ragged mattresses on them, their stained ticking full of holes from which the dirty stuffing stuck out in hanks and bunches. Randall did not want to understand what had got them into that condition. He moved quickly to leave the room, slamming the door behind him. He hurried downstairs, washed his hands, changed his coat for the brown velvet lounging-jacket which Seymour had given him last Christmas and his boots for a pair of slippers, and settled down in the library with a motet of Palestrina which he was preparing for the choir to sing next week. Studying this should be the most calming of occupations and efface from his mind the impression of what he had seen upstairs. That was not important, he assured himself; he need only forget it. Usually he studied a score with reliable and effortless concentration. But tonight that did not come easily. His thoughts seemed to wander and run in every direction. Some of them were amusing, reflections of his morning with Renata Tosi. Others were less pleasant. He wished now that he hadn't gone upstairs, it had proved to be unnecessary. He sat with his eyes on the score, reading but not digesting it, and with his pencil he scribbled absent-mindedly on the margins.

CHAPTER 9

Seymour woke late the next morning, gloomy and unrested. He lay in bed in his darkened room, vexed by fragmentary impressions of last night's diversion. He was not repelled by his thoughts, but he was bored. When he had really enjoyed himself he was apt to sleep well and wake in good humor, but such moments were becoming increasingly infrequent. Without looking at his watch he knew that it must be about ten o'clock. He had a very sharp sense of time in all its phases, the result, he believed, of the fate which challenged him to get the most out of every hour and every day while he could still see. He measured all things by the tenuous span of his eyesight. And much of his secretiveness had grown from the habit of silence about his eyes. He had never told Randall the truth about this, and he had parried every remark or question which could have led up to the subject. Sometimes he wondered how well he had succeeded; not so well, he feared, as he could have wished. Often he caught Randall looking at him with anxiety, and at his many pairs of eyeglasses with uneasy curiosity.

Well, he thought, rolling over and lying face down, the less I say now the less there will be to say in the end. He could have said more than he had at dinner last night. But why burden Randall yet? The coming years would tell their story fast enough. He would go on, getting as much pleasure as he could until he could have no more at all. A poor show, the better side of his mind sometimes reproved him; after you are blind will this kind of life be anything worth living in retrospect? Could you do better? He turned tense and depressed in the grip of such thoughts. Presently he pulled himself up, sat for a few minutes accustoming his eyes to the dim light filtering about the edges of the curtains, and then swung himself out of bed. Shuffling across the room in his nightshirt he looked even taller and bonier than when he was dressed. Cautiously he parted the curtains just enough to see that the spring morning was sunny and brilliant; so he left the curtains drawn. Strong light was distressing to him, especially in contrast to the dark. He moved about the room, shaving and dressing almost entirely by touch. He was not very meticulous about it, he was in fact becoming careless except at moments when he wanted to make a particularly fine appearance. He was learning how to do these things without looking; a strange, almost perverse secret now as if in practice for the future when he would have to depend on the habit.

When he was dressed he went to the library, where he and Randall took their coffee and rolls every morning. They had fixed up a shelf hidden by a screen, and put on it the gas-ring from the kitchenette upstairs where Mrs. Gerrity had cooked their mother's food. Here Randall made their morning coffee and boiled the kettle for an occasional cup of tea. They never used the abandoned basement kitchen at all. Seymour cautiously raised the dark blinds on the four bay-window sashes, running them up only a few inches to keep the room dim. He lit the gas-ring to re-heat the coffee that Randall had left for him, and putting on the special spectacles which he needed, he sat down with the morning's *Times*. He had grown accustomed to rationing his failing sight; he used it mostly for such work as he could still do and then, able to read only a little, he gave preference to the daily newspaper because a sense of knowing what was happening in the world helped him to ward off the stronger sense, the looming fear of the time when he would be cut off from everything. Today the news was not interesting. He sat sipping his coffee, eating bits of dry crust from a roll, and scanning the columns of print which he realized presently were telling him nothing. He let the paper slide to the floor. These mornings when he rose late and did not go to work were demoralizing. Like so many other things about himself, he kept them as much as possible a secret. Last year he had had to make one exception to his rule and tell Wilfred Minturn the truth about his condition. He had met kindness and sympathetic understanding, but important firms could not maintain their staffs upon partial charity. Upon learning that four or five years was the maximum possible time that Seymour could hope to continue working, Mr. Minturn had arranged that so long as Seymour remained with the firm he would receive no increases of salary but should have freedom to come and go, and be absent from the office as much as was necessary to rest his eyes.

Seymour sighed. He was learning by degrees to live with his fate, but protest and the instinct to strike back were powerful in his nature. Perhaps it was silly to buy an automobile, but he wanted one passionately. He felt confident of seeing well enough to drive easily, and his fingers itched at the thought of such a machine to tinker with. Then, the fun he might have! He knew nobody who would not be twice as amusing when he had the excitement of motoring to offer. This idea grew more intriguing every minute. Why not go out right now and see the Stevens-Duryea people and find out how long they would require to deliver him a car?

He had left their catalogue, along with a stack of others which he had been studying, down in the cellar in his workshop. He wanted another look at them all for a final comparison before he went out to order his car. On his way downstairs he encountered Mrs. McBane listlessly flapping at the tiled floor of the front entry. He bade her good morning and she answered sullenly. "Are you through in the library, sir?" she asked. She was always sour when he stayed in his rooms all morning and made her wait to finish her work.

"Yes," he said. "You can finish up now."

He passed her slatternly bulk, kneeling on the hall rug, and went towards the back hall and the cellar stairs.

"Mr. Holt, sir," she said.

"Yes?" He paused.

"Them rooms up at the top," she said. "I told yer brother, sir, how the roof's leaked and made a mess up there. It had ought to be fixed."

"We will attend to it when we wish to."

"I could get ye a price for the roofing work, sir. Me brother-in-law—"

"I told you we will see to this for ourselves." His tone was sharp. "What difference does it make to you?—do you get a commission for jobs that you give your brother-in-law?"

The woman squatted there scowling, with her eyes narrowed. Seymour was discomfited. Why had he given way to a flash of irritability, and why be scathing? He could not back down now, the thing was said. He heard some muttered remark as he turned away, something that sounded like 'crazy-house'. He swung round on his heel and snapped, "What were you doing up on the top floor anyway? You know your orders."

"Me orders is to clean the halls and stairs. If I get up there and smell wet plaster—and mildew—and—and—other things, I'll not need your insults to know *I'm* in me right mind!" She flung her scrubbing-rag into the pail of dirty water and heaved herself clumsily to her feet. She advanced towards Seymour, wiping her hands on her apron, and said, "If ye'll give me me money to Saturday I'll be quitting now. And well out of it too." She sniffed.

He took a bill from his wallet and held it out to her with the tips of his fingers.

"Give me your key to the house," he said. She lifted her calico skirt to display a red flannel petticoat and a black pocket-book hanging from her waist. She took the key from her purse and dropped it into his outstretched hand. She tossed her head with another sniff. Then she said, "Look close at the key, Mr. Holt. Be sure it's the right one." She gave a queer nasal laugh. "That's the right one, eh? Feel better now?" She walked away, untying her apron.

Seymour went on to the cellar. He was trembling with temper. His rage at the slut was only less violent than his annoyance with himself. The woman knew the house too well, she had been about for a long time. She lived in a tenement the other side of Tenth Avenue, only half a block away, and she would fill the whole neighborhood with snide gossip about the Holts. The hell with her, he thought, remembering his decision last night with Randall to move to a nice flat next year. Next year . . . any year . . . anything which had to do with the future . . . such thoughts, at times when he felt oppressed and upset, were the overture to a sense of panic. He stood in the middle of his workshop surrounded by the massed and stacked collection of objects which had been accumulating here for nearly twenty years. Each of them by itself was a perfectly sensible thing. It was actually or potentially useful for some purpose of Seymour's, something interesting, mechanical, creative. What was the matter with that?

"What's the matter with that?" he shouted suddenly, grimacing. He kicked at an old bicycle leaning against an empty crate. The bicycle fell over on its side and Seymour ran at it and stamped on its rear wheel, stamped again and again until the wire spokes were broken and twisted and tangled like a mass of jackstraws. One of them snagged the right leg of his trousers. He bent down with an oath and freed himself. He stood for a moment looking round, swinging his head, distraught with panic. Then he sank down in a corner, burying his face in his hands with a hoarse cry.

At about the same time Randall was standing in the corridor outside Renata Tosi's apartment, knocking on her door. She had told him to come half an hour later than yesterday, laughing that the ten o'clocks had proved too early for her. So Randall gave her fifteen minutes' grace and a little before eleven he arrived at her hotel. His knock went unanswered. He waited for a moment and knocked again and was not answered. He began to feel annoyed. It might be just like her to have forgotten all about the appointment and gone out. He stood hesitating. It was his habit to arrive at St. Timothy's before noon every day, practise on the organ for an hour, and then go out for something light to eat. After lunch he usually conferred and worked for a time with Dr. Fitzhugh, and most afternoons he had choir rehearsals from three to five. Even though this coaching of Renata Tosi would be finished in a few days, he felt distracted at having his morning routine upset. He decided to go away and forget this nonsense. He had had misgivings from the first, she was as frivolous as the other opera-singers of his experience although he had to admit she was more charming about it. But he had had enough. He turned away and then, to satisfy himself that he had done all he could be expected to do before quitting, he knocked hard for a last time on the door.

"*Avanti!*" came the cry from inside the room, but in a tone so muffled, yet startled, that he knew she had been sound asleep. Drat the woman, he thought; now what am I supposed to do? I wish I had gone away a minute ago. He had no idea of walking in on her as she must be now. But she called impatiently, "*Avanti!—cameriere*—come in, is my *caffè?*"

"No," said Randall through the door. "It is not your coffee."

"*Oh! Dio!* Is you! *Allora*, come in, come in."

What should he do? Stand there arguing through a closed door in a hotel corridor? He turned the handle and the door opened, to his discomfiture, for he had supposed it would be locked.

"*Buon giorno!*" cried Tosi from behind her screen. "You 'scuse me, please, I am so sorry. Must be *quell'asino*, how you say, waiter, I order last night he wake me with the *caffè*. He forget. Is nothing, I order now. We must have the *caffè*."

"Thank you," said Randall stiffly, from across the room, "I've had mine. Since you are not up yet, Madame Tosi, I think it might be as well if I just went along. I really don't feel able to—"

"What you say? For what is this talk? Come here!"

"I—"

"You don't hear? You have the frighten? How is possible talk through a *mobile*? Come here."

"I did not come here to talk," said Randall, exasperated. "Nor to drink coffee either. I came to give you a lesson that you are not ready for, and I cannot wait until you are. The whole idea was a mistake, I think we should drop it. I would rather go now. I have my own work to do today."

"*Sei un bel tipo tu*! Is so important every minute? You didn't never sleep after you amuse' yourself very late?"

Perhaps she would believe him if she saw that he was really annoyed. He made his way across the room, cluttered like yesterday with the débris of the costume she had flung off last night, and walked round the corner of the screen. She was sitting up in bed, laughing, and the courage to rebuke her ebbed away from him as he took in her delighted smile, the freshness of her face innocent of cosmetics and framed in bright brown curls tumbling round her shoulders and hanging down her back. She was wrapped in a cape or some such garment made of lace ruffles and it was as useless to be cross with her as with a talking doll. The woman had literally no notion of convention or manners or responsibility on any terms in common with him. His brother persisted, without ever having seen her, in calling her a toy, and Randall's mind ceded suddenly as he stood there that Seymour was right. I do wish, he thought, that she wasn't a good artist. That's the only obstacle to dismissing her and forgetting her altogether. I still mean to.

Renata Tosi had been sitting with her deep-set brown eyes fixed on his face. He stood looking into hers chiefly because he did not want to seem to notice anything else about her. So he saw a series of expressions follow one another across her lively features; she frowned, she knit her brows, she raised them disapprovingly, she tucked in her chin and pursed her mouth, and suddenly Randall saw that she was mimicking and wickedly reflecting the sequence of thoughts which had crossed his mind. Then her lips began to twitch and Randall heard himself ridiculously confounded as they both burst out laughing. She laughed as she had laughed in the parish house, peal upon peal of childish, unbridled mirth, and Randall laughed as he had never done in his life. He could scarcely get his breath. Each time he tried she pointed a finger at him and made a face and went off into gales and shrieks of merriment, carrying him along with her. Finally she paused and drew a long breath and wiped her eyes on a handful of ruffles. Randall was choking into his handkerchief. He had laughed until his muscles ached.

"*Ecco!*" she said. "Is not only you who can teach!" She flapped her hand at him and said, "Go, wait one moment till I am ready. Drink your *caffè.*" The waiter had come and gone.

"I'll wait," he said, still trying to catch his breath, but shaking his head. "You must be a handful for anybody who—who—" he broke off.

"*Ma che!* I am nice, *molto amabile.* Go! Drink the *caffè.*"

"You may as well know," he blurted, "that I don't want any because I don't like your Italian coffee."

"No? *Come mai?* You don't like? You like your *orribile caffè americano?*" She shuddered. "Like the wash water. *Va bene,* you ring for it."

"Never mind, thanks, really." He looked at his watch. He would not be able to get to St. Timothy's at all before lunch time. "You really will be quick, won't you," he said with a smile. "I do have work to do right after lunch."

"How you are serious! For what you live—*niente altro?* Good, I let you go *prestissimo.*"

And to his surprise, she did. He would not have believed that with all her nonsense yesterday she had mastered the music of the part, however short, and a few of the words in a language that meant nothing to her. Today she wandered round the room, sketchily dressed but at least covered over with clothes, and he could think of no improvement on her suggestion that he pronounce the German words for her while he played the notes of her music. She followed accurately, shaping each syllable exactly as he said it, and repeating each phrase several times before she went on to the next. When they paused he asked her, "Don't you care if you never find out what it means?"

"No! *Basta* I know is a lot of *sciocchezze*—how you say—" she made a senseless babbling noise. "*Così.* You tell me this *storia tedesca,* I laugh out loud on the stage."

"You won't be out on the stage. You are supposed to be up in a tree."

"Well, you think I take *sul serio* such a foolishness? A talking bird? We are reasonable, we Italians!"

"Of course," said Randall drily. "You don't believe in miracles or anything like that in your religion."

"But that is real! Is true! Not like this nonsense from German barbarians."

How surprising, he thought, to stumble on a streak of bigotry in a woman who seemed never to have taken anything seriously, and who teased him when he did. He might have challenged her from his background of German culture, but why trouble? Her stubborn words bore the impress of centuries of prejudice. He had a curious moment of awareness of those centuries, as she stood there with her feet planted slightly apart, her arms akimbo, and her eyes flashing defiant insistence about something she could never have thought out for herself. He laughed and said, "Anyway, you're a quick study and I hate to admit it, since you're so lazy and careless."

She shrugged. "You come again tomorrow?"

"Why, I scarcely think you need it."

"Oh yes, twice more."

"Why twice?"

"What about my cues?"

He could have kicked himself. He had just tossed off—smartly, he thought—a cool reproach for her laziness, and here she was reminding him that while she knew her own passages of the music, she must still learn the cues for her tricky offstage entrances. He was tempted to tell her to keep the score and figure them out for herself. Then he knew it was useless, she would only say something to nettle him. Actually he was beginning to enjoy being nettled, but he did not know it.

"Very well," he said, uncomfortably meek and compliant. "I suppose you will be asleep and unpresentable no matter what time I come."

"Absolutely," she agreed cheerfully. "I will be tired, tonight I have to sing Musetta." She set her features in demure and virtuous lines.

"I don't believe it's singing makes you want to sleep all morning," he said. She laughed.

"Would you like to hear my Musetta?" she asked. "Is no bad."

He was astonished. Could he really have lacked the initiative to think of going to the opera to hear her?

"Why, yes," he said, as if involuntarily.

"*Va bene*. You go to the stage door, you will find the *biglietto*. I arrange it for you."

"Thank you very much."

He must go now, he was in a hurry to get away, not only because the whole morning had gone, but because he felt strangely embarrassed. He never knew when this clumsy sensation would upset the teetering bal-

ance of badinage which was so awkward and so new to him. Not until
he had left her and was on his way downtown did he realize his
gaucherie. He should have asked her to supper after the opera, or at least
said he would come backstage to pay his respects. Now he could not do
anything without its appearing an afterthought, and by the time he had
fumed over this most of the afternoon, he had about decided not to go to
Bohême. But in the end he went only because, he told himself, Seymour
was not free that evening. On his way to the opera house he resolved his
dilemma by stepping into a florist's and sending roses to be delivered to
Renata Tosi in her dressing-room. He could not bring himself to the
decision to call there after the performance, though she did sing beautifully and he could have told her so with sincerity. But he did not know
who or what he might find backstage; he had nothing to go by except
uneasy memories of Vienna.

On the fourth and presumably the last morning that he arrived to
work with Renata Tosi, Randall's knock was answered, not by her cheerful *"Avanti!"* but by the decorous opening of the door, which swung
wide to reveal her standing, soberly dressed, with her hand on the doorknob.

"Good morning," she said demurely.

"Good morning." Randall walked into the room with the increased
confidence derived from his previous visits. Yesterday had been quite
pleasant and Renata gracious and pleased with his roses and his compliments on her singing. There had been more ease and less mischief. He
laid his hat on a stand and took a step towards the piano. Then he stopped.
Seated in an armchair with an air of aggressive proprietorship was a
heavy, florid man with a spectacular black moustache waxed into
needle-tipped curls. He was tightly fitted into striped trousers, a black
jacket, and pointed patent leather buttoned boots with fawn-colored
cloth tops. Randall looked stupidly at Renata Tosi, whose subdued
manner was belied by a taunting twinkle in her eye.

"I present you Signor Ugo Baldini," she said.

"How do you do," said Randall, more nonplussed than he should
have been.

"Piacere," grunted Baldini. But he glowered. Randall looked again
at Renata, who laughed.

"My friend," she explained, with nervous and conspicuously artificial gaiety. "He is so interest', he come listen how you teach me that German bird. *Non è vero*, Ugo?"

Baldini's rude up-and-down scrutiny of Randall suggested total disinterest in German birds. Renata Tosi hesitated; then she said eagerly to Randall, "You have hear' Baldini *al teatro*, no? You have admire' his Ramfis, Ferrando, Leporello?" Randall tried to nod and smile the indicated compliments, though he had never heard the man sing a note and had already told Renata how rarely he went to the opera. She chattered on, reeling off "Sparafucile, Colline, Mefistofele, Angelotti," like an excited barker crying his wares, until Baldini growled, "*Basta! Taci!*" and Randall did not know what to say. He murmured, "Yes, yes, of course," and groping for a quick device to end this encounter he said, "You won't need more than a minute today. I'm sure you've got the cues perfectly now. In fact," he added, "perhaps you don't even need to run through it again."

"But I must!" she cried. "How I have work' to learn that *porco tedesco!*" She cast her eyes and clasped her hands heavenward. Randall could have snickered but for the lowering presence of Baldini. Renata snatched the score from Randall's hand and ran with it to the piano, ruffling the pages to find the place. "*Ecco!*" she cried. "*Andiamo al lavoro.*"

Randall sat down, nervously hitching the piano stool forwards and backwards. He heartily wished Renata Tosi at the end of the earth and Baldini sizzling in hell. The only reason for her fluster must be that every word of Seymour's cynical taunts was true. Since Randall had never had a thought, still less ever said a word, which could have provoked Baldini's behavior, he could only imagine as a commonplace the ugly jealousy which had probably caused a scene before his arrival this morning, and perhaps had followed a night the thought of which turned his face brick red. How he would like to be out of here! But Renata Tosi was standing at his elbow like a docile student with her eyes fixed on the music—which she had never done before—and there was nothing to do but proceed.

She sang the two short passages beautifully, with fluency and perfect grace. Against his will Randall was forced to admire her artistry which was sound enough to lift her above her trepidation and insure her singing admirably. He was surprised at the finish and seeming facility of her German pronunciation. He remembered her ridicule of it while learning it phonetically and refusing to be bothered with its meaning. *"Un ammasso di sciocchezze!"* she had said; "a lot of rot." Now she sang with intensity, telling an absent Siegfried of Brünnhilde sleeping on her rock, and of the miraculous powers of the treasures in Fafner's cave. Tosi had not the remotest idea what she was saying. But she did convey to Randall that for once she must try to seem serious. It occurred to him that she might be afraid of Baldini, and some of his pique disappeared in a sense of concern for her. Then he had a sharp impression of Seymour's comment, could he be here to make one. This woman knows what she is doing. She is about as innocent and as much in need of help as a clever cat. Randall finished the music with a feeling of cool relief that the ordeal was ending. He said, "Very nice indeed," as Renata turned from the piano towards Baldini, arching her pretty eyebrows as if to ask for his approval. Baldini shrugged and made some comment in Italian.

"He is surprise'," she said to Randall, a little too glibly. "He would not think so possible learn a Wagner like that." She moved restlessly towards a table and picked up an Italian macaroon from a dish and began to nibble it. "He would understand better if he hear from in first. But he was away, was engage' for week in Chicago."

So there it was. She was trying to explain her situation now that it had proclaimed itself. She was sillier than he had thought her, and that was silly enough. He saw that Baldini did not know a word of English, for his expression did not change by a flicker until she said 'Chicago', at which point his eyes dilated and Randall felt once more a turn of anxiety for Renata Tosi. Now she had done it—she should never have mentioned the man's absence or explained his presence.

Randall rose and gathered up his hat, and the score from the piano. Renata shook her head as he closed the volume and said, "Oh, please, you leave with me *la musica* until I finish the rehearsals?"

What was she up to? He remembered every word of her mischievous refusals to look at the score or learn a line of it except by ear. He could hardly tease her about that now. He said, "Why certainly," and put the music back on the rack.

"Tante grazie," she said. "The first rehearsal is Monday, at the eleven o'clocks." She flicked an eyelid with a touch of her natural flippancy but he believed he understood a plea in the earnest, quickly-effaced expression which came into her eyes. He acted as if he had

neither heard nor perceived anything. He went over to Baldini who did not move from his chair, and held out his hand, which the man took indifferently. Then Randall shook hands with Renata Tosi, in a manner as American as he knew how, and without another word he opened the door and went away. By the time he was out on Broadway in the sunshine he was entirely decided that he was well out of this potential embroilment, and grateful that he had learned enough since Vienna not to have let himself be made a fool of. He could not see what further use Renata Tosi could have for him, and surely he had none for her. Why had she kept his score and, in effect, asked him to come to her rehearsals? These appeared to be devices through which to see him again, but what on earth for? She was a flibbertigibbet, the mistress of a jealous Italian boor, and he would be well advised by his own judgment, as well as by Seymour should he consult him, to have nothing more to do with her.

But Randall was more naïve than he judged himself. He might have been a little less puzzled by Renata Tosi and her manoeuvres if he could impersonally have seen himself walking down Broadway towards a street-car stop. People sincerely without vanity do not see in their utilitarian shaving or dressing mirrors the personalities which they present to others. Randall had no idea that the young man with the graceful bearing, the broad shoulders, the well-bred head with its wide blue eyes and good bones and its dark blond curls could be of challenging interest to any woman who took a titillative view of life. He believed himself to have ruled all such women and their accomplices out of his orbit when he left Vienna. He had every intention now of ruling out Renata Tosi too. His reason for seeing her had terminated and his reasons for not seeing her were explicit. He walked on, comfortably secure in his decision, and rather smugly pleased with himself.

His self-approval hung on for several days, diminishing all the time though he did not know it. Seymour was preoccupied with excitement and pleasure about his automobile, which he said would be delivered in a few days. He was so full of his own concerns that he forgot to tease Randall about his. In four days they only dined together once, so Randall had three lonely evenings, eating in the cheap places where he went alone, and sitting afterwards in the library with his scores and a pencil, making notations and also filling several sheets of blank music-paper with cramped scribblings. He had a way of not noticing these once he had written them. He stuck them away in his room, between the pages of the scores and musical books which he kept in an old glass-fronted book case which had once been in the day-nursery upstairs. By degrees Randall lost track of the scribbled music-paper. He had accumulated and forgotten a considerable quantity of it in the past two years, and might never have thought to move it, except that several of the sheets fell out of a volume of Bach Preludes one day when he was practising in the church. He decided then to find somewhere else to put them, though this seemed a contradiction of his real intention; he had thought to destroy them. It was on one of those evenings alone that he rummaged through the house to find a place to keep his papers. Nobody ever went to the fourth floor, and there he found the child's desk on which he had done his first lessons. It had a slanting top which closed over several drawers and a row of pigeon-holes. It seemed just the thing and Randall began then to use it as a repository for his music-papers and other oddments for which he had no other private place.

He had a long, dull, and lonely week end, broken only by choir-practice and services at St. Timothy's. From now on through the later spring and even more during the summer, the music at the church would be simpler and take less of his time. When he woke on Monday morning he realized that he had no work scheduled at St. Timothy's until Wednesday afternoon.

The empty time yawned ahead of him. Even with the best will in the world he could not see how to kill almost three whole days—not to mention the dreaded evenings—by practising on the piano and the organ. He did not feel like practising. He felt restless and sick of being alone. Seymour was still asleep and might sleep all morning. Randall went down to the side door and took in the daily pint of milk, the bag of rolls, and Seymour's *Times*. He noticed the dust gathering thickly on the stairs, as it had in the library and his own room, a rude reminder that he ought to go out and do something about finding another cleaning-woman. So far he had ignored Mrs. McBane's absence, making his own bed with a few careless tugs, and washing up the breakfast things in cold water in the bathroom down the hall from the library. They seldom bothered to make a fire in the water-heater in the deserted kitchen. A little shaving-water heated in the teakettle on the gas-ring was as much trouble as any daily hot water was worth. They bathed sporadically, in summer taking sponge-baths in a little cold water in the deep tin tub; in winter occasionally lighting a fire in the boiler. But they regarded that as a nuisance. It was all a messy and increasingly uncomfortable state of affairs, and at the same time Randall felt defiant about it. It was nobody else's business. Proper people didn't live in that way, but proper people didn't have to live in a horrible old warren and try to find ways to keep it from swallowing them up entirely. Randall envied Seymour his stronger will and his clearer sense of what he wanted. He wished he were the one more eager to leave this house, but now that Seymour could not move for a year, Randall was certainly not going to do so. Even this sparse companionship was better than the thought of living all alone.

He felt more and more jangled and disturbed. His coffee was poor, he must have been inattentive and measured it out carelessly; and the prospect of having nothing to do today was almost unendurable. He went downstairs and practised finger-exercises for a while, but he became careless and broke off with a bang. This kind of botch was worse than no practice at all. He wandered upstairs again and looked at the library clock. A little past ten, and not a sign of Seymour. He must have had a night of it.

Randall flung himself into his chair, on the opposite side of the library fire from Seymour's. He took up the folded copy of the *Times,* childishly guilty because of the ridiculous dictum that this was Seymour's newspaper and Seymour was violently irritated if Randall opened it first. He sat holding it on his knee for a moment, then with a shrug he opened it and began to look through it. Nothing fixed his attention until he came to the page of musical and theatrical news. At that point he had a sense as if of the raising of a thin, confusing curtain, something which had drifted across the panes of his mind and obscured the clear view of his intentions which had always been there. His decision to forget Renata Tosi now appeared clumsy and artificial. In truth he had not forgotten her, he had only succeeded in shrouding her behind that figurative curtain. She had been right there all the time. And this was Monday morning and she had tried to convey to him that she hoped he would come to her rehearsal at eleven—or so he thought. He had had no idea of going. Now he sat wondering why he should not. It might be interesting to see how well he had prepared her for something so new and strange to her.

His eye fell on the article about the week's repertoire at the opera. "Last week but one of opera season," was the heading. He found him-

self facing another thought which he must have been holding hidden
for some time. What would become of Renata Tosi when the season
was over? How could that possibly be any concern of his! Then he
glanced at the cast for tonight's performance of *Aïda*. Ugo Baldini was
singing and Renata Tosi was not. Randall sat for a short time and
meditated. The idea which was taking shape almost frightened him by
its bold novelty; he could scarcely recognize himself in it. Timidity
struggled briefly with inclination and retired. He folded Seymour's
Times carefully in its original creases and laid it on the arm of Seymour's chair. Then he went downstairs and took his hat and started
uptown to the opera house.

CHAPTER 10

They were halfway through dinner and Renata was still laughing and saying, "I am so surprise'. How you have thought of something so *intelligente* and *furbo*?"

"What does 'furbo' mean?"

She waved her hand as if trying to pluck the word from the air. "*Oh! Dio!* I don't know. It means, how is it, clever?—but maybe, too clever? Is possible?"

"You mean 'tricky'? 'Deceitful'?"

She pulled a face of mock protest. "*Ma no!*" Her eyes were wide. "I never deceive nobody! Surely you have never deceive' nobody?"

"Not—well, not by arranging it myself, exactly. Until now. You do understand," he added quickly. "I haven't meant to, I mean I was not thinking about your—eh—friend."

"No?" Again the mock surprise. "Then why we are here?"

He put his attention on the piece of chicken on his plate. She went on chattering. "If you don't think about Baldini, why we arrange so carefully come here after *Aïda* begin, and put me home with the *mal di testa* before it end?"

"You ought to be ashamed of yourself," he said, looking up suddenly.

"*Io!*" she gasped, planting her square hand on her breast. "*I* have thought of these *inganni*—what I mean—tricks? I?"

"I mean on account of Mr. Ba—" Randall choked over the name. He swallowed and said firmly, "Baldini."

"*Ma perchè?*" Her surprise appeared sincere this time.

Randall sighed. "Look here," he said. "Is this customary in Italy, arrangements like the one you seem to have with him?"

"That depend'," she shrugged. "In Italy *per esempio* Baldini is not free like here. Sometimes he get away, but—"

"He is married."

"Naturally. Is very jealous his wife and he make many *bambini* to keep her busy."

"How many *bambini*?" He used the word unconsciously.

"Six. In Piacenza."

She drank some of the wine he had almost forgotten to order, and smiled at him charmingly. In the shaded light of the candle on the table she looked particularly pretty. She was wearing one of the blouses to which she seemed partial, made of innumerable narrow rows of fine net ruching, with ballooning sleeves. It would never have occurred to him that she made these things herself, or that she had trimmed the coal-scuttle hat framing her brown pompadour and her creamy forehead, with tiny rosettes of pink feathers. He supposed, just because she was an actress and he disapproved of most things she did, that she must also paint her face, but he could see no proof of it; her complexion had the same fresh, clear pallor and her lips the rosy tinge that he had also seen when she was barely awake in the morning. Her eyes above her wineglass were laughing, but in spite of his opinion that she should be ashamed of her situation, they seemed curiously calm and sincere.

He looked across at her, unaware that his own eyes were much more eloquent than his uncertain tongue. He thought about what he wanted to say, and could not quite say it; then he blurted, "The queerest thing happens to me when I try to talk to you. Either I can't think of anything to say, or else I blunder into personal things that are none of my business."

"Why is not your business? You are jealous of Baldini, you tell it. *E' naturale.*" She shrugged.

"I am not jealous of Baldini!" He felt his face redden. "I scarcely know you. I only said you should be ashamed of your situation with him, and you should."

"*D'accordo,*" she laughed, blinking at him, "Let us agree. Baldini is not your business. He go away soon, back to La Scala and the wife in Piacenza with six *bambini. Anche sette finora, può darsi,*" she added, muttering.

"What did you say?"

"I say maybe is already seven. Why you make me think to talk English? I grow tired. *Invece* better I teach you Italian. For some things is only possible Italian."

"For what things?"

"For making love," she said, as coolly as if she were describing a dance step. "English would be *scandaloso.*"

Oh, God, he thought. She is impossible.

"You would speak well Italian," she murmured, resting her chin on her folded hands, her elbows on the table. *"Bel giovane che sei!"* Randall obeyed his instinct not to notice that remark; he was afraid he had understood it. Had she called him beautiful?

"No, seriously," he said. "What would you do if I asked you questions? Without stopping to think whether they are too personal or not?"

"Answer them," she said calmly. "I only tell the lies to save the trouble. What is so, is so."

"That's the way it seems," he sighed. "I just can't see why you have that—why you—ah—why—Baldini." He drew a breath and summoned his courage and said, "You couldn't be in love with him."

"Ecco! At last you talk the sense!"

"Then, why—?"

She shook her head a little and smiled as if excusing the ignorance of a child. "You were never poor?" she asked gently. "Very poor, like us? Peasants and *artigiani*?"

"I'm sorry you have to ask that." He felt a little ashamed of himself. But he said, "You ought to be better off by now. Isn't that so? And you were fairly well started in Milano before, otherwise they wouldn't have brought you here."

She was eating ice cream in tiny spoonfuls, and she only said, "Ah, Milano. You should taste the *gelati* there. *Una meraviglia.*"

"I don't care about the ice cream in Milano. I was talking about you. Do you mean to say you really need Baldini? Madame, Signorina . . ."

"Renata. And I call you Randalo. *Che bel nome!*" She smiled like a delighted child and his attention was diverted by admiration for her beautifully white teeth. He had noticed them before; her wide but delicately modelled singer's mouth with its fresh red lips was one of her most charming features. She knew how to play on these features for any purpose of her own and she was playing now, turning him away from his solemn aim. He decided not to let her get away with it and he repeated, "Is the whole thing—" he implied Baldini—"necessary?"

"Oh! Dio! You talk like a priest. *Madonna!*" she exclaimed, in sudden horror, "how I know what you are in that pagan church of yours?"

"Nothing," he said coldly. He was resigned that there was no use sparring with her if one could not hold one's own. "I am absolutely nothing in that church but a minor musician employed to work there.

And we are just as Christian as you are, so restrain your insults. Now look here—Renata." He pronounced her name with obvious pleasure and she beamed at him. "Must you really go on with this arrangement of yours? I've been trying to tell you—it's not—well—people in this country don't see these things in the same light you do. We—"

"What people?" she interrupted.

"Why—" he frowned irritably. She burst into a laugh and leaned over and put her hand on top of his.

"*Sei troppo serio*," she said. "People you know, they do not care what I do, Baldini do, all the artists do. We like to play, we like pleasure."

"So you play with me too," he said with bitterness. "I bet Baldini wouldn't be amused. This wouldn't be his idea of play."

"Indeed, no. *E' gelosissimo, lui.*"

"So you are playing with fire as well as with me and Baldini and—" suddenly he saw in retrospect her room as it had looked in the mornings, strewn with the finery in which she had been dressed the night before. "With others too, I suppose," he said hopelessly. He decided to drop the subject. He sat with his head bent, crumbling a wafer and pushing the crumbs with his forefinger into a meaningless pattern. She watched him. He was surely, she told herself, beautiful, a beautiful young man, and different from any she had ever seen. It must be that difference, that foreignness, which attracted her and which had carried her so far as to be sitting here now. His views were preposterous. Anybody else so earnest and serious would seem an intolerable prude and a bore. But this one had some strange appeal, perhaps his looks, perhaps his extraordinary innocence which to her realistic eye seemed virginal although she could not believe that this was so. Up to now it had been refreshing and flattering that he was plainly falling in love with her, which he himself in that very innocence did not yet realize. When he did, he would be afraid to take the initiative and his solemn, puritanical American character would never let him enjoy any pleasure—unless she taught him to. She sighed. Could this be worth all the trouble?— all the questions he had been raising and many which she herself kept strictly out of mind? Perhaps she ought to cut him off right now while it was still soon enough not to hurt him. She had never seen a man whom it would more have displeased her to hurt.

"How old are you, Randalo?" she asked him, speaking low.

"Twenty-three." He did not look up.

Two years younger than herself, her real age which she never stated because no singer ever did. She said slowly, "I think perhaps is because you are young you have so little tolerance. The human nature she is not what you believe should be, only what is."

He was so astonished at her words, spoken in a tone of calm sincerity and, indeed, wisdom, that he raised his head and stared at her in spite of his intention not to do so. He was quite startled at what he saw. There was no raillery in her face, no mischief in her eyes; she had her hands folded on the edge of the table and her face above her high ruched collar had the serenity of a classic mask. She smiled quietly, a smile of kindliness without the sparkle of her constant mirth. She had had the idea of telling him that he would be wise to go his way and forget her. But watching the clear trustfulness which superseded the resentment in his blue eyes, her resolution wavered and she was left impaled upon the pinpoint of one serious moment.

"You think very bad of me," she said. "Perhaps I deserve. But is not for you I would change, not for any man. Life will change me, like you, like *tutti*. When is time, is time. Until come this time, I want to enjoy. You do not like how I live because is *troppo di lusso* and Baldini pay something for it. But not everything, understand," she flashed, with a wink of mischief. "When I tell you I don't like to work hard, you are shock'. Some day I tell you how I have work' hard *da bambina* and you understand maybe why I want the pleasure while I am still young. Also, is my nature. *Basta*. I talk too much."

"Will you really tell me about all that?"

"*Vediamo*. Now is no more the time, you watch your clock?"

He looked and saw that they should leave at once. They went out and got into a hansom and Randall told the driver to hurry. When the apron slammed shut Renata settled into her corner with the certainty, a novelty to her, that this man would not immediately besiege her with kisses as anybody else would do. He sat with his hands clasped on his knees. She copied his prim attitude. They chatted about the opera while the cab jounced up Broadway; about the week's repertoire, which for Randall was tantamount to asking on what evenings she and also Baldini would be singing. He soon had it clear: On Wednesday both were cast in *Rigoletto*, Renata as Contessa Ceprano; on Thursday she was to sing Micaela in a *Carmen* without Baldini, and on Friday

Baldini was down for Angelotti. Renata laughed sharply when she said that there would never be a part for her in *Tosca* unless she aimed at the title role itself. "Me?" she scoffed. *"Troppo lavoro!"* So that left her free again on Friday. Randall looked at her with a question unspoken, and she nodded and laughed again and they dropped the matter there. She sat back farther in her corner. Her eyes sparkled in the dim light of the street lamps but her expression was demure and she sat asking herself what would happen if she should make it clear that she was willing, if not waiting, for him to kiss her, now or very soon. She was also weighing whether he would take the initiative before she should be begin to be bored by him.

"The first *Siegfried* is next Monday?" he asked her.

"Yes, is ridiculous. Two times they do it, only in the last week. All that work."

"It must be that he only wants to make the experiment. If it goes badly it will die off quietly, it won't have been a real part of this year's repertoire. If it goes well he has a start on next year."

She made a face. "No for me. No more Wagner."

"You needn't worry. There is only one other Wagner part he could ask you to sing, the Shepherd in *Tannhäuser*. And he couldn't be planning more Wagner unless he engages all sorts of different people."

Renata shrugged. Randall felt unexpectedly flustered about asking her questions much less personal than those he had already ventured. She must have understood his difficulty, for she raised her brows as if inviting him to speak. So he said uneasily, "I take it, I don't doubt, you've been reengaged for next year?"

"Oh, yes."

"And in the meantime?" That was what was really bothering him. "When the opera closes now?"

"I go in Italy, naturally."

"I see." His voice was dull. It was what he had expected to hear. "Have you engagements there?" (Or, he tried to suppress the thought, are you just trailing along with Baldini?)

"But of course! La Scala continue until June. *Poi*, is many places, Bologna, Genova," she ticked them off on her fingers, "Ravenna, Como— *Oh! Dio!*" She shook her head. *"Poi* Verona, all'Arena. Is terrible so much work."

"You ought to be proud to have it," said Randall crossly.

"*Ma!*" she said.

The cab drew up at the hotel and Randall helped her out. He started to escort her across the pavement to the door, but she shook her head and gave him her hand. He felt the rigidity of her arm, intended to hold him at the greatest distance. She was astonished when he bent and kissed her gloved hand as anybody else would do.

"*Buona notte,*" she murmured and turned quickly away. It had not been made definite that she would see him again on Friday, she had only hinted at it, and she had not said a word about any further rehearsals for *Siegfried*. There was no reason why he should go again. But he felt so agitated of mind that he stepped back into the hansom without thinking, and told the man to drive him home. Ordinarily he would have taken the street-car, just from his habitual frugality. He sat with his arms folded, scowling over the teasing rebuffs she had meted out all evening. But then she had given him a glimpse of a totally different character, and then immediately slammed the door on the person so revealed.

"I ought to forget her," he told himself, half aloud. "I've got no business whatever with such a woman." He could not understand her. Here she had a calendar crammed with tours of provincial opera houses in Italy, and still she insisted that she hated to work and looked on it only as the means to her pursuit of pleasure. "I wonder if she ever tells the truth," he thought; and then he was standing on the deserted pavement, looking up at the dark façade of his house. It loomed at him, bleak, baleful, forbidding. He had a sense of reluctance to walk up the path and let himself in through the heavy, peeling door, and grope his way to light the dim wheezing gas-jet. This place was part of him and part of Seymour, but it was alien from everything else that could ever touch their lives. It was as if when they turned their backs on other associations and occupations they disappeared through the door of this house into a world as darkly legendary as the farther shore of the Styx. Yet, once inside, the rest of the world became unreal. Seymour was right, they must get away from here. He was also right that it would be a waste of their capital, as well as a mad gesture of ceding a hostage to fortune, to spend a penny or lift a finger to make a repair on this house. Better let it rot until it collapsed, their best defiance of any fate that might connive to keep them here.

Randall climbed the front steps slowly. One of the most oppressive things about living here was the way in which his thoughts about it rose up and obliterated other thoughts which he preferred to pursue. Sometimes he could control these skirmishes and sometimes he could not. He felt now the small legion of ugly plaguers forming to assault him. Not since the night he had been up on the top floor had he allowed the impression of it to recur. Now, with urgent concerns to compel his mind and his retrospective ear, he could not blank out the small vile remembered sound of scratching and scurrying. This is damnable, he thought; I won't let it get to me. I won't hear it. I don't have to hear it. He went into the drawing-room and lit the gas in all the fixtures, and took off his coat and sat down at the piano and plunged into a Bach fugue. He played with vigor and big sonority, and he intended to keep on playing until Seymour came home, no matter what time that might be. He had decided not to go upstairs tonight alone.

Next morning Seymour appeared early for breakfast, full of unusual good humor. Randall was distracted and glum. It was a beautiful morning and he went to the bay windows to raise the blinds. He had put the coffee pot on the round table and was filling the jug with hot milk when Seymour drew the blinds partly down again.

"Why do you do that?" asked Randall. "Isn't this place gloomy enough for you?" He moved towards the windows again.

"I'm sorry." Seymour's voice was unusually gentle and Randall paused, his hand on a blind, and looked over at Seymour who was just sitting down. He had turned his chair as much as possible to cut off the light and still sit facing Randall. Randall left the window and walked across the room and put his hand on Seymour's shoulder. He looked down at him.

"Brother," he said slowly, "does the light hurt your eyes very much?"

Seymour laughed a little. "Oh, it's nothing. You know I've never liked strong light. Come on, drink your coffee."

Randall sat down, still looking closely at Seymour. "Do you know," he said, "I have a feeling as if I've been awfully stupid about you lately." He leaned forward. "Tell me something, Seymour. Are your eyes getting weaker? Are you worried about them?"

Seymour said, "Of course not! Don't imagine things. You know my eyes have never been very strong, and I suppose the light seemed brighter than usual this morning because we've had a lot of rainy days lately. Forget it."

Randall raised his brows suspiciously, but he could say nothing more without upsetting Seymour, which would be especially a pity today when his spirits were so high. So Randall asked, "When do you get your automobile?"

Seymour beamed. "Today!"

"Gee, I hadn't realized. You must be awfully excited." Randall ate some bread and jam and then said with his mouth full, "What about driving it?"

"I've been learning. When you order a car they send one out with an instructor for a few days to show you what to do, and there's really nothing to it."

"Really? I'd be afraid to try."

"I don't think I'd let you. The thing you have to watch out for is horses shying. Sometimes there's quite a mess."

"Lord, I'm not even sure I'd ride in the thing with you."

"You haven't been invited yet."

"Whom are you going to take for the first ride in it?"

"Well, how about you? I'm going up to the Stevens place to get the car this morning. Any time after eleven o'clock, they said."

"Oh." Randall could perfectly well have gone, he had no work to do until tomorrow afternoon. This was surely the greatest moment of Seymour's life, and he would like to share it. He had already decided not to go to the rehearsal of *Siegfried* this morning. He opened his mouth to tell Seymour he would go along to fetch the automobile, and instead he heard himself say, "That's too bad. I'd love to go, Brother, but I have to work." He was such a poor liar that he felt his hands go clammy as he spoke, and he almost held his breath in the effort to keep his face expressionless. Inwardly he was calling himself a fool, why should he have harbored this buried intention to go to that rehearsal and hang about in the back of the darkened theatre to catch a couple of glimpses of Renata Tosi? He would be swamped in mortification if Seymour should catch him out now. But Seymour was far too excited and preoccupied about his automobile. He only said, "That's too bad. You'll see it this afternoon, or some time soon."

"Sure," said Randall, drawing a breath. "I won't be your favorite guest in it, though, not by a long shot. I wonder who will be—or do you stick to your usual doctrine of safety in numbers?"

Seymour laughed. "I hope I do," he said. "But I suppose if I follow the line of least resistance I'll be taking out Miss Marietta Pawling a good deal. I'm trying to taper that off though."

"Oh?"

"Frankly," said Seymour, "I'm beginning to wish Miss Marietta Pawling at some distance such as Mount Everest." He looked rather shamefaced, but nonchalant; he smoothed the long blond drooping wings of his moustache with the knuckle of his forefinger.

"Marietta Pawling," said Randall. Most of Seymour's ladies were anonymous but he knew a few, the result of the sporadic late suppers to which Seymour had dragged him. "Is that the pretty one with the reddish hair, the night we went to Mouquin's?"

"That's the one. Pretty and reddish hair and would you like to take over my moderately vested interest in her? I'd quite as soon write it off altogether, you know, but she seems to have other ideas."

"None of this is the least like you. You've never had any trouble getting rid of them."

"I know, I never have, have I?"

"Then what's the trouble now?"

"Oh, one or two moments of uncharacteristic indecision on my part. Usually one leaves them in no doubt at all of one's ultimate intentions, but I'm afraid I've botched this a bit. Oh, well." He lit one of the Turkish cigarettes that he had taken to smoking instead of his pipe, which he now liked only when he was working, or when out on a boat. "How are *you* getting on, by the way? How's your lark?"

"Leaving for Italy in a couple of weeks." Randall discovered a sharp wish to keep his concern with Renata well concealed. Perhaps the best move would be to tell Seymour about Baldini, which would prove sufficient reason to drop the subject and also give Seymour the pleasure of having been right. So he said, keeping his tone as casual as possible, "You were right about that hot-tempered Latin. He's there and that's the end of it."

"Too bad," said Seymour judiciously. "She sounds amusing."

"She is, rather." Randall shrugged. He was determined to keep out of his voice and his face any such expression as the 'gleam' in his eye about which Seymour had teased him last week. "But I've finished the job I undertook to do and that's all there is to it."

"Did she pay you?"

"Of course." The subject of pay had never been mentioned.

"Well," said Seymour, stretching his long legs and smiling, "it's a pity she's due to go back to Italy with her paramour. What would you bet she'd rather stay here? He's pretty awful, I take it?"

Randall described Baldini.

"Good God!" said Seymour, shuddering. "Can't you save her from that?"

"Certainly not. Stop talking nonsense, among other things she doesn't want to be saved. She likes him."

Seymour stood up with a mocking sigh. "Wasted opportunity. No initiative. Couldn't I help?" he asked, swinging round.

Randall stopped himself short of a brusque reply. He was aware that any word of this conversation could prove to be a snare; Seymour was trying to catch him off his guard in some admission of interest, or even involvement, with Renata Tosi. Randall knew he lacked the skill to parry this any further and he was distinctly surprised to find how strongly he felt about it. He only laughed, with the best imitation of Seymour's cool derision that he could manage, and changed the subject. Gesturing at the breakfast dishes and the unkempt room he said, "We've simply got to find another cleaning-woman."

"Yes, I suppose we should." Seymour's mood changed. He moved his shoulders as if the thought made him uncomfortable. "It's a damned nuisance, some woman poking and prying about the house."

"If we tell her she's not to go anywhere except this floor and the halls and the drawing-room—"

"How are you going to prevent her? The last one—"

"Oh, I guess we'd just better lock all the doors, all the ones that aren't locked already. Unless we really pitch in and go through the house and sort everything out."

"Why?" asked Seymour. "It would be damnably tiresome and what are you going to do with all the—oh, you know—Mama's things and—"

"I know. It's more trouble to decide what to do about each thing than just leave it the way it is."

"Especially since we're sure to get out of here in another year. If we were going to sell the house eventually, there'd be a reason for going to all that trouble. But since it's the way it is—"

"Oh, let's lock the doors and forget it. We'll just tell the woman to clean wherever the doors aren't locked."

"It might be a good idea to find somebody who doesn't live right in the neighborhood," said Seymour, trying to keep a tinge of uneasiness out of his voice. "That McBane woman—" He paused. "She's cracked," he said.

"They gab, don't they, people like that. About anyone who's the least bit different."

"I don't want any gab about us." Seymour spoke gruffly. "Remember that."

"Oh, I don't want it either. I'll find somebody or other. Aren't you going to the office now, before you go for your automobile?"

"I should." Seymour's mood changed swiftly and he grinned. "But I'm not going to."

"Why, Brother." There was not only surprise, but anxiety in Randall's voice. More and more often recently he had noticed Seymour's absences from his office. No matter what the reason, Randall found this hard to understand. If Seymour was becoming lazy and irresponsible the consequences would soon enough have to be faced; but Randall doubted that. Seymour liked his work and was good at it. He seemed to be on the best of terms with the members of his firm. His absences from the office apparently caused no criticism. Then what was up? At times lately Randall had succumbed to his uneasiness and turned a more inquisitive eye on his brother than he would have dared admit. All he had learned was that Seymour spent more time than formerly down in his workshop in the basement, so Randall had made the only possible conclusion: Seymour must be designing something as a model rather than on paper. Well enough; this morning's truancy must be sheer excitement about the new motor car. Randall put aside his disquiet and said lightly, "I guess anybody would be too excited to go to work today. You're lucky they don't seem to mind, though."

"Oh, they love me," said Seymour, with sufficient irony to raise fresh questions in Randall's mind. "They think I'm indispensable—so anybody but a fool would know how to make the most of that. Why don't you come along with me now, Ran, I'm going shopping."

"What for? Why should I go?"

"You might as well get motoring clothes too. You'll need them."

"My word. I hadn't thought of it. Won't just clothes do?"

"Of course not! Come on, Ran, leave this mess for the time being, let's walk over to Stern's and look at these dusters." Seymour pointed to the morning's advertisement in the *Times*—fine crash dusters for three dollars and a half. "Come on."

Walking West on Twenty-third Street Seymour said suddenly, "See here, why don't you dine with me and Marietta and somebody else one evening this week? Maybe we could undertake a quiet transfer manoeuvre. She's not bad, you know," he said critically. "In her way. I'd just rather—"

"You'd rather get clear without any fireworks. I see perfectly. But—"

"Oh, don't 'but' about everything. How about Friday?"

"Sorry," said Randall, "I can't." He took a deep breath of resolution and lied stoutly, "I've promised to dine with Dr. Fitzhugh on Friday and lay out the summer work afterwards."

"H'm." Seymour looked slyly at Randall from behind his thick glasses. He too had stopped to take note of the week's opera casts in this morning's *Times*. He smothered a small laugh.

When the salesman had ridden along with him twice up Central Park West and back down Broadway to the showroom where he dropped off, Seymour drove his automobile slowly and proudly down Seventh Avenue. It was a busy hour of the day. The street swarmed with drays, delivery wagons, cabs, and the carriages of ladies out on their shopping trips to the department stores grouped in Sixth and Seventh Avenues around Twenty-third Street and below. Seymour had got deep into this stream of traffic before he realized that he should have chosen a less crowded avenue. He drove at the same pace as the horse-drawn traffic, nervous about making the attempt to overtake any cart or carriage and startle its horses. He was relieved that his new goggles, a strong special prescription for distance lenses, enabled him to see well, rather better, he thought, than he could under any other circumstances. The car moved along quite smoothly, which was also a relief; he did not want to have to shift gears often while he was concentrating on all this traffic. Bystanders on the pavements pointed and waved at the spectacular scarlet car, and occasionally, in spite of his careful effort not to frighten a horse, he had to pass one, which almost always shied. Its driver then volleyed a string of curses at Seymour, and this had not happened many times before he was cheerfully thumbing his nose at the truckmen. He gained confidence so fast that by the time he reached Thirty-fourth Street he negotiated a right-hand turn without any mishap in spite of the horses, and continued on to Ninth Avenue, where the more critical business of a left-hand turn was safely dispatched. He sighed with relief. The next ten blocks were effortless, he turned right on Twenty-fourth Street, and in a moment had drawn up at the curb outside his house. He shut off the motor and sat there feeling like a king on his throne. Up and down the street heads appeared at windows, slatternly women ran down the high-stepped stoops, delivery boys and passers-by stopped in their tracks, the postman who was making his second round came up to Seymour and congratulated him. Sitting there the master of this wonderful and costly thing, Seymour looked at its gleaming bonnet and all its fascinating instruments, then turned his glance up the walk, past the mournful front yard with Randall's hyacinths bravely budding, to the drab brown face of the sandstone house. Every window except those of the second floor was covered by a drawn blind, and while there was surely no other way to keep a place which was mostly shut up, Seymour thought what a forbidding sight it was. Lord, he muttered, will I be glad to get out of there! If it weren't for *this*—he ran his hand over the beautiful red varnish of his car; but then he smiled. It was worth it. It was worth anything he had to put up with, to possess this one treasure for as long as it would be possible for him to enjoy anything.

And we are right, he thought, not to pay attention to the mess in that house; not to give a damn whether it falls apart inside or out. By the time I—here his mouth trembled and he bit his lips and tugged at his moustache—by that time we'll be gone from there. I won't want to live in a place with stairs to worry about, with gas lighting to be groped for—you fool, his sharp, cruel mind rebuked him. You fool, will you know whether there is lighting or not? Drop it, cut it. Leave it to—to what? Randall? No. He had been resolved for years that he would not be an incubus on Randall. Then how will you live? God damn, he said half aloud. Why think about this now? Can you do anything about it? Is there any use hurrying to meet it? He shook his head angrily as if to dash these thoughts out of it, and sprang down from his throne.

He had a fascinating job planned, something he would delight in doing himself when most people would have hired a mechanic. Inside the doorway of the house stood a wooden crate, and in it a windshield which he had bought last week for his automobile. Seymour laid aside his long duster and changed his coat for an old alpaca jacket. He brought up tools from his workshop and opened the crate and took the windshield out to the street and set to work to mount it on the car. He felt so happy that once he paused in the midst of drilling the holes for the bolts and said to himself, "You're just a damned fool. You're acting like a kid on Christmas."

Just then he heard a sniff and an Irish voice saying something scathing, a few scurvy words ending in "bug-house". He turned his head and saw Mary McBane flat-footing by with a market basket, her hips flapping.

"Bitch," he said aloud, and went on with his drilling.

When he thought about it later Randall marvelled at Renata Tosi's way of fixing the time and place of appointments without appearing to have said much of anything. On Friday evening he picked her up at a florist's shop a block down Broadway from the opera house. He knew that she must have stopped in to see Baldini in his dressing-room before the performance, and he summoned up the boldness to ask her, "I suppose you said you'd be at home afterwards?"

"No, tonight is a party. I must be back in the *teatro* before the finale because afterwards we go in the Ristorante Brunetti, many artists, because today is the saint's day of Giorgio Morosini."

So there was not much time and he supposed she would not want to dine when she would be going to a supper party afterwards. But she said, "Is necessary to go somewhere, no? Where do you live, Randalo?"

He was startled. Surely she was not suggesting going to his house? He parried the question by saying vaguely, "Oh, downtown. We'd better go and have a bite to eat somewhere, you would be hungry long before your party."

"*Va bene,*" she said. Her tone was non-committal.

He was about to say that they would go to the same quiet French restaurant near Madison Square where they had dined on Monday, when he remembered that he knew of this place through Seymour, who sometimes dropped in there. Something warned him away. He decided on the Murray Hill Hotel, a place he had reason to know that Seymour never patronized. They were given a table in a secluded corner, and Renata grimaced a little when he asked what she would like to eat.

"Is Friday," she sighed. "I don't like the fish. Is perhaps no fish on the *carta*?" she asked hopefully.

He laughed. "I'd know better what to answer if I knew how seriously you take this. Are you very devout, Renata?"

"But yes! Is only when exists no fish I make the exception."

"I'm afraid New York is still a seaport. But perhaps there's some good American fish you've never tried. Maybe you only dislike Italian fish."

"Fish is fish," she said. "But I try. Which is good, the American fish?"

"Shad roe?"

"What is that?"

He explained. She squinted disgustedly. "*Schifoso!* Eggs from fishes. No, no, better I eat the real eggs. Is light. Later they give us meat, nobody care at a party. I am home soon anyway, I confess everything." She laughed carelessly.

"Everything?"

"Absolutely." She lifted her chin with bravado.

"My!" he said. "You've got more courage than I would have."

She shrugged. "My sins are like everybody else. Not better, not worse."

"Are you sure? What about Signor Baldini?"

"*Dio santissimo!* Once again we have the *predica*, the how you say, preach, about Baldini? *Povero* Baldini! You make me sorry for him."

"Oh, I didn't mean to do that," he said hastily.

"Well. Then you must accept the reality. I have decide' I will not betray him." Actually she had decided that this statement was the only device likely to precipitate something interesting. But Randall surprised her by asking sharply, "And how sure are you that he doesn't betray you?"

She sat back and widened her eyes, leaving Randall in silence for a moment. Then she said, "Is not the same thing. Like the fishes, the men are the men. They betray everybody. But a woman only protest when she is *innamorata*, she is *gelosa*, is natural, no? Otherwise—" she shrugged. "Is the life, *cosa vuoi*?"

He looked at her sadly. "It would be wonderful if you could be serious once in a while," he said. He started to recall her single such moment and then thought better of it.

"It would not be wonderful," she said, frowning a little. "It would be *noioso*."

"Then I suppose you think me '*noioso*'—I take it that means, a bore?"

"No—not entirely. Sometimes yes. But you are beautiful," she said.

"Please!" He could have covered his face with his hands. "We don't use that word the way you do. And one doesn't say such things to a man, Renata. Haven't you been in America long enough to realize that?"

"In America is no different the nature from Europe. Is only different the *commedia*, nobody tell what they think. *Mi piaci, tu*—I like you—how long you think is necessary make a secret?"

"Suppose I said something of the sort to you?" He looked at her boldly and tried with the weight of real feeling to quell the mischief which sparked from her like electricity from a cat's fur.

"I would say '*Benissimo*! For what we wait longer?'"

"For you to get rid of Baldini," said Randall slowly. "And the kind of ideas that go with all that."

"Then you could wait forever!" Her face was pink with temper and her eyes larger and darker than he had ever seen them. She had been toying with her omelette; now she pushed the plate aside and folded her arms brusquely. Nothing was said for a time, each stared away from the other and Randall waited as long as he could before stealing a sidelong glance at her. Her lips were tightly closed, her perpetual laugh was erased, and the line of her chin was a fine angle of defiance.

"I see you mean what you say," he said at last. "You will not allow a decent man to have serious feelings about you. My God!" he exclaimed, "I'd have more respect for you if you were even in love with Baldini!"

"Such a view is your misfortune," she said with a cold shrug. "Is different what I think is honest and what you think. I tell you already, is also different love, amusement, responsibility. *Tutti diversi*. Some I want, some I not want. So I choose. I am not confuse'. But you—you are like they tell about Americans. Is all confuse', pleasure, *l'amore*, *il matrimonio*—no thank you." She brushed her hands crosswise before her. Again they fell into silence but this time it was she who looked first at his hurt, baffled face, his mouth set downwards, his eyes fixed on the table. Suddenly she leaned over and put one hand quickly on his and said, "Do not feel so hurt, Randalo, believe me is not that important. I am sorry surprise you in such a way."

"Oh, I'm not surprised," he said. "And you don't know everything about Americans. I've got—" he stopped.

"You have what?"

"Nothing." He had been about to say, "I've got a brother just like you." But as quickly he thought better of it. The truth was so disconcerting that he saw in clear perspective his real reason for trying to keep Seymour out of Renata's orbit. He was horrified. Surely one's own brother was nothing to be afraid of. Then he saw that he would not be afraid of anybody unless his feelings were much deeper than he had admitted up to now. Good God!, he thought, I ought to have the sense to pull out of this. I would be a fool to stake anything on a woman like this even if she weren't involved as she is. Utterly frivolous, utterly superficial . . . he raised his head slowly and came back to the reality of the moment, to see Renata Tosi smiling at him, her good humor restored but with it a tinge of wistfulness. Her head was bent a little to one side, and the comic twist of her pretty mouth suggested a disappointed pout.

"Is no use we quarrel," she said. "We are different, is better we remain like now. *Così* nobody regret nothing."

"When do you sail for Italy?" he asked abruptly.

"Monday eight days."

"The first ship after the opera closes?"

"Yes. Sometimes I don't feel please' to go. I like very much New York."

"Don't you like Milano?"

"Oh, yes, in some ways is better. But—" she gestured.

"You said you'd tell me about Italy," he said.

"That was before we agree is better not continue this—this—" She laughed. "For what you want to know about me when we don't meet not any more?"

"Don't we?" He leaned forward and overcoming his timidity, he took her hand across the table and looked into her eyes. She saw in his face a sincerity which her realism knew to be a warning; she had better give up the attempt to play with this curiously appealing young man.

There was no promise of a game here, there was only the probability of defeat for her or of hurt for him, or of both. "That would make me very unhappy, Renata," he said.

She did not answer at once. Then she shook her head and sighed, "Why you don't understand?—I tell you already, is not for me the serious things. I don't want to repeat any more."

"I suppose you are right," he said slowly. She sat watching his face, drooping with disappointment and even still, after all her talk, with bewilderment. He was looking down at the tablecloth, he was resisting the instinct to raise his eyes and meet hers, which so long as he could not see them, were soft with unconscious tenderness. Then he startled her by raising his head suddenly and she saw the glint of unshed tears blurring the clear bright blue of his eyes which, she thought again, were truly beautiful. She was disturbed to discover herself on the verge of some similar feeling, and she took the matter quickly in hand, determined not to be deflected from her views.

"Yes," she said, gathering up her gloves and her gold mesh bag, "I am right and is better not meet like this to talk many times the same thing. I go in Italy, you make here the life, you have the *famiglia*, your own—"

"But I haven't," he said, with a sense of bleakness as if a cold draught had whistled down a dead chimney.

"No? What you say? How is possible? You have nobody?"

"Just my brother."

"And he? He is older? He is married?"

"Older, and we live together. There's nobody else."

"*Pensa!* I, *invece*, we, we have always the many family. *Quanti!* Everybody in San Bernardo is my parent."

"What!" He leaned forward, with his mouth open. "What did you say?"

"*Ma, niente!* For what you look so funny? I say only is everybody in my village, the cousins, the aunts, the uncles, how you say, *parenti*? What you say here?"

"Relatives. Oh, Renata!" Randall's dejection was blown away in a gale of laughter. "You are killing. When we say 'parents' we mean your mother and father."

"Oh, *i genitori*. Well, I see, is funny. But was not funny mine when they die and leave me *bambina*, I must live with these *parenti* which make you laugh. But I did not laugh. *Basta.* Now we understand, we say *'addio, senza rancor'.* I return in *Ottobre,* maybe then is something different. Who knows?"

"You mean," he said, as she groaned in mock desperation, "you might have decided to leave Baldini?"

"I mean you will maybe learn should not be always so serious the life. Or you either."

And on the short drive back towards the opera house she said nothing to mitigate her decision, or to encourage him to come to hear her in *Siegfried* or in her one other appearance next week. Once as the cab paused on the corner of Fifth Avenue, where the street lamp shone upon her face, he checked himself in a sudden sharp impulse to seize her in his arms and kiss her. Then he wove his fingers together and shut his mouth hard. He would do no such thing. That was what she wanted, and he had already made his decision that he would have nothing more to do with her except on his own terms. He was no longer surprised to find that there were such terms, that he knew all too well just what he wanted.

CHAPTER 11

On Sunday, after Evensong, Randall went from the church to the parish house to put away the music, change his clothes, and lock up. He walked slowly through the linoleum-floored passage that connected the two buildings, staring at the toes of his shoes. He felt despondent beyond endurance; lonely beyond anything he had ever known. During the service the first soprano had sung *Bist Du Bei Mir*, Randall's great favorite of all Bach arias, and the noble melody, the clear and trusting words had seemed literally to wring his heart. He had not felt so near to real helplessness in all the time since the bad weeks after his mother's death.

And why, he thought, should this be so? A man doesn't really fall in love with a silly flirt like Renata; I don't honestly think I have done so. She stirs me in some way when I am with her, but perhaps any woman as pretty and amusing would do the same. She doesn't want anything I could offer her, and wouldn't know what to do with it if she did want it. She wants what she's got; she's quite right that I should forget her. No, he thought, his trouble was sheer loneliness. He shrank at the thought of leaving even a place so austere as this parish house, whose saving grace was that he kept busy here, to go home to that silent emptiness, that mustiness, that knowledge of massed inanimate secrets accumulating only because one could not decide to disperse and dispose of them. Most of the time he did not feel this, he warded off the possibility of feeling it, because the practical reality was Seymour's intention and his too, to leave the house so soon. Only his unbearable loneliness, whose cause he knew perfectly well to be his own inertia and diffidence, plunged him into desolation like this that he was suffering now.

It was a soft and beautiful April evening, not yet dark; and while changing his clothes he stood looking out the high west window at the pinkish sunset sky. A young maple tree outside was just breaking into leaf, and its sharp delicate outline struck him as personifying the wistful fragility of all new feeling. He stood there, hearing footsteps and voices thin out and fade away as the choir left the building; the light dimmed slowly and presently there was the familiar enclosing silence which told him that he was all alone. He lingered at the window, trying to decide to go somewhere and do something, if only to Seymour's club, rather than to skulk at home alone. He thought about Renata, imagining her among the rowdy, high-colored companions of her special world, presided over by Baldini; this was what she liked and he had made his last attempt to separate her from it. Probably this evening they would all be holding forth in some Italian restaurant in the West Thirties, drinking chianti and singing and making outrageous jokes, some of them perhaps at his expense if she and Baldini were as capable of cruel wit as he suspected. She was right, she and Randall had nothing in common and it was better that the thing had ended where it had.

He had spent forty-eight hours telling himself this and his reason believed it. But his heart accepted nothing, he was disturbed and hurt and puzzled, and if he must resign himself to eliminating Renata it loomed an appalling impossibility to find anything or anybody to re-place her. I ought not to have seen as much of her as I did, he thought, pulling on his coat and settling his possessions in his waistcoat pockets. All that foolishness and foreignness has no relation to this. "This" meant emptiness; "this" meant standing as he was standing now, desolate in the face of beauty like the lovely spring evening which was painful when one had nobody with whom to share it. He stood at the window sunken in his unhappiness. Suddenly he jumped. The silent Sunday evening, the quiet Chelsea side street, were shattered by the shrill blast of a motor horn. Randall peered out the window; nobody should do such a thing. Around the corner came Seymour in his Stevens-Duryea, proudly steer-ing with one gauntleted hand while the other squeezed the rubber bulb of the horn. The scarlet car glittered with polish and brilliant brass. Riding beside Seymour in front was a laughing woman in a long duster and a big hat tied down with a chiffon veil; a second one sat alone in the back. Seymour stopped the car in front of the parish house and once again squeezed the horn, looking up at the windows. Randall threw up the sash and called softly, "Hush! I'll be right down."

He hurried out, locking the door behind him, and in the street Sey-mour whipped off his motoring cap with a bow. "Miss Lillian McCoy," he said, with a courtly gesture at his companion. "Miss Marietta Pawling, whom of course you know." He waved at the girl in back. "I have brought along your duster and cap, Randall." He produced them. "Put them on and let's be on our way."

"But," said Randall weakly.

" 'But' nothing. We are going out to Glen Island for dinner and you," Seymour raised his goggles and gave Randall a sharp look, "are coming along."

"Glen Island! Why, that's way out on the Sound."

"Yes!" cried Marietta Pawling. "Almost all the way out to New Rochelle. Isn't it exciting?"

"Thrilling!" said Miss McCoy.

"Why it must be twenty miles," said Randall incredulously.

"All of it," said Seymour with pride. "It shouldn't take much above two hours." He looked at his watch. "Quarter to six now, we'll arrive just in time to dine comfortably."

"But it will be dark when we start back."

"It usually is dark at night."

"And you mean to drive in the dark?"

Miss Pawling said, "He's got lamps on the car. Really, you know, it's not dangerous, Mr. Holt. Quite a lot of people are doing it."

Randall had no wish to seem ridiculous, so he opened the door of the tonneau and climbed in. The seats were comfortably barrel-upholstered in black leather, and he settled into the right-hand one behind Seymour, with Miss Pawling on his left. She greeted him enthusiastically and almost immediately he caught her stealing a glance from Seymour to himself and back again, a comparison that a child might have had more wit than to make. The result, however, was apparently favorable to Randall and once again he smothered the memory of Renata Tosi calmly remarking, "You are beautiful."

Suppose it's true, he thought, with queer detachment. If it is, I guess they all think the same thing. But only in Renata did he find such an attitude shocking. If anybody else thinks it, he decided coldly, I might as well give them their head. He put Renata Tosi resolutely out of mind, and threw himself into the spirit of the excursion. Seymour was in fine form. They proceeded up Madison Avenue, the motor proclaiming their progress with a solid but subdued roar of which Seymour appeared to approve. He drove very well, threading his way past horses and slowing down to watch for cross traffic at the corners. But there was not much; on a Sunday evening there were not many people out. "Week days," said Seymour, "I see almost as many motor cars as carriages now."

"Why, yes," said Miss McCoy, "the other day I rode in a motor taxicab. Imagine!"

"Those have been around for quite a while."

"I wonder if they'll ever replace hansoms entirely."

"Seems hard to imagine, doesn't it?"

"Have you ridden in this automobile before?" Marietta Pawling asked Randall.

"Just short distances. I think this must be the first real trip Seymour has taken in it, isn't it?"

"Well, yes. I've had it as far as Van Cortlandt Park. But I want to get out in the country where I can really see what it will do." Seymour honked at a fat man who stood in the middle of the street waiting for a trolley-car, though none was in sight. The man shook his fist and yelled, "Get a horse!"

"Why, he's way out of date!" giggled Miss McCoy. "They stopped yelling that two or three years ago."

"How fast do you think it will go, Seymour?" Randall hoped his voice did not betray apprehension.

"Oh—maybe thirty-five. With four of us in it."

"*Goodness!*" cried the girls. "You wouldn't frighten us, would you?"

Seymour laughed proudly. They snorted along, through Harlem and over the One Hundred and Twenty-Fifth Street Bridge. There Seymour drew over carefully to the curb and stopped the car.

"What's the trouble?" they all asked at once. "Is anything wrong?"

"Of course not! I just think it's time to light the lamps."

"Oh." Randall jumped out to help Seymour. While they were lighting matches, opening the glass, adjusting the flames, and snapping shut the brass frames of the lamps, Randall said, "You aren't really going to try to drive fast tonight, are you, Brother?"

"Why?" asked Seymour in a queer tone. "Are you scared?"

"No, I'm not." Randall shut the red pane of the rear lantern and took off his goggles and looked Seymour in the eyes. "You know what's on my mind. I guess you can see as well as anybody but sometimes I'm beginning to wonder about it. I just want you to be careful, that's all."

Seymour had shut his mouth with a hard grimace and for a moment stood flushed with anger. Then he twitched his shoulders and drew in his breath and said, "I'll be careful. Don't worry."

"I know you will." Randall closed his hand for an instant on Seymour's forearm. "Please don't mind what I said."

"You're all right. Come on now, here we go." They climbed back to their seats and Seymour carefully let out the clutch and put the car into gear. "Isn't she a beauty?" he gloated. "Didn't stall while I had it stopped. I guess the mixture's just right."

It was a gay evening. They arrived in good time at the Glen Island restaurant and Seymour ordered a fine shore dinner, champagne, and afterwards sweet liqueurs for the ladies. Randall observed that Seymour drank very little, which proved his good sense, and he was skilful in entertaining the two girls. Whatever he had said or hinted to Marietta Pawling, it was clear that she knew she could only continue to see him on the contingent basis of accepting Randall at times as his substitute. But that, Seymour was relieved to see, was going to be no hardship for her. My God, he thought, while the orchestra played the current favorites from *Mademoiselle Modiste*, if that kid realized how attractive he is he could have them lined up in rows for the whistling. He studied his brother's face, apparently absorbed in the girls' chatter, but to Seymour's shrewd judgment a partial mask which did not conceal immense wistfulness. Seymour sighed. Was it possible that the lad had really been hard hit by that Italian woman? From everything he knew, Seymour could think of her only as a thoroughly expert proposition, skilled in a realm where Randall Holt was helpless. No two episodes were ever alike, he knew well; the preposterous story of Vienna could not have been repeated. Whatever had happened, Randall's evident distress evoked real concern from Seymour, and the resolve to do what he could to ease for his brother the lesson that it was useless to lay sincere emotion at the feet of such a woman. At the same time Seymour found himself inordinately curious to get a look at her. While he was talking with Marietta Pawling and she exclaiming, "My, I hadn't realized your brother is such a stunner," he said, "You be nice to him, Marietta. He's better stuff than we are, either of us."

"Oh, I'll be nice," she assured him.

"I mean what *he* thinks is nice. Never mind what you think."

Seymour had scarcely been inside the opera house since his boyhood. He cared little for music and nothing for opera as such. But on Thurs-

day evening when Renata Tosi was singing Musetta, he invited himself
into the box of old Mrs. Waterworth, to whom he had not paid his
respects in years. The dowager was flattered. Seymour had brought
along the smallest of his pairs of binoculars, which had extremely powerful lenses. Standing in the back of the box he used them inconspicu-
ously. He watched Renata Tosi's entrance, and her bewitching acting,
almost without listening to her sing. His face was a tableau of astonishment and knowing appraisal. He had expected nothing like this. During
the curtain-calls he trained his glasses downwards on the house and in
a moment saw what he expected: Randall among the standees at the
rail, with everything there was to know plainly written on his face,
there where he thought himself alone and unwatched and unknown.

The Stevens-Duryea meant that Seymour would be away over the
week end. Even before the car was delivered he had begun to assemble
maps and information about roads and places to stop. He was very
systematic about it. He had bought a leather portfolio in which to keep
these things and carry them in the automobile. He had spent much of
the week equipping the car with extra luxuries like the windshield; also
with an elaborate tire-patching kit and a newly-invented pneumatic
pump which he hoped he would not too soon have to use. He was even
considering a detachable folding carriage-top which could be set up
quickly in case of rain, but that was too expensive, he decided; mackin-
toshes would have to do for the time being.

He was so absorbed in his new treasure that he forgot the prosaic
details of time and place and work, his own and Randall's. On Friday
morning he asked Randall to come along on the week end trip he was
planning, and simply stared when Randall answered, "But Brother,
you know I can't be away Saturday and Sunday. That's when—"

"Oh," said Seymour. He laughed ruefully. "You know, I really am
acting like a ten-year-old about this machine."

"Well, why not? It must be wonderful to know so exactly what you
want and be able to have it."

Seymour gave him a sidelong glance. He was much more concerned
for Randall since his visit to the opera last night than he had been
before. With Renata Tosi gone, after Monday, it would be easier to
throw diversions in Randall's way, and there might even be the natural
reaction that he would begin to amuse himself with some other woman,

once the thread of his intensity about the Italian was cut. It was just too bad about this gloomy week end looming up for him but there was nothing to be done about it. Seymour reminded him, though, of the many summer week ends to come. "You get busy and set up a decent vacation for yourself," he advised. "You need to practise a little self-preservation. Don't let Fitzhugh grab the best of the summer."

Randall smiled a little sadly. "All right, Brother," he said. "I'll try. Seems to me you're being awfully brotherly these days, aren't you?" He looked hard at Seymour.

"I don't know. Maybe I'm just too un-brotherly most of the time. I'm a selfish pig, who should know better than you?"

Randall gave him an affectionate pat on the shoulder as he went away to let in the new cleaning-woman, who was ringing the bell of the side door downstairs. Seymour had suggested not giving her a latchkey until they felt sure she was a person they wouldn't mind letting walk in and out; not like that prying McBane woman. Randall agreed. It was a nuisance to have to deal with such people at all, but somebody had to clean the rooms where they lived.

Saturday and Sunday dragged by. Randall had accepted the invitation of the Rector and his wife to lunch after church on Sunday. It was stiff and boring in a way, but at the same time remotely consoling. The Rector was pompous and wonderfully conceited, his every word and every gesture a careful study; but a glimpse at his house, his elaborate plush-embellished drawing-room, his dark, ceremonial dining-room where they ate the traditional roast beef and Yorkshire pudding and chocolate ice cream of classic Sunday memory, reminded Randall that there was a world and a way of life and a point of view more natural to him than the turmoil in which he had lately been floundering. He even found himself thinking, as they sat over a glass of port after lunch, that it would be a relief to have Renata Tosi gone after tomorrow, and every possibility of seeing her cut off for good. Next autumn seemed such ages away that it had no reality.

He went away from luncheon in a calmer, much improved frame of mind. He had succeeded pretty well in his stubborn effort not to think about Renata's last evening in New York, and this was the more difficult because he had seen (after trying not to look at it) the announcement of the opera's "Grand Gala Finale", the last Sunday evening concert of the season. Renata Tosi was not billed, but Baldini was, since the programme consisted entirely of favorite concerted numbers from the repertoire and Baldini was one of the leading bassos. Randall propelled himself through the remaining hours of the afternoon and the early evening, concentrating hard on his work and grateful that Merion Fitzhugh had gone off and left him again to play Evensong. When he was through, he stood again at the window in the parish house as he had a week ago, contemplating a lonely evening. He counted off the ten long days since he had last seen Renata (except for his surreptitious visits to the opera when she was singing) and once more he told himself that if he was not to see her again, it was much better that she go away to Italy. Then he had a struggle to thrust aside the knowledge that it need not have been impossible to see her again, or to expect to do so in the future. He need only have accepted her on her terms and he could have been with her as much as trickery could contrive. "I don't want that," he said, half aloud; "I don't want any part of it. I'm through. *Through*."

He took his hat and walked away home through the quiet streets. He was not hungry enough to think of eating again today, after that huge unaccustomed midday dinner, and he decided to try to spend the evening putting his mind on something absorbing instead of letting it dwell where it would. He settled down in the library with a brandy and soda and Spitta's *Bach*. Once or twice he found himself reading lines which bore no meaning; then he would sit up, shake his head hard, and drive his thoughts back from their wandering to the sturdy confines of the Cantor and his world. Several times he glanced unconsciously at the mantel where the old ormulu clock had ticked ever since he could remember, but it had broken down recently and Seymour had removed it to his workshop, saying he wanted to try the experiment of installing a new set of works in it. Seymour had bought for the purpose a cheap American clock of the same dimensions. Randall had laughed at him for thinking himself capable of clockmaking. Well, he thought now, he probably makes more sense than I do—and certainly gets more out of life.

He found himself with his watch in his hand, and Spitta sliding off his knee. He caught the book, scowled, and put his watch back in his pocket. It was five minutes past nine. If he went out and picked up a cab right now, he could drive past the opera house and if Renata Tosi was not there, he could go on up Broadway to the Ansonia where he would surely find her, finishing her packing. Her ship was to sail at noon tomorrow. Without doubt she would be up late tonight at a farewell party after the concert. The more he thought of it the more certain it appeared that she must be at her hotel now. Would she see him if he went there? He knew that she would, he knew also that if he had not taken her at her word ever since last Friday, she would have seen him at any time he had contrived. What would have happened? He sat struggling not to think; the heavy book slid from his knee with a thump; he ignored it and jumped to his feet and began to pace back and forth across the room. He heard again her lovely, rippling voice, her ridiculous English, the outrageous things she said which left him confounded by their unabashed truth.

"Oh, my God!" he exclaimed aloud, "how I wish I'd never seen her."

He went to the door; he went back to his chair; he looked at his watch again; he sat down; presently he stood up. He left the room and started down the stairs. There he paused. What would happen if he should go to see her now? A quarrel? A surrender? A few moments of passion which would amuse her and shatter him? Whatever that hour might hold, her departure tomorrow would grieve him the more. He ran his fingers nervously through his hair, stood a little while on the stairs, then slowly turned and went back up to the library.

He got through Monday better than he had hoped, for he slept unusually late and had to hurry to get Seymour off to the office. Then he turned his attention to Mrs. Quinn, the new charwoman, who demanded coal for the seldom-used boiler so that she could have hot water for her scrubbing. He went out and attended to that and other domestic errands and when he reached home again it was past noon and he knew that Renata's ship had sailed. He felt distinctly better; not happier, but less distraught. She was out of reach and this should help him once for all to put her out of mind.

Seymour came home early from the office, unable to resist his automobile, and they started off by themselves to cross the river on the Twenty-third Street ferry and drive up the Jersey shore of the Hudson until they found some attractive place to dine. They never reached one because they spent most of the evening patching a punctured tire in a streaming April cloudburst, and when Seymour went round to crank the motor afterwards the car would not start because a spark plug had got wet. By the time Seymour had remedied all this and, to Randall's vast admiration, proved himself the master of everything concerning the Stevens-Duryea, they had to take the ferry back again, and they wound up at Jack's at eleven o'clock with a beefsteak and a quart of ale. They had laughed so much that Randall's stomach ached. Cronies of Seymour's kept coming over to their table to admire and discuss the Stevens-Duryea, which was parked outside in Sixth Avenue in care of the proud door-man who was busy shooing away young spawns and limbs of the devil who wanted the glory of having touched the wonderful red machine.

They went to bed in high spirits and Randall woke late on Tuesday morning in a better mood than for a long time past. There was no doubt about it, Seymour when things went right was the best company in the world. He was full of plans for the coming months, and taking Randall's share in them for granted. Several times Randall had hesitated over the question which he could not bring himself to ask: how could Seymour possibly be away from his office as much as his talk seemed to suggest?

This morning, like yesterday, Seymour did get off to work, and Randall went to the drawing-room to shut himself up with his practising. I'm not much of a one to think Seymour is lazy, he thought; look at me. I haven't done any real work for weeks. He settled down and worked hard; an hour of scales and arpeggios and octave exercises, then he got out the Prelude and Fugue in C Minor, and dug in for an hour at that. Though all his work at St. Timothy's was satisfying, his great delight was the constantly widening study of Bach, and the fine organ on which he was playing it increasingly well.

A little past eleven o'clock he took the score and walked over to St. Timothy's to continue working at the organ. He was just coming up the walk to the parish house when the door opened and one of the curates hurried down the steps.

"Ah, here you are, Holt," he said. "That's good. There is someone asking for you on the telephone in the office."

"The telephone!" Randall stopped, almost gaping. He had scarcely ever used a telephone and could not imagine being called to it. Unless something should be wrong with Seymour? Grew and Minturn had a telephone, he knew, so did most business offices; but he was bewildered. He hurried into the Secretary's office and picked up the receiver hanging by its wire from the brown box on the wall.

"Yes?" he said nervously. "Yes?"

"Hello? Is that Mr. Randall Holt?" A man was speaking.

"Yes. I am Randall Holt." He wondered if the man could hear him. He heard clearly, to his amazement. The man said, "This is the Ansonia Hotel, Mr. Holt. The manager's office."

Randall's pulse began to pound; he felt as if it must drown out his hearing and he strained to listen.

"Yes," he said again. "Yes, what is it?"

"It's about Miss Renata Tosi, Mr. Holt. She is very ill here."

"But she sailed for Italy yesterday," said Randall stupidly.

"She was to have sailed. She could not leave. She was able to give us your name when we—ah—asked for—"

"Is she dead?" Randall had no idea what he was saying.

"No, no, I'm sorry if I alarmed you. But she is very ill, as I said. We were going to notify someone at the opera house but she insisted we send for you."

"I'll be right there. I'm coming at once." Randall dropped the telephone receiver and turned away in a daze. He went out to the street and ran to the nearest cab stand, leaped into a cab and shouted at the man to hurry. All the way uptown he sat on the edge of the seat twisting his hands together and trying to make sense of what he had heard. Was she all alone? Had she had no care? What was the matter with her? Where was Baldini?

When he entered her room with the hotel manager, it was dimmed by drawn blinds, but he saw the disorder of last-minute packing, the open trunks and valises which he had imagined on Sunday. He walked quickly round the screen in the corner and stood rigid, terrified at the change in Renata. He saw that she had been hideously sick, and he would have quailed at the vile odor around her but for his greater concern at seeing how she looked. She lay on her right side, absolutely still. Her face was ghastly, very pale, her cheekbones jutting sharply, her eyes wide open but sunken. Her legs appeared to be drawn up beneath the bedclothes, and her hands, usually so firm and smooth, looked like white claws picking spasmodically at the soiled sheet. Randall bent and touched her forehead timidly. It was dry and burning. He heard her breathing queerly, as if she dared not use her lungs. He kept his hand lightly on her forehead, amazed that in spite of her condition she was not unconscious; she recognized him. Her lips moved a little and he thought she spoke his name, but he shook his head, trying to give her a reassuring smile. He knew nothing of illness, but it took no knowledge to see that she should not try to speak. But she fixed him with her brown, staring eyes and said faintly, "*Paura. Ho tanta paura.*" Her mouth went down in a grimace of terror; then she stiffened in a spasm of pain.

"Don't be frightened, Renata," he whispered. "Just try to be quiet. I'm so glad you sent for me, everything will be all right." Even while he spoke he felt swamped with helplessness; how could he know what to do about all this! "I have the frighten," she muttered stiffly. "Frighten. No *ospedale*."

"Just be still," he whispered. "Please, Renata, dear. I'm going to take care of you." He must get to that wonderful telephone. "Will you just lie perfectly still and try not to worry for a minute? Please!" He smiled at her and gently pushed the tangled mass of her hair back over the pillow. "Just five minutes."

"*Oh! i dolori,*" she moaned. "I will die."

"No, no." He shook his head gently and put his finger on his lips. "I'm just going to telephone," he said. "Only a minute."

There was no time now to ask the hotel people questions. He slipped from the room and stood for a moment in the corridor trying to decide what to do. He had never dealt with illness, but Seymour had. He could ask Seymour what to do. Then he realized that Seymour would get hold of Doctor Slade, and he could save time by doing that himself. He had once sworn never to speak to Doctor Slade again, but that was nonsense. The manager took him to a telephone in a little cupboard down the hall, and in an instant somebody told him, "We have Doctor Kenneth Slade on the wire."

Slade listened to Randall's description of Renata's condition and said, "I'll send John Whitby up immediately. This isn't my sort of thing, you know, and somebody must get there at once. Don't let anybody touch her and above all, don't move her."

"Oh, thank you." Randall tried to get his breath. But he was so upset that he blurted, "Couldn't you come too, Doctor? I'm so—I don't know anything about this. I'm—" he was almost in tears.

"Very well. We'll both come. But do nothing meanwhile."

In the hall Randall asked the manager how long he had known about Renata.

"Only an hour ago, that was the first we knew about it. I had our house physician up here then. Yesterday morning we were told she wasn't well and had put off her sailing for a week. We heard nothing more from her room and of course we thought she was resting. This morning the maid found her like this and when I brought up the doctor, he said she must be taken to a hospital at once. But she was terrified. I've never seen such fear. That was when she asked for you."

The two doctors arrived almost immediately. While Doctor Whitby was examining Renata, Randall tried to explain to Doctor Slade who she was.

"Just a professional acquaintance. I see."

"Well—yes." Randall tried to bear that out. "But she hasn't got anybody in this country and she's terribly frightened, Doctor. I said—well, I mean, I want to take care of her."

Whitby came from the patient. He looked very dubious.

"Peritonitis, of course," he said. He glanced meaningly at Slade. "No time to lose. I'll go and telephone."

"You will take her to the hospital?" asked Randall.

"If we don't!—where's the telephone?" Randall showed him and came back to Doctor Slade who was standing looking down at Renata. She lay as before, even more ghastly pale, and from time to time she whispered, "I have the frighten. Very frighten to die in *ospedale*."

Randall tried to quiet her. Slade beckoned him outside the screen. He started to take his leave, since there was nothing for him to do. But Randall said, "Oh, please, Doctor. What really is the matter? What are they going to do?" They moved away out of earshot of the bed. Slade explained. "She has a burst appendix. It may even be too late to operate, but that's the only thing they can do."

"Then will you tell them at the hospital that I want her to have—" Randall took a deep breath. "You know, what you'd do for us. Don't let them put her in a ward or anything like that."

"You can have what you ask for, Randall. But if you put her in a private room, with all the special nursing she will need, it's going to cost you a lot of money."

"I don't care. I can pay it."

"Very well." Slade smiled kindly. "I'll see to it." Probably, he thought, it will not cost so much because I'll be surprised if the woman is alive tomorrow.

"She's so terribly frightened," said Randall again. "About the hospital."

"All foreigners are like that," said Slade. "They think any hospital is the pest-house where they are just sent to die."

"Then I'll try to explain to her that it's different here."

Whitby came back to the room, saying, "They're on the way. I'll go straight over now and start getting ready. You realize," he said to Randall, "her condition is grave. Very doubtful, I can't promise anything."

Randall nodded slowly, his eyes wide and strained. Whitby said, leaving the room with Slade, "Keep her exactly as she is until they get here. It will only be a few minutes."

"Shall I go along in the ambulance?"

"Better not. There won't be room, there's an extra nurse coming." He nodded quickly at Randall and hurried away.

Renata had not moved when Randall went back to her. She was still muttering her terror and repeating in Italian, "I don't want to die in a hospital. Don't let them send me to a hospital."

Randall bent close to her and gently took her burning hands, their fingers still picking weakly at the sheet.

"Let me try to explain, Renata," he said softly. "Our hospitals here are not dreadful places. Please believe me—please." He touched her forehead carefully. "We are never afraid of a hospital, everybody goes to them in America. Truly."

She stared in pitiful apprehension. Her lips moved again, but he said, "Don't try to speak. I just want you to believe me. You'll be safe and comfortable there. They'll take the most wonderful care of you." He had a sudden gruesome vision of a place to fit Doctor Slade's word, 'pest-house', and he said, "This isn't a big horrible public place, Renata, dear. American hospitals are entirely different. You'll have a nice quiet room by yourself and you'll see, the nurses will take such good care of you. You couldn't have such care anywhere else, do you understand?"

He could not tell whether he had relieved her mind at all. But he tried to smile encouragement and keep her soothed for the few moments until the door opened and the ambulance staff arrived, noiseless and swift and efficient. When Renata saw them Randall realized that his reassurance had done some good; nobody could be afraid of the calm, smiling young white-clad doctor and the nurses in their starched uniforms and smart blue-and-scarlet capes. Renata was wrapped in blankets and on her way down the hall on a stretcher in less than five minutes, and as they carried her into the elevator Randall stood nearby and said, "I'll be there in a little while, Renata. You'll see, everything I told you is true."

He went back to her room, dazed and bewildered. Mechanically he looked at his watch. It was a little past one o'clock, a bare two hours since he had been called to that telephone in the parish house. He sat down slowly on the edge of a chair and looked at the mess around him and tried to make himself believe that he had not dreamed all this. The last feeling that he remembered was a mixture of sadness and relief because Renata had sailed for Italy; and now he had become the one person in the United States who was responsible for her. He could not believe it and he sat there shaking his head. Presently the hotel manager came in, and once again Randall was faced with details and decisions that he had no idea how to resolve. But something had to be done about Renata's possessions, and with the help of a maid he did it. They rounded up all the things which remained unpacked and strewn about the room, and the maid packed them. When she had nearly finished, Randall stepped into the bathroom to see whether she had overlooked anything. On the shelf above the basin he saw an empty medicine bottle labelled Castor Oil, and the mashed halves of a sucked lemon. Poor girl, he thought, I'd hate to have taken all that castor oil, but he was so ignorant of illness that he had no idea that this had precipitated the disaster.

He went down to the office to pay Renata's account, but he was told that it had been paid on Monday morning and for a week in advance besides. Well, he thought, Baldini didn't go off without doing what he could for her; he expected her to come along on the next ship. He accepted the refund due from the hotel and then, when the clerk asked what was to be done with Miss Tosi's luggage, he had no idea what to answer.

"Knabe's will come anyway to take back their piano," said the clerk, "but where are the trunks to be sent?"

Randall could think of no other place, so he gave his own address. Then he tipped the hotel staff who had helped him and went out and got into a cab and hurried off to the hospital.

CHAPTER 12

He had refused to listen to the doctors and nurses who told him to go home and get some rest, and long past eleven o'clock that night he was still sitting in the visitors' room, his head in his hands. He heard someone come in and felt a hand on his shoulder. He looked up. The surgeon, Doctor Whitby, was standing there, pale and exhausted. Randall got slowly to his feet and murmured, "Is it—she—?" He was afraid of words.

Whitby shook his head, but not reassuringly. "She is still alive," he said. "But it's going badly. I can't deceive you, Mr. Holt. I don't have to tell you we're doing our utmost. These cases, most of them—"

"Doctor Slade warned me too."

"Well, it's better that you understand. Frankly, I think you ought to go home and try to get some sleep. I'm spending the night in the hospital and if there's any change either way I'll telephone you."

"We haven't a telephone, Doctor. But if you don't mind, I'd rather wait here. I'm all right, really I am."

"Well, do as you choose. If you want to lie down on the sofa there, I'll have someone bring you a blanket. I wish I could give you some hope."

"Oh, you've been wonderful. I just—" Randall stopped speaking, overcome by shyness. He should not bother this man with his own feelings. But the surgeon smiled in spite of his fatigue and said, "What? Say it."

Randall swallowed. He said, "It's just that—if she can't pull through I wouldn't want her to be all alone. She was so afraid of that." He felt that he sounded silly and added quickly, "Of course, I suppose she is unconscious, she wouldn't really know . . ."

"Not unconscious. But somnolent and extremely weak. You try to rest for a while now. There may not be any change for a long time." He thought better of saying that a change would almost surely come before dawn; and for the worst. He smiled wearily and went away.

Randall dozed brokenly on the hard horsehair sofa. But much of the night he prowled round and round the stiffly impersonal room, dark except for one heavily-shaded electric light bulb. Sometimes he heard the muffled footsteps of nurses up and down the corridor; then he went and stood at the open door waiting for someone to come and tell him that Renata was dead. But nobody came near him. He knew which door was Renata's, he could see it down the hall, and the silent nurses and internes who went in and out carrying things swathed in white covers. By three o'clock he was wide awake and standing most of the time in the doorway, watching down the hall. As long as they were still doing something, he told himself, she could not yet have died.

He left the door and threw himself into a chair and sat staring at the dun-colored wall, trying to relate this experience to the Renata of the laughter and teasing and mischief, the funny English, the flippancy, the maddening refusal to be serious. He tried to summon up the emotions which had kept him in a turmoil about her for a fortnight past, but he could feel nothing at all. That Renata could just as well have sailed away to Italy. All he knew now was a crushing degree of concern that the woman dying in the room down the hall somehow not be allowed to die. Every idea apart from that had been swept from his mind as if a hand had dragged a cloth from a laden table, leaving it bare. Once tonight he had had a passing thought for Seymour, who might have wondered where he was, but that too had vanished into unreality.

He fell at last into another sleep, which he did not know until he found himself on his feet, rubbing his eyes. Doctor Whitby was standing before him and the sky was light behind the roof of the clinic across the street. Randall said nothing, he waited for the doctor. Whitby said soberly, "No change. But I am really surprised." He took out his watch and said, "It's nearly seven o'clock, you see. I wouldn't have dared believe it."

"Do you think—"

"Let's not think anything, Mr. Holt. She's still hanging on. That's enough for the moment. I must say, those Italians have iron constitutions."

"Oh, that's wonderful," said Randall. "That's wonderful."

"You really should go home now and get some rest," said the doctor. "You can't stay here twenty-four hours a day, you know."

"Very well." Randall looked at him with such pleading, plainly not daring to ask, that the doctor said, "You wanted to ask if you could see her?"

"Not unless you think so, Doctor."

"Well, I don't see why not. Only for a moment, of course. Just let her see you're here."

They walked down the hall to the closed door. The doctor opened it and motioned Randall into the room. The nurse moved from her chair beside the bed and Randall walked over on tiptoe and looked at Renata. She looked much as she had yesterday, but her eyes were closed. Her hands were hidden by the bed-covers drawn up to her chin, and her face against the white sheet was a dreadful yellowish grey. Randall could not see that she was breathing. He looked round at the doctor, and was surprised that he stepped forward and said, "Miss Tosi. *Miss Tosi.*" He was not afraid to rouse her! Randall watched and saw her eyelids tremble and roll heavily open in their sunken sockets. Her eyes were dull and stunned. Randall leaned forward and looked at her, hoping to make sure she could see him. Her eyelids fluttered again. Her lips were grey and dry. He saw her nostrils flatten in a difficult breath. He managed to smile, and he said softly, "It's all right, Renata. You see, I told you it would be all right here. You're going to be all right."

He could not tell if she had understood. But there was no doubt that she had seen and recognized him. Her eyes closed slowly and she sank back into somnolence. Randall stood for another moment looking at her face so queerly shrunken and sharpened. Then he turned and left the room. He felt as if he had lived a century since yesterday. He walked away through the halls of the hospital, full of early morning noises and the smell of coffee and breakfast; past young nurses in blue and white stripes carrying trays and pushing carts laden with all sorts of things. When he rang for the elevator he saw through the iron gratings that it could not stop at his floor; it was filled by a patient on a wheeled stretcher, surrounded by nurses. He ran down the stairs instead and went out to the sun shining in Fifty-ninth Street and the incredible fact that New York was going about its morning business unconcerned who had lived or died during the night.

When he walked into the library at home, Seymour dropped his newspaper on the floor and looked up with a chortle. "Well, I'll be damned," he said. "Baby Brother has gone and done it."

"Shut up." Randall flopped into his chair and told him what had happened.

"Good God!" Seymour sat with his mouth open while Randall talked. "God Almighty! What a thing to happen to you."

"To me? You ought to see her. She's awfully sick, Seymour. She's very likely to die."

Seymour whistled. "For a good little boy who stays home and keeps his pants buttoned, the damnedest things happen to you."

"I guess they do." Randall felt a little dizzy and was overcome by an enormous yawn. "I'd better go to bed," he said. He looked dully at the crumbs on Seymour's plate.

"When did you last eat?"

"I haven't the remotest idea. Now that you mention it I suppose I'm hungry."

"You ought to have something more than a roll. Look here, you go and get your clothes off and I'll go up to the corner and get you some food."

"Thanks." Randall's eyes were so heavy that the room was a blur. He leaned back in his chair with his hands hanging over the arms. Seymour went away. When he came back in a quarter of an hour Randall was sound asleep. Seymour had brought sliced ham, eggs, butter, cheese, a tin of tomato soup, and a jar of potato salad. He was very clumsy with the gas burner but he managed to assemble the queer meal on the table and woke Randall up.

"It's a horror," he apologized, "but eat it."

"It's fine." Randall sopped up fried egg with the crust of a roll and said, "I'd rather have it than oysters and terrapin. Brother," he said, "don't you think we'd better have a telephone put in here?"

"Well—" Seymour was surprised. "I never thought of it before."

"Neither did I. But after yesterday—"

"I suppose it might be a good idea. But you want it during this emergency. By the time they get it installed—"

"Couldn't you order it this morning? Couldn't you say it *is* for an emergency?"

"Why, yes, I'll try. I'll see about it on the way to the office. Now you get to bed, you're dead. You'll sleep for twelve hours."

"Oh, sure."

Randall went away to his room, but he stopped on the way to find Mrs. Quinn at her cleaning, and told her to wake him up before she left the house at noon.

It was four days before there was sufficient change in Renata's condition for the doctor to concede a real chance of her pulling through. After the second day Randall stopped trying to keep himself rationally pessimistic. One could not be the bystander at a fight for someone's life without believing passionately that the fight would be won. The days went by as if they had been lifted from the calendar, nameless and wrenched from their design. On Wednesday when he ordinarily took the week's first choir rehearsal he forget it completely and was appalled at what he had done. But Dr. Fitzhugh was wonderfully kind; he told him on Thursday to stay away from work altogether until his friend was out of danger.

So day and night, morning, evening, the routine of sleep and food and daily habits dissolved and ran together like a series of colors whose mixture produces nothing but grey. All during that time, he would remember later, Renata was not the woman he had known before and was to know much better afterwards. She was 'she'; or 'the case'. She was the instrument through which, for the first time in his life, he was stubbornly, fanatically absorbed in the attainment of something that he wanted and would stop at nothing to win. Even after Doctor Whitby began cautiously to admit that she was gaining, Randall took no account of hours or days or the matters that ordinarily filled them. And then one sunny morning he was sitting beside the narrow, high bed, with Renata raised a little on her mattress, still pale but not ghastly, still heavy-eyed, but smiling. Her face which he had first learned to know in a frame of ruffles and wavy pompadoured hair, was a different face above the ugly white hospital gown, and her hair, parted in the middle, fell over her shoulders in two long brown braids. Her hands quietly folded on the covers, had also changed; their square firmness was gone. They were blue-white and fragile. She looked, he thought, like the kind of pictures he had seen in art and history books; he did not know enough of painting to realize that she looked like a model for Giotto. She was too weak to speak with any of her verve and sparkle, her voice like the rest of her was thin and wavering, but she said, "How you are good! Such a goodness is never before."

"Nonsense," he said. "You have a wonderful doctor and your nurses—!"

"Is true. Is very different everything here, why they are not the *suore*?"

"I'm afraid I don't know what you mean. But don't try to explain," he added quickly. "You mustn't use your strength talking."

"*Le suore*," she said again. "*Le monache*. Long. Black. Sometimes—" she wrinkled her nose.

"Oh," he said, laughing, "you mean nuns. Well, this isn't a Catholic hospital, Renata."

"No?" She crossed her hands on her breast, dismayed. "You mean I nearly die among heathens? *Oh! Dio!* How I confess that?"

"I'm afraid that's not the worst thing you'd ever have done. I think we're very nice heathens. But I admit I should have thought of calling in a priest for you. I'm sorry, I've been pretty distracted."

"Never mind. If I have seen the priest then, I know absolutely I must die. *Basta* now if maybe he come soon one day. I tell him is no my fault."

"It wasn't your fault," said Randall.

He was surprised, as she improved day by day, that she seemed to give no thought at all to her plans, to questions which he would have supposed must be on her mind. She lay in bed like a contented child, submitting to treatment, obediently doing what she was told, even to eating the soft, milky, slippery food which she told Randall was disgusting.

"What would you like instead?" he asked her; and when she told him he had to admit he had never heard of anything that she mentioned. But he remembered her speaking of the Ristorante Brunetti, so he sought out the place and found it in West Thirty-seventh Street and asked the proprietor if there was anything he could make for Signorina Tosi within the limits of her strict invalid diet.

"She is here? She is sick? She didn't go in Italy? *Mamma mia!*" The man clapped his hands to his head.

Randall told him.

"*Ah poveretta!* You leave to me, Signore. Every day I make for her something very good, very light. Like we give the *bambini*. I make her well quick."

So every morning on his way to the hospital Randall stopped at Brunetti's restaurant and collected a parcel. There was always a bottle of pastina in brodo or some other delicate soup; there was a risotto or dainty boiled chicken or pasta in a little casserole. Sometimes there was a cup of what looked to Randall like custard, but when he wondered why Renata might not as well eat the hospital's custard, she laughed and hugged Brunetti's dish to her bosom.

"Oh, no," she said. "This is the zabaione. You didn't never taste? Here!"—and she made him finish it.

She gained strength on the food she liked, and the daily pint fiasco of wine which the doctor approved to the astonishment of the nurses. But at the end of the second week she had still not mentioned Milano, where she should be arriving in a few days if she had left New York when she was to have gone. Doctor Whitby had told Randall that it would be out of the question for her to sing before next autumn, and better if she did not travel at any distance for at least six weeks. Not knowing how to tell her, Randall put off the subject until almost the day when she should have arrived in Italy. Then he asked her if she did not think he should cable somebody there that she was not coming. She seemed surprised.

"*Pensa!*" she said. "Is true! I am not going."

"But hadn't you thought of it?"

She smiled weakly. "Sometimes is very hard to think. But you are right, Randalo, is necessary inform La Scala."

"And all your other engagements?"

"Oh, Santorelli, alla Scala, he tell them."

Randall wrote down the name. He thought for a moment and sat looking at Renata. She saw that he was waiting for her to speak and she let him wait until a puzzled look came into his eyes. She said, "What you think, Randalo? Is something?"

"I was wondering if you would like me to cable Baldini too," he said. To his surprise, she did not toss off an answer in her usual way. She said quietly, "No, is time enough I write him. Thank you."

Randall sat wondering what she meant. In a way he did not really dare to think. He wanted to ask and lacked the courage. She lay there looking at him with a little smile, that newly childish expression in her eyes to which he was not accustomed; was it gentleness or trustfulness? Whatever it was, it meant to him that she was changed. He said a little uneasily, "I hope Baldini was good to you that day when you were taken ill."

"He was good. He did the best he could. He could not remain, I tell him to go. An important artist cannot abandon the engagements." She thought for a moment and then she said, "But he was not good like you,

Randalo. Nobody I have ever seen, nobody is good like you." And two great tears rolled from her eyes and slid down her cheeks.

"Oh, Renata, dear!" He took her hand and put his cheek to it. "Don't tell me things like that, it isn't true. I'm so glad I was here." He bent over her and dropped to his knees and kissed her hand and held it to his cheek. He took her other hand and held them both clasped in his and looked into her eyes and tried to smile. "Don't you see, Renata, I—" he gulped and stopped speaking. He laid his face on their clasped hands.

"*Tanto buono,*" he heard her whisper. "*Un angelo, sei tu.*"

"No," he said, his face hidden. "But you know, surely you know, I—" This was not time to say it. She was weak and very far from well and nothing should agitate her now. He stayed for a moment as he was, then he raised his head and looked at her, and gently freed her hands and stood up.

"I'll go and send the cable now," he said. "You should be resting. I'll be in again later."

In more than two weeks he had scarcely seen Seymour. Every day he went out early to pick up Renata's food and make a quick visit to the hospital before he went downtown to St. Timothy's. Seymour was usually asleep when Randall left the house, and they never met for dinner because Randall spent the evenings at the hospital, sitting with Renata until it was time for her to go to sleep. When he did see Seymour for a moment, their talk consisted of quick reports: Renata was improving and Seymour was having a wonderful time with his automobile. He offered to take Randall and Renata out in it when she was well enough to go for an airing, and Randall said that would still be a long time off. He would let Seymour know. The *Times* was lying on the floor between them and Randall looked at it absently. "It's so queer," he said. "I've never been one for the news like you, but these past couple of weeks I have absolutely no idea what's happened anywhere."

"You haven't missed a thing," said Seymour. "Nothing's happened. San Francisco's been destroyed. Vesuvius has erupted. A—"

"What? What happened to San Francisco?"

"Oh, nothing much. Just a little earthquake. And a little fire."

Randall stared. "That just goes to show. I've been practically in another world." He looked at his watch. "I must go now."

Seymour pointed out that since the telephone was already installed, it could as well be used to inquire about Renata. But Randall said, "They only say the same thing: she is doing well. It's routine."

"It's true, isn't it?"

"Yes, but I want to see for myself."

Seymour could see for himself too. He was more curious than ever about Renata Tosi. Randall was so wrapped up in her that he had no idea how he appeared, and if he had realized, he would not have cared. He was a different man. He showed an ability to plan and manage, a degree of purpose which nothing had ever evoked before. Seymour's curiosity probed beyond the self-evident fact that Randall was deeply in love, and that his romantic, childlike nature would consider no dénouement other than marriage. Seymour wondered. The Devil a monk would be, at this particular time. But one grave illness and a burden of gratitude which to her would first be welcome but later oppressive, would never make a wife out of the minx he had seen coquetting on the opera-house stage. Very probably she had no interest in marriage at all unless—and that thought worried him almost as much as his fear of Randall's being hurt—she thought there was money involved. He wished he knew a tactful way to sound out that question; and when Renata was about to leave the hospital and Randall, with surprising efficiency, was arranging everything, her move with a nurse to a quiet hotel for a week, then a long stay at a comfortable boarding-house in the country, Seymour asked him, "Are you sure you can afford all this, Ran? Aren't you spending an awful lot of money?"

"Not as much as you've spent on your automobile," said Randall. "And I had a lot in my account, too. I told you I've never used all my income. What have I had to spend it on?"

Seymour felt uncomfortable. He had not expected such an answer, though he doubted that the implication of his own extravagance, or even selfishness, was intentional. He only said, "Well, you couldn't have had the bill from that surgeon yet. It's going to be a whopper, you know."

"Is it? Well, it'll be worth it. How do you know how much it will be, anyway? Have you had such a lot of experience with doctors?"

Seymour froze up and went away saying, "Why don't you get those trunks and valises out of the drawing-room?"

"They aren't in my way there," said Randall. "Do I interfere with what you keep in the cellar?"

But he had a bewildering morning with Renata's luggage the day before she was to leave the hospital. Enough of her clothes had to be produced to dress her to move to a hotel. Then Randall pointed out that she could hardly want to be encumbered with all those opera costumes and winter clothes now and while she was in the country. So she thought out a list of things that he should sort and pack and bring to her. He wrote down each item of the clothes and other articles that she would need; and between his unfamiliarity with the names of such things in Italian or English either, and his intense embarrassment at her graphic explanations what some of them were, she laughed until her nurse became alarmed and said she would rupture her stitches.

She was enchanted with the country. Randall had remembered a place where he had spent a summer with his mother in the years after Hare Island was sold, a dairy farm in Putnam County east of Lake Mahopac. It was owned by people named Maynard, who took one or two summer boarders every year, and gave them comfortable rooms in the big farmhouse, and abundant, delicious food. When he told Renata where she was to go her eyes sparkled and she said, "Ah, a *lago*. I will feel like myself very quick."

"You like lakes especially?"

"I am born *sul Lago di Como*. Is my *paesino*, my village there. What beauty!"

"Oh, Lord. Well, look, Renata—don't expect anything of Lake Mahopac. But it's as far as you ought to travel now."

"Must be beautiful," she said. "Is a lake."

The Maynards soon said she was the nicest guest they had ever had. At first they had their misgivings about an Italian opery-singer who didn't speak good English, was recovering from a long illness, would probably put on airs and throw tantrums and be temperamental and a nuisance. Instead she amazed them by her lively interest in everything around her and her ready comments about the farm which sounded to the Maynard family and their hired hands like madness. But she kept them laughing.

"Is so fine the *erba* here," she exclaimed, pointing to the rich stand of meadow grass west of the house. It was the end of May. "How is you are not already cutting?"

"Cutting! For land's sakes, why?" Tom Maynard was appalled.

"But," she said, astonished, "you leave to grow high such beautiful grass, will soon begin to dry. Would be a pity, no?"

"A pity? Gee." The farmer scratched his head. "A field o' hay like that?"

"Hay? What is, hay?"

Randall was there and he explained. She listened, squinting with bewilderment.

"Never I hear of such a thing," she said. "We would cut it now."

"What do you know about it anyway? How do you know when they cut the hay in Italy?"

"How I know! *Madonna*, I am *contadina*, peasant, if I didn't go to work in Milano I never know anything except walk four *chilometri* up and down the mountain every day carrying the milk on my back to the *latteria*, and sew the *fazzoletti* like my aunts."

"What are *fazzoletti*?" asked Randall, dumbfounded by this glimpse of her origin.

"Like this." She took out her handkerchief. "But bigger, pieces of silk like you buy everywhere for the presents. We sew on them the hems, all the women. *Dio mio*! how many dozens—for two lire the week."

"How much would that be in our money, Renata?" He spoke watching the strangely harsh expression of her face.

"Oh, I cannot count, let me think. Maybe thirty-five, forty cents?"

"Good God. And what did you do in Milano?"

"I was *collocata*, how you say that?—to a dressmaker. *Così* I learned, I was the *piccinina*. I was thirteen years old." He stood staring at her, watching her leaning there on the barnyard fence, slender— too slender—and a picture of freshness in her long ruffled dress. She looked off in the distance where the fields sloped away towards a clump of woods, and then back at the big red barn, solid and important with its gilded weather-vane and its towering silo. "How is different here from us," she sighed. "So rich, so much of everything. So much land!" She smiled then. "But not so beautiful," she said. "In all the world is nothing so beautiful like my country. But," she shrugged, "is no good to be poor there."

"When did you start to sing?" he asked. "How?"

"A *cliente* of the place where I work. She hear me singing while I am doing something and she become interest' and when I am sixteen

she send me to the *Conservatorio*. Also her husband. Eh, the husband!"
She lifted her chin with a telling gesture. *"Ma, cosa vuoi?* Is like I tell
you, the men are the men."

Randall plucked a long blade of grass and leaned on the fence
chewing its sweet white tip.

"I'm not that kind of man," he said quietly.

"No, is true. You are different and you are good. But you demand no
pleasure and this I cannot understand. You are young, you are b—"
she stopped and her laughter rang across the barnyard. *"Ecco,* I didn't
say it again. You are please'?"

"It is you who are beautiful, Renata," he said. "And I am in love
with you."

"No-no-no," she said quickly. It was as if she had sprung back
upon touching a hot iron. He turned his head and tried to fix her eyes
with his, but she was standing very straight, looking away towards the
distance. He knew that his hand was trembling, he felt that the last
grain of his courage had been dashed to nothing at her feet; but he put
out his shaky hand and took her left one and held it hard while he said,
"You act as if you were shocked, Renata. But it's not a shocking idea
and certainly you can't be surprised by it."

"I am not surprise'. But you give me pain."

"But—please look at me!" He grasped her hand tighter and waited
until her head turned slowly and she looked at him. "What do you
mean?"

"Perchè non capisci? Is so difficult? Is not for me the love like you
say, so *profondo* . . . for me is better something different. I have tell
you before, I do not want to become confuse'. I am so grateful, I feel
such a goodness for you, a goodness like you are. If you let me give you
pleasure, what I understand, I make you happy. If is love like you mean,
something so *grave*, I make you unhappy."

Her voice trembled and he turned sharply from thoughts of himself
to say, "You are tired, you've been standing too long. I didn't mean to
plague you, Renata, dear." He drew her hand through his arm and
began to walk slowly with her towards the house. "I was selfish, I
shouldn't have said that now, so soon, when you are still shaky."

"How you are good!"

"Let's not say that any more. I'd rather just feel—I don't know.
Perhaps time will make a difference. Anyway, you have to get well first.

I won't say another word until you can run everywhere the way you used to, instead of walk."

"You watch me close then," she said. Her old deviltry flared. "I run quick right after you."

He was not sure whether her contented settling down to rural life was a concession to her weak condition or a reversion to the habits of her childhood. He suspected the former, for whenever she saw some heavy piece of farm work under way she made a little mock shudder and said, "This we had to do *così*—" spreading her handsome, square-tipped fingers, "or *così*—" moving as if to lift a load onto her slender back.

"My land!" exclaimed Mrs. Maynard, when Renata did that, "you mean women do that kind o' hard work, too?"

"But yes! Why no?" Her brown eyes were full of surprise.

By the time she was strong enough to walk out over the fields, at whose spaciousness she was amazed, the corn was over a foot high and she was shocked at what she considered Tom Maynard's wastefulness. Three feet of rich loam lay between the rows. Renata could not understand, and at the noon dinner-table she asked why they wasted all that priceless land.

"In my *paese*," she said, "is planted the *grano turco*—you call corn? —between the grapes. We do not waste the precious ground," she said virtuously.

"Hanh? What's that? *Grapes* in the *corn*!" Tom Maynard sat with his mouth open, a forkful of food poised in the air. "Miss Tosi, you must be teched. How you goin' to get a horse and cultivator through there?"

"A what? A which?"

Randall looked at her and laughed and shook his head. Neither she nor Tom Maynard had the means—the vocabulary, the least grasp of another world's necessities and habits—to explain that they were not both crazy. They got along delightfully because nobody could resist Renata's laughter and her funny language and naturalness.

Randall was scarcely ever in New York now; the summer services at St. Timothy's required little preparation since the skeleton choir sang no special works. He was able to stay at the farm most of each week. The days went by, lovely rich June days, long, glowing evenings when the light lasted until after nine; exquisite fragrant nights. He was very careful of Renata, watching to see that she did not overdo, always ready with a light shawl in case the air should turn suddenly cool. They explored the farm and the surrounding countryside, the shores of the prosaic lake which only evoked from her the wish that he could see her native paradise—and in the next breath she laughed, "How I was fortunate to escape from there!"

"Weren't your relatives good to you, Renata?"

"They were good," she said thoughtfully, "but what means good, that depend on many things. For poor *contadini* is good a different thing from you, *per esempio*. You are good—and also rich," she sighed.

"No I'm not. Not at all."

"You have spend' such *ricchezze* upon me, is no use to deny."

"You don't know anything about it."

"I know very much. Is impossible conceal from a person like me. We always know."

"You did have a hard childhood."

"Not more, not less than the others. But my uncle Gandolfi, when my mother die he has already the many family. A fine, good man. He is like the *papà* for me, my zia Paola like the *mamma*. They are very good, very pious. But already they have the many sons and daughters, and this is not easy, you understand. Is not better I work in Milano?"

He indicated his doubt. "I should think the country—"

"Oh, no," she said with a little laugh. "I like too much enjoy the life. In the city is more—you know."

More opportunity, she meant. She had certainly made the most of hers. He was beginning to wonder uneasily how soon this existence would pall on her.

He was lying awake in bed late on a June night, his hands clasped behind his head, his eyes wide open, watching the full moon ride slowly, high past the top of the big maple tree outside his window. The sky had the live, warm luminosity of summer, and he felt warm and alive too, alive as he had never been before. But he was worried. He had not found a way to tell Renata what he had made up his mind to say; she had parried his few cautious beginnings and he was full of the increasing sense that not only could matters not stay as they were now; Renata would soon begin to be restless; he must seize the initiative. He was wondering what to do, how to appeal to her. His eyes had been circling the room; now he stiffened as they saw the door open slowly, very clear in the moonlight. There was not a sound. Renata came into the room, wrapped in a long pale robe. She shut the door noiselessly and walked lightly towards him. Her hair hung dark and long around her.

"Renata!" he whispered, drawing himself up. "You shouldn't be here."

She ignored that and sat down lightly on the edge of the bed. "You are not sleeping," she said, her voice so close to a whisper that she could not have been heard a foot away. "I do not sleep either."

She sat looking down at him, quite calm and quite as frank in her silence as in any words she had ever spoken.

"I wish you hadn't come in here," he said.

"No, that is childish. I come because I decide is ridiculous, how we are. Randalo," she said, putting her hand on his arm, "why you will not cease to be *così*? You are a man, I am—I. You do not like me?"

"Like you! Oh, my God." He flung his forearm across his eyes. "I love you desperately."

"*Non esagerare*. I tell you many times, is not wise, is not *prudente* be like that. *Basta* we enjoy together the pleasure, the *gioia*. Believe me, I know. I learn too much already. I would like to give you pleasure, because not only I like you, I am grateful. Is every reason why I am right."

He did not speak for a time, and then he moved his arm from his face and looked at her and said, "Renata, I want you too. But not in the way you say."

"Why no?"

"Would you even try to understand me? I don't want to touch you because—just because you *are* grateful. In fact—" he raised himself on his elbow and thrust his chin forward stubbornly. "I don't want you as my mistress. I want to marry you."

She drew away, with a hurt, blank expression. She thrust her fingers into the hair at her temples. "*Sei impossibile, tu!* Is impossible to content you. First, you say must be gone Baldini. Now is gone Baldini you say must be first the *matrimonio*. Why you don't understand I am not such a woman? I am honest, you should thank the God for it. Why you don't understand?" she said again.

"Because I love you. You might try to understand too. If I didn't

really love you I'd have—we'd have—had already what I had once before." He shut his mouth hard. "I didn't like it and I'm not cut out for
it."

"You are a man," she said quietly. "You don't want what wants a
man?"

He looked at her and she saw him struggling with some decision. Then
he said, his mouth nearly closed, "I want you so much right now that
I'm in agony. But I'm not going to take you except as my wife. I wish
you'd go away now, Renata. Go back to your room."

"I have never know' a man like you." Her voice was dull.

"Well, you know one now."

"But I do not," she said. "Why you think I will not marry you?
Because is too different, what you are and what I am. Will not make a
matrimonio, such a mixture, also you are a stranger."

"A stranger! Good God, Renata, after the past two months?"

"Yes, a stranger. Is so different your country, your *mondo*, is everything I am not. Also I tell you before, the marriage is *una responsabilità
tremenda* and I do not want. Even," she said, the protest going out of
her voice and a tenderness coming into it that he seldom heard, "I do
not want to hurt you. If I am a bad wife, I hurt you very much."

"You hurt me enough right now."

"That seem to me is your fault. But is *inutile* stay here and talk
like this." She bent close to him and laid her hand on his cheek.
"Randalo," she whispered. Her hair brushed his face and she saw his
jaw tighten. "You are sure I must go away now?"

"Yes." She heard him breathing very loud. "Go away. And think
about what I said. One of us has got to give in and I'm not going to.
If you do this again, I'll go away. You haven't really thought about
marrying me. Think about it enough to see if you won't change your
mind."

She shook her head a little and moved, saying, "Well, I try to think."

He would not look at her, he lay there turned away with his hand
covering his eyes. "Please marry me, Renata," he said, choking; "but
for God's sake go away now."

When she had gone he lay with tears on his cheeks, looking at the
closed door.

CHAPTER 13

On a lovely evening a few days later they were all sitting after supper, rocking on the farmhouse porch. Tom Maynard was resting after his heavy day, with his feet up on the porch railing, smoking his corncob pipe. Mrs. Maynard was hemming a tablecloth for the hope chest of her daughter, Emma, who was going to be married in the autumn. Renata too was sewing. She had surprised and delighted the Maynards by picking up one of the plain white petticoats for Emma's wedding outfit, and whipping onto it yards of pretty ruffling which she made lightning-fast by hand. When Mrs. Maynard asked where in the world she had learned to do that, Renata only winked at Randall. He was leaning back in his chair, silent and pondering what to do about the impasse he had created.

Renata, with other people about, was as lively, chattering, and funny as she had ever been before her illness. When she was alone with him she was subdued and distant. He was worried; the strain between them was increasing. He went out of his way now to avoid being alone with her. Times like this were better than the blank stretches of mid-morning and early afternoon, when everybody except the boarders was hard at work; and he had begun to dread the evenings after the Maynards had gone to their early bed. There were moments then when his hands ached to touch her, when he did not dare speak lest his voice gave him away. And sometimes she raised to him her dark, deepset, gentle eyes, full of bewildered chagrin and protest. Whatever was to come next, Randall doubted that she would want to stay here much longer.

Nobody was saying much; there were comfortable comments about the weather or the young stock or the coming Fourth of July fireworks on the village green; then there was a roar, a popping noise, and a great puffing somewhere beyond the bend of the road along the row of big elm trees. Randall held his breath and looked at the ends of his fingers. He heard Mrs. Maynard exclaim, "Land o' Jerusalem, what's *that*?" and as Tom Maynard got heavily to his feet, the scarlet Stevens-Duryea hove around the curve and stopped with a snort at the Maynards' mailbox. Renata's eyes grew round as saucers, her mouth dropped open, and she clapped her hands. Seymour sat high on his throne with the usual laughing lady in motoring costume perched beside him. Randall could have groaned as he recognized Marietta Pawling. The Maynards and their son Walt and Emma and her young man and the hired hands and Renata all stood in a row on the porch, staring and wondering. But Randall sat still. Seymour leaped down from his seat, lightly vaulting the gear and brake levers at his right, and started up the walk to the house. Randall sighed faintly, rallied his manners, and got up to go and meet Seymour. They shook hands affectionately.

"This is my brother, Seymour Holt," he said, and gravely named the row of wonder-struck faces along the porch, coming last to Renata whose eyes were dancing. Seymour greeted everybody with his usual elegant flair and said, "May I go and fetch Miss Pawling?" He presented Marietta, and Mrs. Maynard who, after years of city boarders, was used to anything short of automobiles, hospitably urged them to sit down.

Randall asked where they had come from, and when Seymour said, "From town," there was a chorus of incredulous questions.

"Oh, it didn't take so long," said Seymour. "We left at eleven this morning. I made pretty good time considering three punctures."

"How far you reckon it is by road?" Tom Maynard was still eyeing the red monster with suspicion and dislike.

"Just fifty-five miles. I'd have made better time if some of the roads hadn't been so bad." He smiled at Randall and said, "We thought we'd take you and Miss Tosi off somewhere for a jaunt tomorrow. My brother must have bored you to death by this time," he joked, turning to Renata.

"Oh, I am never bore'. Sometimes he is very serious, is true—" She tipped her chin towards Randall and gave him a wink that was a mixture of mischief and tenderness. "But we accept with pleasure, you agree, Randalo?"

"Why, yes. But where are you going to stop tonight, Seymour?"

"Well—" Seymour looked at Mrs. Maynard. "I wasn't sure there would be room here, but I just thought I'd find out when we arrived."

Mrs. Maynard said, "Might be a tight squeeze, but if you don't mind sort of squaring around I guess we can manage it. Emma, you move your things up to the loft and fix up your room for Miss Pawling.

And I s'pose you wouldn't mind doubling up with your brother, Mr. Holt? That's about the best we can do."

Randall watched Seymour, knowing how he loathed sharing a room. But Seymour beamed and said, "That would be fine. It's awfully good of you, isn't it, Ran?"

"Awfully," said Randall. "Thanks ever so much, Mrs. Maynard."

"And how about your supper?" asked Mrs. Maynard. "You wouldn't have had a chance to eat, driving that thing, would you?"

"Oh, we had a big luncheon at White Plains." Marietta Pawling turned from her inconspicuous scrutinizing of Renata to thank Mrs. Maynard. "I'm not a bit hungry, really."

"Well, Mr. Holt must be. I'll have something ready in a jiffy. There's cold fried chicken left, and cherry pie and lots of fresh buttermilk and a coconut cake. Come on, Emma." She went away. Randall did not trust himself to look at Seymour: cherry pie and coconut cake and buttermilk!

When they were going to bed Randall asked Seymour why he had not sent word that they were coming.

"I never thought of it. I just did it on the spur of the minute, I thought you'd be glad to see me."

"Oh, I am, Brother. But what about Marietta?"

Seymour gave a benevolent chuckle. "What can I do, Ran? She's all right if I keep my foot on her neck. You know. I told you, I'm fond of her. I threw one scare into her and it worked. She's been behaving herself ever since."

"You—you've—I mean—"

"I am still privy to her not inconsiderable favors, if that's what you're trying so tactfully to ask me. I must be getting old, I simply find her less trouble on that footing than on any other."

"Well, just see you don't try to palm her off on me again."

"On you!" Seymour widened his weak, milky-grey eyes. "You're sealed off in your paradise as if there were nobody else on the planet. She's enchanting, Ran. Absolutely bewitching." He did not expect, knowing his own instinct to hide emotion, and Randall's in lesser degree, that Randall would vouchsafe any measure of his feelings about Renata Tosi. But much less did he expect the sense of anxiety, of uncertainty and strain which he felt in Randall as surely as he could have smelled it had somebody been peeling an orange in the room.

What in God's name has gone wrong, he thought. If the boy hasn't settled into it in this feathered nest, he must be the clumsiest damn fool in Christendom. That was too cruel a verdict to believe; and whatever the truth might prove to be, it was already a challenge to Seymour's curiosity.

All the next day they laughed and bantered and bumped their way cross-country to Cold Spring and back. They chose Cold Spring because Seymour estimated that it would not make too long a trip; Randall had reminded him that Renata was not yet perfectly strong. They set off after breakfast with Tom Maynard's assurance that the weather could not possibly change today. It did change, of course; they were caught in a thunderstorm which would have drenched them to the skin except for Seymour's quickness in spotting an empty carriage-shed by the road and driving the car straight into it. They sat there listening to the rain pelt and rattle on the tin roof. It fell rhythmically in a certain pattern to which Renata was soon beating time, making a pompous, scowling face like a conductor. With her left hand she made florid gestures at imaginary instruments and when her pantomime introduction was unmistakable she made an equally unmistakable burlesque of the classic fat tenor and broke out, *"Bella figlia dell'amore"*, filling in the other voices as they came along and finally leaning towards Seymour to growl in a mock basso, *"Taci, il piangere non vale."* She patted him on the shoulder, nodding wisely.

She was so funny that she herself joined in the roars of laughter that drowned her out. Then they began asking her to sing this and that, and as she was recklessly in the mood she sat there singing like a bird in a tree. Anything, everything, snatches of *The Barber* and *Faust* and *Sonnambula* and *Lucia* and suddenly, fixing her eyes on Randall, she began to sing *Vissi d'arte*. She sang with a warm, pulsating urgency he had never known in her before, her head thrown back, her expression intent. In the cramped shed her delicate voice took on richness and volume. Seymour and Marietta Pawling in the front seat were turned to watch her, he with a fascinated glaze in his half-closed eyes, she frankly open-mouthed. She had never heard a fine singer before. Randall was tense and very stirred. He wished he were alone with her. The presence of the others was a rude intrusion. Her pleading, her phrasing even more poignant than the pitifully appealing words, went through him like a chill. Nobody spoke when she finished. The last perfect notes echoed in their ears. Then as Seymour and Marietta Pawling began to clamor their appreciation she said to Randall under her breath, "*Hai capito?* You have understood the words?"

He only looked at her and said, "I thought you said you'd never learn *Tosca.*"

"*Vero!*" she cried delightedly. "*Non mi piace lavorare. Ecco!*—I call you out the sun!"

And she had—the sun was shining into the shed and every trace of the storm had vanished, leaving a washed, brilliant blue sky and the delicious pungency of wet earth and leaves and grass. Seymour set the spark and the hand throttle and switched the magneto and felt carefully to make certain that the gear was in neutral, and with a hearty, "Get set, everybody!" he jumped down and went round in front to crank. The motor turned over with a pop and a roar, and they all held their breaths while Seymour skilfully and carefully backed out of the narrow shed and manoeuvred round into the road again.

"We're off!" he cried, and they rolled and jounced and slithered away through the film of mud churned up by the rain on the dirt road. Renata was fascinated, she sat up very straight eagerly looking to this side and that, her charming face with its laughing brown eyes like a bright light between the folds of the chiffon veil tied under chin.

"Is *bello*, no, Marietta?" she cried. She had already said there could be no such name as Poll-ling, it sounded like something to do with the poultry business and Marietta was a pretty, civilized name that anybody could pronounce. So this put them all on a first-name footing and at lunch in the hotel at Cold Spring, in a bay-window overlooking the splendid view of West Point down the river, Renata asked, "I cannot understand for what saints are such names like yours? Si-morr! Randalo! In America exist such saints?"

The brothers shook with laughter. "We aren't named for saints, Renata," said Randall, and Seymour said, "We'd be a fine travesty of the poor chaps if we were."

"But what is? What mean such names?"

"They are family names, last names—"

"*Cognomi?*" she asked, frowning a little.

"Yes," said Seymour. "That's it. Family names."

"You mean your own family is full of saints? Must be everybody saints to make enough names!"

Marietta Pawling was giggling.

"Look at her," said Renata. "She has a name like a Christian, taken from the *Santa Vergine*. Is no nonsense about saints in her family!"

Seymour guffawed into his napkin.

After lunch they went out on the porch of the hotel and strolled up and down and Seymour, finding himself beside Renata, answered her questions about the turreted fortress across and down the river. When she learned what it was her eyes danced and she said, *"Oh! che bello!* So many beautiful young men! Must be wonderful."

She heard Randall sigh hopelessly behind her. "I like very much the beautiful young men," she rattled on. "Like *i nostri carabinieri*—such a *bellezza* you cannot imagine."

Randall was explaining awkwardly to Marietta that Italian adjectives were very different from English ones.

"Oh, I think she's killing," said Marietta. "I never saw anybody like her."

"Neither did I," said Randall heavily.

Renata turned and looked over her shoulder at Randall. Then she said in an undertone to Seymour, "I think Randalo he is the most beautiful man I have ever seen."

Seymour gave her a look. "I trust he knows you think so?" he murmured.

"He is—" she moved her shoulders delicately. "Very young. Too serious."

"I would hate to see him hurt." Seymour contrived to speak tonelessly.

"I too. I have tell him so. I have try' explain many things."

"I see."

"You understand, *anche*?"

"Perfectly." They were strolling round the corner of the wide veranda and he looked once into her eyes. They were not laughing now; they were also not serious; they were communicating in a direct and definite language. "I should say we understand one another very well."

They got back to the farm at nightfall, having been stopped twice on the way by punctured tires which Seymour had patched with skill, and what they all told him was remarkable good humor.

"I would never have the *pazienza* for all that trouble," said Renata; and Seymour, jacking up the car and looking coolly at the three figures standing in the muddy road, said, "Have you got much patience about anything?"

Renata was yawning at supper, unaccustomed to such a long day and so much company. She appeared not to be listening while tomorrow's plans were discussed, but she found herself surprised when Randall said, "No, thanks, Seymour, I can't ride back to town with you and Marietta tomorrow because I always have to go over the music on Friday afternoons. You wouldn't get there in time."

"Well, we'd have been glad to have you along."

Renata had forgotten that tomorrow was Friday and that Randall always took the morning train to New York. She looked up and said, "I think I go to New York with you tomorrow, Randalo."

"Why Renata! What for?"

"I must buy some things to make me clothes, something for summer. I come from Italy not prepared." She flipped her hand at the sleeve of her blouse. "I am tired of these few, I wear them too much."

Randall was surprised and also, he found, somewhat troubled. Why should she decide so suddenly that she needed summer clothes? She did need them, she had been makeshifting all this time, but she had not seemed to mind it before. He was apparently right in suspecting that she was beginning to be bored here.

"Then *you* can ride in with us," said Marietta. She said it only to please Seymour, which she was sure it would; she would much have preferred to be alone with him.

Renata considered for a moment and then said, "No, is very *gentile*, thank you—also Simorr—" for he had seconded the invitation. "But I think is better I go in the train with Randalo. *Così* I can make the shoppings in the afternoon, also on Saturday, and I do not grow too tired."

Seymour dropped them next morning at the railway station before starting the trip back to New York. Randall went inside to buy the tickets, and Seymour helped Renata down and escorted her to the platform, leaving Marietta in the car. "I'll be right back," he said to her.

"Where will you be stopping in town?" he asked Renata, walking to the platform.

She named the hotel that Randall had chosen for her when she left the hospital.

"If I can do anything for you—" Seymour spoke gravely.

"Oh, thank you. Only I may require some things from my trunks which Randalo sent to your house."

"I will come and fetch you after lunch tomorrow," he said.

"But where is your automobile?" she asked Seymour next day, emerging from her hotel. She pronounced the word in Italian.

"I am having some work done on it." He had thought it better not to drive up to the house with Renata in the car. They took a taxicab instead, and when they arrived at the Holt house, Seymour paused on the pavement as the cab drove away. He saw the whole place, the bleak blind-windowed house, the drab yard, the scaling paint, the rusty iron gratings, as they must appear to Renata's surprised eyes.

"I'm afraid it's an ugly place," he said. "And rather a queer one. We keep most of it shut up, you see, because Randall and I live here all alone and we couldn't possibly use all the rooms." They were walking up the front path, between the plots of sparse, weedy, gritty grass.

"Naturally. But why you don't rent many rooms? Never I have seen a house so large just for two people. In Italy is no such thing like this in a city."

Such a thought had never entered Seymour's head. "Why—I don't know," he said. "It never occurred to us. But I don't think we'd like to be all surrounded with roomers. Our house would be like all those others—" he gestured back at the rundown mansions on both sides of the street. "Anyway—" he took out his latchkey and opened the front door. "Please don't mind how it looks. We're hardly ever here."

"I told Randalo last night you have been so kind to offer to bring me here for my things today while he was working."

"Yes, he spoke about it this morning. He said he'd be home by five o'clock." Seymour stepped aside and bowed her into the house. The dim, musty hall was a strange contrast to the brassy summer sun outside; Renata blinked, trying to adjust herself to the darkness and Seymour stood for a moment revelling in the relief to his eyes. He put his hat on the rack and turned to open the drawing-room door.

"The trunks are here," he said, and lied, "I had them brought here from the storage room to make it more convenient for you."

"Ah, thank you very much." She advanced into the room, eyeing it curiously. In her sweeping black-and-white striped gown and her big hat trimmed with roses she was an incongruous sight against the streaked, ragged wallpaper, the dingy woodwork, the swagged plush curtains, the tufted magenta upholstery, the Brussels carpet, all threadbare. She was puzzled, Seymour could see. On the one hand she had concluded, between Randall's generosity and Seymour's automobile, that they must be millionaires. On the other, what could they be doing in a place like this? Real poverty would not confound her, nothing on earth was more familiar; but this was not poverty, real or simulated. This was something else, which she could not understand. It was also not like her to brood about anything. She turned cheerfully to Seymour and said, "It will not take me long to find the things I need."

"No," he said, standing close to her and looking down, from his two inches of height greater than Randall's, at her vivid face. At this moment it bore an expression of mischief; her lips were set in a remote smile and her slender, slanting nostrils flared faintly. She did not raise her eyes and look at him. But she did look at the hideous old tombstone clock on the mantel, which still ran, still timing Randall's practice hours. Seymour said, "I told Randall I would bring you here about four o'clock."

It was not yet three. Renata laughed and walked lightly across the room and sat down on the high-backed Victorian divan, shabby like everything else in the room. Seymour stood with his elbow on the mantel, looking at her.

"Of course you are an irresistibly fascinating woman," he said.

She made as if mockingly to pull her features into a serious expression and said, pointing to the piano in the corner, "This is where Randalo practise? This is his piano?"

Seymour nodded. "I'm afraid he practises, or used to, too much."

"Is true. I tell you, he is too serious. It is not—" she changed her remark to a question. "Is good for a young man? I ask you!"

"As I said, you are extraordinarily fascinating and I am afraid Randall doesn't know how to—shall we say, appreciate it?"

"Randalo is good like the God. But a child."

"And you are not quite the plaything for a child?" He strolled across the room and sat down beside her on the divan.

"What you think?"

"Oh," he said, "I make a great point of never thinking."

She gave a small laugh and said, "Italian men do not think either. A man beautiful like Randalo in my country—!"

"Such a man wouldn't have Randall's virtues, either. He would only want pleasure."

"And who does not?" Her eyes opened wide. "What kind of man is it you describe?—or what woman?"

"Anyway—"

"Anyway." She looked at him with frank curiosity. "I wonder."

After a silence he said, "You are surely not wondering if I am like my brother?"

"All Americans."

"You could try and see."

"I could?" Her eyebrows rose. Her hand lay on the divan and he picked it up and turned its palm to his lips. Presently she raised her other hand to the back of his head. They did not speak again, absorbed in the exchange of subtle pleasures. Light tentative caresses were followed by greater, and those by a graceful, melting motion which joined their figures prone on the divan. Half an hour passed. When they spoke again, Seymour was sitting in one of the low parlor chairs, smoking one of his Turkish cigarettes. Renata, casually making order of her hair and costume before the glass over the mantel, smiled at him with approval as he said, "You do know how to give pleasure."

"Is true," she said, "and *perchè no?* Also I like to enjoy."

"Your frankness could be disconcerting, you know."

"But not to you!"

"Oh, to me!" He took off his heavy glasses which he had only a moment ago put on, and polished them with his handkerchief. "I am hard to embarrass, Renata."

"I too. But I want no problem, this could very easy become one."

"Not," said Seymour, tweaking his moustache, "if we chose to consider this episode forgotten. A moment, isolated, you know—"

She turned from the mirror, pretty and dainty and very self-possessed.

"*Vediamo,*" she said lightly. "What has nothing to do with nothing else—"

"Naturally that is my own view too. But—" he made a gesture at the room and shook his head. She nodded and laughed shortly and tilted her chin, saying, "I am sure you are clever. Already you prove—" she broke off and took from her purse the keys to her trunks and went over to unlock them and begin to find the things she wanted.

Randall came in a little before five o'clock. Renata was packing into a suitcase the things she had sorted out and Seymour was still sitting in the tufted chair smoking cigarettes. Renata turned to Randall with a delighted smile and seemed almost about to embrace him.

"*Ah, eccoti!*" she cried. "How is, in your *chiesa pagana*?"

"Cooler than anywhere else, thank goodness." Randall looked at the things she had strewn about and asked, "Can I help you?"

"Oh no, *caro*, thank you is nearly finish'. What we do this evening?" she asked, including both brothers in her question which assumed that there was some plan to include them all. Seymour answered, "The car should be ready by now. I'll go and get it and pick up Marietta and we'll drive somewhere for dinner."

"*Benissimo*," said Renata. "I like Marietta. She is your *amante*, no?—" she asked Seymour. Randall made a sign of despair for her lack of reticence. "Your mistress?"

Seymour laughed noisily. "I must say," he said to Randall, "*your* lady is a caution."

Renata seemed glad to return to the farm on Sunday night. Walt Maynard met them at the station and drove them home under a darkly starlit sky. The air was delicious after the steaming cauldron of New York, but Randall had already remarked how little that seemed to bother Renata. "Is like Milano," she shrugged. She sat contentedly in the wagonette, her hand in Randall's, like that of a child. She had been very sweet in the train, perhaps a little tired, he thought, but gentler and less flippant than usual. He wondered if she had really given any serious thought to his plea. Perhaps it was a good thing that she and Seymour appeared to have hit it off so well. Almost every word she said in his presence and Marietta's kept them rocking with laughter. She adored the wonderful scarlet motor car and the excursions it made possible. Randall would have liked to keep her to himself all summer at the Maynards' farm but he had never believed she would stay in retreat so long. If she must have gaiety and convivality, better they all have it together.

The next evening, when he and Renata were alone after the Maynards had gone to bed, he was surprised when she asked, "Randalo, tell me, why is so strange your big house in the city?"

"How do you mean, strange?" he asked. The question made him uncomfortable.

"Oh—is not necessary explain. I have seen it was once very *elegante*, but is now so—I don't know what is. For somebody else would be poor, but you and the Simorr, you are not poor."

Randall wondered what to tell her, and decided on the truth. He explained about their grandmother's will and their intention to leave the house as soon as possible without having wasted a penny on repairing it or anything in it. Renata considered for a moment and then said, "Well. Perhaps you are right. But is so strange leave a rich property go in ruin. In Italy would nobody do such a thing."

"Well, we can't help it, Renata dear. She was a very peculiar old woman and we have no control over what becomes of the house. We both hate it and we hated her. That's why—" he took her hand and drew it through his arm and said, watching her face, "Look at me, Renata. Please." She turned her head and gave him a vague, patient smile. "That's why I want—you know what I want. A life of my own. Someone to live for, to love. I love you," he said timidly, afraid that she would spring away again at the mention of the word. Instead she sat quite still. Then she put her hand softly on his cheek and said, "*Abbi pazienza*. Do not say this again, Randalo. I have promise' think what you ask me. Until now I cannot be different from what I said. You are so good," she murmured, shaking her head sadly. "Why you want the only thing I am not prepare' to give?"

"But can I hope?" he pleaded. "Why do you go on—like this—without any other plans—" he stumbled on, trying to express himself and terrified lest she take offense. "Unless you—want to be with me—in some way?"

"I want," she said simply. "I told you."

"And I told you. I am too much in love with you to think of you as—" he made a motion as if to describe Seymour's concept of women. "Don't shut your mind to it. Will you at least let me hope?" he pleaded.

She sighed and hung her head and because she gave no audible answer he told himself that he had received an unspoken one. He held her hand to his cheek and kissed its soft sunbrowned skin, and presently she turned her head and kissed him gently on the mouth. He put his arm round her and drew her head to his shoulder and sat for a while in the dark without moving.

But a few days later, as the week end was approaching, she said, "Randalo, I think would be a good idea I move now to New York."

Though this was not unexpected, he felt as if a hammer had struck him. "Why, dear?" he asked, which was a stupid thing, he knew, to say.

As usual she was perfectly honest. "Because I begin to be bore' here."

"Bored with me?"

"*Ma no, caro*! But is here very far from the life, the *divertimento*. Look how much trouble is we make a little trip on Wednesday." It had been; they had gone by train to White Plains where Seymour and Marietta had met them with the automobile, and they had returned the same way because Seymour dared not make many runs as far as here on account of his tires. "If we are in New York, is possible do many amusing things."

"I was afraid you'd soon be getting bored alone with me here."

"But I am not alone with you! Not even like I have offer'. If is to be with you among others, is more amusing your brother and his *amante* than these *contadini* here."

Randall said wearily and with uncharacteristic irritation, "There are no peasants in America, Renata."

But he could not prevent her going, and perhaps it was as well. He would have extra work to do in August while Dr. Fitzhugh was away, and if she was content to remain in New York, he would be nearer to her that way than otherwise. He said, "Where would you want to go in New York? To the Hotel Westwood again?"

She looked doubtful. "I think is expensive, no?"

"But—well, what difference does that make?" He looked at her with the silent assurance that he expected to go on taking care of her until— until what? He had not yet dared ask himself plainly. Would she one day capitulate and marry him? And if not, she had her profession, by which she could very well support herself. But she surprised him by saying, "I have a little money, Randalo. I would like now not be so—" she smiled ruefully. "So to depend on you. Already you have done so much, *Dio mio*!" As they had before, tears welled into her eyes; she seized his hand and said with passionate sincerity, "Nobody was ever good and *generoso* like you. You are an angel."

"Well," he said awkwardly. "You seem to overlook the happiness it gives me. And if you did save some money last winter you hadn't expected to use it up this summer. You thought you'd be working. I wish you'd just keep it, Renata, it makes me feel you're safer."

"*Vediamo allora,*" she said. "I would like a little apartment—" she astonished him by blushing, which resolved into a peal of laughter and her flinging herself on his neck with a hug. "I start to say 'like in Ansonia' but then I feel ashame' because you were so shock' about Baldini. But now," she cried, like a child delighted with a new discovery, "is my Randalo no better than Baldini! *Ecco*! I find such a little apartment which I like and I pay what I can and you—" she waved her hand with a wink. "Maybe I make you my *amante* yet."

"Oh, Renata." Randall shook his head and tenderly pushed her away. "Maybe I'll make you my wife. One is beginning to look as unlikely as the other."

CHAPTER 14

Seymour moved, luxuriously deliberate, from the wide bed to a chair nearby, and sat down, stretching his long legs. He clasped his hands behind his head and gave himself the pleasure of looking at Renata, slightly propped on her pillows, with her dark hair falling round her shoulders. She was smiling a little, with a sensuous twist to her lips. Her brown eyes, deep-set below the low white forehead, were mischievous.

"Is the pity you cannot smoke," she said. "You would enjoy it now."

"My Turkish tobacco is both pungent and lasting," he said. "For the first I can accept a more piquant substitute and for the second—" he laughed a little. "You are extraordinary, Renata, something too delightful. I suppose you know it?"

She shrugged. "I have heard. Is very nice you think so. I am please' too. You please me very much."

The mid-afternoon sun was gratefully shut out by the drawn blinds, and Seymour enjoyed the special pleasure of looking at Renata when his eyes were not assaulted by strong light, either out of doors in the automobile, or indoors in the brightly lit places where they all dined together on most evenings. He reached round and felt for his spectacles in the breast pocket of his coat hanging on the back of his chair. He wiped the spectacles carefully and put them on; "The better to see you, my dear," he joked, like a Nannie telling the story of Red Riding Hood.

"I have observe' many times," said Renata, "you have not the strong eyes. Is something grave the matter with them?"

"No," he said, with a mocking downward turn of his mouth. "Of course not. Just a little myopia, you know, and it makes them a bit sensitive to light." ('And you will be well advised to be more careful of exposure to strong light, Mr. Holt. This is not the first time I have warned you. It can be as destructive as close application. The prognosis is increasingly unsatisfactory.') He rammed the raw, recent memory back into its dungeon and turned a cool smile on Renata. In that moment her expression had become serious. "Please don't give it a thought. I never do," he assured her.

"I was no more thinking of that," she said. "Is very *noioso* when somebody worry, and I wish not to be like that." She pursed her pretty lips and peaked her eyebrows in a vivid reflection of doubt.

"I should guess, then, that you are worrying about Randall?"

She nodded a little sadly. "With the words, you understand, we can do no good. What is so, is so. Only I have always the frighten he will be hurt."

"One calculates one's risks, my dear."

"*D'accordo.* But what begin with a single *giuoco* take sometimes not many comedies to make a tragedy."

"Well?" Seymour raised his straggling pale eyebrows and looked at her with cynical inquiry. "If you wish—of course I should regret—"

"Oh, you make seem so complicate'. Is not what I meant. Is not right I marry Randalo like he want. Who understand better than you?"

"Who indeed? I think you are enchanting but I don't want you for a sister-in-law. You oughtn't to marry anybody."

"You see. Is true. I am like—like this." She spread her hands. "But would be so sad the pity if this hurt Randalo after all his goodness. I am so grateful to him!"

"Which is distressingly different from other attitudes that Randall cannot understand. I am just as concerned about him as you are. He would be smashed to bits if he should learn about something which actually—though he could never believe it—can do him no more harm than if he had never known the people involved."

"Is a *pericolo tremendo.*"

"As I said, a calculated risk. How much pleasure do you want, and what are you prepared to pay for it? Or do you prefer to repay Randall's devotion, so long as you do not break with him, by turning celibate—which is your only alternative unless you marry him?"

"Would be easier not see none of you any more," she said abruptly.

"Easier, no doubt. But kind to Randall?"

"*Taci!*" she cried, seizing her head between her hands. "Is too confuse'."

"I should think we might simply be prudent enough not to do any stupidities and in time—" he shrugged and she laughed.

"Time change everything," she agreed wisely. But she said, "Is also another *pericolo* you must think." She raised a forefinger and shook it slowly.

"Oh," he said.

"*Sì, la Marietta.* If you do the least *stupidaggine* she become suspicious, *poi* follow something *orribile*."

"My dear, you must think me really clumsy."

"You are clever, *davvero*? You make her the love very often, you keep her well satisfy? If no, she become *gelosa* and make the terrible mischief."

Seymour chuckled. "I like a clever woman, Renata," he said, unfolding his lean length from the chair. "You are a delicious devil." He sat down on the edge of the bed, and bent his head to her throat.

"Is too bad I dare not please you with the skin *molto profumata*," she murmured. "But this would remark immediately the Marietta."

"The nose police," said Seymour, laying aside his spectacles.

"*Appunto.*" She smiled lazily and flicked his long moustache with her finger.

That morning after Seymour had left the house Randall took a bunch of keys from a concealed compartment in the black walnut secretary-bureau in Seymour's room. He went up to the fourth floor to the old day-nursery. He unlocked the door and went into the room and locked the door again from inside. The atmosphere was suffocating. On a blazing August day like this any closed room would be cooler than the scorching heat out of doors. But the least motion stirred up a cloud of acrid dust, which settled and stuck to one's damp skin on a hot day. In winter when he came occasionally to this room the mouldy chill turned his lips and fingers blue, and the smell of the mildewed wallpaper, its pattern long since unrecognizable, was sickening. In summer the damp dried out, leaving crumbling plaster and streaks of dry greenish fuzz on the walls. Randall believed he had thoroughly hardened himself against concern about this; in fact, his attitude when he came here was defiant, as if to tell the place repeatedly that he and Seymour were almost through with it, almost ready to consign it forever to its corruption.

He went to the rickety wardrobe in the corner, whose key he kept always on his own watch-chain with several others, and he opened it. Inside, face against the back of the wardrobe, was his old child's desk.

He turned that around and unlocked its drop lid and took from his inside pocket a bundle of papers. He glanced them quickly through, a mixture of receipted bills from hospital and hotel and doctors and the Maynards, his bank statement and other financial papers at which he never looked when they came; the usual bundle of music-manuscript paper minutely covered with his miniature handwriting. He rolled the lot together and thrust it tightly into a section of the desk and stuck a couple of childhood animal-tracings in front of it. Then he locked the desk and replaced it face backwards in the wardrobe and locked that too, and with a glance round to make sure that nothing appeared to have been disturbed, he left the room, carefully locking the door behind him, and started down the stairs.

On the third-floor landing he stopped at the door of his mother's room. Something had been going through his mind for weeks, rising almost to the point of his accepting it, then being thrust away, back down into the turbid vault where the bad memories of two and three years ago were sealed. Other and older memories were there too, and among these the impediment which had stopped him on the few occasions when he had been on the verge of talking to Seymour about Renata. It should be infinitely simple to state that he wanted to marry her. But in some deeply disturbing way, the wish lost its simplicity on the brink of telling it to Seymour, and became entangled in murky memories of trouble and cruelty. If he should search closely enough in this morass he had a dim fear of coming up with the startling fragment of Seymour's resemblance to their grandmother. It was not even a real resemblance, there was only a suggestion. But that was enough to remind him that one could never have thought of telling Grandmama that one wanted to marry. Must he hover now over a dead and buried fear—merely because Seymour's jaw happened to have a certain length and angularity? He sat down on the top step and put his chin in his hands and stayed there thinking for a long time.

Then he stood up and shut his mouth hard and chose a key from the bunch and unlocked the door. He had never been here since that afternoon when he had railed and protested to Seymour, and had been led shivering back to his room. He would not be here now, except he had come arduously to his decision and he intended to effect it. He was going to choose a piece from among his mother's bits of modest jewelry and take it to Renata and plead with her upon this talisman, which could not help but touch her heart, to give up her reservations and marry him. His hand shook as he opened the door, and the courage to enter the room almost failed him. He forced himself to take a few steps inside, and then he had to stop, because his way was blocked. He stood still, hiding his face in his hands for a moment. All of this took so much courage, all of it demanded so inexorably the facing of everything that he had learned, painfully, deviously, not to face. He remembered his mother hovering and whimpering through the last clouded years of her life, and earlier he remembered himself, frightened of everything in his little world except her, clinging to her over there on that divan where they used to look at the old memory-books and albums, listening all the while for the old woman's pounding step and thundering voice.

He raised his head with a faint groan, and began to clamber his way across the room, pushing or lifting aside boxes and cases and parcels whose ancient paper and brittle ribbons fell apart at a touch. The ravages of moths were everywhere; no bit of wool, no cuff or tippet of now unrecognizable fur, was anything but bare brittle leather or a crumbling mess of holes. Oh, he thought, we must clean it out, we must, we must, we should carry it down and make a great fire in the boiler and burn it all and leave her memory clear.

He inched and twisted his way to the high rosewood bureau, and lit the gas-jet above it, and began carefully to search for the mother-of-pearl inlaid box that he remembered, where she used to keep her trinkets. He found it quite soon. Poignant memories stabbed him as he sorted through the things; this cameo brooch she always wore on Sundays; that pair of onyx earrings set with seed-pearls when she dressed her hair as he had liked it best, very high. Piece by piece he turned the things over. Her only valuable jewel had been the big diamond which had bought his piano downstairs; he looked across at its predecessor dumb in the corner, whose felts had surely all been eaten away; and he thought of the burnt hulk down in Seymour's warren in the cellar, of the defiant boy glaring at the old woman and roaring, "I DON'T KNOW."

"I don't know either," Randall sighed, looking for an instant into the crackled greenish looking-glass. "I don't know anything, least of all why we are as we are." Distorted though it was, the face in the glass was handsome and even had he not thought so before, he reflected that Renata with all her flippancy had made him believe it. But it was a long time since she had said he was beautiful; perhaps she was learning. She was quieter and gentler and more serious when she was alone with him. Dare he hope that this meant the change he had been praying for? He turned back to the inlaid box and after much deliberation he decided upon a small brooch in the shape of a butterfly, of deep blue enamel, embellished with tiny stones and seed-pearls. It was charming and surely a butterfly was the perfect symbol for Renata. He found a worn purple velvet jewelry-box and shut the butterfly in it and put it in his pocket. As he did so, he thought he should probably make sure that Seymour had no objection to his doing this; then he rejected the question altogether and, to his own surprise, angrily. He turned out the gas and worked his way to the door again, and making sure that everything was as nearly as possible as he had found it, he locked the door and went away.

On most mornings, instead of practising he went to see Renata, but as this was Friday he went straight from the house to St. Timothy's. In Dr. Fitzhugh's absence he had a full day preparing the Sunday music. August was deadly in a city church; the Rector and Fitzhugh and two-thirds of the choir and almost all the congregation were away, but the services must continue no matter how few straggling souls rattled about the empty church. The two curates and Randall were left to make the best of it and of the other duties which had been assigned them. One of these was to make the arrangements for the annual Church Picnic, which took place on Staten Island in September to mark the opening of the Sunday School year.

Against the realities of his anguished suspense about Renata, of flamboyant expeditions in Seymour's motor car, of dinners and suppers in racy places with hilarious company, the church picnic seemed the last straw of implausibility. Five months ago he would have thought it important. Now it was absurd except to the degree that it piqued his conscience. It was hard enough to try steadily and doggedly to win Renata; it was made twice as hard with Seymour and Marietta Pawling constantly inciting her love of frivolity.

Yet, he thought, at half-past five, ringing the bell of the little flat that she had sub-leased from an opera colleague, she was a good deal changed when she was alone with him. It could not be his imagination that she was gentler and quieter, he remembered too vividly her flaunting ways only a short time ago. She still crackled with mischief when the four of them were together, she still teased Randall and waited, the cat with the mouse, for his protesting blush and Seymour's snorting laughter. Fingering the velvet box in his pocket, he thought again, she is different, really different. She opened the door and greeted him. There, you see? he asked himself. Her voice is different, too—affectionate—tender.

"*Caro!*" she said. "How you are? Is hot, no?"

The little flat was in perfect order, the blinds raised and the windows open to catch the bit of breeze from the east. Renata looked fresh as a strawberry blossom, dressed in a flowered muslin gown that she had made, frothing with her beloved ruffles. Her bright brown hair rose in springy waves from her forehead, piled high on her head. Randall held her hand to his cheek for a moment.

"You are tired," she said. "*S'accomodi*, take here the nice chair by the window. I bring you a *bevanda*."

He leaned back in his chair, listening to her hum while she chipped ice in the kitchenette. Presently she brought him a glass of Campari with ice and seltzer and a twist of lemon peel. She had a second glass for herself. She put it down on a stand beside her chair and sat down near him and took up her sewing again. He watched her.

"You really sew beautifully, don't you, Renata?"

"*E perchè no?* Is not it please me so much, but is like the second nature. Is not worth go to a *sarta* make me things like this—" she fingered her new dress. "When must be *molto elegante*, is different."

"You always look elegant to me."

"Like you," she said, with a sidelong glance as if to see how far she dare go. "Always—you look like what to me, Randalo? Guess!"

He shook his head. "I'm not in the mood for that. I'm sorry I couldn't come this morning. Have you had a very long day all alone?"

"Oh, no," she said. "Was no bad. Sometimes I like to remain alone—when I know is only for a short time."

"So you don't want to remain alone all the time."

"*Per carità!* I?"

"Well, neither do I." He put down his glass and looked at her so meaningly that her hands dropped to her lap. She sat silent, then she made an awkward effort and said lightly, "Who say you are alone? You have your brother who is *molto divertente* and give you always the company. Now we have all together very often much amusement—" she paused. He wondered if she had been about to ask if that was not enough to satisfy him.

He said, "Renata, don't talk a lot of nonsense. You understand exactly what I mean even when I don't say a word." She was silent. He leaned forward and put his hand on her forearm and sat looking at her until she raised her head and looked him in the eyes. "I *am* alone," he said slowly. "You can surround me with all the brothers in Christendom and all the tomfool things you all think of to do. I do them too because I want to be with you. But that still leaves me alone, do you understand? Utterly alone. Unless you marry me."

She sat there with her brown eyes gentle and tender, yet baffling. He tried to find in them some clue, some sign by which to hope that he had moved her. Many times before he had looked into those eyes so deeply set under classically-modelled brows, and many times he had wondered at the sculptural fineness of the high, straight nose, suggesting a contradiction of her peasant birth. But he had learned that when she wanted to make her eyes inscrutable it was useless to search them; and so she looked now.

"Why do you make it so hard!" he cried suddenly, as if a gash had been torn in the difficult web of restraint behind which she forced him to hover. She sighed heavily; words for this sort of talk came very hard to the irrepressible chatterbox.

"I suppose I know what you're thinking," he said unhappily. "We've been all over this endless times before and you're tired of saying the same thing over and over again. But so am I! Don't you see—I can't go on like this? Where is it getting us?"

She had bent her head and because he wanted to make her look at him again he slid from his chair and sat down on the floor close to her, close enough to reach under her chin with his fingers and gently raise her face until he could see her eyes again. But they told him, if he could bring himself to believe it, even less than before.

"If I didn't know you so well," he said rather bitterly, "I'd think you are just being cruel to me."

"That would be impossible," she muttered. "To you—?"

"Then—then—" He reached into his pocket and took out the threadbare velvet box. "I've got something here that—oh, God!" he said, trying to control his voice. "*Please* understand!" He opened the box and took out the little butterfly. He held it on the palm of his hand and said, "It was my mother's, Renata. She used to wear it sometimes when she was young and pretty, before—" he drew a long breath and said with difficulty, "before her life became something that—something very sad, dearest Renata. Something pitiful . . . tragic." He tried again to keep his voice level. She saw the butterfly trembling on his hand. His blue eyes were glassy, suffused with tears. He said, "Don't let such a thing happen to me too. Sometimes I'm afraid it will, if you won't marry me." He gave up the struggle with himself and hid his face, in tears, in her lap. He felt her hand touch his hair, a touch of infinite, lightness, benign, remote. After a time he looked up and took her hand and laid the butterfly into it. "For her sake," he said, almost whispering. "Say you will." He held her hands clasped between his, intently watching her face. He saw a deep blush travel slowly from the ruffles of her collar, up her slender neck and her face towards the roots of her hair. For this he had no precedent, he could not understand it, nor the unspoken phrase in Italian which moved her silent lips. He waited, holding his breath and gripping her hands. She did not speak and finally he had to beg her to.

"I don't know what to say," she said slowly. "I am very move'. I am not *degna*—you say, worth—?"

"Oh, no. Worthy has nothing to do with it. Only what you are to me. I love you, I need to love you. I need you. But in my own way, Renata. I know there are other ways, I don't want to hear another word about them. I only want my answer from you."

Suddenly she gasped and burst into tears. This he had never known her to do; she sobbed helplessly, with the abandon of a child. He got to his knees and took her in his arms and held her tightly, and she wept with her head in his shoulder, until her sobs began to subside and he took the handkerchief from her belt and gently wiped her eyes and her cheeks. He blotted them with the handkerchief and then with his lips, covering her face with tender, adoring kisses. When she was quiet again she said, "*Almeno* I feel is no longer possible leave this like before, *tutto sospeso*. Randalo, *caro amico*, tell me—you would suffer also we do not see each other not any more?"

"Oh, my God," he breathed, wincing.

"But also I make you suffer. Also you make me suffer, is so difficult such a decision. You do not know how difficult!" she exclaimed, as if to a third person, and left him wondering. *"Senti,"* she said. "I am finally convince' is impossible not decide never. *Hai ragione.* Also is impossible, like before, decide now, today. Maybe would be better not be together but—" they both shook their heads helplessly. "What you say," she asked speaking very slowly, "if I promise give you the answer in three months?" She did not wait for him to comment, she went on, thinking as she spoke, saying, "In three months I promise is definite everything. Either I agree to marry you or we all agree not meet together no more, nobody, none of us. *Così,* if I must do that, *almeno* is no surprise. No shock. You can agree, Randalo?"

He sat looking at her helplessly. He tried to say something and failed, and said, miserably, "What else can I do?"

She leaned forward and kissed him on the forehead. She took his right hand and put the butterfly carefully into it and folded his fingers round the brooch. *"Intanto* this remain with you. In three months if I can feel I deserve, you give it to me then."

One day early in the following week they spent the afternoon at Brighton Beach at the races and afterwards dined at the adjoining hotel. Marietta Pawling had a passion for races and was avid for all gambling. Renata had enjoyed the excitement and the crowds and the splendid view of the ocean. Now, on the glassed-in terrace overlooking the beach, she gestured at the surf-capped breakers and the Atlantic horizon, and said, "Is very *imponente,* but I can enjoy only from a distance comfortable like this."

Seymour's face expressed mock exasperation. He turned to Randall. "Can't you appeal to her?" he asked. "Haven't you any influence?" For Renata had stubbornly refused his repeated suggestions that they drive out to Larchmont, where several clients of his firm kept boats which he had standing invitations to use. Half a dozen times he had proposed a sail on the Sound and Renata had shrieked, "No! Never. Never you get me in any *battello a vela.* I am terrify'!"

"But Seymour is a wonderful sailor," said Randall. "Truly, Renata. He's been doing it all his life, in fact—" Randall nodded derisively at Seymour, "boats and machinery are all he knows anything about."

"H'm," said Marietta Pawling.

"Non importa," cried Renata. "I don't care. Can be the Simorr *più bravo* than Amerigo Vespucci, Marco Polo, Cristoforo Colombo, *tutti*

tre. I don't go on that—" she pointed at the Atlantic— "unless is necessary cross it in *bastimento.* Then already I am praying to die."

"The Sound is not the ocean—" Seymour began.

"Is the salt, no? Is the same *acqua* like the sea? I am sick like the dog. This year I have vomit' already enough in the *ospedale,* no thank you, *basta.*"

"But you said you love the water," Randall reminded her.

"I said I love the lakes, is true. But even *il mio Lago di Como,* he become sometimes a wild animal."

Seymour guffawed.

"No, is true," she said seriously. "Sometimes come *subito* a storm terrible like I cannot describe. Is drowned many people every year."

"Smart sailors you must have there," said Seymour. Renata flashed him a look of genuine scorn. Randall saw it with surprise, and he noticed a curious narrowing of Marietta Pawling's eyes as she saw it too.

"Well," said Seymour, "I've got to go out to Larchmont anyway the day after tomorrow, to check up on some work on the Robinson boat. You lubbers can ride along if you like and kill time at the Yacht Club."

"I can't go," said Randall. "I've got an appointment with some people at the parish house."

"My God, what a bore. In August—what for?"

Randall explained about the imminent church picnic.

"Pic-nic?" mimicked Renata. "What is, such a funny word?"

They explained. Renata began to smile and nod, more enthusiastic every minute. *"Che bello!"* she cried. "Is the first thing I hear about your *religione pagana* which I can understand."

"It has nothing to do with our religion," said Randall. "It's a way of raising money for some of the parish work, and getting the kids in a good mood to go to Sunday School."

"Ecco!" she cried. "I tell you, just like us. The *bambini* they always march in the *Processione,* is very pretty. With the *bandiere* and the flowers and the holy images."

Seymour began to laugh. Randall said uncomfortably. "You're just silly, Renata, you don't know what you're talking about."

Marietta said, "There are no holy images in Protestant churches."

"No? *Pensa!* Never mind, we all go anyway, I must see this *Processione.*" She turned to Seymour. "You take us all in the *macchina, va bene?*"

Seymour and Randall exchanged a look. Renata watched them and saw consternation in both faces, but particularly in Randall's.

"*Perchè no*, Randalo?" she teased. "Why you act so funny?"

"But Renata, this isn't what you think it is. A lot of stuffy old ladies and their starched-up grandchildren and the Rector and—no, Renata. It's out of the question."

She appealed swiftly to Seymour. "You make him say yes," she said abruptly. "I want to go."

Randall looked from one face to the next and saw Marietta Pawling weighing something carefully before she spoke. She had that shrewd look in her eyes again. She said, "We'd look like damned fools, Renata. And what's worse, make a fool of Randall." She put her attention on digging a bit of lobster meat from a claw. She had caused a moment of uneasy silence into which Seymour rushed with the scoffing assurance that they'd all be bored to death. "Besides," he said, "Renata, this place can only be reached by ferry-boat and you've made your feelings about all boats crystal-clear."

Nobody knew just why the trips in the Stevens-Duryea and the jolly foursome dinners began to be less frequent. The postponements or changes of plan were always impromptu. Seymour went to Larchmont alone in the train because he found that the car needed two days' work on its brakes and its radiator. That evening Randall dined alone with Renata, and on a sentimental impulse took her to the same restaurant where they had first dined together on that Monday last April, which now seemed like years ago. The evening was not a success. Randall was ill at ease in some way far beyond the restraint that he had learned to impose upon himself, and Renata was strangely silent. Either she was bored, which he was too unhappily ready to believe, or she was disgruntled. Surely she could not be harboring a grudge about that preposterous picnic? He was afraid to reopen the subject to find out.

The next time they went out in the car they were caught in a tremendous thunderstorm, with rain falling in cascades like the spill from a great dam. Instantly they were soaked to the skin and, halfway up Riverside Drive to Claremont, Seymour turned the car around and started for Renata's flat, the point nearest to where they were. "I'll take Marietta on home," he said, jumping down, "and come along and collect you in an hour or so when we've all changed our clothes."

"No," said Renata. "Is too far across the city drive the Marietta *tutta bagnata così*. She catch the terrible cold. I keep her here with me," she said, taking Seymour's hand and stepping from the car, holding her soaked skirts in a bunch.

"Then we'll pick you both up here," said Seymour.

"No. You cannot know is no more the rain. We stay here alone, I and the Marietta. I have *in casa* the eggs, I make a *frittata*, we eat some cheese and fruit. *Basta*, I am no longer in the mood to go out. *Buona notte*, Randalo, you 'scuse us, please? Come, Marietta."

Randall gave his hand to Marietta to help her down. She had not given a sign of agreement, disagreement, or anything else. Barely moving her lips she murmured to him, "Are you beginning to catch on?"

He stood shivering on the pavement, his thin summer clothes plastered to his body. Through the curtain of water he watched the two women disappear inside Renata's door and Seymour, as ridiculously drenched as himself, start back across the sidewalk to the car. All three looked to Randall like puppets moving at the behest of some monstrously incomprehensible imagination. There was absolutely no sense in anything that he had drawn from a word or a look of Marietta's, tonight or any other night. No sense. She doesn't mean anything, his mind concocted, she's talking to hear herself talk. She doesn't mean anything, there's nothing to mean . . . she's . . . He jumped as the automobile started with a bang. He had forgotten it and the torrential rain streaming over his head and shoulders.

"Come on," shouted Seymour. "For God's sake get a move on, what are you dreaming about?" He had had to push his goggles up on his forehead when the rain pelted them, and he drove slowly, sitting nervously forward as Randall had never seen him do, cautiously peering ahead.

"I don't want anything to eat," said Randall when they had left the car in its shed which had once been the Dysons' carriage-house up the street, and had run home and changed to dry clothes. All the while he had wilfully held his retrospective ear and eye and mind closed to Marietta's words. Or he thought he had. Now he stood at the library window, staring at the bleary spectacle outside, the abandoned back yard churned by the rain to revolting black slime, the ailanthus tree graceless and dripping, under which he had played with Seymour while their grandmother from this window watched their every move. They had both learned to loathe being watched, they had learned beyond any other lesson never to watch one another. Now, what did she mean? *Nothing*, he snarled at himself. Nothing. She's a cheap, silly . . . why? Why did she say those things? What's she got against . . . *No*, he thought. I won't think about it any more. How can I find out what she meant . . . except by watching Seymour . . . *No I won't* . . .

"I'm not hungry," he said, turning from the window when Seymour urged him again to go and have something to eat. The rain had stopped; let's walk over to Cavanagh's, he had said, it's the nearest place.

"No thanks," said Randall for the third time.

"What's the matter with you?" Seymour came across the room polishing his spectacles. His thinning fair hair and his moustache were still wet, carefully combed into place.

"Nothing," muttered Randall.

"Well, damn it, then, don't be so grumpy. It wasn't my fault the evening turned out like this."

"Oh, all right." Randall turned indifferently from the window and started to follow Seymour from the room. If I'm going to watch him I'm not going to let him know it, he thought.

They had not dined alone together in months. And now that they were here they had nothing to say. Seymour made desultory stabs at talk and Randall answered in monosyllables. He ate nothing but a bowl of fish chowder and not all of that. He sat crumbling a pilot biscuit into it and dabbing at the thick porridge with his spoon.

"You know," said Seymour, "you were absolutely right when Renata made that silly fuss about your picnic. Of course it's out of the question.

"Why bring that up now?" Randall moved his shoulders irritably.

"Well, because she began to harp on it again last Friday when I picked her up before we came for you." Randall had been kept later than usual at the parish house.

And she had harped on it on each of the three afternoons that Seymour had been with her since the dinner at Brighton Beach. He had warned her that she was being madly unreasonable, reckless, in fact; that a caprice like this could make a disaster as terrible as the worst capitulation to jealousy. "You are clever enough never to be that kind of woman," he had said to her. "What the devil has got into you now?"

"I want to go to that *Processione*," she said stubbornly.

"What you want," he said, "is to pit Randall against me to see if you can get something you consider essentially innocuous—which it is. But this time we're both impervious to you, Renata, and I warn you to drop it. I warn you not to mention it to him again."

"*E' una bella cosa* you warn me something about your brother!"

"You'll do as I say about my brother." Seymour had stood over her with his long face reddening, his weak eyes glaring in a show of temper which she had never come up against. She turned away contemptuously, muttering something in Italian.

He decided then himself to mention the subject to Randall to shut it out of discussion once for all.

Randall said now, "She needn't harp on it any more. To anybody. That's the end of it."

What Seymour did not know was the strength of Randall's urge to hide the tokens and the symbols of emotion, as powerful in a different way as Seymour's own fanatic secrecy about his eyes. He did not know that Randall too had his violences of mind, stranger, more devious, more inexplicable than Seymour's own secret bawling rages. He did not know what touched off detonations in the depths of Randall's being, which no eye resting on his lovely face could guess.

Nor did Randall know. He only knew that when Renata in her unwonted perversity had begun a few mornings ago to tease and wheedle him about the church picnic, he had once for all said, "Stop it. It isn't fair to ask me for something I can't consent to. Why don't you ask me for something I can give? Those are the things I wish you would ask, Renata dear. And you never do."

He had gone down to St. Timothy's in an agitation of mind all out of proportion to the silliness of the question. And there on his table in the parish house he found a pile of boxes. The tickets for the picnic had come. He opened the top box and picked up a bundle of tickets and stood and looked at it, weighing it on the palm of his hand. Now, he thought, if these things didn't exist there couldn't be any picnic and if there weren't any picnic Renata wouldn't want to make a fool of me and if she didn't want to make a fool of me she would really love me and if she really loved me . . . . . he stood there, dreaming or imagining, detached from any sense of the immediate and the real. He had no idea how long he stood there or how far his fantasy carried him. He only knew that when he looked at the clock on the wall it was half-past one, and that the two curates and the Church secretary were all out at lunch. He was entirely alone in the parish house with six boxes full of tickets for the picnic. It doesn't matter what I do with them, he thought, still spinning his dream. It doesn't matter a bit. But if nobody can find them it's going to settle the question of that picnic. The whole dream was irrational, but why should he know that: it was a dream.

He found a piece of cord and tied the six boxes together so that he could carry them, and he put on his straw hat again and calmly walked out to the street. There he stood for a moment wondering what to do with the boxes. I can't throw them any place, he thought, they'll only be found. I might burn them but where can I find a furnace going in the middle of August? No, there was only one thing to do. Randall hailed a cab and got into it and went home. He got out the keys and went up to the fourth floor and opened the boxes and began carefully to stow the bundles of tickets away. He was well satisfied; in three or four crammed bureaus and wardrobes in various rooms up here he could hide every bundle of the tickets so that nobody until kingdom come would ever know they were there.

Whenever he was alone in the following days he found himself remembering those words or glances of Marietta's. Only his will not to understand spared him the agony of understanding all too clearly. He told himself that she was disgruntled; what could that be but that Seymour once again was growing bored with her? Why need it mean anything else? She must, he thought, have said something to Renata about it, and that was why Renata had been so kind to her the night of the rainstorm, as a way of reproaching Seymour. Well, yes, he argued, but why did she make me think, that night, of watching Seymour? What is there to watch? Nothing, he told himself, *nothing* . . .

But he watched. Though they were gay on Thursday evening, when they drove up to Yonkers and dined at a new restaurant on the banks of the Hudson, he watched all three of them with every sense sharpened to catch any meaning look or word, not alone from Marietta; from Seymour or Renata as well. But there was nothing. Renata was in her funniest mood; even Randall, full of hopeless yearning for her, was convulsed like the others when she fell to mimicking certain of her more celebrated colleagues at the opera, and graphically telling some of their seamier secrets. Only once all evening did Randall feel a pang of concern, and that was for Seymour, when he saw him wince and strain to keep his eyes open as they were entering the gaudy restaurant ablaze with electric lights. His eyes must be worse, Randall thought, they must be much weaker. I wonder if he's careful enough of them. He had never tried to question Seymour about this without meeting a rebuff. I suppose he knows best, Randall thought uneasily. He put his attention on the party again.

On the way back to town the air was chilly and Renata let him wrap her shoulders in the light shawl that she had brought along. He was surprised when she settled back in the seat, close to him for warmth, with her hand lying quietly in his. Very seldom was she ever in a mood like that. He kept her hand in his all the way, sometimes raising it to his lips. She smiled at him, and he thought wistfully of the peaceful days at the Maynard farm, before Seymour and Marietta and this snorting red intruder had broken in. He tried to weave a dream of such a time to come again.

Not only did the dream elude him; so did sleep, most of that night. He tossed and thrashed; one after another his worries writhed and bored to the surface of his mind, like snakes emerging from a hole where they had hibernated, to weave their ugly heads about and vie with one another to command his notice. At first they were separate, each a color and a type of itself. Then they began to tangle and merge into a twisting mass, every one a factor in the compounding of some awful evil which, though its different parts were as unrelated as his fear of the rats in the attic and of the deferred crisis which must break over the lost picnic tickets, still came to the same festering head, his suspicion of Seymour. But of what did he suspect Seymour? . . . nothing that he could bring himself to face. Then one snake weaved apart from the others and to his horror said in his own voice, I've got a brother just like you. *No*, said Randall into his pillow, no I won't hear it, I won't think it . . . a brother just like you just like you just like you . . . *stop it*, stop hearing that . . .

He tried to sweep it all away with the great clean tender beauty of his love for Renata, the love he believed would win her and bring them together and take him away from all this, all these rats and snakes of his imagination, which had their nests deep in every corner of this house. Please help me, he breathed in the dark, please, please, though whether he prayed to Renata or to some deity who had no place in St. Timothy's Church he did not know. He could not lie still any more, he rolled off his bed and stumbled to the window and stood there trying to calm himself with a breath of the damp dawn air.

He did not want to face Seymour in the morning; a glimpse of his own sickly grey face in the glass was enough to decide him. He did not want any coffee, nor any food; he did not want to go to St. Timothy's, because St. Timothy's was no longer the pleasant place where he worked, it was the place where something dreadful was going to happen on account of those picnic tickets. His horror was not a fear of disgrace; it was a fear that they should ever discover his deepest secrets. He would simply not go there any more. He would go to Renata and tell her some of his sufferings of the night, and get from her company the consolation that only she could give.

Then he thought about her unusual gentleness in the car riding back from Yonkers, the unaccustomed tenderness of leaving her hand in his and sitting so close to him because she was cold. It had warmed and reassured him then, but now he stood weighing and pondering it, and he saw, as if it moved on two axial screws like this old-fashioned mirror in its frame, the whole thing roll slowly over and show him its reverse. No, he began to tell himself again, while he stood trembling in his nightshirt, no, I'm not going to believe that. Nothing will make me believe that. *She did it to fool you. She did it to throw you off the track.*

He put his hand across his mouth as if he were afraid that he might scream, and he stood looking at that mirror which had taken on the dire power of showing him what he did not mean to see. He stood there until he was swaying on his feet. Then he wrenched himself away, pulled off his nightshirt, threw on the first clothes that came to hand and rushed downstairs and out of the house. He did not know where he went all day long. He tramped the streets and sat in parks with his head clutched between his hands, and tramped again, and stood for he did not know how long at the railing of Brooklyn Bridge, gazing at the swift tangled currents of water far below. Then it was three o'clock and he was walking up Broadway, past an office of the telephone company. There was a row of booths inside the door. He went in and looked up the number of Grew and Minturn and dropped a nickel in the box and asked Central for the number.

When somebody answered he asked to speak to Seymour Holt.

"Oh," said the voice. "He is not here. Mr. Holt is never at the office in the afternoon."

He went out, walking fast and with sharp accuracy of which he was unaware. He took the subway and got out uptown at the corner nearest Renata's apartment house and walked there, still like a wound-up toy. There was an open ironwork elevator shaft running straight up the centre of the building, and a stairway winding round it all the way from the ground floor to the roof. Some people used the stairs as often as the elevator, because they lived on the lower floors and the elevator was so slow. Randall walked into the lobby, past the elevator shaft which was empty because the car was up above somewhere, and began quietly to climb the stairs. He met nobody. He climbed to the fifth floor where Renata lived, turning his head away when the elevator passed him on its slow descent. He was not conscious of a plan, no part of this had he thought about more distinctly than about anything else today. It was still a great mixed writhing inside him. He stopped at Renata's door and though he knew it would be locked, he tried the handle anyway. The door was locked, of course. He looked round the hall; nobody was there; he put his ear tight against the door. He could not hear anything, but he thought of the layout of the two rooms inside and the unlikelihood that one could hear sounds out here. He put his hands over his face for a moment, sick and bewildered and uncertain what to do. But that passed; he knew now with frightening clearness what he meant to do. He went back to the stairway and climbed to the landing on the half-turn of the stairs between the fifth and sixth floors. Standing there, in an angle behind a fire extinguisher on the wall, he could look down and see Renata's door.

And there he stood, for an hour which he measured because he was dully surprised to find that he had put his watch and chain in his trousers pocket when he rushed out of the house this morning. He stood with his watch in his hand, moving his eyes from the watch to the door, from the door to the watch. The full hour passed. He was drawing long breaths half-strangled by the pounding of his pulse. Then the door opened. Randall stood stock-still, watching Seymour come quietly through the doorway, shut the door behind him, and walk to the stairs. He'll ring for the elevator, Randall thought, knowing Seymour's ways; but Seymour did not. He started down the stairs, with Randall flattened in the niche behind the fire extinguisher watching him and thinking, "He probably thinks he's less observed that way." Randall leaned forward and watched Seymour going down and down, turn after turn, his footfalls growing fainter. Then Randall left his corner and ran down the few steps and put his thumb upon Renata's doorbell and pushed it hard. For a moment he heard nothing. Then her voice said, "Is you, Simorr? You forgot something?"

"Yes," said Randall in a voice pitched enough lower than his own, and enough like Seymour's for the monosyllable to have deceived anybody. The door opened slowly. He threw his weight against it, flung into the hall, and slammed the door behind him. Renata stood, naked except for a nightgown sheer as glass, dead white and silent. She was barefoot. Randall strode past her into her bedroom. The bed was in wild disorder, the pillows on the floor, the coverings tumbled everywhere. The blinds were drawn. Flung across a chair was a thin silk summer dressing-gown of Seymour's.

He stood and looked at the room and for a long time did not move at all; then his hands went slowly to his eyes as if to cover them from shame. Finally his hands dropped to his sides. He turned and went towards the hall and saw Renata standing as he had left her. Her face was still chalk-white. He raised his right hand and lashed it across her cheek and said, "Go in there." She moved ahead of him into the bedroom, walking slowly with stiff steps like a doll.

She stood in the middle of the room, looking neither to one side nor the other. Her eyes were fixed on the drawn blinds at the windows. She held her head up; he saw the sharp young angle of her chin and throat. Her right cheek was mottled with red where he had struck her.

"So this is what you tried to tell me you were," he said. His voice was loud and rough and later in hideous retrospect he would hear and not be able to recognize it.

"I have tell you many times," she said dully. "For you, may not seem so, but for me I am honest."

"Honest! Yes, like an animal. Why didn't you tell me *that*?"

"I did tell you. Everything, I have try' to make you believe. Can I help if you are a child, also a *puritano*? Always I know is the terrible mistake I have anything to do with you."

"Why did you, then?" he shouted. "Why?"

She shrugged, not contemptuously, but with the resigned heaviness of an old woman. She did not answer him, except with a long, grave, eloquent look.

He began to rave at her, pouring out a stream of cruelty, of reckless injustices, of insane protests against what she could have reminded him he should have known. She never said a word. "I loved you," he shouted. "I thought I could make you a woman worth loving, worth marrying, I dreamed of a life with you, I—"

She shook her head slowly, reminding him of all her refusals and all her warnings. He took no notice, but went on raving. "I worshipped you, I believed I could make you want what I wanted, what I could love, not what I am sickened by. I've had that too, you slut, that filth you call pleasure, you and my rotten lecher of a brother. Two of a kind. He saw what you are, he sized you up fast enough!"

She stood looking at him with an expression which he was too frenzied to recognize as infinite regret and infinite pity.

"I have try' to tell you myself," she said with astonishing dignity. He scarcely listened. He shouted, "Yes, I see you did. And I wouldn't believe you, I thought I could make you worthy of real love by loving you. But I guess you knew better, you and Seymour. *Seymour* . . . All right!" he roared. "I'll show you too, I'll show you what you're worth." He began to rip and tear at his clothes. "I'll take you at your own estimation. Slut! Strumpet! Whore!" He seized her by her shoulders and flung her violently on her back on the bed.

CHAPTER 15

The place was dim and evil-smelling. Raising his head from the gritty spot where it lay, Randall peered dully round. He recognized nothing of the little he could see: a leaden-grey wall, a barred rectangle near the low ceiling, something shuffling past it outside. He turned his head heavily the other way: a row of objects like this lumpy cot where he lay, each with a shape sprawled or flung upon it. Snores and snuffling sickly breathing, a belch, an undertone of witless mumbling, were all he heard. He stayed for a moment raised on one elbow, squinting at the dirty wall. His head weaved slowly, right to left, left to right, up and down. Presently it fell once more on the rough soiled ticking.

When he roused again he heard a harsh, steady splashing. He pushed himself up on his hands and looked about. Now he recognized what he had seen before. The rectangle was a window, and the splashing was rain, and some of the cots along the wall were empty now. As if with some faculty that he was afraid to use, he began to try to understand where he was. Those were feet stumbling and dragging past the window. The trousers above them were dripping rags. This must be a cellar, he thought, which was his first thought about anything in a length of time which had no span. Like the reluctant turning of an unoiled wheel, his mind began stiffly to go round. Each fragment of thought was like another hard push on the wheel; it moved barely at all, creaking, grating; but it moved. This is a cellar, he thought innumerable times, and there he stuck until the shove which made him ask, what cellar? Slowly he sat up and swung weakly round and felt for the floor with his feet. His elbows fell on his knees, and his head into his hands, and he sat there for a long time.

When he raised his head it was because the smell was so evil, a strangling sour smell which had settled in his belly and would soon make him sick. So he thought of air. Slowly in painful jerks his mind, like that rusted wheel, began to gather feeble momentum. Could he stand up? It was a long time before he tried. It was longer before he dared let go of the iron footrail of the cot, to try his balance without holding on; longer still before he put one shaking foot ahead of the other and shifted his weight. But he could walk. Then he must find a door, he must see how to get out of here, since that was why he had decided he must walk. The door was down at the end of this long stinking place, down to the right of the high, barred window.

Then he was outside, standing in a pool of water to his ankles, with rain sluicing down to plaster his ragged shirt to his body. This sensation was familiar. This belonged with something that lay on the other side of the high black wall that cut off everything he knew except that that place in there was a cellar. Standing in the rain, shivering, watching people hurry into a house; standing in the rain cold and soaking wet, and somebody saying something. Standing in the rain, he heard it again, he was sure he heard it, then he was not sure; no, why had somebody said something? Who had said it? What had he heard, standing in the rain? *Are you beginning to catch on?*

The high black wall collapsed. Randall Holt raised his filthy hands to his temples and staggered towards the side of the building behind him and leaned against it and the wheel spun, greased and swift and cruel. Now the other balance of a scale loaded with nightmare came riding up, while the time since that Friday afternoon sank down, lost, drowned, forever gone. His hands slipping down his cheeks touched heavy stubble, he wore nothing but a tattered shirt and trousers. The rain streamed down and he gave a cry of terror at a brutal roaring noise bursting suddenly overhead. Cowering, he looked up; it was the elevated; a train of cars crashed by. He turned, wavering on his feet, and holding on to walls and ledges, made his way to the corner. He saw that he was on the Bowery. Other figures like his own stumbled and shuffled past him, their broken shoes squelching water. Nobody looked at him. On the corner there was an eating-place, spewing out a reek of stale frying-fat and bad coffee. His stomach heaved, but he was empty too. He hesitated on the pavement, looking through the dirty window at a few ragged men humped over cups and bowls. His hand went to his pocket. Then he remembered standing before the mirror in his room, a Friday, what Friday—how long ago? He had flung on some clothes—he looked down at the same shirt and trousers—and stuffed some loose bills and change in one pocket and his watch on its chain in the other. And rushed out—to the beginning of this. His hands groped in the trousers pockets. In the left one there was half a dollar. In the right one he touched metal, and pulling it out, he saw a short piece of the chain from his watch with his bunch of keys at one end. He stood with the keys in his hand wondering why somebody had left him fifty cents and torn his watch from its chain, leaving his keys. But they're *my* keys, he said half aloud. My keys.

The keys meant his things and his little desk and his locked secret places, and those meant the house and the house meant Seymour. He could not think about Seymour, and all the rest of it was dim; very far away. If he should let it rush at him it would come crashing down, a savage thing like that train up overhead, driven by some devil who would as soon kill a dozen Randall Holts. But he meant to outwit that devil. He would not let the whole train run him down, car after car crushing his mangled body after the first one had struck him. He could avoid that, and the avoiding meant also protecting his things. They were safe so long as he had these keys. He must remove everything from the house, watching to be sure when Seymour was out, keeping his visits secret until he had got all his things and taken them to some safe place. This would be an exhausting job and take a long time; to do it would be like uncoupling one car from that murderous train, in which he and his things would be safe, while the rest of the train hurtled on anywhere. He would never see Seymour again, never see any part of that train or any passenger in it.

Should he go now and begin the long, secret task of carrying away his things? Shaky on his feet, he stood and weighed the question. The smell from the eating-place bored at his nostrils and twisted his empty gut. It was repellent, but he was weak and knew he should eat. After that, he thought, I could go to the house. It is afternoon, he saw by the clock on the wall in the eating-place, and Seymour will be out. *Mr. Holt is never at the office in the afternoon.* He is never at home either. Randall's mind swung wildly away from the thought of where Seymour might be, or with whom. He tried to think of something else, something concrete. I have money in the house, he thought. Clean clothes, several suits. He would need them. He hesitated on the corner for a long time. Then he turned into the cheap restaurant and clambered unsteadily onto a stool at the counter and ordered food and coffee.

When he came out into the wet cavern of the street he had two dimes and a nickel in his pocket. He started to walk north on the Bowery. The cold rain wrapped his thin shirt and trousers round his body and legs and soon he was shivering. The greasy food and bad coffee lay uneasily in his stomach; he had got a moment's warmth from them but no strength; he was still weak and now he felt sick besides. He began to wonder whether he was strong enough to walk all the way to the house, and presently he decided it would be better to take a street car. But I can't get into a street car looking like this, he thought. And I haven't money enough for a cab. Even if I had there are no cabs in sight. He leaned against the side of a building and stood with his hands to his temples, trying to make sense of all this. A while ago he had decided something, but now he could not remember exactly what. He was becoming more confused all the time. What had he figured out about Seymour—that he would be in the house or not? He could not recall. It seemed to him that whatever it had been, Seymour stood facing him at the end of some enormous effort he had meant to make. No, he thought, his head swimming, I can't go through with that. I don't want to see Seymour. He said the words aloud several times. Ragged, drunken men staggered past him, taking no notice of a derelict talking to himself in the streaming rain. Oh, I'm not going to the house, he muttered. I didn't mean to do that. He was unsure what he had meant when he was trying to decide something before.

He began to walk again, blindly, and oblivious of directions and street signs. He turned several corners in the maze of slum streets east of the Bowery, and having nothing to do instead, he kept on walking. After a time the narrow streets crammed with tenements and swarming people began to look different. They widened, and he walked out suddenly onto the river-front, faced by the hulls and stacks of a long row of ships at their piers. He was bewildered. He was not sure where he was, but these were certainly not the North River docks only two blocks from home. I couldn't have got there so soon, he thought; and I didn't mean to go there. Where am I? He thought then to look for a street sign and he wandered about, peering, until he saw one: Peck Slip. From its very unfamiliarity he knew; this must be the East River. Those dirty-looking small ships were freighters. Some were high in the water, some low, loaded and ready to sail.

He stood gazing dully at the rusty stern of a loaded ship. It was marked *Comanche*, Galveston. That's a long way away, he thought. Texas. How would a ship get from here to Texas? He was not sure. He was wondering about it when a man appeared at the taffrail and hailed him.

"Hey," he yelled. "You want to ship?"

"What?"

"Want a job? Deckhand?"

"Why—" Randall stood shivering, not knowing what to say. "When?" he asked stupidly.

"Tonight. Need three hands. Look like you want a berth, do you?"

"Why—yes." Randall spoke without any volition at all. "Where do you go?"

"Coast. Gulf. Galveston. And back. Hurry up, make up your mind. I'm goin' ashore to sign on two more. Want the job or not?"

"Why—sure." As soon as he had said it Randall wanted to take it back. This was a nightmare. He could not go off on any ship, he would die of seasickness. But, he thought, if I don't do this I'll have to go home. The idea of any alternative eluded his confused mind. This is the way not to see Seymour. I'll do it. "How long will you be gone?" he called up to the man.

"Three-four weeks. Plannin' a cruise? Don't fart around now, take it or leave it. I'm in a hurry."

"I'm coming," said Randall.

The man jerked his thumb back over the side at the gangplank leading into a square black hole. Randall walked round as if he were sleep-walking, climbed the gangway, and disappeared into the hold.

Four weeks later, on a sunny afternoon at the end of September, he walked down the same gangway to the same pier at Peck Slip. He wore a soiled blue shirt and denim trousers, his face was deeply tanned, his hands stained and calloused. His hair was bleached almost white. In his pocket he had four dollars and sixty-eight cents. He was thin, but muscled and toughened as he had never been before, and though he had no wish to repeat the experience, it had not been too bad a one. On both voyages, out and in, he had been desperately sick between Norfolk and Cape Fear. Last week off Cape Hatteras they had roped him into a dirty bunk and left him like a corpse for twenty-four hours. But otherwise the sea had been calm. Coasting around the Gulf, with calls at Pensacola, Mobile, and New Orleans, had been interesting enough to compensate for the hard labor, the bad food, and the half-dozen toughs among whom he had lived, imitating their habits and their speech for

fear of being different. The best of it had been that it had amounted to
an anaesthetic. He had almost entirely succeeded in his intention not
to think. Whether he had really put his brother, the past months, and
above all, Renata Tosi out of mind; or whether he had only managed
to stave off their reappearance, he had at least had a respite. He felt
calm, unconfused, and certain what he meant to do. He would go
straight to the house, sure that Seymour would not be there at this time
of day. He would clean himself, get properly dressed, pack his clothes
and his most important possessions, and go and find somewhere to live.
Then, taking care always to avoid Seymour, he would go to the house
every day and gradually he would take away his things, carrying as
much as he could at a time until he had removed them all. Beyond that
he had not taken thought or made a plan.

He reached the low iron gate at the pavement and stood for a
moment, fingering the keys in his pocket and looking up past the littered
front yard at the blank blinded face of the house. I might, he thought,
be looking at the family tomb. He heard the feet of people passing up
and down the street behind him. He wondered if they thought him a
tramp; they could not know that he belonged here—that he once had, he
corrected himself. He walked up the path, selecting from his bunch the
key to the front door. He unlocked the door and shut it quietly behind
himself; he was always quiet by habit, but now, even with Seymour
out as he must be, Randall felt stealthy because in some way that
seemed important. He stood for a moment in the front hall, noting that
nothing seemed changed and wondering for the first time exactly how
long he had been gone. Twenty-seven days on the *Comanche*; how many
days before that in that fearful place which was only an ugly, clouded
memory? He would never know. That had become a scab, the material
of tough scar-tissue, beneath which lay the wound . . . he must not
let himself feel . . . or even think . . .

He mounted the stairs, quietly, wondering at the musty smell of the
house and whether it had always smelt like that, and he turned at the
top to go to his own room. Then he jumped and gasped, gripping the
newel-post; and almost fled.

"Who is there?" said Seymour's voice from inside his own room.
The voice was frail and low. It held Randall still when he would have
run. You don't mean to see Seymour, he told himself, and put his foot

on the step to go down. "Who is there?" he heard again, weaker and with a frighteningly helpless note. Randall swallowed and passed his hardened hand across his eyes. He meant to go, he meant to go straight back down those stairs. Against his will he turned and moved and said, walking into the room, "It is I."

Seymour lay on his bed, with his hands folded on his chest. His eyes were closed. When he heard Randall's voice his right hand flung out; he stiffened as if to raise himself but he kept his head still and Randall heard him choke or sob in a hoarse low cry. Randall strode to the bed and took Seymour's hand and said, "What is it? What's happened to you? Look at me, Seymour!"

Seymour moved convulsively; his left hand together with his right closed on Randall's, but his eyes remained closed. He said, and Randall heard that he was in tears, "Oh, Randall. Randall. God bless you."

Randall fell on his knees, his free hand touching Seymour's face. "Please," he said, "Brother, open your eyes and look at me. Tell me what has happened to you."

"Are you all right?" Tears slid from his closed lids down Seymour's cheeks, and he clutched harder at Randall's hand. "Tell me, are you?"

"Yes, yes, never mind about me. I'm fine." Randall stared at Seymour's face. A terrible idea was beginning to work into his mind, a suspicion so frightful that he dared not face it. "It's you that matters," he said. He passed his free hand lightly over Seymour's forehead, watching the white, set face; watching, wondering. Suddenly he cried, "Seymour! Open your eyes!" He saw Seymour's mouth tighten, the long jaw move in an effort at control. "Seymour," he whispered, "can't you open your eyes?"

There was a dreadful sound, a groan or a sob; the eyes remained closed. Randall shook with terror, watching Seymour struggle in what he would understand later was the last stand of fanatical pride and courage in defeat. "Please," he begged, "can't you open your eyes, Brother?"

"I can open them," said Seymour in a hoarse whisper, "but I am blind." He began to sob like a child.

"Brother . . . Brother . . ." Randall bent over him. "Oh my God, my poor Brother . . . And I left you alone. Oh, Seymour, what have I done?"

"I drove you . . ." Seymour tried to master his tears. "It was I who—think what I did to you! I deserve this. Worse than this."

"No. No." Randall put his fingers against Seymour's closed eyelids, a curious reverent gesture as if to make contact with a talisman. "No, Brother. I left you alone; oh, I can't bear it! Tell me. Tell me what it is, when it happened. Tell me everything."

"Haven't you always known, Ran?" Seymour spoke only after a long silence. "I thought you had."

Randall shook his head wretchedly. He said, "How could I? How could I imagine it would end in this? I only thought—" For a moment he could not speak. Then he said, "Have you known for a long time, Brother? Do you mean you've gone on for years?—with that much courage, knowing this was hanging over you? Oh my God."

"What else would a man do?"

"I don't know. I'd never have been so brave. When did you first know, how long—?"

"For years, since long before Mama died. I've known, and when I haven't wanted to know, Willingdon has reminded me. But you fight a thing like this, you fight hard."

"What is it, Brother? What happened to your eyes?"

"Oh," said Seymour drearily, "does the name of it matter?"

"Of course it does. Everything matters. I have to know. Oh, to have left you alone to face this! Tell me what it is."

Seymour sighed. "A condition called high grade myopia with eventual detachment of the retina, which is what has finally happened. It's progressive and incurable and for years he's warned me to stop doing this and that and every other damned thing until I've done them all almost out of—oh, hell. You understand."

"Was the—all the driving and being outdoors this past summer? Was that very bad?"

"Probably. He says the end wasn't precipitated by too much exposure to light, that it would have happened anyway. But it certainly didn't help."

"And now? Brother, is it—you know what I mean."

"Final? Hopeless? Yes. I'm not quite totally blind yet." Seymour's voice began to regain some of its normal firmness. "I will be soon. It doesn't matter how soon any more, because I can't see enough to use my eyes for anything. I can see—oh, shapes, if they're very large. Or the difference between light and dark, that's about all. And it hit me just the way he said it would. One day I just couldn't see anything any more."

"When was that?"

"Oh—" Seymour paused. For the first time he let his eyelids roll slowly open and Randall looked with piteous anxiety at the grey eyes, visibly no different than before. It was inconceivable that they could not see; looking at them he pressed Seymour's hand hard and for one moment was about to insist he could believe none of this; it was on the tip of his tongue to cry "Look at me, Brother! Say you see me!" Then he bent his head in abashment, such an exclamation would have been the greatest cruelty. Seymour lay perfectly still, as if staring at the ceiling overhead, and Randall stayed close to him and presently repeated, "When was that, Brother?"

Seymour did not answer immediately. He turned on his side, facing Randall, and closed his eyes again and Randall suspected he had begun to weep once more. He felt the tremor of his muscles. But when Seymour spoke he said steadily, "Five days after you—went away."

"Did your doctor say it was brought on by shock?"

"You mean, do I know everything that happened?"

"Yes," whispered Randall.

"I know. Everything. But if you say 'shock', just be sure we mean the same thing. The shock was my anxiety and remorse about you and my terror when you disappeared."

"Remorse!" said Randall. "Oh, Brother, I'm the one who's dying of that. I'm so desperately ashamed."

"No, Ran. You mustn't feel that way. You did what any man— never mind. The provocation was inhuman and I did it to you."

"We must stop talking about this now, Brother."

"If we can. But I can't let you stay a night in this house without asking you with all my soul to forgive me. I'm a selfish bastard, Ran— nobody knows it like you. But I love you and I ask you to forgive me if you can. It was a criminal thing I did. And my only reason was the same damned one I had for everything." He sighed and made a despairing motion towards his closed eyes. "I wanted every pleasure while I could still see to enjoy it."

"I know that now. And I realize that's all she—" Randall stopped and forced himself to go on. "That's all she was anyway. She always tried to tell me so."

"That doesn't minimize what I did to you. Can you forgive me, Ran?"

"Need you ask?" He leaned forward and lightly put his hand on Seymour's forehead.

He answered briefly when Seymour asked where he had been, even drawing a faint smile and an incredulous exclamation or two at his description of himself as a deckhand on a freighter. Seymour marvelled that he had had the nerve to do it, plagued by seasickness, but Randall said, "I wasn't making much sense at first, and when I got used to it I rather enjoyed it." They talked for a long time, Seymour lying always in that pathetic, still position, with his eyes closed and his hands folded. Randall asked if the doctor had ordered him to do that.

"No," sighed Seymour. "There just hasn't been anything else to do."

Randall asked how he had been managing about his food. Mrs. Quinn, said Seymour, had been cooking him a meal of sorts at midday and in the evening he ate only fruit. "I can feel my way for that," said Seymour. "I'll get used to it all, in time."

"I need something more than fruit myself, tonight," said Randall. "I know. I'll go and get cleaned up and take a basket over to that German bakery-restaurant place on Tenth Avenue and have them give me whatever they've got. I'll bring it back and we'll eat it here."

"Fine," said Seymour. He had no appetite, but he had felt Randall's jutting bones through his coarse shirt.

"I'll be back soon. Oh, by the way," said Randall, because he knew how much it had meant to Seymour, "what did you do about your automobile?"

"Well—" Seymour hesitated. "I—I'm afraid you'll think me a damned fool."

"Why should I? I couldn't."

"Well—it's down in the cellar." Seymour laughed nervously and said, "I *am* a damn fool. But I just couldn't bear to part with it and—"

"Of course not! I know just how you felt. But goodness, Brother, how did you get it into the cellar?"

"Those last days before—before my eyes gave out. I knew it was going to happen and I got a mechanic to help me and we dismantled the car and took the parts down cellar and assembled them again down there."

"Well, I think if that's what you wanted, it was the thing to do," said Randall, and he took the basket and went to fetch their food.

There was peace of a sort, and a sense of purpose in life, rooted in tragedy where its opposite had brought only turmoil. Randall's days were not long enough to give him time for everything he wanted to do for Seymour. He was surprised to see how Seymour managed, how he could walk about the house, all over the second floor and down the front stairs and the cellar stairs to his workshop, where he was beginning the experiment of making a ship model by touch. He could shave himself to as much nicety as he cared for, and dress himself and do many other commonplace things.

"I'm so surprised," Randall said more than once, when he had sprung to help Seymour and found it unnecessary. "One would almost think—"

"One would altogether think, unless one were a damn fool. Do you suppose I haven't been practising for this for years?"

"Oh, I'm so stupid," said Randall quickly. "I'm the one who's got to learn."

"Oh, no. You don't realize what this is yet. So far it's like an illness —I stay in the house and lie down with my eyes closed most of the time. But when Willingdon for some pompous reason of his own advises me to let up on that, where am I then? Outdoors taking a nice constitutional? Not on your life."

"But, Brother—"

"That's it, Ran. What the hell do I want to go out of doors for? Tapping my way along with a stick, or being led by you? Or seen by anybody? Christ!"

"Oh, Seymour, it won't be like that. It can't." Randall put his hand on Seymour's arm and held it for a moment. "I don't believe Doctor Willingdon will say there isn't a chance. I can't believe it. You look absolutely the same to me."

"But I can't see those big blue eyes of yours. Or anything else about you except lightish where your face is and darkish where your clothes are. No, Ran. Willingdon's been saying this for seven years. And since he is an unsentimental scientific son of a bitch I can't see him changing his mind."

"This seems to be bringing out all the profanity in you."

"You haven't heard anything yet. Wait till I get one of my bad spells. You know me. Did you think I was meeting this with Christian resignation and fortitude?"

And yet in a startling way he was. He had had three soul-crushing weeks abandoned in his Gehenna, alone with his guilt and the consequences of his transgressions. He had writhed in a hell of anxiety about Randall, sharpened by the frustration of his helplessness. He had not thought that Randall was "lost" in any sense where an appeal to the police would solve his dilemma by producing his brother. They could have found him, doubtless. But Seymour knew that Randall had fled in a frenzy of loathing for himself, for her, for Seymour, for all that had been polluted. Wherever he was, Randall was swamped in the muck of that pollution and must be left alone to make his own way out. To hound him, drag or force him here, would have been the most heartless of Seymour's selfishnesses. He lay and met his castigation alone.

It happened that only Marietta Pawling had telephoned him in the first days of his blindness and, not being a stupid woman, had sensed in his refusal to see her something other than the irritable evidences of surfeit which he had shown her in the past. His iron cincture of pride had bent only enough for him to admit some minor illness, but she was not deceived. She knew something to be seriously wrong, and she offered to be of help. He had put her off rudely.

"Then Randall is looking after you?" she had asked in a guarded way which apprised him that she had been in touch with Renata.

"Naturally he is," Seymour had replied, "and I don't want to see anybody else." He broke the connection and said half aloud, "There, let them make what they can of that." He had done what he could to shield Randall.

And now when Randall with heartrending tenderness and a timidity which made Seymour wince, apologized for the simple food that he produced for the erstwhile gourmet, Seymour could not show appreciation enough. Though he cringed inwardly at the bitter humiliation of letting Randall help him to eat, he conquered his stinging pride and smiled and thanked Randall, joking whenever he could think of a silly thing to say. Every morning Randall read the newspapers aloud to him, almost completely through, omitting only the pages whose contents bored Seymour. He handled and read the papers as if there were no such thing as a page of musical and theatrical news, and Seymour never remarked it. Not once had Randall stopped to glance at one of those pages. He also read aloud in the afternoon or evening magazines and books that might interest Seymour.

"You'll ruin your own eyesight, Ran," Seymour protested, "you aren't used to reading as much as that."

"I love it, Brother," said Randall. "I really do." His voice was so warm that tears gathered in Seymour's blind eyes. He thought, what the poor chap really loves is someone to take care of and be necessary to. How bitter that I am the only wretched, twisted means of his having it. But Randall seemed quite happy. The nightmares had faded, those before and those afterwards, and for the time being he did not brood. He did not worry either about the fears that had plagued him before he came home here; that great crashing train of cars no longer assaulted him. He did not worry about his things. Now that he was here and all his things locked away in their places he did not need to go and look at them unless he wanted to. They were safe.

So Seymour never left the house at all, and Randall only when he went to do errands, all of which were part of taking care of Seymour. It was early in December now. Very much of the memory of recent months had blacked down in a vault, inside which it would be madness to look. Seymour, with his dreadful future already marked out for him, knew the urgency of holding to this modus vivendi, whose only compensation, a pitiful one, was giving Randall an occupation which at this time seemed good. But how could that continue, how could he let it continue, how could this be the end of his brother's life as well as his own?

"What about your church, Ran?" he asked one day. "Wouldn't you like to go back there, at least part of the time?" He could not see the dull terror which whitened Randall's face and swept his blue eyes wildly towards the ceiling. "Don't you miss your work, your music?"

Randall was clever enough to wait with his answer until he felt sure his voice would betray nothing. Then he said, "Oh, no, Brother. I was getting bored with it anyway—and really I'm so much happier just staying here with you."

"We'd be in fine case if we hadn't any money between us," said Seymour. "Both without jobs."

"But as for music—wouldn't you like me to play for you sometimes?" Randall asked. He found himself facing the amazing fact that this had not occurred to him before. He ran his knuckles up his forehead as if to knock at the door of his wits.

"Why—yes." This time Seymour was slow with his answer. He had never cared much for music but in these circumstances it might turn out to be a wonderful resource, and it might also be good for Randall. But he was worried. Those trunks were still downstairs in the drawing-room, she had done nothing about sending for them, and in the few days before he collapsed he had been in no frame of mind to trouble to send them to her. And Randall ought not to see those trunks. Or had he? Seymour did not dare pursue it. He did know that Randall had not struck a note of music since he had been back in the house. It looked as if he had not gone into the drawing-room, or more probably, had done so—enough to see the trunks still there and flee.

"I tell you, Ran," said Seymour slowly. "This is a funny house. I only like the rooms in it that I've always used myself. You know what I mean? Not the ones that are full of—what do I mean? Memories? Personalities? Anyway, I've never liked that drawing-room ever since the days when you used to be shut up there with Mama practising all the time and getting all the attention."

"Was I, Brother?" Randall's voice was bewildered.

"Why, sure. I was jealous of you, didn't you know that?" (God forgive me, Seymour thought, any rot I can think of will be a good enough reason for staying out of that room.)

"I never knew that," said Randall slowly. "But I guess it's true. I do remember the way you wouldn't let her go to Europe with me."

"Well, we're queer dicks, we always knew that. Anyway, I don't much want to sit in that drawing-room."

"Of course not," said Randall quickly. "We'll—" he paused. "That wouldn't do. I was about to say we'd move the piano up here. But it's so big. There wouldn't be room for it on this floor."

"Never mind," said Seymour. "Some days I'll be in a specially unjealous mood and then we'll go downstairs and you'll play for me."

But Randall went out a few days later and bought the smallest upright piano he could find, and had it hoisted up to the second floor and put in the wide part of the hall outside the library. There it wouldn't be in anybody's way and he could play for Seymour while he sat in his own chair and was comfortable.

Seymour, when Randall was out next day, stood in the hall gingerly feeling the new piano. "God Almighty," he said, shaking his head. "This makes five." At that moment the telephone rang. Startled, Seymour gasped out an oath. This almost never happened. The bell rang again and Seymour groped along the hall wall until he found the telephone and as it rang the third time, he lifted the receiver.

A week later Randall was on his way home in the afternoon. Over on Twenty-third Street where he had been doing errands, the big shops were so brightly lighted, and the street so crowded with busy people, that he had not noticed the early dark which at this season closes in on New York while one thinks it is still day. He began to walk faster, he did not like the thought of Seymour alone in the dark house. He cannot see it is so dark, Randall thought, but I don't want to think of him there in his chair, not even knowing. It was cold and he wanted to get home and replenish the library fire and light a gas globe and make sure that Seymour was comfortable. He turned into his own block on Ninth Avenue and walked quickly west on Twenty-fourth Street. He was almost at the house when a figure appeared beside him, and his ears, his whole head rattled with shock as he heard, softly, "Randalo."

He stopped walking, and looking straight ahead he said, "Go away." Something pounded in his throat.

"Please let me speak to you," she said.

"No, I don't want to have anything to do with you. Go away." He was still looking straight before him, he had not seen her at all. He took a step forward but he felt her hand fall lightly on his arm.

"Randalo," she whispered, "for the love of God. I pray you, let me speak."

"I don't want to listen to you. I don't want to hear anything." He shook off her hand. "Get away from here. Haven't you been enough of a—a—" he had no word. "Without loitering here?"

"I come because is the *disperazione*, I must tell you something, I—"

He turned and looked at her in the dim light from the arc-lamp up the street. Her face was ghostly, her eyes enormous above her pinched cheeks. He let her see he remarked her looks. He said, "If you're hungry, go and ply your trade in some other block."

Her face fell into her hands, and though he meant to step ahead again and get away from her, he could not escape her words.

"I am not hungry," was what he heard. "I am *incinta*. I am to have a child."

He stood for a moment, overwhelmed. First this had no reality, then it had the terrible reality of the last he had seen of her. That reminded him. He said, "I called you three names the last time I saw you. They're true. Take your choice. Nobody gives a damn when such a woman has a child. Why should I?"

"*Abbi pietà!*" she moaned softly. "This is not you, Randalo."

"I am not the man you knew. You took good care to destroy him."

"But the child—"

"Stop talking. The filth of it, to tell *me* about your child."

"Can be yours, Randalo." She whispered the words, her head bent, but he heard. He felt sick and cold; a vile bitter taste flooded his mouth.

"It can be anybody's. Anybody's at all. Why pick on me? Because I was a sucker before? Or because you were too smart to try to tell my brother?"

"I have try'."

"What!" He felt his fists clench, a spasm of rage seize his stomach. How had she tried? What had she done, how had she contrived to vex and mortify his afflicted brother? He was infuriated. One of his hands gripped her upper arm until she quailed with pain and he saw her lips bitten hard together. "Shameless! You dared to go near that house? You've just been there?"

"No. I have talk' to him once on the telephone." Her eyes were closed, she was visibly faint from the pain of his savage grip on her arm. He shook it once contemptuously and flung it aside. She staggered a little. He saw this now as an assault on Seymour. No other part of what she said mattered at all, compared with the vehemence of his passion to protect Seymour.

"What did he say?" He bent over her, speaking in a snarl. "What did he tell you?"

"Tell me?" Her face was unnaturally stupid in her bewilderment. "He tell me—" she choked. "The same like you. He say he kill me if I tell you."

"Well—and so you took a chance on your precious life and told me anyway. Would you be interested to know he can't kill you, or do anything else about you because he is blind?"

"*Oh! Dio! Madonna Santa!*" She crumpled against the iron railing nearby and began to sob, praying the while in a throbbing moan.

"And if you ever try to bother him again, I swear to God I will kill you, and I'm not blind. I was. But never again. Now clear out."

He turned to go towards his house but she stumbled after him and caught at his sleeve. He tried to shake her off but she held his right arm tightly between her hands.

"Is not for myself," she said. There was a note of solemn desperation in her voice that overreached the peak of his anger and held him there, scowling. "You didn't understand? Is for the child I am praying."

"Then go and bother the other men who've had you."

"There have been none. Nobody."

"Pah!"

She bent her head, but she still held his sleeve like a vise. "I have been alone. Absolutely alone. Is not what I did with my body or what anybody has done has made me live in *penitenza*, but what I did to you *moralmente*. You can believe or not believe. Is not probable you believe. I only ask from the heart should not be punished the child."

"You are what you are, you always said so. Now I know it. Women like you get rid of these—things. Go and get rid of yours."

Her hands fell from his arm, and though he could now have walked away he was abruptly compelled to stand and watch her head come up with a motion of unflinching conviction.

"I will not kill a child," she said. She looked him straight in the eyes.

He wanted with all his strength to turn on his heel and walk away and leave her there. He could almost have done so, propelled by the waves of his rage and disgust. But he had made an error, allowing himself to look at her eyes. Against the whole force of his anger, his brutal disillusionment, his passion to protect Seymour, the silent intimation of truth in that glance shook him profoundly. In his mind he struggled to hold shut a figurative door, behind which swarmed the memories that could undo him. He was right now; he had been wrong then; for Seymour's sake he must remain right. As he had done at other crises in his life, he reached for the one prop which could get him through this and beyond it. He invoked the thought of Seymour and what he would say or do; and having grasped it clearly, he spoke in what he conceived as Seymour's words.

"And how long," he sneered, "have you been in this consecrated state?"

"Three and a half months." She still looked him steadily in the eyes, commanding rather than pleading that he make for himself the simple calculation which would state exactly what she had come to tell him.

"And you have the extraordinary idea that I—that—"

"Or one or the other," she said. "You or your brother. It makes no difference about me, I tell you I think only of the child."

"We will both be damned in hell before we will lift a finger for it or for you either. How could you have been such a fool as to think anything else?"

"I have know' you when you display a goodness, a *generosità*, like I have never hear about in all my life. In that time you do it for a woman, you are *innamorato*. In this time I ask that same man do something for an innocent child."

Struggling to keep his voice icy he said, with stiff lips, "And what do you suppose can be done for the child?"

"I am not sure," she said. "Only I know is a terrible thing for a child to find itself a *bastardo*. I am *straniera* here, in America is nothing I can do, I do not know enough to think how to help my child. Only I could take it in Italy, and in Italy is a tragedy to break the heart, it follow all through the life such a child, how it is born."

"There have been plenty of other such children in Italy," he said. "Yours will just have to be another. I don't know what kind of idea you may have had, thinking there was anything we would do about it. Surely you couldn't have thought—" his mouth hung open, silent, and he felt himself sinking down again into the quicksands of revulsion. "You go away from here," he said, breaking into irrationality. "Go away and don't ever come near either of us again."

He swung away and hurried almost at a run the short distance to his own place, and turned in there and got into the house and shut the door behind him. He stood with his back against the door, staring into the hall and towards the dark staircase. He heard Seymour's voice at the top of the stairs.

"Is that you, Ran?"

"Yes, Brother." Randall stood there taking long breaths, trying to get his voice under control so that Seymour should not hear he had been upset.

"Are you all right?" asked Seymour gently.

"Why, of course! I'm sorry I was so long, I was trying to find some specially nice crisp apples for you, the red and white kind you like. Now I'm just lighting the gas, I'll be right there."

He was careful all evening while he was reading aloud, to keep his voice light and clear, and not to let it betray his agitation in any way. He looked constantly at Seymour's face, watching for the scowl or the nervous sag of the mouth or any tense expression which would reveal that Seymour too was struggling with this knowledge and trying to keep Randall unaware that he knew. But Seymour sat quiet, his face like a mask, except at the scattered moments when he laughed—Randall wondered with how much difficulty—because they were reading *Mr. Dooley*.

Randall had one of his worst nights. Hour after hour he lay remembering other nights as bad, garnished with shreds and fragments of horror; bad, searing memories from which he would fling and toss and twist away, only to find worse ones on the farther side of his bed, the other side of his pillow. He was harrowed with misery about Seymour, but sometimes Seymour, or an image which caricatured him, rose in the midst of all this wreckage to glide forward, cynical and elegant, at the side of a laughing Renata, both together to mock at Randall until he could have screamed for surcease. Then he swung around, groping and snatching for something to drive this away, and came face to face with the newest of his chimaeras: Renata abandoned, alone in the dark street, pleading with him for help, for mercy, for—no, he groaned into his pillow. No, that can't be so. And if it is, it's Seymour's fault. Why? Didn't she tell me, how can she know, what do we all know . . . *what difference does it make*? Does it matter which of us was the worst? What can we know? Now in the ugly December dawn he knew only that he had turned on her, his cruelty complete and final. And I meant it, too. Did you? Were you speaking for yourself or for Seymour? Oh, Christ! he snarled. He leaped to his feet and rushed at his clothes. He went up to the fourth floor and spent an hour in the old day nursery.

When the day was half over he had convinced himself for the hundredth time that he had done right and that there was nothing else he could have said to her, no other attitude he could have taken. There, he told himself, that's settled. *What's settled?* How could he be sure that she would stay away from him, and how could he know that she would not again entreat Seymour? He could fix that at least. Seymour was lying down in his room. Randall ran down to Seymour's shop in the cellar. He knew nothing about tools but he clambered his way over masses of stuff to get a screw-driver and a pair of pliers. He went quietly upstairs to the hall and examined the telephone on the wall. He was not sure that he knew how to remove it, but, he thought, even a fool like me can find a way to put it out of order.

He had the box off the wall and was twisting away with the pliers at the wires he had exposed, when he heard Seymour's soft step behind him, and looked over his shoulder to see him groping quietly along the wall. Seymour's hand fell on his shoulder and he said gently, "Randall, are you trying to disconnect the telephone?"

"Yes."

"So she reached you too. Come here, Ran." He drew Randall into the library and sat down and pulled him down on the hassock near his chair. "What did you say to her?"

"About the same thing you did, I suppose." Randall sat doubled over, his head in his hands.

"Then you think—" Seymour spoke uneasily—"I did right?"

"Oh—oh, how do I know!" Randall's voice broke shrilly. "It's all such a hideous, tragic mess."

"It is. But you know yourself what she—" Seymour shook his head with a sigh.

"She swore there's been nobody else."

"I'd be afraid to take her word for anything, Ran."

The memory of her eyes yesterday, level and curiously fearless even in the midst of panic, gnawed at Randall. He only said, "Did she tell you how long she's been pregnant?"

"Eh—yes."

"Well."

"There's something I hope you know," said Seymour slowly. "After that day, that day last August, you know the day I mean. I never—"

"Oh, don't talk about it!"

"I think I should. We never have. When you disappeared then, I realized what had happened. Although the very first night, when you didn't come home, of course I thought—" he shrugged. "If that was so, God knew I wished you well and wouldn't for the world have touched her again. But when days passed and you didn't come home, I was beside myself. I was so alarmed that I went and asked her if she knew where you were. She was very upset, and I can tell you, no two people ever hated the sight of each other more. We hated ourselves and each other and what we had done to you. That was the end of her so far as I was concerned."

"Brother," said Randall, in a high, tense tone frightening to Seymour's sensitive ears and nerves, "do you realize what all this means?"

"I suppose so."

Randall's voice turned louder. "She's been pregnant since the end of August. She swears she's been alone ever since, but even if she's the biggest liar in the world it doesn't make any difference. One of us— oh, my God!" He broke down.

Seymour leaned over and put his arms round Randall's shoulders. He held him so for a moment and then said, "The chances are that it is I, you know. I don't want to make you think about it—" as Randall winced, "but since it will be your nature to try to lay the blame on yourself, I'd rather you put it on me right from the start. It will help you to put it out of mind, eventually."

"But how can I do that when it can exactly as well be I?"

"Can it?"

"Can't it?"

Seymour let go of Randall's shoulders and shrank down in his chair, covering his blind eyes with one long, bony hand. He said, "It's unendurable, to have done this to you. Now, especially—when you're—" he cringed, "trapped with me. Oh, Randall, how you must hate me."

"But I don't, Brother! Maybe I have at times—or even still might, in a way. But it has nothing to do with what I really feel for you. Don't you know that?"

Seymour was silent.

"Don't you know it?" cried Randall again. "Brother, you must believe me. I love you, more than I ever feel—ever felt—anything else about you. Won't you believe me?"

"Of course I believe you." Seymour's hand groped towards Randall and rested for a moment on his cheek. The cheek was wet and Seymour let his fingers lie there as if he had not felt that. "Of course I believe you. But I don't deserve it."

"I'm so confused," said Randall, suddenly giving up the struggle to control his voice. Seymour heard it break. "The whole thing, all mixed up like this. I don't know. I talked to her yesterday just the way she said you had, but I couldn't do that again, Brother." He looked at Seymour as if to plead with those unseeing eyes. "I couldn't."

"But you did right," said Seymour. "There wasn't any other way to treat her. You know what she was when you first knew her. How she behaved with me. I'm not trying to duck any blame. But, Ran, it takes two to hit it off. She knew what she was doing. She wanted to do it."

"Oh, I know that."

"Then she's got to take the consequences. And if you should begin to weaken about it and think you owed her anything, you'd end in a mess worse than this. If that were possible."

"I know." Randall sat with his head down, his clasped hands hanging between his knees. "But I just can't keep on feeling so—so raging— as I was yesterday, and all those months before. I feel as if it had all been emptied out of me at once."

"You feel sorry for her. You would, with that tender heart of yours. I wronged you worse than she did, and see how you are with me!"

"You weren't any worse than she—than any of us."

Seymour sighed and said, uncharacteristically, "Judge not. But now what's done has got to stay done, Ran. We mustn't back down. If you won't believe me for any other reason, you will admit I know more about women than you do. We did the right thing yesterday and we've got to stick to it."

They were silent for a long time. Seymour wished wretchedly that he could see Randall's face. He could imagine all too vividly its pitiful, drooping bewilderment, but only his eyes could have told him whether he had convinced Randall to any lasting degree. After a while he said, "Ran, did you take the telephone off the wall, or what?"

"Just about. It's hanging by a wire. What do you want me to do about it?"

"Why, finish what you started. What do we want it for anyway?"

The weeks went by at a dead-march pace, one blank stretch following on the next. Seymour lived in terror that Renata Tosi would return to importune Randall, which he would be helpless to intercept. Randall lived in tormented anxiety because she did not. Having emptied out all at once, as he had said, the seething poisons of his outrage, he felt as if he had also broken the vessel that had held them. They did not seep back; he had no place in which to retain them. The catharsis had left him his truest, simplest self, a person whom Seymour knew minutely but could never really understand.

Seymour could take a decision effortlessly and live by it without the least further concern either that it might have been faulty or that wisdom might suggest revising it if the circumstances should change. For Randall any decision was difficult, and a radical one, agony. This one in whose jaws he was caught was brutal, and he could not rest on the accomplished fact. His thoughts of Renata did not hang upon her cruelty to him, but upon his to her. His mind was permeated by memories which he loved even while he could no longer love her. He had loved standing by her when she was helpless; now his imagination saw her more helpless still. Why was he alive, if not to act in the only way his nature knew? The enormity of her situation hounded and haunted him. How was she living? Where? What about money? What about her health?

He had abandoned the self-deception of never looking at the music news in the papers and he followed minutely the casts billed in the opera announcements. She was singing about three times a week. So long as she could keep this up, he calculated, she could support herself and if she was careful, save enough to live on for a time after she must stop singing. But that would be soon now; this was the end of January. When would it be impossible for her to appear any longer on the stage? Then what would she do? Go to Italy? She had made it pitifully clear that that was what she most dreaded. He remembered fragments of her talk at different times; he saw her sitting across a restaurant table, or standing in the Maynards' cornfield, scattering shreds of knowledge which he pieced together to envision the stringency of her childhood. Where could she go but to her native village, to throw herself and the child on the mercy of her relatives?

"I have work' hard *da bambina* . . . I did not laugh . . . for poor *contadini* is a different thing . . . . walking four *chilometri* up and down the mountain . . . carrying on my back . . . thirty-five cents a week. . . ." He did not need to think further what her life would be; he knew. Well, she will go away afterwards and sing again. Yes, but the child? "In Italy is a tragedy . . . how it follow such a child . . ." But what could he do? Even if he could decide to do something, what should it be?

He knew, because anybody would know; only money could help her through the worst of her ordeal and shield her from the total impact of everything she most feared. She had not asked him for money but it was the only help he could give; he was inclined to agree with Seymour that the child was the consequence of her own voluntary acts, and she must find her own solution for it. Her own voluntary acts . . . for a moment the burden of his deadly guilt came sweeping back, but he held his ground against it because his memories were so clear.

Now he must contrive to send money to her in such a way that Seymour should not know, and she should understand this was all that Randall would do. Anything beyond that could bring her back into their orbit to harass his helpless brother and make discord between them. That must not be. No: it had to be money. He was pondering that the next morning, when he went downstairs to take in the newspapers and the morning mail. Few letters ever came to the Holt house, but today was the first of February; the post had brought his bank statement, and Seymour's and a sheaf of bills which he sorted as he walked slowly upstairs to the library. Perhaps because he had been thinking for several days about money, to which he ordinarily never gave a thought; or perhaps because up to now so many greater concerns had preoccupied him in his care of Seymour, he had not really noticed these bills as they went unopened through his hands on the first of each month. It was part of the slow lesson of learning to care for Seymour, to act out the ghastly farce of respect for his privacy. Randall had handed him his mail when it came, and never yet had Seymour submitted to the humiliation of asking to have a letter read to him. Randall had somehow never wondered why. Now he stood in the library doorway, with his right hand full of envelopes addressed to Seymour, and he saw suddenly that Seymour in these four months had received scarcely any other mail at all.

He went over to Seymour and said, "Here's your mail, Brother," and laid the pile on Seymour's knee. He sat down in his own chair and ripped open his bank statement. He had never kept close track of his balance, and he was startled to see how it had shrunk. He sat back and ran his fingers into his hair and began the futile mental back-tracking of trying to understand where the money had gone. Most of it on Renata, between last April and August; her illness had eaten up the accumulated income that he had not spent before. And since then he had quit his job, and now he realized, turning over his cancelled vouchers one by one, and thinking about the past four months, he had been paying all the living expenses which he and Seymour had always shared before. The gas and the coal and the food and Mrs. Quinn's wages—it didn't amount to so very much, but four months of it made quite a total. And then he had bought the small upright piano so that he could play for Seymour. Well, he would have to find a tactful way of suggesting that he write out the necessary checks for Seymour, and guide his hand while he signed them. But, he saw, picking up the yellow bank statement again, even after Seymour had reimbursed him, he would have to be extremely careful—penurious, in fact—if he were to send Renata even a little money; as little as would help her at all. He was digesting this in worried silence when Seymour said, "Randall." He looked across at his brother. "Yes," he said.

Seymour was sitting with the pile of unopened envelopes clutched between his hands as if he were about to tear the lot in half. His fore-head was stitched in a nervous scowl, and his whole appearance was so tense that Randall had for a moment the illusion that Seymour had been able to read the mail which had upset him. Seymour dragged at his moustache and started several times to say something, and shut his mouth again while Randall sat watching him and waiting for him to speak. Finally he dropped the pile of letters on his knees and felt them over until he found the large envelope from the bank. He opened it. His long precise fingers made as neat a job of it as they did of everything. He drew out the statement and unfolded it. There were no cancelled checks enclosed. He thrust the yellow paper at Randall and said, "It's a damned bloody nuisance . . . . would you mind telling me what it says? The balance?"

Randall took the paper slowly and looked at the solitary figure in the right-hand column. Without thinking, completely flabbergasted, he said, "Why—there must be some mistake, Seymour." The balance showed less than two hundred dollars.

Seymour was silent. He did not ask what Randall meant. He sat for a while with his fists clenched on the letters in his lap. Then he stood up with a jerk, scattering them, and began to pace up and down the room, cursing. Randall sat and watched him, afraid to say a word. Presently Seymour swung round and snapped, "Why should there be a mistake? Surely you aren't surprised?"

"Well—" Randall was embarrassed. Whatever he said would be wrong. "I guess I just supposed—"

"Ah, the gentleman of means," said Seymour acidly, "who can afford to suppose!"

"You—you stop that!" Randall was in no mood for this. "What's got into you?"

Seymour stopped pacing and shut his mouth hard. Randall saw a flush of embarrassment come over his face. "I'm sorry, Ran," he said. He patted at the space to his left until his hand found Randall's shoulder. "Please forgive me. I'm nervous."

"Oh that's nothing, forget it. But isn't there some mistake about this?"

Seymour shook his head. "No. That's the trouble. I'm in a good deal of a mess as a result of this bloody thing—" he passed his hand across his eyes. "It damn near kills me to do it, but I'm afraid I'll have to ask if you can help me out for the time being."

"I suppose you mean those bills." Randall's voice was dull.

"Yes. I don't give a hang about most of them, they can just damn well wait. But there's a bill from Willingdon—"

"You mean you haven't paid him for a long time?"

Seymour tweaked hard at his moustache. "I—no." He paused as if waiting for Randall to comment, and when he heard nothing he snapped, "It's a damned outrage. The man's a millionaire, those fees of his. He ought to be ashamed of himself."

"You mean—he's been pressing you?"

"What the hell else would I mean? The bastard had the gall to dun me to my face the last two times he was here."

"How else could he dun you?" Randall muttered. "How long is it since you've paid him?"

"How should I know!" Seymour's voice was shrill.

Randall said nothing. Seymour set to pacing again. The silence pressed on them like a pair of giant hands pushing them down against the floor. Randall waited until he saw that Seymour was not going to say anything, and then he asked, "How much do you owe Doctor Willingdon, Seymour?"

"Oh, open his goddam bill and look for yourself."

Randall sat with the open envelope in one hand and the bill in the other. Several times he started to speak and then shut his mouth again. Each time he looked at the bill once more, and then at Seymour. "Gee," he said, finally.

"Well, what are you so surprised about?" Seymour's fingers twitched and he groped for a cigarette and matches. "Where do you suppose I found out what these muckamucks charge? You remember how I warned you when—when you had that surgeon?"

"Yes, but—" Randall ran his fingers through his hair again. "This must have been running on for a long time. Seymour," he said, "what did you do with your money? Oh, the automobile." He answered himself.

"Why, sure. I told you what I was going to do."

"Of course I never realized you had this—piling up long before."

"Well, I did. And since I had this fella telling me, in effect, that if I didn't buy a car then I'd never have one at all, I damn well decided I'd have one. How should I know he'd turn into a bloodsucker?"

Randall looked again at Seymour's bank statement. He said uneasily, for he was afraid of another outburst, "If you haven't paid your doctor in such a long time—I don't quite understand—maybe it's none of my business," he said uncomfortably.

"Oh, hell," said Seymour. "If I'm going to ask you to help me out, I suppose you've got a right to ask about it. I got the money for the car from a crook by signing notes ordering the bank to make over my income to him every quarter until he was paid up—with too much interest, you can be sure."

"And he'll still be getting your money—until—?"

"Figure it out for yourself. You know I bought the car last Spring. He gets my money next month and the quarter after that—before I'm shut of him."

"June." Randall sat shaking his head. "That means you won't have any more money than this—" he tapped the bank statement— "until next September."

"That's right," said Seymour with the slashing note in his voice again. "Bright boy. Go to the head of the class."

"Seymour, will you shut up?" Randall's voice rose dangerously. He pulled himself together and said, "This bill of your doctor's—why don't you ask the Trustees to pay it?"

"My dear Randall, you ought to know the terms of those trusts as well as I do. The Trustees have no authority to pay out a dime more for us than the will says without a special order from the Surrogate's Court. Do you think old Dickinson and that desiccated Judge Bronson would even think of going to the Surrogate's Court without first skinning us alive of the last shred of our privacy? As soon as they find out I bought a car instead of paying some son of a bitch for the privilege of going blind—"

"Oh, Brother!" Randall jumped up, scattering the papers from his lap. He put his arm round Seymour's shoulders and held him tight and said, "Of course I'll help you. I don't quite know how we'll manage, I can't possibly pay Doctor Willingdon all at once. But I'll talk to him and work it out. I haven't got much leeway myself, you know. I—spent a lot of money, too. But we'll manage somehow."

"Ran, I feel like such a hound—"

"Oh, no." Randall stood patting Seymour's shoulder, wildly calculating inside a head not only unused to this kind of thing, but reeling as if the ceiling had fallen on it. Between now and next September he would be paying every penny of Seymour's expenses and this enormous bill besides, if not—his eyes fell on the rest of Seymour's mail strewn across the floor. God knew what those envelopes contained. There would not be a penny to spare for anything . . . anybody . . . anywhere.

Every day after Mrs. Quinn had cooked their deadly plain midday dinner and cleaned up the kitchen, now reimpressed into use, and gone home, Seymour went to his room to lie down. Randall usually went out at that hour to do the frugal marketing. He had found this the way to effect the strictest economy. Cooked food brought in from restaurants was now out of the question, although Seymour liked it so much better. It cost twice as much. And Randall found that he saved money by marketing himself, instead of leaving it to Mrs. Quinn. She not only spent more than he did, but he had to pay for more of her time.

So his days were an endless succession of petty details, the mornings filled by reading the newspapers to Seymour, the early afternoons by his patient searches for food at the lowest possible prices. He would walk blocks out of his way to save three or four cents, carrying a market basket on his arm in oblivion of the inquisitive or scornful stares of the neighborhood women. If he saved a quarter on a whole week's food he thought it worthwhile. Seymour not only could not see the notebooks and account books in Randall's room, filled with anxious budgeting in his tiny hand; once Randall had taken over Seymour's .debt to Doctor Willingdon, and all their joint expenses with it, Seymour did not give the matter another thought.

Each brother had withdrawn to a degree behind the screen of his own trouble. Neither sought, nor would have sought, the separate truth about the other. Both wondered secretly at times, and both shrank from discovering. Randall dared not plumb the wreck of Seymour's life buried beneath his blindness and locked behind his pride. Was he desperately bored and lonely? What had become of his friends? None of them had been friends in a real sense, they had only been the companions of his pleasures, and those would be the surest to fall away in affliction. And Seymour, listening to Randall while he read aloud with angelic patience, hours upon end, or chatted about the trivial things which took up his unnatural days; Seymour soon built the evasive defence of assuring himself that Randall did not think about that—or her—or it, any more. Better that he was busy, even if only in pursuit of potatoes for a penny less a pound than he might have paid.

But when Renata's name disappeared from the Opera's billings in the *Times*, Randall brooded heavily upon what had become of her. Had she gone back to Italy? He could imagine no alternative. He would have been thankful for the relief of not thinking about her at all, but that was not within his will-power. Well, then, would it lift him from his morass of wretched, guilty uncertainty to go to the opera house and inquire about her at the stage-door desk? They knew him; they would tell him. But when they did tell him, what good would that do? What could he do for her?

April dragged by and May too. Seymour was often short-tempered. He snapped at Randall, he scorned the dull food, he made thoughtless requests for this and that which Randall could not buy on his stringent budget. Seymour had apparently outgrown his contrition about the disaster and his concern for burdening Randall. His only concern now seemed to be himself, which Randall found too pathetically easy to understand. But mere understanding made matters no easier to manage. One hot night in the first week of June he was reading to Seymour in the library, conscious that Seymour was restless and not paying attention. When he was in that mood he made it hopelessly difficult to read to him. He would spring from his chair, pace the floor for a time, worry his moustache, light a cigarette, crush it out (while Randall thought of the price of that Turkish tobacco), stride up and down again. And if Randall paused, supposing him too bored to listen any more, Seymour said snappishly, "Well? What are you stopping for?"

But this time when Randall paused for breath at the end of a chapter Seymour stood with his elbow on the mantel and said, "Ran, I've been thinking of something."

Randall sighed. That remark usually presaged a suggestion that money be spent. "Yes?" he said.

"I think we ought to have the telephone put back."

Randall only said, "Why?"

"Thoughtful, aren't you," said Seymour. "I should think you'd be able to see for yourself that it's the only way I could ever have a human being to talk to."

"I see." Randall's voice quavered.

"Oh, I don't mean to be rude," Seymour hurried to apologize. "Of course—of course I appreciate all you—"

"Never mind that," said Randall. "Maybe I ought to have thought of it myself. But now that it's gone, that's a few dollars we aren't spending each month. We can't afford it now, Seymour."

"God damn it! Is there anything we can afford? I'm getting so sick of your pious penny-pinching—I think you like it. I think you actually like that vile boiled dog-meat with cabbage in it."

Randall sat stiffly with the closed book gripped in his fingers. He sat imagining what it would be like to feel even more angry than he was now hurt. His mouth was shut so tight that his jaws ached. He had no intention of saying anything. Seymour, perfectly aware of this, stood hesitating for a moment; Randall saw him struggling with his temper. Then he muttered sullenly, "I'm sorry. I guess I get pushed pretty near the edge at times, Ran."

"I know."

"Well, I didn't mean it, anyway. But I do think we ought to have the telephone again."

"You were ready enough to have me take it out."

"My God! Do I have to explain why?"

"No." Suddenly Randall did feel angry, and he decided that for once Seymour was not going to have what he wanted. "But since you were glad to have it gone because that put you out of reach of your creditors and also of—of—"

"Well, what kind of damned fool do you think I am? When there's a reason for something, it's one way and when there's no reason—Randall, don't be so childish. Naturally, now that you've salted things down so those bastards won't try to bother me, and we can take it for granted that—that—" he paused, embarrassed.

"What can we take for granted?" asked Randall, in a tone as icy as one of Seymour's own.

"Why—that she, well, she's out of the picture." Seymour made rough gestures in the air. "If she was telling the truth she'd have had the child by now and whatever she was telling, the chances are she went back to Italy and won't ever bother us again."

Randall for a moment sank down in his chair, his face in his hands. Then he looked at Seymour, standing there with his eyes narrowed cynically, exactly as he used to do when he could see.

"So you've been thinking about it too," he said bitterly. "And such wise, generous, compassionate thoughts. Sometimes I think you are the most selfish, diabolical—"

"Sure!" Seymour let his voice go in a scream. "Try this over on one of your crazy pianos and see how you like the music! Try being blind yourself! It's wonderful! Nothing to do all day but worry about little brother's—" he stopped short with a gasp and a shudder. Through the house, peal after peal, they heard the hoarse clang of the front doorbell. Somebody was pulling again and again at the rusty knob. Randall turned pale. Seymour stood with his mouth open, his hands trembling before him.

"What was that?" he said, choked.

Randall stood up, holding onto his chair. He licked his lips. "The doorbell," he said.

"Nobody ever rings the doorbell at night." Seymour stood squinting, bracing himself against the mantel. The bell clanged again. He cowered.

"I'm going down to see—" Randall began to move towards the hall.

"No," cried Seymour. "Don't go down there, Ran."

"I'm going."

"No, no. Stay here. What time is it?" The bell rang again.

"A quarter to one," said Randall, and left the room. He went downstairs. He heard Seymour come out on the landing behind him. He looked back once and saw Seymour crouching there, holding onto the banister.

Slowly Randall opened the front door. Nobody was there. He looked, puzzled, out at the walk, and right and left as far as he could see. He saw nobody. Then he heard a sound, a tiny, utterly unmistakable cry. He looked down at his feet. There on the doorstep stood a basket. He dropped to his knees. The basket was oblong, like his market basket, with rounded corners. It was filled with a pillow and knitted wool shawls and there was a bow of pink ribbon tied to its handle. He saw the color of the ribbon in the dim light from the street. He saw the tiny, red, wailing face carefully hooded by a shawl; the child's cry was thin and fretful. He lifted the basket, holding it tight in his arms, and took it into the house. He put it gently on the hall table and reached up to light the gas. The puny, choking wail continued.

Randall looked up the stairs. Seymour was still crouching at the top. His ears, thought Randall, his ears were always sharp and have been much sharper since he was blind. He has heard it already.

"What is it?" asked Seymour. His voice was strangled.

"You can hear," said Randall, in tears.

"No, no, what do you mean?"

Randall bent over the basket. A piece of paper was tucked among the shawls. "There is a note here," he said.

"What? Note? Well, what does it say?"

Randall did not speak, doubled over with the note crushed in his hand.

"The note," said Seymour hoarsely from upstairs. "What does it say?"

"It says: *Here is my child. Renata.*"

CHAPTER 16

When John was two years old, Randall had a sand-pile made for him in the back yard, a square of smooth boards, filled with clean white sand which did not cost very much over at the building-supply dealer's at the foot of Twenty-fourth Street by the river. Randall bought a toy spade and bucket and with these and a handful of clothespins, John kept busy and happy all the afternoon. Randall usually sat watching him under the ailanthus tree, on a wobbly kitchen chair. The little boy was stocky and sturdy, with a firmness and accuracy about all his movements, and a solemnity in his baby face that reflected the concentration with which he played. Even though his aim when he did something might be incomprehensible to anybody else, he seemed to Randall always to have a definite purpose. He was a silent child, not given at all to prattling, which Mrs. Quinn and her daughter Maggie said was that different: most children were after making some kind of noise all the time. John spoke when he had something to say, and then slowly, thinking while he said it, in few words, clearly pronounced.

Randall watched him as he stuck his clothespins into the sand, patting them firmly into place. Then he began to shovel more sand around and between them, moulding it with his fingers into something that looked like a low Chinese wall, punctuated at intervals by the knobs on top of the clothespins. I wonder if he knows that he's actually making a design, Randall thought. It looks much too orderly to be an accident. But he couldn't know, at that age . . . John looked over his shoulder at Randall and gave him a beaming silent smile and went on with his wall. The sun was warm, and Randall sighed with recurrent relief that this back yard had turned out to be as good a place for John's airings as it had. The board fence had been repaired and painted dark green, the bare black grit had been planted with sod, and Randall had even induced a few flowers to grow in the narrow border against the fence. What would we have done without it, he thought, imagining as he often had before the impossibility of sending the child out in its pram to be pushed up and down Twenty-fourth Street under the coarse stares of the neighbors . . . people who whispered or giggled or pointed or . . .

why think about it? He had long fixed the habit of not thinking or caring about such people, or any people. But he had to be alert at every moment to protect John. He was always one step ahead of himself when it came to problems.

He heard the back door open; Seymour came slowly out to the yard. He was feeling his way up the steps from the basement entry, dragging behind him an old zinc wash-tub, which banged on each step. Randall said, "What are you going to do with that, Brother?"

"I've made a boat for John to sail, a very simple one. I thought we could sink the tub in a corner of his sand-box and put some water in it, and I think I can feel around well enough to show him how to sail the boat."

"That's fine," said Randall. John was much too young to sail a boat, but why spoil Seymour's pleasure? "I only wonder—well, I'm a little worried he might fall in. That's a pretty big tub."

"You may be right. Damn," said Seymour, "why didn't I think of that? I know. You tie a clothes-line around his waist and hold one end of it while you watch him. If he gets too near the edge of the tub you can yank him back."

So Randall helped Seymour to put the tub in place and put water in it, and Seymour brought out his boat, the simplification of an old one that he had made when he was a boy, and they tied the clothes-line round John's waist. Randall guided Seymour to the corner of the sand-pile and put him on his knees where he could reach the boat, and John scrambled along beside Seymour, following the boat and clapping his hands with delight while Randall sat holding the end of the rope. He marvelled to see how Seymour managed; how sensitive he was to the faint play of the summer breeze, how his nervous, delicate fingers adjusted the miniature rigging and set the boat on a true course across the tub. He is at last, thought Randall, beginning to be a little easier, a little reconciled. It is making him happy, or giving him a moment's illusion of happiness, to do this with John. Thank God, Randall thought. In the beginning he could never have dared to hope for a time like this afternoon.

When Randall was restless and wakeful in the night, when the bad memories came back at him as they had done through all these years, he lived again those terrible hours and days, the climax of all the disasters that had gone before, when Seymour raved and stormed and threatened and Randall for the one time in his life had been adamant. Now it seemed an impossibility that they could have got through that crisis and that John had survived it. Like so much else from which it was inextricable, Randall managed most of the time to keep it rammed away in the dark pit of wilful oblivion; but sometimes even now it broke out, horrible and vivid and worst of all, pregnant with some threat for the future. He had that to conquer too; it strode always beside him, a grey, powerful ghost. Seymour had raised it that very first night, had blown into it the breath of its hateful vitality; and Randall must struggle with it forever, holding John beyond its reach.

The argument had been savage; never had a thing of such ferocity touched them before. Seymour had said he would not have the child in the house even for the night. Randall had said, "Either it stays or I leave with it." Seymour had said, "You can't go, you can't leave, there must be some kind of law that will keep you from abandoning me for a nameless bastard."

"Nameless. But one of us is its father and both of us are going to take the responsibility."

"Bastards don't have fathers. It can be anybody's spawn. It's not mine."

"Then it's mine. And I'm keeping it."

"You're not," screamed Seymour from the top of those dark stairs, while the child wailed and gargled in the basket on the table. "If you try to keep it here I'll kill it."

"If you do I'll turn you in. I mean that."

And Seymour had known from Randall's voice, a tone of voice he had never heard before, that this was true. So he turned to argument again, talking, talking, while Randall down in the hall ignored him and tried to quiet the screaming infant. He sat on the bottom step in the hall, holding the child bundled in his arms, clumsy, helpless, frantic, not knowing what to do. And upstairs Seymour stood clinging to the banister and talking.

"Take it to a foundling hospital," he said. "Get it out of the house. Take it to that convent over in Twenty-third Street. Go and take it now."

Randall ignored him. Seymour talked until he was sick and sweating, wildly repeating himself and no longer coherent, and Randall sat rocking the child and saying nothing. Little by little the child became quieter. Randall did not know that it was too hot, that he should have unwrapped it from the knitted blanket, he knew nothing, he could not see how to manage until morning when he would get help; but he paid no attention to Seymour. The child slept at last from exhaustion and Randall laid it back in its basket and said, "Seymour, shut up and go to your room. Not one word you've said makes the slightest difference. Shut up and go to bed."

Then Seymour said, "I suppose you realize that its sainted mother must be here in New York, that she stayed here plotting to do this. I'm damn well going to see she gets it right back."

"You're going to see nothing," said Randall. "You're blind."

He heard a gasp from Seymour behind him up the stairs; he had not known he could be capable of such cruelty. But he had hit the mark.

"At least," said Seymour, "try to make sense enough to think about what I said. She obviously is here. And maybe we made a mistake, not giving her any money. If you go and talk to her now and tell her we'll give her money, she'll take the child back. You can't keep it, Randall, you must be out of your mind."

"In or out of it, I don't care. I'm going to keep the child."

All that night he stayed downstairs in the drawing-room, watching and hovering over the child. Hour by hour his helpless desperation grew, as the child howled weakly from hunger and discomfort and heat, none of which Randall knew how to assuage. Towards morning he grew frightened, the child was quiet, but he thought, too quiet. Suppose it should die. He knelt beside the divan where he had placed the basket, and put his head in his hands and prayed, though to whom, in what words, he could never have said. As soon as it was light he began to watch from the window for somebody out in the street whom he could hail, and after a time he saw a boy walking along on his way to some early job. Randall threw up the sash and called to him. The boy came to the window and Randall handed him out some money and told him to go to Mrs. Quinn, who lived in Twenty-seventh Street near Eleventh Avenue, and ask her to come at once, because there was an emergency.

Randall heard her come in soon through the side door. He went out to the hall and called her into the drawing-room. The child was wailing feebly. She stood in the doorway in her shabby clothes, a cracked straw hat with a red rose pinned to her topknot. Her mouth was wide open with amazement. Randall only said, "I won't explain anything, Mrs. Quinn. But please—please—take care of this child. I—" he turned away, unable to speak.

The woman crossed the room and looked into the basket and with a capable scoop lifted the child out and unwrapped it from its shawls. "Oh, the poor thing," she said, and then, "Mother o' God, Mr. Holt, it can't be much over a week old."

"I know." He was standing at the window with his back turned. "Can you—look here, it isn't going to die, is it?"

"Die? I should say not. Here, now." She sat down on the divan, rummaged in the basket, and was soon busy changing the child's diaper and making it comfortable. "That's better," she said, in her fat brogue. "Lord, what a mess. He'll be feelin' better now."

"He?"

"Yes, sir. He. There's the little man." The child was quiet.

Later in the morning Randall had a talk with Mrs. Quinn. He intended to say as little as possible, but looking at the woman's plain, common-garden face, her eyes which would see such a thing only in its brutal elementary reality, he said, "Mrs. Quinn, there is no use my telling you the story behind this. If I tell you lies, you'll know they are lies, and the truth you can guess for yourself. Which of us is the father—that is what I'm not going to tell you. Nor who the mother is either. The child is here—and I intend to keep it. Will you help me?"

The woman said slowly, "Mr. Holt, sir, I don't mean to be steppin' out of me place. But I don't think it would be fair to a child to raise it up like that. It's an awful odd situation, sir."

"I know that. You may as well know my brother thinks as you do. He wanted me to take it to an orphanage last night."

"Well, sir, in a way he's right. Them childer, the poor things—"

"And you honestly think I can't give this child a better life than the foundlings in an orphanage?"

"Why—" her mouth hung half open.

"There you are. That's what I mean. I don't know anything about this yet, but I'll learn. The minute you saw what I meant, you began to think so too."

She stood silent, twisting a corner of her apron. He saw that she was weighing something which she hesitated to say. He nodded at her and said, "I know what you're thinking. We're pretty queer here. Both of us. This house—" he motioned overhead to indicate all the locked, derelict rooms. "And my blind brother. You may be thinking this is no place for a young child. You may be right. All I know is the child is here," he was unconscious of repeating himself, "and I mean to keep it."

"Very well, sir," she said quietly.

"Thank you. Now what should we do about taking care of it?"

"I should say it had ought to have a nurse, sir. Someone's got to be with it all the time while it's so little."

"You couldn't do that yourself? You couldn't just move in here and stay?"

She shook her head. "I've got me husband, sir, and the three younger childer. I'm needed at home, the hours I'm not here. But—"

"Then find me a nurse. I'd rather have somebody you know. Somebody who—" he smiled lamely. Somebody who will be trustworthy with the child, he meant, and charitable about this grotesque house and its occupants, and perhaps even decent enough not to blab about them too maliciously. He asked Mrs. Quinn in a burst of helpless frankness if that was too much to hope. She wove her hard red fingers together in her embarrassment, and bit her lip; then she said, "That's awful hard to answer, Mr. Holt."

"I suppose it is. A woman used to work for us, named McBane—"

"I know. She's no different from most. But you can't be like— excuse me, sir, like you are, and not have everybody in a neighborhood know it. I tend to mind my own business more than Mary McBane, but—" her unfinished sentence told him the uselessness of wanting human nature to be other than it was.

"Well, the important thing is a nurse now. Can't you find me somebody, Mrs. Quinn?"

She said slowly, "I was thinkin' about me daughter Maggie. She works as nursemaid for Mrs. Worthington over on Gramercy Park—"

"Then get her! I hadn't hoped for anything as good as that. How quickly could she come?"

Mrs. Quinn looked embarrassed again. "Oh, quickly enough, I suppose. But you see, sir—" she hung her head. Randall stood and watched her and once again her awkward silence told him what she could not find a way to say.

"I see," he sighed. "You wouldn't feel too good about having your own daughter work in such a—an—unconventional situation. I understand. I wish it could be different. But don't you see—I must have help? If it were anything but a child—"

"I know. You see, good jobs depends on always havin' good references —the best. And Maggie's been near two years with Mrs. Worthington, it's her first job. If she left it for—" Mrs. Quinn shut her mouth, then sighed and said, "for a place like this, what would happen when she went to apply for the next one?"

"I'd give her the best reference in the world," he said quickly.

She looked at him as if to ask who, upon verifying a reference from him, would think it anything but an obloquy. Overcome by mortification, he said with his eyes averted, "I understand. But this is—you do know, don't you, that I'd pay your daughter, and you too, much more than ordinary wages? And—" he managed a tone of such innate, well-bred authority that it slightly reassured the uneasy Irishwoman, "when it comes time for a reference, something can be arranged, I'm sure."

She stood biting her lip, swayed by the promise of extra money. He said, "Please, Mrs. Quinn. Please do it for me." He put his hand on her forearm and looked into her hard grey eyes with such pleading that she yielded to what her better sense had told her from the first would be a mistake. She sighed. A body would have to have a heart of stone, she thought, and went away to see Maggie.

Seymour was furious. The first he knew of the arrangement was when he heard Randall upstairs that afternoon, dragging and pushing furniture around the old spare-room above the library, the rear bedroom on the third floor where their mother had lived in the front. He felt his way upstairs and along the hall until he stood in the room, smelling the warm air from the open window, which, mingling with the dust and must of a decade, carried a mouldy miasma to his nostrils.

"What are you doing?" he asked Randall, though he knew perfectly well.

"Getting this room ready to be used."

"There isn't a room in this house fit to use."

"There will be when I get through with this one."

"You can't get this room fit to be lived in. It stinks like a sty."

"It won't." Seymour heard a crash and Randall said, "If you don't want to get hurt, get out of the way. I'm piling up the furniture in this end of the room. Move."

"Why?"

"Seymour, go downstairs and mind your own business."

"Are you going to have any repairs made?" Seymour's voice twanged.

"Yes. Whatever's necessary. I'm going to have the roof fixed so no more damp comes down the back of the house. And I'm going to have this room plastered and papered. Thank God it's the one room in the house where there isn't a lot of old stuff I'd have to stop and sort out."

"You're going to ask the Trustees to pay for that?"

"I certainly am. At least when *I* want them to spend some money they don't have to go to court to get permission."

"I won't have any of my money used this way!"

"Don't. I'll tell them to use mine."

"And I'll tell them," Seymour shouted, "that you're fixing up this room to keep your bastard in."

"Ours. I can always tell them that, and I will if you force me. Or I'll just pay for the repairs myself. Instead of paying your doctor's bill for another three months. In fact I don't see how I can carry it any longer anyway." He walked over to Seymour and put his hands on either side of his face and said, "Now you listen to me. You've used that word for the last time. Understand? I mean it, Seymour. God help you if you use that word again."

Seymour swore and said, "If you don't take my advice and go and look for her before you let yourself in for all this, you're a bigger damn fool than you ever proved yourself before. And that was spectacular." He turned to go away.

But next day, when Maggie Quinn, detached from Mrs. Worthington by a fictitious family emergency, was settled temporarily in the drawing-room with the child, and Randall had seen a contractor and ordered the repairs, he was nonplussed to find that he could not get Seymour's words out of his head. He tried to keep too busy to think at all, but even while he was buried in the details of furnishing the third floor room, digging out from the shut-up fourth floor pieces of old nursery furniture which could be cleaned and painted and put to use, carefully leaving his own things hidden and locked up there, he found his mind uneasily turning over Seymour's remarks about Renata. Was it possible that Seymour could be right? If she had stayed in New York it struck him suddenly that he ought to get some kind of assurance from her that she would never try to see the child. He sat down heavily and began to ponder the possibility that some day she might walk into their lives again and demand to take the child back. It did not fit with anything he knew of Renata, but he had read of far stranger happenings in situations with the elements of this one. Presently it became clear that he would have no peace of mind until he had found out whether Seymour was right about her.

It was surprisingly simple to trace her. That had not occurred to him at all. The Opera was closed, but he reached its booking-manager, who had sent Renata to St. Timothy's those unbelievable fifteen months ago. The man gave him an address to which she had evidently moved from the flat she had sublet last summer. She had left there to go to another place, whose address was readily given him. He followed two more such moves, each a shabbier descent, and at the end of the day found himself on a doorstep talking to a heavy, sullen Italian woman with wary black eyes. He supposed this must be a musicians' boarding-house, but if it wasn't, he did not want to know what it was. The woman was a clam at first, she did not even admit that she knew anyone who fitted the description of Renata Tosi, and she shrugged indifferently at Randall's assurances that he wanted to know nothing except where the young woman was. Then, damning his own naïveté he took out his wallet and offered the woman a bill. Once again he asked if she knew where Renata Tosi was—if, perhaps, she was not right inside the house now?

"No," said the woman. "She went away."

"When?"

"The day before yesterday."

"Do you know where she went?"

The woman shook her head. But her black eyes shifted. "Not even for another five dollars?" he asked, "you don't know where she went?"

The woman shrugged. He handed over the second bill and she said, "She went in South America. The *piroscafo* leave the day before yesterday. In the afternoon."

"Did she go alone?" The question dropped unintended from his lips.

"No." The woman turned to go into the house. "She go with a Signor Baldini."

Seymour made his way down to his workshop in the cellar. He was so familiar with the walls, the banisters, the number of steps in each flight of stairs, that he went quickly and surely. He had spent more time down here in the past six weeks than ever in his life before. His quarrel with Randall was still bitter and open, though largely silent. He acted as if the child were not in the house, nor any of the innovations that had come with it. His habits were disrupted, and he ignored Randall's efforts to get back on their previous footing. Every morning Randall asked in the same gentle tone if Seymour would not like him to read the newspapers aloud, and every morning Seymour snapped, "No, thank you," and stalked away to the cellar.

"Very well, then," Randall said many times. "I'll just keep the papers in case something ever comes up that you want to ask about."

This day was like all other days, a yawning void, and Seymour heard the tombstone clock in the drawing-room striking nine as he went through the hall. Nine o'clock, he thought, and shuddered as he started down the cellar stairs. Nine o'clock and the day is over—but never over. Fourteen, fifteen hours to drag through, to count off when the clocks strike, to guess at between: this blank was twenty minutes, that lump of dead time forty-five. He never slept soundly because he was never physically tired; he was resigned to any mess they gave him to eat because he had no appetite. He reached the bottom of the stairs and felt his way between the stacked and jammed objects which filled most of the space between the stairs and his workbench under the window. He had told himself, and he had in past months told Randall, that he was able to do a good deal with his hands; he could experiment and begin to make mechanical things, working by touch.

"But it's a lie," he thought now. "I could, if I cared enough. But I cannot care enough about anything—not even enough to want to die. Why don't I want to die?"

He climbed into the driver's seat of the Stevens-Duryea, where he spent hours of his time, and sat there with his hands on the steering-wheel, touching from time to time the gear-lever and the other instruments as if for reassurance. "Why don't I want to die? Why don't I commit suicide?"

He often thought of a talk that he had had with Doctor Willingdon in the latter days of his failing sight, before he had put himself beyond reach of the man's confidence by his behavior about the bill. Panic-stricken, and in spite of years of reluctant preparation, unbelieving that this fate was really to befall him, he had asked the doctor what people

actually did when they found themselves blind. Did they not immediately decide that death was preferable? Did not many of them resort
to suicide almost automatically? He would, he said; he could not conceive of dragging out an existence, a burden to himself or anyone else.

"You will not feel like that when it happens," Willingdon had said.
"Blindness is a strange thing, like many other permanent handicaps.
There is sometimes terrible despair and panic in the beginning—but
most people make the adjustment and very few indeed, almost none, in
my experience, ever try to end their lives."

"But they should," Seymour had cried. "I know I shall feel like
that. How can I become an incubus upon my brother all the rest of
his life? And my God! what a horror my own life would be."

And so it was, a horror beyond anything he had imagined. He could
hear his own voice in retrospect, protesting to Willingdon that he would
feel it his duty to free Randall of this burden; protesting too that a
man could not accept such an ignominy and drag out a lifetime, clut-
tering up the earth. Well, he thought, that was so, it made sense then
and it makes sense still. But why do I do nothing about it? He had no
answer. He sat there in his ghostly motor car, abandoned to his darkness and indifferent to the tragic absurdity of the spectacle he must be,
and wondered whether a time would ever come when any propellent
would make a change in his present state of living death. Something
might make him resolve it, one day he might really decide to end it.
And, he thought, on the other hand, when I get past this immediate
financial jam it will not make much difference to my life, but it might
make some. In September, only six weeks from now, he would have his
income again—he ignored the fact that he would owe all of it for a long
time to come. In three years he would have twice as much. Nine years
after that he would be a rich man. It might make a difference, he
thought. Perhaps one can hire somebody to read to one, to go about,
possibly even to find some lovely and benign place to live. From the
corner where his soundest instincts lay hidden much as once-functioning
objects now rusted and mouldered in this cellar, his best sense asked
him where he could ever expect to hire devotion like Randall's, rendered
so warmly with such genuine love? Would anything less be other than
repellent?

Nonsense, he answered himself brusquely. I will have to change my
ways and my habits because Randall has forsaken me anyway for

that blasted infant, that insult to our decency and our privacy. Has he forsaken you? Well, it amounts to that, he almost shouted aloud. I have no other choice anyway. I shall have to fill my shadow-world with something else, something I can have by cultivating the use of my other senses. If I do that, will the loss of my sight mean I must always be what I am now?

His other senses: what were they? Nothing, he thought, sitting there gripping that dead steering-wheel, driving to nowhere; nothing that is not a mockery. Taste and smell? He had already lost interest in food. Touch? What should he touch for the sake of human consolation which would not shrink from the thing he had become? His ears? They had never contributed markedly to his pleasure. And now he thought of women, a thought once sufficiently challenging to give a sense of life even to a blind man; but that had been before the nightmare of this past year. Now it meant this grotesque thing that had overtaken him and his brother, this exaggeration of all preposterous insistences that the price of pleasure could be too high. But nobody except a sentimental fool like Randall would have insisted on paying this price. A sentimental fool! Seymour had nothing but scorn for that. And the other side of his nature was desolate for the care and tenderness and companionship that Randall had lavished upon him.

He put his head down upon his crossed arms on the steering-wheel and sat there in his cellar, in his darkness.

The contractor had done the roofing work without entering the attic rooms at the rear of the house. When he saw how dampness had rotted spots of the plaster in the third-floor back rooms which he was to repair, he had suggested to Randall also putting the rest of the rear rooms in order. But Randall had put him off by saying that this much work was all he could afford now, and as the other rooms were never used, they could be left alone to dry out by themselves once the roof was sound again. So he got a good clean room for John and his nurse without anybody having intruded either on the fourth floor where his things were, or the attic where he had not brought himself to go since that eerie night a year and a half ago. Almost completely he had succeeded in his will to forget those attic rooms and the smells and the sounds up there which could give one the horrors if one were so susceptible as to think about them. He had had plenty of other things to think about in the intervening time. Less than ever was there reason to worry about all that now, except that Maggie Quinn was living in the house. She appeared to take it for granted as willingly as her mother that there was no need ever to enter any of the disused rooms. "They are just storage rooms," Randall told her truthfully enough. "And it would be a lot of wasted work to try to clean them. So we just keep them locked." She was pleased enough to have no stairs to climb beyond the third floor; she was a nice decent girl anyway, understanding of his problems which he had once for all frankly stated, saying that her mother knew as much as was necessary about the place and everybody in it.

But once the new nursery was ready and Maggie Quinn settled in it with John, Randall thought a good deal about those attic rooms. Some-times late at night he went up to the fourth floor, to shut himself in the old day nursery and stay there, listening carefully, to see if he heard any of those small scuffling sounds overhead. He heard none, to his relief. Maybe it was my imagination in the first place, he thought. And maybe if there was anything there, it—they—would long since have gone away, because there was nothing for them to eat. But there was nothing at any time, and they were there. Or was it my imagination? Rather than build up any further picture of what might be there now, he began to think what he might do to insulate the two small rooms in such a way that nothing inside them, nothing of any kind, could make itself known to anybody elsewhere in the house. Suppose, he thought, they were solidly filled up with something heavy and inert, something like paper, for instance, which would deaden any sound and obstruct any passage-way across them. It seemed a good idea. And, wondering where to find a lot of paper, he thought of the daily newspapers which he had kept for a long time, day by day, as Seymour refused to have them read to him. He had been putting them each day in the old dining-room downstairs, which they never used, and now a good many of them had accumulated.

He waited until mid-afternoon when Maggie Quinn had John out in the back yard, pushing him slowly back and forth in his pram. Her mother had gone home for the day. Randall took a ball of strong twine and tied the newspapers tightly in bundles, so as to make good solid packs like blocks. He carried these up to the top floor and when he had them all up there, he unlocked one of the attic rooms and, beginning at the back wall, stacked the bundles of newspapers as tightly as he could. There were not nearly enough papers to finish the job as he meant

to, but he would simply go on keeping them and tying them up in
bundles like this until he had filled up both these nasty little rooms
so that they ceased in fact to be rooms and were solid cubes in which
there was no space for anything. He felt much better.

"Why, of course, Mr. Holt!" Maggie Quinn set John down on a
blanket on the nursery floor and watched him proudly while he thrashed
his sturdy arms and legs. Lying on his stomach he could brace himself
by his arms, and now he was trying to pull his legs up until he could rest
on his knees. He turned his head from Maggie to Randall and back to
Maggie again, each time with a delighted toothless smile. "Of course
he's old enough to enjoy a Christmas tree. They love shiny things and
all the pretties. He's smart, he is, sir; he'll be crawling in no time."

"Is that so remarkable?" asked Randall. He knelt down and rolled a
ball across the blanket into John's hands and John collapsed on top of
the ball, squealing with pleasure.

"It is that, indeed, Mr. Holt. He's not seven months old yet. Many's
the one won't try to crawl till it's nearly a year."

"Well, Maggie, I guess that's pretty smart, if you think so. So we'll
have a real Christmas for him."

"I wouldn't get him any fancy toys yet, sir—just soft things he can
toss around. Excuse my mentioning it—but usually the—the gentlemen
—they want to get such comical things for a boy baby—toy trains and
hobby-horses and I wouldn't know what all."

Randall laughed a little wryly. "I don't think you need worry about
that this year, Maggie," he said. He went down to find Seymour. He had
been trying for a week to make up his mind to tell Seymour what the
Trustees had been writing to both of them during these last two weeks
of November. Randall had asked Seymour every morning if he did not
want to have his mail read to him; and Seymour, after asking from
whom the letters had come, curtly said, "No, thank you." But the first
of December was tomorrow and Seymour really ought to be told before
the news reached him as a shock. Randall found him in the library,
gloomily sitting with his chin in hands. It wrung his heart to see Seymour like this, frozen and bitter and visibly tortured by loneliness. He
was feeding on his own spleen; sometimes Randall suspected that he
had actually forgotten much of the reason for this bitterness, but was
wallowing in the habit of it. Something ought to push him out of it.

Randall went over to Seymour and for a moment put his hand on his shoulder. Seymour flinched; this was sheer stubborn pride, for in the past year an occasional caress from Randall's hand had come to take the place of the smile that Seymour could not see. Randall stood still and said gently, "Seymour, I've been trying for over a week to tell you something you really ought to know, and you just won't let me. But I'm afraid if you have to find it out some other way—"

"Is it about—about—that child?"

"No, Brother. It's about money."

"What about money?" Seymour's voice was sullen; he knew perfectly well that he owed Randall a lot of money. Why remind him? But Randall said, "It's those letters that they've been writing us, that you didn't want me to read. They've told me that my income is to be drastically cut this quarter and I suppose—I'm afraid—"

"God damn it, why?"

"Well, you know about the panic. Even with my scarcely ever reading the papers to you any more, nobody could help knowing about that."

Seymour clenched the arms of his chair. "Are you trying to tell me that those mealy-mouthed walking corpses have lost all our money?"

"No, Brother. That's what they've been writing about. I don't understand enough to know all the ins and outs of it—but they say they're very pleased because they saved the basic capital value of what we've got. But most of the stocks are passing their dividends—and except for a few things, we're not going to have much income. At least that's what they've written me—I suppose your letters say the same."

"Well, get them out and read the damned things."

Randall glanced through the letters and said, "They're just the same as mine."

"Wouldn't you know it? As soon as I begin to get my money again." Seymour swore.

Randall shook his head slowly. It was like Seymour to have expected to keep all his money, even though he owed it to Randall. What was the use of reminding him now? But there was nothing else to do. Randall had spent every evening for days past figuring, adding, dividing, and trying to budget the next three months' money over the expenses which were so much larger on account of John. He had expected that Seymour would pay some of his heavy accumulated debt. Now he could not see how to manage unless he could add nearly all of Seymour's reduced income for this quarter to his own. Reluctantly, and anxiously feeling his way, praying to avoid a new outburst, he told Seymour. For a while there was silence. Then Seymour said, "I could almost say you're as determined to keep on punishing me as Grandmama would have been."

"Oh, Brother, can't you try to be a little bit fair? You know me. You know perfectly well that if we were going to get our regular income I would have spread those payments to Doctor Willingdon and all—all the rest—over any length of time you wanted. I can't help this, Seymour. Truly I can't."

"Running a household for a—"

"Seymour, I implore you to stop saying such things. And thinking them, too." Randall put his hand against Seymour's cheek as if to try to fix his attention, as he would do by looking him deep in the eyes if Seymour could see. "I know how you feel. But John is here now, and if you could only know how I feel about him you'd realize he has nothing to do with everything that happened before. He makes you forget it if you get attached to him the way I am. Whatever happened, whatever we all did—it's not his fault, Brother." Randall got down on his knees and took Seymour's hands and held them tightly and said, "Please. Please, Seymour. Listen to me. You're good, you know. Good and generous and much wiser about life than I am. Be your own self, Brother. Ask yourself if it's right to take out your bitterness on that little boy. Don't make him pay for our mistakes, Brother. He can't know your reasons, he shouldn't know them. All he knows is that there is some big tall stranger here who never takes any notice of him. He's old enough to realize that. It's going to be bad for him. Seymour, if you'd only let him know you the way he does me—and Maggie, and even Mrs. Quinn—it would give you happiness. Believe me." Randall put his face down on Seymour's clasped hands. "Please believe me. If only for your own sake."

Seymour sat silent. His face, as Randall raised his head and saw its leathery pallor, was drawn and rigid. His grey eyes which in recent months had lost their power of expression and turned into blank symbols of hopeless tragedy, were quite as blank now, but as Randall watched them, a film of moisture spread slowly across their pitiful imperturbability. Randall knew sharply that he must not sear this open wound by the humiliation of watching it quiver. He got to his feet and with his fingertips gently closed Seymour's eyes and, more gently, bent over and put his lips upon the lids, one and then the other. Seymour sat tense, grasping Randall's hands. Presently he said hoarsely, "You call him John."

"Yes. Don't you agree?"

"Yes."

"Take your time, Brother. I haven't asked for anything—only for you to be yourself."

"No," said Seymour. "Time is a mistake. Now or never. Bring him here."

Randall went and fetched John and carried him to the library. "I won't put him on your lap," he said. "Wait until he wants to sit there himself. We're right here." He sat down on the hassock close to Seymour's chair and reached over and took Seymour's forefinger and put it in John's hand. The fat fingers closed tightly and John shook the hand up and down, gurgling cheerfully. Seymour leaned forward slowly and put his other hand on John's head. He felt it gently, with the butterfly lightness that was teaching his fingers to see. The hand passed softly over John's hair, across his broad forehead, down one fat cheek and then the other. John liked that. He crowed.

"What color is his hair, Randall?"

"Brown. Sort of bright shiny brown. Maggie says it's going to be curly."

"And his eyes?"

"Well—I think that depends on the light. Sometimes they seem rather blue and sometimes they're grey."

"Not so blue as yours?"

"Oh, no."

"And not so grey as mine?"

"No. Sort of in between."

"And his coloring? His skin?"

"Well, he's just a baby still. He's so rosy you can't tell what his skin will really be like."

"It's so soft," said Seymour, as if unconsciously. He passed his hand down over the child's body and caught one of the energetic kicking feet. John thought it a game and kicked harder with the other foot. Seymour caught that too. John screamed with amusement. He bounced up and down on Randall's knees. Seymour said, "He's awfully hefty, isn't he? And full of energy."

"And bright, Maggie says. I don't know how they tell about those things, but she insists he's much brighter than most babies. But nurses are like that about each one, I suppose."

"Does he really know you? By name?"

"Well, of course he doesn't call me anything. But he knows Maggie and her mother and me and we call ourselves by name and he makes a noise that Maggie says will turn into a word pretty soon."

"Show me."

Randall said, "Where's Uncle Ran, John?" The child had been sitting facing Seymour and playing with his finger. Seymour felt him turn and fling himself against Randall and gurgle a delighted unintelligible noise. Randall hugged him and then gently leaned forward and said, "That's Uncle Seymour. See? Hold out your arms, Seymour. Speak to him."

"Will you come here, John?" Seymour's voice was as soft as he could make it. John sat still, not sure of this unfamiliar person who had never been anything but a silent moving statue before. He did not make a motion to go to Seymour, and Randall said again, "That's Uncle Seymour. Nice. Nice Uncle Seymour."

Seymour thought suddenly of the bunch of seals on the end of his watch-chain, big heavy gold seals which had belonged to his father and his grandfather, which he had worn for years. He wore them still, from habit, just as he wound and carried the watch he could not see. He took out the seals and dangled them before John. They tinkled and glittered and John reached for them with a peremptory cluck. Seymour put them in his hands and held the other end of the chain. John shook and jangled the seals and Seymour jerked the chain gently as if he were playing a fish. Randall moved closer, hitching the hassock along. When the seals were back almost in Seymour's hand John plunked forward with a gurgle and found himself in Seymour's lap. This appeared to please him; he had the bunch of seals in one hand and something equally new in the other, a long, bristly, handle sort of thing which he tugged sharply. The face on the other end of the handle bent his way and Seymour laughed, saying, "Ouch!"

John gave the thing another tug and Seymour said "Ouch" again. This was a new game. John was delighted with it. He let out one of his shrieks of pleasure and flung himself against Seymour's chest. Seymour's arms closed round him and Randall got up from the hassock and went away.

CHAPTER 17

The tune continued, repeated a second time and a third. Seymour concentrated on his counting and folding, but he scowled and hunched his shoulders irritably. It was a silly little tune, something about a nut tree, which Randall often played and sang to John, and it was beginning to get on Seymour's nerves. Even sitting at his desk in the library, with Randall and John downstairs in the drawing-room and all the doors closed, Seymour's ears were so sharp that he was conscious of much that another person would scarcely have heard. He went on counting and carefully putting away his money. He had finally found a way to manage, now that his income and Randall's were restored and some of their worst financial worries past. Since he could have no privacy if he must depend upon Randall to write checks and keep accounts for him, he had ordered the bank to deliver him one-third of his quarter's income in cash on the first of each month. The bank's messenger would lay out the packages of bills in the order of their denominations, and later Seymour would fold them, each denomination differently, in such a way that he knew exactly what it was. He left the one-dollar bills flat, and folded the fives in thirds, the tens in quarters, and the twenties once lengthwise. Then he put them all away in a steel strongbox which had belonged to his grandmother, and he kept that in the bottom drawer of his desk. The keys to both box and desk were always in his pocket. He felt much less helpless after this, and better still when without consulting Randall he had a telephone reinstalled in the house. He could now buy what he liked and pay for it when it was delivered. Not that he bought much. But it had been intolerable to be dependent upon Randall for every piddling trifle.

Seymour finished his counting and locked the strongbox away and sat for a moment listening, but trying not to listen, to that fool tune downstairs. Ever since Christmas this had been going on. First it had been that sickly sentimental German stuff, *Stille Nacht* and *Tannenbaum*. John's second Christmas, three months ago, had certainly been the best time they had had in years, but Seymour had not altogether liked Randall's arrangements. Randall had put the Christmas tree in the drawing-room, where John would have plenty of room to play with his new toys. That was his stated reason, at any rate. But the house for so many years had been apportioned on the basis that the library was Seymour's and the drawing-room Randall's that Seymour felt jostled by the latter's becoming the centre of the Christmas stage. Of course the trunks and valises had long ago been removed, Randall had never said to what part of the house, but Seymour was still uncomfortable in the drawing-room. He never ventured far inside it. He stayed near the door, sitting on one of the fussy Victorian chairs which flanked it. Perhaps he had been particularly irked because so much of a child's Christmas was the wonderland of its visual discoveries; its shouts and squeals of pleasure at the Christmas tree, its constant cry of "Look! Look!" He could still feel John staggering up to him, placing a wooden elephant from his Noah's Ark in Seymour's hands, crying, "Look, Unc' Seymour. Look!" John at nineteen months could not know the meaning of blindness but he knew already that communication with Seymour lay in appeal to the long, perceptive hands, and in the sounds by which he fixed Seymour's attention when a mere smile, which always drew a response from Randall, seemed not to get any notice from Seymour at all.

> "I had a little nut tree,
> Nothing would it bear—"

Seymour sat taut with fretfulness. Why did he dislike that harmless tune? His conscience troubled him; but he was uncomfortable anyway because he so often felt cross or critical of Randall, and he was too astute not to realize why. Randall had been right about John; nobody could help growing fond of him. It was fascinating for Seymour to hear and to feel, even when he could not see, how the child grew and became more interesting month by month. But Seymour knew perfectly well that in order for the child to be interesting it had to be interested; and there Randall had all the advantages. He read to John, and Seymour heard them talking about the pictures in the story-books, with John responding intelligently as soon as he could articulate at all. Randall played and sang with John; Randall took care of him on Maggie's Wednesday afternoons out. When John made a discovery, when he wanted something, when he bumped his head, it was always Randall to whom he turned. How could it be otherwise? And how could it help but exasperate Seymour?

He did not want John to be the soft and too-sensitive little boy that Randall had been. He did not want them down there in the drawing-room, exactly as Randall in his own childhood had sat for hours with their mother, playing music and singing sentimental nursery songs. He wanted John to be a real boy, active and boisterous, good at sports and strong and quick and not afraid of rough games. It was one thing to want all this for John and quite another to know how to obtain it. Who was to teach him to roller-skate and ride a bicycle and play baseball and above all, sail a boat? Seymour did not know, and he could not even grope towards the outlines of a future which could make of John what he wanted him to be. He only knew now that there had been enough of that maddening tune down in the drawing-room, and entirely too much of all this playing and singing in the weeks since Christmas. He got to his feet and felt his way quickly downstairs.

Randall looked up as the door opened and was disconcerted to see the scowl on Seymour's face. Randall's hands paused on the keyboard and John cried, "More, Unc' Ran. More." He dropped his baby fist on the keys with a discordant bang.

"No, John," said Seymour from the doorway. "That's enough music for today."

"Why, Seymour." Randall's blue eyes were puzzled. John began to bounce up and down with impatience, clamoring for the music again.

Seymour said, "No more music today, John. Time to do something else. Why isn't he out of doors this afternoon, Randall?"

"Because the weather is bad," said Randall. "What's come over you, Seymour? I'm perfectly capable of deciding whether he should be indoors or out."

"Sing," said John. He banged the piano again. "Nut tree."

Randall folded John's arms quietly inside his own and sat there holding the child and looking up at Seymour. "Why the interference?" he asked. "I'm going to bring him upstairs to play with you in the library at five o'clock, just like any other day. Leave him alone now, Seymour."

"I don't want him mixed up in so much music all the time." Seymour's voice was waspish. "You're going to make a sissy out of him."

"Oh, nonsense. Look at him. He's as husky as a horse. He's too active ever to turn into a sissy. But he loves music and I'm going to see he hears all he wants."

"You are not." Seymour came slowly across the room with a tight, drawn look on his face which even John perceived, for his forehead began to pucker in a bewildered frown. Randall stared at Seymour as if he were looking at something he had never seen before. "It's about time you stopped being so important around that kid," said Seymour.

"Why?" Randall's face was flushed and his usually mild expression had disappeared in tight lips and a sharply set jaw.

"Because I don't like it, see?"

"That's too bad," said Randall, very angry. His voice was low. "Under the circumstances I think you would be wise to shut up, Seymour, and stay shut up. Do you understand me?"

Seymour scowled and said, "I know how that kid ought to be brought up. I know why, too."

"Do you?" Randall rose from the piano and stood holding John, who put his arms about Randall's neck and looked from one brother to the other with huge round uncomprehending eyes. "Well, I know exactly the same thing you know. And neither of us can ever prove what he knows." His voice trembled and his face was pale and grave. "Now you go back to your library and think that over before you do anything you'll be sorry for. We're not going to have any more of this."

"Sing," said John again, kicking his heels. "Play. Nut tree."

"Just a minute, John." Randall put the child down on his feet and took one of his hands and put it in Seymour's. He spoke quietly. "You've got to do something to reassure him, Seymour. You frightened him and by God you're not going to do it again. I don't like talking this way in front of him and that's not going to happen again either."

Seymour's face worked. John stood looking up at him, the little pucker back again between his baby eyebrows. He tugged at Seymour's hand and said, "Horsie, Unc' Seymour. Play horsie."

"Do it," said Randall, barely aloud. He saw Seymour moisten his lips and bite them and swallow several times. He was imagining all too clearly the savage turmoil which but for John's presence would have exploded in a raving temper. Seymour stood rigid, with John dragging at his right hand, looking up in bewilderment at the face he had never seen in this guise before. Seymour gritted his teeth; Randall saw his jaws flexing; suddenly Seymour got down on his hands and knees.

"Horsie!" cried John, jumping up and down. He clambered onto Seymour's back and locked his arms round Seymour's neck, and Seymour lumbered slowly across the room, with Randall watching to see that he did not bump into anything.

After that there was no trouble for a time. Seymour even tried to make silent amends for what his better sense knew to have been outrageous behavior. And Randall was surprisingly conciliatory. He saw now that in his early anxiety to melt Seymour's bitter opposition to John he had not taken realistically into consideration the fantastic nature of the problem itself and of Seymour, growing more possessive and didactic all the time. This was part of his terrible fate, inseparable from his increasing self-absorption. How could one expect anything else? Yet once he grasped the situation in all its actual and eventual gravity, Randall could think of it only in terms of protecting John. He must be protected now from any further assaults of Seymour's temper; and still more must his future be considered, a problem too portentous to grasp. John was two years old now, and the two years had moved fairly slowly, but time was beginning to frighten Randall, time was speeding up. He knew that children began to go to school when they were about six. School meant people, school meant identity, school meant the facing of questions which for Randall on the night he had taken John into the house and into his heart had been non-existent. I wouldn't have done any differently in the beginning if I had realized every single problem ten times over, he told himself; but that made their realization no less worrisome now. Certainly it was a mistake to antagonize Seymour. I must keep him with me, he thought; we must act in partnership to make a solid footing under John no matter what it may cost each of us in effort and self-denial. He could understand how special emphasis on music might alarm Seymour; he would try to hold it to a proportion of John's interests no greater than anything else. He would encourage Seymour in every sort of activity that he could share with John.

So he was pleased about the boat-sailing in the wash tub, although John was too young for it. And so he was helpful when Seymour said one day, "There is something I need and I don't quite know how to go about getting it."

"What is that, Brother?" They were at breakfast in the library.

"An electric motor. It sounds perfectly crazy, I know, but—"

"Well, you must have a use for it. What do you want it for?"

"I want to see if I can rig up a power-lathe at my bench downstairs. I could use it for various kinds of work that's tedious by hand—and I haven't got too much patience, have I?" Seymour laughed ruefully.

"I don't know anything about such things," said Randall. "What do you suppose is involved in it?"

"Well, I'd have to have access to electric current, for one thing."

"You aren't suggesting wiring the house for electricity?"

"God forbid! I have as much intention of our getting out of here as I ever had. All we need now is the patience to sit out the money question until we can afford to do it. Don't you agree?"

"Absolutely."

"Well then, I should think we could get a single electric line run in the cellar window from outside somewhere and then I could use a motor and hook up any power tools I might want."

Randall said, admiringly, "Can you really do things like that just by touch? It seems incredible."

"Not well enough," said Seymour, with a grimace. "I might grind off a thumb or something. But at least I'd like to try. Only it isn't worth spending much money on, and I just don't know where to start."

Randall said, "Do you suppose they sell such things second-hand?"

"Why not?"

They sat thinking.

"I know!" exclaimed Randall. "Here I read through all these newspapers every day and I simply ignore the pages we aren't interested in." He opened one of the morning papers to the last page. "Listen to this. A whole page full of notices of auctions and second-hand sales of everything under the sun. Leather. Contractors' Supplies. Hardware. Chinaware & Crockery. Bicycle Manufacturing Plant." He looked over at Seymour whose expression was fascinated. "Grocery Store. Upholstery Findings. Here you are, Brother. Miscellaneous Job Lot Machinery and Electric Equipment. Generators. Dynamos. Assorted Tools. Lathes—why, this looks like just what you want."

"What do you know about that. Where is this place?"

"It says an address and Abraham Bromberg, Auctioneer. Do you want me to go there?"

"Why, sure." Seymour looked as delighted as John with a new toy.

"How will I know what you want to spend?"

"Oh, find out what the lot is likely to go for and telephone me and we'll decide on our outside bid."

When Randall got to the place he found that the job lot had come from a small commercial warehouse in Brooklyn which was disposing of remnants of stock of various bankrupt manufacturers. There were a number of other things beside the electric motor and two generators and enough assorted machine parts and tools to keep Seymour busy for months. Randall got the lot very cheap, and not until it was delivered to the house did he realize that among the other stuff he had bid in were two upright pianos and a small organ. Seymour was so excited about his haul that he scarcely remarked the instruments, but Randall was flustered. He told Seymour that he would find some way of re-selling them, and in the meantime he had them stored in the closed dining-room which nobody ever entered anyway.

Maggie and Mrs. Quinn were having one more cup of tea to wash down their midday dinner. John was asleep upstairs. It would be an hour before time to take him out after his nap. Mrs. Quinn dunked a piece of stale cake in her tea, to favor her bothersome gums, and Maggie sat with her black cotton legs hooked round the legs of her chair. She held her cup in both hands, braced by her elbows on the kitchen table. She looked thoughtful and her mother was not surprised when she spoke, for she said something they had said often enough before.

"Ma, which one do ye think it is?" she asked.

"I've told ye what I think, Maggie, and sure it's a waste of breath to repeat it. Why do ye harp on it so? It's the younger one, of course. The way he loves that child. Pitiful, it is."

"Maybe. But I ain't so sure."

"It seems to be worryin' ye more all the time. But it needn't. It's no business of ours."

"I wouldn't say that! It's all the business I've got. Ye can't help wonderin' about it, Ma, a body wouldn't be human."

"Well, the blind one didn't pay no mind to the child for so long, and raised all that cain about havin' it here. He hated it. He wouldn't be the father."

"That's just it. He might. He'd be ashamed and have a bad conscience."

Mrs. Quinn made a mouth. "Not the way the younger one loves it."

"But now the blind one loves it too. He's gettin' jealous of the way John loves Mr. Holt, Mr. Randall, I mean."

"Maggie, ye're imaginin' things."

"No I ain't, Ma. Ye don't see 'em around the child all the time like I do. The blind one is tryin' to be the boss instead of his brother, and he'll start makin' trouble one o' these days, you mark my words. They'd do better to say right out which one is the father and not be headin' into the kind o' scrap they are. It's bad for John, too."

Mrs. Quinn poked anxiously at her dental plate and said slowly, "Which one do ye think he really looks like?"

"That's got me stumped, Ma. I can't decide. I look and look at John and sometimes I think I see one in him and sometimes the other. That would be just a family resemblance, of course—look at our James. He's the dead spit of Uncle Terence."

"Well, I guess they got their reasons."

"Oh, I know their reasons. If they'd just stick to 'em they'd probably be all right. I heard 'em talkin' only last week. They were sayin' how when John is old enough to start school they're goin' to move to some small town where nobody knows 'em, and say he's the son of a dead brother o' theirs and his mother died when he was born. That's why they've taught him to call them both Uncle. It's a good idee."

"Maggie," said Mrs. Quinn slowly. "Do ye really believe that?"

"What, Ma?" Maggie poured out the dregs of the mahogany-colored tea and began to spoon sugar into it. She did not look across the table.

"Why, that they're ever goin' to move away from here. Out o' this house."

"Well—" Maggie raised her eyes uneasily to her mother's face, which had taken on a sharp expression.

"They've been talkin' about it all the three years and more that I've been here, and the whole neighborhood—"

"Ma, ye ain't been talkin' to that McBane woman again?"

"I never talked to her willingly. Can I help it if I bump into her on the street?"

"Ye oughtn't to listen to her," said Maggie.

"That I don't, Maggie, honest. She's a sluttish sort and I want none of her. But she's sure filled this block full o' tales about them brothers."

"Well, they are pretty odd, Ma. I wouldn't have stayed this long but for John. He's a lovely child, ye can't help gettin' that fond of him."

"I know. I wouldn't have let ye come here except I was so sorry for the poor mite."

"Ma, do they talk about him too?"

Mrs. Quinn said, "Maggie, I tried to bring ye up decent and thanks be to the Blessed Virgin I succeeded better than I knew. Ye must be real innocent not to imagine how they talk."

"Oh, I'm not that innocent. I just meant—do they talk like they knew which one is the father?"

"No, how could they? They just blab about both of 'em. And the poor child. They see over the back fence when he's out gettin' his airings."

"It'll be a good thing when they do move away, then. They'd have to, for the child's sake."

"I tried to tell Mr. Randall what to do for the child's sake the day it came into this house."

"Oh, Ma, ye wouldn't have had it left at an orphanage! Why, any home would be better than that." Maggie's lips trembled a little.

Mrs. Quinn heaved her knobbily corseted bulk from her chair and prepared to tackle the washing-up. She looked over her shoulder at Maggie and said, "Any home? Even one like this?" She jerked her chin upwards and turned one thumb downwards as if to encompass the upper and the nether reaches of this house. She shook her head slowly and tapped her forehead with her red forefinger. And Maggie sighed and went to have a look at John.

For weeks past Seymour had been preoccupied by his new installation in the cellar. Randall felt well satisfied at having bought the job lot of stuff. He had no idea just what Seymour was making down there, and he was not at all sure that Seymour knew either. Perhaps he was not making anything, only teaching himself gradually to use the lathe and the unfamiliar tools. It was not the sort of thing about which one questioned Seymour; nor, indeed, was anything else. But when Seymour emerged from his cellar and materialized in John's room or the drawing-room or the back yard, and began to ask peremptory questions about John's occupations or his habits or his food, Randall found it hard to be patient. Seymour was interfering and didactic just for the sake of being so. Randall often saw a resentful flush sweep across Maggie's face when Seymour gave her some order concerning John which was very apt to be a contradiction of her own way of doing things or of what Randall had previously arranged with her. She evolved a quiet manner of saying, "Yes, sir," to Seymour and ignoring what he said. Randall not only agreed with her; he backed her up in every way that was beyond Seymour's observation.

It was raining one afternoon in October and Randall had John in the drawing-room reading *Little Black Sambo* to him. John sat in Randall's lap, holding his beloved teddy bear. Teddy was John's inseparable companion. He slept in John's bed and sat in a toy chair beside John's high-chair while he ate, and rode on the Kiddie Kar in front of John, strapped on by a blue leather belt. He had been loved bare in spots and his stuffing had leaked at some time before Maggie had sewed him up, for he was rather limp. John clutched him in his left arm, and with his right hand he pointed to the pictures he knew so well, chiming in whenever Randall made one of the classic pauses: "Now *I'm* the grandest Tiger in the Jungle." He knew much of *Little Black Sambo* by heart; and *Peter Rabbit*, too, and *The House that Jack Built*. But *Little Black Sambo* was his favorite.

" 'When Black Mumbo saw the melted butter, wasn't she pleased!'," Randall read. " ' "Now," said she—' "

" 'We'll all have pancakes for supper!' " cried John. The door opened. He saw Seymour come in and he shouted, "Pancakes for supper, Uncle Seymour! Pancakes for supper!"

Seymour stood by the door for a moment, then instead of sitting down there as he often did, he walked over to Randall and John. He put out his hand and felt John's thick curls against Randall's waistcoat, and Teddy tight in John's arm.

"Don't you think, Randall," he said, "that he's getting too old to sit in your lap that way all the time?"

"He doesn't do it all the time. But he wants to look at the pictures while I read to him, Seymour. That's how he learns—he knows the words that go with each picture."

"He can look at pictures sitting in a chair by himself. You baby him too much. He oughtn't to sit in your lap. And always be clutching that teddy bear. That's a baby's toy."

"He doesn't think of it as a toy," said Randall, in a tone so careful that it should have warned Seymour. "It's a companion to him—he thinks of it as a person."

" 'Flour and eggs'!" cried John. "Finish the story!"

"You know that story by heart, John," said Seymour. "You're too big to hear the same story over and over."

"Finish the story," said John again, ignoring Seymour.

"Uncle Ran isn't going to finish that story," said Seymour. "He'll read you a new one."

"Don't want a new one. Finish Little Black Sambo, Uncle Ran!"

"Seymour," said Randall, "would you mind going upstairs? If there's anything to say about this let's wait until later."

"I'll have something to say later," said Seymour, "but first will you please put him down off your lap and stop making such a sissy of him? He oughtn't to be so attached to that fool teddy bear, either. Give Teddy to Uncle Seymour, John." He put out his hand and took hold of one of the bear's arms.

"No! Leave Teddy alone." John's eyes widened and filled with tears and he clutched his bear tighter and huddled against Randall.

"Give me that teddy bear, John." Seymour's voice was hard.

"No!" John was beginning to cry.

"Seymour, I implore you. I can't say anything with him here, but will you please—"

"You must obey, John," said Seymour. "Give me the bear."

"No!" John was howling.

"Give me that bear!" Seymour jerked sharply on the bear's arm as John pulled it frantically away and buried himself and the bear in Randall's arms, screaming. The arm came off in Seymour's hand. John screamed in such terror that they heard Maggie flying down the stairs and into the room. She stopped in the doorway, gaping. "What—what's—"

Randall was holding John tightly, looking over the child's head at Seymour. His face was white and Maggie Quinn put her hand to her open mouth as she saw his expression. He took a long breath and forced his voice to an ordinary tone and said, "It's all right, Maggie. Something happened to John's bear. He's frightened, but he'll be all right. I'll bring him upstairs in a few minutes."

"Yes—sir," she said, and went away.

"Now you go, Seymour," said Randall. His face was still white with rage. Seymour stood there with the bear's arm in his hand. "Give me that and get out of here."

John huddled against Randall, sobbing.

"You put him down off your lap," said Seymour.

"You give me that thing and clear out." Randall shot out his right hand and seized the bear's arm from Seymour. He bent over John and said, "Teddy'll be all right, John. We'll get him fixed right away. Nobody meant to hurt him. He says it doesn't hurt him. He says it doesn't hurt a bit."

"It *does* hurt," screamed John. "Teddy hurts."

"He'll be all right. He told me so." Randall sat and comforted John and did not look up when Seymour turned and left the room. After a while John stopped sobbing and Randall wiped his eyes and blew his nose and began at the beginning and read through *Little Black Sambo* again.

But late that night he had it out with Seymour. He had not seen him since afternoon, leaving him to go to the kitchen by himself and feel around for whatever fruit or left-over food he wanted for his supper. Usually Randall carried something up to the library where they ate. This evening he stayed in his own room until the late hour when he heard Seymour go to bed. He did not want to talk in the library because it was directly below the room where John and Maggie were asleep. But from Seymour's bedroom he was sure voices would not carry to the other end of the house.

Randall tried to speak with restraint, but in a moment they were deep in their worst quarrel since the first days that John had been in the house. They quarrelled savagely, but each stopped again and again on the verge of saying the one thing that justified him in his own mind, yet the thing he could not prove and therefore dare not say.

"It's all your fault," said Seymour. "You ought never to have kept him in the beginning."

"Because I wasn't afraid to take the consequences and you were? Just remember how you acted about it."

"And I was right."

"Then why don't you leave him alone now? What are you trying to do to him, Seymour?"

"Keep him from being the sissy you're making of him."

"He's not a sissy! The whole thing's your imagination."

"He is. You spoil him and coddle him—he's got to have some discipline."

"At the age of two and a half? Your cruelty today—you call that discipline?"

"He's got to be deprived of things. Somebody's got to be strict with him. He must obey."

"He does obey—for a child of his age. He obeys reasonably. But when you want to interrupt him in the middle of something he's interested in and take away something he loves and make him obey just for the sake of having your own way with him, that's not teaching him obedience. That's bullying him."

"You're a sentimental sop, Randall, you always were. With this child's heredity—"

"If you'd think more about his feelings and less about his heredity—" Randall paused and stood staring at the floor, as if gazing into a pit which had yawned suddenly before his eyes. Down in its depths if he should dare to look, he would find everything he most dreaded. The grappling roots, the twisted wills, the bitter, futile efforts of weakness to hold its own against bullying force; the pitiful image of his mother, the despotic old woman whom Seymour—no, he thought, no, you must never see that in him. You must wipe it out, like the memory of Renata, of Seymour then; of us, of what we did; you must forget it all for John. No, he thought, putting his hand to his eyes, you must never see the past in Seymour, never the resemblance, never be reminded. But his hand went down and he looked at his brother, lying grey and sightless on that ugly bed; he stared until the strength went out of him and he could not muzzle the words that he heard, appalled, coming from his own mouth. His voice was thick and strange. "Seymour," he said. "Do you know what's the matter with you?"

Seymour made an ugly sound. Randall bent over him and said, close to his ear, "You want to believe you are his father. You act—the way She used to—Seymour, this is horrible! Stop it, stop for God's sake before you destroy us. You'll hate me. Perhaps you hate me now. You want to believe you are his father and you hate me because I may be. Oh, my God . . ." He turned away, chilled and sick.

It was out. Seymour lay with his eyes closed, his mouth locked contemptuously, his long bony jaw jutting. Randall saw wretchedly, as never before, the resemblance to the old woman whose room this had been, the likeness emphasized by the gloomy shadows and the flickering light of the single gas-jet overhead.

"No doubt," said Seymour, with his mouth almost closed, "you feel exactly the same yourself. A fine, sane, healthy state of things. And you brought it all down on us."

"Yes. Absolutely single-handed, I did. So I'll take it off us too. I'll take him away."

"Oh, no! You can't do that."

"But you've as good as suggested I should. What do you mean?"

Seymour turned on his side and put his right hand over his eyes, a curious gesture as if to hide from their blindness something that even blindness could see.

"Don't you understand?" he said, with an uncharacteristic tremor in his voice. "I—I love him too, Randall."

They were silent. Randall struggled with the impulse to say, "If that's what you call love, it's nothing but destruction." Instead, when he could speak with control, he said slowly, "If you really love him, Seymour, you'll have to show it in ways that he can understand. He's used to trusting the people around him and knowing where he stands with them. It's no good if you do what you did to him today, and then give him some expensive toy tomorrow and think that makes up for it. He's confused about you already. If you make him afraid of you I swear to God I'll take him away. I mean I'll do it before he gets frightened."

"You'll spoil him to death in the meantime."

"He's not spoiled! He's just a normal child who's fond of the people he's dependent on. Maggie and I happen to do everything for him, but that's no fault of yours. There isn't much you can do, on account of your eyes. That's too bad, but it's nature. It's fate. Stop fighting it. Stop it before you do something you'll be terribly sorry for."

He stood for a moment, looking round the dim, stuffy room, every object and its position part of the pathetic scheme of the blind man for managing his existence. It was a forbidding room, it had always been; and though some of the furniture was changed and the old woman's belongings replaced by Seymour's, it was permeated by her personality. Memories came sweeping over Randall, memories of her heavy step and booming voice, memories of himself clinging to his mother in terror while they listened to her giving orders, browbeating Seymour, scolding the servants, bullying Lily. Mama, thought Randall. Mama literally went off her head on account of that old woman. That's all ancient history. That's supposed to be forgotten and done with. If it were, he thought, would we be the way we are now? Would we? Against his strongest efforts he had set a train of thought in motion, everything shoved by the single propellent, moving swiftly along, through the trail of his life, gathering and storing the tokens that were part of it. He had kept the things he had, and written what he had written, and hidden what he had hidden often without a purpose at the moment. But he had felt that the purpose would ultimately make itself known. He believed he had one in sight now. He would go and find out. He said, "Good night, Seymour, I've turned out the gas." He left the dark room and went noiselessly up to the fourth floor and shut himself in the old day nursery. There by another dim gas light he took his little desk from its hiding-place and opened it and sat slowly leafing through his papers. He did that for a long time, reading, and then he took a blank sheet of music manuscript and in his minute hand began to write. He thought and pondered and scribbled, and sat and thought some more, all night almost until daylight.

The pattern repeated itself more and more often. Each time that Seymour made trouble and Randall forced him to back down, there followed an interval of uneasy peace. During these periods Seymour was contrite and Randall was conciliatory. And John, with his happy disposition, seemed too cheerful and interested in his busy little world to harbor any grudge or fear of Seymour, if he were old enough. But one could not really know, Randall felt. He watched John carefully to see whether he ever shrank from Seymour or otherwise unconsciously showed that the outbreaks had left their mark. Apparently not. But it was growing upon Randall that this house was no place to be bringing up a child. What Maggie had overheard—indeed, what Randall had deliberately said to Seymour in her presence—about their moving away to a small town was not only his intention for the future; he was beginning to feel that they should go soon. The move had first been associated in his mind with school, but he saw now that very soon, long before beginning school, John must have playmates. He could not play with the ragtag-and-bobtail that lived in the neighborhood. He could not know the children of anybody else, people from whom the Holts were forever cut off. Randall spoke about all this to Seymour one night shortly before Christmas, sitting in the library. Seymour reflected for a while and said slowly, "I suppose you're right."

"Anyway," said Randall, "even if it weren't for John's sake, it was always you who wanted most to get out of here."

"I know. Curious, isn't it, that such a succession of things happened to make it impossible."

"Well, it's only three months now until you start getting your doubled income. That's going to make a big difference."

"Oh," said Seymour. "So you're counting on my income. That's thoughtful of you."

"Oh, Brother, be reasonable. You know what I mean. I'm willing to put up practically all of mine, and if you match that, we'd have enough to live quietly in some place like we've been talking about and you'd have about two thousand a year left over for yourself. Doesn't that seem fair?"

"I suppose so," said Seymour grudgingly.

Randall stared at him. Could it be possible that Seymour resented paying his share of their expenses? Randall saw no reason for reticence and he asked him outright.

"Well—no. I don't resent it. But after taking a couple of years to get out of debt to you and waiting all this time to have enough money to be of any use to a man—"

Randall shook his head. He said, "I just hadn't realized you had any plans of your own. In the circumstances." He spoke gently.

"Oh, I haven't," said Seymour. "I only mean I'd like the feeling of having some money for a change and having the satisfaction of keeping it without spending it all on this household you've saddled us with."

"But Brother, we've got to make a home for John."

Seymour smoothed his moustache. "Yes. But does it have to take everything we've got?"

"I just told you it would only take half of what you'll have. I don't care if I use all of mine, I like to. What else have I got to do with it?"

Damn him, thought Seymour. Those pious virtues of his. He uses them to rebuke me. He got up from his chair and went away to his room without having committed himself.

A few days later, Seymour waited in mid-afternoon until John had gone out with Randall to make a snow-man in the back yard. His accurate ears informed him that Maggie was ironing in the kitchen. Standing in the passageway at the top of the cellar stairs he heard the thump of the sad-irons when she changed them, and smelled the crisp warm odor of starched linen. Mrs. Quinn had gone home. Seymour went quietly up to the third floor to John's room, and felt around in his crib to find the teddy bear tucked against the pillow. It was never taken out in wet weather so it "wouldn't catch cold." Seymour took the bear, whose arm had been mended, and started downstairs with it. He intended to take it to the cellar. At the top of the stairs on the second floor he heard Maggie, unexpectedly coming up, proclaimed by the rustle of her skirts. He stood still and swore silently.

"Why, Mr. Holt," she said. "Did John leave his bear in the library?"

"No. I got it from his room." Unable to see the quick anger which suffused her face he heard her say, "I'll take it along with me, sir." She paused; he knew she was considering something. She said politely, "Or perhaps ye wanted to measure it for another thing like its toy chair? For Christmas?"

"No, Maggie. I'm going to throw it away. John is too old for it. He's turning into a mollycoddle and this bear is exactly the sort of thing that's doing it to him. He ought to like different toys, real boy's toys. He's got some and I'm going to give him more for Christmas. He—"

"Excuse me, sir." Seymour heard the girl's voice tremble and he supposed she must be afraid of him. Let her be afraid. He even shrugged as a commentary. But she said quietly, "Mr. Holt, I'll have that bear from you, if you please."

"Just go on upstairs, Maggie and—" Seymour's voice turned glacial, "shall we say—mind your own business?"

"This is my business, sir," she said. Her voice was also cold, and now perfectly controlled. "As long as I am in this house, John is my business and nothing else is. I know what is best for a child of his age."

"You might know if he were a girl. I have no intention of letting him turn into anything resembling one. He is not to be babied any more."

"He is not babied now, sir. Seeing as he has no mother, he gets less babying than any child I ever heard of. He's got to be let to love something the way he loves that bear. Ye'll do him serious harm if ye take it from him, mark my words."

Seymour, who appreciated spunk, could not help admiring the girl for standing up to him. But that feeling, which could have saved the situation, was quickly submerged in the backwash of pent-up acrimonies which wore for him the guise of legitimate concern for John. His jealousy of Randall; his passionate, possessive love for the child, frustrated by his physical inability to do much for him or with him; his obsession that John become quickly—too quickly—a real boy, all coalesced into a hot spear of protest against this feminine way of doing things which, he thought, grew from Randall's sentimentality.

He said, "Get out of my way, Maggie."

"Not until you give me that bear, Mr. Holt."

"Damn you!" Seymour could have lunged forward on the stairway and knocked the woman down and in his rage stood there, trembling on the brink of doing it. She looked up at his red, twitching face, the blind eyes suffused, the muscles taut and cordlike. The veneer of her restraint broke sharply and her own Irish temper burst through it. She raised her strong right hand and brought it down like a cleaver across Seymour's wrists. He yelped a shocking curse. The bear flew out of his hands and over the banister down to the ground-floor hall. Maggie turned, seizing her skirts high, and dashed down the stairs and through the hall, retrieving the bear on her way. She ran to the back door and shouted, "Mr. Holt, sir, Mr. Randall. Please come here at once."

Randall looked up from the snow-man's buttons, lumps of coal which they were putting in place; and seizing John by the hand, he ran towards Maggie as fast as their heavy galoshes and John's short legs could manage. "What is it, Maggie? What's happened?"

She told him, trying to talk above John's comprehension. But John, thinking she had brought Teddy down to see the snow-man, was not interested in talk anyway. He dragged at Randall's hand, saying, "Show snow-man to Teddy. Teddy wants to see."

"Yes, John," said Randall. "Right away. Take him over yourself and show him the snow-man and then come back." It was the best way to keep the child from listening. "Oh, Maggie, I'm so sorry. This is terrible."

"Yes, sir. I'll be leaving now, Mr. Holt. I couldn't do else."

Randall stood dumbstruck. He gave Maggie a look more eloquent than all the pleading words he could have spoken. Then he bent his head in a gesture of overwhelming discouragement and murmured, "What on earth shall I do?"

"I'm that sorry, sir," she said. "But ye surely knew this would happen sooner or later. It's been awful trying, Mr. Holt, the way yer brother has been interferin' and bossin' me around these past months. A body couldn't have stood it no longer. Nobody'll work for two masters. But after what I just did—"

"You were right, Maggie. You did right. But—" he looked at her with utter misery in his eyes. "What shall I do?" he said again.

"If ye're really askin' me, I can only say one thing, Mr. Holt. Take John and get out o' this house with him as fast as ever ye can."

Randall took off his mittens and ran his right hand over his forehead, thrusting his fingers into his hair. "My God," he said. "Maggie this is awful."

"I know, sir." She was shivering in her cotton dress.

"Go inside," said Randall. "I'll bring John right upstairs." In the nursery, while Maggie was pulling off John's leggings, Randall paced up and down saying, "It's going be so hard on him when he realizes. He's going to be so unhappy."

"They always are when their first nurse leaves. He'd have to go through that some time. That ain't the worst, sir, it's that ye can't go on livin' like this, in this house and—and all."

"I know it. Just the thought of how to manage—the food, and everything." The thought of Seymour was the real trouble, too frightening to mention.

"I know, sir. Ma wouldn't stay without me. Not after this."

Randall sat down and put his head in his hands and said, "I feel just about desperate. I haven't got any right to ask you to stay—"

"It wouldn't do any good if ye did, sir. When it happens, it happens."

They began to make shift with a colored woman named Essie who lived up in San Juan Hill and had never been in this neighborhood. She did the work that Mrs. Quinn had done and was a better cook. She prepared their midday dinner, and the broths and cereals that John ate for supper, and went home in the afternoon carrying with her things upon which Seymour and Randall were accustomed to depend for their light evening meal. She also cheated them through the marketing which Randall had to leave to her, as he had long left it to Mrs. Quinn, because he was entirely preempted by John. He had broken the shock of Maggie's departure by moving upstairs to take her place in John's room, and he replaced her in every other way as well. At first he was too stunned to think of looking for another nurse, and by the time he began to weigh whether he should, he saw that no nurse worth having would be willing to work here. Maggie's parting advice was the echo of his own best judgment. The time had come to make the move he had been talking about. But how could he even set about looking for a town to settle in, or a house in which to live there, unless he took John along wherever he went? For Randall had arrived with foreboding at the conclusion that he was unwilling—or was he afraid?—to leave John alone with Seymour. If fear was at the bottom of his feeling he did not know what he feared Seymour would do. But he had learned long ago that fear of the intangible was infinitely worse than fear of the concrete. He was swamped in misgivings and immobilized by his unwillingness ever to take John out on the street. Nothing seemed to him more unendurable than the thought of running the gamut of those diabolical eyes and tongues. The result was that John, who would be three years old in five months, had never been outside this house or its back yard since he had first come into it. One need know nothing about bringing up children to realize that this state of affairs must be changed quickly if John were not to become more eccentric than any Holt who had preceded him. All of Randall's adoring and protecting love could not spare him that—indeed, it might commit him more irrevocably to it unless Randall found the determination to act now.

Because everything integral with his deepest feelings lay hidden among his papers and the other things locked away in his warren on the fourth floor, he took to going up there oftener than ever, very late at night when John was sound asleep and Seymour too. He read and re-read the crackling pages of music manuscript-paper on which he had recorded in his curious hand all that he had lived and shared, and everything that had been said to him, through the recent but weirdly remote past. It was, he felt, the earth and substance out of which John had grown, some of it as common and crudely odorous as the mixture of loam and animal manure in which he had seen good plants flourish and flowers bloom. His thoughts were drawn persistently towards memory of the Maynard farm, and of Renata as she had appeared there, part and parcel despite herself of the elementary life of the place even though she saw it from the viewpoint of another world. The lives of such people made sense, lives of hard work and limited outlook, to be sure; but Randall was repeatedly startled to find himself comparing that with the life which lay ahead of John—even the best future that imagination could contrive. Whatever that might be, there was not only Seymour, blind, jealous, increasingly domineering, to threaten it with strife and stricture. There was Randall himself, and here he had to plumb bitter depths to come up with the brute immutable fact that his own emotion about John could not exist and permeate the child without smashing head-on into equal emotion, equally intense and possibly violent, in Seymour. This was what they hid between them, this was what lay irrationally veiled by a plan to move to a small country town and construct a façade for existence behind which they would deceive themselves that John could grow up to be a normal if not a happy man.

Randall sat for hours up in that clammy, dirty room, sometimes reading, sometimes not, staring at the streaked and peeling wall, or holding his head between his hands while he tried to reach the awful conclusion that lay beyond the last limits of his courage. Very long before he brought himself to face it, he knew what the answer was. He could not keep John to grow up in the house with Seymour. One day, a day looming imminently near, he would have to choose between them. And he would choose for John's sake alone, he would make the choice that most nearly promised a good life for John. For weeks that choice appeared to be the simple departure from this house, to anywhere that would serve as the setting for the life that John should have. Then he touched the last barrier in the maze of thoughts too awful to be faced: are you sure that you, either, are the means to fulfillment for John? What have you to offer him, beyond love so great that it could smother him? Is Seymour right? Are you too soft, too protective, because the boy has no mother? Will you make him into a replica of yourself, and if you do, is that any better than a replica of Seymour? Are you so free of strangeness, of fear, of the secrets and tokens of a burdened past? Look about this room. Think what is in it, in the next room; think of Mama's room, think of the attic, think of the *things*—the things—will you be a different man if you burn them all and go away to make this life for John? Will you burn them? Can you? Do you mean to? For any reason, even for John?

That was when the simple strength of the world of earth and growth and hard-working people emerged as a thought so powerful that Randall knew it had always been there, a factor one could not ignore in facing one's bounden duty to John. It is half his heredity, he thought, and because I and my brother are what we are, it might be the half that will save him.

Now he understood why he had not only written down, but long since memorized, the names, the small words, the broken phrases, that were all he knew of that half of John. Poor they were, those people, yes, and poverty was the reason for such stringencies as could make their lives intolerable if they were so; but poverty; not fear, not queerness, he told himself; not being afraid, not being secret, not being bound by walls and locks and things and memories. Poverty was tangible, poverty one could do something about. Remove that as the real obstruction, and would there not be the chance, perhaps the only chance, that this plant, from its roots deep in earth and warm reality, might bloom? He could not know, it was a thing impossible to guess. But he could try to find out. He could find out too just what she had meant when she said, "in Italy it follow all through the life such a child . . ." She had spoken from her knowledge of unremitting poverty. Had that been her fear? Had it been to solve that one tangible problem posed by poverty that she had pleaded with him that night in the street? And if he had solved it, would she have turned desperate and left the child as she had done?

These questions no longer mattered and she was no longer a reality. But the earth was, and the strong people who belonged to it, whose blood was half of John's. Randall knew now that he could not truly do his duty to John until he had learned what they might be able to tell him. It had taken him weeks to labor through the maze and the mass of memory and instinct, carrying about his neck the albatross of his fears. When he emerged with knowledge and the elements of a decision it was none too soon, for Seymour was becoming impossible.

There was no real reason for his obsession that Randall was spoiling John and coddling him and that Seymour must therefore be strict and exacting and train John to instant obedience. But with this obsession he made John's third Christmas a torment, nagging, criticizing, and interfering at every turn. He contrived an inexhaustible string of reasons for interrupting each time that Randall sat down at the piano with John to play and sing the Christmas music which the boy loved. He catechized Randall to the last detail about every toy that John was to receive, and he infuriated him by trying to destroy John's blissful belief in Santa Claus. Randall had taught John that Christmas toys always came from Santa Claus. Seymour this year turned full of importance about his own very expensive present to John. It was a hobby-horse, large and lifelike, covered with real piebald horsehide. It had flaring red nostrils and an alarming glitter in its glaring glass eyes. John did not like it. He shrank away the moment he saw it. When Seymour said, "Uncle Seymour has given you the horse, John," the child burst into tears and said, "Then Santa Claus didn't come!"

Seymour's face reddened and from that moment he began to force John to ride the horse, which at first merely bored him, but soon became something he dreaded. He was not allowed to go a day without a session on the horse. Inside of a week the child was screaming, "No! No!" when Seymour led him to the horse and lifted him up to mount it. Randall stepped in and said, "Seymour, if I were you I'd let the horse go. He'll take to it of his own free will after a while if you leave him alone."

"And play with clothespins and rag dolls in the meantime?"

"He hasn't played with such things for a long time," said Randall wearily. "If you paid any real attention to him you'd see how interested he is in his new building blocks. You could make things with him— you'd be far more fun for him in such a way than I am."

"And let him go on being afraid of a hobby-horse? He's got to be a boy! He's got to be active. He's got to—" Randall had taken John's hand and quietly led him out of the room, leaving Seymour talking to himself.

But he still tried to balance things by taking John to Seymour in the library every afternoon to play there for an hour before his supper. He had bought a box of thick colored crayons and an outline picture book to give John something to do in the library, since he was beginning to be bored there. John lay on his stomach on the floor, crudely filling in the outline pictures with crazy-quilt colors whose selection had some meaning for him, but no relation to the objects he was coloring. Since Seymour could only participate by hearing about it, he questioned John from time to time what he was coloring, and how; and at one point John said, vigorously daubing away, "It's a lion. Blue lion."

"Lions are not blue," said Seymour. "You must make your lion brown."

"Don't like brown."

"But John, that is silly. You can't make a lion blue when there is no such thing."

"This one is blue." John rubbed harder with his crayon.

"And I tell you you've got to make it brown."

"I won't."

"John! Give me that book."

"No."

Randall was coming up the stairs with John's supper of barley-broth and milk and junket on a tray. He heard the argument in the library and John's shrill, stubborn "No!" He heard Seymour say, "John, obey me at once. Bring me that book."

"No! You'll hurt my lion."

"You come here with that book." Randall, nearing the top of the stairs, could see into the library, see John there on the floor with his knees drawn up under him, and his square little hands planted flat to protect his book and his lion. Seymour rose from his chair and strode towards John and seized him by the shoulder. "Give me that book!" he said, in a tone which ripped from Randall's mind the last curtain that had hidden the full face of the thing he feared. He hurried in and put the tray on a table near the door and said, "Seymour! What are you trying to do?"

John turned and flung himself against Randall's knees, holding his arms around them. Seymour reached after him and tried to drag him away. "Go 'way!" screamed John. "Uncle Ran, make him go 'way."

"That child is going to obey!" shouted Seymour. "John! Get up off that floor and stand on your feet. Do as I say."

John took one bewildered, terrified look over his shoulder at Seymour and began to bawl. Randall bent over and lifted him gently aside, a little behind himself, and holding John in his left arm, with his sobbing face hidden against his leg, he said, "I've been watching it happen. I've been a damned fool. I've been watching it, seeing it right before my eyes."

His voice turned hoarse; he swallowed. If Seymour could have looked at him he would have been the blue eyes dilate in slow horror, the color drain from the gentle face, the mouth drop slowly open. There was a long, tense silence while John sobbed with his face hidden against Randall's leg. Seymour spoke finally, furious, contemptuous.

"What have you been watching?" he said. "What do you see—you with your precious eyesight?"

"What a thing to say! Do you mean you don't know? You can't feel it yourself?"

"My blindness does not extend to my mind, which remains considerably more balanced, I venture, than yours."

"Oh, God." Randall bent down and tried to comfort John, but Seymour took a step towards the child and he began to scream louder. Randall looked up at Seymour's bony face, set and ugly, the blind eyes giving the illusion of an angry glare, the bitter mouth dragged down between the wings of the moustache. Randall tried to deny the terrible truth hammering at his raw nerves. "You mean you don't know?" he breathed, staring at Seymour.

"What?" Seymour's voice was a snarl. "What the hell are you maundering about?"

"You're—just—like—*Her*," said Randall very slowly, breathing hard between the words. He stood aghast, watching Seymour's face tighten into a scornful, weirdly male replica of the face at the root of all fear. Seymour made a sneering sound and took another step towards John. The child shrieked so piteously that Randall knew this to be nothing momentary; it was cumulative, a long-wrought crisis. Randall felt him shaking all over, stamping his feet in fright and temper.

"Make him go 'way," he screamed, clinging to Randall's leg.

Randall picked John up and stood for a moment holding the heavy child and looking round the room. Every corner, every shadow, every object, a hell's crew of memories, and Seymour there in the midst of it, invoked the sources of terror and threat and heartbreak his whole life long.

"You heard me," he said, almost whispering. He scarcely recognized his own voice. "You're just like Her, I said. Seymour—" he tightened his arms round John; his face was grey and haunted. He stared wretchedly at his brother. "You've turned into Her—oh!" he gasped, burying his face in John's neck. "Oh, how horrible. God help you."

He turned away and carried John out of the room. Behind him he heard, "And God damn you!" Seymour lunged forward, there was a crash, Randall gave a brief look over his shoulder at the smashed dishes and the mess on the floor. He held John tightly and took him upstairs.

His hesitations were past. He had only one more decision to make now, and that was about his things. He had got John to sleep, holding him in his arms, and tucked him up at last in his crib. Then he lay down on his own bed, to get some rest and make up his mind. Should he go up and get all his things now and take them down and burn them in the boiler? Everything? That would take courage, he did not know exactly why, but it would be very hard to bring himself to do it. It would mean that the future, whatever form it might take beyond the impenetrable veil of this moment, might be much harder for him; he might feel lost, he might founder without his things. He could not carry them with him, he did not want to. He wanted them to stay hidden.

He went downstairs and telephoned to a locksmith whose shop he had often seen over in Twenty-first Street. Day and Night Service, said a sign across the window. Randall found the number in the book and told the man what he wanted. In a little while a workman arrived, and under Randall's direction he installed strong tumbler locks on the little desk, the wardrobe where it was hidden, and the doors of both old nursery rooms on the fourth floor. After a moment's hesitation Randall had him put a Yale lock also on the door of his mother's room. Then he paid the man, put all the new keys in his pocket, and went upstairs and packed a large valise with John's clothes and his own. Then he roused John, who was too sleepy to ask questions, and dressed him and put on his own best suit. He had already left the valise down in the front hall beside his hat and overcoat. When John was ready, still half asleep, Randall picked him up.

"Teddy," said John drowsily. "Teddy come along."

Randall put the bear in John's arm, turned out the gas, and carried John quietly downstairs. It was half past one in the morning when they left the house.

CHAPTER 18

At first when the cart wheeled round the steep serpentines, with the driver trudging ahead leading the straining mule, John clung to Randall in amazement and fear. "Don't fall over," he cried, his eyes big and round. "Don't let him fall over, Uncle Ran!"

"He won't, John. He's used to it, he does it all the time. Don't be afraid." He pointed down as they rumbled along, higher and always higher. "Look. Isn't it beautiful?"

The air was cold, but not biting. Below them lay a spectacle of splendor, a triangular sweep of brilliant sapphire water; spring-like green slopes; villages whose yellow and grey walls and deep red roofs were picked up like jewels by the morning sunlight. Beyond rose the mountains, proud and glistening in full winter dress, folded in ranges up and away into the bluest sky Randall had ever seen. "This is a beautiful place," he said to John. "Remember, that's what I promised you?"

John nodded solemnly. The driver bellowed, the mule took another turn, and they came round the next bend. Each time the view widened, dropping into grander perspective as they climbed, Randall felt more keenly the sensation of soaring into pure beauty. Once as they turned he made a loud exclamation of delight and the mule-driver looked back with a smile. "It is so beautiful!" said Randall shyly in Italian, and the man nodded as enthusiastically as if he had never heard this before.

"*E' molto bello!*" echoed John proudly. For in the twelve days on the steamer he had done what the Italian stewardess had said he would do: begin instinctively to imitate the sounds he heard and put them to use. In the rough winter seas Randall had been helplessly seasick and Donata the stewardess had promptly adopted the child and taught him simple words and phrases. John had a wonderful time and landed at Genoa in possession of as many Italian words as he had English ones. He interchanged them without effort and he was far more at ease among the Italians than Randall, timidly consulting his pocket self-teacher. He was timid not so much about the language itself as about the purpose for which he was going to need it. Sometimes lying in his bunk, queasy enough from seasickness, he felt sicker still from doubt about the wisdom of what he had done. My God, he thought, was I out of my mind to go off like this with nothing but a couple of names in the back of my head, and no real idea of what I meant to do? What on earth am I going to prove? Then he told himself, as he had been doing for weeks past, not to try to anticipate. You cannot guess, he thought. You want to see them, you want to learn something, you want advice. Wait and see.

He looked at John, happy and interested beside him. The boy's cheeks were apple-red in the pure winter air. His eyes, clear and wide-spaced, were sparkling; his brown curls peeped from the edges of his cap. His lips were parted over little new white teeth. He was sturdy and chunky in his warm clothes. He clapped his mittened hands as the mule swung out for another turn. He had lost his fear of the curves and sat as eager as Randall, watching everything.

There was a narrower road going downhill at the right, and the driver turned into it. The road descended a little way, very rough, jouncing them in the two-wheeled cart; then it widened to a small, bare piazza and the mule stopped. Randall sat looking round at the bleak houses and the humble church. Faces appeared at windows and went away again. Randall jumped down from the cart and held up his arms to John.

"This is San Bernardo di Bellagio?" he asked the driver slowly in Italian.

"Yes, Signore. You know where you want to go here?"

He could scarcely help but know, once he saw anybody to talk to. He remembered too vividly those then funny words: Everybody in San Bernardo is my parent. He preferred to manage without the help of the driver, a cheerful, mannerly peasant whose polite curiosity made him uncomfortable. He knew that a *signor inglese* arriving in midwinter with a small child, asking for the tiniest village in the Comune, would hardly be considered a tourist. He told the man he might be here an hour or two, and the man said, *"Va bene,* Signore, I will go home for dinner and come back afterwards and wait until the Signore is ready to return to Bellagio."

"You live near here?"

"The next village," said the man, pointing up the mountain.

He led the mule away and Randall stood in the middle of the piazza holding John by the hand and wondering how and where to begin. He looked at the houses forming three sides of the piazza, with the church the fourth side. In one corner there was a small shop with a dark doorway, through which an occasional woman came or went, carrying a straw bag or a basket. Each looked curiously at the man and the child, and then went her way. Randall was beginning to wonder whether he had better go and knock on some door and find somebody to talk to when John said, "Where are we, Uncle Ran?"

Randall looked down at him and smiled. "In a village called San Bernardo," he said. "We came all the way from New York to find it. Now we'll find someone to talk to here."

He walked towards the tallest house, not knowing why he had chosen it, leading John by the hand. He was beginning to feel very uneasy, unsure of himself, worried about his scant Italian, anxious because, though there were few people about and those few had hardly spoken in his hearing, he had not understood a word that they had said. Mostly the village appeared deserted and he wondered whether the time of day had anything to do with that. He looked at his watch. It was half past ten in the morning. Well, he thought, I suppose the men are at work and the children are at school and the women are indoors doing their housework. Just then he heard clattering footsteps inside the entry of the tall house, and a woman came out on the doorstep carrying a heavy iron pot. She was small and spare, elderly, with iron-grey hair in a knot on top of her head, dressed in black, with her feet thickly woolclad and thrust into wooden clogs. She paused on the step and looked at Randall and the boy. Her eyes were deep-set in a worn brown face. Randall stood still, hoping for luck with his Italian; then he took a step towards her and said slowly, "Excuse me, I am looking for the Famiglia Gandolfi. Can you—?"

"Here there are many families Gandolfi." She spoke as slowly as Randall had done and he understood her well.

"This one has a Zia Paola in it, Signora."

She drew back a little, knitting her thick eyebrows. She looked from the man to the child and again at the man, with a half-cognizant, half-suspicious expression. He saw that she was weighing what to do. He had divined already who she was. She said, as if reluctantly, "They call me Zia Paola."

Randall smiled timidly and put out his hand. She did not move for a moment. Then she put her iron pot down on the doorstep, slowly ran her right hand down the side of her black skirt, and laid it in Randall's. It felt rough and hard. She did not say anything, but after the hand-shake she stood staring at the boy. Randall put his arm round John, drawing him forward towards the woman, and said, "I think you will know whose child this is, Signora. Is it not so?"

Her mouth was shut tight, her whole face stern and controlled. But she nodded slowly. Her eyes began to soften as they rested on John's bright face and sturdy little body. She had apparently nothing to say and was far from knowing what to do. John smiled at her and said, "Is this the lady you were looking for, Uncle Ran?"

The woman's eyes went uneasily over John's head, across the piazza where Randall, though he could not see behind him, knew there must be women standing by the shop, watching this scene with natural curiosity. "Let us go into the house," said Zia Paola. She picked up her iron pot and motioned them inside. She led them up two flights of dark and very cold stone steps; Randall carried John most of the way. She opened a door into a small room with a single window on the piazza. It was fur-nished with a rough square table and several hard wooden chairs, a home-made set of shelves which held crockery and kitchen utensils, and a low cot in one corner covered by a grey blanket. In another corner there was a small brick stove, merely a firebox with a round hole in the top. On the whitewashed plaster walls were several religious chromos and an illustrated calendar and a crucifix with a dry sprig of olive thrust behind it. The scrubbed board floor was bare. The woman went over and put some faggots into the stove and blew on them until they flamed up. "It is probably colder here than you are accustomed," she said.

Randall stood in his overcoat, holding his hat in his hand, looking slowly round the bare, clean room. John surprised him by leaving his side and trotting over to the woman at the stove, to watch what she was doing. She turned from the fire and looked down at the boy with an expression which could not conceal that he charmed her. But when she looked at Randall her face was different; remote, closed.

"Why have you come here?" she asked. She did not make the ques-tion sound rude as it might have done. Randall knew that she was feel-ing her way.

"I came to see you. To talk to you." He paused and added, "But, as you see, I speak very little Italian."

She did not answer at once. Then suddenly she shrugged. She said, "My son Domenico speaks English. In summer he works at the Gran' Albergo. He will be able to explain. He comes home soon for dinner."

"That is good." Randall felt a little better. He took courage and said, "Signora—you are, indeed, Renata Tosi's aunt?"

He had the impression that the woman would have avoided answering had that been possible. As it was, she stayed silent for a moment and her face was cold. Then she shrugged again, assenting to the self-evident. Randall knew that she was not pleased to hear him speak Renata's name. She was embarrassed; so was he. But she kept looking with increasing interest and warmth at John. Presently she put out her hand and took the cap off his head and ran her rough fingers over his thick brown curls.

"It is a beautiful child," she said, almost as if against her will. Then she looked hard at Randall and her level stare demanded to know once for all why he had come here. "Why did you ask for me?" she said. "Why not for the boy's mother?"

"Renata?" Randall was surprised. "I did not come to find her." He had no wish to give his reasons. "I know nothing about her since she went to South America. Is she not still there?"

The aunt did not answer. She sat down and lifted John to her lap. She began to take off his warm coat and leggings. "He will be too hot," she said. "You will stay and eat dinner with us."

Randall did not know what to say. He had not expected this, and he felt he ought to refuse. They might not have enough food on hand for two extra mouths; they were surely very poor. But if I act as if I were thinking this, he knew, she will be offended and that is the last thing I want. He looked at her face, bent over John; it was austere and patient, the forehead curiously unlined in contrast with the toll that years and hard work had visibly taken of her. She was making friends with John who appeared to be pleased.

"Thank you very much," said Randall shyly, and stood by listening as John told her his name, though she had asked the question of Randall. She broke into a smile as the boy spoke and exclaimed, "But he understands Italian!"

"A little," said Randall, and explained in a few words about the ship.

"He must be intelligent." She studied John's face. "He is—what? Not quite three years old?"

"In four mouths." He did not know how much she knew.

"John," she said phonetically, shaking her head a little. "That is Giovanni, is it not?"

"Yes, Signora."

"Who chose San Giovanni?"

Randall was nonplussed. Here was a whole aspect of life with its imminent impact upon John which in his preoccupation with everything else, he had never thought about. He realized now its supreme importance to these people here. He was afraid to answer, unwilling to say the wrong thing.

"John was my father's name, Signora. I—"

"But San Giovanni is a saint, first." She looked suspicious. "When was he baptized?"

Randall was not perfectly sure of the word *battezzato*, but he guessed at it. My God, he thought, how is it possible this question never entered my head before? How can I tell her I don't know? What does she know about Renata's actions beyond the fact that she had this child? Randall did not want to prejudice the aunt. He decided to take refuge for the moment in simulated confusion about the language. He said, stumbling over his words, "Signora, there are so many things to talk about, many important things like this. Perhaps a little later, when your son—when I can—" he broke off.

Zia Paola got to her feet, not very well satisfied as he could see. "I must start the polenta," she said uneasily, and then stood listening to the sound that Randall also heard, the clattering of wooden clogs on the stairway. Her face had turned tense, her mouth was closed hard, and John, who had begun to take to her quite cosily, turned to Randall with a puzzled look on his face. Randall was standing there wondering what had happened, whether his pretense about misunderstanding Italian had not only failed, but had offended her. He was thinking about her, and not about the footsteps which rattled along the passage, coming closer. Then the door opened. He was stunned. Without volition his astounded eyes stopped short of the face, and took in first a long black skirt, a coarse grey blouse, a little knitted shawl. Then and only then did he look up straight into the face of Renata Tosi. She stood enormous-eyed, dead-white, bent a little forward, staring at John. She was holding a straw bag in her right hand and he saw the hand tense until the tendons swelled. Her mouth opened, she dropped the bag, he saw her pale lips form the syllables: *mio bambino*. She fell on her knees with her arms round John, holding him in a vise of an embrace with her face buried in his neck. Randall heard her weeping. He turned aside, almost equally overcome himself. He covered his eyes with one hand, not only to avoid the heartrending sight of Renata and the portentous scrutiny of the old woman over by the stove; he was utterly bewildered. He stood trying to fight down the turmoil which catapulted through him. He was beyond thinking, torn in mind, aware only of his enormous blindness in not having foreseen this. When he could think at all, he asked himself how this could never have occurred to him. I never once imagined she could be here. She went to South America, I always thought she stayed there. Why? My God, his mind went round in a circle; my God, why didn't I think of this, what have I done? What have I done . . .

He had to raise his head then because John was asking, "Who is it, Uncle Ran? Who is *this* lady?"

Renata Tosi knelt with her arms tight round the child, looking up at Randall with tears running down her white face. No particle of his memory could find a parallel for the way she looked now. The features were the same, the deep dark eyes beautiful behind the tears; but she was a different woman.

"You brought him," she said in Italian. "You brought him." She raised one hand in an unconscious gesture; it might have been pleading. "May God bless you," she said. She laid her pale cheek against John's fat red one. "God bless you, my friend."

"But who is she, Uncle Ran?" John's piping voice pierced the solemnity. He seemed content with her embraces, but his little face was puzzled. The aunt stood in the corner watching; her face was expressionless but Randall heard a telltale sniffle. Randall put his hand for a moment on John's head. He looked hard at Renata Tosi.

"She is your aunt, John," he said slowly. "Your Italian aunt." Her eyes widened in surprise, he saw what went through her mind. "Tell him, Renata," said Randall. She bowed her head slightly with a suggestion of obedience.

"Zia Renata," she said tenderly to John. She spoke in Italian; she looked at him with adoration, and told him to repeat her name.

"Zia Renata," he said, with his usual interest in anything new, and she wept again and covered his forehead with kisses. When Randall looked at the old woman, she was standing there with a frown on her face, squinting. She might as well have asked aloud what was in Randall's mind, what did he mean? Why start off by telling the boy that his mother was his aunt? Randall gave Zia Paola a meaning look which conveyed clearly, "I knew nothing. It was you I came to see."

She turned to her cooking. She had a hot fire burning now. Renata was still kneeling with her left arm round John. Her right hand caressed his cheek and brushed the curls back from his forehead. Zia Paola came across the room, carrying her empty iron pot; she had been on her way to fetch water when she encountered Randall on the steps. Renata started to rise and take the pot, but her aunt waved her back and went on out of the room. Randall stood and watched Renata. Her tears had stopped and she was gazing with delight at John. She smiled once tremulously at Randall, raising her head, and as she did so her glance fell on the calendar on the wall. The renewed color drained from her cheeks. Once again she turned perfectly white, her mouth opened wide, she stared as if at something altogether extraordinary, which nobody else could see. She pointed, trembling, at the calendar; then she crossed herself slowly and bowed her head and began to weep again. Randall was mystified. He waited; John started to squirm with impatience; Renata said nothing. At last Randall asked, "What is it, Renata? What do you mean?"

She looked up, kneeling there, and crossed her hands on her breast with unaffected sincerity. "It is a miracle," she said quietly in Italian. "A true miracle."

"But why? How?"

She kept her eyes on the calendar and said, "Today is San Sebastiano. The twentieth of January. You could not know—" she blushed with shame and hung her head and whispered, "That is the name I chose when he was baptized."

"You had him baptized, Renata?" Randall did not know, and for some reason also did not care, how much John could understand of this.

"But of course, yes." She spoke quickly. He had always understood her when she spoke Italian, his feeling for her had filled what might have been gaps in his understanding of anyone else. "You could not know," she said, her head still bent. "But you should have guessed. Already so deep in sin, I could not imagine how I could ever atone. But one sin I need not commit—allow his immortal soul to be lost? No, of course I had him baptized."

"Why didn't you—" he broke off. He could not bring himself to refer to the note in the basket.

She shook her head a little. "The name was not the most important thing. He would be American. I—" she made a gesture which meant, "I left everything to you." She had been right, he thought. Suppose she had told him the Italian name she had chosen; would he have paid any attention to it? Not any more than he would have consented in the beginning to raise the child as a Catholic. She had been realistic and knowing and consistent; she had always been so.

John had left her side, tired of standing still, and had begun to trot round the room, examining everything within his reach. Renata still knelt there, genuinely unconscious of the saintly picture she made. Randall was touched by it, but baffled when he tried to relate her to the woman he had last seen. There was no time for questions now, he knew her aunt would return in a moment. He only said, because other questions of greater urgency would require more time and more thought and more privacy, "Why did you choose the name Sebastiano?"

She smiled a little. "It was always my favorite name. I like it because it is so musical, so harmonious. But how could I know it would be the miracle that would bring him here? You do understand what I mean? To me this is—" she broke off, shaking her head with wonderment. Then she said, a complete afterthought, "But what have you called him?"

"John. And it would be difficult to change now, to explain to him."

"That is unnecessary. He is used to it. Let him be called Giovanni, John—here they will call him Giu'an in the dialect. But his baptismal name is Sebastiano. Thank God," she said softly. She rose to her feet. She had spoken with such simple conviction that there was no question in Randall's mind of differing with her. Although he was confused about every aspect of this situation into which he had blundered, he felt an instinct that it would be best to let these questions take the direction in which she had—innocently or wisely—set them. She had not spoken a word of English and perhaps in that too she had known the right thing to do.

She began to take things out of the bag that she had carried in. She said, "We must hurry, we should not be late with dinner."

Randall realized that he still had his overcoat on. He took it off slowly, looking round the primitive kitchen. He asked softly, "Do you stay—do you live here, Renata?"

She pointed to the cot in the corner. "I sleep there. This kitchen belongs to my uncle and Zia Paola. They have two other rooms along this passage. In one they sleep, in the other my cousins, their two youngest sons. All the rest are married."

Randall was afraid to talk any more, he was listening for Zia Paola's return. His thoughts were a turmoil, everything had been swept from his hands by this wildly unexpected ending to the journey whose purpose from the first had been, he saw now, much too vague. He could not see beyond the next minutes, beyond the aunt's return; all he could think was, "What have I done? What have I done!" He folded his overcoat slowly and laid it with his hat beside John's coat on the end of the cot. He looked at Renata with such visible bewilderment, sweeping the room and her plain poor clothes with his eye, that she said, "I will tell you later, another time. Now my aunt—"

"How much does she know?" he asked. "Did she—does she—"

"They all know," she said quietly. She looked at John, who was standing at the window watching something outside. "They have not been pleased with me. But they will love him. I told you long ago, they are good. Such people are not confused."

Zia Paola came in. She carried her pot and a metal milk can. She said something to Renata in dialect which Randall did not understand. Renata smiled and said to Randall, "She says we will cook the polenta in milk today because it is a special occasion, also it is good for the boy. Later I will tell her what a special occasion it really is. She will be moved."

John turned from the window and stood on tiptoe by the table and peered at the things on it. Zia Paola smiled at him, saying, "He is hungry, he has a good appetite." She sliced a heel off the round crusty loaf and offered it to him.

"*Grazie*," said the child gravely, and the woman bent down and kissed him delightedly. Randall was uncomfortable; he should be relieved, but he found himself troubled by her unquestioning acceptance of the boy. It did not seem even so pliant a thing as acceptance, it more resembled seizure. Love any or all children as she might, he knew she regarded this one as her own flesh and blood. He was uneasy. He had given neither her nor Renata any reason to suppose that he had come here to hand over the child. He wanted to warn them right now not to think so. He wanted to invoke Renata's help, and he saw that in Zia Paola's presence, from every motive of discretion he must keep a wall between himself and Renata. Then suddenly, in utter consternation, he saw the most appalling thing of all. The aunt knows none of the story behind this. She can suppose nothing except that I am John's father and have brought him here because I am unequal to taking care of him by myself. He felt the sweat breaking out on his forehead and the palms of his hands, he was quavering inwardly with nervousness. He told himself he must stop any such misapprehension right now, before it was too late. He bit his lips and swallowed and said, "Renata."

"How?" She turned and looked at him. For the first time he caught in her face something of the vivid expressiveness which in the past had held him fascinated, had kept him watching every mood of her deep-set eyes under their level brows, every angle of her fine high-bridged nose whose slanting nostrils had spelt mischief like the smiling curves of her wide mouth, now closed so firmly that in this strange moment he knew one certainty which she would not have to tell him. She no longer sang. How he knew this he could not tell, nor whether she was silent from choice or because she had lost her voice. Why else, he asked himself, looking at her peasant's clothes, her hand stirring the polenta with a curiously-shaped wooden paddle, would she be here? She was looking over her shoulder at him, her arm working the paddle in a slow steady rhythm. "How?" she asked again; "*com'è*?"

"Would you," he said uneasily, speaking English. "Renata—would you please explain something to your aunt?" He gave her a kind of smile which was meant to be reassuring, but this was difficult because he felt so nearly helpless himself. "All this, you see, is so unexpected. I didn't realize—I wasn't sure—just who I would find here." He thought for a moment and said quite flatly, "I didn't expect to find you. But I came because I wanted to see your people and talk to somebody here."

"You must have had a reason," she said in Italian.

"It was very difficult in New York. I had to take him away. This isn't the time to talk about that. I just want all of you here to know I haven't made any decisions about anything. This is a visit, do you see?"

She nodded, sighing.

"I'm awfully grateful to your aunt." Randall's face was solemn; drawn. "She's been so good. I wish you'd explain to her."

Renata told her aunt quickly, in dialect. Zia Paola frowned a little, perhaps more puzzled than annoyed. So long as this had appeared to her a clear-cut situation she had reacted directly and naturally, in spite of her original hesitation. Now if it were going to become clouded or complicated she would be less approving. But, with her eyes on John happily munching his bread, she said in Italian, "In any case, it is almost midday and you will eat with us, you and Giovanni. Afterwards—?"

"Where would you go after dinner?" asked Renata. "From where did you come this morning?"

"From Bellagio. I have a room in the small hotel there, the one that is open all winter. We arrived last night by the boat from Como."

Renata shook her head slowly in wonderment. He saw that his warning had made her too timid to ask him any further questions. He said again, "I just haven't decided anything. But I might stay a while in Bellagio."

His voice sounded slack and tired, and his few words told the Renata who was no longer visible, the hidden woman who knew him well, that he had been struggling with a burden much too heavy for his gentle nature. His bare hint at the impasse of strife and worry from which he had fled caused her a painful twinge of conscience. But this was not the time, as he said, to dwell on any of that. She smiled a little and said, "I hope Giovanni will like our food. He has surely never eaten this before." She indicated the polenta and a second pot, giving forth a savory steam.

"He loved the Italian food on the ship. I was sick most of the time," Randall laughed, "but Donata the stewardess told me he ate everything he was given and often asked for more."

Renata told her aunt, and Zia Paola, who had been listening to Randall's English with an uneasy expression, relaxed a little and nodded her head.

The hoarse, humble voice of the church bell in the piazza began to sound noon. It had not finished striking when the door opened and three men trooped in, Renata's uncle Gandolfi and her cousins Nino and Domenico. They were strapping, brown-faced chaps with brilliant white teeth, smiling and curly-headed; Nino about eighteen and

Domenico somewhat older. Zio Gandolfi was a bent, dignified peasant of indefinable age, with a straggling moustache and abundant white hair. All three men stood staring at Randall and the boy. For a moment nobody spoke. Then as Renata with a helpless look turned away to attend to something at the stove, Zia Paola said in dialect in a flat, heavy tone, "This is Renata's boy, Papà. And its father."

Randall understood her but hoped that John had not; in the same moment he saw the uselessness of these devices of his. He might as well chuck them all aside. He knew he had turned red, his face was burning. He did not know where to look; surely not at Renata, more surely not at the Gandolfis standing there agape. John had sidled close to him, faced with a new influx of strangers, and stood there chewing the last of his bread. Domenico was the first to recover, perhaps because he was used to the sight of new faces, and always ready to show off his English. He glanced at his mother for a cue, and when he saw her shrug faintly as if to say, "What can we do about it?", he went over to Randall and held out his hand.

"You are American, Signore?" he said in English as they shook hands.

"Yes." Randall managed a smile. "How do you do? My name is Randall Holt."

"Gandolfi Domenico," replied the young man politely, with a slight bow curiously elegant in a peasant, dressed in his rough working clothes. "My father, Gandolfi Luigi. My brother Nino." Papà and Nino made noncommittal sounds. "You have just arrived? You come from Bellagio?" He offered the banalities that one always had ready for travellers. Randall answered briefly, aware that Renata in the corner was keeping her back turned, and that Zia Paola was putting dishes and spoons on the table with a good deal of noise, as if to cover the awkwardness.

John pulled at Randall's hand, solemnly eyeing the three men, and asked softly, "Who are they, Uncle Ran?"

Domenico heard him and raised his eyebrows. Without thinking, he blurted, "He calls you 'Uncle'?"

Randall looked him hard in the eye, deciding that now or never he must get the English-speaking member of this family on a basis of understanding. "Naturally," he said. "In the circumstances—"

"But naturally, Signore." Domenico smiled lamely, by way of asking pardon for his tactlessness. He bent down and put his hard, stained hand on John's curly head. "You are my little cousin," he said. "You must learn to speak Italian."

"*Posso parlare italiano*," said John quickly. "*Ho fame.*"

"*Eh! Bello!*"

"*Carino!*"

"*Che bravo!*"

"*Che intelligente!*"

They all spoke at once. Their faces warmed, they began to smile and nod, they closed in on the table drawing Randall and John with them while Zia Paola and Renata approached from the stove, each carrying a steaming pot. Randall had the feeling that but for John's artless, charming remark they might have remained suspicious and chilly for a long time. Also, he saw once again, he had not reckoned with the delighted love of Italians for children. Suddenly, standing shyly by their poor, rough table, about to share their coarse food, he felt himself teetering on the brink of tears. He had struck a lode of human kindliness which in spite of all the problems, all the difficulties which still lay ahead, proved that his instinct in turning with the child to these people had been the right one. It was a staggering relief to feel, after the frightening, furtive, desolate years in New York, that there was in the world a fund of natural love upon which John could draw. Renata's face did not altogether bear that out. She kept her eyes lowered and did not say a word. But her own shame, like his, and whatever means they found to come to terms with it, were not the concern of these Gandolfis. They had taken in the child because it would be against nature to do anything else.

Randall first saw the pink house a fortnight later when the weather turned so warm and soft, as it often does early in February, that Domenico suggested taking him and John out on the lake to enjoy the view from a boat. There had been a certain amount of visiting with the Gandolfis, but Randall was careful not to overdo it. He wanted no issues raised, and only by degrees had he discovered how enormously tired he was in every way. He was too tired to decide what he wanted to eat, what necktie to put on, what John should wear; he felt and acted like a sleep-walker and was content to have it so. The quiet, the remoteness, the timelessness, and the completeness of his escape enclosed him in a caressing mist. Until this should begin to disperse of its own accord, he had no idea of deciding anything, or even of learning anything, such as what had happened to Renata in the past three years. He kept his distance and still more she kept hers. They had scarcely exchanged a word alone. Even had they wanted to talk privately it would not have been feasible. There was no privacy in the Gandolfis' kitchen and Randall in fact had been only a few times there. Nothing would have induced Renata to go out walking, or to sit with him somewhere in a public place in Bellagio or in one of the villages. Thus she had avoided him, but never her own thoughts which she had hidden with consummate success. His lifelong refuge in self-delusion had worked to hide from him the truths that behind her impassivity lay passionate, gnawing anxiety as to his intentions about the boy; that her calm tenderness with the child was a prodigy of self-control. In her downcast eyes, her deferential bearing towards her relatives, her austere reserve with himself, Randall could not sense her torments of suspense, sharpened by guilt, heightened by her adoration of the boy.

Domenico was the member of the family who appointed himself a kind of host, or guide, or courier, not having much farm work to do at this season and greatly preferring something that resembled the summer work which brought him into contact with foreigners. Randall was a bit uncomfortable with him at first. He wanted neither the subservience which Domenico would have proffered a real tourist, nor the intimacy that belonged to a real relative. Gradually they struck a medium and became, within a certain careful formality, friends.

It was chance that took them round the tip of the peninsula and into the eastern branch of the lake. From Bellagio Randall had not seen it and Domenico said, "It is beautiful too, you understand, but different. It has not got big hotels and beautiful villas, it is more simple." He smiled lightly. "It belongs more to us."

"I'd like to see that!"

So they drifted round the point and down the winding shore, with its tiny bays and coves, its softly terraced hillsides, their grass as green as April—but it is always so green here, said Domenico—its twisted silvery olive trees leaning tenderly to the sun, its dark patches of cedar and spruce, the tall solemnity of cypresses.

"One would never believe there could be so many different shades of green," said Randall. "I've never seen such lovely soft variations of a color." They floated along, Domenico barely plying the oars. To their right the hills were only moderately high, but on their left across the lake rose the Grigna, rugged and peaked with snow. Towns clustered along the shore at its feet; above and behind them the range turned rocky and grim.

"I suppose everybody remarks about that mountain down there that looks like a face," said Randall pointing southwards.

"Yes." Domenico laughed. "They call it the Profile of Napoleon. I think they call every such mountain in Europe by the same name."

"Oh, look," cried John suddenly. "A pink house! What a funny pink house, Uncle Ran."

He pointed at a little cove, where a tall, narrow, shrimp-pink house nestled among grey olive trees and leafless, pale-trunked poplars, close to the water's edge. On the rocks nearby were stretched some nets to dry. "I like it!" cried John. "I never saw a pink house before."

"Pink houses are not admired in this region, Giu'an," said Domenico. "You will not see many of them."

"Why?" asked Randall.

"They are considered ordinary. In most places anyway, pink stucco is only for contadini. They say that only in Genova the nobili and rich people color their houses pink."

"Oh, that can't be true," said Randall. "Every book you read about Italy is full of pink houses."

Domenico shook his head. "I have never travelled," he said. "I only know what we think here."

Randall was looking at the house with a curiously sleepy kind of interest. The air and the springlike sun made him feel so relaxed that he held his eyes open with effort. Yet there was something peculiarly pleasing about the sight of the pink house. He asked Domenico to whom it belonged.

"To an old fisherman whom everybody calls Zio Pepe. He must be nearly ninety years old and he has always been there."

"The place looks quite well kept."

"Yes. Zio Pepe is a busy old man. He could never earn a sufficient living at fishing, for our fish are too wily to let themselves be caught in such numbers. But he owns a sandpit across the road back of his house which gives a certain quality of sand that the capomastri prefer for making stucco, and he sells enough sand to keep him going. But the real difference with him is that some ten years ago an English painter mooning about the lake in a rowboat fell in love with Zio Pepe's house and wanted to live in it."

Randall's eyes were opened wider now and he listened carefully, looking at the shore and the nets and the house.

"They did a lot of talking and there was some expense for the Englishman, but not very much because he was a poor man. Still he had more money than Zio Pepe, who had none, and between them they fixed up about half of the house into the kind of place the Englishman wanted to live in. It is not like a real villa, you understand, but much more comfortable than our houses. They say there is a stove in every room. It has not got a bathroom such as my cousin Mauri the idraulico installs in rich people's villas, but the Englishman contrived a way to get water into the house without carrying it, and heat enough of it at a time to fill a tin vasca da bagno like they all use, those inglesi."

Domenico always showed off what he knew of foreigners' habits and he never needed much prodding to encourage him to talk. Randall said, "Go on," and Domenico said, "He was a good gardener and when he was not painting he was raising flowers. Lots of them are still there."

"Where is he now?" Randall's voice was husky, with a note of suspense in it which Domenico appeared not to remark, or anyway, not to understand.

"He lived there until a couple of years ago, then he had to go back to England in the winter because of some family matter, and naturally the climate killed him, poveretto. He should never have gone."

"And the house, his part of the house—"

"Why, it has been empty ever since." Domenico looked sharply at Randall. "I don't know why, one would think that somebody would want it."

"I do," said Randall.

"You?"

"Do you think I could rent it?"

Domenico stopped rowing and sat resting on his oars, a few strokes offshore from the house. "I don't see why not," he said, but he was surprised.

John clapped his hands and said, "I want the pink house, too, Uncle Ran!"

"Can we go ashore now?" asked Randall. "Is Zio, what's his name—Zio Pepe—there?"

"I suppose so. You can see his boat is there." Domenico was finding himself not quite so used to foreigners as he had thought. Most people would not take such a decision in this sudden way.

"Let's go and talk to him now, Domenico," said Randall. "You do the talking and be sure you get me the house."

It was a milky, windless morning in the middle of February when they moved in. Domenico brought them from the landing in Bellagio with their big valise and a basket of provisions. Randall was happy about the move, even rather excited; but that was tempered by his doubts about the wisdom of what he had done. He sat in the boat with his coat-collar turned up, for the air was chilly, watching the odd whitish tinge of the sky and the reflecting water, and so preoccupied by his doubts that he took no notice of John's chatter with Domenico, mostly in the dialect which he was picking up very fast. The house might prove to be the haven of peace for which Randall had reached with the instinct of a hungry man for food. But he might too have ruined that possibility and done something disastrously unwise when he had followed the line of least resistance and consented to a startling resolution of his strange situation with Renata. He could not keep his feelings in balance. Each time that he arrived at reacceptance of the idea, his anxiety began to undermine it again.

Well, if it proved impossible, he would simply leave. At times in the past weeks he had had difficult moments, discomfited by the knowledge that the Gandolfis, while perfectly at ease about John, were always on their guard, always reserved with Randall himself. How could they be otherwise; indeed, how could he wish them otherwise? He did not. He thought they had attained a remarkable compromise and shown surprising poise in view of the gap of class and language and nationality. Renata had answered one of his infrequent questions by explaining that this was only because he was not Italian, only his foreignness enabled them to accept his presence on his terms. But he felt constantly their silent questions and the weight of their unmistakable views about him and about Renata and the child. They found it hard to understand why he should have come here merely as a drifter, a temporizer. He knew the source of Renata's profound sense of natural truth: it was these people behind her. He knew that they expected one of two alternatives as the outcome of his presence here, either that he would turn over the child to Renata and go away, or that he would stay here and marry her. This indeterminate course of his, caring for the boy as no ordinary man would do, hanging about here without resolving anything, became more puzzling to the Gandolfis as time went on.

He wanted so much to live in the pink house and lose himself in the dreaming beauty of the place that he pushed those questions aside. He had been adept all his life at hiding what he did not want to see; nobody could know how adept. He had long recognized that one could hide thoughts, ideas, memories, intangibles, quite as well as paper and stuffs, a box, a locket, a blank-book, a desk. How could he be here at all if he could not fairly well keep hidden the thought of Seymour? It was when he was most impelled by this knowledge that he cared least how he appeared to the Gandolfis. He became then more commanding of himself, more decisive of manner. Inevitably they reacted with a certain increase of distance but also of respect. It was at such a moment last week that he had asked Zia Paola in Renata's presence how he could go about finding a woman to keep house for him, or whether she would be willing to find him one.

She had first raised her shoulders in a slow shrug and made a sound which might mean anything. Then she said, "*Ma!*" and put on her shawl and said, "Talk to her about it," jerking her head towards Renata; and she took her marketing-bag and went out.

Randall stood by the table, looking down at Renata who was hemming a silk handkerchief. He was thoroughly surprised and ill at ease. John was outside playing with some children in the piazza, he could hear their prattle through the open window. Renata kept her head bent over her sewing. She did not speak. After a time Randall said in English, "What did she mean?"

Renata's muscular fingers whipped stitches and she did not look up. She said in English, the first time she had spoken it, "What you think? It seem clear enough." Her voice was dull, muffled.

"But," he said. He drew up a chair and sat down near her, across the corner of the table. "I wouldn't dare think. It would never have occurred to me."

"No," she said, "probably not. Is like you, Randalo, not see what is the most simple, most natural."

He was silent, weighing this extremely problematical idea. He had barely got used to the fact that Renata was here at all, instead of lost forever in the nowhere of South America—another piece of his characteristic hiding. And here was this astonishing proposal that she come and live in the house with him. Why was it not impossibly shocking, how could her aunt of all people have suggested such a thing? Embarrassed and confused, he asked Renata.

She looked up then, and he thought sharply of other times when she had given him this cool, almost patronizing stare. It was when her view of a situation, the rational, the factual one, had come up against his tentative or his evasive or his romantic idea.

"Is not natural," she said, "its mother is the best woman to be with a child? You think Zia Paola care about something else? Whether is good the cooking or—or—" she shut her mouth for a moment, then opened it again and said, "Who you suppose she care about—you or Giu'an?"

Her use of the name in dialect struck Randall hard.

"But if I let you come," he said slowly, "won't they all think—"

She sighed, shaking her head, and dropped her work in her lap. "How you have not change'," she said. "You don't see what they think from the moment you arrive?"

"They think we are John's parents," he said reluctantly. He spoke more slowly, almost whispering. "They assume I am his father."

"Well?" In spite of her self-possessed mien up to now he saw her pallor giving way to a slow, dark blush. She turned from his gaze and muttered, "You would have them think—otherwise?"

"My God—" the thought came back at him for the first time in weeks, a brutal, sickening thrust. "No."

"Well," she said.

There was a long silence. "Do you really want to come, Renata?" he asked finally.

"You have brought Giu'an here. Nobody understand why, but you imagine I don't want to be with him?"

"But with me too?"

She shrugged, the ancient, infinitely redundant gesture of her aunt and all the women like her. "Why not? If to be with Giu'an means also with you, very well."

"And you don't care what they, the village people—"

"You think they say anything they have not said already? You do not understand them well. Like me, they are the realists. Like I always tell you, we—"

"I know. But—" he stopped. This he did not know how to say. But somehow he must force it out, there was all too much of this living with things he was afraid to talk about, afraid to face. "They will all be saying I ought to marry you." He was uncomfortable. "And I—" he swallowed, and she looked up and saw the uncharacteristic hardness of his jaw. Something flashed through her mind and was reflected in a frown, but he was either too preoccupied or not in the mood to see it. It was a long time since he had been given to studying her face and hanging on what he might find there or hope to read into it.

"You have not the intention," she said, perfectly calm. "Nor I." Her level brows were still; her lips, her delicate nostrils; the deepest of inscrutable expressions darkened her eyes. "I never had it. Is no different now."

His memory wrenched out an echo of the pleading woman who had stopped him in the December street. That had been the single chink in the solid wall of her consistency. Had time filled it in, could he be sure that hardship had not breached it? He wanted no new problem posed by her. She sat watching his face and watching him look, as he had done that first day, all round this poor, bare kitchen, and then at her hands, hardened by work, and at her ugly clothes; and last at her closed, silent mouth.

"You have not told me how any of this came about," he said slowly.

"I tell you if it seem necessary," she said. "Is little to tell. Perhaps is enough you know I was very sick, I lose my voice, I return here." She paused, but not to give him a chance to ask questions. Her expression kept him silent. "Was my own choice," she said, and picked up her sewing again.

He sighed over another long silence. "Well," he said, and she heard the doubtfulness in his voice, "if you really want to try it, Renata—"

"I want," she said. "And to Giu'an I am always the Zia Renata. And," she added sharply, "also he will not know I can speak English."

Randall tried to smile, as if to give agreement, or thanks, or encouragement. Instead he turned his head quickly, overcome by another stabbing memory. He saw the lovely, laughing face framed in ruching, across a restaurant table, and heard the rippling voice saying, "Better I teach you Italian." For what a reason then, he thought; and for what a reason now! She sat with her head bent humbly over her sewing.

Domenico beached the boat on the narrow strand of pebbles and lifted John out and put him down to run up to the house while they unloaded the boat. A short flight of crooked steps led up to the small loggia which enclosed the entrance to the "English" part of the house. Renata stood in the open doorway, smiling. John clambered quickly up the steps and threw his arms round her. "Ciao!" he cried. "Ciao, Zia!" She kissed him and swung him up in her arms and put him down again. He ran inside and round the rooms which he knew well already, for they had been here much of the past week during the daytime, putting the house in order.

Domenico shouldered the heavy valise and ran lightly up the steps with it and Randall followed with the basket. The house smelled clean and fresh and the rooms were pleasantly warm. There was a small red terra-cotta stove in each room, as Domenico had said, and a better stove in the kitchen than the primitive firebox at Zia Paola's. There had been a good deal of head-wagging over the amount of firewood that Randall would have to buy if he meant to use all the stoves, but everybody agreed that fire for an hour or two a day would keep the place more than warm enough.

John came and seized Randall's hand and dragged him to the kitchen. "Look!" he cried. He pointed to the things ready on the table which Renata would soon begin to cook. "Risotto!" His eyes danced. This was a treat, a luxury, according to the Gandolfis, whose invariable polenta even at a few meals had become wearisome to the child. John continued his tour of inspection, pulling Randall along. The place looked welcoming and comfortable. Nobody knew the status of the Englishman's furniture and possessions, no one had come to claim them and Zio Pepe had simply kept them locked up here. Now, aired and cleaned, they looked very cosy. In addition to the pleasant kitchen there was the large room which had been the painter's studio, with a high window cut into the north wall; and upstairs there were two bedrooms with good beds and more sheets and blankets than most people would know what to do with. "They come from such a cold country," Domenico had said when they were carrying the bedding outside to air. "They can never believe it is not the same everywhere."

"It's much colder where I come from," said Randall, "and I haven't noticed any balmy southern nights around here yet. It's only warm here so long as the sun is out."

Domenico laughed. "Winter is winter," he said. But he tipped his chin at the lovely green hillsides that Randall so much admired. "Is it like that all winter in America?"

This morning Randall thanked him for all his help and the use of the boat, which Domenico borrowed whenever he needed it, and with a good deal of embarrassment on both sides, payment was offered and accepted. This was the sort of thing that made the situation awkward. But, thought Randall, in such ways at least I can be as matter-of-fact as they are. His resolution stopped short, however, at Renata herself. He had not found a suitable way to broach the subject of payment to her and something told him he had better not try, at any rate not yet.

He waved at Domenico as he pulled away in the boat, and went into the house to unpack and put away his clothes and John's. Upstairs in the larger bedroom there was an ample wardrobe and a chest of drawers, a wash-stand, a small bed for John, and the wide one in which the Englishman had slept, which would be Randall's. When he had put all their things away he stepped out onto the narrow balcony, with its waist-high iron railing, upon which the long window opened. This seemed a luxury, an elegance out of proportion to what he had understood of the Englishman's small means; but it was commonplace on any house about here, as he had seen. He loved it. The balcony seemed to hang directly above the water, though actually the house stood some yards from the shore, tucked into the steep hillside at the bend of the cove. The white haze of this morning was burning off, the sun was glistening through and a light breeze from the north was blowing off the thin layer of cloud. It swept the sky a brilliant blue. The water reflected it. Oh, he thought, the blessing of this water; the sense it makes of quiet and space in the mind. Morning is a lovely thing here, each morning is a newly-washed face. In the town there had been noise, the ordinary comfortable noise of people beginning their day. Here he heard not a sound, except a boy singing out of tune far off up the road behind him. That was good; silly; human. And he was so grateful for this view. The other branch of the lake was more imposing, grandly spectacular; the view from the height of San Bernardo was panoramic like a great relief map. This was intimate, gentle, cosy. Even the stern peaks of the Grigna had an humble quality, they did not seem to have been put there to overawe humanity like the vaster ranges sweeping up to soar into the Swiss Alps. This was very, very good, he thought, sighing with a bottomless sense of relief.

He turned and went inside. He heard Renata and John talking and moving about downstairs. He decided to look into the second bedroom to make sure, he told himself, that Renata would be comfortable. He stood on the threshold and examined the room; small, plain, white-walled, scrupulously neat, the room of a person of few possessions and no habit for comforts. But, he thought . . . and stood there lost in time. People change; he knew how people change. But those had always been his people, his mother, Seymour. *Himself?* That he did not know. But she, Renata? Was there a way to reach back through all those turns of the wheel of time to bring forward a place and a moment; a late morning; a laughing, teasing, careless woman; scented steam, fading roses, gimcrack furniture strewn with laces and feathers and ruffles? He heard again the crystal peals of laughter, saw the brown hair damp and curly, heard the patter of running slippered feet. She always ran in those days. She never runs now. She walks: remote, sedate, resigned. To what? She said she chose it. What else could she do? His thoughts swerved from the unknown, he could understand only that for which he had a measure. He groped for it. *Life will change me, like you, like tutti. When is time, is time.* His jaw dropped, he stared at the bare white room, the blank walls, the crude furniture upon which she had put no mark of the butterfly whose rooms he had seen in the past.

Moved by an irresistible impulse he stepped softly to the low chest and drew open the top drawer a little. Inside were a few articles of clean, plain white underclothing, neatly arranged. He shut the drawer quickly. Memory could serve him as much and as far as he would let it. But his memory was a plateau, high and sweeping, which ran to the edge of a fatal precipice and stopped there dead.

He backed out of the room and went to the stairs, just as he heard the sound that he had thought relegated forever to that far plateau, the ripple of her quick, delighted laughter. He paused and listened, swallowing a lump in his throat. He had not heard this once since coming here. He tried not to think it remarkable, he ignored the beating of his quickened pulse which seemed to augment the sound in his ears. Slowly he descended the steep stairs, which wound down a corner of the studio room and ended opposite the door into the kitchen. He stood looking in. Renata and John were playing a game of tag round and round the kitchen table. John had snitched one of the fancy horn-shaped rolls that had come for the special occasion in the basket from Bellagio, and eaten part of it while Renata's back was turned. She had pretended to be cross, and had given chase. John kept a jump ahead of her and they were circling the table, trying to double back and outwit one another. John was excited as much by surprise as by the game, he had not known her in this mood; and Randall had not seen in years the sparkling face, the mischievous eyes which he had supposed forever beyond recall. He turned sharply, drawing a breath and struggling to ignore the tingling of his own eyes which he had no idea of allowing to betray him. Renata stopped the game by catching John and giving him a mock spank on the seat of his breeches. She said, wagging her forefinger, "Eat your bread if you want to, you little pig, but you will spoil your appetite!"

She had set the table with the crude, gaily colored Italian pottery left by the Englishman; in the centre stood a bowl of delicate greenish-white flowers, interspersed with clusters of red berries in spiked glossy foliage, which Randall had seen children carrying round the country-side. They gathered them on the hillsides all winter, and Renata said that the little daughter of her cousin Ambrogio had brought these this morning.

"What do they call them?" he asked, as she brought the food to the table and started to serve it.

"The white ones are bucaneve," she said, "and the red ones we call pungitopo." She ladled the steaming yellow risotto onto the plates.

"What a funny name. Did you understand that, John?" he asked in English. "Sting-a-mouse. Isn't that a funny name for a plant?"

Renata's face was inscrutable as she sat down and they began to eat.

"The risotto is good!" said John, with his mouth full. Randall raised his eyebrows, and Renata leaned towards John and said softly, "Swallow your food before you speak, Giu'an."

"It is good," said Randall. He thought it as well that his Italian was still so limited, else he might have blurted, "I had no idea you could cook," making the sort of impression they wished not to make on John. By the time Randall had attained any fluency, John with a child's short memory and quick adaptability would be well over the possibility of asking questions that they did not wish to have to answer. Meanwhile Randall had to think slowly as he spoke, translating from the English in his mind; his conversation was accordingly commonplace.

"I would not like to eat polenta every day," he said.

"No," said Renata. "Neither do I. When you have lived in Milano or other cities, you grow spoiled and want variety. I prefer risotto, by far—but rice is expensive and the polenta costs us nothing."

Randall had never been at the Gandolfis' in the evening and he asked what they usually ate for supper.

"A minestra—a soup. Made of anything there is, vegetables and such. With beans, usually. And we throw in a handful of something farinaceous to make it filling."

"Nothing else?"

She shook her head. "Bread, of course. Always bread."

"And for breakfast?"

"Whatever was left of the minestra from supper."

"No coffee?"

"Coffee! Every day? Never, except on the greatest occasions."

"But," he said. Once again he was caught in the toils of memory. Once again he heard the voice which, speaking its ludicrous English, had seemed lighter, higher, effervescent compared with the calm, cool tone in which she spoke her own language now. Countless references to coffee; slavish dependence on coffee; first we drink the coffee . . . a part of her like ruffles and perfume and laughter.

He looked up from his empty plate and said, "We will have coffee every morning for breakfast, Renata." He would willingly have used the thought and the deliberate order he had given to overreach the stony uncommunicativeness of her expression. She rose to clear the table, keeping her eyes on what she was doing.

"As you like," she said.

Only in the evenings after John was asleep was there any occasion to talk with her, and it was then that he saw her reserve close down like the shutter on a window. All day long she was busy with the house and with John. At meals they spoke Italian, with Renata at Randall's request correcting and teaching him. The rest of the time she and the boy chattered in dialect or in Italian. Randall was not much with them. He had become interested in the Englishman's garden and discovered that Zio Pepe had always had as much to do with it as the painter.

Randall thought dimly of the few miserable bulbs he had once planted in the gritty yard in New York, and of the lawn and the stiff geometrical flower-beds which had preceded it very long ago, when he was a little boy like John. Even then things had not seemed really to grow there, only to be on display until they were overcome by city grime, when something fresh would take their place. He had not realized that he really loved flowers and was capable of gardening. Here it seemed to him that one need only stick a root or a seed in the ground, for some lush green thing to burgeon or sprawl or climb like magic. Zio Pepe soon relieved him of that delusion. Gardening here was work, and the old man was ready enough to show him how to do it.

When Randall had spent the morning out of doors, pruning shrubs, cutting back roses, tying vines, or spading beds and turning in manure, he came in hungry for dinner and ready afterwards for a nap. The air exhilarated him in the sunny hours of the morning, but Renata and Zio Pepe both told him, wagging their heads, that this was tranquil air, soporific air, and that life moved here accordingly. It was true; nobody hurried, nobody travelled, nobody planned. One just went along, keeping regular hours, sleeping more than Randall had ever heard of sleeping, going to bed early and getting up early, digging oneself by easy degrees into the ancient mood and tempo of the place. Only in the brief evening hour or two between supper and bedtime did he hold to the old habit of sitting down to read. He would put a few sticks of wood into the stove in the studio room, and sit down in an armchair beside the round table where there was a student lamp with a green shade, which gave good light. There was a smaller oil lamp in each of the other rooms, as well as candlesticks; the Englishman had, as they said, known how to make himself comfortable. Randall read the *Corriere* which a boy brought every day from the post-office at the nearby village, along with the bread and the milk. When he had finished he was more than sleepy enough to go to bed.

The first few evenings he sat alone in the studio, appearing more absorbed in the newspaper than he was, for he was wondering what Renata was doing and whether she would not presently come in and sit for a while, which would be natural, would it not? He heard her finish the work in the kitchen, and sat waiting for the light to be extinguished there, and Renata to appear. She did not; as soon as the kitchen was dark she went quietly upstairs, pausing only to say "Buona notte, Randalo." He answered and she disappeared. After several evenings he said, as she paused on the stairway, "Why don't you come and sit here for awhile, Renata? It is very comfortable."

She hesitated. For a moment her stern and remote look made him feel rebuked. But why should he not have said this? Why should she expect him to treat her like a servant now when her attitude all day long, in spite of her reserve, was nothing of the sort? To keep such a distance in the presence of John would have been preposterous, and confusing to the child. Randall looked up at her and said, "Please don't mind what I said. After all—" he smiled wryly. Any kind of silent appeal was better than the clumsiness of words. He saw her eyelids droop slowly and widen again, a tremor cross her face. It would be better, he thought, with a sharp, painful grasp of what she felt, if I did not look at her. This is not reproof that she is showing. She is afraid, abashed, unsure. We have mountains to climb, higher than any peaks to be seen from here, and depths to plumb, deeper than the fathoms of that lake, before we can meet again where we can feel at ease. He dropped his eyes and said quietly, "I understand, you know. I would like you to sit here with me awhile if you are willing."

"I will bring my work," she said, and presently came with one of the gaudy silk handkerchiefs. She took a chair on the other side of the table and began to hem the silk square. He read desultorily; from time to time his eyes followed her fingers. His memory once again had stepped in and seized the initiative. He could not see her do anything now which she had also done in times gone by, without rousing to these stabs. He had often seen her sew; he remembered the white ruchings on Emma Maynard's petticoats, the dimity dresses that she had made for the hot summer in New York. He sat now and listened to the echo of the past, clear against the quiet crackle of the fire. *Sew the fazzoletti*, she had said, *sew the fazzoletti like my aunts. Two lire the week. Maybe thirty-five cents?*

He put aside his newspaper and leaned over and looked at her, rejecting any notion of trying to keep from his eyes the emotions brimming in them, the burden of memory against the sight of her poor clothes and the drudge's work in her hands. He spoke to her and she raised her head and looked at him, and he knew from her face that his blue eyes had moved her as he had suddenly and forcefully intended that they should.

"That work you are doing," he said quietly in English. "I remember, Renata. I remember all sorts of things, everything." She was silent; he saw her draw a deep breath. "So do you," he said, gathering courage. "Please don't do that any more. I assure you, it is unnecessary."

She paused in her sewing and was plainly thinking what to say. Then she said it, in English almost whispered.

"Is not better keep the work I am sure of," she asked, "when is not sure anything else?"

For a moment he could not speak. Then he said, "I know. I wish—I wish I had the answer to anything. I know I am hard to understand. I'm feeling my way, Renata, you do realize that. Some things I just cannot decide yet, and some I don't know anything about. But this I do know." He put out his hand with a surge of daring and laid it on her forearm. It was the first time he had touched her, he realized, since coming to this country. He felt her arm stiffen and then slowly relax. At that he patted it gently and took his hand away and said, "You can be sure of one thing. It will not be necessary for you to do that kind of work any more." He bent his head, overcome by the thought of his actions in New York, by the thought of Seymour saying, 'There wasn't any other way to treat her . . .' He shivered inwardly. He said, "No matter what I do, you won't be—" he was lost for words. He waited awhile and said, pointing to her work, "Dependent on that. Never."

She sat with the cheap silk crushed in her hands, her head bent. He picked up his newspaper and rattled it and made a show of reading. He heard her speak and pause and speak again and he stopped pretending to read and looked at her.

"How you are good!" she said, and pleased him by raising her small head, with a motion of pride that was sound and reassuring after so much humility. "You have always been good," she said. Her eyes were glistening.

"No," he said, "I haven't. Let's not pretend about that. But whatever I think I am doing here, I can try—" he stopped.

"You have not tell me why you really came," she said.

"It was Seymour."

"Oh?"

He sighed. Better tell her, he thought, hoping to find words which would not too gravely mortify her. Until he told her she must remain bewildered and doubtful. He began to talk, at first brokenly, little by little with more ease. Sitting there, listening to an east wind which had blown up outside, lashing the lake against the pebbly shore, it seemed not weeks, not even months or years, but a fantastic length of time, a planetary distance, since that last dreadful scene in the library and the long parade of previous dreadful scenes, stretching back into the dark, breathless night when their quarrelling was interrupted by the clanging of the rusty doorbell. Long before he could have got as far as that, she was sitting with her face in her hands, breathing *"Dio! Dio! Madonna Santa!"*

When he described Seymour's behavior about John's bear, which was upstairs now hugged in his arm while he slept, he heard her whimper as if she had been slapped; and when he told how John had been parted from Maggie, she gave a sharp sob and looked up, pale, her mouth dragged down at the corners, her eyes enormous. She laid her hands, clenched in fists, against her breast and said, "My fault. It is all my fault."

"No," he said. He too was deeply upset. "It was fault, Renata, God knows what awful fault. You call it—sin. But it was nobody's alone. It almost seems," he said slowly, looking at the small grating through which gleamed the embers of the fire, "as if we had all been destined to commit it. And we are still, I am still, anyway, condemned to keep on wronging somebody. Whatever I do, whichever way I turn—" he shook his head.

"It disturb you leave the Simorr as you have done. It worry you very much?"

"Oh, God. Blind. All alone. That house." He shrank down in his chair.

"Ah, Randalo." She shook her head. "I am very sorry. But he is not poor, the Simorr, he can pay somebody to care for him?"

"If such care can be bought," said Randall, muttering. "But we have become . . . I too . . . when I am there . . . that house," he said again, and drew a long breath and shut his mouth hard. She sat looking at her hands clasped in her lap.

"And by comparison," he said after a long time, "the things you had told me about the life here, and your people and the way they felt about what men and women did—" He paused and made a gesture of a kind of surrender, of finality. "I knew I had to get John out of that house, away from Seymour. And I thought I'd come and see your people and learn what the other half of John's blood really was. Because my half—ours—" he turned brick red and was careful not to meet her eye. "As you know," he said lamely, "I never expected to find you here."

They were silent after that. Each sat thinking of questions he could ask, of thoughts he could voice, of gaps in time and space to fill; both knew they had talked enough tonight and both knew that there was time to come, unhurried, unmeasured, tranquilly spread before them.

CHAPTER 19

A year later the three occupants of the pink house had become as unremarkable to the countryside as the wistaria which curtained the loggia, or the olive trees leaning from the hillsides, twisted to the sun. It was said at first that the couple were married. It was said that they were not married. It was said with shrugs that Renata Tosi had got far better than her deserts; it was asked by others why she should not deserve as good and decent a life as this: had she not shown the penitence and humility that her youthful sins had exacted? She went faithfully to church at San Bernardo on every Sunday and every feast and fast day, bringing the boy with her. She was raising the child a good Christian without regard to the fact that the americano was a heathen: no, said some, only a Protestant; the languid argument usually wandered into the maze of whether Protestants were Christian at all. Yes, said Don Stefano, the parish priest, they were; but he gave as little further elucidation to that subject as to whatever he knew about Renata's boy. It became for a time a mild titillation, a matter of small local pride, to have something in the community so original as the ménage in the pink house. Beyond that lay the slow steps to complete and amiable acceptance of it. People approved of Renata's modest bearing and intense devotion to the child. They approved of the americano's hard work in his garden, his quiet friendliness, his unfailing generosity to the good works of the church. Presently he could have learned, if he had thought of it so concretely, that local opinion had lifted him over the barrier which divided the village people from the travelling foreigners who gave many of them their living, and welded him into the life of the place with little further remark.

He had achieved a balance of sorts in his thoughts about the past or the future, about this identity or the one that lay hidden under lock and key in the mouldering rooms four thousand miles away. He was helped by the sight of John, by his vigorous happiness and the unmistakable evidence of his unusual intelligence. He was helped by Renata, who brought to her life with him a tranquil profundity, set alight at moments by wonderfully natural expressions of passion, which gave him extraordinary wellbeing. He was not helped at all by the sparse reminders of his other self that came at long intervals in the post which usually brought nothing. There had never been a word from Seymour although Randall had tried to calm his aching conscience by sending a message when he had first come to this house. He had written his bank in New York a letter to be telephoned to Seymour, to which there had never been a reply. Thereafter the post brought only his bank statements and a communication now and then from the Trustees or, as time went on, their successors. Once Randall had yielded to a sense of acute concern for Seymour and had written to Mrs. Quinn, asking her to find out if she could, and send him word, how Seymour was doing. He knew that she would have to go and dabble in gossip among the people in the block; it was a bad thought, but he felt driven to it. Her short, illiterately scrawled reply said only that Seymour had never been known to leave the house and that "a black, sir, not the same one, goes in and does for him."

The thought was harrowing, at times almost intolerable; and when such times came round, irregularly cyclic but prompted by the arrival of mail from New York, Renata acted with delicate perceptiveness and understanding. At such times even more than ordinarily, she kept a distance sensitively adjusted to all that the easy-going people of the countryside could never know and never be allowed to learn. Once she had seen Randall, sitting with an opened letter in his hand, stare hard at John who was lying on his stomach, absorbed in copying the alphabet. Randall's face, red-brown from the sun, had hardened into a mask of grievous consternation; he had shaken his head slowly and leaned it on his brown, calloused hand, and Renata had moved silently away. It was on such a day that she would find a reason for going up to Zia Paola's for the afternoon, returning quietly at dusk to prepare the simple supper, and retiring afterwards to her original bed in the smaller room to which John's cot had long since been moved.

Her innate tact, clothed in tender warmth and naturalness, had eased them past those steps which Randall inevitably wanted, yet had been afraid to take. She knew him better than he could know himself; she knew too how to use her knowledge. He would never forget her gentleness in those first days after she had consented to sit with him in the evenings after supper. Sometimes they talked; quite as often they were silent while he read his newspaper and she sewed on the first of the dresses which he had persuaded her to make for herself, to replace the coarse skirts and blouses to which he could not become accustomed. She bought some simple stuff on market day, which in the hand looked as modest as the grey flannel of her blouses, but when finished had the flair of the pretty things she had worn years ago, though tempered, quieter.

She had been, he would always remember, sewing a double row of tiny covered buttons onto the bodice of that new dress, when he had laid down his newspaper and looked at her and said, "Renata, I always think it such a pity that you people close all the shutters on the houses every night." He spoke English as they usually did in the evenings alone; in the daytime when John was about they spoke only Italian.

"Why is the pity?" she looked up, smiling. "Is our habit. In America I could never understand. No shutters, sometimes open the windows— we believe is poisonous the night air."

"I know," he said. "It's not poisonous, you know. But it's not the air I was thinking about. It's the beauty here. It's so beautiful at night, sometimes I spend an hour on that balcony of mine, just looking at it all. Why—have you ever seen it at night?"

She laughed. "Is beautiful, yes. Of course I have seen. When I was younger—eh!" she made a quick gesture of mischief with her eyes and her chin. "But the beauty, you know—when you have lived always here —you grow used to it."

"Nonsense. You people know every rock, every tree, every ripple of that lake and what the wind does to it, and all the changes of light, and the stars and the moon—"

"How you are becoming poetic!" she murmured, sewing hard.

"I am thinking about the moon," he said. "It is full tonight."

"Really?" He had not seen such bantering in her face since years ago.

"Really. You know it better than I do, like everybody else here. Why, nobody does a thing without consulting the moon."

"Really?" she said again. She was laughing softly.

"I stayed awake most of the night four weeks ago when the moon was full," he said. "I opened the shutters wide and lay in bed and looked at that moonlight on the water and watched the lights over on the other shore, and the mountains going dark again when the moon went down. It was the most beautiful sight I ever saw."

She made no comment. Presently he said, "Do you remember the night at the Maynards' farm when you came to my room? It was full moon then too." He spoke without looking at her, his eyes on the green globe of the lamp.

"I remember," she said, barely aloud. After that there was a long silence, so long that when she came to the end of her thread and had to look up at the lamp to rethread her needle, she met his eyes fixed there. Slowly her hands went down to her lap and he leaned forward across the table, looking into her eyes. The lids fluttered faintly, he saw that she was groping for the curtain of reserve which she meant to draw again across her features. She looked as if she could not find it; as if it must be impossible to look away from his face which in times gone by had evoked her startling, ingenuous tributes to what she called his beauty. He had never seen her so unconscious of her own looks, the low forehead serene, the lips quiet, the deep eyes not quite smiling.

"Renata," he said, finding it hard to keep his voice level.

"Yes?"

"If—" he drew a long breath. "If I should ask you now to come to my room the way you did that night . . . what would you do?"

"I would come," she said quietly.

She looked at him steadily, as if to say that she followed every shade of his thoughts, all the clamoring components of his memory, everything which he was dredging up, but thrusting back, into the unforgotten past. Here he was, turned and moulded by the potter of fate, hardened in the kiln of suffering; and he had asked her what the man of earlier days, the youth soft in the unformed clay, would never have asked. Now though she saw goodness in his face, vast relief, glowing warmth, gratitude, she saw no passion, no surge of eager love. Some of that might come, she thought; if not? Well: she would give him what she could. She saw too the serious look of question.

"It is Giu'an?" she asked. "You are wondering about him."

He nodded.

She smiled gently and raised her head, tilting her fine chin at that angle which it gave him pleasure to see.

"Do not be worried about him. With what is natural, with the sincere feeling, a child is not hurt. He is at the right age now, too young to question, young enough to take us as we are. He love us so much, he accept whatever we do." She put her work together and laid it on the table. "Come," she said, rising. "I show you."

She led the way up the stairs, carrying a lighted candle. She went first to her own room, took the counterpane off the bed, and turned down the covers. Then she went to Randall's room where John was asleep in his cot, both arms tightly clasped round his bear. She put the candle on the night-stand and knelt down beside John and put her cheek against his. He stirred a little but did not wake. She slipped one arm beneath his head and raised him and whispered in his ear. He let go the bear and put his arms round her neck. She kissed him.

"You are going to sleep in Zia Renata's room," she said, "you and Teddy. You will like it very much."

She motioned to Randall to take the bear and the candle and go ahead of her. He looked back over his shoulder as he crossed the narrow passage between the rooms. She was carrying John, still sound asleep, in her arms. She laid him in her own bed and put the bear back in his arms and he rolled over with a small grunt. She tucked the covers round him and kissed him again and looked up at Randall.

"Go and open your shutters to the moonlight," she whispered, with a curious wistful smile. She looked down at John. "I will be with him here when he wakes in the morning."

The barriers went down slowly. His impression persisted, his disbelief that he could ever have known an earlier incarnation of this woman who had been all play, froth, teasing, verve; who bore to this calm, warm, tender creature the relation that whitecaps skipping in a gay wind bore to the deep water beneath. To her he seemed even more changed, but she took the work of time and tribulation without surprise. He had never held, not once comprehended, the key to her nature: that she was incapable of astonishment at the manifestations of human character. In this she was born old, which is to say, born a peasant of an ancient race, in whose view everything has happened before, for whom men and women cannot devise acts or wants, betray faults, discover instincts, that have not always been known in them.

So she not only took him as he was: tentative, withdrawn, sometimes moody, occasionally demonstrative; she let him sense that she was content. Once she had sparkled with talk which had spiced every motion of her animated face, her graceful body. Now she said singularly little;

she had, he thought, evolved to finer nicety an art of communicative silence. Now it was his gratitude which surrendered him to her wise and benevolent arms; not hers which he had repulsed in the days of his rhapsodic delusions. It was natural to attain a sense of profundity, of timelessness, simplicity, of human inevitability, surrounded by spontaneous beauty such as no contriving with art or money could ever have achieved.

The spring months were hardly credible in the completeness of their beauty, the enchantment that they lavished upon the senses. Had he never heard birds sing before, or were these as rare in their amazing music as the wildflowers which grew only in the Alps? Renata laughed when he asked her. He had sat for an hour on the top step of the loggia, whistling first to rouse, then to lead on, the bird whose song most enchanted him. He had never heard such a song, he said. "Listen! It's an aria! What *is* that bird?"

She was leaning on the balcony railing upstairs with a duster in her hand. The May sun was hot on her shining hair and her face was framed in the mass of climbing roses. Bees buzzed and bustled all around her; she stayed quite still, unperturbed. She laughed again.

"Silly!" she said. "That is a merlo, a common merlo. Yes, he sings charmingly but wait until those cherries are ripe."

"What is a 'merlo'?" he asked, too lazy to go inside and get the dictionary. She shrugged. "How should I know?" she said. It proved to be a blackbird when he looked it up.

"It can't be!" he said. "A common blackbird. Whoever thought they had such a fascinating song?"

"We never thought otherwise."

"And the one that sings this? The one I call the bel canto bird?" He whistled its song, two ridiculously Italian grace-noted turns, followed by a triplet in a preposterous, unrelated key.

"Also the merlo."

"You mean he has a whole repertoire?"

"Oh, yes. He is the most original and melodious of them all."

"A common blackbird," he marvelled. "And which is this?" He whistled again, a simpler song on a single note.

She laughed. "That is the fringuello."

"Oh, dear." He found it to be the chaffinch. "I don't even know one bird from another in English."

"What difference does that make? Are you not content that these are Italian?"

He looked up at her. The sun was in his eyes, he squinted, and took a sort of refuge in the grimace. "Yes," he said almost under his breath. "And you too."

In the night they lay in bed with the shutters and windows open, which she had learned to accept, to please him, and listened to the nightingale.

"He is like many singers," said Renata lazily. She must, he thought, be off her guard; this was the subject she usually abjured. "His reputation is more spectacular than his song."

"Sometimes he is very profuse with his music, quite excited, like yesterday."

"Like anybody. But really he only sings hew-hew-hew-hew-hew."

"With variations." He rolled over on his side and lifted the dark mass of her hair and raised himself on his elbow to see her face. "Renata," he said. "Do you know I have never asked you to forgive me?"

She did not speak, she lay with her eyes wide open but this was not a bright night, one did not see every expression. She said after a time, "Nor I you."

"That is not—that is different. You may have been—never mind all that. I have damned myself every day since, for the way I treated you when you, we, talked in the street in New York."

"Was entirely natural what you did."

"It was entirely inhuman."

"I do not think so, really. Was equally inhuman when I went—" she stopped and even in the dark he perceived the grave hardening of her features. "Away," she said. "To Buenos Aires."

"It was panic. Despair. At the time I thought you utterly irresponsible, but now, as you are with John—"

She turned her head and he knew that the barrier was up. She was silent for a long time and at last she said stiffly, "Was part of my *penitenza* you must think that. Was not a sudden thing I did. Many months I had in which to think about it. Was necessary decide only for the best of the bambino. I could not know," she said in a way which flooded his eyes with tears, "how would be the *disastro* with the Simorr. Is impossible know everything." She had not spoken as much as this in all the months since they had come here. Afraid to embarrass and silence her, he said nothing. He remained braced on one elbow, from time to time gently stroking the hair back from her brow.

"Only I knew, like I have try to tell you there in the street," she said, her voice as dull as if a film of lead had come over it, "what would be like the life for that child if I bring it here. Without money."

He did not need to remind her that he had seen how good her people were, and how difficult this was for him to understand. She continued as if he had said that. She said, "You have seen only the life of my village, my *parenti* who are good, like I tell you. You have not seen the real life of the poor in Italy, the towns, the cities. It was necessary to think. I must think, what can become of this child? A *contadino*, you would want him like the Nino, the Domenico? They will ever be different than now? Is good enough for them, *va bene*—but that child? Or he should be an *artigiano*—or an *operaio*—work perhaps in a factory in Sesto?"

"How could you know?" he murmured. "Before he was born."

"A woman know," she said. "Many things. I knew him."

"And also, you had a premonition about yourself? You thought you would not be able to sing always, to earn enough money—"

She nodded, with a bitter set to her mouth. "Was never a strong voice," she said. "Never a real career. Always I knew that, why you think you found me never serious? Even," she said, "when I had so bad the diphtheria in Buenos Aires and it leave me without the voice any more. I was not surprise'." After another long pause she said, "Probably because I have deserve' it."

"I have wanted to ask you something ever since I came here," he said slowly. Then he was afraid to say more. But she said, "Well? Go on."

"You said, that awful time, 'In Italy is a tragedy to break the heart, it follow all through the life such a child, how it is born.'" He had quoted her exactly, keeping his eyes averted; he had already exposed her too much to cruel memory. "What did you mean, Renata? I have been wondering about that ever since I came here."

"I meant," she said slowly, "what you find when is to be educated a child, when you hope he will become a person—how you would say— a person of consequence? Something not *ordinario*."

Randall nodded gravely. "Yes. What happens?"

"You can see," she said, "if you understand how is the question here of *identità*. Every person, he is known not alone with his own name and the *cognome di famiglia*, but with his father's name too. Always there are the *documenti*, every kind of paper that make possible go to school, to work, to marry, whatever concern the life. To everybody is tied always the name of the father. If is living the father, is called *per esempio* my cousin, Gandolfi Domenico di Luigi. If was dead the father, would be Gandolfi Domenico fu Luigi. Always is fixed in this way every Italian."

She stopped speaking and the ensuing silence was gravid with the next question, which it was unnecessary to ask. Randall had not even been so ignorant as he seemed of what she had already explained; one could not live a fortnight here without having remarked it. He forced out at last what they both knew he must say.

"And when the child has no—when its parents were not—"

"Then," she said, her voice perfectly toneless, "is called the person by the *cognome* of the mother, with afterwards N.N. *Anonimo*. So, *per esempio*—" He saw her nostrils flatten; she drew a deep breath as if to reach for greater control, "—Tosi Sebastiano di N.N. Then everybody know all his life long, is the person a *bastardo*."

Slowly Randall turned away; his hand which had been curved at her temple fell lax on the pillow. He had never heard of anything so cruel. He had never felt until this moment the whole terrible enormity of what they had, all three, done. Renata in some way seemed diminished, wafted a spectral distance away by the beating of the great dark wings of his anguished conscience. Close before his eyes and, he felt, his very heart, was the beloved innocent face of the boy. He had never loved and could never again hope or want to love a human being as he loved that child. It was my love that made me bring him here, he thought; I brought him to shelter and shield him, to find a little timeless peace in which to let him grow. It is timeless, infinitely peaceful, more than I thought to find. But it too like all the rest is illusory. Behind this smiling softness lies as she always said, reality; the last grey crag of the inexorable. He lay with his eyes closed, following the dark beating wings as they flailed first at one mute door, then at another. Which, he thought, will be the one that opens; or are they locked, one upon the other, like the doors that I have sealed upon my secrets? One by one, space by space, room by room, he faced them all; and chained in the deepest dungeon of the spirit he came upon his brother, helpless, abandoned, condemned, alone. He lay with his eyes closed, struggling with the furies, but still as if in sleep. The woman beside him watched for a time, motionless as he; then she moved very gently away, intending to go to the other room. He turned, roused, and with a rending cry, flung himself upon her breast.

"It is the effect of the place," said Renata on a December night, when Randall had been reading the *Corriere* aloud and laid it down, saying, "It seems so unreal, so far away." Yesterday had been Santo Stefano and he had read the music critic's exhaustive review, and the elaborate chronicle of Society and fashion at the great night of the Milanese year, the opening of La Scala's season. "It seems impossible to imagine you ever there, Renata. Simply fantastic. Or else all this is a dream."

She laughed a little. "Is only sixty kilometers away," she said, "but I agree, is another world. Here has changed nothing in so many *secoli*, it seem the air keep the people always the same too."

"You could say that of all of Italy—any of Europe—"

"Perhaps. But is more than a *leggenda*, what we say about the Lago. It has something make nobody wish to move or go away or be changed, if he stay long enough to catch this *malattia*. Or if he was born here."

"But you left."

"In a certain time. I was young, I have tell you long ago how I was. But after I have no more the instrument to make possible the life of art and pleasure, is time to forget it, no?"

"You came straight back here from South America, you didn't think of anything like your former work in Milano?"

"You mean, to sew? To work for a *sarta*?" She shook her head, then turned it slightly and stared at the far wall of the room. "You do not know how much earns such a woman in Milano?" She named a figure. He winced. "So what you suppose she do in order to eat or maybe keep clean?"

"I can imagine."

"Well." She shrugged. "Besides, as you found me here was the life I earned by what I did."

"How you have changed," he said slowly after a time.

"No, *caro*, you are mistaken. Is not I have change', but that the life change everybody. Like also I have tell you long ago. Like you too."

"Still," he said, ruminating, "don't you ever miss your former life? All that activity, and the music and the theatre which does get in one's blood, doesn't it?"

She looked at him. "How much you miss your own music?" she asked.

"Why—" he stared. "You know, it's true, I never think about it." He looked round at the sparse but comfortable furnishings of the room. "Do you know, if there were a piano here, I don't think it would ever occur to me to touch it?"

She sat back and laughed, looking at him quizzically. "There, you see? Like I say."

"What I see," he said slowly, "is that I was never really a musician at all. I never had the least thing to do with deciding it."

"And you think is strange how I can forget when I was singing!"

He thought it far stranger, he sat inwardly chilled by the thought of music as it had seeped and penetrated into the dark closed corners of his own life about which she had no idea. What would she say, he thought in sudden horror, if she knew about the pianos . . . pianos . . . he clenched his hands on the arms of his chair, as if to cling to something tangible while the wave washed up, heaved, broke upon his mind . . . how many pianos? What is that, what are you thinking? Five? Seven? An organ . . . No. This is beyond reason, what are you thinking about? How did it all happen? He sat rigid in his chair, holding his mouth closed hard, fighting off that wave, his head turned sharply to keep her from looking at his face. It is, he thought, like being sick, like being at sea, you feel that frightful plummeting inside, there is the cold sweat and the green feeling and the bitter taste in your mouth. What has all that to do with being here, what has it to do with anything? Does it exist or do I only think so, and if it does, then what of all this here is real? He did not know it, but he was breathing hard exactly like a person on the verge of a burst of nausea. She heard the loud, quick breaths, she had the urge to leave her chair and go and touch him and see if he had really been taken ill. But she was afraid to move, certain that she must not look at him, at least not let him know that she had stolen a glance. She sat very still. Gradually his breathing slowed, became quieter. She moved her eyes under her downcast lids enough to see when his left hand relaxed its rigid grip upon the chair. He sat back limp and said, "That's queer, I really felt quite ill for a minute."

"Is better now?" She was careful not to seem alarmed.

"Oh, yes, much. I think I must have eaten too much minestrone at supper."

"Was a little heavy," she agreed. "In winter we use more pork fat."

After a time he glanced at the newspaper, lying where he had dropped it, and asked, "Renata, would it give you any pleasure to go to Milano? For the day, I mean, or the evening."

"You mean to La Scala?"

"Well, yes. It's one of those notions that don't really matter. The kind of thing where you probably have a strong feeling about it one way or the other and I—" his expression was shy and rueful "—am just too clumsy to sense which it is."

"It had not ever occur' to me," she said slowly. "Now you have mention' it, I feel the surprise. For myself, I think I would not wish to hear La Scala, but if would please you I could accompany you, without doubt. How you feel about it yourself?"

"I feel," he said, "to tell you the truth, something quite strange. I feel as if I ought to want to go, but the fact is, I don't want to. I'm sure I am very lazy and ignorant and peculiar—who on earth would have lived here almost a year and not even thought of going to Milano, much less the Scala?"

She made a gesture of casual assent. "Who would want," she said, "would be either a tourist or a *musicista*. For them would seem necessary, would be important. For you—"

"That does really sum it up. I'm not a tourist and I'm certainly not a musician any more. I'm just—" he looked at his toughened hands and then at his warm flannel shirt and then round the room and then at her. They laughed.

"Besides," she said, "to go to La Scala is necessary the proper clothes. I have not such things any more and you, you brought the dress for evening, Randalo?"

"Good God!" He thought of his departure from the house. Then his thoughts stayed, like flies tangled in a film of glue, inside the house and up and down and through the rooms whose contents only he could know. Something occurred to him, prompted by her remarks about clothes, and he said slowly, "I wondered for a long time and I used to try not to think about it."

"About what, Randalo?"

"Those trunks of yours that were, that you—"

"That were in your house in New York. Well?"

"They were full of opera costumes and pretty clothes. Why did you never send for them, Renata?"

She did not answer at once. She happened not to be sewing this evening, and he was aware that if she had had some work in her hands she would have kept her head bent over it. Instead, she sat very still, looking past him, her dark eyes fixed on the farther wall. He wished he had not brought this up, he would have given his tongue not to have asked the question. When she did speak, her voice was so low and strained that he was careful not to look at her face.

"Was because," she said, "I thought if I leave them, you maybe try to find me and return them to me. After—after you not feel so angry any more." She had whispered the last words. He turned his head to look at her and saw the pained, deep red which had swept across her pale face. He made a sudden motion which brought him to his knees beside her chair and he said, folding her hands inside his own, "You knew? You knew that I wouldn't—couldn't—stay as I was to you that time, that terrible, cruel—" His face was hidden over their hands clasped in her lap.

"Dear Randalo," she said. "Always I knew. Have I not tell you, you are good? Nobody, I have said before, was ever good like you." He shook his bowed head, and felt her cheek bent for a moment to caress his hair. He looked up and into her face and no longer cared whether he could hide the tears in his eyes. Hers too were wet; very beautiful, with tears standing in them which did not flow to mar the classic stillness of her features.

"Oh," he said softly, "Renata, my love . . ."

Her head moved faintly, the merest shadow of abnegation. "My dear, dear friend," she said.

Zio Pepe, who descended from a time when peasants were untaught and had not learned to speak the national language easily, always replied in dialect when Randall spoke to him in Italian. It became, by force of habit, fairly easy to understand him. Once in a while Randall went out in the boat with him to draw in the nets, in place of his nephew who was usually the helper. It was a charming, picturesque procedure; lovely to watch from the shore, as two boats or three, working together, floated from the full circumference of the net towards a central goal, gathering in the net as they approached. One man stood up in the stern and rowed, backing water, leaning forward to his oars with a slow rhythmic jerk; the second man stood in the bow drawing in the net. At first Randall's eye had been bewildered by this curious method of propelling a rather heavy boat, but when Zio Pepe asked how else should one row it, he had no answer. Could he suggest the only alternatives he had ever seen, the sail or the small steam engines of the fishing craft around Hare Island? Those tough sea-going boats had no relation to these, up-pointed at both ends, canoe-bottomed, arched overhead by the frame of the canvas awning. They looked heavy and clumsy and were not easy to handle, yet they had a certain natural grace in their own setting, which he knew to be the heritage of two thousand years. When he really thought about it he could find no reason for supposing that these were markedly different from the Roman barks that had first plied these waters. He wondered what Seymour would think; it was impossible to contemplate boats without including Seymour in the same frame.

He did say to Domenico that rowing anything by standing up and backing water looked ridiculous to him.

"We would think it much more ridiculous to row a barca like a row-boat. Looking over your shoulder like a thief running from the cara-binieri? How is a man to see where he is going?"

Now that he knew about the fishermen and their ways he could join in Renata's teasing which had made him feel so foolish in the early days of his first summer. Standing in the loggia on a beautiful warm night, breathing the perfumes borne on the mild, fresh wind, he had exclaimed at the loveliness of all these seductions to the senses; the visual beauty, the fragrance, the obbligato of softly lapping water. "Even those cow-bells," he had said, "they sound so sweet, so gentle and silly . . ."

"Those *what* did you say?" Renata's laughter rippled in the dark.

"Why—cowbells. I never understand why we hear them from the direction of the water, but—"

"Oh, Randalo! *Come sei buffo!*"

"But why? What have I said? Only that it seems queer you people never let out your cows until night when they—"

She had been convulsed. "The cows spend their nights like their days shut up in their stalls, until they go to the mountains in summer to the grass. Those bells you hear are the bells on the nets, so nobody will strike and tear them in the dark."

"Buoys, you mean!"

"What? *Ragazzi*? Boys?"

Then it was his turn to explain. But always after that, the tinkling of the bells on a soft summer night made them laugh before they lay still to enjoy the sights and perfumes and sounds which grew more treasurable the longer one stayed in this persuasive place.

Once they went away for a day, to Como, to buy books for John. This was suggested by Renata, though it had been with Randall's help that the child, then not quite five, had learned to read. He had long since mastered the handful of nursery favorites that had come with them from New York; now he could read with equal facility in English or in Italian, and was beginning to write as well. The natural reaction to this early show of intelligence was wondering smiles, stares, and head-waggings on the part of the Gandolfis. But as Randall watched the emerging evidences of real mentality in the child, he—or was it his heart, or some part of himself which this nirvana could not hold in its spell—moved steadily closer to the brink of what he had always dreaded: a profound, irrevocable decision. Its components eluded him. Sometimes he felt suspended, groping, nudged by blind instinct as he had been in the days in New York when the looming problem hung by Seymour like Damocles' sword over the child's head, had driven him to the sources of the only escape he could then devise. He had from the first called this time here a visit; he had implied and once or twice even plainly said, that one day he would take John back to some kind of life, inevitably in the United States, but irrationally free in his mind of the menace posed by Seymour. Renata had never uttered a syllable of comment. But one evening he saw in her expression more than hours of talk could have conveyed, when he said on the heels of their speaking of John's absorption in reading, "Next year he ought to start school, oughtn't he . . ."

And from her pallor, her closely set lips, he knew that she too was struggling with the terrible questions at the heart of this simple event, which should be a commonplace in any child's life, but a milestone also of pride and hope and rejoicing when one's child was as bright as John. She only looked at Randall, with a burden of pitiful anxiety in her eyes. He could not speak for a moment either. He sat watching her, sitting there in the lamplight with her work in her lap, her hands crossed on top of it in such a way as to suggest that if she moved them she would betray her agitation.

"Randalo," she said, after a long time. "You have thought? You have been thinking?"

"All the time. More and more . . . every time I look at him. Oh, Renata," he sighed, "there is so much I am afraid to say."

She nodded heavily. "I too."

"Even to approach it . . . to begin at the beginning . . . the very first question. Where is he to start school?"

He had to bend towards her to hear what she said, her head was bowed so low. "Is for you to say, Randalo."

"It means. It means that a number of things have to be decided," he said, with all the reluctance which proclaimed his loathing of such crises.

"I know."

"If I take him back to America soon—"

Her head came up slowly; he saw her swallow and strain to hold a posture of imperturbability. She said, "In America is the Simorr, Randalo."

"Oh, not again with him," he said quickly, with a note of panic. "Not anything like that."

"How you know?" she asked in the same still voice. "How you can say? Is the Simorr *afflitto*, a tragic man, helpless. You suppose he remain always alone like this? Such a thing could not be. One day needs you very much the Simorr. With your good heart you think you refuse him?"

"If I have to choose between him and John."

"Is not reasonable what you say. Is not what happen in the life. Will become the boy a splendid man, a man able to make the life for himself."

He put his head in his hands and sat bent over, his elbows braced on his knees. She said only, "What you decide, should be only what seem the very best for—for—" he looked up and stared at her because of her hesitation. "Sebastiano," she finished firmly. He dropped his head again. He spoke from behind his hands.

"Is that your way," he asked, "of suggesting you think he ought to stay in Italy?"

"Not necessarily. If were different some things, is possible I would suggest it. You yourself, many times, you have say he is happy here, is not like you have keep him hidden in New York."

"But I wouldn't be in New York—"

"No," she said, with something ominous in her voice. "Not until the Simorr he need you."

"And if he—John—were to be educated here," said Randall slowly, "there is the question of—everything. His name, his identity."

"Yes."

He looked up at her and she almost shrank from the bewildered, suffering look of his blue eyes. They seemed unnaturally dark in color. "I suppose," he said, "it would be solved if—if we married?"

He had not expected to see the cold curtain of evasiveness which immediately veiled her face. He was nonplussed. At the same time he was aware of his own deep sense of uneasiness, a startling realization that he had forced himself onto ground where he would have preferred not to step. He waited for her answer in miserable suspense; he found he was afraid to hear it. She said, "Would be solved that question, Randalo, but it is not something I would do."

He looked at her in great surprise. "But, Renata—"

She shook her head, very slowly and with a strange suggestion of age.

"But, Renata," he said again, "you have just said this thing has got to be decided entirely for the sake of John. You are right. If you mean that, I don't see how you can refuse to marry me since that would give him the name he must have if he were to be brought up and educated in Italy."

He heard her say something so softly that he missed her words altogether and had to ask her to repeat them.

"I asked," she murmured, "if you have overlook' my reason for refusing?" She raised her eyes to give him a long probing glance, and dropped them again and whispered, "You do not want to marry me either. For the same reason."

A gulf of pain lay open between them, a spectre in its depths.

"Oh," he breathed. "Oh, my God . . ."

After a time he raised his head and sat looking at her, opening his mouth to speak, and shutting it again because the words would not come. Then he pulled himself upright in his chair, rose quickly, walked around the table and put his hand under her chin. He raised her face and stood looking down into it. His own skin was pallid beneath the warm color dyed upon it by the sun. He could have closed his eyes to avoid the sight of hers, dark with mortification and suffering. But he forced himself and said slowly, "Have you any way of knowing, Renata? Can you possibly tell me—for sure—which one it was?"

She put up her hands and seized his right one holding her chin, and thrust it away so that she could bow her head and not have to look at him any more. He saw her head shake heavily, right and left. She said nothing. Never had her simple, rational fortitude struck him as so heartrending as at this moment. He stood there for a long time, looking at the top of her bowed head, himself so drained of strength that he felt the numbness of his feet and knees. He heard again the beating of the dark, heavy wings, once more he felt the flailing at the sealed doors; the prison of himself, the prison of his heritage. As he had done in other awful urgencies, he fell upon his knees and took her hands and said, "Renata, help me. Help us both, all three of us, John too. Tell me. Say. Say—*anyway*—" he put his face upon her knees. He felt her trembling. "Tell me that you know," he pleaded in a throbbing whisper. "Say whose he is."

He felt her hands move and fall softly upon his head. "I cannot," she said, her voice laden with tears.

"You have no way of knowing? Not even by instinct? Does not something tell you?"

"I only know," he heard her say, "whose I wish he were."

He gave up the struggle with himself. When he could speak, he said, "And that is why you will not marry me?"

"And also why you will not marry me."

"Oh, I don't know," he said. "I don't know. I believe I would do anything to solve this, to retrieve our wrongs. To make it up to John. Wouldn't you?"

"If I can believe is right what I do."

"Renata, has your church, your priest told you we cannot marry?"

"On the contrary."

"Then who are you to set yourself above—"

"I am not doing that. I am trying to think what is the best for the child. Is most important he have a name, a fine education, the opportunity for the place in the world. He has a brain, Randalo!"

"But you are contradicting yourself. He must have a name, you are right, and I do not see how you can refuse to—"

"A name, yes," she said, looking up suddenly with flaring resolution. "But why yours?"

"*Why mine*?" He sat back on the floor, leaning on his hands, squinting with bewilderment. "What are you talking about? What do you mean?"

"If you will try to understand me," she said, with a faint, wistful smile. "If you will have the patience. First you must have guess' I have not lived here like this not thinking about this question? Is not so?"

He nodded, wondering that she had so much determination where he lacked it. He could not say he had put thought on the matter; he had kept his head in the sand.

"Naturally," she said, "I cannot know what is your intention—even if you have any intention. I cannot ask you, I would fear to ask. But also I cannot help to think."

"Well?"

"If you go in America and take the child with you, is the end of the situation here. What you do there cannot concern me. But sometimes it come to me—Randalo, you understand, is very hard what I am trying to explain." She put her hand on her breast as if to assuage a pain.

He nodded again, slowly, watching her face intently. He said, "Go on, Renata. This is no time to be afraid to speak."

"*Dio ti benedica*," she murmured. Then with a long, uncharacteristic sigh, she said, "Sometimes it come to me, this feeling, like—like, oh I do not know the word in English. Something you see in the future."

"A premonition."

"I suppose, yes."

"What is it you see?"

"The Simorr," she said, her voice trembling, low and dark. "Only because we do not speak often about him does not mean we do not think about him."

"You know me as well as that," he said, shaking his head.

"I know you. And so I know, if happen something which make you feel you must go and take care of the *afflitto*, the blind Simorr, I think you will not take the boy again into that bad place, that life of tragedy. Is not I would ask," she said, slowly putting her hands on either side of his face and looking deep into his eyes. "Is you would choose."

He felt helpless in the presence of her wisdom. He could only stare at her, searching her face as if for proof that she had become indeed the woman who was speaking now. Where was the person who had led him into all this, where the will-o'-the-wisp, the sparkling creature of his illusions? He felt for a time as if lost in the spaces of his search; then he came back to her grave, tender face looking so earnestly into his.

"I love him so, Renata," he said. "I love him—oh you cannot imagine how much. More than I ever loved anyone, my mother—more than I ever loved you."

"That is right. It should be so."

"And I cannot bear to think of life without him. To give him up—" he turned away, burying his face in his hands. He felt her touch his shoulder, the nape of his neck, his tense, clasped hands. There was a brooding silence. At last he raised his head. It was only with effort that she could sit so still, inwardly harrowed at the sight of his suffering. She spoke very quietly.

"Is your love," she said, "will tell you what to do for him?"

"Even—oh, merciful God!—even to giving him up?"

"Even. If is best for him." Her eyes were heavy.

He knew that she did not think his anguish unmanly, nor anything that he did a cause for shame. When he was able later to go on talking, he said, "Now is the time to tell me what you meant by what you said about his name."

"It occur to me when I have thought of all this. When came in my head the possibility he might remain here. Then I see is not so surely the best thing for him we marry and he have your name—especially if you must go away. If he should be Italian," she said with great deliberation, "could be better he have an Italian name. An Italian identity. Everything to make for him most *normale* his situation."

"An American—an English—name; would that be a handicap?"

"Not precisely. Only he would be something different, something always to explain. Here in the *paesino* would never be necessary explain anyway. Everybody know the truth, everybody love him, *di fatti* everybody protect him. But outside—in the cities—in the world. If he is Italian, he should have with pride a good Italian name."

"And how would you give him that?" Randall's imagination had moved with some revulsion to what he expected to hear her say. Instead it was with amazement that he heard, "I would have adopt him my Zio Matteo."

"Renata! *What?*"

"My Zio Matteo," she repeated, perfectly impassive. "The younger brother of my Zio Gandolfi. You have seen him. You know him."

"But—" He stared. "I don't understand."

"If adopts him my uncle, then he become like everybody else, what is good for a child when it begin to go to school. He would be *registrato* the son of Matteo Gandolfi, which would understand everybody here. And—"

"But *I* don't understand," Randall repeated, shaking his head. He was astounded that she had so plainly thought this all out. "Why your Uncle Matteo?" he asked. "Why not—"

"Because is the law here that is only permitted to adopt a child a person who has no children. Also must be at least fifty years old the person. Always they have lamented, Zio Matteo and his wife, that they had no children. *Cosa vuoi?* For Sebastiano—" again she pronounced the name with profound import "—would be the best thing. And when he go on to the better schools, where is necessary to be in towns, in cities, when he make his place in the life in Italy—then he have a good, respected name. A name knows everybody is an honest *cognome* from Lombardia."

He sat stock-still on the floor, silent for a long time. Then he said, "All this?" His forehead was puckered, his chin taut with incredulous surprise. "You have thought of all this?"

"Oh, yes," she said, with her sad smile. "Is not necessary tell you how much I love him too. For this I have study a very long time what I could do if should be given me the opportunity—" she drew herself up as if with one last effort at perfect control; suddenly it was too much; she broke, burst into tears, and sobbed, "The chance to atone. To him. To my son who—" she wept piteously "—must not know the world to be my son."

The spring moved on, too dry; the birds turned silent and were followed by the grating racket of tree-crickets. The summer was un-naturally hot that year, bringing swarms of predatory insects and pretty, scuttling lizards with their curious charm. The grass was burnt for the first time in years; there was little fruit and little grain. Autumn came early and furiously, preceded by ferocious hailstorms. Then the heat fled; they had torrents of relentless, persistent rain. The lake erupted in savage tempests. October, usually the most magnificent month of all with its glorious radiance, was a sodden mess. November was worse; dank, dark, and cold. Randall had seen two Novembers past, wonderful interludes of the year's last color; the blinding brilliant blue borne by the north wind, the golden glory of the poplars, the ripe persimmons glowing like orange-colored lanterns on their graceful, leafless trees. This year they dropped away and rotted in the cold, streaming rain; the hood of clouds never rose from the shoulders of the Grigna, and many people fell ill.

In their house Randall kept them warm and dry with an extravagance of firewood which quite shocked Domenico and Zio Pepe, who helped him to stack it, and Renata whom he told to burn it. Anxiety was in the air, and misfortune; and because these people and their land were what they were, resignation. Neither for him when the shock came, nor for Renata when she knew about it, was there any real surprise. She looked into the studio room late one morning after the neighbor's boy had brought the infrequent post, and saw Randall standing, dead white, with a letter crushed in his hand. There, she knew, is the thing I have foreseen, there is the substance of my premonition. He turned his head towards her at that moment and holding out his hand, said, "Here." The hand was shaking helplessly. "Read this and see. You are always right."

She read the letter. Seymour, wrote the person whom she interpreted to be the family *avvocato*, had fallen down a flight of stairs, "the whole length of the first-floor staircase," she read. "His left arm was fractured and is now in splints. Much more seriously, there appears to be an injury to the lower spinal column which has affected his legs. Whether the resulting paralysis will be permanent, it is impossible for the physicians to say as yet. Your brother is almost entirely uncooperative with them. He is in poor condition, and the contingent circumstances are such that I feel obliged to inform you, even though your brother, who never lost consciousness at any time, had categorically forbidden me to cable you, and now does not know that I am writing this letter contrary to his express instructions. His situation in that house, however,

with no reliable person constantly in attendance, and his absolute refusal to be moved to a hospital, make me unwilling to accept further
responsibility for not having apprised you of the facts."

Renata looked up at Randall, staring, with a gleam of something in
her eyes very like terror at the accuracy of her own intuition. He was
still standing as if asleep on his feet, but with his eyes stretched blankly
open. She looked down again at the paper in her hand. There was a
final paragraph; he watched her read it, and was conscious of the preposterous irrelevancy which wormed through his mind: how easy for an
Italian eye such English must be. He watched her lips moving a little
as she finished the letter.

"It appears to be unknown by any person of whom I have inquired
at your bank, or at the offices of Payne, Morrison, and Jerrold, successors to the late Judge Bronson as co-Trustees with me of your grandmother's estate in trust, whether it is your intention at any time to return to the United States. Since I have also never been informed, I am
taking it upon myself to suggest that should you have it in mind to return, your brother's present condition might be a determining factor in
your plans. I am, etc . . ."

The paper fluttered to the floor. The fire in the stove snapped and
crackled; there was a sudden hissing and splattering from the kitchen
where something had boiled over; John, coming in from the loggia, exclaimed at the burnt smell which the two of them standing there had
not noticed. Renata without turning stretched one hand towards the
boy and caressing his head said, "It is too early to eat, *tesoro mio*, you
have time to go upstairs and read for a while."

They stood listening to his footsteps climbing the stairs and pattering to his room where his books were kept. Still they said nothing. The
burnt smell grew stronger. Renata made an exclamation of annoyance,
went to the kitchen, and presently returned. Almost grey of color Randall said tonelessly, "Of course I have to go."

Her head went up and down slowly, nodding like that of a
jointed doll. She still had a strange, possessed, staring look in her
eyes.

"It is too much of a coincidence," he said, bent and shrunken together as if threatened by something. "It's unnatural."

"That is the trouble," she said, speaking slowly and very low, in
Italian. "That is why we are so horrified. Randalo, listen to me—" she

went close to him and her white face came forward, almost touching his. "It is no coincidence. You can believe me or not—*but this is something I knew*. For a long time past."

"I believe you," he said. "You've had me expecting it ever since—" he looked up at the ceiling "—the talk we had about him." Suddenly he wheeled round and seized her by the shoulders and said in a hoarse whisper, "If you have so much intuition why can't you tell me—" he jerked his head towards the room upstairs where John was "—that? Why don't you know?"

"Ah," she breathed. "*Abbi pietà*! Do you think I would not like to say? I would give my immortal soul if I could do so in truth. But I cannot, and that is part of my penitence. I do not know. This I must suffer to the end of my days."

"Forgive me," he muttered. "I had no right, I less than any of us. We shall never speak of it again."

"We shall not speak of much at all, any more," she said, shaking her head. "That is unnecessary when one's duty is so clear."

He watched her, the gentleness in which he could see her enclosing every word, every expression of her face. She bent her head a little and put out her hands and took his and said, holding them clasped against her cheek, "Dear, dear Randalo. Beloved friend. I will pray for courage for you."

He could have screamed at her, in a flash of panic, that he did not want her prayers, her faith, her doctrine. He wanted John. He wanted to keep him, here or somewhere, anywhere that was not the looming, mouldy, rat-ridden prison to which he must return, cringing, burrowing; a prison webbed in prehensile memories, crammed with things which would not stay things, but which came alive to snare him and twist him and mock the frightened furtive shadow to whom this man standing here was a stranger. No, he said, almost aloud, they don't stay things; they come to life, they are alive, and they get their life from me . . . boxes . . . crates . . . papers . . . wheels . . . shoes and cloaks and kettles and lamps . . . the pianos, the noises, the motion, the wave . . . there is the wave. They get their life from me. And I want only to have given it to him.

He was shuddering in her arms, then she was holding his head against her breast. He heard her whispered words, felt the cool benison of her closed lips touching his eyes.

"I know," he heard her breathe. "Oh, I know. Did you think I did not understand?"

He raised his face and she looked at it, into a wrack of suffering. He tried to speak, choked, and tried again. "I cannot bear to leave him," he sobbed.

She did not speak for a long time. When he looked at her as if to ask her, she said, "Is it given to us to choose?" Her voice was somehow very beautiful; he thought of the notes of a viola. "I would seek to comfort you," she said, "if it would give you consolation to know that I too will be living a life of sacrifice. I," she said, "forfeited my rights to the full joys of being his mother. If I should ever forget, and try to seize what is not mine, I would harm the future of the child, his best interests which must always be my only aim."

"You are sure you know what to do, Renata?" He spoke in English. She answered likewise, "I think I know. Mostly I have explain' before. For the adoption I will consult the finest *avvocato* in Milano, first of all."

"Do you," he asked slowly and with some embarrassment, "know any such people, Renata?"

She nodded, with a sad, worldly smile. "Eh! You forget? I was—" she shrugged. "*Non importa* how it happen you meet somebody long ago. When is a question like this, are people very serious here."

"You will have plenty of money. Always."

"Yes." Her quiet assent, unembellished by awkward thanks, reassured him with the sense of his own share of the responsibility.

"And you will—how can I say it—compensate your uncle? Make their life better somehow, in appreciation—"

"Do not worry, Randalo. They all love the child, that matter the most."

"And his schooling? The very best? You will get good advice?"

"The very best. Only we know now he is *straordinario* in his intelligence. Gradually will come the discovery what he may best do."

"He wouldn't—you wouldn't keep him here in a village for long?"

"Only the first years, the *Elementare*, in Bellagio. After that will be necessary he go to a town for the *Scuola Media*. Such a town like Como, or larger."

"You would be with him?"

She nodded, with a solemn expression. "His aunt. But only until he is an age not to be tied to a protector."

"And then after the—what we call high school?"

"Is different here. After the two lower schools comes the *Liceo*."

"Yes, I remember it was something like that in Austria. I hadn't thought. And that would be where?"

"Should be Milano, or some big city. And finally, the University."

"I wouldn't want him to be a musician," said Randall suddenly and he knew, irrelevantly.

Renata laughed a little. "Do not fear," she said. "He has too much brains."

"Will you write, Renata? Will we? Are you going to teach him to write to me?"

She rested her chin on her clasped hands and looked at him deeply, letting him see that she did not know what to answer. He shook his head a little, frightened and puzzled by her silence.

"What do you mean?" he asked in a bewildered way.

"Only that I do not know," she said slowly. "I answer you yes, naturally. But only so far as I can see. This is a question can change very much with time, Randalo." She sighed sadly. "How can I make such a promise? How can I know for how long?"

"But," he said, with the bright, heartrending self-deception of a child, "I will be back—when—you know, when I can leave Seymour. There's no real reason why he has to go on living in that way. If—" he bit his lip. "If he—"

"He will live," she said.

"Of course," said Randall too quickly. "But that house, Renata. The whole thing." He grimaced, thrusting away the images that clamored and battered behind their walls. "We always meant to get out of that house. Now when I go there I'll see that we do."

"Yes," she said. Her tone was without any meaning at all. His mind made a quick, frightened circle round the core of the subject. That house. Why we stayed before. What we waited for. How it will be different now. What were we always waiting for? Now he was not going to know, he was not going to allow himself to know. Behind the refusal to know lay what he would never see, never say, never feel. A good life for John was not too high a price, even if it meant his own imprisonment. A good life for John, for John the broad road outwards where the doors and the walls, the rooms, the locks, the dark, the hiding, the blight, the things, could never capture him. He will be free and will never have known that; that nor any of us who brought it to pass. Back in the farthest spaces of his memory hovered the predatory old woman, closer his mindless, shattered mother, closer still the imperative burden of his helpless brother. Yet they were far away. They might drift for the moment to hover and darken the spaces in which the spirit existed here; they floated away, back behind their doors and locks, and were unreal. Here there was a small clay stove, a bare table at his elbow, the splashing rain outside; before him the woman who had foreseen his duty and given him the courage to do it, and upstairs the boy whom he loved with the greatest love that the heart could know.

After a long time he bent towards Renata and took her in his arms and said with his face against her hair, "Help me to go without making him sad, Renata. Help us to act as if it were not good bye."

CHAPTER 20

Huddled in the corner to avoid seeing out the window Randall did not move when the cab slithered to a stop. He sat still, wilfully ignoring his whereabouts until the driver said, "Hey, Mister, ain't this the address you told me?"

"Yes." Randall opened the door, stepped out unsteadily, and dragged his valise after him. The ground appeared to heave; the voyage had been a nightmare and he was still plagued by the motion of the ship. Inattentively he paid the cab-driver, leaving him all the change from a dollar rather than bothering to count it. He stood on the curb with his back to the house, conquering an impulse to shout, "Stop! I'm going further!" as the taxi drove away. It just would, he thought, be this time of day and this time of year, the gloomiest possible. The bad weather of months past had persisted all the way across the Atlantic and reasserted itself here in the form of driving sleet falling on streets ankle deep in filthy slush. It was almost dark, but only a little past four in the afternoon. The street lamps were not yet lighted. But across the street in the "terrace row" of drab rooming-houses, people had lit the gas here and there, which shone with a dim ugly gleam. He stood gazing stupidly at a lighted window where a small Christmas wreath hung between frayed curtains.

What a dreary time of year, he thought again; and clapped his hands to his ears, violently startled by the blat of a tin horn. He glanced round; two dirty small boys were capering behind him, hooting "Happ-y NOO Year!", delighted to have frightened him. He ignored them. It must be the thirty-first of December; he had not really noticed. He sighed. Slowly he picked up his valise and raised his head for a first, painfully reluctant look at the house. It did not seem any different; blinded, blankly brown, every window like a closed eye. The top floor and the fourth floor, he thought; nobody could have been in those rooms, nor in Mama's room on the third floor either. Seymour's on the second floor might as well be sealed like the others; its windows looked just the same. So did those of the drawing-room below; Randall had left them that way. When, he thought, slowly lugging the valise up the littered walk, how long ago was it? Some part of his mind refused to say; another part refuted that with the icy fact: two weeks short of three years. You knew it all the time, you knew it to the day. No I didn't, I don't want to think about then, or about this, or over there, or them, or anything. I don't want to think . . . Most of all I don't want to think about the other time I came back here.

How could he help it? Like then he had his keys, like then there was no question about getting into the house. But that time I thought I was going to leave Seymour forever. Yes, you thought so another time too. And now here he was. I'm not going to stay this time, he repeated, as he had been doing ever since his pathetic assurance to Renata. I'm going to find a way to . . . get Seymour taken care of . . . get out of here. . . . get rid of all this . . .

He was standing in the front hall with his valise at his feet and the door closed behind him. It was pitch dark and he reached by old habit towards the brass match-safe on the wall near the hatrack. It had always held sulphur matches which Seymour as a boy had delighted in scratching on the seat of his pants, as he had seen Reilly the coachman do; a forbidden thing of course. Why think of that now? He stood in the dark with a match in his hand, wondering that he had found some in the brass holder. Who must buy them and put them there? He put off lighting the gas, because he did not want to begin seeing anything around him; whatever he saw would look the way this place smelt. It had a dead, dry, yet vaguely putrid odor, compounded of dust and bad air and sickness and other smells that he could not identify. Several times he swallowed uneasily. Then from upstairs he heard Seymour's voice. It called, "Haggerty, aren't you early? What time is it?"

Randall lit the gas and started quickly up the stairs, saying, "I'm here, Seymour. It's not somebody else."

He stopped on the second-floor landing to light the gas there. The door to Seymour's room stood open, and by the light from the hall Randall saw, in the dark, the pallid face in its frame of hanging moustache, the high bald forehead, the blind eyes staring not only as if they could see, but see something horrifying. The mouth was wide open. Seymour sat in a wheelchair, facing the open door. Randall stood silent, shocked, gazing at Seymour's left hand lying limply on his covered knees. The right one gripped the wheel of the chair. Randall's eyes moved slowly from the hands to the blind eyes, back to the covered knees and the crippled hand.

"What in hell are you doing here?" asked Seymour. His voice grated with scorn.

"I came when I heard about you."

"Who told you?"

"I—never mind. Did you suppose nobody would tell me?"

"Why didn't you say you were coming?"

"Why should I?"

"Where is the boy?"

"None of your business," said Randall, amazed at the curtness of his own voice.

"Have you left him in Italy?"

"I didn't come back to report about him. If there's anything I can do for you, tell me what it is and I'll do it. I won't talk about any of that."

"Charming of you to walk in and be high-handed with me."

"That's not my intention, so far as you yourself are concerned. I'm extremely sorry you've had this accident and if you don't mind telling me how you are, and how you're being looked after, naturally I want to know."

"Oh," said Seymour, with a disgusted flap of his right hand, "it's a hell of a mess."

Randall moved slowly into the room, taking off his overcoat. He was swept by consternation and pity as, he thought, any human creature must be; he would stick to his refusal to discuss John and everything concerning him, but beyond that, Seymour's condition would melt a heart of stone. His left hand was visibly disabled; there was an ominous look of stillness about the legs hidden under the blanket; worst of all, Randall felt now as if he had forgotten that Seymour had been blind long before he went away. The blindness had a terrible immediacy, as if to reproach Randall that nobody in his right mind could have gone off three years ago and abandoned this man. Randall put out his hand timidly in the instinctive gesture of touching Seymour lightly on the shoulder or the arm, a thing which had had to take the place of the glances that Seymour could not see; but he could not bring himself to touch his brother. He might hate it, he thought; and if he did, he'd have good reason.

"Brother," he said, and Seymour heard for the first time Randall's natural voice, "won't you tell me about it? At least—who's been taking care of you?"

Seymour shrugged. "An orderly from the Post Graduate Hospital. The doctor has him come here twice a day and move me from the bed to this bloody chair and back to the bed again. And do the other usual things." He waved at a stand upon which stood basins and vessels. "I didn't want any part of the filthy business."

"So," Randall asked slowly and with audible distress, "you—you are—"

"Helpless," said Seymour abruptly. "Now are you satisfied?"

"Brother—please! I want to help. Don't be so—"

"Oh," muttered Seymour, "the hell with it."

"No! Why wouldn't you go to the hospital? Where you could be properly looked after?"

"And be Exhibit Number One? I told you, the hell with it!" Seymour was almost screaming. "If I'm going to rot alive, I'll do it shut up here."

Randall did not speak. He was fighting with the echo of Seymour's words, overcome by the sensation of grappling with a writhing mass like the serpents setting upon Laocoön, monsters whose deadliness lay not in touch but in sound; murderous, strangling echoes, worming in from every side: shut up here shut up here . . . Randall twisted his cold hands together, slowly raising their blue knuckles towards his mouth as if to be ready to ram it shut should the torrent of his fears burst out. His eyes were fixed with incredulous horror upon Seymour's long, hairy face. Seymour sat there silent, his head sunken between his shoulders, thrust a little forward in a position which bespoke eternal listening. Around his bitter mouth there played a faint, twitching look of devilishness. But when he spoke his voice was matter-of-fact. "There," he said, "is my keeper coming in now."

Randall had not heard the door downstairs opening with a latchkey.

"I hated having to give that man a key," said Seymour. "I hate his knowing where I keep my money."

"But doesn't he make you at least—well, less uncomfortable?"

"He keeps me from having bedsores, or so the doctor says. That's what all this damned shifting is for. Clear out now, Randall. Your homecoming can be spared the spectacle of my functions."

Randall went to his old room, the small one next to Seymour's which he had occupied in the immeasurably long ago, before Maggie Quinn had fled and left him to care for John. He opened the door and stepped inside the dark chamber, and fumbling for the gaslight, almost choked on the dead, dust-laden air. When he had light, a glance round the room told him it had not been cleaned since the last time he had been in it. It was a revolting sight. His hand came away from the top of the bureau black with dirt, leaving behind a print like that of an animal in sand. The room smelt, not alone of dust and dead air, but of something that suggested a search for its source, a search that nobody would want to make. He supposed he would have to do it. He stood looking at the old glass-paned book-case, empty because everything that had been in it was locked away up on the fourth floor. All his things were there. His hand went to the bunch of keys in his pocket, the guarantee that his things were safe; his things which, even had Seymour not existed, were still the indissoluble link to this place. He had more things downstairs in his valise. I shall have to get to work tomorrow morning, he thought, and put them safely away too. He sat down slowly on the edge of the sagging bed. From the next room he heard the sound of Seymour's voice, subdued, saying something not meant to be overheard, and the clink of glass or something metallic. He sat there for a long time, lost in the kind of thoughts which are weirdly unrelated to memory.

Next morning he saw with revulsion the breakfast, in chipped kitchen dishes slung upon a dented tray, which a giantess of a Negro woman, slatternly and insolent, brought to Seymour. She did not offer Randall anything and he went down to the kitchen to get a cup of coffee. The filth that he saw there, the long-accumulating traces of rats and mice, the cockroaches, the rotten boards under the leaking sink, drove him away shuddering and thinking of the bare clean sunny kitchen, the little morning cup of strong coffee, the beckoning garden outside. Of John and of Renata he would not think, not now, not yet; that was his vow and he had sworn to keep it. He went to Seymour to say he intended to get rid of the woman. He had no chance because Seymour spoke first. Lying in bed, he said, "You may as well begin, Randall. If you don't know what to do, I'll tell you."

"Why, of course. You mean, do something for you?"

"Quite. Now I'm used to being up in that damned chair all day, I suppose I might as well continue. But I mean to boot out that twaddling doctor the way I did his nursemaid."

"Oh. The man from the hospital?"

"Yes. I fired him last night. Why should I pay anyone to do something you can do?"

"That's so," said Randall slowly. "Of course I want to take care of you, Brother. Didn't I say so last night?"

Days had no meaning as time wheeled slowly by, and months rolled in the wake of days, and years seemed infinitely less noteworthy than the least of momentary concerns. Any day was the pattern of a thousand others, the year in which it fell of utter insignificance. Any morning saw the same drab sights, echoed the same querulous, drilling monotone:

"Randall!"

"Yes, Brother."

"Where are you?"

"Just in my room. I'm coming."

"I called you before."

"I'm coming." Randall shuffled to the library where ten minutes before he had pushed the wheelchair into the bay window when Seymour said he was cold, he wanted to feel the sun. It was May; several Mays had gone before; it was quite hot.

"I'm too warm here," said Seymour.

"Then we'll move you." Randall took the bar of the chair and drew it back into the dusky room. All the blinds were down except the one that had been raised a little to the sun.

"Not too far!" Seymour put out his right hand and felt expertly in the spaces round him. "Not by the table."

"Yes, Brother."

"And draw that blind again."

"Very well."

"What were you doing?"

"Why—oh, nothing. I don't know."

"Isn't it time for my orange?"

"Not quite. Not unless you want it now."

"No." Seymour sniffed in an aggrieved way. "But I shouldn't have to think of it before you do."

"I—" Randall shut his mouth again. "You can have it any time you want it."

"I want it when it's time for it. *You* can see the clock."

When the clock struck eleven Randall was ready with the orange, peeled, carefully freed of every shred of white rind and filament, separated into segments. Seymour ate the pieces nervously, his mouth working in small twitches which agitated the shaggy shanks of his unkempt ash-colored moustache; had his nose been shorter, Randall often thought, he would have resembled a hairy rabbit. He spat out the seeds into the palm of his withered left hand, then brushed them anywhere on the theory that most of them would land in the plate on his lap. They fell, in fact, on the floor and Randall did not always bother to sweep them up.

"How much did you pay for them this time?" asked Seymour, nibbling.

"Twenty-one cents the dozen."

"That's a penny more than before."

"I must have gone to fifteen places, Seymour. I got these off a stand down near Mulberry Street somewhere."

"You'd get better ones if you went for them early in the morning. Of course if you go in the middle of the night you have to take what you can get and I—" the voice rose shrilly "—have to pay for it. Like everything else." The blind eyes which held no expression gave the illusion of glaring palely.

"Thank you. I'm willing to walk anywhere I have to go to find the cheapest oranges in New York for you but I'm going when I want to. Do you hear me?"

"Yes. I never hear anything else."

"All right. I'm not going out except at night and that's the end of it."

"Why?" asked Seymour, as if he had never heard of the subject before.

"Do you want me to explain? If I start—"

"Oh, no." Suddenly the spate of ill-humor was spent. "I understand. In fact I don't blame you."

After a time Randall came back from upstairs where he had been doing whatever it was that sometimes echoed in a thick, but distant dragging sound, interspersed with an occasional thump. He asked, "Would you like me to read the newspapers today, Brother?"

"What are the headlines?"

"Oh, a lot more about all that palavering at Versailles."

"Peace Conference," sniffed Seymour. "Good God, the greatest brain since Plato wouldn't be able to make head or tail of all that gabble. I'm sick to death of it."

"Well, then, I'll just put the papers with all the others."

"That's right. We'll always have a file of them, at least. God knows there's room enough for them."

"Of course there is. And oh, Brother, wouldn't it be wonderful—" At moments the pale shadow of Randall's present haggard face reflected the warmth and hopefulness of long ago. "It would be a miracle, but—"

"It wasn't written up as a miracle. The man you went to talk to didn't claim it to be a miracle. He just proved the cases where it had worked."

"Yes," said Randall. "He certainly had the proofs. Three different cases, where he fed them the oranges and their sight came back. Oh, if it does that for you, I'd walk a hundred miles every night to buy the oranges!"

"You are a good soul, Randall. Look here, I'm cold."

The wheelchair was moved back to the bay window. There was not much space to manoeuvre it, the room was very crowded with all the appurtenances of their daily existence, which Randall had been moving into it by degrees, partly to put them all within Seymour's reach, partly to save himself the trouble of going elsewhere in the house to fetch them. Fetching anything meant a long, patient, exhausting search. Even with the top floor completely blocked off now, the job of packing and stacking it solidly with newspapers neatly finished, there were so many other rooms to deal with if something had to be found. The things already in them were very important. Randall did not want to move them or change anything. So he had been assembling everything here which Seymour might ever need. Seymour was here all of the time except the brief span of the night when Randall pushed him into his bedroom, and by a process of skill and ingenuity, partly lifted, partly slid him onto his bed. In the morning the procedure, with greater difficulty, was reversed, and the chair cautiously steered along the cluttered hall and through the crowded library back to the corner between the windows and the fireplace where Seymour spent his days.

"By the way," said Seymour after they had finished their midday meal of tinned soup, bread, a piece of cheese for Randall and another orange for Seymour, "you said there was a letter this morning." He had been in a temper at the time and had not wanted to have it read to him.

"Yes." This year there were a good many letters for Seymour, as the result of his becoming forty years of age. His grandmother's trust had terminated and he had received his inheritance outright. He had immediately severed all connections with the successors to the original Trustees, and chosen a lawyer of his own, whom he had known at his club long ago. He never saw the man, whose name was Cullom; everything was attended to by letter, with Randall writing Seymour's dictated instructions, and reading him Cullom's replies and other communications. Until Seymour's securities, to which he paid the most minute attention, were all reinvested and his affairs arranged as he wished them, there would be a good deal of this correspondence with Cullom. Several times a week there were letters from him to Seymour. But there had not been a letter for Randall for quite a while, not since . . . he was hazy about dates. Italy had entered the war a considerable time before, there had been infrequent brief notes, opened by the censor, and after a space they had stopped.

Randall did not know why; nor when he had stopped answering the notes, nor how long it had been since he had written at all. But it was much longer than he would have believed if some keeper of records had been able to tell him. Perhaps he thought he had always continued to write; in his mind he had, the secret compartment of his mind which was the counterpart of his other secrets guarded under this roof. One did not leave one's things unlocked, accessible to accident or prying eyes; one did not write one's closest, deepest thoughts on paper, only to cast them to the glaring exposure of a world at war. A censored letter was a picked lock, a terrible assault on the treasure-house of his secrets; somebody might as well smash the locks on his desk, the doors of the rooms where his things were safe. No, he would not write; or if he did he would not dream of committing his letters to the dangers of censorship and the possibility that they might not reach their destination at all. Letters became by slow degrees integral with all other sorts of paper, something to be hoarded, hidden, guarded, locked. It was better for the link to lie safe and cherished in his mind; he would not violate it by any exposure.

Six years had blunted the spike of memory. It became steadily more difficult to go about, like the paper-collector in the Park, spearing this or that, lifting it up, looking it over to trace beyond the dust and the rain and the evanescence of paper itself, whatever had been printed or written upon it when it was new. He had become better satisfied not to try. He had made one sharp, concrete effort when the daily newspapers, sometimes read aloud to Seymour, oftener put aside for the promised day when he should be able to read them for himself, forced the violent reality of war upon Randall's attention. By a means whose details he could not understand, he had made sure that his money would still reach its destination, routed in some complicated way through Switzerland. He felt safe about that. He liked the feeling that the money was going there. He had liked it even more since 1914, when his income had doubled and he had been as choleric as Seymour himself with the Trustees when they had remonstrated against sending every penny of it abroad. All his intensity spent itself in that outburst. Thereafter the subject began to fade, back, back, a recession into a dream where he had left in good care the greatest treasure of his heart, which had no place in the house here with Seymour.

He read Cullom's letter aloud to Seymour, and they had some acrimonious discussion about their daily expenses, which Seymour doled out from the steel strongbox locked in the bottom drawer of his desk. Randall was required to stay at the far end of the room whenever Seymour had the box open, while his long grey fingers, the right hand an acutely sensitive instrument, the left feeble and atrophied, slowly felt and counted and re-counted the money. If Seymour suspected that Randall could see into the box there was a burst of temper. He would place the few bills that he had chosen on the edge of his desk, carefully close and lock the box and replace it in the drawer, which he also locked, and then propel himself to the corner of the desk again, using his right hand to turn the wheels of the chair and his left to guide himself. That manoeuvre, from the locked drawer to the corner of the desk, was the only one he negotiated by himself. Otherwise Randall must always push and move the chair.

Randall had grown used to Seymour's interminable, drilling sarcasm about money; his meanness was a fact like his blindness and his paralyzed legs. They had had one tremendous quarrel in the beginning, when Randall first came back from Italy. It bore the strange perversion of reversing the situation of former days, when Randall had paid all their expenses and Seymour had dragged and weaseled with his debts. Now Seymour had held out a few dollars to Randall and said, "Here, this is what it costs me to live . . ."

"And me?"

"Why, you pay for yourself, of course."

"No, Seymour, I can't. I have no money."

"You—*what*?" The long, bony face had twisted and grimaced.

"I tell you, I have no money."

"What do you mean? What have you done with it?"

"None of your damned business."

"I know what you've done! You imbecile!" Seymour had screamed, "You bloody, blathering, sentimental—"

"Shut up. I came back here to take care of you, and a fine state I found you in. If you want me to stay, you can pay for everything. If you don't, I'll leave."

"You—"

"It's no use calling me names. Take it or leave it."

Seymour had gone into a tantrum of the utmost frenzy, screaming a tirade of protest and rage. Randall had not stayed nearby to hear it. But all the way upstairs in the fourth-floor room where he locked himself when he wanted to be alone with his papers, he could hear the stream of monstrous imprecations. They did not speak for several days after that. In the interval Seymour contrived by means of the telephone, which he later had removed, to learn that Randall upon returning from Europe, had closed his account with the Seaboard Trust Company, and ordered the Trustees to send all his income abroad, depositing nothing in New York. Seymour had to choose. If he wanted Randall to stay, he must pay for everything, support him entirely. He paid with grudging, taunting bitterness, nagging, carping, droning a stream of the pettiest possible abuse. Every imaginable way to pinch a penny was pursued with avidity more than preposterous in a man of his means. The second removal of the telephone was followed by a refusal ever to buy any coal, except for the grate in the library, so that hot water became altogether a thing of the past. One could shave in cold, if one troubled occasionally to shave. Seymour had not been able to have a tub bath since his accident; gradually Randall too had lost the habit of using the old tin behemoth in its mahogany wainscot. Why plunge into that much cold water all at once? Easier, he thought, to wash himself if he cared to, in patches as he sometimes washed Seymour, using a dribble of cold water from the hand-basin tap. The whole idea became steadily less important. There was no longer any tiresome charwoman to demand hot water for scrubbing; the last of a succession of brutal slatterns who had come in to do housework was dismissed and after that Randall did any housework that was done.

"I'd rather," he said, not meaning to take the wind out of Seymour's sails, but doing so. "I don't want anybody rooting about in here. I don't want any intruders."

"Neither do I." Seymour was surprised to find himself wholly in agreement, and approving of Randall's view. "We're much better off by ourselves."

His inconsistencies did not seem extraordinary to Randall, nor difficult to accept. Occasionally after he had made a frenzied scene while counting out money for food from his strongbox, the whole paroxysm collapsed; he would sit for a moment bowed in his chair with the closed box clutched on his insensible knees; Randall would hear the slow snorts of his diminishing passion; finally his bony, greyish right hand, its fingers tactile as antennae, would feel the quarter-folded paper which meant a ten-dollar bill, and hold it out towards Randall. "Here," Seymour would say, his head turned sharp the other way, "take it . . ."

Why refuse? Pride had no more meaning than money itself, a thing of distant import, confusing, vaguely shelved. Randall did not thank Seymour, the words would have implied an importance that the subject did not have. He walked about for weeks on end with forgotten ten-dollar bills in his pockets, then sometimes in his nocturnal searches for oranges he saw a thing in the basement lair of an old-iron or other second-hand dealer, and sometimes he bought it. In certain parts of town there seemed little distinction between night and day: poor parts, queer parts, foreign parts. Their inhabitants lived the whole clock round, working at the times they could get work, buying when they had the price of an article or the time to haggle over it. He drifted to those parts of town, not knowing why, but drawn beyond his knowledge by the fact that nobody looked at him. Nobody noticed straggling uncut hair, days of beard, a threadbare coat, soiled linen, cracked shoes: everybody looked the same. If he saw a broken trombone sticking out of a pile of old brass at a junk dealer's in Essex Street, and thought,

"There! when Seymour feels like tinkering with something, I'll get him to fix that; I might try to play it," nobody cared or remarked that he went in and bought it for ninety-six cents. He took it home and laid it away in case Seymour should ever feel like tinkering.

One hot summer night—was it ten summers that he had been back here?—twelve?—he let himself out of the house after Seymour was settled in bed. It was about half past nine, a dark, moonless night when he faced his hours of prowling and searching with a sense of refuge in the heavy blackness of the sky. Here in Chelsea where the last traces of respectability had vanished in the wake of ragtag rooming-houses, the street lamps were far apart and dimly lit. Downtown in the directions where he usually walked, there was more or less illumination, depending upon the neighborhood and the extent of its nocturnal activity. Where shops were open and the streets crowded with noisy people escaping the foetor of their tenement rooms, bargaining with pushcart vendors for trashy articles and decaying fruit, nobody noticed him and he did not shrink from such light as there was. On his long, maundering walks down to such districts the streets were very dark, echoingly empty, almost abandoned, as if recovering from the daytime assaults of traffic and commerce. He liked the feeling of their belonging to him when they were of no use to anyone else.

He stood on the top step of the stoop, his basket on his arm, deciding in which direction to go. The basket was the same rather odd and invariable shape as several others which he used; the shape of *the* basket, which was carefully stowed away in a safe place on the fourth floor. He saw fewer and fewer baskets of this shape; oblong, with rounded corners, the willow bent as if to puff them out, in contrast with the commoner square corners that most baskets had. Whenever he saw another basket of his own sort, he acquired it, acting upon some impulse which was deeply urgent in him, like the physical necessity to relieve himself. He was compelled, but the habit was so long established that he never recognized it as a compulsion; it functioned of itself. If the basket were for sale, he bought it; if it could be had for the taking, he took it. He always carried one of the baskets on his arm when he went out at night. In it he brought home Seymour's oranges and whatever other food he bought, and anything else that he acquired, if it was of a size to fit in the basket.

He was just beginning to descend the sandstone steps, some of which were jagged like broken teeth at the edges, when a figure leaped from the shadow of the areaway, uttering a long, shrill howl. Randall gasped, clutched his basket, and sank down terrified on the steps. There was a second howl, a snarling noise which could be the caterwaul of an alley-cat but was not.

"Yanh," shrilled the voice. "Looney! Loo—oo—ney!" It hooted like an owl.

"Yanh! Shame! Shame on you!" A second voice joined the caterwauling. Figures began to creep towards the steps, dark figures, undiscernible.

"Go away!" Randall's voice broke high. "Get out of here!"

"Loo—oo—ney!" The wailing rose and fell. Randall cowered on the broken step, hiding his face from the skulking figures.

"Crazy house . . . Looney people . . . Bughouse . . . Yanh . . . Yooooooooooh . . ." Two voices, three, four. . . .

"Stop it!" Randall tried to stand, shaking so helplessly that he dropped the basket and it rolled down the steps. Something jumped on it. He heard crackling, splintering, loutish laughs.

"You stop that," he screamed. "Get out of here. Leave that alone."

"Aw, come off," roared a hoodlum's voice. "Lay off, Smitty. Leava poor nut alone."

"Looney! Bughouse!"

"Sharrup. Getta hell out. C'mon, Skinnay."

"Whooo—ooo—"

"No," sobbed Randall, cowering on the step. "No . . . no."

"Dat's enough, getta hell out. Hey you, McBane, scram . . ."

"No!" screamed Randall again. The figures swarmed in the yard. One approached the steps, he saw two hands, the forefinger of one brushing the forefinger of the other. "Shame!" chanted a hooligan's voice. "Shame on a loon! Shame on you . . . yanh . . . yanh!"

"Lay off, ya hear? Ya done it, beat it."

"Yanh . . . yanh . . . shame on you, shame on you . . ." The hoots and calls moved off, there were shambling figures out by the gate, a hoarse bass snigger, rough guffaws, shuffling steps, obscenities. Randall sat still, bent into a trembling ball, his face buried in his hands. He cowered there for a long time, long after he had heard the last of the dragging footsteps, the coarse bawling voices. Then, still crouched, looking neither right nor left, he crept by inches down the steps, picked up the splinters of his basket, slowly climbed the steps again and let himself into the house. With a groan he slammed the door behind him and stood with his back against it, panting. From upstairs he heard the high tremor of Seymour's voice, frantic, panic-ridden. He too was crying, "No, no . . . stop. *McBane*, I heard them yell McBane . . ."

Randall went up to him and found him shaking, his hands beating the air, his face contorted. He said, "It's me, Brother, I came back. I—"

Seymour began to whimper. "They said McBane," he cried again. "That woman, that terrible—"

"Oh, she's dead," said Randall in a strange matter-of-fact voice at which he himself was astonished. "That hoodlum must be her son."

"They said McBane," whined Seymour again. "You've got to keep them out, Randall. You mustn't let them near us. They're devils, they want to—" he choked and chattered incoherently. "Keep them out, keep them away . . ."

"Yes," said Randall, smoothing Seymour's forehead. "Yes, Brother. You're perfectly right. We've got to keep them out. We've got to be safe."

"Oh, how can we do it . . . what will you do?"

"Try to be quiet, Seymour," said Randall gently. "Try to get calm. I'll find ways to do it, stop worrying about that. I won't let them in here."

"Don't let them in," said Seymour, lost in his fear. "Don't let them in. They'll get my box, they'll steal my money."

"No, Brother." Randall sat on the edge of the bed, gently stroking Seymour's tangled hair. "Try to stop worrying now. They shan't get in."

He had no box, he had no money. But he had his things. He could not endure the thought of intruders either.

If it had not been for the newspapers they might have had no idea at all of the passage of years, instead of the crepuscular impression that they received but did not retain. The seasons had more reality, the necessity to buy more kerosene when the weather was cold, less bread when it was hot, because bread went mouldy so fast. They had not used gas for years. After they knew that nothing would ever again induce them to allow a person to enter their house, they said they could as well get along without gas, meaning more exactly, that they would never again admit the man who came to read the meter. After that Randall found a second-hand two-burner kerosene cookstove, which he put behind the screen in the corner of the library; and two old-fashioned kerosene lamps, which with occasional candles were all the light they wanted anyway. One day they asked one another why they should bother any longer with coal for the library grate. If they did not want the man from Tony's in Tenth Avenue even to enter the yard to bring small sacks of coal and dump them down the chute in the areaway, Randall would have to carry them himself. He was not strong enough. Besides, it was becoming too difficult to get through the blockade of massed stuff to get to the coal-bin in the front of the cellar. He said it was much easier to carry home the filled gallon can of kerosene whenever they needed it. He bought a couple of round sheet-iron kerosene room-heaters with which they managed, they said, perfectly well. He was pleased to be able to find them in a junk shop for less than two dollars apiece.

But the newspapers came regularly, morning and evening, the full complement of every daily paper published in New York. The brothers never asked each other why they had no objection to the newsboy's approaching the house to fling his bundle of folded papers at the disused side door. Randall used the front door when entering or leaving the house, but the newsboy had always brought the papers to the side door; he must continue to do so. It was years since Randall had unlocked and opened that door. Morning and evening he waited in the ground-floor hall, hovering behind the glass-paned ebony curio cabinet that he had dragged from the drawing-room and set against the door. When he heard outside the thump that meant the landing of the bundle of newspapers against the door, he waited a moment until the boy should have reached the street again; then he ran quickly out the front door, down the steps, round to the side, seized the armful of papers, and hurried into the house, bolting and chaining the front door behind himself.

In actual fact he seldom read the papers aloud to Seymour. The promised day when Seymour should have recovered his sight and become able to read for himself was so cogent a talisman that they felt, and sometimes said, they did not want to impede it by the least doubt of its eventuality. So they clung doggedly to the cure, which meant Seymour's eating about a hundred oranges every week, and Randall's keeping very busy supplying them.

It was only when Seymour was unusually restless, late on the nights when he refused to be moved into his bed, and stayed instead in his chair in the library, that he asked Randall to read a newspaper aloud to him. The rest of the time Randall assembled the papers downstairs in the old dining-room and at regular intervals bundled and tied them and methodically continued what he had long termed in his own mind, his work. What had begun as a means of obstructing the attic rooms to the passage and the audible presence of rats was continuing because it seemed so practical a way to effect other results that he wanted. After filling up, blocking absolutely solid the entire attic floor, rooms, hall, and stairs, he had found that the front rooms of the next lower floor, the fourth, were mildewing, peeling, moulding, and giving very disagreeable evidence that the upper front wall, or the roof over the front of the house, was leaking badly. It did not even occur to him to bring up the question of repairs. Seymour with his violent tantrums at any demand for money, would only go into one of his bad states, and Randall was too hazy about the notion of any money of his own to think of a use for it. The mere idea of any repair to the house ruled itself out because only once in all his life had there been a reason for doing such a thing. Now the reason did not exist. He took the place as it was, and he felt capable of dealing with it in his own way. He felt secure and satisfied with the solid soundproof block he had made of the top floor; he would start in the front of the fourth floor to make another such block. The papers would absorb the slimy damp that greased the walls and must be the reason for that nasty smell. His own special place, the old day nursery on the same floor at the back of the house, seemed to be just the same as ever. Of course his accumulation of papers had long since become too much for his small hidden desk. He had sorted them all through and put in the desk the very most important, most secret, most treasured of his things. The rest he kept in the wardrobe, the bureau, and various other pieces of furniture which he had dragged to the room, each thing supplied with its own lock and key. He carried a very large bunch of keys in his trousers pocket and it took a long time to find the right key when he wanted to open something. Once in a while he stood in the remaining space, little enough, in the centre of the room, estimating how much more place there was for his papers as he accumulated them. He had years ago used up the last of his music-manuscript paper, and, already fixed in the habit of buying nothing blank or new, he had simply moved to the room his collection of printed music, whose margins provided enough space for jottings in his miniscule hand. It was when he had no further pieces of furniture in which to lock up the sheets and volumes of scribbled-over printed music that he took to finding suitcases, valises, any sort of old luggage, in which to keep them. Nothing was easier to pick up at junk shops or in rubbish dumps than old luggage. He required only that it have locks. If the keys were lost he was always sure of finding some key in his enormous bunch which would fit.

What year was it now? If Seymour asked him—and occasionally Seymour did—he had only to look at a newspaper. When he read out such a date as November 19th, 1925, they murmured in dull surprise at the passage of time, but actually the span had little meaning. They had never been given to talk about time, the past, the assembled identities which hovered in the dusk of intentional oblivion. From the first days of Randall's return to share this life with Seymour, his brother had maintained a silence concerning the interval of Randall's absence, and all that had brought it about, as dogged as the avarice which dictated every detail of their lives. And, with the same sharp breaks of inconsistency that tossed at Randall an occasional sop of pocket-money, Seymour at rare intervals ruptured the crust of silence with a question about the past.

On such an evening, when Randall that day had done him some particular kindness, Seymour sat on in his chair past the hour when he ordinarily went to bed and Randall ventured out on his nightly errands. Randall said something about its growing late; Seymour put him off, asking if there were not enough oranges on hand to last through tomorrow? Randall had found a special bargain last night and bought an extra quantity.

"Yes," he answered, "I guess there are."

"I don't feel like going to bed," said Seymour. "It might be like last night again. I got to—thinking."

"You did?" Randall did not ask what Seymour had thought about. But Seymour said uneasily, "Yes. About you. And—all that."

"There's nothing to think about me."

"Rot. You mean you never think about it yourself?"

"About what, Brother?" Randall's eyes at a moment like this could glow as blue and innocent as ever, even though they shone from a pale, stubbled face, rising from a dirt-encrusted neck and a soiled paper collar.

"About that life you lived in Italy. And her, and the boy."

Randall's lips trembled for a moment; his muscles tensed, his face worked. He swallowed, twisted his hands uneasily and felt weak and dizzy; but Seymour could not see him; a good deal of calm could be achieved in the face of that.

"Well," he said slowly, after a time, "I don't believe I think about it very much. I don't believe I have," he said, "ever since I came back here."

"Twelve years," said Seymour, drawling. "Don't you ever wonder what's—what's—happened?"

"I know what's happened," said Randall, very quiet.

"Oh. So they write to you."

Panic swept Randall for an instant, a sense of being spied upon. But Seymour cannot spy, he cannot see. They do not write. Why don't they write? I must have told them not to. But they're all right. He knew that, he had never had any doubt about it. "It's just that I know," he said.

"Strange," said Seymour slowly. They sat silent for a long time. At last he said, "Don't you ever think about that place over there? It must have been to say the least a lot different from this."

"It was, of course. But you know, Brother, I never have been able somehow to think much about it since I came back here. I don't remember it very well. It's queer. It was beautiful." Randall's voice turned very soft, much softer than the quiet tone in which he usually spoke. "It was so beautiful that I feel as if I didn't think it was real while I was there. Ever since I left, when I've tried to reach back and touch the memories of it I've scarcely ever been able to do it . . . I get all sort of hazy. Much more as time goes on."

Seymour did not comment. Suddenly Randall said, "But the curious thing is that when I was there, I used to get—" he waved his hands as if to draw the words he sought from the air. "Sort of waves, fits, I don't know how to say it."

"Of what?"

"Of remembering about here. I can remember being there and having all these feelings about here. But after I came here—well, I guess I just lost the power to remember about it over there. Anyway, it's always seemed so very far away, like something I dreamed."

"It wasn't too much of a dream for you to do something concrete about the boy. And I suppose, her."

Randall sat swallowing, breathing hard, relieved that Seymour could not see him. He said, with great effort, "Let's not talk about that."

"Why?" Seymour leaned forward, his narrow shoulders hunched, his gaunt hairy face peering between them like something reptilian. The lids twitched over his blind eyes. "Why?" His voice was sliding, veiled in the faintest hint of a snarl. "Why? Isn't it as much my business as yours?"

"Please." Randall turned away and sat swallowing the sick feeling, the lump in his throat which he did not want Seymour, in the form of choked words, to hear.

"Isn't it?" asked Seymour again. Randall did not answer. Suddenly Seymour said, cruel and swift, "Randall, did you marry her?"

"No!" It was almost a scream.

"Well . . ." The bony body sank back slowly in the cripple's chair. "Why not?"

"I don't want to talk about it," said Randall. "After all these years, this is no time to bring it up. Let it be."

"I have a right to know," said Seymour abruptly.

Randall sat crushed with miserable surprise. Seymour repeated, "I have a right to know," and Randall said, unendurably goaded, "Why?"

Horribly, Seymour gave a short, nasal laugh. He said slowly, "Could you prove he was yours? Could you prove he wasn't mine?"

"Oh . . . Oh . . ." Randall buried his face in his hands and spoke from behind them. "Be still. Stop talking about it."

"Now that I've started? I don't see why. I'd like to know I'd had a son," he reflected. "She ought to be able to say."

"Seymour, I can't bear it! Will you be still!"

"You always were a sentimental fool." Seymour ignored Randall's agonized protest. "I wouldn't have married her for all the rice in China but I suppose you asked her to marry you. It would be just like you." He leaned forward again, the slow movement which reminded Randall of a turtle thrusting its head from its shell. His sense of place and sound and contact was so acute that he had at moments the power to fix his sightless eyes as if they were staring hard. He did that now, leaning straight towards Randall. He asked, "Why wouldn't she marry you?"

"I didn't say I ever asked her to," said Randall through his teeth.

"But you did. Why did she refuse?"

"Oh, Brother," cried Randall, in a frenzy, "why are you tormenting me?"

"Because I want to know. I have a right to know. Why did she refuse?"

"You know the answer as well as I do." His head was bent and turned away.

"You mean she didn't know? Or wouldn't say?"

Randall made a sound; assent or denial, let Seymour deduce his meaning for himself.

"She was a damned fool, then. I wouldn't have thought it of her. You mean to tell me, for such a reason, she wouldn't marry and legitimize the child? I can hardly believe it."

"The child is legitimized. The child has a better identity than we have—for where he is."

"No! What on earth did she do? Marry somebody else, for God's sake?"

In a few words Randall explained. Seymour sat slowly shaking his head, incredulous and astonished. Suddenly he said, "Why didn't I ask you all this long ago? When you first came back?"

"I suppose it's just as painful for you to think about as it is for me."

"I'm not a damn fool sentimentalist. I want to know whose child it is."

"You'll never know, Seymour."

"Don't be an idiot. I'll make her say." He gave a sharp, unnatural laugh. "I'll make her say he's mine."

"She'll never say. If she could, she never would."

"She wouldn't, eh?" Seymour made that menacing sound again, a cracked laugh that had no laughter in it. He banged his clenched right fist upon his useless knees and laughed again and said, "She wouldn't? Well, you watch—I'll find a way to make her say."

Randall was too harrowed to hear another word. He got up and went away to his room and flung himself on his bed, from which something sprang away in the dark without his knowing it. The bed was a tumbled mess of moth-eaten blankets and pillows covered only with stained, bare ticking. By what process laundry had drifted out of their lives they were not very clear . . . was it because the last of their grandmother's sheets had fallen to tatters? He was lying there lost in a great misery of mind and spirit, the dark howling corners of the long-forgotten filled with clamor, closing in; his face was muffled in the evil-smelling pillow whose odor he could no longer smell, like other odors, and sights, and the feel of his own unkempt body, senses that had atrophied. But like Seymour he could hear, oh how sharply he could hear! sounds and echoes of the real, and the faint imagined voices of very long ago. There was a violent crash downstairs, glass smashing, and Seymour screaming in terror in the library. Randall ran to him. Seymour sat gibbering in his chair, his hands clutching for Randall. There was another crash, then the voices, hooting, yowling, the same loathsome words, the same brutal roars of animal laughter.

"Don't let them in," shrieked Seymour, a twitching bundle of bones clinging to Randall. "They've broken in, they're in the house . . ."

"Sh—sh—" Randall's throat was locked, he was sick with terror but trying to quiet Seymour. They clung together.

"C'mon fellas, let's smash up da bughouse . . ."

"*McBane*" sobbed Seymour, panting. "It's them, it's . . ."

"You go away," shouted Randall, raising with effort a voice he did not know as his own. "Get out of here. We're upstairs, we've telephoned for the police. Get out of here." He bent down and whispered to Seymour, "I've got to go down, I've got to see—"

"No," moaned Seymour, "don't leave me alone, don't leave me, they'll come for my box . . ."

"I've got to get them out, Brother. Before they come and find out there's no telephone." Downstairs there was pandemonium, the same voices, the long taunting howls. "I've got to go. Let go of me, Brother."

He broke the grip of Seymour's right hand on his forearm, and wrenched himself away. He gave a frantic look round the room; in a corner there was an old Webster on a wheeled iron stand. He seized it with one hand, turned and picked up the lamp in the other. Holding the lamp high he dragged the stand with the enormous book on it out to the hall and to the top of the stairs. He peered down; they were everywhere, kicking, roaring, smashing; the terrible bawling guffaws, the indescribable obscenities. The place was an uproar.

"Get out," he shouted, bellowing to overreach the noise. Then he shoved the iron stand to the top step and braced his foot against it and pushed. It went down with a tremendous crash, splintering some of the banister-rails. The howls and the jeering stopped. Randall held the lamp high above his head and slowly started down the stairs. At the bottom two faces stood staring up, horror-stricken, mouths hanging open.

"Jeest," he heard. "Looka da loon . . ."

"Jesus Christ. Getta hell out . . ." The others were leaving the drawing-room, they were jumping from the windows through which they had climbed after throwing in the bricks. The two stood gazing up at the ghostly face in the circle of lamplight, the floating colorless hair, the staring eyes. He kept on moving down the stairs.

"C'mon, for Chrissake," rasped a voice. "Ain't ya had enough . . ."

"Jeest," hissed the other one, turning away. They were gone.

Randall moved all the way to the bottom step and set the lamp on the hall stand before his knees gave out and he collapsed. He was sitting there shaking, soaked with the sweat of terror, when Seymour's wails and cries recalled him—Seymour alone and helpless there in his chair in the pitch dark—but it's always dark for Seymour, said some detached echo in Randall's mind, always dark. But this is different, the terror, the fear. They've broken in, that was what we feared, I wasn't quick enough to find a way to stop them, I should have done more after that other time, that time outside. He stood up, mopping the sweat from his face with his harsh frayed coat-sleeve. I'll start to do something now, right now, this minute. First he must quiet Seymour. He turned and began slowly to climb the stairs, leaving the lamp behind, edging away from the broken banister-posts and the gaping, rising space as he mounted upwards. He climbed laboriously, breathing hard, moving his hands before himself up the peeling papered wall.

Next day he had a glazier to replace the broken window-panes, and after the man had gone, uneasily looking back over his shoulder at the house he had been afraid to enter, Randall set about making it impossible for them ever to break in again. For the time being it would have to do to drag the biggest pieces of furniture up against each of the ground-floor windows. It was a long, exhausting job and he was not nearly strong enough for it. But somehow by nightfall he had managed to set some object to block every window. Upstairs later, lying spent in his chair in the library with Seymour, trying to rally the strength to go out and do the errands, he listened while Seymour sat and pondered aloud what they could do to make the house impregnable.

At first he was too tired to attend to what Seymour said, but by degrees he felt a little better, and when Seymour said, "If we could just pack it, make it perfectly solid everywhere except where we want to go . . ." Randall found himself answering in a flat, commonplace tone, "Why that's what I've been doing upstairs for a long time, Brother. It's not so difficult." And he explained about his work.

Seymour listened carefully. This was not all news to him, he had merely not realized exactly what Randall had done because he had never had occasion to go up there in the days when he could have gone.

"That's just fine," he said slowly, weighing the situation. "You had a fine idea, Ran. All we have to do is keep on with it. We don't care how long it takes. You ought to start now on the ground floor where they broke in, and by degrees you'll get it filled up solid the same as the top . . . and then if we think we'd feel better you could keep on working from the bottom up as well as from the top down . . ."

"But of course I have to be able to get from certain places to others, Brother . . . and be able to move you . . ."

They were both thinking aloud.

"Yes," said Seymour musing. "You've got to consider that. You could plan it in such a way as to leave passages for yourself . . ." and he went on slowly, with the ingenuity of his mechanical mind, to devise the idea which was to result, after years of painstaking, backbreaking labor, in a system of intricate tunnels. Randall sat and listened, nodding from time to time, saying, "My, I could never have thought of that, you always were a wonder at building things."

They talked so late that Randall's shopping was forgotten and when at last, trembling with exhaustion but reassured by Seymour's cleverness, he suggested they go to bed, he was astonished to see the raw grey of early dawn as he peeped fearfully round the edge of a drawn blind.

Randall was so accustomed to think all mail was meant for Seymour that he almost gave him the long envelope which came on a certain day in 1928. But there were not nearly so many letters for Seymour nowadays as there had been long ago, and this one, he saw, peering at it in the murky light of the barricaded front entry, was addressed to him. He sat down on the bottom of the stairs and opened it. Several times he read through the papers inside. They were confusing, disturbing, meaningless. He let them fall to the floor and sat with his head in his hands trying to realize what they meant. There were so many words and such worrisome references to long ago that he had to think quite hard to get to the point, the fact that he was about to reach his forty-fifth birthday and that, on that day, the trust established for him by his grandmother would terminate. Whoever it was that had written the letter was asking for an appointment in which to discuss all this and—a lot of writing that Randall could scarcely understand—render the Trustees' accounting and turn over to him the securities in the trust.

He did not know what to do. He had no intention of seeing anybody, reading anything, signing anything, bothering with any of this. It had no meaning. He had no money. He was a poor man, a penniless fool, Seymour was always telling him so. Seymour had been saying it for years . . . why did Seymour say it? He sat there trying to understand, slowly shaking his head between his grimy, scaly hands. Did this stuff here have anything to do with Seymour? He tried to get it straight and find the answer to that too. He was not clear. Somehow he sensed that this letter would interest Seymour, dimly he remembered the year or two when Seymour had had all that correspondence about something which had probably been like this, but he could not recall very clearly. All he felt about this was the impulse to hide it, like everything else written on paper. He stooped slowly, scraped together the papers, put them back into the torn envelope, huddling them inside his coat, and climbed to his place on the fourth floor. He put them away, down in the very bottom of a battered, steel-banded sample case which he had got somewhere. It had a tumbler lock and a padlock as well. When he had put back all the other contents of the box on top of the letter, and locked the case again, he felt he had put the whole nagging thing out of mind.

But then the postman began to plague him. Like the newsboy, the postman had always been tolerated; he seemed to be on their side. He came and pushed the letters through the slot in the front door and rang the bell once and went away. After the bell broke Randall did not need to hear it to know that the postman had come; there were the few, infrequent letters lying on the entry floor. And nobody could have walked up the steps of the stoop and down again without Randall's knowing it, wary and anxious on the other side of the front door. Even though he knew the postman's step, and the hour of early morning when he made his rounds, Randall was sick with fear the day he heard the heavy pounding on the door, the Irish voice calling, "Hey! Hey, in there! Your bell's broken, it don't ring. Registered letter, here."

Randall put his hand on the bolt, trying to get up the courage to slide it back, but the hand fell away again. It struck the heavy chain below the bolt and set it jangling.

"I hear ye!" shouted the postman. "I don't want nothin', I've only got a registered letter to deliver and ye have to sign for it."

"I—I don't want it," said Randall hoarsely.

"Aw, it ain't nothin'," said the burly voice. "It's only a letter. But I got to do me duty, don't I? I can't hand it in without ye sign for it."

Randall gulped and began, trembling, to unlock the door. He opened it a crack, holding it in such a way that the postman could not see past him into the entry. He scribbled his name on the book that the man shoved through the crack, and took another long, thick envelope, and shut the door again. Outside a woman watched the postman trudge down the walk, shaking his head.

"They're bats in there, ain't they," she mumbled, leering.

The man tapped his forehead with a shrug and went on to the next house.

Randall did not open that envelope at all. He simply put it away upstairs with the first one. But others came after that. He never knew at what intervals they appeared, but a good deal of time must have elapsed because one day Seymour, who heard every sound inside the house, and many at some distance outside, said, "I suppose they've turned over your securities to you, Randall? It's been over six months since you were forty-five."

"How did you know that?" Randall's face, surrounded by a dusty, colorless mass of uncut hair, was pinched with disquiet.

"Why, just that I knew. Among other things, do you expect to go on sponging on me the rest of your days?"

"Oh," said Randall. After a long time he muttered, "I haven't any money. I gave it all away."

"You couldn't," said Seymour crisply. "At that time. You could only dispose of the income."

"Oh."

"So I just want to warn you, in case you're giving away the principal now, or mean to, you'd damn well better reconsider and hang onto something for yourself."

"But I don't need any money," said Randall vaguely.

"No? Now that you've got some, do you think I'm going to pay all the taxes on this house, and all the food you eat . . . everything?"

"Taxes? Why I thought—"

"You didn't think. You've never thought. Now you listen to me." Seymour leaned forward, gripping the arms of his chair, posing his face rigidly in Randall's direction in the eerie way which made it seem he was staring. He explained, in a few cutting words, that the house had always been incorporated into the two trusts, that in the years since his trust had terminated he had paid the part of the taxes proportional to his share of the house, and that Randall now, instead of his Trustees, must pay the other part. "Otherwise," said Seymour, "they'll seize the house one day for unpaid taxes and you don't think I'd stop them, do you?"

"But—"

"Oh, stop 'butting'! Pull your wits together. You're going to find yourself liable for your share of all our expenses, not to mention your own income tax, and—"

"*Income tax*? What's that?" Randall's forehead was puckered with perplexity.

"Damn it to hell!" snarled Seymour. "Go and find out for yourself. I'm warning you, that's all. You're just damn fool enough to make yourself penniless. And if I died," he added, with a tiny cackling laugh, "you wouldn't get a dime . . ."

Perhaps if he could have seen Randall's trembling, helpless bewilderment he would have spoken more kindly. As it was he sank back in his chair with his head squeezed between his shoulders, his yellowish moustache trailing along his skinny jowls, slowly stroking the back of his atrophied left hand with the long, dirty, nervous fingers of his right.

After that Randall spent days on end, how many days he had no idea, nor that they had dragged out to a string of months, trying to compose a letter to those people who had been pestering him, telling them what to do to settle the questions about his money. He never wanted to think about the subject again, once he had taken care that the amount he stipulated—and it was nearly all—should go where all his income had been going up to now. He thought he had about got it clear, he was almost ready to make a clean copy of this letter over which he had worked so long, he was even beginning to look for writing-paper on which to copy it, when he found another letter on the entry floor one morning, quietly delivered without intrusion. It lay face up, addressed to him in purple ink in a slanting, distantly familiar hand, and its foreign stamps were blue, from Italy. He bent and looked at it without touching it, squatting there over it for a long time. At last, with his hand shaking very badly he picked up the letter, so thin and light by comparison with those horrid things that had been plaguing him, and he put it in his inside pocket and took it away upstairs. He sat all morning, brooding, before he took it out and opened it. He unfolded the single sheet of crackling thin paper and, beginning to read, blinked and squinted and cupped his forehead in his hand, and wondered what to do. The letter was written in Italian. But I know Italian, he thought. I did. Don't I still? I cannot read it. Oh, he thought, that can't be true, of course you know Italian. No. How shall I know what it says? Perhaps I'd better not read it at all. Perhaps that's why it's written in Italian, so I needn't know. But that, he thought, that's nothing you have to hide from. You never had to hide from anything there. He drew long, rattling breaths, trying to get past the choked and beating feeling in his throat; and when he was past it, he started again to read the letter. It was not the least hard to understand. He read:

"My dear, good Friend,

"The time has come to tell you of the results of your wise generosity and benevolence. I have had it in mind to write to you, but I am not in the habit of communication and might have put off longer the effort of writing a letter, except I have received notices from New York which I do not fully understand, but which appear to concern the funds which all these years you have deposited for me in Switzerland. It does not matter that I do not well understand these recent letters, since I have been ready in any case to tell you that it is no longer necessary for you to send money.

"Sebastiano six months ago was awarded his Doctorate in Physics at the University of Pavia, with the highest honors ever accorded in his science. His record was brilliant at the Liceo

Scientifico in Milano, and he has completed his undergraduate and postgraduate courses at the University in such a way as to assure his future in the work he has chosen to do.

"He has been retained at Pavia for a certain amount of lecturing and graduate instruction, but most of his time will be devoted to independent research. He will be paid a stipend upon which he could live modestly. But your generosity for so many years, and the advice of Avvocato Stucchi in Milano, have enabled me to save such a portion of funds in Switzerland that Sebastiano now possesses a competence sufficient to establish him in life.

"As for me, my requirements are extremely small and Sebastiano particularly wishes to be the only person who provides for them. I am sure you will consent to this request of his, since he makes it from a sincere and grateful heart. He charges me to assure you of his profound devotion and his loyalty which is beyond the power of words to express.

"Dear Friend, it is with assurances of the deepest regard that I take leave of you now. It has long been my habit to live in solitude and you will understand that any further effort at communication would be beyond my strength. I implore of you therefore the goodness not to reply to this letter, nor to expect that I will write again. May the blessing of God be with you all the days of your life."

"R.T."

He never knew how many times he had read the letter before he folded it carefully back into its envelope, and slowly, painstakingly took apart a mountainous accumulation of things in order to reach his old childhood desk, which was so deeply hidden in this room. He put the letter away in the innermost recess of the desk and covered it with all his most private things, and having once again packed it solidly in this way, he laid back over everything the crumbling yellow animal-tracings that had always been there, and closed and locked the desk and began once more the slow labor of replacing it where it had been hidden before. It was nightfall before he finished. He was standing inside the door of the room, holding the tips of his fingers to his head as if to pull back his thoughts or his senses to recognition of where he was instead

of where he had been, when he realized that Seymour two flights downstairs was calling and crying in sharp, panicky wails. He shook his head
a little and felt suddenly as if he had jogged his ears to recognize a noise
that had been going on unheard for a long time. Why . . . it *was* Seymour . . . he must have been alone, untended . . . how long? Randall
looked blankly back into the room, shut and locked the door, and
moved down the stairs, feeling his way in the dark, to where Seymour
sat whimpering and quivering with panic and temper and discomfort.
Randall lit a candle.

"Look at the mess you've let me get in," cried Seymour. "I've been
screaming at you for hours . . . my bottle, my bottle . . . you . . ."
He beat his knees.

"Oh, I'm so sorry," said Randall, hurrying and fussing and doing
everything he could. "Forgive me, Brother, I was . . . There," he said,
his hands busy. "There. You'll feel better now."

"Better!" squealed Seymour, dithering and furious. "You and your
blather! How would you feel if you had to wait for some damn fool to
attend to you, instead of walking down the hall to the toilet!"

"Toilet? Why—" Randall stood with his mouth open.

"Yes! Don't you understand English any more or do you want me
to use a politer word?"

"Why, Brother. Didn't you—why, I just took it for granted you
knew."

"What?" Seymour snickered suddenly, but pulled his long face into
a scowl again.

"The—the toilet. It's been broken for a long time."

"It has? Why didn't you say so?"

"Well, I guess I just thought . . . the way you always hear everything . . . didn't you notice when you didn't hear it any more?"

Seymour was giggling, with the witch-like expression which meant
not mirth, but mischief. "It was damned funny you didn't tell me," he
said.

"Why should I?" asked Randall dully. "You don't want to hear
about things like that, you only get angry and yell at me that you won't
pay for any repairs, so . . ."

"So what?"

"I—oh, I—Seymour, I manage. I know we don't want to spend any
money on repairs."

"True enough," said Seymour, nodding hard. "Good little Randall. What do you do?"

"Oh—" Randall was too distraught to talk about it any more. "What did people do before there were such things?"

"I don't give a damn. I'm asking what *you* do. What do you do with that bucket you empty my bottle and the pan into? Where the hell do you go yourself?"

"I don't want to talk about it!"

"I do. I'm curious."

"Oh, Seymour. . . ." Randall tried to get out of the room quietly but Seymour heard him and cried, "Stop! Tell me."

"The back yard . . . there's a . . . a hole . . ."

"You dug a hole?"

"No," shouted Randall. "Just a hole that's there. Now *shut up*." Seymour cackled brittlely, muttering to himself. "Down a rathole," he snickered. "You'll do." He spouted wicked laughter. "You're not as stupid as you seem."

A familiar but infrequent commotion was about to take place, the arrival of a van bringing something which Randall needed. There was no doubt that he did need each object that he brought into the house. Most such things were necessary for his work, but also he felt obliged to take care of certain others if nobody else appeared to want them. That seemed to be the case nowadays with pianos. When he went on his long walks he was quite shocked to see how indifferent people had become to pianos, particularly to uprights. What a pity! Such a thing ought not to be. All pianos were valuable; all his life he had considered them important not only of themselves, but to practise upon and to play to Seymour, which he intended to begin doing again just as soon as he was caught up with his work. But Seymour too had needed pianos, even old and damaged ones, because they were full of stuff he could use when he wanted to make something. Seymour had been following his cure so faithfully for so many years that Randall expected its successful result very soon now. One day, any day, Seymour would be able to see again. And when that happened, he would not only want to read the papers that Randall had saved; he would want to begin to make things again, and he would be perfectly delighted to see how much useful material Randall had collected for him.

But it was difficult to keep him quiet on the days when a van was to deliver a piano or some large object which Randall could not carry home. The brothers scarcely ever had arguments any more, like the quarrels they used to have about money long ago. There was no reason for such quarrels now, since Randall had had to comply with Renata's refusal to accept any more money and therefore possessed his inheritance outright. Seymour, consumed by curiosity, had tried hard to learn what Randall had done about it, but had not found out. Each paid his own share of what they considered it unavoidable to spend. And Seymour's earlier agitation about money was exceeded by his present panic if he ever thought that anybody was trying to break into the house. Any unusual noise suggested that, so it required a good deal of careful, soothing preparation to reassure him beforehand when a van was to come. Randall often wished Seymour's ears were not so sharp; it would all have been so much simpler.

This time, however, Seymour took it more quietly than usual. He did several times call down shrilly to Randall while the front door and the entry door had to stand open, with the men moving two poor mal-treated uprights into the house where they would be safe. "Haven't they finished yet?" he cried from upstairs. "Haven't they gone?"

"Just a moment, Brother. Everything's fine. Just one minute more. Yes," he said to the bull-faced ruffian with whom he had chaffered to move in the pianos, "just over against the doors there. Both of them, side by side."

"Den how ya gonna open'a goddam doors?"

"Will you just please do as I say," said Randall. "That will do nicely, thank you very much."

Quaking with his haste to get them out he urged them along to the open front door and nervously gave each of them half a dollar. Before they were down the stoop he had got the entry door and the outside door closed and was beginning again to stack the crates and boxes, the empty tin cans, the dishpan, the soup-ladle, the pot-lids, the broken dictionary-stand, and all the other things in their places in the vestibule. He was so used to doing this each time he went in and out of the house, and it was so important to Seymour's peace of mind, that he did not mind the trouble at all. It did take a lot of time, of course, but it was important. Seymour had insisted on some kind of arrangement which would make it impossible for anybody to get an inch inside the house without making a tremendous noise to warn them. Randall had some dim recollection now of wondering what use it could be if Seymour heard this alarm at night while Randall was out doing his errands. But that was the sort of question one did not bring up with Seymour.

This especial terror of intruders was perfectly justified; they had always found the idea unbearable, but then there had been all that trouble two or three years ago about the old gas meter. They had not used any gas for longer than they could remember, and they ignored the small monthly charge for the meter installation, convinced that they did not owe the gas company a cent. But the company had decided that they wanted to take the disused meter out of the cellar. There had been letters which the brothers had torn up, and notices posted on the front door, which Randall indignantly removed, and several times the terrifying experience of somebody pounding on the door, right out there in broad daylight, while the brothers clung to each other in panic upstairs. The ultimate shock had been the shouting of a rough voice outside, between thunderous knocks on the door; somebody who shouted that he was the police and had come with an order from the gas company for restitution of its rightful property. If they did not open the door he would go back to the Precinct and report that the owner of the house was dead and come back with a warrant to break open the door and enter.

Though Seymour was usually more terror-stricken than Randall at the mere thought of intruders, he stiffened suddenly in his chair, folded his hands on his lap and said in an icy voice, "Randall, let them in."

"Brother . . . no . . . you can't mean that . . . I . . ."

"Go down," snapped Seymour, "go downstairs and let them in. Tell the fool from the gas company to take out his ——— meter and send the one who says he is a policeman up here to me."

Randall was unnerved, quavering on the brink of tears. He stood trembling by Seymour's chair.

"Go and do as I say," bellowed Seymour, without a trace of his habitual whine. The shouting and pounding were still going on outside. Randall turned and crept, shaking, down the stairs. He let three men into the house, two in overalls, with pipe-wrenches in their hands, from the gas company, and the policeman. Randall shuffled to the cellar door underneath the front stairs and opened it and pointed silently.

"Where's the light?" asked one of the men, feeling for a switch on the wall.

"There is none," said Randall, with stiff lips.

He turned to face the policeman and heard an oath behind him and saw one man, with an electric torch, peering down the black steps.

"My brother wants to speak to you upstairs," he said to the policeman, who was standing there with his mouth open and a pinched look about his nose.

"Never mind."

"Bring that man up here!" shouted Seymour from upstairs.

Randall made a motion and the policeman shrugged and followed him up the stairs, eyeing the broken posts as he climbed past them. Seymour sat drawn as high as he could stretch, motionless in his wheelchair. The policeman stood, a stupefied hulk, gaping at the sight before him; the long greyish-yellow face, the stained moustache, the staring colorless eyes, the ragged grey hair hanging to the shoulders. Seymour's face was hard as granite. He said, in a voice Randall could scarcely recognize, "You claim to be a policeman?"

"Yuh—yes."

"And you took it on yourself to shout in the public street that I am dead? I am not dead." The voice was level; icy. "I am Seymour Holt, marine architect. I am not dead. I am paralyzed and I am blind. I want your name and your shield number."

"Uh," said the policeman.

"Write them down and give them to me."

Randall was afraid to look at the policeman, but he heard heavy breathing and the rustle of paper, and saw the slip put into Seymour's hand. Seymour held it towards Randall and said, "Is the number correct? Look at his badge and—"

"Hey," said the policeman suddenly. "Who's the law around here?"

"I am," said Seymour. "In my own house. Now get out. Stay out."

Randall led the way downstairs again, scarcely able to walk in his frightened amazement at Seymour. The men from the gas company were out on the step with the ancient, rusty meter between them; their faces were pale and they looked at the policeman with sickened eyes. Randall slammed the door behind the three men and stood leaning against it, dripping all over with sweat.

"Holy suffering Christ," he heard, and a sound like somebody choking.

"I never seed the beat o' that. Jesus, what I seed in that cellar . . ."

"*You* seed? Listen, I was down there too. A automobile, for Crissake, a whole automobile . . . older than me."

"Automobile . . ." said the other voice, less loud as the footsteps moved away. "The hell with the automobile. Rats," gulped the voice. "Rats as big as cats . . ."

It was after that that they held a council of war and Seymour said they must rig up a system of alarms to warn them in case anybody ever tried to get into the house again. The first and most important place was the front entry, of course. Then by degrees, as Randall went on painstakingly, and more and more expertly, with his work, they decided that they would punctuate the tunnels that had to go through the stacked newspapers with contraptions that would make a frightful noise if anybody other than Randall tried to pass through. Randall knew his way and knew exactly which pieces of old iron and brass, which bottles and empty tin cans and broken kitchen utensils he should move to clear the way for himself. On the other hand, he also knew which ones not to touch.

But from time to time Seymour had particular spells of fretfulness which were—Randall thought, quite naturally—set off by the occasional arrival of a van bringing things that Randall had needed. He did not want to upset Seymour unnecessarily, and he had about decided anyway not to bring any more large things to the house, no matter how useful they seemed to block spaces, not even if they were pianos. He thought Seymour would be relieved to hear that, so he told him about it the evening after the last two pianos had arrived and been set to block off the drawing-room doors. The room inside was finished now; solidly packed from floor to ceiling, all the old furniture and Randall's big Steinway completely engulfed; there was not even a tunnel because he never expected to have to get through the room. He felt good about it; calm and pleased with a sense of a job well done. He told Seymour; and also how he had finished off the whole thing with the last two pianos.

"That's fine," Seymour agreed. "You're doing wonders, Ran. I'm sorry I get so nervous when things come to the house."

"I'm sorry, too. And I don't really have to send in any more. There's enough, and I don't like the disturbance any more than you do."

"How many pianos have you put in?" asked Seymour, in a tone that sounded unusually vague.

"Why—" Randall was much vaguer. There had been six. He said, "Four—I guess."

"Well, yes," mused Seymour. "That ought to be enough. How much did you pay for them, Ran?" This time his voice was quite different: prying.

"Oh—they don't cost much of anything, you know."

"I suppose not. I'm just surprised you have money enough even for that, the way the damned income-taxes are now."

"Oh, I don't pay any income-taxes," said Randall blandly.

"You *which*? What?" Seymour was at last on the brink of finding out what for years, he had no idea how many years, but more than ten, Randall had done about his money. Time and time again he had almost wormed it out of his brother and somehow they always ended up talking about something else. But this evening they felt unusually relaxed, intimate; perhaps because Randall was so relieved and pleased to have finished his work downstairs. "What did you do about your stuff?" asked Seymour, in the mildest, laziest tone he could contrive.

"Why—I just put it in the bank."

"In the bank? The income yes, but—"

"Oh," said Randall brightly. "I have no income. I didn't want any . . . . that time I finally decided to go and talk to those horrid people and they told me all the things I'd have to do. Like you, Brother. You still do it, or tell Mr. Cullom to do it for you. But I'd never bother with anything like that. My goodness, I'm too busy!"

"I see," said Seymour faintly. His mouth hung open. "So you—"

"I just told them to put the money in the bank, that's all."

"So they just sold all the securities," said Seymour beginning to cackle like a hen, hunched over in his chair, "and you put about a hundred and seventy-five thousand dollars cash in the bank!" His bony shoulders heaved. He laughed and laughed until Randall took hold of his wheelchair to steady it and Seymour wiped his streaming blind eyes with the back of his hand. "Oh, God. Oh, Lord. In the Seaboard, Randall?"

"Oh, no!"

"Why not?"

"I don't know."

"But what bank?"

"I don't know."

"You *don't know*?" Seymour went into another paroxysm. "Well," he gasped, when he could speak again, "of course you don't have to say."

"I really don't know," said Randall earnestly. "I mean I never can remember. I know it when I see it. It's over on Eighth Avenue somewhere. I just go there once in a while and get a little money."

"Oh, God." Seymour was convulsed again. "Out of the mouths of babes! And you've never paid a dime of income-tax."

"No," said Randall, genuinely innocent. "Why should I?"

As time went on, Seymour slept less and less. He had taken a dislike to being wheeled to his bedroom and moved into bed for the night. Randall was concerned because he always felt a bit reluctant to go out on his errands, leaving Seymour sitting up in his chair in the library. But Seymour had other matters on his mind, he could not imagine why Randall thought he was any better off in bed than here in his chair. Sometimes they argued about it. At other times Randall put off his nightly expeditions and sat quietly in the library with Seymour. He kept the day's newspapers handy in case Seymour wanted them read aloud, and on rare occasions Seymour shrugged, sighed, and said, "Oh, all right. Read if you want to. If there's anything worth reading . . ."

Then Randall would turn the pages slowly, looking for something interesting. The front pages were full of war news, but this war had no reality compared to the other one. It was dispersed and diffused, happening all over the world in places that had no meaning to the brothers. Randall would read this headline and that, watching to see if it caught Seymour's attention; but Seymour sat with his head sunken between his shoulders like a turtle half-retracted in its shell, his eyelids nearly closed over the sightless eyes, again in the manner of a dozing tortoise. He would sit in this way while Randall murmured along, fragments of this and that; only occasionally would Seymour's eyebrows go up grudgingly in a suggestion of response. Now and then something caught his interest sufficiently to evoke a snappish, "Well, go on. What are you stopping for?"

So Randall read, one night, about a fire in a house somewhere near Hoboken, which had been occupied by a solitary aged man, who died of suffocation while the firemen were pouring tons of water into the structure.

" 'That water,' " Randall read, " 'dug into the old man's secrets, flushed them out of their hiding-places, and exposed them for all to see. Today police and fire crews, on hand to drain ten feet of water from the cellar, found floating on the surface bills of $10, $20, and $50 denominations. When the water was pumped out they discovered heavier wads of money that had stuck to the cellar floor.' "

"Damned fool," observed Seymour. "Well—go on."

" 'That money was not the end of Mr. Fayer's wealth. Searchers found stocks and bonds too . . . the bills and securities are being turned over to the Coroner . . . so far a total of well over $100,000 . . .' "

"Damned fool," said Seymour again.
"But Brother, listen to this:

" 'Money and securities were not all that Mr. Fayer had hidden squirrel-like in nooks and crannies. From floor to ceiling all seven rooms of the house were piled with what the recluse must have considered precious possessions, saved for some distant date or awful emergency known only to him. . . . Perhaps most inexplicably of all . . . towers of popsicle sticks, some as high as ten feet . . .' "

"What the devil are popsicle sticks?" barked Seymour, listening intently.
"Why—those little sticks that come in ice-cream—like lollipop sticks. You remember, we used to have those when we were boys. Well, now they make ice-cream lollipops, on a stick. I see the children eating them downtown."
"And what did this chap do with them?"
"Why, he seems to have collected them." Randall looked through the article again. "That entire house was crammed full of these towers he had built of popsicle sticks. Millions of them, probably. He had been doing it for years."
They were silent for a time. Then Randall said, "Brother, do you

suppose there are really people like that? Do you think somebody made this story up?"

"Well, you've just read it in the *New York Times*. I don't suppose they made it up."

"How queer," said Randall, in his gentle, thoughtful voice. "It does seem hard to believe, doesn't it."

Seymour shrugged. His momentary interest in the story had already evaporated because he thought he heard a noise downstairs. He sat forward in his chair, sharply concentrated, his face intent. Randall watched him, listening too.

"I don't hear anything, Brother," he said presently.

"Go down and see anyway."

"But—"

"Don't 'but'! Are you paralyzed too? God damn it, go down and see!"

Randall came back to report that everything was absolutely all right. But Seymour was excited; it was a long time before Randall got him quiet enough to settle down for the night. He had been brooding incessantly ever since the intrusion of the policeman; he was obsessed with the possibility that such a thing might happen again. Day by day he questioned Randall minutely about the progress of his work, and about every detail, many of which were Seymour's ideas. Randall thought they made a fine team, Seymour doing the planning and Randall carrying it out. By now the work had advanced both upstairs and down, to the extent that the entire fourth floor, like the attic one, was solidly packed except for the room where Randall kept his things. Most of the third floor was finished too; so far Randall had left just enough unfilled space to be able to worm his way up the stairs to the old day nursery. Downstairs, the old basement kitchen and service rooms were partly done. The dining-room, of course, was Randall's workroom and the place where he stored the newspapers until enough had accumulated at a time to be bundled. On the ground floor he had to leave a certain amount of space for passage past the blocked doors of the finished drawing-room. And he had to leave the stairs clear enough to go up and down to the second floor, where they lived.

Seymour mused about all this to the exclusion, at that time, of speaking about anything else. He often said he could think better sitting up in his chair than lying in bed, and with increasing frequency he never went to bed all night, but stayed in his wheelchair in the library.

"But doesn't your back get very tired, Brother?" asked Randall on one of these nights.

"Your solicitude is touching," replied Seymour. "You so easily over-look the reason why I am in this condition at all. Paralysis," he snapped, "usually means that the affected parts are insensible . . ."

"Oh, forgive me, Brother." Randall put his hand on Seymour's arm, and touched his cheek gently. "I didn't mean to hurt you."

"Oh, you can't hurt me. I just told you—"

"I only meant," said Randall, fumbling for words, "I thought it rested you a little to be p— to be in a different position for the night."

"Well, sometimes it does," said Seymour. He flapped his hands nervously to dismiss the subject. "But just now I'm too busy thinking, I don't want to be distracted. Look here—about those tunnels."

And he began to talk slowly, intently, with the unhesitating exactitude that had never left him in any degree, and least of all when the subject was a technical one. Step by step he set forth what for months he had been designing in his mind with infinite precision of detail. At moments, keeping a block of paper on his lap and a pencil in his hand, he even drew a crude but intelligible diagram of his design.

"It's a question of leverage," he said. "And of balance. Do you see?"

He had explained so explicitly that a ten-year-old boy could have understood him, and Randall had been accustomed for years to working with the materials of this plan. "Yes," he said, nodding slowly and pausing to confirm that he felt perfectly capable of carrying out each step of Seymour's design. "Yes. I follow you exactly."

"Well, then, if you stack the bundles in the remaining unfilled spaces in the way we have been talking about, and plan about four of these traps at equal distances through the tunnels, there isn't a chance in heaven or hell that anybody who did break in could ever get as far as this room. They'd be killed on the way." Seymour chuckled through his nose. "About twenty of those bundles of yours—heh heh heh—" He seemed delighted. "It would squash 'em flatter than a bedbug."

"I wish you'd invent something as smart that would squash our bed-bugs right now."

"Why, Randall! Why Brother—dear! Surely you don't—" Seymour wriggled the upper half of his body with mischievous pleasure.

"You mean they don't bite *you*?"

"I don't know," said Seymour carelessly. "I'm much more comfortable since I stopped that damnfool washing you used to try to put over on me. Clothes are clothes." He sat thinking for a moment. "By the way," he said, "what's the use of that bathroom down the hall?"

"Why—nothing, I guess."

"You've been bringing in water from the hose-tap in the back yard for a long time now."

"Yes. Ever since that pipe burst to the washbasin. After that I took one of your wrenches and turned them all off—the kitchen sink too. So we wouldn't have them leaking on us if anything happened again."

"That's right," said Seymour, nodding agreement. "Absolutely right. Well, then, you might as well start work in the bathroom too. Sooner or later you'll have the rest done, above and below this floor. And we'll finish it off with whatever space we don't really need here. Then let 'em try to get in here again!"

"Well," said Randall. He was thinking about his things on the fourth floor. He had more or less intended to leave that room as it was, and the means of access to it. But if he did that, and then wanted to go up to the room at times, Seymour would hear him and begin to nag. He wondered now why he had not thought of the disused bathroom sooner. If he moved to his own room the things that he might ever want to look at, and hid safely in the bathroom the most private things like his desk, he would feel that they were near enough so he could protect them, and he could go ahead and finish all the space upstairs. A great deal of music and other stuff would still remain on the fourth floor, of course. But he would not worry about it.

"That's fine," he said to Seymour. "Just fine, Brother. I'll keep right on working."

"Good. And you know, you'll have to buy some good strong rope. New rope. I don't mind paying for *that*," Seymour added hastily, and slewed himself round in his chair to get at his box in its drawer. He still kept to his old system of identifying his cash, but the messenger from the bank for years past had not come into the house. Randall met him at the front gate on the first of every month, and took in to Seymour the sealed package from the Seaboard. "New rope," said Seymour again, and told Randall exactly where to go to get it, a ship-chandler's in South Street. "Tell him I sent you. And tell him just what I have specified." He sat and thought for a moment. "But Randall, for God's sake don't start rigging the rope until I've thought a little more about this. It's got to be foolproof, and safe for you. And not too much trouble for you to move and put back whenever you want to go through."

"Oh, it won't be too much trouble, Brother!"

Nothing seemed too much trouble because each thing he did had such a compelling reason. Although Randall himself really never read the newspapers, there were moments when words caught his eye, either when he was stacking and tying the bundles, or on the rare evenings when he read aloud to Seymour. Once in turning a page he had seen a small item at the bottom; something about a blind woman miraculously cured. She ascribed her restored sight to a certain sort of whole-wheat bread which she had been told to eat. Randall determined to find out where this bread could be had, and after weeks of inquiry, he found that it was baked by a German over in Brooklyn. He walked that night downtown, across the Brooklyn Bridge, and then, patiently asking his way in the maze of strange streets, he tramped a couple of miles, sometimes circling back on himself, until he found the bakery. Only as he approached the dark, closed shop, a long time past midnight, did it occur to him that it would be closed; but he sat down on the step and waited until he saw a light go on behind the barred basement window. He smiled happily; he had not wasted his time. Bakers got up in the small hours to do their baking. He banged on the window until the man came and opened it and listened, dumbfounded, to Randall's request.

Thereafter, he walked every Tuesday night all the way to the bakery in Brooklyn to buy a week's supply of the bread which was cheaper than any bread he had bought before, and cost still less when he took it stale. Seymour was inclined to scoff, but Randall begged so hard that he eat it! It was impossible to refuse. Like everything else, the whole-wheat bread gradually became a habit and Seymour would have been indignant had it not been there. He never asked why Randall did not take the subway to Brooklyn and back; the question would have had no meaning. Randall had not gone anywhere except on foot for something approaching thirty years, a span of time that he had long ago lost the ability to count. The immeasurable miles and hours of his nocturnal walks were lost in the mazes of habit. His only tangible concern in that realm was shoes: he wore out an increasingly alarming quantity of them. Leather, he told Seymour sadly, was not what it used to be. Very often the cobbler told him crossly that the uppers of his shoes were not worth the repeated re-solings upon which he insisted. At intervals he actually had to go and buy shoes, a detestable ordeal. He knew a block down on the East Side where vendors sold shoes from pushcarts. Those cost less than any others and suited him better. He had not bought any other article of clothing since he could remember. The house seemed to be an inexhaustible reservoir of trousers and jackets and other perfectly useful things. Seymour had once been a real dandy, and had accumulated a large wardrobe before his sight failed. And Mama of course had carefully treasured every stitch of Papa's clothing. Randall had always found something he could wear. But his favorite clothes were a pair of striped oxford-grey trousers and the brown velvet smoking-jacket that Seymour had given him one Christmas long ago. He did not like hats. They were uncomfortable. He preferred caps, and one particularly, a peaked tweed cap which Seymour had used for motoring. Randall had found that if he turned it round and wore it backwards it kept his hair from straggling and floating over his forehead, and held it down snugly on the back of his neck.

It was quite satisfying, Randall thought, how much less effort he seemed to have to make about things as the end of his work drew in sight. The tunnels were almost finished, and Seymour, when Randall described the workings of the noise-alarms and the delicately-balanced booby traps, was delighted. He took so much satisfaction in the plan that he decided finally to abandon his bedroom altogether. If he should stay day and night in the library, snug in his corner between the bay-window and his desk, he would be more comfortable and Randall could go on and finish the work in Seymour's bedroom. Everything that Seymour needed was at hand in the library, where he could touch it or Randall could give it to him. And Seymour felt safer, for some reason, if he never had to be moved to the front of the house. That was where intruders had come whenever they had threatened. Let us, he said, finish it off, block it entirely: we shall never have to worry again. In the library they blocked up all the sashes of the bay-window except the one beside which Seymour was accustomed to sit. Sometimes if the sun shone he liked to feel it for a few moments on his shoulders; and once in a great while on a summer night he even asked to have the sash raised an inch or two. But most of the time he wanted it shut and latched and the three layers of tattered blinds drawn down.

He appeared to have developed an even acuter degree of hearing than in all his life before. "I need it," he explained, when Randall remarked about it. "Now that you've got the papers right into this room, and the tunnel all rigged with the booby-trap, the papers deaden sound, of course, and I must listen extra carefully to be sure of what I hear. Fortunately," he said, with one of his rare smiles, "it's always you."

The summer was very hot, that year that Randall's work was finished. He had no idea how long he had been at it, nor of any other measure of time. But he supposed he must be growing old because he did not find his long nightly walks so easy any more. On days after he had walked to Brooklyn for the bread he felt quite tired. He was content to stay in the library with Seymour all day, and not make the effort of setting and unsetting the big booby-trap, a nerve-racking procedure which was necessary whenever he went in or out. Once inside, it was effortless to peel Seymour's orange, or open a tin of baked beans or tomato soup, which was all they cared to eat, along with the whole-wheat bread. In hot weather they did not like their food warmed. They ate it with spoons right from the can. After a time they grew so used to this that they never thought to heat the food again at all.

Then at night, because he had so long been fixed in the habit of going out after dark, Randall sometimes took the trouble to clear his way through the big booby-trap and past the two noise-traps in the library tunnel, and then through the other traps of various depths and sorts, all the way out through the barricaded entry to the front stoop. He would come out slowly, carrying his basket, having conscientiously blocked the entry behind himself; and if it were a very hot night, or he felt unusually tired, he would lower himself stiffly to the top step and sit there, not thinking about anything, not deciding whether he would later go on and walk; just resting.

The neighborhood was more crowded than it used to be, but the faces, if he raised his eyes to look at them, were all strange, and there was a feeling of safety in that. Any person who had ever troubled or tormented him and Seymour, those hoodlums of long ago, anybody who had ever known them before, had vanished in the flux of slum life. He never heard a catcall now, he never heard the hissed and snickered words which long ago had set him quaking. He knew that people stood, two or three at a time, down at the bottom of the steps, sometimes staring, sometimes venturing a remark about the heat or the rising rents or some other commonplace. He wondered why they dared come through the gate out by the pavement and then found without surprise that the gate, he had no idea when, had disappeared. The low iron picket fence lay any-which-way between the bare black yard and the broken sidewalk. Well, he thought—and thought no more about it.

Shabby men and fat, blowzy women lounged up and fell to talking when he sat out on the steps, because that was what everybody did on a hot summer night in such a neighborhood. Some were curious; some were mean; some asked questions by which they would later determine, in arguments over a beer, whether that long-haired guy in the funny clothes was real crazy or just a little bit off his nut. Randall had no idea what they thought. When they asked him how his brother was feeling, he smiled, grateful for their interest, and said, "Splendidly, thank you. Improving all the time."

He had lived so long with his faith that the oranges and the whole-wheat bread would restore Seymour's sight that it seemed perfectly natural to express this belief to any person interested enough to ask.

"Is that so!" a neighbor would say, shaking his head. "Waddaya know about that?"

"Oh, yes," said Randall, courteous, naïve, convinced that at last the neighborhood people were friendly. It was dark and he was up on the top step and could not see the winks and the nudges. But there were those who said that them brothers in that dump of a house were not as crazy as they acted. "The one comes out," they said, "he ain't crazy no more than you. He's a real old-fashioned gentleman."

Randall knew all the time that if Seymour should ever discover he was acquainted with people in the block, he would go wild with panic. It was necessary to be very careful, not to say much, not to speak above a murmur. Up there in the second floor back in the library, barricaded with the papers, not even Seymour could hear quiet voices out on the front stoop. But there was a danger, just the same. When the weather cooled Randall stopped sitting out there. He merely nodded and said "Good evening" if he passed somebody on his way to do the errands.

In these recent weeks, somehow, it was becoming more and more of an effort to go out and do the necessary walking. Sometimes he had not gone very far when he would stop in his tracks, moisten his lips once or twice, and try to swallow down the weak queer feeling that seemed to come up from his middle somewhere. Sometimes he would be heading for a certain street, walking along just as he had always done, and a little later he would find himself leaning against the side of a building, shaking and wet with sweat and his basket on the pavement where he had dropped it. He would look up at the lamp-post and not be able to read the street sign for a moment, because the letters were jumping and running together. Then when he could read he would see he was far away in the wrong direction. He began to worry secretly because he simply had to stay well in order to take care of Seymour. Perhaps the long walks were too taxing. He would try to change his ways and learn to do his errands near here, in Ninth or Tenth Avenue, where some shops were open at night. He could manage. He worried very much about the whole-wheat bread. Then when he came to the momentous decision not to walk to Brooklyn any longer, but to find a similar bread near here if he could, Seymour never noticed the difference!

It was a long time since Seymour had been moved from his corner; since, in fact, he could have been moved, for the papers had been stacked two-thirds of the way solidly across the library. Randall sometimes thought a change had come over Seymour in that time. He did not know exactly what it was. At moments it seemed almost as if Seymour had become the tortoise which he had so long resembled. Unless something provoked him to slide his head forward from its position sunken between his shoulders, or to move his hands with a sinuous reptilian motion from their twisted clasp on his lap, he sat for the most part without moving. It was an unimaginable length of time since he had last allowed Randall to wash him, cut his hair, or change his clothes. He had years ago stopped shaving himself, which he had once done accurately by touch, but his beard had never grown long like his stained, hanging moustache, or the thin strings of grey hair falling from his crusted scalp. His chin was long and hard-angled beneath the dirty stubble that masked it. And all of that, thought Randall, creeping with breathless caution through the big booby-trap to get into the small space around Seymour, I can scarcely see anyway because it is always so dark. The kerosene lamps had been abandoned years ago. If he needed light, and he almost never did any more, he lit a candle, placing it carefully away from the stacked walls of paper. Light: what use was light? He was beginning himself not to think in terms of seeing. He could not remember such a thing as a looking-glass ever having been in this house, so long ago had the last of them been swallowed in the papers. And if, when he was out, he passed anywhere a mirror or a polished plate-glass window, which gave a reflection of a stooped, shaking, bearded figure, shuffling and trembling in ragged clothes, he had no idea who it was.

Now that his work was done he often sat in the corner with Seymour, silent, still, lost in the spaces of no thought at all. Memory lay beyond his reach, like his things, the tokens of memory, many of them hidden where he could never touch them any more. He had not quite intended that, but it had happened in the course of his work. He was content; so, it seemed, was Seymour.

He came in not very late one night, since his walks had been so much shortened, and prepared to take food upstairs to Seymour. He could only carry a few things, a couple of tins, two or three oranges, through the tunnels at a time. The big booby-trap in the library was very narrow and even when the ropes were unrigged, it was dangerous to touch the steep, perilously-balanced, stacked paper walls. He knew exactly how to go through, his elbows tight to his sides, one foot straight ahead of the other. He put some oranges in his pockets and took some bread and a tin of soup for Seymour. Then he started the long, tortuous journey, stopping to take apart the noise-traps and, much more cautiously, to unfasten the ropes in the booby-traps, every strand of which he knew. When he was inside the tunnel in the library, approaching the big trap, he heard Seymour shrilly calling, "Is that you, Randall? Is it you? Answer me!"

"Yes, Brother," shouted Randall. "I'm right here. Just a few minutes now, don't worry."

"I'm hungry," he heard Seymour whining. The voice was reedier, with a higher, more querulous twang than before. "I'm hungry."

"Coming, Brother." Randall was about to unrig the ropes. On the other side of the tunnel he heard Seymour, fretting and shrill. He would do his best to hurry.

He did not know, in the close pitch-dark of the tunnel, whether that queer feeling was just his being in the tunnel—he had felt it before—or whether it was like the weakness that had caught him several times in the street, and left him gasping, all in a sweat. He tried to draw a long breath, and told himself he was all right. He groped for the knots and when they were not right there, he felt rather relieved. Why, he thought,

I was all mixed up there for a minute. I've unrigged them already, I've got the way clear. He picked up his things again, holding his elbows close and his right hand a little advanced, and calling, "I'm coming, Brother," he took a step forward.

The crash was a vast thundering temblor, rocking the rotten floor, shaking the cracked walls. Seymour's chair was shaken like a rat in a terrier's teeth; he clung to its arms and shrieked "Randall! *Randall*—!" He crouched, gibbering and shrunken with terror. "Randall—"

Thick dust floated into his open mouth, he choked and hawked. He tried to scream again, but only a drooling gargle came from his throat.

"Randall!" He spat and gagged. He beat the arms of his chair. "Randall, speak to me!" He thrust his head forward, his acute left ear towards the tunnel; he listened, holding his breath. There was no answer. The old man twisted in his chair, strangling on the dust, crying and calling. "Randall!" he squealed, in a long cracking wail.

There was silence. Seymour whimpered.

PART III

PART III

They found the body of Randall Holt on the thirteenth day after I had joined the searchers in the house. I was upstairs in what I now knew to be the old day nursery on the fourth floor, sorting out fragments of crumbling music from the impacted mass of other paper which two men from the Department of Sanitation were cautiously taking apart. From time to time one of them would carry down the stuff that I had weeded out and put it in the old basement dining-room, from which all the newspapers and loose trash had been cleared, leaving only the wreckage of the furniture and of two upright pianos and an organ. Every afternoon when I left the house I took the day's accumulation of material in a taxi to the main office of the bank, where a room had been set aside for this purpose. And every evening until late into the night, I sat there sorting, reading, cogitating, checking against the calendars of almost half a century the scattered clues which at that time were far short of weaving a consecutive record of what had happened.

Up on the fourth floor we heard the commotion, the exclamations, and the sounds very like groans of horror or disgust, which told me before I seized my electric torch and started down the stairs that the search was over. Deering heard me coming down and shouted, "Say, Mr. Wycherly, I wouldn't come in here if I were you."

"Have you found him?" I asked.

Deering came out to the second floor hallway and stood at the bottom of the rickety stairs. The light from my torch showed his heavy square face a sick yellow; his forehead was damp with sweat. I did not need any answer to my question. Deering stood there making a sign to me to stay away. The stench was overpowering, more so than ever before. I said, "I see. But I am supposed to be a witness even if I didn't want to look."

He shrugged and turned back to the room, the old library. I followed him. The room was still very dim with towering stacks of the newspapers which they had not yet moved. It was just as well. All I could bear to see before I closed my eyes in horrified revulsion was a foot; a shoe, more exactly, an old-fashioned high boot with straggling laces and a gaping hole in its sole. It was twisted back from the bones of a decomposing ankle.

When I felt I could keep a grip on myself I opened my eyes, holding my handkerchief before my nose and mouth, and looked at what they had found. Randall Holt's body lay on its side, facing towards the bay-window corner where Seymour Holt had been found dead in his wheel-chair. The right hand was extended in what looked to our appalled eyes like a gesture of pleading; just beyond it lay a tin soup-can, squashed flat. The foot that we could not see was doubled underneath the oozing mass of rotted cloth, tangled in the rope that had sprung the booby-trap. I cannot bear to describe the head, the hands, whatever I saw uncovered, which had been gnawed by rats. The body was partly decomposed, and they had not yet moved away a crushed, tattered suitcase and two smashed tin bread-boxes which lay on top of it. The whole thing was not ten feet from the spot where Seymour Holt had been found, and for three whole weeks they had searched this house inch by inch, while a general alarm for Randall Holt had been on police dockets across the country.

The Medical Examiner had been sent for when they first saw the tip of the boot and knew what they were about to uncover. He arrived while we were standing there, accompanied by those men with the long, narrow, covered basket. I did not watch while he made his examination; indeed, during that time I had to go downstairs and outside for some air. When I went back to the library they were using something like shovels to scoop the thing into the basket, and as they carried it away we followed them down the stairs and out to the desolate front yard.

"At least a month," said the Medical Examiner. We stood out there in a little group, shivering in the raw November wind. But, as Blyfeld said, we all felt sick enough to have shivered had it been a hundred in the shade. "He's been dead at least a month," said the Examiner. "After the laboratory work is finished I'll be able to tell you to within a day or so."

Thus I had my facts. How could anybody have guessed in the beginning the sequence of this horrible thing: that Randall Holt had died first, caught and killed in his own booby-trap, and that Seymour Holt had lived on for several unthinkable days, dying at last of slow starvation. I had two or three very bad nights following this. I slept scarcely

at all, tormented by gruesome, indescribably revolting nightmares. But I
managed to pull myself together, chiefly because we now had the facts
to enable us, Cullom and we at the bank, to do the work that it was our
responsibility to do.

Bowen Dugdale had had me transferred temporarily from the Foreign
Department to the Trust Department, so that all my time could be
assigned to the Holt case until it was cleared up. We had many confer-
ences about it, together with Rodney Cullom. The discovery of Randall Holt's body put a different light on the situation, especially after we
had made sure that he had left no will. We did not have to search for
his bank records, because I had found them packed into a japanned tea-
chest buried under a mass of broken crockery and bundled newspapers
in the bathroom. Now as I write about this, I find myself constantly
drawn back into the frame of mind of those days, a strange state which
consisted, as nearly as I can describe it, of the hard core of the facts
that had involved me in this fantastic situation, surrounded by intangibles, clouds, mists, dreams almost, which I knew to be the story of
the lives of the Holt brothers and Renata Tosi as it came to me through
the crumbling archive of Randall Holt's hoarded papers. The hard-core
element kept me searching single-mindedly for my original objective,
anything which would induce Renata Tosi to answer the question required by Seymour Holt's will. The rest of it, the nebulous part, the
part which grew and took pitifully human, moving form, impelled me
away from the reality of trying to settle a will, and carried me into those
haunting spaces of the imagination which I have tried to describe
heretofore.

I worked for four weeks in the room assigned me at the bank, reading, sorting, and classifying Randall Holt's things, since we had decided
that I ought to prepare a careful and consecutive transcript of every
word of reference to Renata Tosi. With this, we decided, I should go
back to Italy and once again confront the old woman. We could not
imagine how, in the face of this compendium of facts, she could refuse
to make the statement which would enable her and Sebastiano Gandolfi
to inherit the property which we considered rightly theirs.

The day came when I had finished this transcript to the best of my
ability. As I worked through Randall Holt's papers, through the things
that he had saved and hidden as well as through the tremendous mass
of his tiny scribblings, mostly on the margins of musical scores, I had

put aside those whose meaning was so categorical that I believed Renata Tosi, confronted with them, could no longer refuse to speak. Yellow, dry, and crumbling as they were, I felt the only thing to do was to show them to her. I sealed them in padded envelopes to keep them from crushing to powder in transit, and I packed them, together with my long, typewritten transcript, in a boarded attaché case, safer for such fragile material than a brief case. I was ready to leave. I was due at the airport at four o'clock; my plane would take off at five. I looked at my watch. It was a little after two. I had meant to do an errand of my own in the hour at my disposal, but I had a different impulse and decided to follow it. There was no reason for it and it was unnecessary; but that did not matter. I got into a cab and drove to the Holt house.

It was three weeks since I had been there, having taken over then the last of Randall Holt's things that I had been able to find. After that the work of clearing out the house had gone quickly and was now finished to the extent that it was possible. As they had worked down to the walls and floors of the decayed, crumbling, rat-ridden rooms, the plaster disintegrated, the floors in places as pulpy as cheese, they had seen the real condition of the riddled shell. The Department of Housing and Buildings had within recent days taken the legal steps necessary to pronounce the house a public menace. And Rodney Cullom had told me that he and the bank, as Seymour Holt's executors, and the Public Administrator acting, in the absence of a will, for Randall Holt's estate, had moved to obtain authorization to demolish the building. So I knew that I would never see it again.

I stood in the barren, filth-littered yard, with the case in my hand that held the story of fifty years of life in the condemned house; with threads weaving and pulling all through my imagination, back another twenty years to the childhood of those brothers born to a hopeless destiny. When I had first seen the house, in the early days of suspense and of gruesome discovery, I had been shocked and at the same time, almost titillated by a sense of raw excitement at being involved in such a sensational thing. Now all that was past. I held in my hand the text, as it were, of the tragedy for which this had been the stage-setting. The house as I gazed at it was utterly, irrevocably mute. It had nothing more to tell. Its windows, behind whose filthy crust I had first seen the tattered blinds, the dark massed blocks of mystery, were dull blanks now, blank, I thought like my image of the eyes of Seymour Holt himself. I thought about him, with pity, with censure, with bitterness, even with amusement; with consternation at his awful death. Curious, I remember thinking; curious that he is in my mind now, just when my real concern is with the others.

A solitary policeman was there on duty, guarding the sealed house from curiosity-seekers. He looked uncomfortable and bored, there in the early December cold. I knew him; he had been there from the beginning. He said, "Good afternoon, Mr. Wycherly. Do you have to go inside?"

I said, "No thanks, Leary. I just thought for a moment I'd forgotten something." He nodded and I turned away and got into my cab and drove to the airport.

Faced with another twenty-four-hour blank it was inevitable I should pass the time remembering my first interview with Renata Tosi. Against what I now knew of her story the old woman might, I thought, have been a minor creation of Dante. Her surroundings intensified the illusion, for San Bernardo is one of the crumbling villages dating from about the eleventh century, perched in the crevices of the mountainous promontory which divides the Lake of Como into two long, thin arms. The village looks as if little had ever been done to change it or its inhabitants either. It is the dead end of the narrow road and it consists of a small bare piazza surrounded by a handful of buildings and an humble church. The houses are uniformly pale, faded grey, thinly stucco-faced over the rough-hewn stone which is the native building material, and perhaps yellow-washed at some time or other, but long since allowed to weather. The roofs are eloquent of tremendous age, their ridges and humps like the knots on gnarled, aged hands, and their red color darkened to a winy brown. The church is the real measure of the antiquity of the place, for it has not received in seven or eight hundred years the inconsequent face-lifting which overtook many Italian village churches —a baroque façade casually stuck upon the front, with the other three walls left untouched in their mediaeval nudity.

I had left my car, that first day, in a corner of the piazza and walked away from it, looking up at the house in whose shadow I had parked: a tall bleak building five stories high, quite large, and obviously very old. It had small, crooked windows and I could tell from the lower ones that they were set in immensely thick walls and that the casements were a late addition—originally such windows had no glass. I had not been able from inside the car to see the whole façade of the building, but now I stood in the middle of the piazza and looked up to the roof. Off at the farthest corner, in a tiny top-storey window, I saw a woman. I could see her head and neck and the curve of her shoulders, that was all. She held herself so still that one could tell even at a glance that this must be her habit. She had not come to the window for any passing reason, it was strangely clear that her time was spent sitting motionless there. She was very old.

I stood there in the sun staring up at the woman, and she sat in her window staring, but not at me. Her eyes when I first saw her seemed to be fixed on some distant object and as long as I watched her, I never saw them shift their focus. It was that fixedness of her eyes which made me sense, as if through some special nerve, that there was something peculiar about her. She sat turned slightly so that I saw her head a little more than in profile, a remarkable head, the white hair in flat wings framing a low forehead, the nose high and carved, slightly beaked; the mouth tightly closed and not fallen in, which would mark the typical absence of teeth in most such faces; the chin perhaps the most surprising feature, for though everything about the head showed distinct old age, the chin was a firm sculptured line, flowing without blurs or wattles into the high black collar which encased the throat. The face was the nutshell brown of the elderly Italian, but from the distance where I stood I could not discern further details except the sharp contrast between that deep-toned skin and the pure white hair above it. I must have stood for well over five minutes, frankly staring at the old woman, and she remained fixed in her remote, dignified position, oblivious of me.

From the size of San Bernardo I knew it could not be difficult to find Renata Tosi if she were alive. And I was not surprised when the padrone of the dusty little *trattoria* answered my question with a flap of his hand towards the woman at the window, saying, "*Eccola lì.*" He shrugged when I asked if he knew her.

"Nobody knows her, Signore," he said. "She never speaks."

"Not at all?"

"Never. She never leaves that room. She speaks to nobody. She is—" he tapped his forehead.

And with this I turned and crossed the piazza to the house where she was sitting at her window.

The stairs were dark and steep and it was a long climb to the top floor. Though the air was so warm and clear out of doors it was dank and foul here and one knew one was breathing the tomblike effluvia of centuries. The rough stone steps were worn to deep hollows at the middle. And the place had a strange smell—not so much that of primitive habits untouched by sanitation, which rather surprised me, but a sour stench of sheer age, overlaid by the smells of noonday cooking seeping from each household. From my scrutiny of her window outside I thought I could place Renata Tosi's door correctly, and I did; it was the last one along the low, cramped attic passage. I knocked. I had the disturbing sensation of anticipating what was to come, for there was no answer and I knew I had expected none. I knocked again—two or three times. Each time I waited, listening carefully. I knocked once more, a sharper rap with a rat-tat-tat urgency that I had not ventured before. That time I heard, with the greatest difficulty, a muffled sound, a whisper probably, but it sounded like a sigh.

"*Avanti—*"

The door was not locked and I opened it and walked in.

The woman's back was turned, she had not changed her position at the window, and in spite of what I had heard about her I was surprised that she had not the curiosity to turn and look at the intruder. I stood with my hat in my hand, not feeling so rebuffed as I might, for her attitude gave me time to examine the room. It was a cell, nothing more or less, furnished with a pallet in one corner, a stand with a basin and ewer for washing, a table on which stood a candle in a tin holder, a tattered prayer-book, a cup and plate, and a photograph frame so placed that I saw only the back of it from where I stood. The only chair was the hard straight one upon which Renata Tosi was sitting. And finally, to my amazement and again, my discomfiture, because it was all part of anticipating the incredible, there lay across a corner of the bare floor a series of copies of the *Corriere*, all folded back to the third page on which the story about Seymour Holt and his shocking house and his vanished brother had been running every day. My mouth felt dry and I swallowed and wondered how on earth to begin doing what I had to do. At that point, while I was looking first at the woman's back and then at the newspapers and then at her again, she said in the same sighing whisper, "*Chi è*? Who is it?"

"Someone who has to speak to you, Signora," I answered, "I

have been sent from Milano—from New York. I apologize for intruding."

There was a slow reluctant movement of her shoulders, and she did not turn her head. When she spoke she never raised her voice above that strange breathy sound which was almost a sigh.

"What must you say?" she asked.

There was no way of creeping up on a subject like this. I said, *"Mi dispiace,* but the death of a Mr. Seymour Holt in New York has raised a certain question which his will, in fact, the law, makes it necessary for you to answer."

There was not a sound from her for a long time. Finally she said, "Who are you?"

"My name is Richard Wycherly," I said. "I work for a bank—the Seaboard Trust Company of New York. They are the executors of Mr. Holt's will. They have instructed me to come here."

"Well?" she breathed, again after letting me wait.

Cautiously I began to explain. I might have been speaking to an effigy. So I said sharply, "Seymour Holt has left you a fortune on condition that you state truthfully who was the father of your son, known as Sebastiano Gandolfi."

Then she looked at me. She turned her head and stared at me with a pair of extraordinary brown eyes. They seemed penetrating and yet she made me feel as if they ignored my presence. She said, "I have no son."

I looked at the framed photograph, standing at such an angle that by bending forward I could see just enough to discern that it was a picture of a man. She watched me. I said, "Signora, do you really mean that?"

"I have no son," she repeated.

So I said again, "There is a great deal of money involved in this. And your son would inherit it after your death."

"Money! *Per che cosa?"* This was the first I had seen of her hands, as she lifted the right one from its hiding-place in her loose sleeves, and made a scornful gesture at the room. "I need no money. You should go now."

"It is not so simple to drop this matter and walk out of here," I said. "It was as part of this same duty that I learned something about Professor Sebastiano Gandolfi before I came to see you. I am afraid,

Signora, it will be very difficult to accept your word that you are not his mother. There is much proof to the contrary."

She sat like stone.

"And perhaps, if it becomes necessary to prove that you are his mother, he might feel you had no right to deprive—"

She moved quickly, she turned upon me with the speed of a lizard.

"If I had a son as distinguished as Professor Gandolfi, would I have the right to shame him before the world by such a *scandalo* as you want me to confess now? Go, I tell you. *Go!*" Her voice was a hoarse rasp, the sigh extinguished.

Once again I stood in Renata Tosi's room in San Bernardo. It was wretchedly cold, clammy, the piercing chill borne by days without sun, which can be more penetrating than a real winter temperature. The old woman sat as if she had not moved a muscle in the seven weeks since I had seen her. The ochre tint of her skin had a lifeless look, her colorless lips were firmly closed, her eyelids lowered. She wore the same shapeless high-collared black garment, with a knitted shawl about her shoulders. There was a rough grey blanket over her knees. A small charcoal brazier smouldered near her. It gave scarcely any warmth. She sat in precisely the same position as before, staring out the window, her hands hidden in her black sleeves, and she gave no evidence of hearing the few words I had just said. I had hoped, pessimistically to be sure, that because I had been there before she would in some way be less forbidding. But that was not so. She contrived to make me feel as if she had immured herself in a new coating of ice. There was now nothing in sight so betraying as the newspapers that had lain across the floor. The framed photograph was gone from the table. This was a way of informing me that against her will she had expected me to return; that she knew of Randall Holt's terrible death in the same way that she had learned about his brother's. But when I said, "Signora, will you allow me to speak? I have been sent back from New York to see you again," she only shrugged in that faint way which bespoke total indifference.

I stood there, wondering whether it would offend her if I should sit down on the edge of the pallet in the corner, since she occupied the only chair in the room. I took a step towards the cot, and saw by an icy twitch of her eyebrows that this would be presuming. So I stood still, certain that my cold feet would soon be benumbed, not only by the damp draughts across the floor but by the discomfort deliberately imposed by her.

"Signora," I said. "Like the first time when I came, you make me feel that it is useless to look for a tactful approach to what I have to say."

By her stony silence she plainly agreed.

"And this time," I said, "I have here the whole record of your relations with—" I remember I had to stop and take a breath before I managed to say, "—the Holt brothers. Both brothers, Seymour Holt and Randall." I held forward the attaché case in such a way that she could not avoid seeing it. She saw it. Not even she could control the emotion which distended, then flattened, her slanting, narrow nostrils. If she had made it difficult for me to speak the first time I saw her, she was making it virtually impossible now. I had done what I could to tell her that I knew her story, and now again I groped for the device with which I had hoped to disarm her before. I said, "Believe me, this is not a matter of passing judgment upon anybody. I told you before, Signora, that men like myself, bankers, lawyers—our only concern is the rightful and legal disposition of people's property. We feel now, more than ever, that the Holt property is rightfully yours. And—Professor Gandolfi's. It remains only for you to make the statement necessary to claim it."

"I have nothing to state," she said in a steely voice.

"But your—please! Won't you consider him? Your son?"

"I have no son."

"Oh, Signora!" I looked once round the room, I suppose as if expecting a chair to materialize from space; and since there was no other way to manage, I put the attaché case on the floor at her feet and dropped on my knees beside it. She sat staring straight over my head at the empty place on the table where the photograph had been. Not even my involuntarily dramatic motion had moved her. Slowly I opened the leather case.

"I have here," I said, picking up the thick, blue-bound folder of the transcript, "a copy of the notes, something like entries in a diary, which Randall Holt was in the habit of writing throughout his entire life. Did you know he did that?"

She made no answer.

"He did," I said, and went on to explain as best as I could what I had found in the depths of the appalling mess of the Holt brothers' house. Now that I knew so much about her, all of which had been a sealed book before, I felt stirred and pushed by my own recollections of Randall Holt's notes: here was the lovely, careless, curiously wise, infinitely tender creature who had held his life in the palm of her hand, and shared enough of it with him to have moved me, the utter stranger, time and again, to intense feeling. This very morning, on the road skirting the eastern branch of the lake, I had stopped the car on the little height above the cove where stood the pink house, dreaming and unchanged in its soft frame of green, and the sight of it had filled my heart with vivid pity for the gentle souls who had lived in it, and for the awful sacrifices that had torn them from it, which they believed to be retribution.

I tried to suggest that to her, but she seemed to have the power to parry my appeals with ever-increasing imperturbability. I had talked much longer than I believed her strength could stand, and in one last, despairing effort I lifted the sealed, padded envelopes from the case and, though she shrank at the approach of my hand, I laid them gently in her lap.

"Those envelopes, Signora, contain the things which Randall Holt treasured above everything in this world. They are not copies. They are originals—and all of them concern you. Some are written by you. I consider them your property."

"I do not want them," she said.

I went on as if I had not heard her. "The letter is there," I said, "which you wrote to Randall Holt in 1928, telling him it was unnecessary any longer to send money for the education of Sebastiano Gandolfi."

She was silent, her dry lips pressed tight, her eyes averted. I marvelled at her control. I let her wait; she would outwait me. I said softly, "Your son. John. The boy whom Randall Holt worshipped. You used to call him Giu'an."

I saw the muscles strain against her black collar. She would not give a sign. I bent closer to her, pointing to the envelopes in her lap. "The note is there," I whispered. "The note that was in the basket."

"*Taci!*" she cried, a sudden raucous shriek.

The bare room seemed to echo her agony.

"I am so sorry," I said as gently as I could. "I do wish you could believe how I want to help you. Signora, don't you understand? It does not matter by the terms of the will whom you state the father to have been. Only that you state it." By every effort of suggestion and will-power I was trying to advise her to name Randall Holt. She only sat there with her head bent, as it had been since her despairing cry. "There are many reasons," I said very quietly, "why it does not matter which one you name." I let the silence stay for a long time between us. "Will you not say?"

Her head was bent, I could not see anything but the flat cap of white hair, the angle of the wrinkled cheek and the long-lobed ear. I leaned closer to her, sensing for the first time that her cloak of stone was about to crack. "Will you not say?" I asked again, almost whispering. Barely at all, her bowed head moved in refusal. "You cannot say?" The head moved again. "You never knew," I whispered. She cringed; her emaciated shoulders rode up as if to engulf her head in shame. In spite of the piercing chill of the room my own face was hot; I felt almost suffocating with the import of what I had forced myself to say, and her to hear. I rose from my knees and walked over to the other side of the room and stood with my hands in the pockets of my overcoat, deter-mined to get the thing back on its original footing and make my last, obligatory, coldly rational appeal.

"I understand everything implicit in your refusal," I said. "But we do not feel that you have the right to deprive Sebastiano Gandolfi of a fortune. You do not realize, perhaps, that the situation is changed by the death of Randall Holt. He died before his brother Seymour, and without making a will. This means that the estate of Seymour Holt has inherited Randall's money. All this, upon your meeting Seymour Holt's condition, will eventually go to your son."

"I have no son."

This time I could have screamed. Instead I managed to say, "It is possible you have lived so long in retirement, Signora, that you do not quite realize the extreme changes in the present-day world. Neither indi-viduals nor public opinion are shocked by what used to be considered very shocking. Even if some matter does appear to be scandalous, the pace of life is such that people almost immediately forget what we may call yesterday's sensation. This question before you could be arranged in such a way that your declaration about the paternity would scarcely be remarked."

For the first and only time that day she raised her head and looked straight at me. Her face was graven with scorn, her eyes black and enormous.

"*Siete ignoranti tutti!*" she said. "All of you. You understand nothing. Not alone would I not disgrace Sebastiano Gandolfi by a scandalous declaration of paternity. *I have no son.* Have you heard me?" The gnarled claws of hands shot out from the black sleeves and beat furiously upon the shrunken breast. "*I have no son!*" The voice was a strident screech, torn from the lungs. I stood there dumbstruck.

After a time the shaking claw held towards me the envelopes that I had laid upon her knees.

"Take these," she said. She pointed to the leather case at her feet. "Take all of it. And go."

I returned to Milano and telegraphed to the Council Minister for an appointment. His reply came immediately, and I flew to Rome by the next morning's plane. The flight was a troubled interlude for me. I believed I could present the matter in such a way as to convince any rational man—let alone a brilliant one—of his own interest in persuading the old woman to meet the terms of the will. But it would confound me personally and embarrass me professionally if I should fail. I had had too much of horrors and eccentricities and I did not want their consequences to remain as a mark of failure on my record at the bank.

I arrived at the Ministry at half past two and was ushered through the stupendous columned halls of Bernini, and the anterooms hung with Raphaels and Caravaggios, to the office of the Minister. He rose as the doors closed behind me, and came from his place to shake hands. Then he returned to his desk, a neat, simple writing-table austerely in contrast to the baroque room. He indicated the chair on the farther side of the desk, facing his own, and we sat down.

It was in its way an awkward moment, for I had to begin talking, but he encouraged me with a warm smile. His manner was natural and gracious. I had been told that this scholarly man, one of the world's most distinguished in his field, had been prevailed upon only after repeated, urgent appeals, to take this post in the Cabinet at a time when Italy, like every other nation, desperately needed the services of its best brains; so many had perished in the depredations of our time. It was only to be expected that I should look at Sebastiano Gandolfi with extraordinary interest, and I suppose he understood that, for he put me quite at ease during those moments of silence. He was one of the handsomest men I have ever seen, in his middle forties, with a head of nobly-sculptured proportions, clean-shaven, the mouth and the brow serenely reposed, the eyes a clear greyish blue, deep-set and intensely perceptive. His skin was a sunny brown, his curly brown hair threaded with grey. But his hands were the most remarkable feature of all; they were uniquely beautiful. They were square and masculine, the fingers straight, fairly solid, blunt, cushioned, strongly suggesting the hands of a musician. The skin looked silky-smooth, and the fine muscles were visible beneath it. In every line and every motion they were hands of the utmost sensitivity.

I raised my eyes from his hands and looked at him and said, "Eccellenza, do you know why I am here?"

"I may as well tell you that I do," he said, in perfect, unaccented English. "It will save us both a considerable amount of explanation?"

"I think so. And may I speak freely?"

He inclined his head in a gesture of consent.

"I saw Signora Tosi at San Bernardo yesterday," I said slowly. "I had come directly from New York where I have been working for six weeks on the papers found in the house of the late Seymour and Randall Holt."

First he said nothing; then he said: "Yes?"

"I am speaking upon the assumption, Eccellenza, that you know of the condition in the will of Seymour Holt, upon which depends the bequest of his fortune. If I am mistaken—"

"You are not mistaken, sir."

"Then you know of my conversation with Signora Tosi in October, when she refused absolutely to meet that condition . . . to answer that question?"

"I know."

We both smiled, a little wryly, I suppose, for nobody could help feeling a sense of admiration in the presence of that man, and he understood that I was finding my assignment a difficult one.

"The situation is changed now," I said, "because of the fact that Randall Holt was proved to have died before his brother—he died intestate—and his property therefore went to Seymour Holt's estate. This about doubles the original amount involved and we in New York feel very strongly that you are the rightful heir."

He made a little gesture almost of humorous indifference.

"But, Eccellenza," I said, "I have failed absolutely to persuade Signora Tosi to make the necessary declaration which will meet the condition of Seymour Holt's will." I stopped and wondered how to put the next thing, and then, laying my cards face up, I said, "Frankly, I cannot feel that Signora Tosi is competent—mentally competent—to decide what she should do about answering that question."

"And you came here, sir, thinking to ask me to persuade her?"

"In your own interest."

"My dear sir," he said, leaning a little forward and smiling faintly, "I would not think of doing such a thing."

"But can you believe that she is doing right in refusing?"

"Yes, I can believe."

"You agree with her position in this matter?"

"I agree."

Hopelessly discouraged, I asked, "You support entirely Signora Tosi's insistence that she is not your mother?"

"Entirely."

"You know how much evidence there is to the contrary?"

"I suppose I know."

"I have uncovered in New York and brought here a mass of incontrovertible evidence." I looked him intently in the eye.

"With which Signora Tosi will not agree," he said gently.

"And the village people in San Bernardo, their memories of your childhood, your visits to Signora Tosi, your photograph which she appears to treasure—"

"I love Signora Tosi very dearly, sir. She has been all my life the person nearest and dearest to me. I owe her everything. I would do anything she wished."

"Even to refusing a quarter of a million dollars, which is rightfully yours?"

"Even."

"And you refuse to state that she is your mother."

"I have no reason to state that she is. I have every reason to support her word, agree with her, and give her peace of mind."

The Minister folded his beautiful strong hands with a motion of finality, and his warm Italian face with its gentle grey-blue eyes smiled at me across his desk.

X